Violet Storm

A Novel of South Carolina During Reconstruction

By

James A. Huston & Anne Marshall Huston

Book One: *Southern Crosses*

Book Two: *South Wind*

Book Three: *Carolina Phoenix*

ISBN: 0-7596-8922-9 (E-book)
ISBN: 0-7596-8923-7 (Paperback)
ISBN: 0-7596-8924-5 (Dustjacket)

This book is printed on acid free paper.

1stBooks - rev. 07/02/02

Although few battles were fought within her limits...South Carolina made many sacrifices in the interest of her section. With a white population of 291,300 at the beginning of the conflict, the state put into the field during the four years 62,838 effective men...of whom 22 percent were killed on the field or died in prison. General W.T. Sherman's march across the state (February-March, 1865) was accompanied by an enormous destruction of property by fire and pillage.

All the misfortunes of the war itself are insignificant when compared with the sufferings of the people during the era of Reconstruction (1865-1877).

Encyclopedia Britannica, 11th ed. (1910-1911)

Reconstruction, rather than the Civil War, destroyed the Old South.

William B. Hesseltine, *The South in American History* (New York, 1936, 1943)

Accept, then, this book, which to those who care only for history will seem but an idle romance, while to the lovers of romance it may look strangely like the mustiest history.

-Maurice Thompson, *Alice of Old Vincennes* (1900)

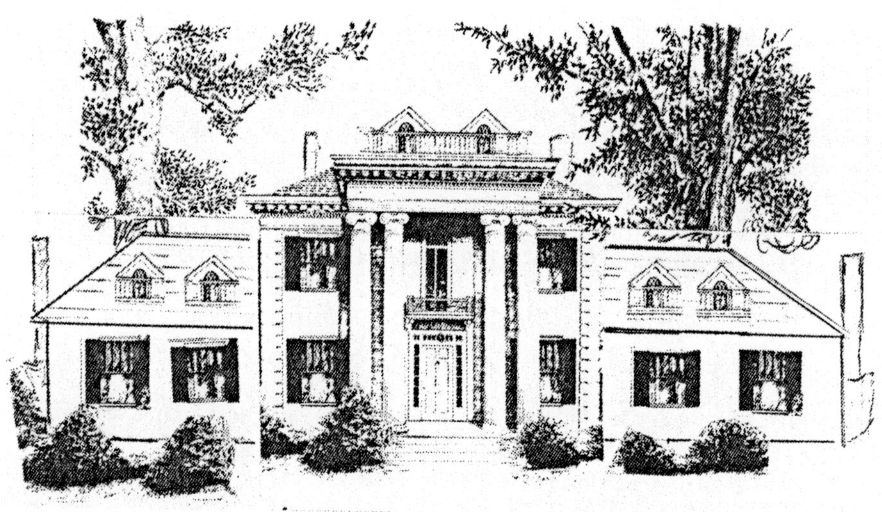

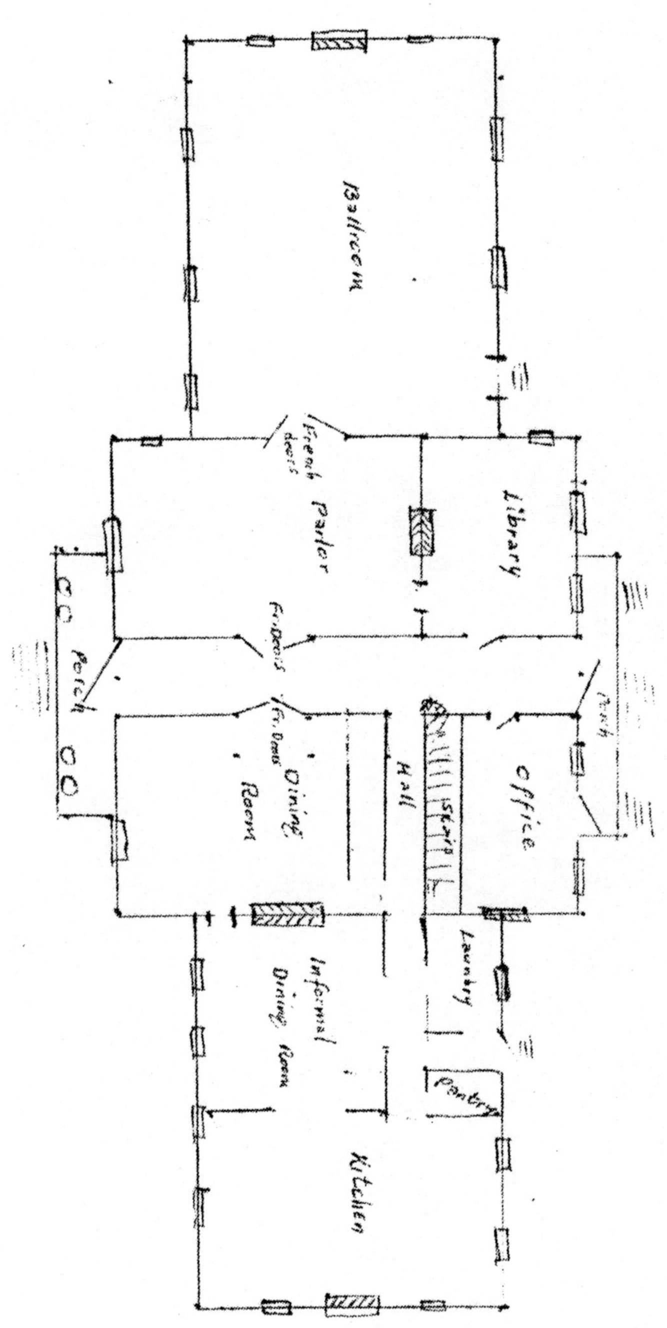

Ballroom
French doors
Parlor
Library
Fr. Doors
Porch
Fr. Doors
Dining Room
Hall
Stairs
Office
Porch
Laundry
Informal Dining Room
Pantry
Kitchen

Table of Contents

Book Three: *Carolina Phoenix*

Characters

Fair Oaks

Violet Violet	Lee Storm, b. 1843. Eldest daughter of Major Alexander and Rosemary Storm of Fair Oaks plantation, Sumter County, South Carolina. Married Brent Sutler April 8, 1862.
Brent George	Brent Sutler, b. 1837. Oldest son of James and Isabel Sutler of Charleston, South Carolina. Married to Violet Storm. Joined Confederate Navy July 15, 1863.
Bonnie Anne	Bonnie Anne Sutler, b 1863. Violet and Brent's young daughter.
J.J.	Jonathan Jackson Sutler ("J.J."), b. 1864. Violet and Brent's son.
Little Wade	Wade Hampton Sutler, b. 1875. Violet and Brent's younger son.
Major Storm	Alexander Fox Storm, b. 1813. Violet's father. Owner of Fair Oaks Plantation. Fought in Mexican War; now commissioned in South Carolina militia.
Rosemary Storm	Rosemary Lee (Clark) Storm, b. 1820; d. 1860. Violet's mother. Originally from Virginia.
Charlotte	Charlotte Rose Storm, b. 1846. Violet's sister.
Susan	Susan Phlox Storm, b. 1849. Violet's sister.
Christopher	Christopher Alexander Storm, b. 1844; d. 1863. Violet's brother. Killed at Gettyburg.
Grandmama	Catherine Victoria Lee. Violet's maternal grandmother who lives in Virginia, between Williamsburg and Richmond.
Gilbert Hudson	Yankee officer who marries Susan.

Fair Oaks House Servants

Uncle Jarvis	House man (Head house servant).
Mammy	Housekeeper, cook, nurse.
Aunt Sheba	Mammy's elderly sister and helper.
Evelina	Mammy's young helper; nurse maid.
Aaron	The Major's manservant.
Hattie	Washing, ironing, sewing; later becomes head housekeeper.
Little Josh	Boy helper.

Fair Oaks Plantation Workers

Leo	Black overseer of Fair Oaks plantation.
Rachel	Leo's wife
Supervisors:	
Amos	Machinery
Avery	Hay, oats, and wheat
Carter	Cabinet maker
Enoch	Maintenance
Fabian	Driver, gardens and orchards.
Henry	Cotton
Isaiah	Corn and tobacco
Jason	Animals
Zeke	Blacksmith

Elijah Jackson	Minister, teacher at church/school in workers' village; later headmaster at *The Joshua School.*
Esther Jackson	Elijah's wife and assistant at church/school and later at *The Joshua School.*
Jesse Wallace	Succeeds Elijah Jackson at church/school in workers' village.
Flora Wallace	Jesse's wife and assistant.

Columbia Town House Servants

Uncle Job	House man.
Aunt Beulah	Housekeeper, cook.
Raymond and Cora Martin	Helpers

At Charleston

James and Isabel Sutler	Brent's parents
Phoebe	Brent's sister
Bruce	Brent's brother, now out west.

Friends and Neighbors

John and Sarah Frierson	At Cherry Vale plantation, across from Fair Oaks.
Andrew Thompson	At Glenmerry plantation, adjacent to Fair Oaks.
Leland Thompson	Andrew's son, at Glenmerry.
Harrison and Patricia Stuart	At Midlands plantation, beyond Thompson's Glenmerry.
Will and Mary Anderson	Friends at Stateburg; Will is a physician.
Victor Shelby	Lawyer in Sumter.

Virginia Shelby	Victor's wife.
Mary Chesnut	Camden, Columbia.
John Dargan	Banker in Sumter.
Charles Rhett	Confederate lieutenant in Sumter.
Scott Carson	Confederate lieutenant in Sumter.
Edith Carson	Scott's wife.
John Fraser	Manager of the railroad, Columbia.
Cedric Johnson	Brent's mercantile assistant in Columbia.
Wade Hampton	Columbia, Lieutenant General, Confederate Army.
John Manning	At Milford Plantation, former governor of South Carolina.
Henry, William, Jr., and Reuben Ellison	Black owners of a large cotton plantation near Stateburg.
Father Roberts	Rector of Holy Cross Episcopal Church, Stateburg.
Father Shand	Rector of Trinity Church, Columbia.
Father Wilson	Successor to Father Roberts at Holy Cross Church.

Antagonists

Blake Farley	Scalawag, storekeeper in Sumter.
Caleb Duprey	Carpetbagger, supervisor on the railroad
Clifford Montgomery	Scalawag, banker in Sumter.
Franklin Moses, Jr.	Scalawag, lawyer, later governor of South Carolina.

Officers of the Aura Lee

Captain	Brent Sutler
Mate	John Hawkins
Boatswain	Owen Douglas
Boatswain's	MateEdward Jones
Quartermaster	Henry Young
Quartermaster's Mate	Charles Caldwell

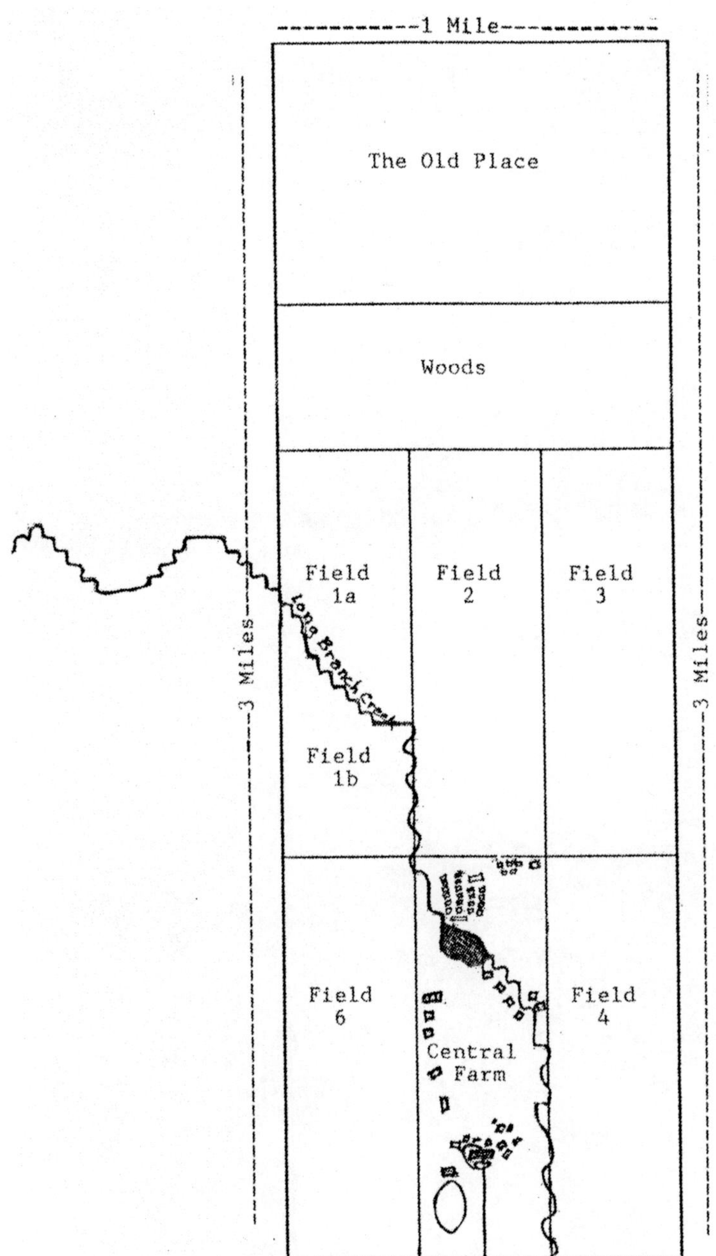

Fair Oaks Plantation

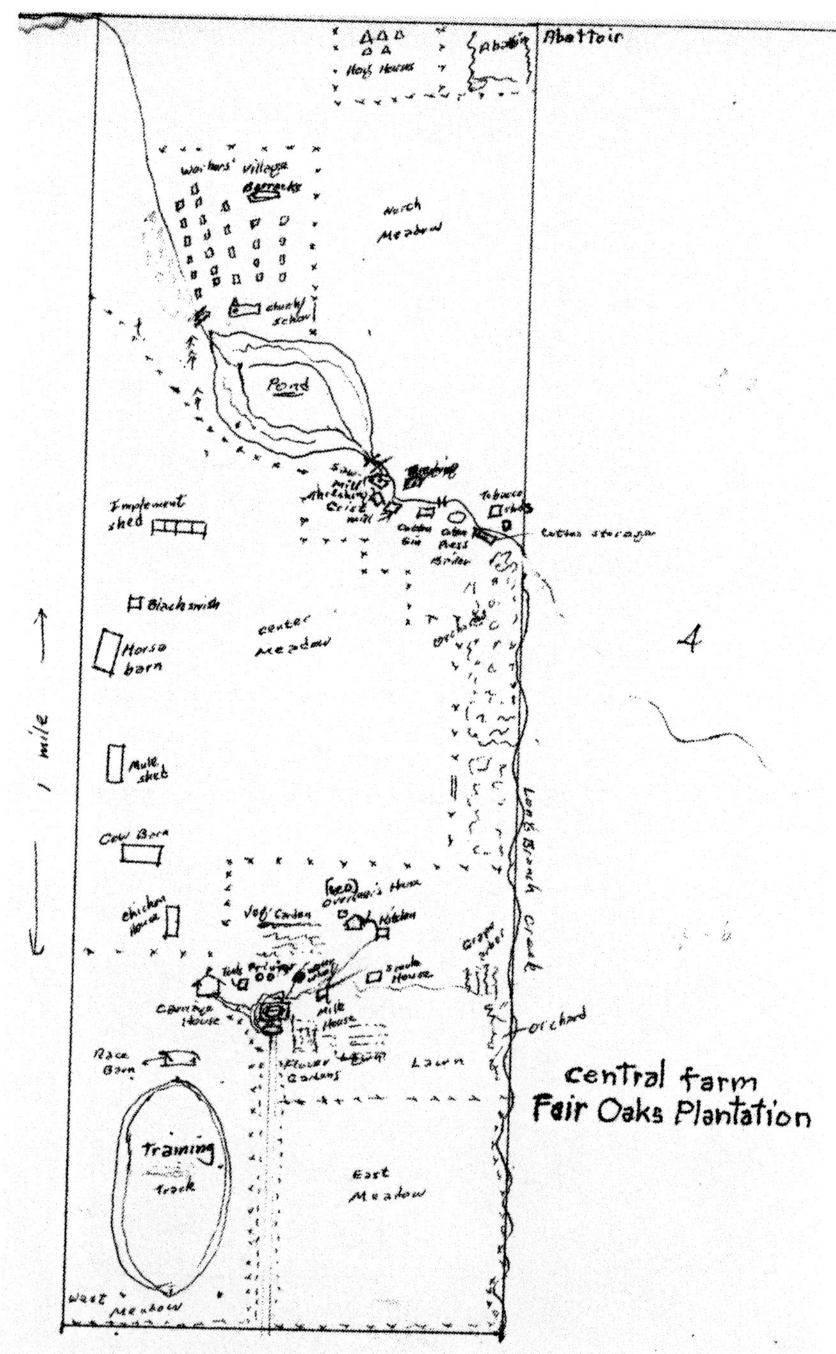
Abattoir
Hog Houses
Workers' Village
Barracks
North Meadow
church/school
Pond
Implement shed
Tobacco sheds
Cotton storage
Blacksmith
center meadow
Orchard
Horse barn
4
1 mile
Mule shed
Cow Barn
Long Branch Creek
Overseer's House
Kitchen
Chicken House
Smoke House
Carriage House
Milk House
Orchard
Race Barn
Flower Gardens
Lawn
central farm
Fair Oaks Plantation
Training track
East Meadow
West Meadow

Book One

Southern Crosses

Chapter 1

Christmas Eve at Fair Oaks

1864

Purple, lavender, lilac, magenta. She was each of these at times—bearing a purple wrath, a lavender sweetness, a lilac melancholy, a magenta daring. But mostly she was all of these together. She was Violet. Violet Lee Storm. And she bore herself as born to the purple.

Actually she was Violet Sutler now and had been since April 8, 1862, but she had not seen her husband, Brent, in seventeen months. He had gone off in mid-July of 1863 to join the Confederate Navy, and she had not heard from him since.

Now twenty-one years of age, Violet radiated a beauty that was a magnet for every man and the envy of every woman who encountered her. The combination of the curved lines of her slender figure, the sculptured contour of her fair-skinned face, the dark hair falling in tantalizing curls to her shoulders, a wide, bewitching smile, and above all her sparkling blue eyes that under soft light seemed to turn to violet, provided a breathtaking picture. She had an effervescent personality spiced by a sharp wit. Her beauty and her bearing gave Violet a commanding presence whenever she entered a room or approached a group.

Violet and Brent had two children. The older, Elizabeth Anne, affectionately known to everyone as Bonnie Anne, would be two in March. Jonathan Jackson, called J.J., was just ten months old. Brent had never seen his little son. He had left before knowing that a child was on the way. Violet, at first not certain that she was pregnant, had said nothing. When Brent told her that he was joining the Confederate Navy, she still said nothing, not wanting to worry him.

Violet had managed the house for her father since the death of her mother, Rosemary Lee, four years earlier. On this Saturday, the day before Christmas, 1864, Violet and her sisters were scurrying about the great house of Fair Oaks plantation, working hard to finish decorating the house before their father returned from his weekly trip to Sumter to pick up the mail and the newspapers. All three wore gray muslin dresses, though of different patterns, with white aprons. Charlotte, 18, who looked like Violet but lacked her flair and had lighter eyes and hair, and Susan, 15, who had her father's blonde hair, greenish-gray eyes, and outgoing nature, broke small pieces of green pine and holly to place over pictures. The house servants were also helping to decorate, bustling with as much excitement and good humor as the others. Mammy, known to outsiders as Aunt Bertha, and who now did the cooking and looked after the children, sat in a wooden rocker and twined thin leafless vines around strips of pine to make ropes of garland. Aunt Sheba, Mammy's elderly sister who grudgingly helped with the cooking and the children, was showing a seldom-seen industriousness, as she broke portions of pine for Mammy.

Evelina, Mammy's sixteen-year-old protegée, was energetically and cheerfully running back and forth, helping everyone who called for her help. Every now and then she ran upstairs to check on the children who were taking their afternoon naps. Uncle Jarvis, the houseman, was cleaning the chandeliers until the crystal pendants sparkled with each movement and the brass shone like mirrors. Aaron, the father's manservant, was helping Mammy by gathering up the garland in large circles, and cleaning up the fallen debris.

Although war clouded the security of their world, the spirit of Christmas was upon them all.

Though given and received in good cheer, Violet was barking out orders like a first sergeant. "Get that bit of evergreen over there"..."Bring me some string"..."Hold this spray for me a minute"..."Mammy, where is the fruit for the dining table centerpiece?"..."Jarvis, will you get the candlesticks for the windows?"..."Aaron, we'll soon be needing a bit of cedar, more sprays of holly, and some pine cones to decorate the garland."

Susan, knowing very well Jarvis's attachment to his silver pocket watch, would teasingly ask him the time repeatedly. Just now she called, "Hey, Uncle Jarvis, what time is it?"

As always, Jarvis immediately dropped his work and with a big grin on his face and a twinkle in his eye, he pulled out the watch and held it at arm's length. "Why, Miz Susan, she say ten minit' after three–jes ten minit' mo' dan w'en ya axe ten minit' ago!" He had saved up his own money over a long time to buy the watch, and he didn't mind how often he was asked the time because each look gave him a sense of pride.

At four o'clock, Violet looked out a front window to see her father riding up the long lane on old Fred, his favorite gray Andalusian mount.

Major Alexander Fox Storm had been a captain of volunteers in the Mexican War. He had met both Grant and Lee in Mexico. Since then he had held a commission in the South Carolina militia, but his age (he now was fifty-one) and the size of the plantation that he was operating, had kept him out of military service thus far. Exactly six feet tall, he had a sturdy build and was in robust health. Only a few specks of gray dotted his blond hair and his short, neatly trimmed beard. He was confident that he could make a worthwhile contribution to the military forces, but he was torn between the need to keep the plantation going for support of the troops and his family, and the need for his military service. Increasingly the thought was on his mind that since it was now winter, he might be better spared from the plantation.

"Susan," Violet called, "run out and meet Daddy and lead him in the front door so he can see the Christmas decorations!"

As Susan opened the door, their faithful collie, old Dan, bounded out to bark greetings to his master. Susan and the dog raced down the lane. Susan jumped up on the horse behind her laughing father to ride with him around to the stable. Then she led him back to the front entrance of the house.

As they approached the porch, Major Storm stopped in his tracks to take in the sight that greeted him. "Ahh," he sighed audibly. He turned to Susan with a wide smile and said, "The house is beautiful indeed."

His eyes followed draped, thick pine and cedar garland ropes around the front door, and again around the outer edge of the frame bordering the English panes of glass that surrounded the front door. He noted with satisfaction other ropes of garland were draped in loops along the side porch railings. Upon the oversized door hung a huge wreath of twisted pine, dotted with holly, cedar sprays, and pine cones, and a large red velvet bow added a bright touch of color.

Violet flung open the door. She and Charlotte rushed out to hug their father, while the other workers peered from the doorway, beaming in anticipation of the Major's pleasure at their handiwork.

Standing in the doorway, Major Storm savored the aroma that burst upon him—mixed scents of fresh cedar and pines and spices. Stepping inside he glanced down the big hall and then through the double French doors into the parlor to the left and toward the dining room to the right. In the hall, a large arrangement of poinsettias and greenery sat on the mahogany card table against the left wall. On either side of the arrangement red candles rose from brass candlesticks of filigree design. On the Major's right, just down from the French doors stood the grandfather clock. A small wooden ornament hung from the key that opened the door to the brass pendulum and two weights. The colorful ornament had been designed and painted by Rosemary Storm as a special Christmas gift to the Major on their first Christmas together. Each Christmas since then it had hung from the clock door key.

Overhead, short branches of pine had been tied with red ribbons around the chain of the sparkling crystal chandelier. A kissing ball hung from the brass end knob of the chandelier. Tucked here and there in the thick sprigs of boxwood were clusters of holly berries, mistletoe, and thin red ribbons. Looking toward the back of the hall, the Major sighed again from pleasure as he noted the curved staircase. The girls and servants had draped loops of garland from the lower railings to the upper railings on the third floor.. The whole effect was one of grace and curves and color and warmth.

From the doorway entrance, Major Storm could see the Christmas tree, ten feet tall, set in the back left corner of the parlor. The family would trim the tree after supper. Under the tree would be placed presents for each member of the family and for each of the house servants. The presents would be opened on the following day, after Christmas Dinner.

With a smile showing his pleasure at the sight that greeted him, the Major said, "It's good to see that your mother's gift for decorating has passed on to you girls."

Violet looked at her father, tears suddenly coming to her eyes. She knew that her father missed her mother as much as they did. Perhaps more. Her parents had worked as a team in the management of the plantation. Both avid readers, they had kept up with all the news, and had kept conversations flying back and forth at the dinner table, as well as during the long evenings spent by the library fireplace in cold weather. They not only had enjoyed the company of each other but also that of others, and had welcomed all visitors with genuine delight and hospitality. There was a saying throughout the area that no one—*no one*—ever turned down an invitation to the Storms' house.

Fair Oaks plantation was in Sumter District, South Carolina, about seven miles west of the town of Sumter, the administrative seat of the district, and about thirty miles east of Columbia, the state capital. The plantation comprised over 1,400 acres of cropland mostly planted in cotton, 200 acres of woods, and a central farm area of 200 acres of meadows, vegetable gardens, orchards, animal barns and other outbuildings, and slave cabins nestled in a grove of pines, for over a hundred field hands. At the south front was the manor house surrounded by broad lawns and flower gardens, shaded by giant oaks and mock orange trees. Thick magnolias, redbud, dogwood, and holly trees dotted the landscape.

Four hundred acres of the cropland lay beyond the woods. This was where the earlier settlers had come, and the family referred to this area as "The Old Place."

The great house was modern. Built in 1850, it replaced what had been a modest house that had been damaged by fire six years earlier. The old house, with ruined parts cleared away and other parts repaired, now served as quarters for the highly esteemed black overseer, Leo. The old outside kitchen served all the hands who worked in the gardens and with the horses, cows, hogs, chickens, and geese. The house servants had rooms in the basement or attic of the modern great house.

Alexander Storm was proud of his new house. He liked to boast that it was the first house in Sumter District to have a basement furnace, running water, and kitchen with cooking stove inside the house. By only a few months he had been ahead of the house at Milford Plantation with all such modern conveniences.

The style of the house was Greek revival of the Federal period. A high rectangular portico, with four fluted Ionic columns paired on either side of stone steps to the porch, protected the main entrance and a small second-story balcony jutting over the door. The top of the portico, adorned with balustrades along front and sides, rested on the columns and the pilasters set into the wall of the house. The exterior covering of the house was white clapboard weather boarding. The highly pitched, hip roof over the center part of the house was of dark gray slate. A pair of gabled dormers pierced the roof, front and back.

An oblong wing extended on either side of the central portion of the house. Each wing had a second story that was covered by a hip roof whose lines paralleled those of the central house. Each wing had two dormers on front and back. The right, or east wing, had a pair of inside chimneys and an outside chimney at the far end. This wing housed the informal dining room, kitchen, and small laundry on the first floor. The second floor included a nursery, and three bedrooms, and a small unfinished room for the water tank. The wooden water tank received its water from a spring-fed brook a few rods behind the house where a water wheel lifted the water to an elevated wooden pipe connected to the tank. A hose made of leather and bound with cotton cord carried water down to the kitchen. Another hose carried water from the tank down to the laundry room. The tank had a spigot to give direct access for the drawing of water for the bathing room and the bedrooms.

The left, or west, wing matched the other in size, roof lines, and dormers to give a symmetrical appearance to the whole house. This wing contained the ballroom with orchestra and spectator balconies at opposite ends joined by promenades on either side. The polished floor rested on springs to give elasticity under the rhythm of dancers.

The main entrance of the house opened into a large central hall that went all the way through to a back entrance. On the right of the hall, behind double French doors, was the formal dining room. Beyond that, with a door from the main hall and with its own outside entrance was the plantation office. To the left of the hall was the parlor, also with access from the hall through French doors near the front entrance. On the opposite side of the parlor, large French doors opened into the ballroom. Another door across the hall from the office led to the library. An interior door connected the parlor and the library.

On the second floor of the center portion of the house were four bedrooms and a bathing room. The bathtub was of wood, lined with copper, with a high back. Additional rooms on the third floor included Mammy's and Evelina's quarters, and the playroom.

Each room had registers in the floor to admit from below the heat generated from the basement furnace into the lower rooms. Each of the main rooms also had a fireplace.

The house sat on a gentle knoll about a quarter of a mile back from the road. A long lane, lined with live oaks, and covered with pea gravel, ran from the road to a circular drive in front of the house. Another driveway led from the circle around the west end of the house to the stable and shed where the driving horses, buggies, and carriages were kept, and where visitors could park their rigs. A connecting driveway made a loop past the back door.

Violet knew that the family would continue to have a deep feeling of loss during this holiday season. They always missed their mother, but the ache seemed worse at Christmas. Mrs. Storm's enthusiasm for all that the season entailed—decorating the beautiful house, trimming the tree, planning special meals and treats and parties, giving gifts that secretly she had been working on for the past year, singing Christmas carols, visiting with old friends and family members, arranging the Christmas Day appreciation event for the slaves at the Overseer's house—always had brought excitement and sparkle to the whole family. Her attention to the deeper and truer meaning of Christmas, the church services, and missionary endeavors to provide some joy to those less fortunate still served as an inspiration and model to her daughters and to everyone else who knew her.

Beyond the emptiness left by Rosemary Storm's death, the family would also feel deeply the loss of the girls' brother, Christopher. Their eighteen-year-old brother had been killed a year and a half ago at Gettysburg. This would be the second Christmas without their laughing, teasing brother, in whom their father had taken such pride and for whom so many plans had been made. Violet and Christopher had been devoted to each other, partly because they were so close in age with only an eighteen-month difference, partly because they were the two oldest children, and partly because they were so alike in personality. She often had moments of sharp despair at the thought that she would never see her brother again—never be able to tease him, fuss at him, ride with him, confide in him again. He and Brent had gotten along famously, taking to each other right from the first. There was never any jealousy on the part of either man. Brent had also taken Christopher's death hard. Violet felt that Brent's profound sorrow coupled with anger at the cause of Christopher's death had had some influence on Brent's decision to join the Navy.

Violet blinked her eyes quickly to push back the tears and took one of her father's hands in hers. Charlotte took his other hand, and Susan and the servants followed behind as Violet and Charlotte called his attention to the results of all their work. "Come into the parlor first," said Violet, pulling her father into the room. "See, mother's collection of angels is on the mantel where she always put them. Don't you think the background of greenery sets them off?" And before her father could answer, she continued, "And look, on the hearth, the Nativity scene, just as mother always placed it..."

Susan interjected, "And we put Christopher's collection of horses and his stable on the side table...and look at the chandelier—isn't it beautiful?" The girls had twined creeping cedar around the chain, tied with thin red ribbons, effectively enhancing the sparkling of the crystal pendants that Jarvis had cleaned so well.

Arrangements of mixed greenery on tables set off poinsettia plants, brilliant with their scarlet bracts. Major Storm laid his hand on the pot of one of the plants and said, "Joel R. Poinsett certainly discovered a beautiful flower in Mexico when he served as U.S. Minister. Just think, he brought seeds back to Sumter District when he returned, and now this lovely plant can be seen everywhere at this season, and in the southern parts the seeds have grown into large bushes."

Major Storm returned to his inspection. He crossed the hall and stood at the dining room doors. Here, too, sprigs of holly adorned family portraits and mirrors. Here, too, the chandelier—all brass in this room—was decorated with greenery and red ribbon. The chandelier had been designed by a Williamsburg silversmith for the Lee family, and Rosemary's father had given it to her when she left Virginia, saying, "Here's a piece of the family and a piece of Virginia to take with you to your new home in South Carolina." From the chandelier hung a large ball. Years ago, Rosemary Storm had taken varied red and green velvet ribbons and made folds which she attached to the ball. Then she had tucked brightly painted red wooden cherries into each fold. Each Christmas the ball was hung from the dining room chandelier that Rosemary had brought with her from Virginia. The Major reached out and lightly stroked the outer edge of one of the brass arms.

Noting this and wanting to distract her father from sad thoughts, Violet said quickly, "Daddy, look at the centerpiece on the table."

On the cherry Queen Anne dining table a circle of crocheted lace surrounded a small cone-shaped tree of live apples. Charlotte had tucked small twigs of boxwood into the spaces between the apples. In earlier years, a pineapple had graced the top of this tree, but, as was the case with so many items, none was available this Christmas on account of the Yankee blockade. So Violet had stuck a perfect, shiny red apple on top.

"I am proud of you all," said the Major to his beaming admirers. "What I have seen thus far impresses me greatly. Now let's see the rest of the house."

The Major was taken on a tour of the library with its walls of books, the plantation office, and even the kitchen and small dining room. Every room greeted the viewer with decorations of one kind or another.

The girls and the servants, giggling with one another in delight that their efforts had been so well received and appreciated, followed Major Storm back to the parlor. He stood by the fireplace and said to all, "I repeat; the house is beautiful. I thank each of you for your special efforts. I know that your hearts are saying to me and to everyone who enters this house, 'Welcome, and may this bit of hospitality help you to find warmth and some happiness this special season, in spite of the War and the sorrows and the deprivations.'"

He walked over to the silver bowl of hot spiced cider that Jarvis had just brought in from the kitchen. Picking up the silver dipper, the Major scooped up some cider and poured it into a small silver cup that was round with no handles. "I drink to each of you." After taking a sip, he added, "Now let's all have a cup of this delicious concoction."

A tradition of the family was to have oyster stew for supper on Christmas Eve, but the Yankee blockade was no respecter of tradition. As a substitute for the unobtainable oysters, Major Storm was able to get some clams from the tidal flats, and Mammy had used the same recipe with fresh cream and butter, salt and pepper. Every Christmas Eve as Mammy had set the tureen of oyster stew on the dining room table, she had commented, "Dis ain't, hit jes' ain't gwine stick ta ya' stumach." This year as she set the tureen of clam stew on the table, she said distastefully, "Dis ain't, it sho' nuff ain't gwine stick ta *nawbudy's* stumach." Actually, the result was a tasteful broth, but it wasn't oyster stew. Nevertheless they were in good humor after their decorating efforts, and they had developed a habit of having to adapt to shortages during these days. However, Bonnie Anne, in spite of being rested and hungry after a long afternoon nap, refused to eat any more after the first spoonful, and Aunt Sheba had to scramble an egg for her.

"She's not yet two," said Major Storm, unperturbed. "She probably wouldn't have liked oyster stew either at this young age. You girls didn't like it until you were school age. I think one has to grow into oyster stew—er, clam stew. Bonnie Anne will like it, given time."

"Damn those...those...those *damned* Yankees!" exploded Susan suddenly. "They are spoiling everything—*everything*—for us..."

Before she could say any more, Major Storm broke in firmly, "Susan! Watch your language!"

"Oh, everyone calls the Yankees those you-know-what Yankees. And they are! I *hate* them. They killed Christopher, and we can't get lots of food and goods, and I haven't had a new dress for years, and we can't do anything or go anywhere like we used to, and Brent wouldn't have had to join the Navy, and..."

Again the Major interrupted Susan's tirade, "That'll be enough, Susan; hold your tongue. I understand why you feel the way you do, but please remember that this *is* Christmas Eve. We are all carrying the burden of worry and loss. Let's all try, at least through Christmas week, to make this as cheerful and happy an occasion as possible. Our worries will be waiting for us at the end of the week, you can be sure."

Realizing that she had cast gloom on what was an enjoyable day, Susan shamefacedly apologized and set about finishing her second bowl of clam stew. The others kept up light conversation bent upon trying to lift the spirits of each. By the time they had finished their dessert of mince pie, all were in good spirits again and ready for the continuation of their Christmas Eve traditions.

Jarvis brought in the stepladder and set it by the tree in the parlor. Earlier he had carried in the box of candle holders and tree ornaments that the family had accumulated over the years. As always, the first to be hung was the delicate porcelain Christmas angel on the top of the tree. This was the Major's job each year. They all watched as he took the angel from Violet and climbed the stepladder. He gently placed the angel on the tree, securing it carefully so that it would neither tilt nor fall. The one-foot space between the tree top and the ceiling was just enough to allow the angel to stand up straight. The Major descended the ladder amidst applause and exclamations of approval.

"Oh, isn't the angel lovely!"..."It's *perfect*!"..."Daddy, you have it just right!"

The ornaments came next. Major Storm and Jarvis always hung those to be placed at the upper part of the tree, while the others hung ornaments within their reach.

They had momentarily forgotten the War. Remembrances of past times blotted out the present day worries. As each ornament went up, cries of joy and recognition and memories filled the room.

"Look!" called Susan, with laughter in her voice. "See, it's the three little kittens!" She tapped the small bells that hung around each kitten's neck, listening to the faint ring. "And look! Here is Mary and her lamb." She rubbed her finger over the lamb's fur.

The Major laughed. "Your mother and I made those for you the year you nearly drove us mad going around repeating those two nursery rhymes over and over. First one and then the other. Over and over. I cut them out of wood, and your mother painted them. It was her idea to put those tiny bells on the kittens' necks and to glue on cotton for the lamb's wool."

He looked down at the ornament that he had just unwrapped. It was a small, beaded purse with a silver chain. He stroked it tenderly before handing it to Violet. "Here, Violet, hang your mother's little purse where it can be seen by everyone."

Violet took the purse, admiring the red and green pattern on the background of tiny beads. With a lump in her throat and her eyes stinging, she gently hung the small purse on the end of a branch at eye-level.

Charlotte interrupted by exclaiming, "Oh, here is the gold star I made when I was little. And, look, Violet, here is the one you made. Do you remember when we made these?"

"Indeed I do," answered Violet. "I was nine years old, and you were six. It had been raining all morning, and that afternoon mother decided that it was an ideal time to make some ornaments for the Christmas tree."

Aunt Sheba, being the oldest, had the privilege of hanging the last ornament, a tiny carved bird sitting in a nest of woven grey moss. She had watched the others do the work while trying to remain unobtrusive, but this she did with relish, taking pride that she was to hang the last one.

Next, they all, including Aunt Sheba now, attached the candle holders on the tips of the tree branches, taking care to secure each carefully so that it would remain upright. They were also careful to place the holders in locations where there would be no interfering over branch, for they were only too aware of the danger of fire. A few years ago, a neighbor's Christmas tree had caught fire and caused much damage to the house. The Storm's tree had been freshly cut that morning but everyone would be watching this tree like a hawk when it was lighted.

When the group had finished securing the candle holders, they inserted short, slim white candles into the holders. After that, while Major Storm, Violet, and Jarvis, remained behind, the others filed into the library and shut the door. The Major lit the wick of a long taper at the fire, and then lit long tapers for the other two to use in lighting the tree candles. When that task was finished, they put out all the other candles in the parlor.

"We're ready!" called the Major, and those in the library filed back into the now darkened parlor except for the candles on the Christmas tree.

"Oh, just look!"..."Oh, my!"..."Isn't the tree beautiful!"..."It's just so very lovely!"..."Oh, my goodness, look at that!" they exclaimed.

In the light of the tree, Violet served silver cups filled with eggnog from the large silver bowl that earlier had held the hot, spiced cider. For a while they stood in quietness while looking at the lighted tree, sipping eggnog, and thinking their own personal thoughts. A peaceful interlude in a troubled world.

Noiselessly, Mammy took Bonnie Anne and slipped out of the room to bathe her. Evelina took J.J. to do the same for him. Aunt Sheba left to start the dishes. She was displaying more initiative than usual. The Christmas spirit seemed to have energized her. Jarvis and Aaron left to get more wood for the fireplace.

Violet walked over to the large, rectangular-shaped piano and lighted the five candles in the silver candelabra that sat on top of the piano. She sat down on the stool, arranging her skirts in folds around her. "Gather around now. It's time for carols.".

The group moved in. Violet and Susan sang soprano, Charlotte contralto, and the Major was a baritone. Christopher had always sung tenor. Rosemary had sung alto along with Charlotte, and the family were of the opinion that they made beautiful harmonious music together. Many an enjoyable evening had been spent in the parlor with the piano. The absence of their loved ones permeated the air. Violet began playing vigorously, *O Come All Ye Faithful.* Music filled the room. When they had finished the first refrain, the Major said, "Wait a minute. Let's start over. I don't know what Jarvis is doing, but get him back in here to sing bass." He called out in a loud voice, "Hey, Jarvis, we need you! Come back in here! Bring your singing voice. And Aaron, too!"

At that moment, Uncle Jarvis and Aaron reentered the room with arms filled with small logs. They had heard what the Major had said, and their glowing eyes revealed their delight at the family wanting them to join in their singing. Uncle Jarvis, in particular, loved to sing and was one to sing softly to himself as he moved about his daily work. His voice was deep and resonant, and he had an ear for melody.

"Here we be, Massuh. Jes' leb ussan git dese logs in de basket an' a coupl' on de fah an' we be righ' dere. Yassuh, we be righ' dere," said Uncle Jarvis.

"Now let's begin again," said the Major. They sang all six verses, and then followed with *While Shepherds Watched Their Flocks by Night, The First Nowell,* and *God Rest You Merry, Gentlemen,* and ended with *The Name-day Now of Christ We Keep,* sung to the tune of the 16th century melody, *Greensleeves.*

Mammy and Evelina reentered the parlor with the children, now washed and in their nightgowns.

When he saw them, Major Storm said, "Carry the children over here by the piano while we sing one last song. I think we should end this song session with *Away in a Manger.* Don't you all agree?" Heads nodded, and they began singing softly.

After that in silence they moved to the tree to snuff the candles before gathering in the library for the last event of this day's Christmas tradition.

In the library, Violet hung little stockings for the children on the mantle, and Major Storm sat in his big leather side chair to the right of the fireplace. Charlotte sat in the twin leather chair on the other side, and Susan pulled up a small woven bench so she could sit by her father. Violet sat in the rocking chair in the corner cuddling little J.J., and Bonnie Anne curled up on her grandfather's lap. On Christmas Eve the Major always read first the poem by Clement Moore, *A Visit From St. Nicholas,* and after that, from the family's King James Bible, St. Luke's account of the birth of the Christ Child. The next day, Christmas Day, he would read to the family Charles Dickens' *A Christmas Carol.*

By the time the Major had finished reading, both the baby and Bonnie Anne were fast asleep. Susan's head was nestled sleepily on his shoulder.

As they rose to take the children to bed, with Violet cuddling J.J. and the Major holding Bonnie Anne in his arms, Violet stood still a moment and then said slowly, "I wonder what next Christmas will be like. I wonder if we will all be together then."

The Major made no comment. He merely sighed and looked at his daughter with bleakness in his eyes.

Chapter 2

A Christmas Gift

1864

Promptly at 10:15 on Sunday morning, Alexander Storm and his three daughters drove down the lane in the inclosed two-seat, one-horse storm carriage. Major Storm had the reins, and Violet sat beside him. Charlotte and Susan were in the back. A dozen slaves, all dressed in their Sunday best, followed in a wagon. A cold, light mist enveloped the carriage and those inside were glad for the protection. The slaves were shielded by a large canvas cover that they had pulled over their heads.

At the road they turned to the right and headed off at a brisk trot toward Holy Cross Episcopal Church in the village of Stateburg, six miles to the west in a sandhill area known as the High Hills of Santee.

As they approached the church, Violet was thinking of the happier day of her confirmation at age twelve, and then the sad day of her mother's funeral four years ago. Suddenly through the mist, the high steeple rising from the tower at the northwest door came into view, the cross on top silhouetted against the gray sky. The indentation of a cross in the front of the steeple, over the door, caught a touch of light from somewhere. A deep feeling of emptiness spread through Violet.

Built about the same time as the house at Fair Oaks, the church was of Gothic revival design on the cruciform plan. Its sturdy walls were of *Pis de terre*, or rammed earth, made from a mixture of clay, lime, and pebbles poured into wooden forms, a layer at a time, and beaten down by hand with wooden pestles. The walls were painted a light buff color. Cypress shingles covered the steeply sloping roof.

After dismounting from their carriage, the Storms exchanged greetings with several of their neighbors who were arriving at the same time.

"A happy Christmas morning to you," they called to John and Sarah Frierson who lived at Cherry Vale plantation, just across the road from Fair Oaks. Sarah was the daughter of the previous rector of Holy Cross, and though older than Violet, the two women had enjoyed years of warm friendship. Violet noted that Sarah had sewn black braid along her coat front and the ends of the sleeves to cover the fraying edges—a device many Southern women were resorting to because of the scarcity of clothing. Only recently Violet and Charlotte had repaired their coats in the same fashion.

"It's good to see you," they said to Archibald Martin from the adjacent Midlands plantation. He replied in a somber manner, "And it's good to see you on this day of the birth of our Christ." He was not much taller than Violet, and was somewhat chubby with a full face and florid cheeks. Archibald had been a widower for three years, and Violet thought him exceedingly set in his ways even though he was only in his early forties. She noted his sly, sidewise glance that lingered on her.

Turning her back to him, she greeted Dr. and Mrs. William Anderson and their son, William, Jr., and his wife, Mary. Will, like his father, was also a doctor. Major Storm asked him, "What news have you of your brother, Richard?" Richard was a general in the Confederate Army. Christopher Storm had admired him greatly and had hoped to serve with him in time. Now Gettysburg had closed that aspiration forever.

"When last we heard, he said he was in good health with no time to be otherwise. He sends notes when he can, but not as often as we would like, of course."

Encountering Andrew Thompson of Glenmerry Plantation, adjacent to Fair Oaks, Charlotte made it a point to ask about his handsome son, "What do you hear from Leland, Mr. Thompson? Is he all right?"

"Yes, Charlotte, my dear, so far as I know. The last I heard, Leland was still in the 9th South Carolina Volunteer Regiment with General Lee at Petersburg in Virginia." He smiled at Storm's pretty daughter.

Turning toward the church the Storms received an especially cordial greeting from Henry Ellison. He was a black man who, with his brothers, William, Jr., and Reuben, now owned a large cotton plantation and the Governor Stephen Miller house in Stateburg, and at least a hundred slaves. The elder William Ellison, their father, had been a slave who was able to earn enough money to buy his freedom and that of his wife and daughter. Then he had developed a cotton gin that Carolina planters agreed was better than Eli Whitney's. The making and repairing of these gins became the basis of his fortune. All three sons had been educated in Canada, and William, Jr., had married a white Canadian woman, while Reuben had married a Sumter District slave woman. All were faithful supporters of Holy Cross Church.

While the Ellisons filed into the church to take their places in their family pew, number 30, the Storms entered by the southwest door, passed by the marble font and two-thirds of the way down the center aisle to their pew, number 15. The slaves found places in unnumbered pews at the rear of the church.

Light coming from diamond-shaped, beveled window panes all along the sides and the candles in the hanging chandeliers reflected from the highly polished wooden beams of the cathedral ceiling, and made the whole interior seem brighter than the out-of-doors.

Violet glanced up beyond the altar rail to the three tall, sanctuary windows of Bavarian stained glass, duplicates of three of the Bavarian windows in Notre Dame Cathedral of Paris. The center window depicted the figure of Christ, with such piercing blue eyes that she felt He was looking right through her. In the left window, St. Peter was portrayed with a belt, carrying the keys to the Kingdom, and a book, and in the right window was St. Paul holding a two-edged sword representing the word of God. Violet sought comfort in the figures, but found none. She looked up over the sanctuary at the light ceiling decorated with dogwood blossoms and stylistic mistletoe. She listened to the music of the great organ with some appreciation, but without elevation. When the choir sang the *Hallelujah Chorus* from George Frederick Handel's *Messiah,* she was momentarily stirred, but when it was over the empty feeling returned. She went through the motions of the prayers and canticles with an automatic numbness. She listened to Father Roberts pray for a just peace. As he preached of faith and charity and forgiveness, her mind wandered to apprehensive thoughts about the days ahead.

This was Christmas. She wanted to be joyful. Instead she felt anxiety and dread. *I wonder what I'm doing here. How could a loving God allow this awful war?* she thought. In the more than three and one-half years of the war up to now she often had worried about what the outcome might be. She had felt deep sadness in mourning the loss of Christopher. She worried constantly about her husband. She had had no word from Brent, nor any word of him from others.

Up to this point she really had never felt fear. Now fear was creeping over her. *If they could not stop Sherman in Georgia, who can stop him in Carolina if he chooses to come this way? What will happen to our family? What will happen to Fair Oaks? What will happen to all that we treasure in the Old South?*

Violet felt cold and began to shiver. Her father turned to her and placed his hand firmly upon hers, his eyes questioning. The warmth and comfort flowing from his hand to hers steadied her, and she smiled at him. She had no intention of adding to his own concerns. She wanted to protect him as he wished to protect her.

They came out of the church to discover that the sun had come out and dried up the mist. The sky was now a deep blue with only an occasional drifting cloud. Yet the day somehow still seemed dull. The air was a bit chilly, but not uncomfortably so. They walked around the right side of the church to the grave of Joel Poinsett. There Susan placed a large red poinsettia plant at the foot of the tomb, and said in a serious manner, "Thank you, Mr. Poinsett, for the beautiful Christmas flowers."

Everyone smiled, and Major Storm suggested that they drive the two and a half miles up to the Claremont Depot to get the Sunday Columbia paper, *The Daily South Carolinian.* Pleased to find the paper there, the Major drove home in good humor.

Violet hopped out of the carriage and sped to the kitchen to check with Mammy on the progress of the Christmas goose and other meats and all the trimmings that went along with these special dishes. The Major went to ask Leo to assemble, in about an hour, all the field hands, along with their children, in front of the overseer's house for the customary ceremonial Christmas Day appreciation with the slaves.

At the appointed time, the Major and all three daughters went to the overseer's house. There the slaves were gathered in the yard. The Storms and Leo stood on the small porch.

The Major spoke out in a loud, clear voice that all could hear, "This is a very special time of the year. We all want to thank you for your hard work, and as I say to you each year, provided that Leo can make arrangements for the animals to be fed and the cows to be milked, everybody will be excused from any other work for the whole week."

"Hurrah!"..."Dat be good!"..."Tank ya, Massuh!" rang out from the slaves.

Then, while Violet, Charlotte, and Susan handed out little gifts of stuffed animals, stick toys, and pieces of fudge candy to the children, the Major gave to each adult individually a ten-dollar bill, a hearty handshake, and a wish for a merry Christmas.

For those who had responded to calls for occasional Sunday work, he had a dollar for each such extra day's work performed during the past year.

A number of the slaves would be going to the afternoon church service at Holy Cross, but many others would be going to the High Hills Baptist Church two or three miles northwest of Holy Cross. For the rest of the week some of them would busy themselves in making various artifacts such as corn brooms and baskets that they could later sell for pocket money. Others would go hunting. Most would spend some time in playing ball, foot racing, fiddling, dancing, singing, eating, and sleeping. Some would take to drinking.

About four o'clock the family sat down for their Christmas dinner in the formal dining room. A white linen cloth, embroidered with red and green and gold thread, covered the large Queen Anne cherry table. Rosemary Lee Storm had brought this cloth with her from Virginia where it had been used by the Lee family for years. It was used only during the Christmas season. After Twelfth Night, it would be carefully washed, ironed, and folded. Then it would be wrapped in white cloth, and placed on the top shelf of the big linen closet for the next Christmas. The apple tree centerpiece and the red bows on the silver napkin holders by each place added bright color to the table.

Mammy and Evelina served dinner, with Jarvis bringing in the heavier dishes. First came delicious, mellow-tasting peanut soup. This was followed by a light lemon sherbet to clear the palate for the goose, ham, and partridges that followed. Vegetables included braised small Irish potatoes, green beans, peas, okra, and whipped, sugared yams. There was lettuce salad. The blockade ruled out the usual Christmas coconut cake, but they managed a delicious facsimile of their traditional plum pudding. Susan was delighted to find the silver thimble in her piece of pudding. This meant that some type of especially good fortune was supposed to be coming to her during the year. They all had great fun speculating on what that might be—until the ridiculous suggestions changed to more serious hopes.

"The Yankees turn tail and race back up north as fast as they can!"..."Brent comes home safe and sound. "..."Just—the end of the war, the end of this damned war."

Silence fell upon the group.

Then Major Storm spoke, determined to change the direction of the conversation and lighten the atmosphere. "Hear, hear," he said. "How fortunate I am to have my favorite bouquet." He raised his glass of wine to each of his daughters as he continued by way of explanation. "Violet, and Charlotte Rose, and Susan Phlox. I must confess I miss very much the missing flower—your mother, Rosemary."

"Daddy," asked Susan. "How on earth did you and mother come up with Phlox for my middle name? I know it is a pretty flower, but *Phlox*! I'm certainly glad everyone calls me Susan."

"Well, Susan, it happened this way," he said with a wide grin, "your two sisters were named after your mother—Violet Lee, Charlotte Rose. When you came along, I thought it only fair that one daughter be named after me."

"Daddy, what are you talking about? Your name is Alexander Storm."

"Yes, but my middle name is Fox, and that is close to Phlox! So there you are. That's how you got your name. And that's why I sometimes refer to you all as my bouquet. For that's what you are—my bouquet of sweet flowers." With a hearty laugh of satisfaction, he again raised his wine glass in salute to his daughters.

"Oh, *Daddy*!" the three girls moaned, almost in unison.

"Well, I've decided I like my name," said Susan. She turned to Violet and said, "Do you remember how Christopher used to tease you and call you *Violent* Storm when you got mad at him?"

"Yes, and if your name had been Violet he probably would have called you *Shrinking* Violet, little sister dear," Violet answered, mimicking Christopher's voice.

"And why did he call Charlotte *Last Rose*? Why?" asked Susan, good-humorly ignoring Violet's rejoinder.

"Last Rose of summer, I suppose. He had quite a sense of humor all right." answered Violet.

Susan added, "Sometimes when I would tease him, he would say, 'You had better stop that or you'll be a black-eyed Susan!"

"Oh, how I wish he were still around to tease us some more. I wouldn't get mad at anything, not anything, he said," murmured Charlotte, her face suddenly become somber.

Violet had been stirring her food without eating much. Looking up, she said, "As Dickens might have put it, Christmas is the happiest of times and it is the saddest of times."

"What do you mean?" asked Susan.

"Oh, it's a happy time because we are celebrating the birth of Jesus, and there are all the music and presents and good food, and being together. And then it is sad because we are reminded of happy times in earlier years with those who are no longer with us—Mother and Christopher and Granddaddy, and Grandpa and Grandma. And Brent isn't with us this Christmas—though, God willing, he will be with us next Christmas. Remember when we were little and Granddaddy and Grandmama and Aunt Nell would come from Virginia to visit with us? But now, with the war, it seems that each Christmas is sadder than the one before."

Violet knew she should change the conversation quickly or all three girls would be in tears. "It's time to exchange our Christmas gifts! Let's all go into the parlor. Mammy, fetch Evelina and Aunt Sheba and Jarvis and Aaron."

They pushed back their chairs and went into the parlor, their mood brighter in anticipation. Evelina followed with the children, and Mammy, Jarvis, and Aunt Sheba joined them. Susan went to the tree and picked up each present in turn and handed it to Violet, who, taking the role that their mother had played when she was alive, read the name of the recipient. She then handed the present back to Susan who delivered it to the appropriate person. This was a traditional routine that they followed each year. They did not hurry, for they knew that time heightened the suspense. Small individual piles of presents rose beside each person. When the last present had been delivered from under the tree, Violet and Susan took their chairs. Now came the routine of opening the presents. Each took a turn at unwrapping a present, while everyone else looked on in anticipation and exclaimed along with the recipient.

"Oh!"..."Ah!"..."How lovely!"..."Thank you!"..."To think that you made this yourself."..."How did you do this without my ever seeing it?"

"Mommy, see! See!" cried Bonnie Anne, holding up a little rag doll that Violet had made, and then hugging it tightly with joy. She then laid it in a new doll cradle that Santa Claus had left. Violet had hoped to obtain a doll with porcelain face and arms, but the blockade had sealed off any possibility of getting such toys for Christmas.

Oh, well, she thought, *it's probably just as well. She's still young. She can play with the rag doll in any way, and it will hold up. If she drops it, it won't break. Certainly she couldn't be happier than she is with this one.*

J.J. was shaking a rattle that Santa Claus had left in his stocking, and his little face filled with delight at the noise. Around him lay small, home-sewn stuffed animals that would keep him company in his cradle.

The house servants were beaming with pleasure and excitement at their gifts. Mammy had received a blue taffeta head wrap, made from one of Violet's party petticoats. She had seen the petticoat a hundred times, but she was as thrilled as though the material had just arrived from Paris. "I'se gwine look mighty fancy when I'se at church tonight!" she exclaimed. All the house servants received knitted scarves and gloves. Evelina had received a tam to match her scarf and gloves, and she put on all three to show everyone. Aunt Sheba took off her soiled apron and tied on the new ruffled one just received. Uncle Jarvis said he could hardly wait to take his new pocket knife and try it out on a piece of wood. He was skilled at carving animals and birds, and small ships and doll furniture, and took pride in the results of his work. Aaron received a pair of gloves. And like the field hands, each of the house servants received a ten-dollar bill from the Major.

Almost all the gifts were handmade, made from saved bits of material and discarded clothes, or carved from pieces of wood. A few were treasured keepsakes and special souvenirs that had been saved for some years, and now brought out as gifts for others. The family had circumvented the tight restrictions of the blockade. They were determined that the Yankees were not going to ruin their Christmas.

After all presents were unwrapped, and everyone was relaxing and sipping syllabub, Violet felt a deep longing for Brent. His time away from the children and from her could never be relived. If only she could have word of him!

That evening after Bonnie Anne and J.J. had been put to bed and everyone else had had a chance for a little rest and a light supper, the three daughters joined their father in the library. They settled in their chairs in front of the brightly glowing fireplace. Since no kerosene was available for the lamps, Major Storm lit a tall candle, placed a hurricane globe over it, and set it on the end table beside his chair. As Evelina served cups of hot syllabub, Violet glanced around the shelves of a thousand books. Many an evening had been spent in this comfortable room, their father, and at times their mother, reading aloud to the whole family, or each reading in a book of his or her choice. Rarely at the dinner table was some book not discussed, argued about, questioned. There were Shakespeare, Milton, Schiller, Goethe, Thackeray, Oliver

Wendell Holmes, George Eliot, George Sand, Alexander Dumas, Carlyle, Lady Mary Montagu, Marie de France, Sir Walter Scott, and Jane Austen.

And there was a copy of what was becoming a symbol of refinement in the libraries of cultural leaders—*A Dictionary of Flower Interpretation.* From this Violet always was reminded that violets represented humility, though really she did not think of herself as a particularly humble person. And certainly no one that got in the way of her family or Fair Oaks Plantation ever thought so.

Violet thought of how often she had heard from her father's favorites, Thucydides' *The Peloponnesian War*, Cicero's *The Laws*, and *Meditations* of Marcus Aurelius. In fact, she had heard from the *Meditations* so much that sometimes she would jokingly call her father, "Marcus Aurelius." She thought of the pleasure she had had in listening to their brother Christopher's favorites, *The Song of Roland* and Sir Thomas Malory's *Morte d'Arthur*. She remembered how her mother enjoyed reading the poetry of Robert Browning and Shelley and Edgar Allan Poe. Oh, how many times had she read *The Raven* and *Annabel Lee* to them! And Violet recalled how her father had given her mother a small book by Elizabeth Barrett Browning called *Sonnets from the Portuguese.* At night, when everyone was in bed and the house was quiet, Violet could hear her parents in their bedroom, taking turns reading aloud to the other the beautiful love poems in that little book.

Her eye fell on Harriet Beecher Stowe's *Uncle Tom's Cabin.* She understood that this book was a great hit up north, and the play based on the book had had an even greater impact. She had read that Mrs. Stowe wrote the book while in Maine, after living in Cincinnati. She had also read that as far as anyone knew, Mrs. Stowe had never ventured south, but had drawn her material from her experiences and circle of friends in Cincinnati. Yet the book had created a stir in both the North and South. *She certainly gave vent to her imagination in the name of philanthropy*, thought Violet, *yet there are kernels of underlying truth in what she says.*

Neither Violet nor her father felt comfortable about the concept of slavery, yet the plantation could not exist without the necessary workers. Violet had heard tales of some slave owners who mistreated their slaves, but her father held fast to the rule, like that of Jefferson Davis, that no slave would be whipped on his plantation—not for any reason. Other types of punishment might be used when called for, but none that would be unfair nor mistreatment of the person. Their overseer, Leo, was of the same mind and thus presented no difficulties in this respect.

Her thoughts returned to this evening of Christmas Day. It had become a tradition that on Christmas night the Major would read excerpts from Dickens' *A Christmas Carol.* He picked up the book, turned a couple of pages, and began to read. "Once upon a time—of all the good days in the year, on Christmas Eve—olde Scrooge sat busy in his counting house..."

At the end, as they got up to go to their rooms, Violet said in soft firmness, "I wish some nightmare could cause those Yankee Scrooges to have a change of heart!"

Since Christmas fell on Sunday this year, Monday would be a continuation of the observance with businesses in town closed and the display of fireworks if any were to be found. The family dinner on this day consisted of left-overs served in the informal dining area adjacent to the kitchen. Attempts to keep the conversation light-hearted became awkward. Each knew that all the others were thinking about the War. Everyone knew now that General Sherman had made good on his promise to Abraham Lincoln to present Savannah as a Christmas present. All knew of the path of desolation that Sherman had left from Atlanta to the sea.

Violet broke the silence. "Father, where will Sherman go from Savannah?"

"Well, he will probably stay there for a while, resupplying and resting his forces. Then, as I see it, there are several possibilities. One possibility would be to go south to Pensacola, though I rather doubt that. Secondly, he might board ships and move up to Wilmington, then move up to attack General Lee from the rear. Or he may go on up to the James River and join Grant directly. Or he may march for Charleston and then on up the coast. This would give him an opportunity to wreak havoc while being resupplied by sea. That probably would be the wisest course from his point of view. Or again he may throw caution to the wind and strike inland to Augusta and then up to Greenville. Or he just may head straight north for Columbia and then Charlotte and Greensboro, North Carolina. Frankly, I strongly suspect that South Carolina will have a price to pay for two reasons–being the first to secede from the union and firing the first shot at Fort Sumter. Vengeance is like strong wine. It can go to one's head and lead to rash behavior, and then have the same kind of bitter aftereffect."

"Daddy, you frighten me! Do you think Sherman might come right through *here*?" gasped Charlotte. "I certainly hope his objective is *not* this Charlotte!"

"Certainly not," the Major smiled at his daughter's pun, "but frankly we don't know what to expect."

Violet pursued her concerns. "Truthfully, do you think that there is any way now that the War can be won? Are we not in for it?"

"Well, I would say the ox is in the ditch, but all is not lost yet."

Violet returned to a constant worry of hers, "I keep wondering where in the world Brent could be. His mother in Charleston has no word, I have no word. What has happened to him?"

Her father sought to reassure her. "Now hold on, Violet, we know that he joined the Navy, and he probably went off on one of those Confederate cruisers that has been destroying the Yankee commerce."

"Oh, my God!" exclaimed Violet. "He might have been on the *Alabama* when it was sunk off the French coast!

"No, no, I doubt it. If he were a casualty I think we would have heard something by now. He's probably on some other ship, far out to sea, where there is no way of getting any word to us."

"Anyway this is a worrisome Christmas," Charlotte broke in, "not knowing if we shall have another."

"It is a troubled world," the Major conceded. "Listen to this from Friday's *South Carolinian*. It's a comment reprinted from a French paper:

> *Three-quarters of humanity...are living in the barbarous state of war. There is war in Poland; war in Algeria; war in Tunis; war in Mexico; war in the United States; war in Peru; war in New Zealand; war in China and Zachgari; war in Japan; war in Afghanistan; war in twenty countries in Africa...Italy, Hungary, Denmark, and the Slavonian population of Turkey, are not, it must be confessed, in the most pacific humor, and, to those who study the general situation of our continent, it is quite evident that the general situation, instead of getting better, goes on from day to day getting more and more complicated."*

"You see, things are bad all over," ended the Major.

Susan asked, "Has it always been like this?"

"Oh, some times have been more peaceful than others," he answered, "but I must say we have been suffering through one of the greatest wars of modern history. Here, the Sunday paper has an interesting editorial about the 'good old days.' It says:

> *"The good old times!" This phrase has fallen sadly from the lips of every passing age. Until the last few years the regret which it implied, did a little injustice to the progress of the world...The world lately, in almost every corner of it, took a turn for the worse, and made the phrase legitimate. We have now, especially in the Confederacy, a perfect right to sigh after the "good old times;" not the "times of the Union"—those we hope never again to see—but of that far happier period when we knew no more treacherous foe than the savage of the forest. People who wake up every morning to read of or witness "goings on" which a short while ago they would not have believed possible under any clime, may well be excused if they sometimes entertain themselves with pleasant memories of the tomahawk and scalping knife. Indeed, there are not wanting a few who maintain that if, by some magical spell we could be all removed several centuries back, we would have no small reason to congratulate ourselves. Who would not rather be a contemporary of Alaric and Attila than of William Seward and Abraham Lincoln? Compared with the Yankees, what noble fellows were the Goths and Vandals? Fancy what a relief it would be, after encountering the vulgar butcher, Grant, to cross weapons with Tamerlane! How worthy an antagonist was DeMontfort, the leader of the Albigensian crusade, in comparison with Sherman, Hunter, and Sheridan!*

"Ha, I guess that's right," mused Violet. "But tell me, Daddy, if you were able to transpose yourself to live in some other period of history than this, what would you choose?"

"Mm, well, I think I would choose Rome in the age of the Antonines."

Of course," Violet exclaimed. "our old favorite, Marcus Aurelius. But tell us, Marcus Aurelius, are you going to read us some of your words of wisdom this evening?"

"Yes, just this, one of my favorite passages from *Meditations.* Now remember, the world was mostly at peace, the *Pax Romana,* but Marcus had to spend a lot of his time defending the frontiers from the northern hordes—the Yankees of the ancient world—and he wrote much of his *Meditations* while in the saddle or in his tent while on campaign. Now listen to this." Without notes or props, he then recited this aphorism of the great Stoic Roman emperor: "'Give yourself time to learn something new and good, and cease to be whirled around.'"

Lowering his voice, he repeated, in almost a whisper, "Give yourself time to learn something new and good, and cease to be whirled around."

Quietly he held out his hands as an invitation to all to join hands as he began to hum the tune of *Bonnie Blue Flag.* They all began to sing:

We are a band of brothers, And native to the soil,
Fighting for our Liberty, With treasure, blood and toil,
And when our rights were threaten'd, The cry rose near and far,
Hurrah for the Bonnie Blue Flag, that bears a Single Star!

And then with gusto they sang the chorus:

Hurrah! Hurrah! for Southern Rights Hurrah!
Hurrah! for the Bonnie Blue Flag that bears a Single Star!

The girls glanced at each other as they noticed a tear roll down their father's cheek. They joined him in one more verse:

Then here's to our Confederacy, strong we are and brave,
Like patriots of old, we'll fight our heritage to save;
And rather than submit to shame, to die we would prefer,
So cheer for the Bonnie Blue Flag that bears a Single Star.

This verse and the chorus brought tears to everyone's eyes. With voices choked with emotion, they quietly bade each other good night and filed up to their beds.

Chapter 3

The Storm Cellar

1865

Each day of the new year brought a greater sense of dread and anxiety to Fair Oaks. Absence of any news of Sherman only opened the way for imaginations to fill the void with all kinds of grim suppositions. New rumors arrived with each return of a family member or neighbor from a trip to Sumter.

After ten days of this the Major took the train from Sumter into Columbia to see what he could find out. He returned in the evening with newspapers and personal assurances from friends in high places that indeed Sherman still was in Savannah.

The next morning Violet joined her father in the office to go over the accounts for the end of the year.

"In spite of everything, we did pretty well this year," she observed as her eyes ran down the notations in the day book and in the ledger.

"Yes, I guess it looks good on paper," her father responded, "but the prices of things we buy keep going up so much faster than the price of cotton that we really are considerably worse off."

"I guess there's not much we can do about that, is there?"

"Well, I'm making something of a hedge against that situation. I'm keeping five hundred bales of cotton in the storage shed until next spring or summer when cotton should fetch a much better price than now. That will give us a good start for next year while we are waiting for next year's crops."

Violet returned to the big question on everybody's mind. "Do you think the War will be over by then?"

"It may be. I don't see how it can go on much longer."

"If so," Violet added, "that storage cotton should be even more valuable. It'll give us a good boost toward getting restarted in whatever kind of world we may have then."

"Yes, it should be substantial in any case."

"Now, to get right down to it. We're going to be in for it, aren't we? We are going to lose this War!" exclaimed Violet, closing the books and setting them aside.

"I'll have to admit that it does not look good. We're going to do what we can to save South Carolina, but we don't have much to work with." The Major leaned back and thought for a moment. Then he said, "You remember the reports of Mr. Lincoln's proclamation of a year ago? He indicated that he would grant a pardon to all Southerners—except those who had held office in the Confederate government or who had served in the Confederate Army with a rank of colonel or above—provided they took an oath of allegiance to the United States."

"Would you take such an oath?"

He hesitated in thought for a moment and then said briskly, "We'll worry about that when the time comes. Maybe it would be a good thing for me *not* to get a promotion."

"What happens for those who take the oath? Then what?"

"Well, then, all who are pardoned will be able to vote, if they are otherwise eligible, and when ten percent of the voters of a state have received the pardon, the state can organize a new state government and be received back in the union."

Violet frowned. "That is not very reassuring--to be received back into the Union--but I can see there may be no other way out if we lose this War. Daddy, do you think we can count on Lincoln's word?"

"I would think so. Probably. They call him 'Honest Abe'. The question is whether he can retain control of events in the face of what may be a very hostile and vindictive Congress."

After another long pause, Violet spoke again, "Daddy, just what is *The Cause* that so many of our men are dying for, and that we all give up so much for? Is any cause worth all the death and destruction that this War has brought?"

"As to the death and destruction and heartache caused by this War, we can never know. I guess nobody on either side figured it would last so long or be so costly. Remember what Thucydides wrote of the beginning of the Peloponnesian War?"

He rose and walked over to the bookshelf, then pulled down the well-worn copy of Thucydides, found his place, and read:

> *On neither side were there any mean thoughts; they were both full of enthusiasm: and no wonder, for all men are energetic when they are making a beginning. At that time the youth of the Peloponnesus and the youth of Athens were numerous; they had never seen war, and were therefore very willing to take up arms!*

The Major glanced at Violet to see if she was making the connection and then continued, "And remember how Archidamus, the Spartan king warned: *If you begin the war in haste, you will end it at your leisure, because you took up arms without sufficient preparation."*

He returned the book to its place on the bookshelf, returned to his chair and, settling back in it with a sigh of comfort, continued: "As for *The Cause*, I guess you might call it the preservation of the Southern way of life."

"Whatever that is," said Violet in a pensive manner as she leaned back in her chair.

"I would say that it is a tradition that aspires to high ideals and the good life. Even if a little far-fetched I guess it is true that we admire the values of medieval chivalry in a way--maintaining a sense of honor, holding out a dream of virtue and service, a respect for beauty and the intellect, and even putting our ladies on a pedestal."

"I would say this War has brought ladies right down off the pedestal to some rather hard work."

"You are right about that. It is amazing what our women have done in running the farms, working in factories and stores, serving in hospitals, and in a dozen other ways."

"But to get back, what has the War got to do with that idealistic life you were talking about?" asked Violet.

"Well, to be more specific, as I see it, we are in this thing in the name of liberty, the freedom to pursue those ideals in our own way, and that means we must fight for freedom from Northern oppression."

"Yes...," pondered Violet. "But–"

"I guess what it boils down to is the question of state rights," he continued. "You know, one of our South Carolina militia generals was named States Rights Gist. You can see what his father thought."

"Oh, yes, I've heard of him, Daddy."

"Unfortunately he was killed in the battle of Franklin, Tennessee, just at the end of last month; he was a good man." The Major's voice had taken on a tenseness.

"Oh, no!" Violet gasped, "I'm sorry. I guess we lost a lot of good men at Franklin, didn't we?"

The Major nodded and sighed. After a pause, he went on, "But to get back to your question, please remember, it was not the Southerners who moved away from the original U.S. Constitution, it was the Northerners."

"How was that?"

"Well, it was the Northern leaders, some of them, who began to insist that the Federal government could intervene in local affairs; it was they who began to deny the right of secession."

"Well, Daddy, was there a right of secession in the U.S. constitution?" she asked.

"Everyone assumed it. James Madison, who had more to do with writing the Constitution than anyone else, assumed a right of secession. When someone proposed that the Constitution should include a clause authorizing the Federal Government to use force against any state for failing to act properly under that Constitution, he and everyone else rejected it. Alexander Hamilton of New York, the greatest advocate of a strong central government, completely rejected the idea of coercing the states. And several of the states, including New York and Rhode Island and Virginia, attached statements to their ratification of the Constitution that they reserved the right to withdraw. And Massachusetts agreed with that. In fact, on the eve of the War of 1812 it was the New England states that claimed the right of secession. And John Quincy Adams of Massachusetts still was upholding the right of secession thirty years later."

"Well, for goodness sakes, Daddy, how interesting!" She shook her head in wonder at what her father was telling her, and then had to tuck back a lock of hair that had fallen in her eyes.

He nodded. "Yes, and do you know that even the abolitionist, Horace Greeley, as late as November and December 1860, was still insisting that states had the right to secede and no force should be used against them."

"Daddy, I simply had not realized all that...but...then why did the Northerners change so much? I don't understand."

"I can only surmise that when secession on the part of the Southern states began to appear actual they started to think of it differently." He leaned back in his chair again and pursed his lips in thought. Violet waited patiently, knowing that he was mulling over ideas in his mind that he would share with her. She had not long to wait as he continued, "Earlier when our Senator Robert Hayne of South Carolina engaged Daniel Webster of Massachusetts in that great debate in 1830, Webster had done a flip-flop. Originally he had insisted on the right of secession. Now he spoke for a strong union. From all accounts that debate was quite a show—two of the greatest orators in the country going at it for two weeks. Hayne made telling arguments for nullification and secession, though Webster gained lots of followers in the North for his views."

"My goodness, that really must have been something!"

"Yes, my dear, it was, but now the idea that the Federal government had the right to coerce a state, to force it to remain in the union was ridiculous, utterly ridiculous!" He banged the desk with his fist as if to punctuate his statement.

"Yes, Daddy, I can see that."

"Violet, that was the issue that led the states of the upper South to secede—the Northern resort to force against the states that had seceded earlier. You remember Virginia and North Carolina and Tennessee and Arkansas did not secede until *after* Lincoln's call for 75,000 men to put down what he termed the insurrection. Yes, a lot of our young hot heads were spoiling for a fight, but it was Lincoln's call to arms that amounted to a declaration of war against the South. Even old General Scott, the head of the Army, had said, 'Let the wayward sisters go in peace.' There is no clearer indication of Northern oppression of the South than this resort to war to deny the right of secession." He sighed deeply and rubbed his temples as though the very thought was making them ache.

Violet still had some questions for her father. "But what was it that drove the Southern states to secede? What do you mean by Northern oppression?"

The Major smiled at his daughter. *She has an inquisitive mind just like her mother had,* he thought with more than a little pride. "Let me mention a few examples. First there is the protective tariff. That is a vicious tax that hurts Southern exports, on account of foreign retaliation, and it means high prices for nearly everything we have to buy. You probably remember from your history books the 'tariff of abominations' in 1828 when South Carolina passed a resolution of nullification. I'll tell you, that came pretty close to starting a war right then."

"Yes, I remember reading about that."

"Then there is the issue of internal improvements. The building of national roads and canals has generally been to the advantage of the North at the expense of the South. We think the users should pay for those things." The Major thought a moment and then continued, "Another matter is the big appropriation bills in which senators and representatives from various localities—usually Northern—slip in their pet schemes. Internal improvements are especially susceptible to this sort of thing."

"But what can be done about those things?" Violet asked, somewhat agitated now. "This just isn't fair!"

"Don't you know that under the Confederate Constitution a protective tariff is unconstitutional, and, with a few exceptions, so are internal improvements?"

"Is that right?"

"Yes. Moreover, under this Constitution the President has the authority to veto specific items in an appropriation bill."

"Seems like a good idea."

"It is."

Violet pressed on, "But what about slavery?"

"What about it?"

"I mean, isn't that really at the heart of *The Cause*?"

"My dear, mere defense of slavery would not explain half a million men, most of whom are not slave holders, rushing to armies to defend *The Cause*, or the sacrifices of virtually the whole people of the Southern States for four years of unprecedented war. You know, of over eight million whites in the South only about 385,000 are slave holders. General Lee himself is opposed to slavery. Long before the War he freed all the slaves that he had inherited.

"I've heard something about that."

"And do you realize how many blacks, free and slave, are helping the Southern war effort? They helped dig the defensive works around Charleston. They are helping in the ordnance shops, and they are driving supply wagons. Many are body servants who accompany their masters without trying to flee. Violet, you know the black Ellison boys over at Stateburg tried to join the Confederate Army—"

"Yes, they told me about that when I stopped by their store—"

Her father went on, "They were rejected, but then they turned their land to growing food for the Army, and they hired out many of their skilled slaves for war work. And you know their nephew, John Wilson Buckner; he's free, but he is as black as the ace of spades, and he joined the First South Carolina Artillery and was wounded in battle."

"Yes, that's true. Still, you have to grant that slavery has been the main issue leading to the division of the Union, don't you?" she asked.

"Violet, my dear, I would say that mostly all the talk about slavery in the North has been to use it as a shibboleth for all these other measures of oppressing the South that I have mentioned. If protection of slavery was all the South wanted we could have had that. You know, in February and March 1861, before Lincoln was inaugurated, Congress, by large majorities in both houses, approved a proposed constitutional amendment that would have guaranteed the protection of slavery in all states where it then existed."

"Is that right?"

"Yes, and in fact, in his inaugural address, Lincoln declared that he would not interfere with the institution of slavery in the states where it existed. You see, he made no mention of emancipation of the slaves, but he did say that he would use his power to collect the duties and imposts—that is, the import taxes."

"Daddy, that may be. Still, there is something about slavery, human bondage, that doesn't seem right."

Red coloring rose up his neck and face. Slamming his fist on the desk he jumped up as he exclaimed, "Dammit, girl, have you been reading that damned *Uncle Tom's Cabin* and other Yankee rubbish?" He strode briskly around the room as if to lend emphasis to his words.

Violet lowered her gaze to the desk. She sat in awkward, embarrassed silence. She could not recall her father ever using that tone of voice with her before.

Regaining self-control, the Major stopped and looked at Violet, his eyes apologetic. "I'm sorry for flying off the handle a bit there. An exchange of ideas never should be cut off like that. Please go on, Violet." He returned to his chair.

With some hesitation, Violet continued in a voice now less sure and more guarded, "Oh, Daddy, I know we're all a little on edge these days."

"As you must know, all the Northerners seem to have the notion that all slave masters and overseers are always beating their slaves, forcing them to live in dark and filthy hovels, and so on."

"Well that certainly is not the case here, nor on neighboring plantations."

"Of course not. It would be stupid to mistreat slaves like that if you want to get good work out of them."

"Of course.

"Yes, there are some cases of whipping and so on, just as some men stupidly beat their horses, but those are never the best farmers. You know that Jefferson Davis had a strict rule against the whipping of any of his slaves, and he even set up a court system on his plantation for the trial of any slaves accused of infractions." He paused and then said, "Now as you were saying..."

Rising from her chair, Violet went over to a coffee pot on the sideboard to pour a cup for each. Handing a cup to her father, she continued, "Really, where has slavery gotten us? Don't we have a kind of class system that is not very democratic?"

The Major took a sip of his coffee, then answered, "You know that civilizations from ancient times have been built on slavery. Slaves in ancient Athens performed the menial tasks that allowed genius to flower—that gave time and resources for the great artists and sculptors and architects and poets and dramatists and philosophers and political leaders to do their classical works. And so it was in Renaissance Italy and England and France. In some of those areas the workers on the land were called serfs, but that amounted to the same thing. And in Africa, the source of our slaves, the Africans themselves continue to hold fellow Africans as slaves—all over that continent."

The Major stopped to have another sip of his coffee, and then went on, "We have to have that labor for our plantations to prosper and to provide here the leisure and resources for higher civilization to develop and grow. And our slaves don't have it so bad, do they?"

"No, I guess our workers at Fair Oaks live fairly well."

"Certainly in comparison with where they came from. Do you think they would want to trade their life on the plantation for life in the jungles of Africa?"

"I shouldn't think so." said Violet with a shudder.

"Of course not. Some years ago there was a great movement to relocate free Negroes in Africa—in the new state of Liberia. There was a lot of enthusiasm among the Negroes at first. But I can tell you, when they got over there and saw what it was like, their enthusiasm cooled very quickly. Not many followed. And do you know what happened? This colony of freed Negroes became a slave state. That is, they acquired slaves of their own."

"Isn't that something!" she exclaimed in astonishment, "so was that the end of that?"

"Well, not altogether. You see, Abraham Lincoln apparently always has seen repatriation as the best answer to what he sees as the racial problem."

"That's interesting. Has he been sending them back?"

"No, but he tried."

"What happened?"

"Oh, something over two years ago, I guess, he got an appropriation of a hundred thousand dollars from the U.S. Congress for colonizing freed Negroes of the District of Columbia in Africa or Central America."

"Did he have any takers?"

"I should say not. William Lloyd Garrison's *Liberator* reported that Lincoln called a committee of free colored men to meet with him at the White House to discuss a plan for colonization abroad."

"And what did they say?"

"They would not hear of it. They did not want to go to Africa or Central America or anywhere else. In fact, the colored people of Queens County, on Long Island, held a mass meeting and adopted a very strong resolution against the whole idea."

"I shouldn't think any of them would want to go back to Africa."

"And yes, I suppose we do have a kind of class society, but then remember, people can move from one class into another. Anybody can become a planter—small farmers and merchants who are industrious and thrifty may eventually buy a plantation. Even a slave can become a planter. How about William Ellison? Do you know that there are three or four thousand William Ellisons, Negroes who own slaves? The serfs in Russia are a lot worse off than our slaves. They are bound to the soil with no chance of rising above their lot."

"I thought the serfs in Russia had been freed."

"Well, yes, the process started about four years ago, but they still have a way to go. And you know even the Holy Scriptures, New Testament as well as Old, speak approvingly of slavery."

"Yes, Daddy, I often have wondered about that, too. It makes me feel somewhat uncomfortable to read that, I must admit."

"Then of course we have the po' buckras, or clay eaters. In some ways they are much worse off than the slaves. Nobody looks after them or cares for them. And it takes some gumption on their part, and maybe some good luck, too, to rise out of their situation. But you know, they harbor a strong feeling against the colored folks. The po' buckras don't have any slaves, but they don't want the Negroes to go free either. They fear the competition of the Negro workers."

Violet came back to her pointed questions. "But granted the labor of the Negroes is essential to our economy, to our cotton culture, I don't see why they cannot do just as well, or better, as free workers. Instead of paying all that money to somebody else to buy them, why not just give that money to them in the form of wages?"

"Properly organized and supervised, I am sure free workers could do as well, and probably a good deal better. But you know free workers are not very highly regarded by White workers or by po' buckras, or even by the slaves. There is great concern—even fear—of the prospect of turning three million illiterate, ignorant slaves loose on society."

"But, Daddy, wouldn't they pretty much stay and work where they are, except they would be free to move about? That would give the land owners and overseers added incentive to treat them well. In that case we would be at an advantage because we do treat ours well. I think ours would stay right here with us."

"Yes, we probably would do all right, but I don't know about all those thousands wandering about the countryside and in the city streets. People would be down right scared."

"Would they need to be?"

The Major stood up, looked thoughtfully out the window for a moment, and returned to his chair. He answered, "Sometimes, yes, sometimes no. Now you take Leo. His father was a Coramantee from the Gold Coast of Africa. They have a reputation of being very dangerous. Some people said that they never would accept servitude—that they either would commit suicide or murder their masters. And we do know that they have been leaders of insurrections. Yet, when you treat them well and respect their qualities, they can be the most trustworthy and loyal helpers. Leo is one we can always depend upon. He has a natural inclination for responsible supervision of the workers. I suspect his father was the son of some tribal chieftan."

"I have always been thankful to have him around," replied Violet, "but to get back to the slaves in general, is there anything we can do about it? Hasn't Abraham Lincoln already freed all the slaves?"

"Lincoln's so-called Emancipation Proclamation did not free *anybody*."

"How is that?"

"You see, he said the slaves were emancipated only in those parts of the Confederate states not under control of the Federal armies at that time, January 1, 1863. In other words, he freed the slaves in the areas where he had no control—no power to do so. And in the border states and areas of the Confederacy where he did have control, he did not free any."

"That is strange, isn't it?" She drained her coffee cup and poured another for each.

"It was a political move. Another attempt to weaken the South and gain foreign sympathy without jeopardizing his position in the slave areas under his control."

"But then doesn't that mean that as the Yankee armies move into these areas that the slaves behind them will be freed, like in Georgia?"

"I'm afraid that is the case. Actually, to look at our situation, I must say that I think you are right. In fact, I have been thinking for some time of offering all our slaves manumission whenever this War is over. You know they represent a lot of money. Of course we did not have to buy a lot of them because they were born here, but all together they are worth probably a hundred thousand dollars in old prices. And just where do you think the slaves came from in the first place?"

"Africa, of course."

"Yes, Africa, but who brought them here?"

"Well, the slave traders."

"Of course, and those slave traders were Yankees. They sold them to southern planters at millions in profits. Now they want to foist manumission on us without any compensation at all. It would be more fair if the Yankees would at least pay half of the cost from their millions gained from the slave trade. But no, they are not interested in fairness; they are interested only in more dollars for themselves. If slavery were a key cause of this War, look how much less it would have cost the federal government if they had just bought all the slaves instead of spending millions to make war on us."

"But aren't there a good many free Negroes in the South already?" she asked.

"Well, yes, Violet, I guess there may be as many as two hundred and fifty thousand—a quarter of a million."

"But, Daddy, that's a lot," she exclaimed, "and they don't cause any particular trouble, do they?"

"No, they don't, but you see they were not all turned loose at once. Having three and a half million Negroes suddenly free to roam the countryside would be a different matter. A different matter, indeed." He rubbed his temples again.

"But surely they wouldn't just be roaming. They would have to work to live, wouldn't they?"

"Yes, if our economy could be organized in a way to give them work, and if they were willing to do the work. Key points, indeed." He sighed deeply and continued rubbing his temples.

"It seems to me," said Violet, "that one of the big disadvantages of depending on slave labor is that you have to pay for their services in advance, while you have to pay for free workers only as they produce."

"You've hit the nail on the head there. And I'm afraid most Southern land owners have been tempted to over-invest in slaves. That has tied up their money and taken it away from investment in other things. Well, anyway, there are bound to be lots of changes when the War is over, but if we are careful, we can manage."

Always relishing a chance to talk history, the Major changed the course of the conversation. "And another interesting footnote," he said, as he adjusted his chair so that he could face Violet more directly. "Do you remember reading about the notorious Peggy O'Neal?"

Violet nodded her assent, but asked, "Do you mean the beautiful tavern keeper whose marriage to Andrew Jackson's Secretary of War disrupted the whole cabinet?"

"Exactly. And you know the reason for the breakup of the Cabinet was the fact that the Cabinet wives shunned her, and Jackson vigorously supported her."

"Yes."

"And do you know who was the leader among the ladies in rejecting Peggy O'Neal Eaton?" he asked.

"Who?"

"Mrs. John C. Calhoun of South Carolina, wife of the Vice-President, that's who." He grinned at Violet.

"Oh!"

"And that derailed what appeared to be Calhoun's direct route to the White House. Everyone assumed that, with Jackson's blessing, Calhoun would succeed Jackson as President."

"But Daddy, what did Peggy O'Neal have to do with all that?"

"Well, Violet, Jackson was so infuriated by Mrs. Calhoun's snubbing of Peggy that Jackson turned against Calhoun. He didn't even support Calhoun for re-election as Vice-President, turned to Martin Van Buren of New York instead."

"My goodness," she exclaimed. "that was a turn of events!"

"But now, Violet, just think what a difference it might have made if Calhoun had become President." He looked at her with anticipation, waiting for her answer.

She thought a moment. "Mm, let me see...well, as President, he hardly could have espoused doctrines of state nullification and secession, could he?"

He flashed her a wide smile and nodded. "It surely would have been difficult; on the other hand, he might have moved the North closer to the South. He might have been the one leader who could have reconciled the sections, and perhaps...perhaps...he might have held the South in the Union under acceptable terms and thus avoided this War."

Violet now broke into a wide smile, her even, white teeth contrasting with the pink of her lips, as she exclaimed, "Oh, how wonderful that would have been!"

"Well, Violet, it's doubtful that anybody could have done that, but if there was anyone that person probably would have been John C. Calhoun."

It was a gray, cool morning in early February. As Violet buttoned her coat and tied on her hat, she heard her father call out, "Violet, are you ready for our swing around the circle?" It was the Major's and Violet's habit to make an inspection of the plantation at least twice a week when they were at home.

"Yes, Daddy, I'm coming!" she answered as she ran out the back door to the mounting block where her mare, Bella, was waiting. She mounted her horse, adjusting her right leg between the two pommels while placing her left leg in the stirrup, resting that leg against a pommel. Then she arranged her skirts neatly about her and over her legs. Bella waited quietly, her ears perked to listen to Violet's soft, loving voice, talking to her as she always did when she mounted Bella. On Violet's sixteenth birthday the Major had presented his oldest daughter with the dark-haired filly. Violet's first comment, after catching her breath, was, "Oh, Daddy, she's so *beautiful*! I have never seen such a beautiful horse. I shall call her 'Bella.' No other name would be suitable." And the filly bore her Latin name with pride and dignity thereafter. There seemed to be a special bond between the beautiful horse and the beautiful girl.

Violet rode over to join her father who was waiting on old Fred. Dan, the collie, was prancing around in anticipation of going along.

Taking more or less the route that they usually followed on their inspection tours, they rode out northwestward beyond the carriage house and stables toward the chicken house where some women were gathering eggs. They then curved around in a rough clockwise arc past the cow barn, then the mule shed where some men were repairing the roof, and the horse barn where others were mucking out the stalls. A further curve to the north took them across Long Branch creek and to the far side of the pond that lay half a mile directly north of the main house. Beyond the pond they approached the slave cabins, cheerfully greeting the workers they saw along the way.

From here they took a detour from their usual route. "Let's go back for a quick look at the woods," the Major called out as he spurred his horse into an easy lope along a path at the edge of the middle cotton field. Violet followed his detour with ease, enjoying her ride on Bella. It was nearly a mile to the near edge of the woods. As they approached it the Major pulled up and said, "I want to check the fence along here. I'll meet you at the Storm Cellar." The Storm Cellar was their name for what they planned to use for an underground hiding place just in case the War should reach their area.

"Good!" called Violet as she galloped on ahead, glad for the chance to pick up speed and feel the wind in her face.

Arriving at the woods, Violet rode up to where she thought the Storm Cellar was, but could find nothing. She rode back and forth and in circles, but still could not find it. *For goodness sakes*, she thought in exasperation, *this is ridiculous*! Finally she gave up and rode back to the edge of the woods where her father was waiting, a sly grin on his face as he watched her return.

"Daddy, I hate to admit it, but I must have lost my bearings. I just could not find any trace of the Storm Cellar. Even Dan's sniffing didn't help."

The Major's grin broke into a hearty laugh. He said, "Follow me, Violet. I'll show you." He led the way to an angle about a hundred yards into the woods, then dismounted and tied his horse to the limb of a low maple. Violet did the same and watched as her father took a careful look at a pair of trees. Then he walked thirty steps to his right, counting aloud so Violet could hear him. Stopping, he brushed away some twigs and leaves. "Look," he said as he pointed to a wooden hatch.

Violet laughed at the deception and exclaimed, "Oh, Daddy, this is wonderful! What a hiding place!"

After a rather long pause while he looked at the ground and swung at twigs with his riding crop, the Major looked up with a somber expression and said gravely, "Violet, we have learned that Sherman is coming north."

"Oh, *no*! When did you find that out?" she exclaimed in dismay.

"Yesterday, when I was in town. The newspaper had a report that Sherman left Savannah two days ago, on the first, and is headed north. No one is sure of his destination."

"If he comes this way, how long will it take him to get here?"

"We can't be sure, but with the heavy rains that we've been having, and the swollen streams and swamps, and the woods and rough ground that he will have to be crossing—all these should slow him down considerably. Some of our leaders think he cannot get through before spring, if at all. But frankly, Violet, I would not be surprised to see the Yankees threatening Columbia within three or four weeks."

"Oh, Daddy, *no*!" she gasped.

"Anyway, I brought you here for a purpose, Violet. I think we should move the things we need to hide into the Storm Cellar right away. I want you to tell Leo to get two trustworthy men and a wagon—no more than that because the more people who know about this, the more likely the Yankees will find somebody to give the secret away."

"I understand."

"You will need to tell Leo what should be moved—the good silver—or what we have left after our donations to The Cause—the porcelain, our paintings and other art work, jewelry, the family portraits—all properly covered, of course—our keepsakes, and the like. I also think it would be a good idea to store some cotton seed and some garden seed in the Storm Cellar."

"Yes, all right," Violet responded as a sense of dread swept over her.

Her father added a warning. "This hatch must always be covered with leaves and brush to match the forest floor *exactly*. Be careful not to come too close with the wagon. We don't want any tracks up here. Have Leo and the men carry things in from different directions, and when they leave, always be careful to cover the tracks."

"I'll remember. I'll be careful," she promised. Violet wondered why her father was giving all these directions to her. He usually supervised activities of this kind. A feeling of apprehension began to rise in her.

There was another pause.

The Major took a deep breath and went on, "Violet, there is something else. I am afraid this means that I must join my regiment to help defend Columbia and our homes."

Violet gulped, "Oh, no! *When*?"

"I expect to leave the first of next week to join Hampton's Legion, or what is left of it, in Columbia."

Sadly Violet said in almost a whisper, "Daddy, this is the day I have been dreading the most. I knew it was coming, but I tried not to think about it."

"With me away, it will be your responsibility to look after the family, and the slaves, and the plantation. Of course, you will have Leo. You and I have worked closely together since your mother died. This was by design. I must say that I have been most pleased with the quickness of your taking over the ledger and reports, ordering supplies, and all the rest. I take comfort in your intelligence and ability to assume responsibility, and I must confess that your help has been of great benefit to me in many ways." He cleared his throat that was blocked with emotion and wiped his eyes with his handkerchief.

Violet knew that her father was pleased with the way she had assumed her mother's responsibilities. It had not been difficult for she and her father worked well together. She discovered that she had learned a lot as she was growing up. She often would bring a doll or another toy into the office and play quietly with these, while all the time listening to her mother and father discuss the affairs of the plantation. She had always been interested in what was going on, what needed to be done, what supplies were required, the planning of the crops, the lives of the slaves. But never did she ever even think that one day she might have to take over for her father. She didn't like to think that he would not always be there for them all. Now he was going to war! *Dear God, keep him safe*!

Silently, Violet and the Major returned to their horses to complete their inspection of the plantation. They rode back to the hog houses and the abattoir where some men were cutting meat, then back to the southeast tip of the pond, recrossed Long Branch, and rode southeastward along the creek, past the saw mill, the grist mill, the cotton gin house, the cotton bailing house, and the cotton storage shed. Continuing on, they followed the creek as it curved southward to form the boundary between the lower half of field number 4 and the central farm. They rode along a path between the creek and the orchards—apple, pear, peach, apricot—then turned back westward into the center meadow.

Arriving back at the overseer's house, they stopped to see Leo so that the Major could explain his intentions and give instructions on the work to be done, not only for the week but for the weeks ahead.

"Leo, it's up to you and Miss Violet to keep the place going in my absence. I know I can count on you both."

"Yassuh. Ya' kno' ya' can. Jes' keep yosef safe an' git bek heah soon ya' can. Don' ya' leb dem Yankee' hurt ya' none. I'se look affer Miz Violet an' Miz Charlotte an' Miz Susan an' ebberbody else fo' ya'. Don' ya worry none. Leo tek cah *ebberbody*."

"I know you will, Leo, and this is a comfort to me. I appreciate your concern." With emotion he cleared his throat and repeated, "I know I can count on you."

They said good-by to Leo and continued on their way in silence. Between the overseer's house and the main house, Violet and the Major solemnly rode past the smoke house and the milk house where some women were cooling milk in the water troughs, churning butter in wooden churns, and making wheels of cheese.

As they dismounted and walked toward the main house, Violet stopped as a thought struck her. She said, "Daddy, what about the town house? If Sherman is coming, maybe it should be boarded up. Shouldn't the servants be moved? Shouldn't something be done with the furnishings? What do you think?"

"I am hoping you can do that, but what about the children?" asked the Major.

"I'll take them with me."

"Certainly not! They are our future. If I could I would hide them in the Storm Cellar until this is all over."

"I don't like the idea of leaving them here," she persisted, unhappy at the thought of not having the children with her in Columbia, and reluctantly said, "I guess Charlotte and Susan and Mammy can look after them. I'll take Evelina with me—and if things get too bad, I'll come back here—fast." Violet paused a moment and then added, "You know we always go to Columbia this time of the year and stay in our town house. I always help the women with the Soldier's Rest Wayside Hospital while we're there. Well, I think I *should* go to Columbia. I know the Hospital needs help desperately. I'll stay in our town house, take care of things there, and work at the Hospital for just a short time."

"I don't think it would be wise to stay more than a few days, not with Sherman on his way. Besides, somebody has to look after things here while I'm away. I expect you to do that. Leo should have your help."

"I'll see that Leo gets the things moved into the Storm Cellar, and then he can look after things all right. Charlotte can look after the house. She'll have Mammy's and Aunt Sheba's and Jarvis' help. It's not as though I am going to stay there long. I know you've asked me to look after things here. And I will. I'll come back soon. It's just that right now I have to do *something* to help! Especially with you joining your regiment."

"Yes, that will be helpful, but you must not tarry too long." he said gruffly. Violet knew that the harsh tone of his voice was the result of his concern for her.

They were both silent a few minutes, thinking, and then with some hesitation, the Major said, "Well, yes, you need to get some of our things out of the house and close it up. You'll need to send the servants, both Aunt Beulah and Uncle Job, back to Fair Oaks. I expect I'll be able to stop at the house a few days myself during off-duty hours and give you a hand." Then he stopped and his greenish-gray eyes pierced hers with their intensity, "But hear this, my girl, I want you out of there long before Sherman gets anywhere near—*anywhere near*! Be sure you understand this, Violet."

Chapter 4

Hail Columbia

1865

On Monday morning, February 6, 1865, everyone was up earlier than usual to help the Major get off for Columbia. Mammy had prepared his favorite breakfast of sausage, fried Irish potatoes, and milk gravy. After he and his daughters, along with Bonnie Anne and J.J. had finished, he turned to Violet and said, "I'll be staying at the town house for a few days until we get orders to move out to our positions. So I should see you there in a couple of days."

"Good," Violet answered, "I'll work all day today and tomorrow to finish getting things into the Storm Cellar. Then I'll come in to Columbia on Wednesday. Do you think I should have Fabian drive me to the station to take the train in, or would it be better to drive in?"

"Oh, I think you had better take Daisy and the buggy. If there's trouble around Columbia, I'm afraid the railroads might get cut before we know it. With the horse and buggy you'll be able to get out of Columbia and back to Fair Oaks when that becomes necessary."

"Yes," Violet replied, "that's what I should do. I'll drive Daisy."

"Incidentally," and now the Major was addressing all the group, "I am leaving a carbine, loaded, in the rack in the office, out of the reach of the children. I hope nobody ever has to use it, but you should know it's there—and be very careful."

"I can guarantee that I'll not be touching that thing," Susan exclaimed in distaste at the thought.

Charlotte spoke up, "Don't worry, Daddy, don't worry about anything here. Just you keep Sherman away from Fair Oaks."

He smiled and said, "I'll do my best. Now I had better get on and get after him."

He rose from the breakfast table. The girls gazed at their father adoringly. The Major presented a striking figure in his little-used gray uniform and pointed black boots as he tied his gold sash and buckled on his saber and pistol. He put on his gray great coat and held his hat and cuffed gloves as he gave an affectionate but cheerful hug to each of his daughters and grandchildren. He shook the hand of each of the house servants who had lined up to wish him farewell, then strode out the back door into the light of a pale rising sun. Everyone followed him out. Leo was waiting outside to say good-bye though he had already done this the evening before when the Major and he had finished conferring about farm matters.

Major Storm threw the strap of a knapsack over his shoulder to carry a lunch that Mammy had prepared. Aaron, his faithful manservant, was waiting with old Fred all saddled up, carbine and ammunition in place, and a pack horse carrying bedroll, extra clothing, and other equipment—and in one saddle pocket, a copy of Marcus Aurelius.

A third horse was saddled and ready for Aaron who would go along as a "striker" to continue his duties as manservant in a military setting.

The Major mounted his horse, raised his hand, and called out with a big smile, "Forward, yo!"

Wednesday morning Violet found that the departure was more difficult than she had expected. The children were crying, and it was all she could do to hold back her own tears. The children could not understand why she was leaving, although she had patiently explained it three times already. Charlotte and Susan's faces were full of worry. Even Mammy was not her usual cheerful self, but went about with her underlip thrust out, as was her custom when she was either worried or peeved. Violet wondered if she were doing the right thing. Nagging doubts gnawed at her, but finally her determination returned and with promises to be back in just a few days, she and Evelina set out about eight o'clock.

She had the folding hood top up and curtains buttoned on the buggy to give protection against the cold air. Evelina was beside her on the single seat. Their baggage was stored in the rear extension behind the cab. A lunch box, packed by Mammy, was on the floor at their feet.

Within a little over an hour they were on the ferry, crossing the Wateree River. At 3:00 they entered Columbia from the Stateburg Turnpike into Gervais Street.

Columbia was laid out in squares, the streets running uniformly at right angles to each other, with uniform house numbers, according to the Philadelphia model. The streets were a hundred feet wide, paved with macadam, cobblestones, brick, or pea gravel, and lighted by gas lights. Most were lined with luxurious trees, many of the evergreen type. Lawns and gardens maintained a neat, well-kept appearance even in the absence of the bright colors of other seasons. The houses, some of brick, many of white frame, and the brick, stone, and stucco public buildings, churches, schools, and business establishments made imposing fixtures on the landscape.

Columbia's normal population of about 8,500, almost equal to the population of Charleston and of Atlanta, now was more than doubled by refugees and transients. Although Violet had been here during the previous winters of the War, she was surprised by the number of people and horses and vehicles in the streets.

She drove on as rapidly as traffic would permit until she and Evelina approached the center of the city. Here she slowed Daisy to a walk in order to be able to take in the whole scene. Now each street became a memory lane for her, packed with memories of childhood and school and growing up during all the years that the family had alternated its residence between Columbia in the winter and Fair Oaks in the summer.

When they arrived at Sumter Street, she paused briefly to look to her left to the middle of the block where rose the twin towers of the Episcopal Trinity Church. She thought almost as much of it as she did her home church of Holy Cross in Stateburg. Here, she and Brent were married on April 8, 1862. *Oh, my Love, how I long to see you, to have your arms around me again. I miss you so terribly. If only I knew where you are, how you are.* She shook her head to get control of her thoughts, and then looked to the outer side so that Evelina could not observe the tears in her eyes.

As Violet pulled the buggy into the intersection she cast her eyes down the street beyond the church and caught a glimpse of the buildings of South Carolina College. *How sad the College had to be closed when the students went off to war, but how fortunate that the buildings can be used as a much-needed soldiers' hospital,* she thought. Seeing the College brought rushing to her mind the great Commencement Ball in December of '61 that she had attended with her father and brother, Chris, then a seventeen-year-old student. There she had met the dashing and handsome Brent Sutler who was in Columbia representing his father's shipping and merchandising business of Charleston. A whirlwind wartime romance had led to the altar at Trinity Church.

Violet had been much sought after and courted because of her beauty and wit, especially since her "Coming Out Ball," but she had been content to enjoy the attentions and company of the young swains, without involvement, deftly and tactfully handling those who became too serious or too forceful or too romantic. She was in no hurry—until she met Brent. The attraction between them had been immediate. Brent was serious about wanting to marry her, forceful about no long engagement, and wonderfully excitingly, *thrillingly* romantic.

Across the way to the north from the church she could see the fine new State House under construction—a project that surely was a symbol of confidence in the midst of war—and beyond she could see the Confederate flag—the white ensign—flying over the old State House where, in a ground-level room she had spent many weeks in each of the last two years working at "Soldiers' Rest," the Wayside Hospital.

She turned Daisy into Sumter Street. At the next intersection she glanced to her right up Lady Street to the Presbyterian Church. A trace of a smile came to her lips as she recalled the rivalry of the Presbyterians and Episcopalians, how the latter had supported the theatre, dancing, and the race course, while the Presbyterians generally had opposed all those things.

Crossing Washington Street, she looked to her right toward the female grammar school and academy. Half to herself and half to Evelina, she said, "Many are the times I have walked along here, to and from school. And often in later years with Miss Charlotte and Miss Susan."

Moving on to Plain Street, still looking to her right, a glimpse of Columbia Female College set off memories of her two and a half years there. Those had been some of the most enjoyable years of her life even though she had worked hard at her studies. These had included courses in the classics, English grammar and literature, rhetoric, geography, French, history, botany, chemistry, philosophy, and mathematics, as well as valuable exercises in the practical arts of music, drawing and painting, and "fancy work." The College had been founded by the Methodist Episcopal Church in 1854, and she had had the honor to be a member of the very first class in 1859.

Within the next block their town house came into view. It was on the northwest corner of Sumter and Taylor streets.

"There it is!" Violet called out to Evelina. With excitement in her voice she urged Daisy to quicken the pace. While Fair Oaks was an integral part of her life and she loved it dearly, the town house in Columbia also held a special place in her heart. Here she had done part of her growing up. Here was where she and Brent had made their home much of the time, though he had been content to commute from Fair Oaks in the summers. Here was where Bonnie Anne was born nearly two years ago. The house was in an excellent location–three blocks from the school, four blocks from the church, and only three blocks from the water works and the fire engine house.

The blockade had been slowly strangling Brent's business. Christopher was killed at Gettysburg, and increasingly Brent felt the need to be more active in support of the Confederacy. It was only natural, then, that he had gone to join the Navy, since in earlier years he had spent many months at sea on his father's ships, and he had become convinced that this was the way to take a more direct part in the War. *Oh, Brent, my Love, it will soon be a whole year since you left. When will I hear from you? When will you come home?*

Evelina broke into her thoughts with a happy, "We is heah, Miz Violet! We is heah a' las'!"

They pulled up to the front of the big two-story house constructed of brick below and wood frame and white clapboard above. The house servants, Uncle Job and Aunt Beulah, came running out to greet them.

"We bin lookin' fo' ya," cried Aunt Beulah. "Ya daddy said ya gwine be here taday." And then she added with obvious relief, "We sho' nuff glad ta see ya. Uncle Job and me bin hearin' all kin' of stuff 'bout dis nauthen debil dat migh' come dis way..."

"Now Wuman," her husband interrupted, shaking his head at her, "don' ya be skeerin' Miz Violet none." He began lifting the bags out of the buggy and setting them on the ground. Evelina hopped out quickly to help him with the smaller ones.

As Violet raised her skirts to step from the buggy she asked, "Do you know what time Daddy will be back?"

"No, mam. I sho' don'," replied Aunt Beulah. Her eyes filled with tears as she added, "Ah sho' don' like de idee of de Massuh takin' off ta go figh' in dis war. No, ah don'. Ah sho' don' like it no way. Bad nuff fer Massuh Brent ta be gone all dis time, an' Massuh Chris' he ain't nebber be back no mo'." She wiped her eyes on the hem of her skirt.

"Wuman," said Uncle Job sternly, "De Massuh do what he got ta do. And dat is dat. Now let's git Miz Violet seddle' in da house. C'mon, Evelina."

After Uncle Job and Evelina had carried the bags in, Uncle Job took Daisy and the buggy around to the shed in back to unharness, rub down, and feed and water the horse. Meanwhile, Beulah brought tea, biscuits, and fig preserves into the parlor. Violet had gone up to her bedroom to freshen up. There she noticed a water stain at one corner where the walls met the ceiling. *Now a leaky roof to worry about,* she thought. Evelina had started unpacking some things, but Violet insisted that the young servant stop what she was doing and come down to the parlor to rest a few minutes.

The trip from Fair Oaks in the buggy was tiring, even for the two healthy young women.

"A cup of hot tea and a bite of something to eat is just what we need," said Violet, pouring a cup of tea for each of them from a china teapot decorated with pink roses and green leaves. She handed a cup to Evelina who drank it down quickly, ate two biscuits liberally spread with preserves, and with her energy completely restored, returned to the task awaiting her upstairs.

Violet remained, sipping another cup of tea, nibbling her biscuits, glad to be at the house at last. Her eyes wandered over the room and came to rest on a side window that had a cracked pane. *And now a cracked pane to worry about, in addition to everything else,* she thought. She wondered if she could find someone to replace the pane and fix the leaky roof. After she finished her tea, she went over to the writing desk, sat down, pulled out a sheet of engraved stationery from a drawer, dipped the steel pen in ink, and wrote a note to the director of the Soldiers' Rest Wayside Hospital:

My Dear Mrs. Fisher,

This is to inform you that I have just arrived in Columbia and will be there for work tomorrow morning. Until then, I am,

Your Most Obedient Servant,
Violet Storm Sutler

She enclosed the note in an addressed envelope and handed it to Uncle Job to deliver to Mrs. Fisher, suggesting that he use the buggy to save time.

Major Storm came in before supper time. After a hug and a quick report on their trip, Violet's first words were, "Where is Sherman? Is he really coming this way?"

"I am afraid Carolina is in grave danger," the Major replied, his brow creased into uncharacteristic frown lines. "We cannot be sure yet whether Sherman is headed for Columbia or Charleston or Augusta."

He reached for his bag and drew out a map. Taking Violet's arm, he led her to the dining room. Spreading out the map on the dining table, he pointed his finger to the southern area of the state and said, "Look. According to our reports Sherman's men already have done the impossible and crossed the Salkehatchie River and the three-mile wide swamp that borders it, and they have reached the South Carolina Railroad here, at Branchville, and are in the process of destroying the track from Branchville to Blackville, right along here." He moved his finger along the map to indicate the location and continued, "You see this cuts the connection between Charleston and Augusta. And you see from there that Sherman could move along the track in either direction, toward Charleston or Augusta or both. But my guess is he will head right up the middle toward us." In anger he slammed his fist upon the table.

"I wonder what it will be like if Sherman comes through here," Violet said.

"It is not a pleasant prospect when you look at Georgia. But it is not just Sherman. It is also the Yankee occupation that will follow."

"I can imagine."

Her father continued, "Surely you have read of the antics of the Yankee General Ben Butler in New Orleans."

"I have heard a little about him, none of it good."

"Thank goodness he has been transferred, but before he left he was seizing all kinds of property, imprisoning and executing respectable people on all kinds of flimsy charges, and he even issued an order stating that Southern women who showed contempt to Northern officers could, quote 'be regarded and held liable to be treated as a woman of the town plying her avocation.'"

"Why, Daddy, that's awful!" Violet blurted out. "How far away is Sherman now? How long will it take them to get here if they do come this way?"

"Well, I guess it's sixty-five or seventy miles or so. Originally nobody thought that they could come close to moving as rapidly as they have. They have to stop from time to time to let supplies catch up, and they are building corduroy roads practically all the way. Still, when they are on the move they can make fifteen miles a day. Fifteen miles a day!"

Like her father, Violet was quick at mental calculation. "Allowing for stops, does that mean they might be here within ten days?"

"I would say so. That also means that by the first of the week I'll be having to stay with the troops twenty-four hours a day. And it also means that you should plan to be back at Fair Oaks at that time."

"I suppose so, but the wounded men will be pouring in if that beast Sherman has his way. I hate to leave when they need all the help they can get at the Wayside Hospital."

"Violet, I can appreciate your sentiments but I do not want you to be in harm's way. You must not tarry too long. I have never been strong-handed with you, but I want you to know I am serious about this matter, very serious."

"Yes, Father," said Violet. She always used the more formal address when the Major used that strong tone when speaking to her.

They separated to wash for supper and then returned to the dining room. The Major and Violet sat around the corner from each other at one end of the cherry oval table, while Evelina brought from the kitchen the food that Aunt Beulah had prepared—a menu consisting mainly of beans and cornbread.

Major Storm interrupted the cursory table conversation to say, "By the way, we are invited to have tea with the Chesnuts on Saturday. I understand that General Wade Hampton and Mrs. Hampton will be there."

"That surely does not include me...or does it?" Although Violet knew Mary Chesnut casually from their work at the Wayside Hospital, she felt a little intimidated at the prospect of holding her own with the older, experienced, and famous Chesnuts and Hamptons.

"Of course it does. You are the lady of the house and my hostess. It is expected that you would accompany me. You know Mary Chesnut, then Mary Boykin Miller, was born at Stateburg. She was only seventeen when she married James Chesnut."

"Oh, yes, I know Mary. Who else will be there, anybody else, or anybody we know?"

"I'm not sure who all, except for the Hamptons."

"I thought he was with General Lee in the Army of Northern Virginia."

"And so he has been. But General Lee has given him leave to come home for a few days."

"How can Lee spare him at a time like this? Didn't he take Jeb Stuart's place as commander of the cavalry?"

"That is correct. Actually, Hampton's leave is unofficial. He really is coming to organize and command the cavalry in defense of Columbia and this part of the state. Fitzhugh Lee takes his place with the cavalry in Virginia."

"I guess that should be encouraging for us, but I don't know."

"Neither do I. But I am glad that I shall be working for a commander like Hampton. I would feel even better if he had the overall command."

"It should be interesting to hear what he may have to say."

"Not to mention Mary Chesnut," the Major added.

Violet changed the subject, "I sent word to Mrs. Fisher this afternoon that I would report to work at the Wayside Hospital tomorrow morning."

"That is good, but be sure Mrs. Fisher knows that you will be there only a few days. Do what you can, but remember, you and the servants are to clear out before Sherman gets here."

The next morning Violet walked the five and one-half blocks to the State House to report for duty at the Soldiers' Rest, the first of the Wayside Hospitals organized by the women of Columbia. The women met all trains stopping at Columbia with food and other refreshments and clean clothing for the hungry and tired soldiers. But those soldiers too sick to continue on were taken to The Soldiers' Rest in the State House.

Violet was greeted warmly by both Mrs. Fisher and her co-director, Mrs. Izard. As Violet looked around the room, a feeling of shock came over her. Although she had served here for several weeks during each of the two preceding winters, she was not prepared for the crowding in the room. All cots were filled, and makeshift beds had been placed in the spaces between the cots.

"Soldiers have been pouring in these last several months," Mrs. Fisher explained. "We now are getting them from the south as well as the north–from the fighting in Georgia and Tennessee as well as from Virginia."

"Oh, dear," said Violet.

Mrs. Fisher continued. "Do you know how many soldiers we have served here in Columbia so far?"

"No. I have no idea."

"Nearly seventy thousand–seventy thousand to have wounds dressed, illnesses attended to, given food and refreshments, and fresh clothing!"

"So many! I would never have guessed it"

"Our problems now are the great numbers coming in and the slowness of crowded trains in moving them out. And many of the men are too badly wounded or too sick to continue on, so they are transferred over to the general hospital at the State College."

As Violet began making rounds to attend to the soldiers, she felt a certain sense of pride in what the women of Columbia and South Carolina had done and were doing. In the first year of the War, women of the South Carolina Aid Association had organized eight hospitals in Virginia to care for the sick and wounded. Then in March of '62 the Young Ladies Hospital Association of Columbia, led by Mrs. Jane Coles Fisher and Mrs. Mary Green Izard, had organized The Soldiers' Rest as the first of the Wayside Hospitals. These soon spread throughout the state and through much of the South, set up near railroad stations. Their function originally was to offer sustenance and care and support for wounded soldiers on their way home or to regular hospitals. At first they had served only at the railroad junction, but then later had opened the room in the State House as a haven for soldiers stranded by the inadequate railroad services.

In the summers, Violet, and her sisters, too, sometimes had served at the Wayside Home at the depot in Sumter. In September of 1863, troops of General Longstreet's corps passed through Sumter on route to join forces with General Bragg at Chickamauga in Tennessee. The soldiers had been issued hardtack and bacon for the trip. The ladies at Sumter had fed an entire artillery battalion at one long table beside the track. On other occasions, when there was less time, the ladies went aboard the crowded troop trains to serve hot food to the men as they passed through. In bad weather, time permitting, they used the dining room of the Rev. Noah Graham's hotel. Then, during this past summer, trains seldom had time to stop long enough for the soldiers to go to the food tables, so the ladies took packaged lunches onto the trains while their daughters and young sisters filled the soldiers' canteens with fresh water. Mrs. Moses and other ladies of Sumter were known to have walked with food to the depot in the early hours after midnight to meet troop trains.

Now, in Columbia, soldiers were having to wait for days for trains to take them to their destinations.

In the afternoon Violet drove a carriage filled with six wounded soldiers the three and a half blocks to the general hospital in the college buildings. If Violet had been shocked by what she had seen at the Wayside Hospital in the old State House, she was in for a greater shock here. Leaving her transferees to be checked in at the main entrance, she went on in to the nearest ward. Cries of anguish and pain and heavy odors of putrefaction, chloroform, and carbolic acid greeted her. She was aghast at the crowding—soldiers were on beds and make-shift cots so close together that one could hardly walk between them. And this when everyone knew that such congestion and lack of fresh air was bound to contribute to the spread of disease and infection, and twice as many men were dying from disease as from battle wounds.

The favored remedy for seriously wounded limbs was amputation. Chloroform and ether had made possible even more amputations, though now the hospital was running so short that what chloroform that could be found was reserved only for the most serious cases. Carbolic acid was known to be an effective disinfectant, though nobody was quite sure how or why it worked. Now that was running short. It struck Violet that there seemed to be a contest between the carrying in of sick and wounded men at the front and the carrying out of the dead at the back.

Yet South Carolina has been fortunate, she thought, *thus far it has escaped the great battles of Virginia and Kentucky and Tennessee, and the marches of destruction of Georgia. And it is fortunate that here a haven could be found far from the battle fronts where soldiers can at least have a fair chance of recovery.*

On leaving the ward, she met in the courtyard a friendly sixteen-year-old girl who struck up a conversation.

"Hello there. I'm Emma LeConte."

"I'm Violet Storm Sutler."

"Hello, Violet. Do you live here?"

"We spend most of our winters at our town house on Taylor Street. During the summers we are at Fair Oaks plantation near Sumter. Do you live here?"

"Yes, my father was a professor here until they turned the College into a hospital. Then he went to work for the State to make gunpowder over at the Arsenal and the Palmetto Armory, north of the water works. We were allowed to continue to live here at the College." The wind blew a lock of her brown hair into her eyes. Brushing it back with her hand, she asked, "Are you a nurse at the hospital?"

Violet smiled. "No. I'm a volunteer worker at the Wayside Hospital in the State House. I've just brought some wounded soldiers here."

Then Emma became solemn. "Are you scared?" she asked.

`"Scared of what?"

"Of Sherman and the Yankees. They are coming this way, aren't they? I've heard that they are. Haven't you?"

Violet paused, then replied, "I have to admit to some apprehension. I guess no one knows for sure, but I'm afraid they will be coming our way within a few days."

"Well, I'm not scared, not half as scared as I thought I would be," declared Emma with the bravado of a naive sixteen-year-old. "Anyway I don't want to leave. We should be safe here at the hospital. But my father says we should be getting our valuables out of here." Anyway," she said again, "I've been busy making pockets to wear under my hoopskirt. Surely the Yankees won't search our persons."

"Sounds like a good idea to make those pockets, though I don't trust Yankee soldiers. Not after what they did in Georgia. I've heard all kinds of things about them."

"Are you going to stay if they come?" asked Emma.

Violet sighed. "I'm supposed to get back to the plantation. In fact my father has practically ordered me to be back there by the first of the week, but I hate to leave those sick and wounded soldiers. Still, I did promise him. And I have two young children and two younger sisters at home for whom I'm responsible. I don't know. I really do not know at this moment."

"Well, if you get caught, come on over here. Come up to our house. It's on the college grounds and Father says we should be safe, the buildings being used as a hospital and all that."

"Thank you, thank you very much. I just may do that if it becomes necessary. But I hope it won't come to that." Violet bade her new friend farewell and sped on her way.

Ordinarily Violet would have taken a tea in stride, for teas were a natural and frequent part of her social life. But on this Saturday it seemed a very special occasion to visit the Chesnuts and meet General Hampton and his wife. The previous day Violet had set Evelina and Aunt Beulah to work cannibalizing three worn dresses to try to make one acceptable dress. Then she went, on foot, to the Wayside Hospital to work for three hours and returned to the house at noon. She was pleased to see the dress nearly finished. It was a mixture all right—the bodice of light blue muslin, puffed sleeves of lavender satin, and the full skirt fitted for hoops, of alternating bands of lavender satin, light blue cotton, and deep blue satin. The scalloped neck of the bodice was edged with the deep blue satin. Tiny lavender and deep blue shell buttons alternated down the front opening of the dress. Actually, Violet thought the dress quite pretty and rather interesting in a different way. She slipped it on and twirled around for Aunt Beulah and Evelina to see the results of their handiwork. The dress fit well, and Violet knew she would feel comfortable and confident when wearing it.

"What do you think?" she asked the two seamstresses, her wide smile causing a dimple to flicker in her cheek.

"Lawdy, Miz Violet, ya sho' do look good!" exclaimed Evelina, full of pride at the way Violet looked in the pieced-together dress.

The Major rode up a little before three o'clock, and within half an hour he was ready to go in a clean uniform and polished boots that Uncle Job had been getting ready that morning. Violet put on her cape and bonnet, tying the ribbons in a bow under her pert little chin. Uncle Job helped the Major put on his great coat, handed him his felt hat, and then Violet and her father set out to walk the six blocks to the cottage on Plain Street, which the Chesnuts rented from Dr. John Chisolm as a town house when they came to Columbia from their beautiful Mulberry plantation near Camden.

As they walked out the front gate the Major said to Violet, "You remember the Hamptons, don't you?"

"Of course. I told you that I'm somewhat apprehensive about meeting a big general like that."

"What about me, a lowly major meeting a big general?"

"Oh, Daddy, that's different. You knew him as a planter, and there you were his equal."

"Except he probably was the wealthiest planter in South Carolina." The Major paused a moment in thought, and then said, "You know he's being made a lieutenant general. I guess he's the highest ranking officer in the Confederate Army who was not a professional soldier. He's highly respected by everybody who knows him—never makes tactical mistakes, and seems to be a born leader. He has a great deal of common sense, is level-headed, and has never taken to drink, unlike some of the officers."

"So I've heard," remarked Violet.

"Some say he could take the place of Robert E. Lee."

"Well I don't know about *that,*" declared Violet, "but I remember General Hampton's son, Preston. Whatever happened to him?"

"I regret to say that he was killed about three months ago. Only nineteen. They brought his body home in the flag he had carried in his father's unit." The Major stopped and cleared his throat, for his words had brought back the sadness of his own son's death over a year ago.

Violet, too, thought of Christopher. She knew what her father was thinking and feeling. To help him she asked quickly, "Didn't General Hampton have another son in the Army? What about him?"

"Yes, he does, Wade Hampton IV. The general wants him kept away from his command."

"Well, I can certainly understand that." She returned to the original topic of conversation. "Have you heard of anyone else who will be at the tea?"

"Only ones I know for sure are John Black and his wife, and probably one of their daughters, Malvina Gist. She's your age."

"Oh, good. I know her from school, and she and her mother come to the Wayside sometimes to help out. Malvina married Governor Gist's son, William. Unfortunately, William was killed at Chickamauga."

"Yes, I know. And did you know Malvina's brother is a prisoner up North?"

"Yes, poor lad."

"What does Malvina do now, help run their house?" asked the Major.

"No," replied Violet, "she's in the Treasury Department. She's the one who signs those treasury notes of Confederate currency."

"That's interesting. Bet she has to work pretty fast to keep up with our inflation now."

They arrived at the Chesnuts' house, and the doorman took the Major's coat and hat and Violet's cape and bonnet. Mary Chesnut, an attractive, confident woman of forty-two years, greeted them warmly. She was wearing a dress of black velvet, low cut, with hoop skirt. She wore a gold band on her soft, dark hair which was parted in the middle and pulled back in bun rolls. Her dark, alert eyes telegraphed her thoughts before she spoke them. Mary presented her husband, James, sixteen years her senior. He was wearing a dark gray civilian suit, though he carried the title of major general. Then she led her guests to the parlor. The only others there were the Blacks—John and Henrietta Black, and Malvina. They had hardly exchanged greetings when another arrival came to the door. Mary Chesnut introduced him as Major General Matthew Butler who had arrived in the area three weeks ago with remnants of General Hampton's old Legion from northern Virginia.

"General Butler and his men are supposed to be a cavalry division. They came by train and are expected to find horses in the area," explained Mary.

"Yes," smiled Butler, "and if we don't find some horses quickly, most of us will be fighting as infantry."

Extending his hand, Major Storm interjected, "And, I am pleased to report, his division is the one to which I am attached, and fortunately we do have a few good South Carolina horses."

When General Hampton and his wife, Mary, arrived a few minutes later, a hush fell over the room. It was as though King Arthur was approaching the Round Table. The General was over six feet tall and weighted over 240 pounds. His sturdy, well-proportioned body showed off his neat uniform in the best military bearing. He had dark hair and a flowing but neatly groomed beard. His steel blue eyes carried a twinkle of self-assurance to punctuate the pleasant disposition of his countenance. Mrs. Hampton seemed almost petite beside her tall husband. Her dark hair was parted in the middle and combed back to a series of buns. She wore a light tan and brown dress with a hoop skirt.

The Hamptons responded to greetings all around. The general grasped Major Storm's hand with one hand and his shoulder with the other and spoke as an old friend. "It's good to see you again, Alex." Turning to Violet, he said, "It's also good to see *you* again. And I must say, you make that dress look beautiful. Is it from Paris?"

Violet immediately forgot that she was supposed to be intimidated and smiled in response, "Oh, yes, it's from Paris–and Charleston and Columbia, of vintage materials."

With everyone seated, Mary Chesnut began pouring tea as she called for her servant to offer generous cuts from a pound cake.

"This may be the last cake for a while," Mary said, "so do your best with it." And then she asked, "Does everyone want tea, or would some of you prefer okra seed coffee? The latter is all we can offer in the way of coffee these days."

"Well, if tea is in short supply, I'll be glad to take okra coffee," Major Storm volunteered.

"Oh, get on, Alex. I was being facetious," Mary retorted. "I've been husbanding this tea for months. It's my favorite English breakfast tea. You see my French tea caddy over there on the mantle?" she asked, pointing in the direction of the caddy. "It is full of tea. Just a few months ago in Camden I bought two pounds of tea, forty pounds of coffee, and sixty pounds of sugar. Can you believe the bill came to eight hundred dollars?"

"Indeed. This inflation is incredible." Turning to Malvina, General Hampton inquired, "Are you the one who signs all those treasury notes that constitute our money?"

"Yes, I do that," she answered.

"You have to work pretty fast these days to keep up with our inflation, don't you?"

"You are right about that. Yesterday I signed four packages of fifty dollar notes. But I feel the effects, too, you know. I had to send a check for two hundred due on a new bonnet. And a length of old lilac barege cost me eighty dollars. Can you believe that?"

Mary Chesnut added, "Just a couple of weeks ago Mrs. McCord exchanged sixteen thousand dollars in Confederate bills for three hundred gold dollars. That makes a Confederate dollar worth less than two cents, doesn't it?"

Small talk and banter continued only for a few minutes. The conversation quickly turned to the subject on everybody's mind—the threat of impending disasters of war.

Matthew Butler asked of James Chesnut, "Any news from the Hampton Roads conference?" General Chesnut had been serving as a kind of liaison between South Carolina and the Confederate government in Richmond.

"Nothing good, I'm afraid. They say Lincoln was willing to make a few meaningless concessions, but he would not budge on reunion, emancipation, and demobilization. So that was that, and Grant is on the attack again in Virginia."

"But what of Sherman? Will he be here soon?" asked Henrietta Black of everyone in general. "We've been insisting that Malvina and the others leave, but she insists on staying."

No one said anything for a few moments. Finally General Hampton spoke up. "I am afraid it does not look promising for Columbia now. I guess we have to give the devil his due. Old Sherman has done the impossible. Nobody thought he could cross all that morass of flooded streams and swamps and be here in less than two or three months. Some had thought he never could make it. But he has been coming through the swamps at thirteen miles a day. At Beaufort's Mills the Salkehatchie has fifteen channels. Sherman's men built fifteen bridges over them in one day. At a point where the Edisto is half a mile wide, they crossed it in four hours. Now Sherman is going to make it in just a little over two weeks."

"You mean two weeks from now?" asked Henrietta.

"I mean two weeks from when he started, which is about one week from now. I understand some of Sherman's troops entered Blackville yesterday."

Everyone gasped.

James Chesnut interjected, "A telegram from Beauregard just a couple of days ago indicated that he still could not be sure whether Sherman means to march for Charleston, directly for Branchville, or for Columbia."

Hampton went on, "General Joe Johnston says that Sherman's army is the greatest since Caesar's. Actually he has two armies coming at us—the Army of Georgia which replaced their Army of the Cumberland, and the Army of the Tennessee."

Before she could contain herself, Violet burst out, "Do we have anybody who can do better than Vercingettorix and the Gauls did against Caesar?"

Hampton smiled and answered, "Frankly, just among us, I think we need Joe Johnston back in command. I like Hood. He is a good man, but he just does not have the ability of Johnston. In fact, in my humble opinion, Joe Johnston is a greater field commander than Robert E. Lee."

Mary Chesnut frowned and showed her disagreement in a whispered aside to Violet, "Caw me, caw thee!"

Butler spoke up, "I would feel a lot more confident if General Wade Hampton were in overall command against Sherman."

Everyone nodded in agreement, though Hampton ignored the comment and continued, "I am worried about the scattering of our forces. Hardee is moving toward Fayetteville in North Carolina, Beauregard is directing Stevenson's march to Charlotte, and Cheatham is bringing his division up from Augusta on the west side of the Broad and Congaree Rivers. We don't have much with which to defend Columbia—as I'm sure you're aware—other than a part of your division, Matthew, only Stevenson's division, and Wheeler's cavalry. That all adds up to about five thousand men to throw against Sherman's host of more than sixty thousand."

Everyone gasped again upon hearing these figures.

Hampton continued, "I have been urging a concentration of forces that might do something, but so far, no luck."

Never one to withhold her opinion, Mary Chesnut offered her analysis of the military leadership. "You do the Anabasis business when you want to get out of the enemy's country, and the Thermopylae business when they want to get your country. But we retreated all across our own country, and we gave up our mountain passes without a blow."

Hampton replied, "Probably our leaders are not sufficiently read in their Herodotus and Xenophon, but I'm not sure it would have made any difference."

Mary came back, "Have we no Leonidas to set three hundred Spartans to make the bridges and causeways across the swamps Thermopylaes?"

Hampton went on, "But don't you see, this is different. The Yankees have had no need for a traitorous Confederate Ephialtes to show them a secret path around the defenses. It's not like having a narrow pass between a high mountain and the sea. Our men did burn the bridges over the Salkehatchie, but the Yankees just built new ones. Our men will set up a defense at a bridge site in a narrow place through the swamps, but the Yankees simply move to other crossing sites, right and left, build more bridges or bring up floating bridges, lay more corduroy roads, and pass on around them, and on to their rear. If one of their corps is held up, the others keep moving until the defense is untenable."

General Chesnut agreed. "We do need to concentrate for a stand at a critical point. Otherwise, all is lost."

Hampton concluded, "I feel more like a King Canute commanding the tide to cease its advance. You know how you can stand on a beach with a determination to stand your ground against the flood tide, but soon you will find the sea swirling all around you. That is the situation we are in against the flood of Yankees headed in our direction."

The women looked at one another, chilled with silent fear. Fear for their men and their families, their friends, their Columbia.

Chapter 5

Sherman's Coming!

1865

Sunday was a day of furious activity. After returning to the house from morning prayer at Trinity Church, Violet and her father went to work to pack the things to send back to Fair Oaks, some of which would need to be hidden in the Storm Cellar. They were gathering china and silverware from the dining room breakfront and the buffet when the Major said, "I'll be having to stay with the troops from now on, and I think you should send Job and Beulah out to Fair Oaks as early as you can tomorrow."

"I understand," responded Violet. "I will," she added, wrapping one of her mother's china cups carefully with an old newspaper.

"And as soon as you get them on the train, you and Evelina should set about getting yourselves on the way to Fair Oaks—as quickly as possible. Understand?"

"Yes, Daddy, I shall go just as soon as we can move those wounded and sick soldiers to safety. We are trying to get all the sick soldiers over to the hospital at the College."

The Major stopped his packing and looked directly into Violet's eyes, "I know that is something that must be done. I understand the importance of looking out for those brave men who have fought for our Cause and were wounded in the process, and I want you to know that I am proud of all that you have done to help. But, Violet, heed me. In caring for the wounded let's not tarry so long that it results in other wounded. And you could be trapped in Columbia, unable to leave for a long period of time, unable to come home to Fair Oaks. *Anything* could happen with Sherman and his troops moving into Columbia. Anything could happen to you and Evelina. The troops may even spread out as far as Fair Oaks. Think of the children and your sisters. We don't *know* what the future holds for us at this time."

"Daddy, will there be a big battle here and then maybe a terrible siege like at Atlanta?"

"I'm afraid we don't have enough men to put up a big battle. We'll delay all that we can to allow other forces to come up and then all together we hope to make a stand somewhere north of the city," answered the Major with concern on his face.

"Then if there is no big battle here, will that mean that the city will be spared the fate of Atlanta?" asked Violet hopefully.

"I certainly pray so. But anyway, we must not take any chances. I think you should plan to clear out Monday."

"All right, I'll try to do that. Don't worry about us. You must concentrate on stopping those Yankees, or in Susan's words, those damn Yankees."

After a light dinner of Irish potato soup and corn cakes, the Major again prepared to take his leave. This time the parting was even more difficult. Aaron and Job had the three horses ready at the back driveway in good time, yet the Major seemed somewhat hesitant in mounting.

Giving Violet a hug and a kiss on her cheek, he said, "Now you have a lot on your shoulders. I have no idea how long these military operations are going to be, but don't expect me at Fair Oaks for several weeks at least. I know you can get things organized and keep everybody together there. Call on Leo whenever you need him. You know he is steady and dependable."

"Don't you worry," Violet called out to her father as he walked toward his mount. "Do be careful. You know we all shall be praying for you."

"We sho be prayin' fer ya, Massuh Storm," said Evelina woefully.

"Tek keer yasef," exclaimed Aunt Beulah, blowing her nose loudly on a large red bandanna handkerchief.

With a solemn face Job handed the Major the reins. Alexander Storm mounted his horse, gave a wave, and with Aaron and the pack horse following, went to the street and was on his way.

Violet followed her father with her eyes, tears running down her cheeks, until he was out of sight. She knew he was big and strong and smart and brave. She and her sisters had always thought of their father as being invincible. But she also knew that he was fearless and daring. A chill came over her as she wondered when she would see him again—indeed *if* she would see him again. Then what had just passed through her mind stopped her cold with shock. *Dear God, please keep my Daddy safe. Please let him come home safe and sound. He is such a good man. And we need him so. You have Mama and Christopher. Please don't take Daddy, too.*

"I hate that damn Sherman and his damn Yankee soldiers, and I sure don't like Mr. Lincoln either. He should never have let this happen. So damn him, too," she said aloud to no one, feeling a bit better for having vented her feelings. Then she looked around quickly to see if anyone had heard her language. She was glad to see that they had not. The servants had gone back into the house. She could just hear Aunt Beulah's scolding if her words had been heard, "Now Miz Violet, ya kno' dem words ain't propah. Tain't propah fo' no Lady ta tawk like dat." Violet sighed again. She didn't care what Aunt Beulah said. It was the way she felt. Quietly and slowly, with a heavy heart, she went back into the house and upstairs to begin packing clothing and personal effects in another small trunk.

The next day was the coldest thus far of the winter. Violet put on extra shawls as well as her cape and bonnet for the walk to the Wayside while Uncle Job and Aunt Beulah continued with their packing. They were scared and glad to be getting out of Columbia and returning to Fair Oaks. Rumors had been flying among the servants of the neighboring households, each fueling the fear of the other. Shortly after noon Violet returned to drive them to the railroad station. They were ready and waiting. Evelina would remain at the house to continue preparation for Violet's and her departure.

The light buggy was overloaded, with Uncle Job perched atop the trunks in the back and Violet and Aunt Beulah in the seat, but they made it to the depot through heavy traffic. Crowds of people were milling around the station trying to get on the trains. While Job and Beulah waited in the buggy, Violet waited in line for half an hour to get their tickets.

When she returned, she handed the tickets to Job, saying, "Now, Uncle Job, these tickets are to Sumter. Remember, get off at Sumter."

"Yassum," nodded Uncle Job. "We kno' dat. We git off de train at Sumter."

"And when you get to Sumter, Aunt Beulah, you mind the trunks while Uncle Job goes over to the livery and hires a hackney to take you out to Fair Oaks." Turning to Job she continued, "Do you remember where the livery barn is, Uncle Job?"

"Yassum, ah ain't fergit, Miz Violet. Ah kno'."

Violet took a small purse from her larger bag and handed it to Job, saying, "Here's the money to pay for the hackney." With a grin and a twinkle in her eyes, she added, "And don't you be stopping at any saloon on the way!"

"Oh, no, Miz Violet, ah nebber do dat!" exclaimed Job, with a grin and an answering twinkle in his eyes.

"Here are the tickets for the train, and here are the passes for the two of you to travel," Violet said as she handed them the tickets and the permits that she had written earlier, just in case their traveling was questioned by someone. With all the hustle and bustle of so many leaving Columbia and the crowded trains, she doubted anyone would ask to see the permits.

Then began another wait of an hour and a half before they could load the trunks and board the train. At last the train chugged hesitatingly out of the station, and the servants were on their way to Fair Oaks. Violet breathed a sigh of relief and drove back to the Wayside at the State House for another three hours of work.

That night, with no one else in the house other than Evelina, the house seemed empty and lonely, and even a little spooky. Most of the drawers and closets had been emptied, and portraits and other paintings removed from the walls (a few taken to Fair Oaks and the others hidden in the carriage house loft).

In spite of her youth and good health, and some fatigue from her work at the Wayside that afternoon, Violet found it hard to fall asleep. Her mind was racing with thoughts. *Oh, Marcus Aurelius, I wish this whirling around in my head would cease!* she addressed the Roman emperor in her mind. She thought of her mother, *Oh, Mama, perhaps it's best that you don't have to go through this awful War*; of her brother, *Oh, Christopher, this awful War has already taken your life*; of her father, *Oh, Daddy, be careful wherever you are, whatever you are doing; come back to us safely*; of her husband, *Oh, my beloved Brent, if only I knew that you are safe wherever you are; if you can, please send me some message that you are safe, I miss you so.*

Eventually she fell asleep and dreamed of Brent. He was smiling at her and holding his arms out as if he wished to gather her up in them, but something seemed to be pulling him away—until he faded from sight.

Early the next morning Violet went to the Wayside Hospital. There she heard that Sherman was in Orangeburg, only three or four days' march from Columbia, now obviously his destination. With this unpleasant news plus the commotion at the hospital, no one even noticed that it was Valentine's Day. Most of the work of the day was in getting men to the trains if they could travel and to the college campus hospital if they could not. Continuation of the removals clearly was taxing the capacity of the hospital at the State College. Now there was a report that another hospital would be established at Columbia Female College, so another task was to get together two crates of bed clothes and a barrel of whiskey to send over for the new hospital—if there was yet time to put it into operation.

During the afternoon the distant sounds of cannon fire added an urgency to the evacuation activities. When Violet walked home that evening she could see reflections against the sky of what appeared to be a fire in the direction of the Saluda factory.

She felt somewhat guilty at not following her father's wishes to leave for Fair Oaks after putting the servants on the train yesterday, or certainly leaving by early this morning. Yet she knew that she was greatly needed at the Wayside Hospital, and that this day's work had helped a number of soldiers to be moved out to more safe surroundings. By Wednesday the city was in near chaos.

As Violet drove invalid soldiers to the depot she saw government employees rushing to and fro, military stores being packed, soldiers moving about, messengers on horseback flying hither and thither, and anxious fugitives crowding about the train begging for transportation. She was glad that she had sent Uncle Job and Aunt Beulah to Fair Oaks last Monday.

The turmoils of movement continued through the night and, with increasing momentum, throughout the next day. More people were trying to leave Columbia. That Thursday morning as Violet set out for the Wayside, on foot as usual, she could sense a growing intensity. People in the streets were grim and haggard, sad and hurried. A block from the house at Plain Street, a flurry of activity drew her attention down the street to the east—carriages and coaches and wagons were forming up to relay the three hundred women students at the Columbia Female College who were being returned to their homes. Presumably some would be going to the depot to try to get on trains while others were being returned to their homes in the area.

Along the center of several of the streets Violet noticed strands and rolls of cotton where bales had been cut and the cotton strewn along the way. Evidently this had been done to keep the cotton out of the hands of the Yankees. A fresh wind was blowing strands and balls across lawns, up in trees, and against buildings.

Most depressing was the sight of groups of Confederate soldiers, in disorganized formations, walking northward, in the opposite direction to hers. Some of them appeared to be sixteen-year-old and sixty-year-old conscripts. Others, many of whom were at least that young or old, were members of the state militia. It all suggested to her that no further stand was being made in front of the city against the approaching Yankees.

This was confirmed that afternoon when cavalry units—those would be the ones covering a withdrawal—were seen leaving the city. On hearing hoofbeats at one time, Violet ran out of the Wayside to the street to see if she might catch a glimpse of her father, but this was in vain.

All of this was enough to convince Violet that it was time to leave. That evening she said to Evelina, "We'll be leaving tomorrow. I plan to work at the Wayside in the morning, but you and I should leave no later than eleven o'clock so that we can get to Fair Oaks before dark. Put everything we are taking in the buggy, and be ready to leave as soon as I get here."

"Yassum, ah be ready ta go de momen' ya gits heah." answered Evelina, with relief that they were going to be out of Columbia at last. She was loyal to her mistress but was becoming alarmed that Violet was delaying their departure so long, especially since Master Storm had instructed them to leave for Fair Oaks plantation the first of the week. As it was, he was going to be mighty upset if he found out.

About six o'clock the next morning, Violet and Evelina awoke to a terrific explosion that shook the whole house. Violet grabbed her coat and ran out into the dark, murky predawn to see what was happening. Seeing and hearing nothing more, she concluded that probably Confederate leaders had just blown up some military stores to keep them out of the hands of the Yankees.

All this had set Evelina, usually calm and unperturbed, to running nervously about the house. "Miz Violet," she said worriedly, "Ah don' much like de idee ah stayin' heah by mahsef."

Violet nodded her head with understanding and patted Evelina's shoulder, saying, "We'll get right to work loading the buggy now. Between the two of us, if we work fast we should have it all done in less than an hour. I've just got to help with moving the last of the men. Mrs. Fisher said they need everyone they can get to help. You can help me move the soldiers, and then we'll come back here and hitch up Daisy and be off to Fair Oaks."

When they arrived at the State House Mrs. Fisher greeted them with pleasure. "Oh, I'm so glad you are here. We just have to get these last men moved out and gather up our things."

"Evelina and I will do what we can to help you," Violet said, "but we must leave by eleven so that we can get to our home, in the country near Sumter, before dark."

"I understand, Violet; I'm afraid this is our doomsday. We'll be closing up this place by noon anyway."

After Violet and the other helpers had made the rounds with food and were putting new dressings on old wounds, a whir of artillery shells began passing overhead, and shells began bursting on the grounds. Everyone looked at each other in dismay. Then they began hurrying around, moving patients to one corner and then another, out into the hall and then back. Caught in an artillery barrage they had an overpowering feeling that if they would move, just a little way, over there, or over there, they would be safer. Violet knew that one place that would not be safer was in front of a window, but she looked out anyway. She looked out in time to see two cannon balls bounce off the granite walls of the new State House that was under construction. The balls did no damage to the structure other than leave pock marks on the walls. Then the cannonading ended. That was all. Apparently the Yankees were just announcing that they were coming.

Half an hour later, Mrs. Fisher relayed a report that the Yankees were putting in a pontoon bridge across the Broad River and that Mayor Thomas Jefferson Goodwyn had ridden out under a white flag to surrender the city. This meant that there would be no fighting in the city, and, he hoped, it would be protected from pillage and destruction.

Leaving Evelina behind to help in cleaning up, Violet instructed her to return to the house as soon as she could get away and to try to pick up some groceries on the way. Then Violet took what she determined would be the last carriage load of sick and wounded soldiers to the station. There the congestion was worse than ever. It was after one o'clock before Violet could find anybody to take her convalescents off the carriage and to a train. They took the horse and carriage to help with movement around the depot.

Quickly Violet walked back toward the old State House. Looking up through the trees, she came to an abrupt halt, stunned at what was happening. She saw the Confederate flag atop the capitol being lowered—the beautiful flag with a pure white field and the battle flag emblem of blue diagonal crossed bars, carrying rows of thirteen white stars, on a red background in the upper corner next to the flag pole. As the flag slowly came down, the wind caught it, and it sparkled as new against the dark gray sky. Then it was out of sight, leaving only the naked flag pole. Violet stood as if in a trance, staring at the gloomy sky. Then she saw the Stars and Stripes flag of the Union rising up the pole. She sobbed as though her heart were breaking, without embarrassment, for all around her others were crying at the sight, some visibly trying to control their own outbursts of dismay and sadness. She felt as though she were being invited to the funeral of her own state.

She avoided the State House and continued on up Sumter Street. At each corner she had to wait for blue-clad Yankee troops to march by. Presently a hush came over the people lining the street. She looked up to see General Sherman himself, surrounded by aides, and accompanied by General Howard, commander of the Army of the Tennessee, riding down the street with seemingly endless columns of troops following. There were no cheers, no jeers, just resignation and heartbreak on the part of the watchers. Sherman came close enough for her to see his fiery, seemingly unseeing eyes. For a moment she reverted back to her childhood impulses and wished she had a rock to throw at him. She shook her head to clear her thoughts. She did not care for Sherman's straggly beard, but she had to admit that his uniform was neat, his rounded hat set squarely on his head, and he did look like an officer—if not a gentleman. *I know you're supposed to love your enemies, but I hate you, you northern devil. I hate what you have done to my country and to my people. I hate what you did to my brother. I hate what you are doing right now, riding through the streets of my Columbia.*

Chapter 6

Rivers of Fire

1865

It was mid-afternoon by the time Violet entered the house. Evelina met her in the hall and said, "See whut ah git," as she led Violet to the kitchen. "Look!"

There on the oak table was a small sack of corn meal, some wheat flour, dried beans, bacon, and some bread and cheese.

Violet gasped at the sight of so much food. "How did you get all this?" she asked.

"De stores all be open, an' ebberbody jes' wen' in an' git whut dey wan'."

"Evelina, do you mean everybody, just pillaging?"

"Ah don' kno' whut dat is, buh all de storekeepers say dey don' wan' no Yankees gittin' dere food, so dey jes' gib it all ta us. Hit dint cost nuttin'. Dey jes' said ta hep mahself ta whut ah want. Ebberbudy in sech uh hurry dat lots of stuff wuz jes' spill'd out on de street."

"Well, for goodness sake. We'll eat some of the bread and cheese now and pack the rest to put in the buggy. This is amazing!"

"Yas, Miz Violet. Is we gwine be ta de country now?" asked Evelina hopefully.

"Evelina, you know I had planned to leave today by eleven, but it's so late now that we probably should wait until early morning to leave. I just don't think it's wise to travel in darkness. There's no telling who we might run into. And the roads will be so dark if the sky remains overcast as it is now. We wouldn't have moonlight to guide our way." Violet paused in thought, and reaffirmed her decision as she walked into the parlor, "Yes, we'll leave at dawn tomorrow morning."

Suddenly the front door crashed open and a young Yankee soldier, carrying Spencer rifle, bounded in. His streaked face was more muddy than bearded, and strands of dirty blond hair ran down from beneath his tattered kepi. His dark blue uniform was worn and muddy, and the only shine on his shoes was from water puddles in the street. He looked about quickly and then spied Violet who was standing perfectly still near the center of the parlor. As Evelina ran to a neutral corner, the intruder walked to Violet and said with a slur, "Well, what do you think of the Yankees now?"

Violet answered coolly, "Do you expect a favorable opinion—especially after you have entered my house uninvited?"

"No, dammit, but you are afeared of us and that's enough."

"No, I do not fear you," said Violet in a calm voice, looking the soldier steadily in his eyes.

"Not yet?" asked the soldier derisively, implying she soon would be.

"Not now. Not ever."

With one hand he grabbed Violet's arm and with the other thrust his rifle into the side of her head. Violet did nothing that might trigger the deadly weapon. She had resolved never to panic again, and she held to her resolve.

"Now, 'ere you afeared?"

Violet answered firmly and calmly, "No, I am not afraid of you. I only look upon you with complete contempt. Now I can appreciate why our brave men have been fighting so long—to protect us from the likes of you, you damn Yankee."

"Oh, Lawdy, Miz Violet," moaned Evelina who had sunk to her knees in the corner, trembling with fright.

"Now hold on there," said the soldier to Violet, ignoring Evelina's outburst.

Violet kept right on talking, her voice at a low pitch, "Is this an example of Yankee gallantry and bravery, going around attacking unarmed women?"

"We just want to scare you people so you will stop afightin' and end this war."

"Well, I'm not afraid of you. I'm furious with you." She curled her lips and spewed forth a torrent of invective, "You damned, insolent wretch. You yellow puppy, you infamous dastard. Are you a total son of a bitch, or do you have a mother?"

"Law, Miz Violet, ya done cook our goose now!" whimpered Evelina.

"Now you be careful whatcha asayin'!" the soldier warned.

"Tell me soldier, if that's what you are, what is your mother's name?"

Without even thinking he blurted out, "Edna Murray."

"And where are you from?"

"Iowa."

"Where in Iowa?"

"Cedar Rapids, but why are you askin' me all this?"

"Because I am going to write to your mother and tell her what a bastard she has for a son, a man who would hold a gun to the head of an unarmed woman!"

The soldier looked surprised and then lowered his rifle. He said, "Aw, shucks, Ma'am, I meant no harm. Like I said, we just want to scare you so we can get this war over with."

"Then get out of here," she said. "Leave this house."

Releasing his grip, he said with respect in his voice, "Dammit, lady, you have pluck enough for a whole regiment." He turned and bolted out the door.

Quickly Violet crossed over to Evelina and lifted the girl from the floor. "Stop shaking, Evelina. We're all right. Now come on, we're getting out now! I'm afraid it's too late to get back to the plantation this evening and we'll go tomorrow early, but we are not staying in this house another minute. I'm beginning to understand why Daddy was so insistent about our leaving earlier. We'll go over to the hospital on the college campus where it should be safe."

"Yassum, I be goin' out an' harness Daisy righ' now." She started to leave but Violet stopped her.

"Wait a minute. Listen. It may be hard to get the horse and buggy over to the hospital without someone trying to take them. I think you had better drive over, and I'll walk. If anybody stops you and asks where you are going, you just say, 'I'm going to my freedom.' Understand? Just say, 'I'm going to my freedom.' and drive on straight to the hospital. The Yankees are more likely to let you go on."

"Yassum, I'se goin' ta ma freedom."

They put the top of the buggy up and tucked their food and bags under blankets in the back. When the rig was ready, Violet ran back to lock the doors of the house and then returned to point the way to go. Evelina knew the city and would have no trouble finding her way, but Violet wanted to be doubly sure. "Now do you know which one is Bull Street, the second street over that way?"

"Yassum, ah knows."

"Go there and turn right, that way, and just keep going until you come to the college buildings. There should be a shed in back where you can put Daisy and the buggy."

"Yassum, Miz Violet."

"And if there is a guard at the hospital, tell him you are driving for Mrs. LeConte. Here I have written the name down so you can show it."

"Yassum. Doncha worry. Ah be dere."

"All right, I'll walk through the center and meet you there in a little while."

Sumter Street was still crowded with people, Yankee soldiers, refugees, freed slaves, and local citizens. At the corner of Lady Street, Violet noticed an altercation between a tall Yankee soldier and a frail woman who was pushing a wheelbarrow and leading a little girl.

"Sir, please don't take this food. It is all I have for my child," the woman was saying in broken English. "I've just lost everything else."

"What's in the bag?" asked the soldier briskly.

"Just flour. My husband and I came to this country from France six years ago, to New Jersey. We made application to become citizens of the United States." She thrust papers toward him. "But my husband could not get a good job in New Jersey, and we moved to Charleston. There he died of yellow fever. I came here to get away from the bombardments at Charleston. Now I have nothing. Only the good Dr. Sill gave us food and shelter. I must have food for my child until we can find other help now. Please, Sir, let us by."

The woman dropped to her knees in supplication. The soldier drew from his belt a big Bowie knife and brandished it in her pleading face. Then he picked up the bag of flour, split it open, and let its contents spill onto the street.

"Take, eat," he laughed and moved on, leaving the woman scraping up what spilled flour she could with her hands and crying softly to herself.

Violet hurried on, passed between Trinity Church and the State House, and arrived at the college campus only partly out of breath. Directly she found Emma LeConte.

"Emma," she said, "I guess I'll have to accept your kind invitation to stay here overnight. I'm afraid it's too late to start out for the country." She told Emma about the Yankee soldier breaking into the house. She also told her about the event she had just witnessed on the street with the woman and child.

"Oh, I'm so glad you came here," said Emma warmly. "Did you come alone or is there anyone else with you?"

"I brought my maid servant, Evelina. I had her drive over separately. I've heard that some roughnecks have tried to steal horses so they can get out of town faster, or else the Yankees might grab it—but they might let a 'freed slave' keep on going. She's a smart girl, and I expect she'll make it here all right. I told her to find a shed in the back where we can keep our horse and buggy in safety overnight."

"Good idea. They should be all right there. Let's go find your maid servant."

Walking back to the sheds, they found Evelina just loosening Daisy's harness. Emma knew of a cot where Evelina could sleep, in a room with several other servant girls, near the stable. She said she would have some food sent round to Evelina who seemed satisfied with the arrangements.

"Come, meet my mother and have some supper with us," said Emma.

"Thank you, I'd like that. You are so good to take us in like this."

"Glad to. Think nothing of it. I'm sure you would help me out if I needed it."

As they walked across the grounds they were pleased to see the arrival of a well-ordered Yankee rifle company to post guards for the protection of the hospital.

"My father left yesterday with as many of our valuables as he could carry. Since he's been prominent in the making of gunpowder, he very likely would be taken prisoner by the Yankees. He was sure that we would be safe here at the hospital."

"Yes, I would think so," Violet remarked, "and it looks as though lots of other people are seeking refuge here in that hope."

"Yes, they are."

After a supper of beans and corn bread in the makeshift basement dining room-sitting room of the LeContes, Emma went along with Violet for a walk around the campus Horseshoe.

"I was looking out of my upstairs bedroom window this afternoon when they hauled down our flag over the State House and ran up the Stars and Stripes flag of the Union. I nearly choked."

"I was walking toward that old State House from the station when I looked up and saw it. My heart felt as though it would break. I just stood there and cried. So did a lot of other people around me." Violet told her.

"It was awful. What a horrid sight! I couldn't look at that other flag—that hateful symbol of despotism, and I left the window and went downstairs to tell mother."

"Yes, it seemed as if we were seeing the end of the world."

"I would rather be ruled by England or France, or almost any other nation but the Yankees."

Violet never had been one to despair, but she was close to it now. They completed their walk around the curve and back toward Sumter Street in silence.

Approaching the street, dusk now upon them, Violet was aware of the din of movement of horses and people and the echoes of animated conversations crossing each other. Crisp Yankee accents competed with soft Southern intonations. She heard someone crying in the distance. She put both of her hands to her temples as lines from Dante's *Inferno* rushed through her mind:

> *There sighs, lamentations, and loud wailings resounded through the starless air, so that at first it made me weep; strange tongues, horrible languages, words of pain, tones of anger, voices loud and hoarse, and with these the sound of hands, made a tumult which is whirling through the air forever dark, as sand eddies in the whirlwind.*

After a few more moments of this, Emma said, "Let's go back. I've had enough of this, haven't you?"

"Oh, yes!" exclaimed Violet, wrinkling her nose in disgust.

"We have an extra cot for you in my room. We've been sleeping in the basement since the artillery shells started coming in, but now I think that danger has passed, don't you?"

"Oh, yes, with the Yankees here they won't be firing any more shells into the city. We should be safe from anything like that now, thank goodness," answered Violet, taking a deep breath of relief that the worst must be over now.

At the house, Violet retrieved her valise and followed Emma up to her bedroom. It was spacious with ample room to place a cot' between Emma's high poster cherry bed and the curved mahogany chest sitting against the wall. Violet noted the inlay design set in the handsome chest by some skilled craftsman. She took her dressing gown from the valise and hung it in Emma's large wardrobe. Then she sat down on the hope chest that was at the foot of Emma's bed, facing Emma who had settled in a rocking chair. They talked about one thing and then another for an hour. By then it was only eight o'clock.

"Let's go up to the piazza on the third floor and have a look," said Emma, rising from her comfortable chair and crossing over and taking Violet's hand, pulling her along with her.

They went to the piazza at the back of the house. From there they could see scores of campfires in the woods beyond the city where Yankee soldiers were in bivouac. Then they noticed some flames of a more sinister kind. Off to their right they could see some blazing buildings along the river. To their left there was a distant glow of what appeared to be a major fire.

"That looks like about where General Hampton's house is!" exclaimed Violet excitedly. "I'll bet those damn Yankees have set his house afire!"

"Oh, surely they wouldn't do such a thing as that!"

Before their very eyes they could see other fires breaking out in various parts of the city. A strong wind–almost a gale–began blowing from the southwest and fanning the flames that were leaping from one structure to another. Noticing a reflection of flames to their right, they ran around to a side window. There they saw a house in flames on Sumter Street. It was burning with such intensity that they could feel the heat, and it lit up the scene for blocks in all directions.

They could see soldiers running through the streets. Obviously they were not the ones in bivouac.

"They must be trying to put out the fires," assumed Emma.

"I'm afraid not," said Violet bitterly. "Those are the Yankee prisoners of war that our officers were trying to get out on the trains this afternoon, but they didn't make it. And now their comrades have set them free. Those caged hyenas are out and running wild in the city."

"But look. Emma pointed down the street. "Some of the people are running out to the street and greeting them. What are they doing?"

"It looks like they are offering the soldiers whiskey—a gesture of appeasement, I guess. That's a stupid thing to do."

Violet was right. The whiskey only added fuel to the fire. Soon fuddled soldiers were running with torches formed from cotton balls from one house to another, quickly extending the area of the fire. When the fire engines came rushing up, the soldiers stopped them and threatened the lives of the firemen. Then they cut the fire hoses to pieces.

"Those damned Yankee bastards," exploded Violet.

Momentarily Emma was shocked at Violet's choice of words, but then she turned and yelled out, "You damned Yankee bastards! You must all be crazy!" And then she turned to Violet and whispered, "Violet, that's the first time I've ever *said* such words. But I don't care. That's what they are—damned Yankee bastards."

The young women watched in awe, dismay, and fright as the fire spread. Strands of cotton blazed up in the streets. Soon burning balls of cotton were falling over the city like incandescent snowflakes. The puffs of cotton, now turned into puffs of fire, descended impartially on the shingle roofs of great houses and modest cottages. Burning shingles rose from one building to float down on another. Embers of all kind played across the undulating red and orange night sky. Rivulets of fire flowed gently northward and eastward along the streets, converging to form raging rivers, and then all joined to form an ocean of flame. Now the old State House stood as the fire spout in this sea as its consuming flames leaped skyward. The crescendo of crashing timbers, falling buildings, and crackling fire rose with the height of the flames in a conflagration that was general and almost total. It was evident to everyone when the fire reached the gas works up near the northeast corner of the city. Sheets of flame shot a hundred feet into the sky. Then the arsenal added a signature of a spectacular pyrotechnic display.

Violet gasped, "Dear God! Tonight we are seeing what burning in hell must be like. What a holocaust! What devastation!"

Now, seeing that the hospital buildings were threatened, Violet and Emma raced up to the roofs to join the doctors and nurses who were beating out flying embers and pouring buckets of water on pockets of flames. The patients who could do so limped or crawled out to the Common while others, in dread of burning to death, waited for someone to move them, and prayed that the fire would be contained.

Not until after four o'clock in the morning did the flames begin to subside. Fortunately, the hospital and other college buildings had been saved with only superficial damage. Violet and Emma returned to Emma's bedroom and fell into their beds from sheer exhaustion.

In spite of getting to bed so late, Violet was determined to get an early start the next morning. By the time she awoke the fire was mostly out although still smoldering in many places. The Common in the college Horseshoe was filled with refugees and homeless people looking for nourishment and some kind of shelter.

By nine o'clock, Violet and Evelina were in the buggy. Violet took the reins and drove around past the main entrance in Sumter Street. Almost everything that they had seen the previous day had vanished. A fog of war, formed of low clouds and rising smoke, hung over the city. It was filled with the pungent odors of burnt cotton, burnt wood, burnt paint, and plaster dust.

Violet looked at the devastation. "How could any destruction be more complete? This is the hell over which the devil Sherman presides." She pressed her handkerchief over her nose as if to screen the burning odors. She looked at Evelina beside her. The young girl's face reflected her shock from the events of the previous night and the destruction all around her.

Violet placed her hand on Evelina's and held it tightly for a moment, willing some of her own strength into the hand she held. She said in a steady voice, "Evelina, before we leave I've just got to go over and see if our house is all right, and then I promise we will be on our way. Are you all right?"

Evelina sat up straight and turned to Violet. "Yassum, Miz Violet. We be gotta see whut hopp'n ta dat house. I'se feared dat fah done git our house. Oh, lawdy. Oh, lawdy. Tell Daisy ta git up, Miz Violet."

Continuing up Sumter Street, not a building was standing except for Trinity Church for as far as they could see. Violet carefully guided the horse to step gingerly around the numerous obstacles in the litter-strewn street. The wind whistled around bleak chimneys and blew ashes through the gaping windows of what once had been warehouses and fine hotels and shops and houses. The old State House was indeed in complete ruins, though the new one was intact as far as it had been built. The city market was but a blackened shell hanging on twisted iron arches, and its clock tower had crumbled to the ground.

As they moved up to the more residential area, they saw people searching in the rubble for valuables and other belongings. Others were trudging toward the outskirts in search of some kind of shelter for the next days. Slaves were streaming after Sherman's army in search of their new freedom.

As Violet and Evelina approached Taylor Street, they looked toward the house. Their worst fears were confirmed. The house and the carriage house in back had been completely reduced to ruins. Only two naked chimneys and two partial brick walls that joined at the nearest corner of the house remained standing amidst the still smoldering rubble. One window remained intact in one of the walls. It was the one with the cracked pane.

Numb with shock and anger and disappointment, Violet turned to Evelina and said, "Well, we were afraid of this. I guess our minds told us to expect the house to be gone, but my heart kept saying, 'It'll be all right. It'll be all right.' I suppose because I wanted it to be all right so badly. Well, it's gone. Gone. So many years of memories eradicated by the Yankees." She stopped to take a deep breath and wipe her burning eyes.

Violet turned the buggy around and headed in the opposite direction. Now she noticed, somewhat to her surprise, that the Baptist church was still standing while the Methodist and Presbyterian churches were in ruins.

"Evelina, look, the Baptist church seems to be unharmed. I wonder why the soldiers didn't burn that along with the other two. How strange. You'd think that would be the first to go since that's the place where the ordinance of secession was adopted."

To get a better look she turned east into Plain Street. As she passed the church, she noticed the old black sexton sitting on the front steps. She stopped the buggy and called to him, "What happened? How did this church happen to be spared? Thank heavens it's all right, but I wonder, why wasn't it burned along with the other two churches."

"Well, Ma'am, w'en dem Yankee soldier come up wif dere fah, dey axed me, if dis be de church which de secess'n wuz pass'd, ah say, 'Oh, no suh, dat wuz at dat udder church down dere. Hit ain't be dis church."

Violet smiled and said, "I'm glad they spared this church. It's now part of our history. Good luck to you!" She knew that the secession convention actually passed the ordinance of secession at a session a little later in Charleston, but the convention had held its first session here at this church and then adjourned to Charleston on account of fear of a smallpox epidemic. She waved to the old man as she clicked for Daisy to start pulling the buggy.

Looking on up Plain Street, she thought she caught a glimpse of the tower of Columbia Female College still standing amidst the rubble. She was anxious to see if the whole building was still there. Crossing Pickens Street, she was able to see that it was. She called "Whoa!" to stop Daisy and handed the reins to Evelina. She jumped out of the buggy and ran up toward the main entrance of the College. As she approached she recognized the college president, the Rev. Henry Mood, who, with a couple of faculty members, was assessing damage.

"Hello, Violet," the Rev. Mood said as he turned to greet her with astonishment. "For goodness sake, what are you doing here? I'm certainly glad to see no harm has come to you. Before he left, your father told me that you would be leaving for Fair Oaks on Monday, or at the latest by early Tuesday morning."

"I've been staying at what used to be our house, and then last night I stayed with a friend who lives in the college buildings where the hospital now is. But right now I'm on my way to get back to Fair Oaks."

"I should think so. I take it your town house is gone, along with so many others."

"Oh, yes. Burned to the ground. And everything left in it. It's terrible. Believe me, I'm not looking forward to telling Daddy and my sisters. But how did they miss the College?"

"We have to thank Mr. Orchard for that."

Violet remembered Orchard as one of her music professors when she attended the Female College. She asked, "How did he accomplish that?"

"Well, he heard a report that all unoccupied buildings were going to be burned. He ran over here from his home, gained admission by breaking a window, and lit candles at the windows all along the front."

"And that kept the soldiers away?" asked Violet in wonder.

"That's not all. Then Mr. Orchard ran down and placed himself at the main entrance, and when a group of Yankees came along with their torches, he stood his ground."

"Wonderful! How courageous of him!"

"And then do you know what he did? He wrote a note to General Sherman begging that the College be spared and reminding Sherman that when Orchard was a music professor in Ohio some years ago, he had taught Sherman's sister!"

"Amazing!"

"And apparently the soldiers delivered the note and then went on to other places with their destruction. But, alas, the Roman Catholic convent did not fare so well. It burned to the ground."

"That's awful!" Violet said in continuing dismay.

"General Stone had promised the nuns protection and assured them that the convent would come to no harm. But you see what happened. His word meant nothing. The sisters are coming over here where we are providing quarters for them and for many other people who have been burned out of their houses."

"They are lucky to have such a place to stay. But I'm happy the College was spared. Will it be able to reopen soon?"

The Rev. Mood looked grim as he answered, "Surely not until the city has been rebuilt, and I sincerely hope that won't be too long. As for now, we can't say what is going to happen. Things are so unsettled. We don't know yet whether the Yankees will occupy Columbia as a captive city, or whether they believe they have destroyed us sufficiently and will move on to continue their devastation of other localities." He paused a moment, and continued, "Violet, I preach about heaven and hell. After last night, I believe I have a deeper understanding of what hell must be like."

"I, too. I know just what you mean," said Violet. "Well, I must be on my way. Take care of yourself and give my regards to Mrs. Mood."

She returned to the buggy, took the reins from Evelina who had been waiting nervously for Violet to return. Several rough looking passers-by had given the buggy a hard look, as had a few Yankee soldiers, and Evelina was fearful that they might return and try to take the buggy from her. Violet drove back to Sumter Street and turned toward the center of the city.

As she drove back past Trinity Church she felt a need to go in for a moment of prayer. Again she handed the reins to a still nervous Evelina and promised she'd be gone only a few minutes. When she entered, she saw the rector, Dr. Peter Shand, down near the altar. All of a sudden the experiences of the last couple of days overcame her, and she ran down the center aisle to him.

"Violet Storm! What are you doing here?" asked the astonished priest.

"Oh, Father."

They hugged in mutual consolation. Stepping back she asked, "Father Shand, what is happening to us?"

"I'm afraid more than the chaff has been burning with unquenchable fire."

"Truly, I thought I was in hell's fire and brimstone."

"Yes, but where were you? What are you doing here? Why aren't you at Fair Oaks?"

"I've been helping at the Wayside Hospital and closing up the town house." Then she added woefully, "Little good that did."

"How is your house?"

"Gone. Completely. Everything." Tears welled up in her eyes.

"Not much left anywhere, is there? Have you heard what happened to me?"

"What? Is the parish house burned" Violet asked.

"Mostly, I'm afraid, and so was the rectory." He sighed. "All the parish records were lost. Thank God the church was spared."

Violet glanced around the beautiful church and realized that all the stained glass windows were gone. "What happened to all the beautiful windows? Were they broken?" she asked.

"No, fortunately, we took out all the windows and hid them from the Yankees. Don't worry, they're all right," he reassured her.

"Oh, thank goodness for that."

"Yes, but yesterday afternoon I was in here getting out the communion silver, and a Yankee soldier came in and took it right out of my hands. Just yanked the chalice right from me, grabbed up the rest and ran out, calling back, 'This ain't yourn no more. Everything in this town is ours now!' Obviously he is not of the belief 'Love thy neighbor as thyself' or 'Do unto others as ye would have them do unto ye'." The priest sighed with sadness.

"Much less the commandment, 'Thou shalt not steal'." Violet said angrily. "Those damn Yankees! And, Father, don't, please don't tell me to turn the other cheek."

"I have no intention of telling you that. Jesus himself drove the moneychangers from the temple. There are times when certain action must be taken, my daughter." He smiled at Violet. "But I think that now it would be prudent for you to be on your way home. The sooner you get there, the sooner I can stop worrying about your safety."

"Oh," said Violet contritely. "You're right, of course. I know I must get to Fair Oaks and tell them what's happened here in Columbia and warn them what may be in store for all of us there."

"Thank you, Violet, for stopping by. Rest assured you and your family will be in my prayers."

"Thank you, Father. Do you know that I still remember from my school memory exercises some lines of Dante, as translated by Longfellow, which now have taken on real meaning." She paused, and then softly recited them: "There is no greater sorrow than to be mindful of the happy times in misery'."

"So true, Violet."

As she turned to go, the priest grasped her hand and said encouragingly, "We must hold to the faith, no matter what, hold to the faith."

Withdrawing her hand, she muttered, half to him and half to the bare wall, "Faith? Faith in what? Faith for what?"

It was not until she was back in the buggy that she realized she had not said a prayer in the church. *I've said so many prayers anyhow—and what good have they done? None. Absolutely none. I'm not sure God is even listening to me, to any of us. Otherwise, how could He let practically a whole city burn down? How could a God who cares let someone like Sherman cause such devastation throughout the South? Oh, I don't know what to believe*, she thought in anguish, and was suddenly cold with the realization that her belief had been shaken.

Chapter 7

Sherman Again?

1865

After coming out of Holy Cross Church and getting into the buggy, Violet found that Sumter Street and apparently all the streets running parallel to it were filled with traffic. Hundreds of Yankee wagons were moving northward through the city. Most were canvas-covered supply wagons, each drawn by six mules, but there were also scores of pontoon boats on wheel chassis, each drawn by four mules. There were artillery pieces and caissons and forges, each drawn by eight horses, and ambulances drawn by two horses.

As Violet climbed into her buggy, she reassured Evelina who was getting jittery again and took the reins from her. Violet guided Daisy to circle around inside the churchyard to come out directly on Gervais Street where the traffic was lighter. There they turned right into the street without difficulty. Still, at each cross street they had to wait for an opening to dash through the endless streams of wagons.

They could hear an explosion now and then in various parts of the city as Sherman's men went about their tasks of destroying the railroads and any remaining military facilities in a more studied fashion.

When they crossed Harden Street at the eastern limit of the city and onto the Mill Creek Road, Violet looked at Evelina and flashed a smile of encouragement. Evelina gave a deep sigh of relief and seemed to relax a bit.

Still the way was not all clear. Hundreds of freed slaves were streaming across the fields and the road to follow Sherman's armies. Men, women, and children, with handcarts, horses, cows, dogs, bed clothes, cooking utensils, and whatever else might be of use, rode, walked and ran after the army of freedom. At one point, a large family of slaves came through the fields, the old father mounted on a mule covered with a blanket to which was attached bags that carried four little pickaninnies, two on each side, while the mother brought up the rear with a pushcart. A little farther on, a black woman was leading a cow with a similar arrangement. In this case the cow was covered with an old canvas tent-fly to which four pockets had been attached to each side from which just the heads of eight pickaninnies could be seen. At a road crossing, there was an open wagon with no driver, filled with a dozen darky babies, and an old horse was plodding along the road, pulling the precious cargo, without any apparent directions from anybody.

All the multitude seemed intent on their own business, and nobody interfered with nor even seemed to notice Violet and Evelina. Soon they were away from the Yankee army and its followers and on the Stateburg Turnpike. Violet coaxed Daisy into a fast trot for the next two miles and then settled into a slower, easier gait, alternating between a slow trot and a fast walk for the long journey.

Within an hour a light rain began to fall and quickly turned into a downpour. The buggy's side curtains and lap robes gave only partial protection from the rain. Evelina took some bread and cheese from the food basket resting on the floor between their feet, and the food raised their spirits as well as their energy.

By five o'clock they were at Garner's Ferry. The rain had stopped, but its effects, added to those of several days previously, were evident in the high waters and swift current of the river. The ferryman was not in sight. Violet hopped out of the buggy and ran over to his cottage and routed him out.

"We need to get across the river," she said.

"Yes ma'm," the grizzled, weather-beaten man answered resignedly as he pulled on an ancient pea jacket and set a frayed cap on his head. "Yes, Ma'm, but I'm afraid t'aint safe right now, too fast a current after all this rain. I ain't been operating since one o'clock. 'Better wait till t'marra."

"We *can't* wait until tomorrow. We must go now. Right now!"

"Sorry, but it ain't safe, ma'm. It jest ain't safe with this current."

"I tell you, Sherman is coming after us, and if he catches us here it will be a lot less safe than that river. Don't you understand, Sherman is coming! The devil himself is on the way!"

The old boatman perked up. "Sherman comin' thisaway, you say?"

"Yes sireebob! We had better get out of here as fast as we can!"

"Well, in that case, I'd better see what I can do. Wait jest a minute 'til I can get some things together. Reckon I'll be stayin' on t'other side tonight."

Daisy shied away from the ferry until Violet got down from the buggy and led the skitterish horse aboard. There Violet remained beside the horse, stroking her head and talking to her in soft, reassuring tones. Presently they were underway. A chain that was secured at the opposite bank and lay all the way across the bottom of the river, came out of the water at the boat's prow. The chain was wrapped around a horizontal drum on the deck and then continued on to a fastening on the near bank. By turning a crank on the drum the ferryman could force the boat along the chain to the other side. Although the swift current carried a potential for disaster, it also was an ally as its pressure pushed the boat along. The boat rocked dangerously, but it moved rapidly, and it was an easy matter to get out to midstream. The final yards were the most difficult as now the ferryman had to fight the current. It took all his strength to turn the drum. At times the strength of the current seemed about to master the boatman, but he held fast using all his will and might to turn the drum. Finally they reached the other side. The ferryman secured the boat and sat down to wipe his brow, exhausted from his efforts.

"We thank you, sir," sighed Violet, much relieved that the ordeal was over. For a brief time she had been fearful that they would not make it to the other side, but the thought of Sherman catching up with them bolstered their determination.

"You're welcome, ma'm," said the ferryman, still breathing heavily from his efforts. He was as much relieved to be at the other side of the swollen river as were his passengers. Daisy was eager to leave the ferry, and Violet had no difficulty leading the horse off the boat. Violet and Evelina climbed back into the buggy for the ride home.

"Now y'all take keer of yourselves!" the ferryman called after them, his cap in his hand.

It was nearly dark when the two women drove up the muddy lane at Fair Oaks. The squish-squish of Daisy's hoofs and the swish of the buggy's wheels was music to their ears. As they pulled around to the back door, Charlotte and Susan and Mammy came running out to greet them with laughs of welcome and relief that they were home safely. Jarvis and Uncle Job came out to get the baggage, and Fabian took Daisy and the buggy to the carriage house to rub down the exhausted horse and give her nourishment.

Everyone was talking at once.

"Was there a fire?"

"Terrible!"

"Did you see Sherman?"

"Yes."

"Is he coming this way?"

"Probably."

"Where is Daddy?"

"I don't know."

"Were you scared?"

"To be perfectly honest—yes!"

"Is our house all right?"

"I'll tell you later."

Violet's first concern was for her children. With a promise to answer all questions directly, she raced upstairs to the nursery with Evelina close behind. Bonnie Anne and J.J. cried out with delight when they saw their mother, and Violet drew both children to her in a tight embrace. Tears filled her eyes as she hugged them. It seemed to all three that she had been away for many months.

Violet asked Evelina to take the children downstairs. Then after a few minutes to wash and repair her toilette she joined her sisters in the informal dining area adjacent to the kitchen. Mammy and Aunt Beulah had already begun preparing supper.

"Violet," Charlotte said excitedly, "all last night we could see a dim red glow in the western sky. We ran over to the Friersons for a while. They thought that it might be Columbia on fire. Was it?" And then she added quickly, "Oh, I hope it wasn't!"

"Yes, it was Columbia," Violet answered sadly. "It was Columbia all right, and it was awful. Just awful." A shudder passed through her at the thought, but she continued in a calm and steady voice, "It was terrible. Nothing is left but the houses around the fringes. Rubble. Ashes. Smoking embers." She closed her eyes as if to shut out the sight in her mind.

"But, Violet! What about our house? It's all right, isn't it?" asked Susan, hopefully.

"No. It's not all right. The house is gone, completely gone, along with everything in it except what little we sent back with Uncle Job and Aunt Beulah, and what we were able to bring back with us in the buggy."

"Oh, no...the paintings, the silver, the furniture, our clothes, the jewelry we kept there! Is it all really gone, Violet?" asked a shocked Charlotte.

"Yes...I told you...the house...everything...gone up in flames. There's nothing left but ashes and debris." Violet shuddered again.

"But, thank God, you're all right. And Evelina. But, Violet, how did you manage to keep yourself and Evelina safe and then to get out of Columbia?" Susan asked in wonder and admiration.

"We left the house in the afternoon, after a crazy Yankee soldier burst in—I got rid of him all right, as Evelina can tell you—and we went over to a friend's house at the State College campus where they have a hospital now. There we found a safe haven and we stayed all night, but I must say we did not get much sleep with all the noise and fires burning and people yelling and smoke in the air, and fighting the fires that threatened the hospital."

"Violet, what about Daddy? Did you see him? Where is he? Is he all right?" asked Susan.

"I last saw Daddy on Tuesday when he went out to remain with his regiment. He's supposed to be with General Hampton's cavalry. They withdrew through the city before Sherman's men got there, and presumably they are still moving north and northeast to keep ahead of Sherman. Dear God! I hope they are successful!"

Susan persisted with her questions, "Did you see old Sherman, Sherman himself?"

"I certainly did," answered Violet bitterly, "the Devil himself, riding right up our main street!" She stopped a moment, reliving in her mind the picture of Sherman as he rode by her.

Charlotte spoke out, a worried expression upon her face, "It seems strange that the Yankees should be coming at us from the south, doesn't it? I always assumed that we would have to watch out from the north."

"You're right," Violet answered. "It's like in chess, to be moving away from your opponent's king. To be retreating is not good."

Charlotte continued, with dread showing in her eyes and voice, "But tell us, Violet, have you heard whether Sherman is coming this way? Is he headed in Fair Oaks direction?"

"We can't be sure, of course, but we must assume so. He has two big armies, and they are spread out as far as from here to Columbia, no matter which way they are going. So we must expect that at least some if not many of his soldiers will be passing through the plantation."

"When do you think they will be here?" asked a frightened Susan.

"They could be here in three days—though they usually pause for a while before moving on. So I would say...not less than three days, nor more than seven."

"Oh, what will we do?" both younger sisters gasped in chorus, horrified at the thought of Yankees on their property or in their home.

"Stay here and try to hide everything they might want to take. And listen to me. Remember what Mother always told us, how important it is in times of emergency to stay calm and in control of ourselves. We can think more clearly and logically, and then, too, the darkies will take their cue from us. We don't want them to be running hither and thither in fright. This is *our* home. Mother is no longer with us, and Daddy's off fighting, so it will be up to the three of us to manage and to take care of each other and the darkies. Keep in mind that Leo and Uncle Jarvis and Mammy and Aunt Beulah and Uncle Job will all help us to keep things going. We aren't alone in this."

After supper, Violet went with Mammy and Evelina to bathe the children and put on their nightshirts. In the nursery, she sat in Rosemary Lee's large old rocking chair, and holding little J.J. in her left arm and Bonnie Anne on her lap, her right arm supporting Bonnie Anne's back, she softly sang sweet lullabies. The children were soon sound asleep. Mammy gently picked up Bonnie Anne and laid her in the hand carved youth bed. Violet laid J.J. in his rocker crib. They tucked the bedclothes snugly around the children, snuffed out the candles on the chest, and tip-toed quietly from the room.

Violet took a long, warm, scented bath, soaking and slowly relaxing after her calamitous days of adventure. She climbed out of the tub and dried her body with a large towel. She took hold of either end and flung the towel behind her back, pulling the towel back and forth across her back to dry it. She stopped suddenly, as if frozen in action, at the reflection of her lovely, slender body in the tall looking glass at the end of the bathing room. She began slowly pulling the towel back and forth watching the movements brought on by this action. Her skin seemed to glow in the candlelight. Her full breasts were still as firm as when she was eighteen, and her small waist only slightly larger. Her hips had acquired a sensual curvaceousness that she did not have at that age. *Why, I've still got a figure,* she thought. *I haven't had time to really look at myself since I don't know when, but I've got an attractive body. Brent used to tell me that I was a beautiful nymph from the tip of my head to the tip of my toes. And he would say how he loved to feel the warm, soft skin of his nymph from head to toe, and he would lightly rub his hands over my body...oh, dear God, the feel of his hands!* Violet realized that she had flung down the towel and was rubbing her body in the same way that Brent did. She grabbed her wrapper, blew out the candle, crossed the hall to her room, slamming both the bathing room and bedroom doors in the process.

Mammy had turned down the bedcovers, and Violet climbed into her bed. Just as she pulled up the covers, there was a knock at her door which then opened to reveal her two sisters ready for bed in their ruffled white nightcaps and faded calico wrappers.

"Violet, may we come in for a few minutes?" asked Charlotte.

"We just have to talk to you some more," added Susan. "We still have to hear more about what happened in Columbia."

Violet didn't want to talk. She only wanted to go to sleep and dream of Brent. She wanted to shut out the horror of recent past events and fear of what may be yet to come. She realized she was now in somewhat of a nasty mood, but she bade them enter for she knew that deep down inside they were scared. They had a need to be with her, their older sister. With their mother dead and their father away, they looked to Violet for guidance and security. Violet rose to the occasion, and putting her own immediate feelings and exhaustion aside, she recounted in detail all that she had done and seen in Columbia. The three sisters talked and talked, with Violet answering what seemed an almost endless series of questions. It was not until the early hours of the morning that Charlotte and Susan slipped back to their own rooms to sleep.

The next day was Sunday, but the family had no time for church. Everyone began helping to gather up additional items in the house for transfer to the Storm Cellar. Leo, Job, and Jarvis took the things out in a wagon, the contents hidden from curious eyes by a canvas cover. Earlier Leo had decided that Job could be trusted with the secret of the Storm Cellar. He and Jarvis had moved the items that were stored before Violet left for Columbia, but with Sherman's men on the way he had decided that another helper was needed. At this point, time was of essence.

After the men had finished that task, Violet asked Leo to assemble as many men as necessary to transfer all the cotton from the storage shed to a series of piles in the woods, making sure the piles were placed in different parts of the woods, and none in the vicinity of the Storm Cellar. She instructed Leo to cover each pile with canvas and then cover that with brush to avoid detection.

Over the next three days they were able to remove to hiding half of the five hundred bales of cotton from the storage shed, but then heavy rains interrupted this work, and the rest of the cotton remained in the storage shed.

At night, in spite of the rain, they almost could trace the advance of Sherman's troops by reflections on the clouds of burning houses and barns that lit up their route of march.

Thursday afternoon Violet and Charlotte rode their horses over to see the Friersons at Cherry Vale Plantation, just across from Fair Oaks. John and Sarah greeted them with warm hugs. John told them that he had ridden over to the Wateree the previous day and found the river completely out of its banks and the whole swamp flooded.

"Do you think that may stop Sherman?" Violet asked, her eyes full of hope.

"It just may," he responded. "The main route of their army probably is on the other side of the river anyway, but I have no doubt that if they could get across the river without too much trouble, some of their bummers would be over here collecting food and burning houses."

"Let's hope it remains too difficult for them," Sarah Frierson added dryly.

"Thank God for the Sherman freshet! May the banks continue to overflow!" exclaimed Violet.

Chapter 8

Sad News from Cheraw

1865

On Saturday one of John Frierson's stable hands arrived with a note reporting word from a returning cavalryman that some of Sherman's raiders had burned most of Camden on the previous day, and that the main bodies of Yankee forces were moving rapidly on toward North Carolina. Violet felt almost a sense of guilt in recognizing that the bad news from Camden meant that Sherman had passed them by. They had been spared!

"That Sherman freshet on the Wateree has saved us!" Violet cried out as she ran into the house. "Sherman has passed us by. He's on the way to North Carolina!"

Charlotte and Susan came running. "What does it mean?" asked Charlotte excitedly.

"Are we safe now?" asked Susan, her hands clasped as though in prayer.

"Yes, yes, I think so," Violet answered. "Now we can be getting our things back in the house and perhaps begin living a little more normally."

"But what about the War?" Charlotte asked. "Does Sherman's move into North Carolina mean that the War is almost over?"

Violet's response reflected her mixed feelings. "It probably does," she said, "and presumably it means that we've lost the War. So it's likely that Daddy will be home soon—and Brent, too. We can be glad that the War is about over and that Daddy and Brent will be with us again, but not that the Yankees have beaten the Confederacy."

"Those damn Yankees!" Susan said heatedly. "But oh, I can hardly wait until Daddy and Brent are back. I've missed them so." She ran off to tell Mammy and the others what Violet had said.

Violet watched Susan until she was out of sight and then said to Charlotte, "Thank goodness, soon we should be able to take up our lives where they broke off on account of the War."

"But what will the Yankees do to us?" asked Charlotte.

"They already have done everything. They'll have what they want—forcing us to stay in the Union to be exploited by them. At least now we can look forward to peace and having our family together again—though it'll never be really the same without Christopher, our sacrificial lamb." She felt her eyes sting at the thought but went on, "At least we can be thankful that we were not in Sherman's path of destruction after all. Yes, that is something for which we truly can be grateful."

With Sherman now en route to North Carolina, Violet and her sisters were able to devote the next several days to returning most of their valuables to the house. Now feeling safe and no longer needing to keep the location of the Storm Cellar a secret,

Leo directed a dozen men in bringing the things out of the Storm Cellar—everything but the seed.

"No use moving the cotton and garden seed twice," Violet explained, "we'll get that out when it's time for planting."

The following Saturday, March 11, another messenger arrived from the Friersons. He was carrying a Sumter newspaper that Violet took from him at the back door. Returning to the office, she quickly glanced at the paper. It featured an account of the inauguration of Abraham Lincoln for a second term just a week ago. Her eye fell to excerpts from his inaugural address:

> *Fondly do we hope, fervently do we pray, that this mighty scourge of war may speedily pass away...*
>
> *With malice toward none; with charity for all; with firmness in the right, as God gives us to see the right, let us strive on to finish the work we are in; to bind up the nation's wounds; to care for him who shall have borne the battle, and for his widow and his orphan—to do all which may achieve and cherish a lasting peace among ourselves and with all nations.*

In these words Violet found hope for recovery of life at Fair Oaks, though she could not help but fear that she might be one of those widows of the war.

While taking a much-needed rest on Sunday afternoon, Violet happened to glance out the front window of her bedroom and saw someone riding up the lane. Looking more closely, she recognized her father's man servant, Aaron, riding Old Fred. *How strange*, she thought, *why would Aaron be riding Daddy's horse?* She threw a coat over her lounging robe and raced down the stairs and out the front door. She met Aaron half-way down the lane.

"Aaron! Welcome home!" she exclaimed, and then showered him with questions, "Why are you on Old Fred? Did something happen to your horse? Where's Daddy? Is he following?" She peered down the lane in search of her father.

Aaron jumped off the horse and, avoiding Violet's eyes, he moaned in a quivering voice, "Oh, Miz Violet...Miz Violet, it be de Massuh."

A wave of apprehension rose within Violet. Grabbing both his upper arms, she coaxed him, "Aaron, what is it? Tell me! What's happened to Daddy?"

"La, Miz Violet, de Massuh he ain't nebbuh comin' home no mo'...he ain't nebbuh comin' home no mo"

Violet gasped in disbelief, "What are you saying, Aaron? What do you mean Daddy isn't coming home again?"

"Miz Violet...de Majuh...de Majuh be daid...he be daid frum de big bat'l...daid." With shaking hands Aaron pulled a piece of paper from his inner coat pocket. "Heah, Miz Violet, heah be de ledda frum de gen'l." He handed the paper to Violet.

She grabbed the letter from his hands, unfolded it, and turned deathly pale as she read the contents affirming Aaron's news. Unable to speak at first, she turned, ran back into the house, and then managed to find her voice to call Charlotte and Susan. Aaron mounted his horse and rode over to inform Leo of the sad news.

The sisters met Violet in the hall, wondering at the shrill tone of her voice. Mammy, too, had heard Violet, and her years of caring for the family had made her sensitive to each member's intonations. She knew from Violet's voice that something terrible had happened, and she raced out of the kitchen to the hall as fast as she could, with Aunt Beulah close behind.

Violet stood in the center of the hall, looking at each one in turn, tears streaming down her face. She buried her head in her hands. *I must be strong. I must be strong. Daddy would want me to be strong. I'm the head of the family now. I've got to be strong for the others.*

"Violet, what is it? What's the matter?" the young Susan asked, as tears welled up for no known reason.

Violet took her hands from her face, lifted her head in resolve, and, fighting back her tears, she waived the others into the library.

As soon as they were in the library, Charlotte turned to Violet and said, "It's Daddy! Something has happened to Daddy, hasn't it? Oh, Violet, tell us right now; is he hurt?"

Violet took a deep breath and said, "Yes, it's Daddy." After a pause during which she fought to control her emotions, she took another deep breath and explained, "Aaron brought this letter. Let me read it to you. Let's all sit down while I read it." The girls and the two servants found chairs and looked at Violet with dread in their eyes.

Violet cleared her throat, and said, "The letter is from General Hampton. This is what he wrote." She unfolded the letter and began reading aloud:

> *Dear Miss Violet and Miss Charlotte and Miss Susan:*
>
> *I have been in many battles. As you know, one of my sons was killed in one of them. But I have had no more painful duty—*

Cries of "No!" broke forth from the girls. A moan rose from Mammy's lips. Violet continued:

> *On the 9th Federal troops occupied Cheraw. That night our cavalry made a surprise attack and completely overran their camp. It was one of the very few successes made against any of Sherman's forces during their whole march through South Carolina. Major Alexander Storm, your father, was in the forefront of that attack. His regiment was the key to that success.*
>
> *Unfortunately, we did not have the forces to hold our advantage. In the gray false dawn of the next morning, Federal cavalry in great numbers came roaring back. It was then that your father, urging his*

men to stay and fight, fell. After that there was no stopping the enemy, and we lost everything that we had gained.

The Major's faithful body servant, Aaron, did all that he could to help. Under fire, he picked up a musket from the field and helped defend the evacuation of the Major and other wounded soldiers. Aaron got him back to a medical station, but nothing could be done for him.

I am afraid that the end will not now be long delayed. Be assured that your father gave everything to defend his State and his people. He was a fine officer, a fine gentleman, and a valued friend. Our best way to honor him is to carry his ideals forward in spite of adversity.

Faithfully, Your Obedient Servant,
Wade Hampton
Lieutenant General, C.S.A.

When she finished reading Hampton's dispatch there was silence for a few moments. The shock of the news had left them speechless. They could not at first either believe or accept what they had just been told. Why, the Major had kissed the girls good-bye and ridden away from Fair Oaks only a month ago!

Violet felt that it was the end of the world. How much more could she and her sisters take? First their mother, then Christopher, and now their father, not to mention the horrors of the burning of Columbia. The sisters hugged each other in futile attempts at consolation, and clung to Mammy and Aunt Beulah as if they were again small children suffering from some hurt. Mammy tried to enfold all three in her arms, soothing them as well as she could, as she had so often through the years as they were growing up. Their sobbing eased eventually, and the sisters went up to their rooms while Mammy went to spread the news to the other house servants. She knew that Aaron would have gone straight to Leo after Violet left him.

A sad silence prevailed throughout the house. Violet knew that she had to pull herself together and set the tone for the others. After a short while, she rinsed her face with cold water, smoothed her hair into place, straightened her shoulders, and lifted her chin. Then she went down to meet with the house servants, devastated with grief for the loss of their beloved Massuh. She read the General's letter to them, knowing that they would take pride in what the General said about the Major.

She sent Uncle Job to tell Fabian to saddle up a fresh horse and bring it over to the back porch where she would meet him. When Fabian arrived, she sent him with a note telling the Reverend Roberts at Holy Cross Church of the Major's death. She asked Fabian also to stop on his way back at the Frierson and Thompson plantations and inform these neighbors. She knew that they would spread the news to other friends for her.

After Fabian left, she walked over to comfort Leo. She was well aware of the mutual deep feeling of respect and affection that existed between him and her father.

As she approached the house, Violet could see Leo sitting on his porch with his head bowed as though deep in thought. When he heard her step upon the wooden stairs he raised his head and rose from the chair.

He looked at her solemnly with desolate eyes and, with compassion in his voice, said, "Ah kno', Miz Violet. After seein' ya, Aaron cum ovah ta tell me de bad news. It jes' ain't fair, Miz Violet. It ain't fair fer de Massuh ta be kill' daid. He be sech a good man. Bad 'nuf fer Massuh Chrisfer ta be kill' by dose Yankees." He pulled a large square of cloth from his pocket, blew his nose, and wiped his eyes.

Violet placed her hand gently on Leo's arm. "Yes, it isn't fair, Leo. So much has happened to us. I just didn't think anything could happen to Daddy. He's so—" She stopped, her hand flying to her mouth. "I mean...He *was* so big and strong...and smart, too."

"He be dat all righ'. Now, Miz Violet, de Massuh w'en he be leavin' sed he coun' on me to hep ya an' ta tek care ebberbody an' jes' ya 'member dat ah be heah ta do jes' dat. Jes' ya 'member dat Leo be heah. An' de Massuh now be up in de sky and w'en he look' down he see dat he can coun' on Leo."

His words brought back the tears so bravely held in check. Now Violet pulled a small white handkerchief from her pocket and wiped her eyes. She cleared her throat and said, "Yes, Leo, we all can count on you. Thank you for your reassuring words." She stopped to clear her throat again and, after taking a deep breath, she continued, "But now, we need to tell the hands. I want to get this behind us."

"Yassum. I get dem heah." He went down the porch steps and crossed over to the large Plantation Bell used to summon all hands in from the fields. With astonishment they heard the bell ring and continue ringing for a full three minutes. Those in the fields who had volunteered to work this Sunday looked at the sun and knew it was not the usual time to come in. Those in the cabins and on the porches and in the yards stopped what they were doing and looked at one another in wonder. Even the children paused in their play. Then the bell began ringing for another three minutes. Now recognizing the emergency signal, they all began moving, picking up momentum as they converged in front of the overseer's house. Wonder changed to anxiety as they saw Violet standing by Leo on the porch. The murmur of their voices ceased, and they stood in silence waiting for the others to arrive and for Leo to speak.

When it was time to speak, Leo said in a loud, strong voice so as to be heard by all. "Ah kno' ya be wonderin' de reas'n ya be call'd heah. Well, Miz Violet gotta tell ya sumpin'. And ah gotta tell ya hit be bad. So y'all liss'n now."

Violet waited a moment, looking at the upturned faces now showing worry at what was to come. She wished that she did not have to tell them the news. For a split second she thought she would ask Leo to do it, but then she knew that it was her responsibility—that her father would expect her to do this bravely, in the manner of the mistress of the plantation. And so she said, "Thank you all for assembling here so quickly. Today I received some unhappy news that I must share with you. This past Friday, Major Storm was killed in battle..." She halted as a swell of moaning arose from the group. She turned to Leo and asked, "Leo, can you settle them down? I want to read the letter I received from the General. I think they would want to hear what he had to say about Daddy."

Leo stepped forward and raised both hands. The slaves one by one fell silent. Then Leo stepped back and Violet proceeded, "I want to read to you the letter sent by General Wade Hampton so that you will know the circumstances of the Major's death." She read the letter slowly and in a strong voice so that they all would hear each word. When she had finished, she announced, "Beginning tomorrow, we will observe two days of mourning. Except for absolutely necessary chores, such as milking the cows and feeding the animals—Leo will let you know what must be done—no plantation work is to be done." She paused a moment and then went on, "You know how much Father cared for each of you. I know that you will keep him in your prayers..." She had to stop, for the moaning again burst forth, this time increasing to a roar. They had had all they could take.

That evening as Violet tucked Bonnie Anne and J.J. into their beds, she was thankful that they were too young to need any lengthy explanation of the great blow that had just fallen. As yet she had said nothing. Perhaps in the morning she would tell them.

They had missed their beloved grandfather a great deal when he first left, with Bonnie Anne asking, "Where Gandadee?" and J.J. listening attentively and turning his head at each heavy boot step. At times, Bonnie Anne would go over and kiss the Major's picture.

It seemed as if the children sensed a stillness in their mother and the others, and they quietly settled down to go to sleep. Violet kissed them, turned the wick down low, and as she was leaving the room, for some strange reason Bonnie Anne called out sleepily, "Where Gandadee?"

Violet's heart leaped. *Dear God! The children would never see their Grandfather again!* She quietly closed the door and hastened to her room to regain her control. After a while she went to Susan's room, and then Charlotte's room, to console them individually and to help them confront the loss of their father.

The next morning Sarah Frierson arrived to offer her condolences. She entered the hall and hugged each girl in turn. They knew that she had come to raise their spirits. They also knew her attempts would do little good at this time, but they appreciated her efforts.

"Oh, Violet, my dear...Charlotte...Susan...we are devastated by the news. So many courageous men have lost their lives in this terrible War. And now the Major. We must all be brave. Your father would want you to be brave. And remember, you have friends who love you and will help you to keep things going. Oh...John would be here this morning, but he thought you would want him to spread the news to your other friends. I'm so glad you had Aaron stop by when he did."

"Yes, well come into the library and have tea with us. We'll talk in there." Violet said, leading the others into the library.

Jarvis soon arrived with tea, just steeped by Mammy. He set the silver service on the tea table in front of Violet and then stood aside waiting for Violet to pour the tea.

Violet knew everyone's preference as to milk and sugar or lemon and sugar, but this time everyone would have either milk or nothing. She prepared the tea for each, then handed the cup and saucer, along with a linen napkin, to Jarvis to serve as she said softly to him, "Mrs. Frierson...Charlotte...Susan." When all had been served and had settled back in their chairs, Jarvis left the room to attend to other duties.

As they sipped their tea, Mrs. Frierson did her best. "Time is the great healer, you know," she said. "We always must be patient in times like this and give time a chance to do its healing."

"Yes, that's what people say at times like this." Violet said courteously. "But I have found that is not really so. I still miss my mother and she has been gone over four years. The grief is always with me, though it seems to simmer at times. And then at other times the grief returns with full force—such as at holidays like Christmas or Easter, and at all our birthdays when Mother was so full of life and fun and enjoyment. And Christopher, well, Christopher has been gone only a year and a half—and that has been nothing. Perhaps this is so because the War in which he fought so bravely and died, is still going on. And now Daddy!" Her voice broke and she could not continue.

"Yes, you have a point. I have not even begun to get over the loss of our son last year in this War. Thoughts of him are with me every day. I don't even want to get out of bed on his birthday. Of course I do—he'd want me to go on." She paused and then said thoughtfully, "Perhaps what is meant by that statement is that, with time, grief gets easier to handle. The sorrow is always with us, but not on the front stove plate, so to speak."

"Yes, that's it, that seems to be a good explanation of that saying." agreed Violet.

"Yes, that's what people really mean when they say that 'time heals,' but one isn't really *healed*; the grief is just a bit easier to handle as time goes on," remarked Charlotte.

"Well, I'll *never* get over Daddy's death. I've never gotten over Mother's and I've never gotten over Christopher's and I won't get over Daddy's either. I know I won't. Never!" exclaimed the agitated Susan. The other three women looked at her and said nothing, understanding the young girl's feelings.

They were silent for a short while, and then Sarah reminded them that they should be prepared for the expected arrival of friends to extend their sympathy and offer their condolences. Since it was customary to offer such guests sustenance and other light refreshments as desired, and to lighten the work of the household at this sorrowful time, prepared foods and beverages would shortly be arriving from the neighboring plantations.

As Sarah rose to take her leave, Charlotte said gratefully, "We do appreciate your coming. You have been so helpful. We can't thank you enough."

And Violet added, "Yes, thank you so much for coming over, Sarah. It is always good to know that there is a friend who understands and shares your feelings at a time like this."

They accompanied their guest to the front door where her carriage was waiting, kissed her on the cheek, and waved good-bye as she and her driver, Ramey, went down the tree-lined lane. They returned to the library for another cup of tea from the pot that Mammy refilled when they were bidding their guest farewell.

Except for that one outburst Susan had been quiet, almost as if in a state of shock. She said to her older sisters, "You know something? I've never told either of you this, but one time when I was only about seven, Grandmama Lee was here, and I happened to walk in here where she was sitting alone with a picture in her hand, and I noticed that she was crying. I asked why she was crying and she showed me the picture. She was looking at a picture of *her* mother who had been dead for over thirty years. I couldn't understand it. How could she be crying about someone who had been dead for thirty years? Now, I guess I am beginning to understand. You never do get over it."

Violet answered softly, "No, little sister, we never do get over these things, no matter how much time goes by. Still, after a while we are able to regain some control over our feelings. We have to, because there are others who are depending on us, and somehow we have to keep going. But time *does* make this easier. That is what Sarah was actually saying."

Early in the afternoon on the following Sunday, Aaron called out that a wagon was coming up the lane. Violet, Charlotte, and Susan went out to meet it at the circular drive. Two wounded Confederate soldiers were driving a pair of lame horses with a broken wagon that was carrying a pine coffin.

"We are bringing Major Storm home," one of the soldiers explained, with sympathy in his voice.

Thank goodness, at least we will be able to have a burial service for Daddy. We can visit his grave each Sunday when we go to church. His body will lie beside mother's. It was so difficult for us all knowing that Christopher had to be buried at Gettysburg, and his body will never rest in the Holy Cross cemetery, and, of course, we could only have a memorial service for him, thought Violet.

She called to Jarvis to come out and help Aaron and the soldiers carry the casket into the parlor. She thanked the soldiers and asked Jarvis to take them to the kitchen where Mammy and Aunt Sheba would provide them with a meal and some food to carry back with them. Then she took Aaron aside and asked him to go tell Father Roberts that the Major had been brought home, and that the family would like to have the burial service as soon as it was convenient for Father Roberts to do so. On the way back, Aaron was again to stop by the Frierson and Thompson plantations and tell them the day and time of the service. And again she knew that they would make sure the news reached other friends. She told Aaron not to linger at either plantation but to hurry back and tell the Storms what the rector had said.

Aaron returned with a note saying that Father Roberts would conduct the burial service at two o'clock the next day and that he would be over early tonight to see the Storms and to plan the service with them. After informing her sisters and the house servants, Violet went over to Leo's house. Again the overseer rang the Plantation Bell for three minutes, then paused, then rang the bell for three minutes more. Again the slaves assembled in front of Leo's house, speculating about what dreadful thing could have happened now. Anxiety was so great that this time there were no murmuring voices, only silence as they waited for the news.

Violet announced, "I will get right to the point for I know you are worried about what terrible thing might have happened. I asked Leo to call you together so that I might tell you that soldiers brought the Major home to rest. The burial service will be at Holy Cross Church at two o'clock tomorrow afternoon. Except for the necessary chores, no plantation work will be done tomorrow. For those of you who wish to attend the service, wagons will be provided for transportation. That is all I have to say other than a thank you to those of you who have said such kind things to the family this difficult week."

Family, friends, and plantation slaves attended the service as the Major was laid to rest beside his beloved wife. Violet heard the words from *The Book of Common Prayer* and the reassuring words of the rector, but she pondered the lack of effect of these words. *Perhaps I am just tired. Perhaps I've done too much this past week. We've had so many good people stop by, so much company, so much food shared with us even in these lean times, and extra wagons lent so our slaves could get here. But, if not, then what is wrong with me?* she asked herself, receiving no answer.

The next day, those on the plantation began the arduous task of trying to resume some normalcy in their lives. Workers returned to the fields and other duties, going about their work with muffled voices. The silence was unnatural for usually outbursts of singing were heard, inside as well as outside the house. In uncommon stoic silence, Leo managed the workers. They took no offense, knowing the reason and that the reason had nothing to do with them.

On Wednesday afternoon Violet called her sisters into the office for a reading of their father's will.

"This is always painful, but necessary." she said.

"Yes, let's get on with it. Let's get this business over with," agreed Charlotte.

Violet opened the heavy safe in the corner of the room, and searching briefly through several papers, she drew out an envelope that contained the will. Unfolding the paper, she said, "This is dated September 22, 1862. That was just a few days after the great battle at Sharpsburg. I guess by then Father was convinced that we were in for a long war."

Going directly to the essentials, Violet read:

1. *I bequeath the Fair Oaks Plantation, with all real and personal property thereon to be divided equally between my eldest daughter, Violet Lee Storm Sutler, and my son, Christopher Alexander Storm, or to the survivor between them.*
2. *To my daughter Charlotte Rose Storm, I bequeath the property in Columbia, South Carolina, at the northwest corner of Taylor and Sumter Streets, with all real and personal property thereon.*
3. *My remaining financial assets, including cash, bank deposits and government bonds, I bequeath to my daughter Susan Phlox Storm.*

4. *Provided that peace has been restored to the land, then manumission will be extended to all slaves remaining on Fair Oaks Plantation and on the property in Columbia, South Carolina.*

"Well, there it is," Violet concluded.

Neither Charlotte nor Susan showed any disappointment or any satisfaction.

"I'm sorry," Violet added. "I'm afraid there's nothing left of the town house, Charlotte, although of course there is the lot; and Susan, I have no idea what the financial assets are worth. But I want both of you to know this—as long as I am here, Fair Oaks will be your home, both of you, for as long as you like."

Chapter 9

Aftershock

1865

"Miz Violet, hit be time ta git ta plowin' de fields fer plantin'," Leo was speaking to Violet on the porch of the overseer's house.

Violet had given no thought to starting the spring plowing. That was something her father always had taken care of in the past. It occurred to her that now the threat of Sherman's coming had passed, any delay in preparation of the fields would likely lead to a decline in yields. Already it was the first day of spring.

"Yes, Leo, I see what you mean. You're right. We should begin the plowing. At sunup tomorrow morning let's get the workers to haul manure from the stables and the cow barn to the cotton fields, and then as soon as we can, start plowing to turn it over. We'll go to the cornfield next week and after that the vegetable garden. Didn't you and Daddy let the plowed fields stand for about three weeks?"

"Yassum. An' 'bout de time we git finish wif plowin' de vegeb'l gard'n hit be time ta plant de cott'n seed an' affer dat den de corn seed an' den de vegeb'l seed." Leo said with a big grin at Violet's knowledge of farming.

"And Leo, I guess we're too late for wheat this year, aren't we?" asked Violet wrinkling her forehead in an effort to recall what the Major had said about the time to plant wheat.

"Yassum, Miz Violet. We gwine wait fer nex' year fer dat now." He grinned at her again and said with a twinkle in his eyes, "But cawnbred sho' be mighty good." He laughed heartily, and then became serious again. "Now don' ya worree none, Miz Violet, Leo tek care of ebberting."

"Thank you, Leo. I know you will. I guess we'll all have to work hard if we're going to eat this year." She took her leave, grateful to have Leo as her overseer. He was experienced and dependable, and she couldn't imagine managing the plantation without him.

It was early Monday Morning, April 10th. Seed had been brought out from hiding, and it was time to begin planting. Still in her robe, Violet ran to the window at the back of the upstairs hall. She flung open the shutters to a beautiful spring day of golden sunshine and green meadows. The whole landscape conveyed a disposition of tranquility, exaggerated in intensity by the war still surrounding it. Even the birds seemed to have recovered their songs with a new enthusiasm. Beyond the pond and the creek she could see with satisfaction that wagons were carrying the workers to the fields. Today and tomorrow they would be hoeing weeds and plowing furrows. By Wednesday some would begin planting cotton while others continued the preparation.Violet returned to her room to dress. There she opened a front window for a look in that direction. She took a deep breath as she looked down on the green lawn dotted with bright yellow dandelions and patches of blue-purple violets. Others might think of these as weeds and a nuisance, but she thought these little wild flowers were beautiful. She recalled when, as a little girl, she would see them blooming from her bedroom window and would race out to pick bunches of violets, which she called her namesake flower. Her mother would put them in a cut crystal bowl and place them on the tea table in the library. At first Violet also had picked bunches of dandelions, but soon discovered that these bright sunny flowers quickly closed up when brought into the house out of the simmering light. So when she picked the violets she would pick just one large dandelion and place it in a buttonhole of her dress.

Her thoughts returned to the present, and her eyes fell upon the roses and azaleas along the borders. These were beginning to bloom. In the apple orchard to her left, the blossoms were popping out on the trees, beginning to create a mass of white. But beyond the orchard, in the direction of Sumter, a thin veil of smoke seemed to be rising. There, below the rising sun the sky was strangely dim. Violet wondered if this might mean rain, even a thunderstorm, later in the day.

The threat of storm sent Violet into feverish activity to get as much done as possible. She gave some attention to little Bonnie Anne and J.J., and then, urging her sisters to oversee the house and garden chores, she hurried outside to try to step up the pace of work in the barns and in the fields. The storm, however, never arrived at the plantation.

That evening, relieved that they were able to get a good day's work done without any rain interruption, Violet sought to create some diversion and entertainment for the family. After supper she called on Charlotte to get her violin and Susan her flute and join her at the piano in the parlor. Bonnie Anne sat beside her on the piano bench, and little J.J., beginning to get a bit sleepy now that his tummy was full, played quietly with his blocks and other toys on the floor by the big chair. For an hour the sisters played favorite pieces of music, from Chopin and Schubert to Stephen Foster. By then J.J. was sound asleep. Mammy and Evelina came to get the children ready for bed. Evelina gently picked up J.J. so as not to awaken him, and everyone went upstairs. Charlotte and Susan went to their rooms, after whispering good night to Bonnie Anne. When the children were in their beds, Violet kissed each good night, sang a lullaby, and then went down the stairs to the library.

She read for a while in one of her old favorites, Jane Austen's *Pride and Prejudice*. Then, as if trying to reestablish some connection with the past, she pulled down her father's old, worn copy of Marcus Aurelius' *Meditations*. The book fell open to Chapter IV where she read:

> *Time is a sort of river of passing events, and strong is its current; no sooner is a thing brought to sight than it is swept by and another takes its place, and this too will be swept away.*

She fingered a few pages further and smiled to herself as she read:

> *In the morning, when thou art sluggish at rousing thee, let this thought be present: 'I am rising to a man's work.'*

She closed the book, returned it to its place on the shelf and went up to bed.

The next day was much like the day before—fair wind, hazy sky, good work. Violet heard what sounded like musket shots now and then in the distance to the southward, and she wondered if somebody might be hunting at this time of year. But she concerned herself little with such distractions as she moved ahead to begin planting on the morrow.

"Miz Violet! Miz Violet! De Yankees be comin'! De Yankees be comin'!"

Startled, Violet turned her head as she walked out toward the cow barn on this Wednesday morning, April 12th, to see a young black man riding up at a gallop. She recognized Ramey, the Frierson's horse swipe.

"What is it, Ramey? What do you mean the Yankees are coming? You'd better not be jesting!"

Leaping off his horse the messenger faced Violet and said in a quivering voice, "Massuh John, he say ta tell ya dat de Yankees be in Manchester..."

"Manchester!"

"Yassum, dey be in Manchester and dey comin' dis way."

"Ramey, you are confused. The Yankees already were in Camden several days ago and are heading northward. They could not now be all the way back down here to Manchester."

"Yassum dey be, an' dey be comin' dis way! Dey be in Sumter yistaday, an' dey burned lot uh houses an' ebberting! De Yankees so' 'nuf comin'!" He nodded his head emphatically.

My, God, that haze in the sky these past two days must have been from fires in Sumter! she thought in dismay. She looked around to the south and could see distinctly spirals of smoke in the direction of Wedgefield plantation and Manchester.

"Thank you, Ramey, thank you. Now you had better get on and warn the others around here!" she said as she turned and ran toward the overseer's house, calling, "Leo! Leo!"

There was no answer. Frantically she knocked on his door. Still no answer. She ran from one end of the small porch to the other, and then out into the small yard, looking and calling for Leo. There was no sight of Leo and no reply to her calls. She stopped and struggled to get hold of herself. *Leo must be out in the field! But first I must warn those in the house!* she thought anxiously. Calling Fabian to saddle Bella so she could get to Leo, Violet ran into the house. She called Charlotte and Susan and each house servant by name and telling everyone to come into the central hall. Noting the urgency in her voice they assembled quickly.

"The Yankees are coming this way!" she exclaimed excitedly.

"How can that be?" asked Charlotte incredulously. "We know that Sherman is up in North Carolina...don't we?"

Susan let out a scream and started running from one end of the hall to the other, looking out one door and then the other.

"*Susan!* Stop that. Come stand here and settle down. We aren't going to accomplish anything running around like a chicken with its head cut off!" Violet said sternly. Realizing the wisdom of her sister's words, Susan obeyed and rejoined the group.

"Come on now, everyone, let's quiet down," said Violet calmly. Trying to reassure them she went on, "I have seen the Yankees in Columbia. They didn't murder everybody. I don't know how they got back to this area from North Carolina, but somehow they already have been to Sumter and burned lots of buildings, and then apparently they went down to Manchester–and it looks like they are back up to Wedgefield now."

"How do you know?" demanded Charlotte.

All eyes were on Violet awaiting her answer. "John Frierson sent their Ramey over to tell us. And you can see the smoke and hear guns off in that direction. My guess is the Yankees will be coming up the King's Highway and the railroad–you know how they like to tear up our railroads–to Stateburg and then Camden." She stopped as a thought suddenly struck her and then spoke that thought aloud. "But you know they will have their bummers out this way, taking everything that isn't nailed down, and likely burning everything that is!"

Susan asked with alarm in her eyes and voice, "Oh, Violet, what are we going to do?"

Quivering in fear and remembering the Yankee soldier who had burst in on them in the Columbia town house, Evelina cried, "Yas, Miz Violet, whar we goin'? Whut we gwine do?" The others nodded their heads for Susan and Evelina had asked the question in their own minds.

"Now listen, everybody. It's important that we remain calm so we can think clearly and won't do anything foolish or anything we might regret. Remember what Daddy always told us, `In an emergency, keep cool, calm, and collected,' and that is just what we must do. We aren't going anywhere. I think it will be best to stay right here. But listen now, we have lots of work to do. We *must* work fast so we can save as much as we can before the Yankees get here. If we get the chance, let's put on three or four dresses to save them and tie our personal things under our hooped skirts."

Mammy, always stalwart, and maintaining a calmer disposition than the others, went straight to the matter at hand. "Miz Violet, jes' tell us whut ya wan' us ta do an' we be doin' it jes' as fas' as we can."

"Now listen," Violet repeated, assuming a business-like tone of authority. "It looks like the Yankees are at least up to Wedgefield. That means that, walking across the fields, they could be here in three or four hours. Aunt Sheba..."

"Yassum, I'se righ' chere."

"Aunt Sheba, get sheets, pillows, and pillow cases out of the linen wardrobe and then go down to the basement and fix cribs for the children and then stay there to help look after them."

"Yassum, I go righ' now." She took off immediately. It was one of the few times anyone ever had seen Aunt Sheba hurry for anything.

"Evelina!"

"Yassum, Miz Violet, Ah stay wif ya."

"No, Evelina. You've got to look after the children. You run up and get them now and then take them to the basement. Stay there with Aunt Sheba, and you all make sure that the children stay there with the two of you. They can walk around the halls, take naps in the cribs, play with toys—but they absolutely must not go outside, understand? Even if the Yankees come in here, don't you or the children leave the basement—unless I tell you differently!"

"Yassum, I look affer dem, I tek care uf dem good!" And Evelina took off quickly.

"Aunt Beulah, you go with Evelina to the children's room and gather up some of their favorite toys and take them to the basement—and after that you'd better get some diapers and some bedclothes and other clothes for the children while Evelina and Aunt Sheba stay with the children. When you've done this, come back upstairs. We'll need you to get some things in boxes for hiding."

"Yassum, I be gone now!"

"Susan, I want to take advantage of your sharp eyes and agility. You can be our lookout."

"Where?"

"Go upstairs and move around to all the windows and look for the Yankees—mainly from the southwest, but be sure to keep looking in *all* directions. We must have warning because we are going to be moving things out for hiding, and we don't want to get caught doing this. I'll send Aaron down the lane on a horse for a further watch. And listen, everybody, I'll tell the rest of you what you are to be doing, but first, if you are still working at hiding things when you hear a warning that the Yankees are coming, *stop* what you are doing, cover up everything, and be going about your regular chores." She had more to tell Susan so she continued, "So Susan, you know how important for us to be warned, but the Yankees probably won't be here for several hours, so you can take a few minutes to get some of your things together that you want us to hide—and then start looking and stay alert! Don't you dare go to sleep on your post."

"I couldn't go to sleep if I wanted to," answered Susan, and she was off in a flash.

Violet turned to the head house servant. "Jarvis, you go out and find Fabian—he's just saddled Bella—and the two of you go to the vegetable garden and begin digging holes to bury the bags of things in. We don't have time to take our household goods back to the Storm Cellar. After you've dug the holes, come back to the house and carry out the bags and boxes we will have packed and bury them."

"Yassum, yassum, whar in de gard'n duz ya wan' us ta go?"

"Anywhere. Anywhere that you can dig quickly and where you can find them again."

"Yassum, Ah go."

"All right, Miss Charlotte will show you what to carry out. Go, now! Dig quickly!"

Next Violet turned to Charlotte. "Charlotte, you'll have to be in charge of getting things together to hide in the garden. I tried to see Leo when I first heard the news but he wasn't at his house, so I've got to ride out to the fields and get the workers to help get as much as we can of the cotton still in the storehouse back to the woods. We've got to save all the cotton we can. You and Mammy and Aunt Beulah and Uncle Job will have to bundle things in sheets and pillowcases and get them ready for Jarvis and Fabian to take out to the garden."

"Sure...I'll do what I can, but what do you think we should take out first?" asked Charlotte.

"Probably the silver, because that is what they are likely to steal first. Too bad we brought all this back in from the Storm Cellar after we thought Sherman had passed beyond us. We should have waited a while."

"Yes, I wish we had. But then what? And do we have boxes or crates?"

"There are a few of both in the basement. Use them and then wrap the rest of the things up in rugs—or anything you can find. And listen, while some are packing silver, have somebody else packing the good china. Then maybe some of our art work and our jewelry. Try to get some of our favorite books out, too"

"All right, we'll have to work fast, I know. Come on Mammy. Uncle Job, you go down and see if you can find the boxes. If Aunt Beulah is down there, tell her to join us in the dining room. After you bring the boxes to us, walk around the house and get some throw rugs that we can use for wrapping items."

As the rest rushed to begin their assigned tasks, Violet ran out the back door and found her mare already saddled by Aaron and waiting at the tying post to be mounted. Apparently Aaron had gone on to help Jarvis dig the hiding holes. She mounted quickly and galloped out toward the cotton fields. She found Leo selecting foremen and getting crews organized for the planting. She stopped a short distance away and called out to him, "Leo! Leo! Come over here. I must talk with you. Hurry!"

He walked rapidly over to her, wondering what had happened to bring Violet out to the fields.

"Leo, the Yankees are coming this way. They'll be here in three or four hours. We've got to hide all the cotton we can back in the woods. Forget about the planting. Get all the horses and mules and wagons and all the men to work on moving the cotton out to the woods where the Yankees can't find it."

Understanding at once the urgency, Leo said, "Yassum, Miz Violet, we git out all de cott'n we can. Tell me, Miz Violet, duz ya kno' wich way dey comin' frum?"

Pointing to the southwest, she answered, "Probably from that way. I don't think we can get much cotton in the Storm Cellar, so just spread it out in the woods and cover it up. Aaron will warn you when he sees any sign that the Yankees are approaching. Then you have your men stop hauling cotton, get everybody back here away from the woods, and go back to your regular work of planting."

"Yassum, Miz Violet. Now don'cha worree none. Leo tek care uf ebberting." They parted and within half an hour Violet could hear the wagons shuttling back and forth between the cotton storage shed and the woods.

Back at the house, Violet found everyone working as fast as possible to get things out and buried, as she had directed. She raced down to the basement and found the children napping along with Aunt Sheba who was sound asleep in a rocking chair. Evelina was folding some of the extra children's clothes while keeping an eye on all three. Violet gave her a reassuring smile and ran back upstairs and into the office. Leaving two old muskets on the wall rack, she took down her father's carbine.

"Uncle Job, Uncle Job!" she called.

"Yassum, Miz Violet." Uncle Job came running in, still carrying a couple of items.

"Uncle Job, take this gun and hide it."

"Yassum, whar ya wan' hit?"

"Well, let's see...I know! Take down the stove pipe from the laundry stove. Put the gun in there and then put the stove pipe back in place. Quickly now."

"Yassum, dat be uh good place. Dey ain't nawbudy ebber gwine ta find hit dere!" Job set his boxes down and hurried off with the gun.

Violet grabbed a bundle of china wrapped up in a rug and ran to the garden. Jarvis and Fabian were making good progress with burying the items. She put the rug in one of the holes and noted with satisfaction the extent of their excavations.

Within another three hours much of the household valuables had been buried. As Violet stood in the hall to survey the work, Susan called down from upstairs, "Somebody's coming!"

"Where?" shouted Violet.

"Coming up the lane, right toward the house!"

Violet ran upstairs and joined Susan at the front window of the house.

"Look," Susan cried out, pointing in the direction of the soldiers.

"Yes, I see...but wait...look! They are wearing old butternut jackets and kepis. I believe they are Confederate soldiers...but I see only three."

"Yes, that's all I see. There are only three soldiers coming up the lane."

Violet raced downstairs, ran out the front door and down the lane where she met the three soldiers. They were Confederates all right. Looked like a grandfather and grandson—one too old to fight and the other too young—and another young soldier.

"Who are you?" Violet demanded.

"Me and the boy here are from the Sumter militia," the old man responded. "This one is a soldier from Kentucky. He's left behind by Johnston's army."

"Where are the others?"

"Oh, they're scattered all over. We've been ordered to go on up t'other side of Stateburg and organize a defense line to make a stand along Beech Creek."

"Then we'll show'em, you just wait and see," the young lad chimed in.

"Well, I hope you make a stand somewhere, but that's not going to do much for us here...is it?" asked Violet.

"No, ma'am," the old man agreed. "But there's not much else we can do. The Yankees have got us outnumbered everywhere."

"What's happened? Where are the Yankees now? Are they headed this way?" asked Violet apprehensively.

The old soldier looked at Violet with sympathy in his eyes. He recognized a young lady of courage and strength and he answered, "Ma'am, I regret to say they are just a couple of miles behind us...headed this way for sure."

With dismay and dread at the thought the Yankees might soon be on Fair Oaks property, Violet asked, "Where did they come from? We thought Sherman was in North Carolina. I don't understand."

"Ma'am, Sherman *is* in North Carolina—or thereabouts. This is General Potter. He came up from Georgetown on the coast. We made a good stand on Sunday at Dingle's Mill to defend their approach to Sumter, but there were too many for us to handle. Late that afternoon the Yankee's cavalry rode up Main Street. Then others came. The Yankees set fire to lots of buildings, and they rounded up all the Negroes. The colored folks, they've been following along after the Yankees. The Yankees followed the railroad from Sumter to Manchester and tore up everything along the way." The old soldier stopped, wiped his forehead with his 'kerchief, looked meaningfully at his companions, and continued, "But we've got to be on our way, Ma'am, no time to tarry any longer."

"Of course. I understand. But first can I give you some water or something?"

"Yes, ma'am, a cup of water would be mighty good, thank you."

"Ma'am," the young Kentucky soldier spoke.

"Yes?"

"I'll stay here to guard you folks and your place."

"Why, thank you, soldier. You're a brave young man, I can tell. Thank you. We need all the help we can get."

"Yes, Ma'am. You go ahead and do what you have to. I'll patrol the area between here and the barns." He took off, eager to fulfil his duty to the beautiful young mistress of the plantation.

Violet, the old soldier, and the younger soldier went to the back of the house for a drink of cool spring water. The two men refilled their canteens and were on their way.

Taking no further chances, Violet told those in the house to resume their normal chores, except that Evelina and Aunt Sheba would remain in the basement with the children. Violet ran to the garden and told Fabian and Jarvis to cover all the holes and scatter weeds over them so that no one would suspect that valuables were hidden there. Then she mounted Bella and galloped out to tell Leo to stop hauling cotton and to get everyone back to work in the fields as if nothing unusual had taken place.

Back in the house Violet and Charlotte gathered up many of their favorite books from the library and took them to the basement. They had not been at this more than half an hour when Susan called out from her upstairs lookout, "The Yankees are coming! The Yankees are coming! It's really the Yankees this time!"

Violet did not have to go upstairs to see the action. It was plain enough that streams of blue-coated men were running across the west meadow toward the house and barns.

To her dismay, she could see their animals being turned out and the buildings being set afire. Smoke rose in turn from the chicken house, the cow barn, the mule shed, the horse barn, then from the mills, and soon roaring flames were consuming the cotton storage house and its contents.

Charlotte ran up to Violet as Susan came running down the stairs, each crying hysterically, "What shall we do? Oh, Violet, what shall we do? Those damn Yankees are burning everything! And soon they'll be here! Oh, Violet, they'll be here any minute!"

"Susan," Violet said with studied composure, trying to calm her younger sister, "you run down to the basement and stay with the children and Evelina and Aunt Sheba." Susan took off for the basement in a flash.

"Charlotte, you come with me...quickly!." Charlotte followed her older sister to the office. Violet took down one of the muskets and, handing it to Charlotte, said, "Take this and go stand on the front porch. Don't let anybody–*anybody*–in and don't let anybody set the house on fire!"

"Violet, I haven't used a gun since Daddy took us target practicing!"

"Oh, it isn't even loaded, but they don't know that, and maybe you can scare them off. I'll go out the back door–that's where they are headed right now–and try to hold them off there." Violet took down the other.

They dashed in opposite directions with their weapons and their frantic determination.

Violet did not have long to wait. A squad of six white Yankee soldiers came running to her. As they approached to within about twenty yards, she leveled her musket at each one in turn. They took a few more steps and stopped as a corporal called out, "Lady, you better stand aside. Our orders are to search the house for firearms."

"And my orders to you are to keep out of here."

"Now we don't want to shoot a lady...don't make us have to, Ma'am."

"I don't mind shooting a damn Yankee at all."

"You know that won't do no good. One musket can't stop six men."

"Maybe not, but it can stop one of you. Now, I'll shoot the first man who steps across that brick walk. Which one of you men wants to have the honor?"

Just then there was something of a commotion as four black Yankee soldiers came up with what evidently was a prisoner. Violet shuddered as she recognized the young Confederate soldier who had volunteered to help protect them.

"We found dis Reb'l out dere," one of the Negro soldiers said. "Whut duz we do wif 'im??"

The corporal spoke up, "Where ya from, Reb?"

"Kentucky."

"Kentucky? I'm from Kentucky, an' I ain't no Reb...whatcha doin' here?"

"I'm fightin' for The Cause, like all other right-thinkin' Kentuckians."

"The hell you are. Now, why don't you just take an oath to the United States, and you can come along with us right peacefully."

"I'm not takin' any oath to support the Yankees," the young soldier said with conviction.

"Come now, we've given you a chance to save your life, to get back to your old Kentucky home. Don't you want that?"

"Course I want that, but I ain't takin' no Yankee oath."

"I'm losing my patience. Now, will you swear allegiance to the United States!"

"No, I just can't do that, Corporal."

"Damn it, swear allegiance to the United States!"

"Sir, I won't...I can't do it."

"Shoot him!" snarled the Corporal in frustration.

Immediately all four black soldiers fired. The young Kentuckian dropped dead. They took him back to the garden to bury him in one of the holes uncovered by the soldiers taking hidden valuables.

Violet had witnessed the whole event. She wanted to faint or to flee. Instead she summoned all the courage stored within her, squared her shoulders, and shouted in anger and disgust, "That's the most despicable thing I have ever seen. You are a bunch of savage murderers and barbarians. And if anybody makes one...I mean **one** step in this direction you are going to join that young man. Corporal, your men may run over me, but if they try, I guarantee that you are never going to see your old Kentucky home again either." She pointed her musket right at the corporal's head. He paused awkwardly, embarrassed to be caught in a stalemate, but not anxious to put her threat to the test.

Just then a Yankee captain came riding up. "Men, the colonel wants to use this house for his headquarters, so don't burn it. Lady, we mean no harm to you. I'll put a guard on the house to protect it, but we must search the house for firearms and clear rooms for our headquarters. We'll be needing this only for a day or two. Now if you will surrender your weapon, we shall go about our business." He held out his hand to take Violet's musket.

"How do I know that I can trust you?" she asked contemptuously.

"Ma'am, you have no choice."

With some misgivings Violet handed the musket to the captain. He laughed as he saw that it was not loaded, and he handed it to one of the men, saying, "Lady, you have enough spunk for a regiment!"

Violet recalled that these were the exact words spoken by the Yankee soldier that had broken into their Columbia town house. Somehow this gave her courage. After all, she had driven off that scoundrel! She intended to keep her wits and do the same with these Yankees.

The search for firearms turned into a general treasure hunt. Black as well as White soldiers ran through the house, pulling down curtains and draperies, stripping beds, overturning furniture, scattering books, emptying shelves of porcelain and pewter.

One soldier ran into the house with a bucket of buttermilk and followed three or four comrades upstairs to Violet's room where they forced the lock on her trunk at the foot of her bed. Finding nothing of value, the soldier tipped the bucket and poured the buttermilk into the trunk.

Violet and her sisters kept their distance from the intruders. A glance out a back window brought further consternation. Yankees were digging up the garden and carrying off all the items buried there. From across the center meadow came whole platoons of Yankees escorting all the slaves—some riding horses, some on mules, some driving carriages, many crowded on wagons, others walking. Other wagons were loaded with meat and cheese and grain and poultry. Animals were wandering all through the multitude.

Running outside, Violet found herself in the midst of a wild celebration. Led on by the black soldiers, the slaves were singing and shouting. "It be de day uf jubilo, we be free! We be free!"

Violet approached Fabian who was in the company of some black soldiers. "Fabian! What are you doing?"

"Ah is free! Ah is free! Ah ain't nebbuh gwine haf ta work no mo'—no mo' work—no mo' work!"

"Fabian, what are you going to do for food and clothing and shelter?"

"Oh, Miz Violet, de guvmint gwine tek care uf ebberbudy...de guvmint-de Yankees say we don' haf ta work no mo'. De guvmint gwine tek care uf us frum now on."

"Oh, Fabian, Fabian. Surely that can't be so." But he had passed on and was soon lost in the crowd. She couldn't believe that he was leaving them.

Violet turned just in time to see Leo and asked in a crestfallen voice "Leo, not you too, Leo?"

"Naw, Miz Violet, Ah ain't gwine nawwhar but ta see if'n ah can git our darkies ta come back heah. Ah be back, Miz Violet, ah be back. Don'cha worree none now. Ah be back. Dis here's whar ah belong. Ah ain't runnin' affer dem Yankees like some folks. Dint ah promise yo' daddy dat ah tek cah uf ya and de girls an' de chillen?" Leo followed Fabian down the lane.

With a deep sigh of disappointment, Violet turned around and saw Aaron, Uncle Job, and Aunt Beulah being prodded along by the bayonets of two black soldiers.

Uncle Job called out, "Don'cha worree none, Miz Violet, we be back! Dese soldiers mek us go wif dem now."

"Yassum, Miz Violet," Aaron shouted, "we be prisoners uf freedom, uf freedom...prisoners uf freedom! But we be back."

Except for a smoldering glance at the soldiers prodding her, Aunt Beulah just walked along with her head down and said nothing.

When the Yankee colonel came in later that evening to set up his headquarters, he restored order and went about his work in a military manner. He was civil enough, but Violet was in no mood for civilities.

At one point the colonel approached Violet and asked, "Ma'am, would you favor us with a piece at the piano?"

Violet hesitated just for a moment, then walked to the piano in the parlor as Charlotte and Susan and the Yankee officers followed. She sat at the piano and began playing *Bonnie Blue Flag*. Glancing over her shoulder she saw little sign of recognition, except for Charlotte and Susan who were exchanging amused looks. Then Violet began singing, and that brought reactions of nervous recognition on the part of her audience. After a couple of verses she shifted to a lively rendition of *Dixie,* singing and playing. Unable to control her mirth, Susan ran out of the room.

"That will be quite enough, thank you, Ma'am," said the Colonel.

Violet excused herself and retired to the basement with the children. Her sisters accompanied her there. All the menservants were gone. Only Mammy and Aunt Sheba and Evelina remained.

At midday the next day, the Yankee headquarters moved out. Before the Colonel left Violet went to him to ask that food be left for the women and children in the house. Nodding in agreement to her request, he ordered his men to leave a couple of hams and sacks of beans, potatoes, and cornmeal. He told Violet that in his view the end of the War was at hand, and he hoped there would be no need for further destruction. He thanked her for the use of the house and departed with his men. Violet took a deep breath of relief.

Only minutes later, Violet sped down to the basement and told everyone to come back upstairs and to bring the children for some fresh air. The Yankees were gone! They all let out a loud cheer.

While Mammy and Aunt Sheba went to the kitchen to begin cooking, and Evelina had the children outdoors, Violet, Charlotte, and Susan began straightening the furniture and putting things back in place. They found that while things on the first floor, where the Colonel spent most of his time, were in fairly good condition other than the stripped windows and emptied drawers, the second floor had been ravaged even more by the soldiers after the Colonel had gone downstairs that morning. The sisters looked around in astonishment and dismay. Charlotte was the first to speak. "My lands! Why on earth would they want to do this?"

They looked at the portraits slashed by bayonets, chairs and sofas with holes poked in the fabric, the portieres pulled from the windows and lying on the floor. Even the mattresses from the beds had been turned over and holes jabbed into them. Drawers had been pulled from dressers, tables, and desks, and the contents dumped on the floor.

In answer to Charlotte's question, Violet said disgustedly, "Because they're butchers and bastards, that's what, with no regard to the feelings and property of other human beings."

"Because they're damn Yankees!" exclaimed Susan. "And I'm sure they're going to be damned and go to hell and it'll serve them right and I hate them all." She burst into tears.

Violet put her arms around her younger sister, "No doubt you're right, Susan." She stopped in thought and then added, "I guess the Colonel is responsible for his men's actions, but I'm willing to bet that he was unaware of what his men were doing after he went downstairs this morning. Somehow I think he would have reprimanded them most severely."

They were startled by a noise outside the back hall window. As they crossed over to look out they were chilled by a loud scream. It was Evelina with three black soldiers. She was trying to pull away from them. Violet raced down the stairs with Charlotte and Susan close behind. Mammy had been feeding the children in the kitchen when she heard Evelina screaming. She met the girls in the hall. They arrived at the door just in time to see the soldiers carrying Evelina across the west meadow. Violet ran after them, but it was no use. They were already too far ahead. She looked for a horse, but there was none. The Yankees had taken all the horses with them. She walked back to the house with a heart even heavier than before and with eyes reddened by smoke and sadness and smoldering rage.

Chapter 10

Potter Again?

1865

The next day Violet went out to survey the damage. She found herself heading for the stable to get her horse. But there was no stable. She looked around, stunned at what lay before her. All the outbuildings and most of the slave cabins were in smoldering ruins. No animal, no vehicle was to be found anywhere. The Yankees had taken all the horses for their own transportation and all the chickens, hogs, and cattle for their food. She found the remains, still smoking, of two wagons and one buggy. There was no trace of the carriage, the other buggy, or remaining wagons. She walked all the way back to the woods to see if the hidden cotton had escaped the Yankee bummers. It took her an hour to reach the woods, but she was relieved to find that the cotton was still there. Suddenly Old Dan bounded through the woods toward her, his tail wagging. Violet realized that the hordes of unfamiliar faces trampling around the plantation must have unsettled the dog, and he had sought refuge in the familiar woods where he and his beloved master had often walked and hunted.

She looked down into the Storm Cellar, regretting that she had had all the valuables returned to the house just in time for Potter. She saw a few bags of cottonseed and some garden seed still there. For this she was thankful. Then she noted movement below. *An animal!* she thought, but she shouted, "Who's in there? Come out or I'll shoot!"

A quivering voice responded, "Naw, Miz Violet, don' shoo', hit be me!" and out climbed Uncle Jarvis.

In astonishment Violet exclaimed, "Uncle Jarvis, what are you doing here? You said you were going to celebrate your day of jubilo!" She reached out her hand to help him.

"No, Ma'am, ah stay heah!"

"What happened?"

"Miz Violet, uh Yankee sojuh stole mah watch, he stole hit. Ah say ta dat sojuh dat ah buy dat watch wif mah own monee dat ah save up ovah uh long time. He jes' say, 'Too bad, fellah, hits mine now.' Den ah say ta him dat ah druver stay wif de folk whar ah could buy de watch den go wif de thief dat steal hit..."

"Oh, Uncle Jarvis, good for you!"

He continued, "Den ah afeard dey mek me leave wif dem. Ah wen' thru all de people cumin' ou', an' ah hide in de burnin' mule shed, an' den, w'en nawbudy look, ah run bek heah an' clum down de Stawm Celluh an' heah ah be." He looked around fearfully to see if any soldiers were lurking behind the trees.

"They're gone now, Uncle Jarvis. You'll be all right. Come, you can walk back to the house with me."

As they started walking toward the house with Old Dan following, Jarvis went on, "Miz Violet, dat watch wuz de only ting uf mah own dat ah ebber have. Yas, de Massuh gib meh mah cloves and ebberting, buh de watch ah buy wif mah own monee, de monee dat ah git Chrismuss and dat ah mek workin' extra on Sundays. An' now hit be gone, stole by dat Yankee sojuh." He took a large soiled handkerchief from his pocket and wiped his eyes.

Looking around as they walked back, they could see no chickens, no foodstuffs. They looked inside the still standing smokehouse and milkhouse, and found these empty of all meat and cheese. The overseer's house and kitchen were still there, but they had been ransacked by the soldiers. Leo, of course, was gone.

"Lawdy, Miz Violet, ain't dere be nawbudy buh ussan heah? Whar ebberbudy? Whar Miz Charlotte an' Miz Susan an' de udders?"

"Miss Charlotte and Miss Susan are at the house. So are Mammy and Aunt Sheba. The Yankees took Evelina and Aunt Beulah and Uncle Job and Aaron with them. Fabian took off on his own, saying the government would take care of him from now on. And Leo left to see what he could do about rounding up our folks and getting them back here. But we're all right. I guess you can say we're still in a state of shock by all that's happened to us. And mad. Whopping mad!"

"Yassum, ah sho' be mad, too. Ussan got de righ' ta be mad, Miz Violet."

That night a full moon reminded Violet that Easter was approaching. It was the paschal moon. Tomorrow would be Good Friday. For the Storms, this would be the saddest Good Friday ever. As far as Violet was concerned, Easter carried none of the hope this year that was supposed to be its traditional message. She walked out to the front porch for a better look at the moon. Even as it rose higher in the eastern sky it appeared to retain a tint of orange from the smoke and haze still in the air. She wondered if moonbeams were riding the waves beside Brent's ship somewhere on the high seas—*Brent, we all need you so terribly now. These are such hard times*—or maybe his ship had gone to Davy Jones' locker, and Brent would never see this Easter or any other. *Oh, dear God, no! Don't let that be so!*

Good Friday itself was just another day of work at Fair Oaks. Only Mammy, Aunt Sheba, and Uncle Jarvis remained to help Violet and her sisters in straightening the house, caring for the children, washing clothes, and preparing meals from a steadily declining larder.

At the supper table that evening, Charlotte raised the question of their prospects.

Violet answered her by saying, "I do think that now the War is over for us. We've got to figure out how to keep body and soul together, at least until Brent gets back."

"Yes, but when do you think that will be, Brent's getting back, I mean?" asked Charlotte. She did not want to suggest in any way that he might not be able to return. Her older sister had enough to worry about, taking care of all of them.

Violet replied hopefully, "It might be only a few days if he is in this country, maybe along the coast somewhere. But if he is somewhere at sea, which I'm afraid is more likely, then it could take several weeks or even months for him to get the news and come home."

Susan gasped in alarm. "Oh, no! Then what do we do?"

"Fend for ourselves, what else?" Violet replied dryly. "We can do it. If we can survive the horrors of this war, and somehow we have, then we know we can continue surviving. We can..and we will!" she added determinedly.

"But what about Easter? I don't have anything to wear," Susan asked. "You know we always get new dresses for Easter."

"Forget Easter!" Violet said harshly. But realizing that her sister was still young, and had endured so much heartache, and that she was still somewhat emotionally shaken, Violet added in more gentle tones, "Susan, if you just think through our problems a bit, you'll realize that we have no fabric—we haven't been able to get any for ages because of the War—and even if we had the material there is no one with time to make new dresses."

With a frown Charlotte said, "It doesn't seem right for us not to do something a little special for Easter, like decorating with flowers and ribbons, and coloring eggs and everything."

"Forget it," Violet repeated. "Charlotte, *think* about what's happened. You know we don't have any chickens, let alone eggs, and the Yankee troops and horses trampled all our flowers and shrubs."

"But Violet, if we have no chickens, and no eggs, what do we eat? We don't have any hogs nor any cattle either, do we?" asked young Susan.

"No. We'll continue eating the ham and beans and cornbread and Irish potatoes until it all runs out. Thank goodness, that Yankee officer left us this bit of food when he left. But we've got to scrounge for more, maybe fruit and berries and nuts and edible greens, and the like. And we must plant a garden so that we'll have something this summer. I think I saw a sizeable amount of garden seed left in the Storm Cellar. And we've got to find some way to plant just a little bit of cotton so that we can have a little money for other essentials. We'll have to make do with the clothes we have—there's no one about who can manage the loom. Certainly for a while we're all going to be too busy to sit at a spinning wheel."

"But Violet, how can we do any planting? We don't have any horses or mules to pull the plow. We don't even have a cow that we might use." wondered Charlotte.

"I'm not quite sure how we are going to handle the problem of planting. We'll have to figure out what to do. Jarvis can help. For now, we'll continue our house work. Sunday will be a day of rest, and then on Monday we'll start making a garden.

Rain on Monday delayed the garden project, but Tuesday was a fair day, and the young ladies were out early. They were dressed in worn gingham gowns and wore sunbonnets to protect their fair skin. Jarvis had found some shovels and hoes in the vicinity of the burned tool shed, where they had been carelessly thrown by the slaves when the Yankees soldiers arrived. He distributed the tools among the girls, keeping the heaviest for himself. They worked side by side for about half an hour. Then a hay wagon drawn by a team of horses came around the driveway at the back of the house.

Violet, with Charlotte and Susan close behind, ran to meet their neighbors, John and Sarah Frierson. As John climbed down quickly from the wagon, Violet greeted them, "Good morning! I'm glad to see that you two are all right. What brings you out so early?" She wondered at his haste and the stern look upon his face. She braced herself for more bad news. Perhaps something awful had happened at Cherry Vale.

But the news was even worse. "Girls, I'm afraid Potter is coming back this way!"

Violet and her sisters gasped in horror. An involuntary "Damn!" escaped Violet's lips. "You mean the Yankees are coming again?" she exclaimed. *This can't be happening. I must be dreaming.* "Yes, I'm afraid so," answered John Frierson, shaking his thick mane of white hair in disgust, "and we think it would be wise to clear out before they get here. We heard this morning that they were approaching Balkans Mill and Bradford Springs, and probably will be in Stateburg again by tomorrow—and there's no one around to stop them."

Another "Damn!" burst from Violet's lips. She thrust out her chin and said with determination, "Well, we are staying right here. We've come through all right, more or less, so far."

"Yes!" agreed Susan bravely. "Those damned Yankees! Who do they think they are, anyhow, running all over everybody all the time. Well, we showed them, and we'll show them again, just you wait and see. We're staying right here. They can't scare us off." She put her hands on her hips in a defiant gesture. If Violet wasn't frightened, then she wouldn't be either.

"Oh, no!" exclaimed a dismayed Sarah Frierson.

John said forcefully, looking at the sisters severely, "We may not be as lucky as when they came through last week. You know that young ladies should not be in the midst of an enemy army."

Violet explained, "In Columbia the word was that the houses that had been abandoned were the ones most likely to be burned, and our town house got burned. Here at Fair Oaks we held off the raiders last time and saved the house, and I'm not going to let them destroy it this time."

John Frierson was insistent. "Your lives and the lives of your children are more important than a house, and you know what your father would say."

Violet recalled her father's reaction when she first mentioned taking the children to Columbia with her. She knew he would want them away from any danger, as well as his daughters.

Violet sighed in resignation. "Yes, I know what Daddy would say. And I certainly don't want anything to happen to Bonnie Anne and J.J." Charlotte and Susan nodded their heads in agreement. Uncle Jarvis, standing to the side, but taking in all that passed between the group, also nodded his head in accord.

"Well then," John said with some relief. "Quickly get just a few things, and climb aboard the wagon. Are any of your slaves still here, besides your man, Jarvis?"

"Just two other house servants—Mammy, and her older sister."

"Tell them all to come along if they've a mind to, or let them stay here if they prefer and join Potter's horde of freed slaves."

The sisters rushed into the house and returned only minutes later, each with a small bag, Violet and Charlotte carrying the children. The three house servants followed closely. They had no intention of being left behind when the Yankees were coming again, especially Uncle Jarvis after his experience with the soldier who stole his treasured watch. They nodded to the Frierson's two women servants and Ramey climbed in the rear of the wagon, settling down in comfort on the bed of hay that had been spread on the bottom.

"What about Old Dan?" asked Susan. She had grown up with the family's pet. He was her special playmate and often slipped upstairs to sleep by her bed when her father had been away. They had romped through the meadows and swam in the pond together many times. Susan frequently bragged that the dog was a better swimmer than she.

"How can we take a dog with us?" asked a crestfallen Violet, for she loved Old Dan as much as anyone.

Noting the expression on the girls' faces, John Frierson said kindly, "Oh, I believe there's sufficient room in the wagon for him. Call him."

"But where *is* he?" asked Susan. She ran around the house calling, "Dan! Dan, here! Here, here, come here, Dan!"

The others called, too, but there was no sign of the dog. Sadly, Susan rejoined the group and took her place, tears gathering in her eyes. The sisters knew they had to get going and should delay no longer. Uncle Jarvis helped them climb up on the wagon.

As they settled on the straw-covered wagon bed and John Frierson got the horses in motion, Violet asked, "Where are we going–to Sumter?"

Frierson answered, "At first I thought Sumter may be the best place, but then I thought that would be a likely target for Potter. I think he's coming back just to return to the coast, where he came from. What disturbs me is that I've heard that his men are being even more destructive than before."

On hearing this, the women shuddered at the thought of Potter being even more damaging, Violet asked anxiously, "Well, John, where then? Where are you taking us?"

"I think it probably best to go south. We'll drive over to the King's Highway and turn south toward Manchester."

"This would be fun if I weren't so scared," said Susan.

"Yes, indeed," agreed Charlotte. Her bonnet straps had become untied, and as she slowly retied the ribbons, she thought of past hay rides that were certainly more carefree than this one. She said aloud to no one in particular, "I wonder if we will ever have a carefree day again."

Violet asked the Friersons, "John...Sarah...how were you able to save these horses and wagon? We have no horses, no mules, no wagons, no carriages, nor anything. The Yankees stole the animals and burned the vehicles."

"Hid them in the swamp," Frierson answered tersely. "Good thing I did. The soldiers got everything else. They don't care what happens to us. They don't care if we starve to death or freeze to death or anything else." Then he did an uncharacteristic thing. He leaned over the side of the wagon, cleared his throat, and spit heartily as though he wanted to cover the entire Union army with spittle.

As they moved along the road toward Stateburg, evidences of destruction were all around them. Through the trees they could see that the neighboring Thompson place had been ruined, the big house, outbuildings, and most of the slave cabins burned. It was even worse after they turned onto the King's Highway—bleak, darkened chimneys marked the sites of burned houses, and the burned ruins of barns and cotton gin houses testified to the ruin of a dozen plantations along the way. The James Caldwell house, near the Stateburg corner, had been burned. At the Argyle plantation, all the outbuildings had been destroyed. Wedgefield plantation was reduced to almost nothing.

John Frierson called out, "Looks like we have company." Other wagons were moving along the road some distance ahead of them, and others were coming behind.

About a mile north of the village of Manchester, everyone recoiled at the sight of ashes and debris where the beautiful home of Mrs. Elliott had stood. And here, too, the cotton gin house and all the other outbuildings had been burned.

As they passed the old Campbell home, Mrs. Campbell, seventy-six year old widow of Alexander Campbell, waved from the lawn. John Frierson pulled the team up to a halt, handed the reins to his wife, and climbed down. Mrs. Campbell approached the wagon with a greeting as John called to her, "Mrs. Campbell, you had better come along with us."

"Why, what's going on?" she inquired.

"We've heard that Potter's Yankees may be coming back this way."

"Potter? My stars, hasn't he done all the damage he can?"

"One would think so, but it may not be safe to stay here. I think you should come along with us."

She thought a moment and then said, "Yes, I reckon so; I don't want to see the likes of them again."

John said, "You know the Storm sisters, of course." The women nodded to one another in acknowledgment. Mrs. Campbell had been a close acquaintance of Rosemary and Alexander Storm.

"Well, you gather some things to last for a few days and come along with us. Are your son and daughter here? Any Negroes?"

"Just my daughter and a young housemaid."

"Bring them along. Jarvis here and Ramey will help you." The two men climbed out of the wagon and followed Mrs. Campbell into her house.

Within a few minutes the old lady and her daughter and maid were on the wagon, and they were moving again.

Sarah Frierson asked, "Mrs. Campbell, where is your son?"

The old lady burst into tears before she could reply. Then, taking a deep breath, she said in a quivering voice, "He's gone. Gone. And it was awful."

"Oh, I'm so sorry," Sarah said kindly. "Can you tell us what happened?"

"Oh, it was awful. And I can tell you this. If it had not been for Elsie here," Mrs. Campbell paused as she patted her black maid on the knee, "my daughter and I might not be here either."

"What happened?" Sarah persisted.

"Well, you know that Thomas was an invalid..."

"Yes, we know."

"Well, some of those Yankee Negro soldiers came storming into the house and commenced shouting orders. Thomas could not understand them, and when he could not comply quickly enough to suit them, they just shot him. They shot him dead."

"Oh, my lands!" Violet and the others gasped in unison with Sarah.

Mrs. Campbell went on, "And they left him out in the dust all day and all night while they completely looted the house. They took everything–food, clothing, bedclothes, valuables...everything!"

"That's awful!" they gasped again.

"And I must tell you," the old lady went on, "that no good darky, Jude–Judas is what he was–only made things worse. He egged them on to set fire to everything. When they set the storehouse afire, Elsie here ran out and put the fire out. Then she found an officer and put up such a plea for her old mistress that he set a guard to protect us. So, thankfully we are still alive, and the house is still there, but if they are coming back, it may not be awaiting me."

As they went on, Frierson noticed that some of the wagons were turning off to the left, toward Privateer or Timmonstown, but most continued southward, and he followed their example. After about five hours on the road, he pulled up at St. Mark's church and climbed down to make inquiries. He returned with word that most of the people were going over to Milford House for protection.

"So, over to the Governor's mansion we go," he announced to the group of weary travelers.

"You mean ex-Governor Manning's?" Violet asked, recalling earlier visits to this plantation. The governor and Major Storm had enjoyed playing chess together, as well as hunting fowl.

"Of course," he replied, "to the Milford mansion. It certainly is the sturdiest house around here."

"And probably the most beautiful," added Sarah. "I wonder how it escaped the Yankees' wrath. I suppose we'll soon find out if that's where we are going."

They turned to the west and rode up a narrow, sandy road between tall pine trees. After going half a mile in that direction, they came upon a clearing. Then, in a grove of big trees, the great Milford mansion came into view. Light gray in color, it was built of Rhode Island granite, with six massive, two-story Corinthian columns spread evenly along the piazza that extended all across the front. The house was almost square, with five tall windows (a door in place of a window on the first floor, front and back) on each story along the front and back and on each side.

John Frierson asked the others to wait a few minutes while he inquired about the situation. He climbed down from the wagon, and went to the front door. When he returned, Governor Manning himself was accompanying him. The congenial former governor bade everyone welcome, and as they dismounted with the little baggage that they had, Manning greeted them individually. He was an impressive looking politician, with gray hair just beginning to thin, warm blue eyes, and a sturdy frame. He was polished and gracious in manner, clever, and quick-thinking. He had only recently returned from a visit of the western states under a commission from the current governor, A.G. Magrath. Earlier he had served as a colonel with Beauregard.

"You remember the Storm sisters, Charlotte...Susan...Violet."

"Indeed, I do, three of the loveliest young ladies around here." His blue eyes were twinkling at the sight of them, but quickly turned somber as he said, "I want to say to all three of you how awfully sorry I was at the news of the loss of your father. Good man, Major Storm. Nobody like him. I shall certainly miss him, and you are all most welcome to stay here anytime you choose."

Violet managed a low "Thank you." along with her sisters.

"Glad to have you here anytime," he repeated heartily, "but just now we hope we can keep you out of the way of that mad Potter and his marauders."

While Uncle Jarvis and Ramey drove the horses and wagon around to the back, the others filed up to the piazza. Mrs. Sally Manning met them in the great marble hall and invited them into the parlor to refresh themselves with cool drinks. Though quiet in nature she was gracious as a hostess. Her brown hair was parted in the middle and pulled back into overlapping braids, presenting a complimentary frame to her pleasant, round face. The long ride had not only made the travelers thirsty but somewhat weary.

As soon as they had finished their refreshment, Sally Manning explained to all, "You understand, we'll have to double up a bit."

"Of course," Violet answered. "We are thankful to have any shelter at all. The three of us and the children can find some corner together."

"There is a room upstairs that you may have, Violet, if you don't mind sharing. My maid, Mandy here will show you up to the room. There's an extra bed in there, and we'll find some cribs for the little ones."

"Wonderful, and we have Mammy and Aunt Sheba here, and Uncle Jarvis who is helping the Frierson's servant, Ramey, take care of the horses." said Violet gratefully.

"Yes, we'll find a place for them and the Frierson's servants in the basement. Our loyal Uncle Ben and Mammy, who refused to run off after Potter's troops as so many others did, will show them where they can stay. And they can all help with food preparation."

"Of course. We'll all do anything we can to help."

Sally Manning looked at the Friersons and smiled, "And Sarah and John, you'll take the back corner guest room. I believe you've slept there quite a few times. I'll get Uncle Ben to carry your bags up."

Before evening, parts of over a dozen families, mostly women and children, had become refugees in the Milford House. Governor Manning asked everyone to remain indoors all afternoon as sounds of explosions drifted in from the direction of Middleton Depot and Manchester.

With the help of Violet and her sisters, and other visitors, Sally Manning organized lines for food distribution in the hall and dining room, while the servants—resident and visiting—prepared the food and cleaned up afterwards. Victuals included chicken as well as ham and black-eyed peas and potatoes and Irish potatoes, and even enough coffee for all who wanted it. There was also milk for the children. The Governor's wife expressed satisfaction that there was enough food to go around. "Fortunately, Potter missed us on his foray northward last week," she explained, "but we're not so sure that we'll be lucky this time. Let us hope so."

Food lines were open again early the next morning. Violet asked Charlotte and Susan to take turns staying with the children. It was not yet eight o'clock when someone called out, "There's fire up in the north! Look at the smoke!"

Those who ran to the windows and to the piazza could see columns of smoke rising high into the sky.

Governor Manning already had dispatched one of his hands by horseback to go up and have a look. He returned presently with word that the fire was from the burning of hundreds of bales of cotton four miles away. It belonged to Mrs. Richard Manning, whose husband was killed early in the war, and who with her young children had now sought refuge with her kinsman at Milford House.

It was not two hours later when Yankee soldiers could be seen running through the yard and around the outbuildings. They began driving off horses and mules and carrying off chickens, just as they had done at Fair Oaks and at other earlier raids. Violet came up to John Frierson who looked out an east window just in time to see his team being driven off.

"Damn!" he exclaimed heatedly, "There go my last horses, and I'm afraid they're taking your Jarvis with them."

"Oh, no, not Uncle Jarvis! But I know he'll try to slip away from them if he ever gets the chance." Then another disturbing thought hit her. "Oh, dear, it looks like we walk home—if we ever get out of here. I guess we can take turns carrying the children."

Just then a noisy mob of black soldiers came surging through the back doorway and into the great hall. A black sergeant in the lead called out, "Haf ya got any pertection fo' dis house?"

Governor Manning came striding up and replied, "Our only protection is from the Army of the Confederate States."

This infuriated the Negro sergeant who pointed his musket at Manning and shouted, "Yo' be uh daid man!"

At that moment a black officer entered the back door and shouted, "Halt! De General is at de front do'."

Ignoring the gun in his face, Manning turned about and walked quickly out the front door and onto the piazza. Violet and Charlotte watched with the others as Potter and his aides rode up on horseback.

"I have the honor of greeting the commander of this United States Army?" asked Manning.

"Yes, sir," the General answered, twisting the ends of his full German-styled mustache.

"Well, I only ask for protection for the ladies and children under my roof—though I assume that is always granted in civilized warfare."

With his dark brown eyes peering steadily at the Governor, Potter responded, "That is my object in coming here, and I'll carry out my purpose." He dismounted and, with his staff officers following, walked up to the portico like a bantam rooster.

"This is a fine house," he commented, looking around.

"Yes," said Manning, "it was built by a man from Providence, Rhode Island, by the name of Potter, and now I suppose it is to be destroyed by a man from New York by the name of Potter."

For a moment, Potter seemed taken aback, but his composure returned. "No, sir, I am here to protect your family and your house from injury." Then Potter went on, "No, it is not my intention to destroy your place. It will be protected." Turning to his staff officers, he gave his orders, "Get out word to all units that everything on these premises is to be protected."

Looking over at the adjacent meadow, Potter saw two soldiers trying to lasso a horse and immediately he shouted to an aide, "Tell them to let that horse go, or I'll hang them! Hang them, I said."

Resuming his calm air, Potter followed Manning to the door, and as the General crossed the threshold, Governor Manning announced to those inside, "The commander of the United States army."

As further reassurance, Potter repeated for all to hear, "There will be no destruction on your estate, Governor, and all the ladies and children will be protected."

Why weren't you here when they dragged Uncle Jarvis away, Violet thought to herself, glad to hear the reassurances of the General.

Turning back to Manning the Yankee General asked, "Have you heard any news of the fall of the Confederacy?"

"No. None." Manning answered simply.

"It's imminent, I can assure you."

Manning then presented the General and his remaining staff officers to the ladies in the hall and the parlor. Violet and Susan listened with interest as the crowd broke into small groups to engage in conversation with the invading officers. They learned that a horde of five thousand freed slaves had been following Potter's army during its earlier march northward until the commander had sent most of them back to Wright's Bluff to take boats back to the Georgetown area on the coast.

The conversations continued until all the troops had passed. About four o'clock Potter and his staff mounted their horses and rode away.

They had not been gone more than twenty minutes when Lieutenant Charles Rhett, a Confederate courier and one of Brent's friends, rode up with the news that Johnston and Sherman had signed an armistice. He nodded to Violet and her sisters, but was so exhausted by his long ride that he lay down on a divan in the hall and fell asleep almost immediately. His rest was of short duration. Governor Manning awoke him to ask him to carry a flag of truce and ride on to overtake Potter and give him the news.

As the news of Johnston's armistice spread through the area, people flocked to Milford House for verification. When the courier returned in less than an hour, accompanied by one of Potter's aides, over sixty people had gathered at the house. They heard the Yankee aide deliver Potter's compliments and best wishes to the Governor.

Violet wondered if this meant that they would be able to return to Fair Oaks on the morrow.

John Frierson said that he hoped so–if they could find their horses and wagon.

That night at Milford House was even more crowded than the night before, but it was less tense. Prospects of an end to the War, even with the sting of defeat, elevated spirits almost to the point of joyful celebration.

The next morning brought further sensational news. The rector of St. Mark's Church arrived with a report from a Yankee courier who had passed on his way to deliver dispatches to General Potter. General Lee had surrendered to General Grant at Appomattox Court house in Virginia, on April 9th, and the War for all practical purposes was over. But there was further grim news. On the night of Good Friday, April 14th, Abraham Lincoln had been shot and had died the next day. He had been shot by an actor by the name of Booth while attending a play at Ford's Theater in Washington. A few cheered on hearing that news, but most remained silent, stunned.

"My God!" Violet exclaimed to those around her, "What does this mean?"

John Frierson asked of the Rector, "Was there a conspiracy of some kind involved in the shooting of Lincoln?"

"Yes, there was. The U.S. Secretary of State, Seward, also was shot, though not fatally, the same night at his home."

Everyone turned inquiring eyes upon Governor Manning. His brow puckered in thought as all became quiet. Finally he spoke in soft, measured tones, "I'm afraid this is bad news for the South, very bad news."

"Why?" several asked at once.

One man spoke up. "Yes, why? Lincoln wouldn't call off the shooting. Maybe if he had gone sooner the War would have ended sooner, and the South would have been better off."

"I doubt that," Manning insisted, "and I'm afraid this means more trouble for the South."

"Why do you say that?"

"For two reasons. First, I'm afraid the North will be all stirred up for vengeance. They are likely to think that the Confederate Government or Jefferson Davis was behind the assassination plot, and that will make it difficult for all of us. Secondly, Lincoln had given indications of a lenient policy toward a postwar reconstruction. Now heaven only knows what their vindictive politicians may do."

Chapter 11

On Their Own

1865

"I'm afraid we may be stranded here for a while," announced John Frierson to his wife and the Storm sisters. The women were gathered on the porch while Frierson looked around, hoping to hear that they could return to their homes. "I cannot find your Jarvis, Violet, nor my Ramey, nor my horses and wagon anywhere. I'm afraid the Yankees have made off with them. Too bad they took them before Potter arrived."

As the women exchanged worried glances, Governor Manning came up and offered his help. "Luckily Potter's threats to his men saved some of my horses and a couple of wagons. I'll have my Gerald drive you back to your homes. I know you're anxious to get back and see what's happened—I hope, nothing adverse."

Frierson responded for all, "Governor, you already have given us so much that we hate to impose on you for this further favor, but the only alternative I see is walking, and that would be difficult with the little ones."

"Impossible with the children," agreed Manning. "Think nothing of it. Glad to be of what help I can. Everyone has lots of work to do to get their places back in order, and we should lose no more time. All of us will have hard days ahead, I fear. And we are going to need to help each other so that all of us come through these difficult times in good order. We are friends and neighbors," and he repeated for emphasis, "friends and neighbors."

With that he disappeared around the corner of the house. Within only a few minutes the promised team of horses and wagon was coming around to the driveway. Gerald, the Manning's driver, jumped down to help put the baggage and a box of cold chicken and corn bread on board, and then the passengers. They said goodbye to their hosts and other friends, and Violet and Charlotte each gave a hug to the elderly Mrs. Campbell who would not be accompanying them on the return trip. She and her daughter and maid would stay at Milford Plantation until some means could be found for their sustenance.

It was not yet eleven o'clock when they started down the road toward St. Mark's Church. The morning was bright and sunny and tended to lift the spirits of the travelers. At Manchester they paused briefly to water the horses. About two-thirty, while the horses rested under a roadside shade tree, they enjoyed the nourishing chicken and corn bread supplied by their host and hostess. They found the return trip much less wearying. The group came within sight of Cherry Vale about five o'clock, and everyone cheered to see that it was intact. John and Sarah Frierson wanted to accompany the girls home so he told Gerald to continue on to Fair Oaks to see if it was all right, and then he and his wife would get off on the way back.

Approaching Fair Oaks, all were delighted to see that the big house still was there as they had left it. Another loud cheer arose from the wagon. *Maybe there is just a little justice left in this harsh world,* thought Violet.

"Guess Potter's men didn't get this far east this time," remarked a relieved Frierson. He closed his eyes and said a brief, silent prayer of thanks.

"Thank, God!" Violet and Charlotte said in unison. Susan was looking intently around in all directions and said nothing.

Sarah Frierson sighed with relief, wiping her eyes with her white, linen handkerchief. She said, "I am *so* glad. I have been worrying about what would happen to you all if things had not turned out this way. I know how much you love your home and all the memories here. At least you girls have a solid roof over your heads. And you know that we are nearby to help when we can."

As they drove up the lane, Old Dan came from around the house and trotted up to meet them, his tail wagging furiously. He was barking a joyful greeting. In the three days since their departure, he had become gaunt and bedraggled, but to the sisters he looked beautiful. Susan snatched several pieces of corn bread from the box and jumped down from the still moving wagon. Old Dan took the corn bread from her hand in swift, hungry gulps, and then with his tongue searched her fingers for crumbs. When the wagon came to a stop in front of the house, everyone else got out, stretched their legs, and gave Old Dan a loving pat. Little Bonnie Anne threw her arms around her animal friend and kissed his furry coat. Even Gerald climbed down to pat the dog he had seen off and on for so many years, thankful that the young ladies still had their beloved pet.

Happy to be home, everyone washed and changed clothes—from soiled, worn dresses to worn dresses that were at least clean. Aunt Sheba was not feeling well and could not help with anything, even if disposed to do so. Mammy scurried about to make supper that turned out to be Irish potato soup and more corn bread. Everyone, except Aunt Sheba, ate heartily. Mammy gave Old Dan a generous portion of corn bread which he again gulped hungrily. He had apparently gone to the pond for water since he did not appear thirsty.

It was early to bed for everyone and late to rise on Friday—even the children seemed to need more sleep and slept as late as the adults. And the usually energetic Mammy slept later than was her custom. Aunt Sheba felt weak and said she would not get up for a while, so Mammy fixed a light breakfast for everyone. The sisters played with the children, read while they slept, and sat around as much as they could, still resting. Violet said little, often seeming to be in deep thought. Mammy took a brief nap while the children slept. Aunt Sheba ended up staying in bed all day.

After a dinner of hot biscuits and again Irish potato soup, but with a little ham this time, Violet asked Charlotte and Susan to remain at the table while she outlined plans for work.

"I'm hoping that Brent will be back soon, but whether he is or not it's going to be difficult for the next several weeks," she began, brushing a lock of soft hair out of her eyes. "We are all going to have to learn to do things that we've not done before. We are on our own. We don't have Daddy; we don't have Christopher; we don't have Leo. We don't even have Jarvis now. We have no field hands. We've got to make the best of things. What we are going to have to do will not be easy for us." She stopped and looked at each of her sisters to gauge their reaction to what she was telling them.

"We'll have to do what we can," agreed Charlotte willingly, but Violet was not sure that either she or Susan understood the voluminous task awaiting them.

Susan said nothing, waiting for Violet to say more.

Violet continued, "We at least have to put in a garden so that we can have something to eat, and we had just started the digging when the Friersons drove up to take us away with them, out of harm's way. Charlotte, let's you and I walk back to the woods this afternoon to see if the cotton is still there, and we need to bring back some garden seed from the Storm Cellar—if the seed is still there." She paused and looked at Susan. Then she added, "Susan, you can come, too, if you like. Bring along Old Dan."

The sisters fetched their sunbonnets, Susan called Old Dan, and they took off for the woods, with Susan and Old Dan running ahead.

It was still an unsettling experience to walk out among the ruins of the outbuildings, to see the charred wood and piles of debris. The aroma of ashes still clung to the air, contaminating the freshness of a spring breeze and the sweet scent of flowers somewhere in bloom. They found a few tools scattered in the vicinity of where the tool shed had been. Jarvis had already carried some hoes and shovels to the garden spot. Pieces of harness and rope were strewn about the barnyards. Although all the barns and mills were in charred ruins, it appeared that some scrap lumber might be salvaged from them. Over behind the slave quarters area they found a one-horse plow where it had been left when the slaves dropped their work in front of Potter's sweep. A few of the slave cabins had not burned, but these had been completely ransacked.

They crossed the creek and walked around the pond to what was known as field number 2, the middle field of the three 210-acre tracts that extended back to the woods. Here were some gang plows that were still usable—if there were animals to pull them.

On reaching the woods they quickly ran about uncovering the mounds of cotton bales. "Prices are bound to be going sky high now, and this should give us the wherewithal to get some animals and chickens and everything," said Violet happily.

"I should think so," said Charlotte, smiling.

"Hurrah! Hurrah!" exclaimed Susan, dancing with joy. Old Dan sensed her excitement and began running around barking. Susan went on, her eyes shining in expectation, "Now I can get a new dress! Just think, a *new* dress!"

"Susan! Dan! Calm down!" Violet knew it would be a long time before anybody got new dresses, but she said nothing, not wanting to dampen the spirits of her youngest sister. "Come on, let's go look in the Storm Cellar." She led the way to the hiding place and opened the hatch. They went down the steps. There were bags of cotton seed and all kinds of garden seed. Violet sighed with relief. She had been fearful that these might have been stolen since she was last there.

Violet looked at Charlotte and Susan. "We may as well carry some of this garden seed back now, don't you think?" Each picked up as much as she could carry, and they walked back to the house and set the bags on the back porch. Susan ran into the kitchen to tell Mammy what they had found.

The next morning Violet had her sisters up early for work, but they had no more than finished their breakfast in the kitchen dining room when there was a knock at the back door. Violet recognized the visitor as Blake Farley who operated a farm supply store in Sumter. He was neatly dressed, but not attractively so. He was slight of build—Violet had to look down to meet his eyes—and his dark eyes moved nervously as she greeted him.

"Good morning, Mr. Farley," she said graciously with a smile. "What brings you out at such an early hour?"

"Good morning, Miss Storm."

"It's Mrs. Sutler now, Mr. Farley," corrected Violet.

"Eh? Oh, yes, that's right, Mrs. Sutler. Beg pardon, Ma'am," he answered, and then got right to the purpose of his visit. "I'm canvassing the area for cotton. Do you by any chance have any?"

A buyer already! exulted Violet to herself, but in a calm voice she answered, "Why yes, we do. Won't you come in?" She led Farley into the plantation office and motioned for him to take a seat.

She began with general talk, as her father had always done. "Well, Mr. Farley, do you think the War really is over?"

"I'm sure of it. Washington said that Sherman's terms to General Johnston were too lenient, and they are having to renegotiate, but there's no more war for us."

"I must say I'm glad for that, but what now?"

"Well, the Government is anxious to get business and everything going again." At this his nervous eyes avoided hers again.

"What government?" Violet inquired with great interest.

"Why, the U.S. Government, of course."

"Oh."

"Well, now, Miss...eh...Mrs. Sutler, if you will tell me where the cotton is we can get it out to market."

"When?"

"Right now. I have wagons with me."

Violet glanced out the window and saw a string of horses and wagons, driven, apparently, by ex-slaves. For some reason she felt a faint sense of apprehension. Putting the feeling out of her mind, she returned to the business at hand. "What's the price of cotton now?"

"At least ten cents."

"Good, let's get it out."

"Where is it?"

"Unfortunately, we lost most of the crop. It was burned in the storehouse when Potter's raiders set fire to it." She was unable to hide the bitterness in her voice.

"I'm right sorry to hear that, Miss...eh...Mrs. Sutler, but I assume from your comments there is more?"

"Yes, we stored as much as we could back in the woods. Thank goodness the Yankee scavengers didn't find that!"

"That's nice, that's nice." Farley's eyes sparkled with anticipation. "Will it be easy to find the cotton in the woods?"

"I think so. We have uncovered most of it. There are eight piles, I think, each with half a dozen bales."

"Good. Then I'll be on my way." He rose to leave, tipped his hat in farewell, and left by the outside office door to rejoin his men.

Violet could hardly wait to tell Charlotte and Susan who were still waiting in the dining room. "Mr. Farley is taking our cotton to market! Even with his commission that should be at least a couple of thousand dollars for us. Now we should be able to get horses and cows and chickens, and even maybe hire some field hands. Our problems should soon be mostly over."

"It's wonderful!" the other two said excitedly.

"And I *will* be able to get a new dress!" added Susan, clapping her hands with delight.

Before noon Farley was back at the outside door of the office. Violet asked him in, anxious to get a financial report. She had been too excited to concentrate on anything since he had left. She could scarcely believe their good fortune.

"Well," he began, "it was just as you had said, forty-eight bales. Glad you had counted it."

"Good, now what are the financial arrangements? Will you deposit to my account at the bank after you have sold it—and do you have a receipt to give me?" She recalled her father asking these questions when dealing with the buyers.

"Here's a receipt just to acknowledge how much cotton I found hidden in the woods."

That's an odd way of putting it, thought Violet, but she didn't care—just so she had the receipt for business purposes.

"Thank you," she said, slipping the receipt into a top drawer of her desk. "Now, when can I expect payment? We desperately need practically everything here." She hated to admit that they were almost completely out of food.

"Eh..Mrs. Sutler...I'm afraid this is Confederate cotton."

"Confederate cotton? What do you mean, Confederate cotton? And what difference does it make anyway? Cotton is cotton. I don't understand."

"Evidently it was hidden by agents of the Confederate government, and that makes it subject to seizure by the U.S. Treasury Department." He grinned mockingly at her vulnerability.

"I don't know what you are talking about. Agents! What agents? This is cotton that we grew here, on Fair Oaks plantation, and we hid it so that Potter's scavengers would not burn it. No *agents* hid it. We did—I, and Leo, our overseer, and our slaves. And now what we can get for that cotton is all we have to go on—all we have to live on. I have two small children who need milk and food and clothes." She could not believe this turn of events. A slow rage was festering inside her, but she knew she had to keep her wits and it would not be wise to let her anger show.

"Well, I'm sorry about that, Mrs. Sutler, but what proof do you have that it is yours?"

Violet could not believe what she was hearing. This was a fellow Southerner saying this! She asked, "Proof? It's on our property, isn't it?"

"Of course it's on your property, put there I assume by Confederate agents in a desperate effort to save something to prolong the war."

A chill of recognition crept over Violet as she began to realize what was actually happening. Her joyful anticipation of only moments before was being dashed in what appeared to be a case of blatant robbery.

Her self-control broke and she burst forth with "Why...you sound like a damned Yankee—not a southern born and bred gentleman!" Then with great effort she gathered her composure and remained silent for a moment—but only for a moment. She simply could not maintain her composure, and she let her feelings tumble out again, this time more impassionately.

"Mr. Farley, you are a Scalawag, that's what you are, a damned Scalawag, out to line your pockets at the expense of the widows and orphans of this terrible war. Our men are not even home from the War, and already you are preying on their families like a vulture, taking milk out of the mouths of babies. I don't know which is worst, Sherman or Potter or you!" She paused for breath and then said, "On second thought—*you* are, because you are a traitor to your own people!"

He gave no indication of hearing her. Already he was turning to leave without further words. He had finished what he had come for. Violet called after him, "You'll not get away with this, you damned thief! I'll sue you for trespassing and for larceny, and everything else, even if I have to wait for ten years to get you. I guarantee that, and don't you forget it. If I ever see you on our place again I'll shoot you on sight!"

Violet sank to her chair, laid her head upon her arms, and burst into tears. She could not control her sobs. Charlotte and Susan rushed into the office to see what had happened. Mammy had heard Violet's voice from the kitchen and arrived out of breath to find out what was going on. *Lawdy, nuttin' bet'r hopp'n ta mah chile! Miz Violet still mah baby ev'n if she grow'd up now.*

For a minute or two Violet could not speak. She knew she had to tell her sisters what had happened, the sooner the better, so she sat up and squared her shoulders determinedly. She wiped her eyes with the back of her hand. The words tumbled out in anguish, "That no-good Farley has stolen all our cotton, claimed it was Confederate government cotton that was being seized for the U.S. Treasury. We're right back to where we were early this morning, only with no cotton."

"Oh, no, Violet! You can't mean what you say!" cried Charlotte, shocked at this turn of events.

Susan looked from one sister to the other dejectedly. She sighed deeply. All she said was, "I guess the dress will have to wait awhile."

Mammy was standing by the hall door listening. She didn't understand everything that Violet was saying, but she knew that Farley had stolen the cotton and Miss Violet would not get any money from it. "Duz ya all tink uh cup uh tea would mek ya feel bet'r?" she asked, wanting to help in some way.

"Yes, Mammy, thank you. I think we can all use a cup of tea," Violet answered.

Mammy turned on her heel and left the room, her lower lip stuck out and muttering to herself, "Ah don' kno' whut dis wurl' cumin ta wif dese mean peop'l jes' waitin' ta gitcha, dese damn'd Yankee sojuh an' dese wick'd men who ain't give de monee fo' de cott'n, wurrin' mah babies an' tek'n food frum dere moufs. De deb'l gwine git dem fo' sure, yassum, de deb'l gwine mek dem pay fo' whut dey do ta mah fam'ly."

After some minutes to regain her composure and collect her thoughts, Violet continued, "Well, my dearest sisters, you know we've just lost all prospects for any money. Now we are going to have to work harder than we thought. We don't even have money for taxes."

"Taxes? What do you mean, taxes?" Charlotte asked.

Violet sighed. Her sister had never had the opportunity to learn about managing a plantation or any such business matters. "I'm talking about the assessment that we have to pay to the local government every year, and if we don't pay up on the plantation they'll take it away from us."

"Oh," said Charlotte, disheartened at what Violet was explaining.

Violet returned to the topic at hand. "It will not be enough to plant a garden. We'll have to try to put in some cotton and corn so that we can have at least a few cents by fall for medicine and a cow so that the children will have milk, and, I hope, pay the taxes."

"What do you propose?" asked Charlotte in a business-like manner, sounding just like Major Storm.

"First of all, we'll try to put in a little cotton, and..."

Charlotte interrupted. "Just what do you plan to use for horses and mules?"

"Us," Violet returned gamely.

"Oh, sure," Susan sighed.

"As I was saying," Violet went on, "we must do the cotton first, because it takes longest to grow. You know the fields already were mostly plowed and the soil turned before the Yankees came. We'll just have to plow furrows to put the seed in. That shouldn't be too difficult."

"How do we do that?" Charlotte asked.

"Remember that one-horse plow we saw out behind the slave cabins?"

"Yes, but I don't think I like what you're about to say."

"No, now just wait. I think we can hitch up that old garden plow, and you and I can pull it while Susan holds on to the handle bars and guides it."

"Oh, sure," Susan repeated as Charlotte shuddered at the thought of trying to pull a plow.

"We can give it a try. We can do a little anyway if we don't make the furrows too deep. And even if it's only a little bit, it can mean some essential cash. At least we won't have to be furnishing board and clothing for field hands."

"Nor forage for mules," Charlotte added.

"How about clothes for us." Susan was trying to introduce a touch of humor. Her sisters smiled at her fondly, but no one laughed. This was too serious.

"As soon as we get in as much cotton as we think we can manage, we'll plant a little corn—for roasting ears and later corn meal and grits and big hominy for us, and to have whenever we do get a horse and some chickens."

"Is that all?" asked Susan. Surely there couldn't be more.

Violet shook her head. "Then we put in the vegetable garden, mostly for food, but part of it can be a truck patch for produce to sell in town, along with some of our fruit."

"Go on, Massuh Violet," said Charlotte. This did draw a smile from Violet and a giggle from Susan.

Monday afternoon Violet and Charlotte returned to the Storm Cellar. They carried several sacks of cotton seed to the near edge of the field, then carried what they could along the side and to the opposite end. The sacks were heavy and the walking was tiring. When they returned to the house they were exhausted both physically and emotionally.

The next morning, Tuesday, was for the beginning of the great planting. Shortly after sun up the three sisters were down for a quick breakfast of oak husks and siftings that they called sowens. Then promptly they donned their sunbonnets and cotton gloves and soon were at work. They found enough harness for their purpose—a couple of horse collars and hames that they could put around their waists, and traces to fasten to the plow. With these they dragged the plow across to the field and quickly made ready to begin their furrowing.

At first it seemed a kind of game.

Violet gave Susan her instructions, "Susan, we've got to plow a straight furrow. To do this you need to look at a spot straight ahead and keep us heading toward it—yell 'gee' to get us to move right and 'haw' if you want us to move left."

"Yes, and 'giddup' to go and 'whoa' for stop!"

"You've got it," laughed Violet.

"I don't think I'll ever get it," said Charlotte.

"And don't be kicking up the traces, either," Susan added.

Turning philosophical, Violet said, "Two hundred years ago James Howell wrote, 'One hair of a woman can draw more than a hundred pair of oxen,' so let's to it, ladies."

Violet and Charlotte slipped the horse collars and hames over their waists, and then, with hands against the inner rim of the collar, pushed as they walked. They were surprised at how well the plow worked. The plowshare turned the sandy loam fairly easily, so long as the furrow was not too deep. But it was a heavy drag on young women unaccustomed to rigorous exercise of this type. Light-hearted banter quickly gave way to silence and heavy breathing. It took an hour and a half for them to make the one-mile distance across the length of the field. Turning around, Violet was careful to space the next row about three and a half feet from the first. Now each step was a tortured one. The temperature rose with the sun, and by the time they had completed the second row their muscles were getting numb from strain and fatigue.

"Now we'll take a break from being mules and driver and plant the first two rows before we furrow the next," Violet instructed, rubbing between her shoulders. "Susan, you take a sack of seed—throw the rope over your shoulder, and drop the seeds in the furrow as you walk along. Charlotte and I will follow with hoes to cover them." She had removed her gloves to cool her hands, but now she pulled them on again for the hoeing.

The younger sisters wasted no energy in reply. They just moved to do what they were told. While this task was by no means easy, it was less difficult than the plowing. By noon the planting of the first two rows of cotton was completed. Slowly they trudged back to the house for a bowl of soup, some cool water, and best of all, an hour's rest. Mammy's face was stormy. She knew it wasn't proper for the Storm girls to work like farm hands, but she didn't know what to do about it with no men on the place. She was also worried about her elderly sister who continued to do poorly. Aunt Sheba had not gotten out of bed this day either, although she had taken a little soup and water. Mammy was concerned about Sheba's health, but she also needed her help with the work at the house.

The sisters were back at the field by one o'clock. The sun seemed unusually hot for April, and it seemed more so as they resumed their plowing. With determination, Violet set the pace. An outpouring of perspiration combined with the dust on her face to form rivulets of mud coursing down her throat and between her breasts. *Oh, Mama! You always said that horses sweat, men perspire, and ladies glow. If you could but see me now,* she thought. A hot, light wind tangled even more her already tangled hair below her bonnet and dipped the loose strands of hair into the streaks of perspiration on her cheeks and neck. Violet glanced at her sisters. Their grim, grimy faces reflected her own fatigue.

Old Dan showed up with a stick in his mouth, wanting someone to play with him. "Later!" Susan called to him. "Later, Dan, nobody has time to play right now—or the energy." The faithful dog seemed to understand, picked up the stick where he had dropped it when Susan called to him, and left in the direction of the house, his ears and tail drooping in disappointment.

At one point Susan complained that she had had quite enough, but Violet persuaded her to keep going with an offer to trade places with her. Violet was proud of her two sisters. Here they had been raised in an atmosphere of luxury and unhurriedness and waited on with tenderness and caring, but the strong stock from which they came was evident. The strength and courage and intelligence of Rosemary and Alexander Storm had been passed on to their children.

Before sundown they had completed the planting of another two one-mile rows. The girls barely had energy left to drag themselves back to the house. They ached all over. The hoeing had worn holes in Violet and Charlotte's gloves, and they each had a couple of blisters that had broken. These now burned with pain.

"I used to think just to walk four miles in a day was quite an accomplishment," Charlotte remarked.

Violet responded, smiling in spite of her fatigue and pain, "Yes, and you know we've walked eight miles in the field today while plowing and planting, plus walking from the house and back. Tell me, would you have believed that we could do what we did?"

"Never!" exclaimed Susan, and then she went on, "Oh, how I wish the barn was still here with hay in it. I would stop right here, lie down on the hay, and take a nap."

"I know how you feel," said Violet. "When we get to the house, why don't we rest just a bit before supper." The other two nodded in agreement and with anticipation. They were so very tired. Starting up the steps, Violet added, "As Daddy used to quote from Marcus Aurelius, 'I shall fall and rest."

It was a struggle to climb the stairs to their rooms. In her room, Violet washed her face and hands using water from the bowl in her room, dried them quickly, put some ointment on her burst blisters, and fell onto her bed.

When she awoke, it was morning. She felt unkempt and dirty. When she moved, her muscles cried out with pain. She washed her face quickly and ran a brush through her hair which she pulled up and secured on top of her head. The thick, lovely hair was so hot yesterday. Perhaps this style would be cooler. She tied on her sunbonnet, thinking, *No use changing clothes now—may as well carry the dirt on the clothes back to the field it came from.* She put more ointment on her burst blisters and grabbed another pair of cotton gloves from the drawer. These were somewhat sturdier than those worn yesterday, and she hoped they would hold up better, as well as offer protection for her sore fingers.

A tour down the hall revealed that her younger sisters were in the same condition as she. Mammy had let them all sleep through supper, the evening, and the night. She had put the children to bed explaining they would get double kisses from their mother and aunts the next evening. The little ones were obedient and soon fell asleep themselves.

Violet affected an attitude of shock as she teased Charlotte and Susan about going to bed without any supper and of sleeping in their work clothes. Then, seeing the shame-faced look upon their faces, she laughed and admitted that she had done the same.

"But come on now. Come as you are. We've got to get to work again."

"What a slave driver!" said Susan, grimacing at the thought of another day like yesterday.

"Yas, massuh," said Charlotte with a twinkle in her eye, repeating her answer of the day before.

Mammy had a good breakfast of corn cakes ready, and, after eating, Violet took time to feed Bonnie Anne and J.J., chatting with them about this and that. She told them to be good children and to mind Mammy, that she and their aunts would be in the fields again today, but that she would see them at dinner. Guilt feelings stirred within her. *I must not neglect the children, no matter how much and how hard the work is,* she thought. She kissed the children good-bye, as did Charlotte and Susan, and they left for the fields.

This day was worse than the one before. Now muscles were aching from the very start of their work. Each step, each movement, became more painful, but they kept at it. By the day's end they had done another four rows. They had never experienced such a mass of pain and exhaustion.

As they again dragged themselves back to the house, Susan asked despondently, "How much more are we going to do?"

Always good at figures, Charlotte interjected, "Do you know how long it would take to do this field at this rate?" Then before anyone could venture a reply she answered her own question. "I've got it figured out—about a hundred and fifty days!"

"No use in that even if we could," said Violet, noting Susan's dismay at Charlotte's comment and her immediate relief at Violet's response. "By the time we got finished plowing it would be about time to start picking cotton. No, but I think we should try to get ten acres planted. We can do that in eight days. We've already done two, with three days left in this week. We'll take Sunday off and then go at it three days next week."

"And then we'll be finished," Susan said in relief.

"Yes...with the cotton. Then we'll have to plant the corn and the vegetable garden, and then pretty soon we'll have to start hoeing." She had to give them an idea of what lay ahead.

"Oh, Violet! Is there no end to this?" exclaimed Susan mournfully.

Chapter 12

Farewell to Aunt Sheba

1865

The days ground on, each merging into the one before as though forming an endless furrow of cultivation. A thunderstorm on Friday gave some relief from the field. As in every thunderstorm, Violet saw the fire of Columbia in each lightning flash, and in each peal of thunder she heard the roar of the cannon and felt again the loss of her father in battle.

On Sunday afternoon, though still feeling tired, Susan, with Bonnie Anne, played with Old Dan. He chased sticks and balls for them, his ears perked and his tail looped over his back in happiness at finally getting some attention. He had followed the sisters to the field each day, picking up sticks along the way in the hope someone would play with him. Eventually he had to content himself with lying in the shade of a tree and watching them work. The little ones, of course, would hug and pat him when he was at the house, but there were times when he was in the mood to romp and chase sticks and the like.

Aunt Sheba's condition had improved somewhat, and she was up and about doing a little to lighten Mammy's load, but she tired quickly and had to take frequent rest periods. They all realized that this was something far more serious than her known reluctance to do much work. Everyone was worried about her.

By the following Thursday the ten acres of cotton had been planted. Then beginning the next morning in the same field, but about twenty yards away, they planted two mile rows of corn. In this case Violet instructed Susan to put three or four seeds in a hill, the hills in the row separated by about the same distance as between rows.

The following week they were ready to return to the garden that they had just begun when the Friersons had driven up to take them away when Potter's raiding army was retracing its steps. At first the girls gave up the plow in favor of shovels and hoes but soon concluded that these were slower and actually harder on them. So they used the plow for the garden too. They planted Irish potatoes, yams, peas, string beans, turnips, pinto beans, white beans, spinach, lettuce, carrots, musk melons, watermelons, pumpkins, and squash. They noticed with pleasure that some strawberries and asparagus were coming up from last year. All this done, the labor of hoeing needed to begin, hoeing to thin out the plants where necessary, to clear out the weeds, and to coax up moisture from beneath the surface.

Early one afternoon as the sisters were resting after dinner, they were surprised to hear Old Dan barking and then a knock at the door. Mammy came in to announce that Leland Thompson of Glenmerry Plantation was there.

Violet hurried to greet their guest. "Leland! Welcome home!" she cried at the sight of their neighbor, back at last from the War. Charlotte and Susan joined in the greeting as they escorted him back to the kitchen dining room where they offered him a cup of tea.

He was wearing a tattered butternut uniform, with a shabby gray kepi. Twenty-four years old, he was about average height, rather thinner than they had remembered him, and his hazel eyes showed a dullness of fatigue and hopelessness. His sandy hair was untrimmed and mussed.

"When did you get home?" Charlotte asked happily.

"Just yesterday." He grinned at the sister who looked so much like her older sister.

"From where?" asked Susan.

"From Virginia. I was with General Lee's army at Appomattox. I still have my parole from General Grant in my pocket." He drew out a piece of paper and showed it all around.

"Are you all right? No Yankee wounds?" asked a worried Charlotte.

"Nothing to speak of," he answered. "Caught a Minié bullet in my leg at Petersburg, but it's all healed now." Involuntarily he glanced down at his right leg.

"Did you ever run into Christopher?" Violet wanted to know.

He looked at Violet with sympathy in his eyes. "No, I didn't get up with Lee's army until after Gettysburg. Father wrote me about Christopher. I'm so sorry, so very sorry. The news really hit me hard." He paused, cleared his throat, then added, "And Violet, I was shocked to hear about the Major's death at Cheraw."

"Yes, we all miss Daddy so much. We miss both of them." Violet said sadly. Then she asked, "What are you and your father going to do?" She had seen the devastation of Glenmerry Plantation by the Yankee soldiers.

Leland sighed. "Well, as you probably already know, we got burned out by Potter—the main house and everything in it, barns, outbuildings—all are gone. We're living in a slave cabin that was left standing, though ransacked thoroughly. We've got no animals, nor anything else—nothing—but I guess we'll try to get in some crops somehow."

"We've been plowing and sowing ourselves," Susan said with pride.

"You have? You've got some horses and mules? Do you think you might lend them to me when you're through?" he asked in amazement, and then with hope.

Susan answered drily, "Oh, sure. Violet and Charlotte are the horses and I am the driver, and I doubt that I should sell or lend them at any price."

"*What!*"

"Sure, but I'm sorry, the horses and the driver are not for let," Susan laughed.

"Incredible! You three girls have been plowing and sowing and heaven knows what else...no man around...you young ladies...all by yourselves!" he exclaimed unbelievingly. It was almost incomprehensible to Leland that these gently reared young ladies were capable of such endeavors.

"We can let you have some seed, if you need it," Violet volunteered. "We have more cotton seed and seed corn and vegetable seed than we can ever plant."

"Well, thanks...thank you very much. We certainly can use the seed," he said gratefully. As he got up to leave, he looked at Violet intently and asked, "From what you've told me about your work here, I assume that Brent has not returned."

"No, not yet," she answered, "but we are looking for him any day now...any day now that the War is over."

They escorted their guest to the door, and as Violet headed out toward the garden, Leland followed a short way.

In a voice low enough so that he could not be heard by those at the house, he asked, "Violet, tell me, how long has it been since you have heard from Brent?"

She turned to look at Leland. "Actually I've not heard from him since he joined the Navy two years ago."

"No letters? No messages or word for two years? That's a long time not to hear anything."

"Nothing. But that's probably because he's been at sea."

He looked into Violet's eyes. "Yes, that may be so, but he ought to be home by now." He paused a moment, took a deep breath, and said, "Violet, I've been thinking about you a lot, all the while I was away, and now...now please don't misunderstand me...I pray that everything is all right with Brent, for your sake...but if he doesn't come back fairly soon...would it be all right if I call on you some times?"

Violet looked at Leland in astonishment that quickly turned to disappointment at what their neighbor had just suggested. "Why, Leland Thompson! You surprise me! You should not even *think* such things!" She turned away and strode off as fast as she could, leaving him standing there with a perplexed expression upon his face.

Aunt Sheba was in bed again and appeared to be growing weaker by the day. Mammy gave her lots of attention and care. One night Aunt Sheba developed a high fever. Violet sat with her through the night, planning to have Susan walk over to Dr. Anderson's early the next morning, but by then it was too late. The old woman had expired. They were heartbroken. The girls had known her all their lives. And they had lost so many and so much already. With tears rolling down her cheeks, Mammy had tenderly dressed Aunt Sheba in her goin'-ta-church clothes.

With the children playing quietly on the floor, Violet, Charlotte, Susan, and Mammy sat at the informal dining table discussing what to do about Aunt Sheba's burial. There was no wagon nor horse to take her to the community slave burying ground. There were no coffins about. Even if they used the scraps of burned lumber from the outbuildings, they had no nails, no hammer, no saw. What could they put the body in? Could they dig a deep enough hole?

"We've *got* to figure out what to do. Maybe it'll be easier if we take one thing at a time," said Violet. "First. Where can we bury her? There's no way we can get Aunt Sheba to the community slave burial ground, and—"

"Miz Violet, ah kno' dere be no way ta git her ta de big simmuhterree, but whut 'bout dat litt'l one ovuh dere by de woods, de one whar dey usta buree peop'l befo' the big simmuhterree wuz set up? Ah means de one whar de Majuh usta use fo' ussan?"

"Violet!" exclaimed Charlotte, "she's talking about the one with the iron fence around it–remember, one Halloween we took everyone at the party up there to scare them."

"Yes, you and Susan and I used to ride over there sometimes. I had almost forgotten about that one, it hasn't been used in so long." She thought a minute and then said, "That solves the first problem–where to bury Aunt Sheba. Now here's the second one: what do we bury her in? What can we do about a coffin?"

"Aunt Sheba was not very tall, and so thin by the time she died. I've got an idea," said Charlotte tentatively, somewhat fearful at how her suggestion would be taken.

"Well, let's hear it. We need ideas." said Violet, smiling encouragingly at her sister.

"Do you think she would fit in that empty cedar chest that's at the foot of the bed in the back guest room?"

"It's perfect!" exclaimed Violet and Susan at the same time.

"Yassum, dat be uh mightee fine box for mah sist'r. Hit sho' be purty. Ain't no burryin' box got dat purty carvin' on hit. An' ah kno' she fit in dat jes' fine!" Mammy wiped a tear from her eye, relieved that her sister would have a proper burial box. Indeed, she couldn't think of any slave who had had such a fine box.

"That takes care of the coffin," said Violet. "Now the third question is, how do we get the hole dug? I think sometime or other I recall Daddy saying that graves are six feet deep. That's not a furrow. That's a deep, deep hole. Can we do it?"

"We can do it," responded Susan. "We'll just take turns digging until it's deep enough."

"Ah'll dig too, ah sho' will," said Mammy emphatically. She was profoundly touched by what her babies were willing to do for her and her dead sister. They had been working so hard trying to get food for the table, and now this.

"Does it *have* to be six feet deep? Would it matter if we couldn't get the hole quite that deep?" inquired Charlotte.

Violet answered thoughtfully, "I suppose not really, Charlotte. I'm not even sure about the six-foot figure. I guess the main thing is to get Aunt Sheba buried in as decent a manner as we can, just as soon as we can. We'll just do the best we can." She stopped a moment and then continued, "The next question is–how do we get Aunt Sheba's body and the coffin to the burial ground? There's no way we could carry both at the same time–too heavy. We'll have to carry first one and then the other. Any ideas?" She looked at Charlotte, expecting her to speak.

But it was Susan who asked, "Why can't we make some sort of sled and pull it? I know! In my book on Indians there's a picture showing how they carry things. We could get a piece of one of the sides of a burned outbuilding, find some rope or make rope from old sheets or clothes, tie it on one end and pull it, just like we did the plow."

"A travois, yes, that just might work, Susan. That's good thinking on your part. We'd have to secure the body so it won't slip off."

"That ought to work with the cedar chest, too, don't you think," said Charlotte, looking at Violet.

"It should. We can certainly try it." answered Violet. She turned to Susan. "Susan, I think you should walk over to John and Sarah Frierson's and tell them what's happened and not to worry. Maybe he can help us dig the hole and maybe he's got a hammer and some nails and can make some kind of a liner for the hole. He can use some of the unburned wood lying around here."

Two hours later, Susan was back. John Frierson had returned with her, bringing Sarah's condolences, and carrying a shovel, a hammer, and some nails. While Mammy took care of the children, he and the sisters, each carrying a spade, walked to the cemetery, picked out a spot, and began digging the grave. It took the rest of the morning and most of the afternoon. The girls were thankful that John Frierson was there to help. He was a strong man and worked quickly. He accomplished as much as all three of the girls working steadily. It was also tiring work, but the sisters were used to hard work by now. They returned to the burned outbuildings and gathered strips of unburned planks and carried these back to the grave where Frierson made a workable liner for the coffin. Together they placed it in the hole.

"That's enough work for today," Frierson said. "I'll be back early in the morning to help you move the body and the cedar chest. Sarah'll be coming with me."

They all walked back to the house and John bade the girls good-bye. Then the sisters entered the house and sat down to a dinner of meager helpings of more Irish potato soup and corn bread that Mammy had waiting for them. After dinner Violet rocked and read to the children, then put them to bed. She and Charlotte and Susan went to bed shortly afterwards, tired and weary from their efforts.

John and Sarah Frierson arrived shortly after sun-up, bringing wheat flour and a piece of rope that had been stored in his cellar. Sarah came into the house to extend her condolences to Mammy and the sisters, while John went straight to the burned out buildings to look for wood. He found a piece of unburned side about four by seven. With Susan's help, he secured the rope to the corners of a four-foot end. They got inside the circle of rope and began pulling the slide.

"It'll do, but it'll work better if we can keep the front end up a little. Too bad I couldn't find any wheels."

They returned to the house, and with Violet and Charlotte at one end of the cedar chest, and Frierson and Susan at the other, they carried it down and placed it on the siding. Fortunately, it had handles at either end by which Frierson could tie it on. He also wrapped rope around the chest several times. Frierson and Susan pulled it part of the way, and then Violet and Charlotte took their turn. When they reached the grave, they picked it up again and set it in the hole. Then they returned to the house for the body.

Violet did not want Mammy seeing them tying the body on the make-shift sled and carrying it up to the old cemetery, so she asked Mammy to watch the children and bring them up in a little while for the funeral service. Sarah stayed to chat with her and keep her from dwelling on what was happening. Mammy was dressed in her finest and wanted to talk about her younger days with Aunt Sheba.

When the burial group reached the grave with Aunt Sheba, they gently lifted her off the siding and into the cedar chest, now lined with material from some old satin draperies. John Frierson closed the lid and nailed it shut. Shortly afterwards, Mammy, Sarah, and the children arrived. Frierson read the burial service from the Episcopal prayer book. Susan laid some yellow roses on the top of the coffin, and then all returned to the house with Mammy except for Violet and John Frierson who remained to fill the grave with dirt. Frierson stuck a small wooden cross with Aunt Sheba's name written on it at the head of the grave.

When Violet arrived at the house, Mammy met her at the door. "Miz Violet, mah sistuh, Shebuh, sho' had uh fancee funer'l. She sho' happee now, ah kno' an' ah sho' 'preciate whut y'all do." And she repeated with satisfaction, "Yassum, uh mightee fancee funer'l."

Chapter 13

Little Josh

1865

A few days after the burial of Aunt Sheba, Mammy was taken sick. *How could we ever get along without Mammy,* thought a worried Violet. *Mammy is vital to the whole family. Not just because she took care of all three of us from the time we were born, but she keeps the house going for us. She takes care of all of us so efficiently and so lovingly. A bit bossy, but that's because she wants us to be raised 'proper-like.' Besides, her bossiness is tempered with love and concern for us.*

Mammy's illness may have been a combination of the tragic events of the War, the recent death of the Major, the actions of the Yankee invaders and scavengers, the disappearance of the other slaves, especially the kidnaping of Evelina and Jarvis, the additional physical work load placed on her—coupled by the death of her sister. At any rate, Mammy was basically strong and sturdy with a wiry, muscular frame, and when healthy had an abundance of energy. While her condition was not serious, she was unable to do her work. The real danger was that her present weakness might invite pneumonia. Violet insisted that she remain in bed, and all three girls tended her lovingly.

With Mammy unable to cook, care for the children, clean, or do any of her usual tasks, the sisters found even more that they would have to do for themselves. Other than making tea on rare occasions, or candy, or what they may have picked up over the years hanging around Mammy and Aunt Sheba in the kitchen, the girls knew little about food preparation. They had never even given this much thought.

"Charlotte, you'll have to be our chief cook, at least for awhile, and Susan and I will take turns at helping. We've all got to learn more about cooking," decided Violet, accepting the new challenge somewhat reluctantly.

Charlotte tucked some stray hairs back into place, thinking about what Violet had just said. "Yes...if there's anything to cook...but, Violet, you know more about cooking than I do. I hardly know how to begin."

"Would you rather do more hoeing?"

Charlotte grimaced at the question. "No, thank you! Cooking shouldn't be too difficult when all we have to do is boil turnips and potatoes."

"Let me do it," interjected Susan with confidence. "I know how to boil water for tea. That shouldn't be much different than for vegetables. I don't mind not hoeing either."

Violet smiled at her younger sister. "Susan, we'll let Charlotte keep that task. I'll need to count on you for looking after the children more." Then she added diplomaticallyz "You are so good with them."

She turned to Charlotte and said, "It'd be nice to have a little corn bread along with those turnips and potatoes. Mammy can tell you how to go about making it.

Take a pen and paper and write down what she says to do, and then we'll all be able to cook corn bread."

For three weeks Mammy continued to be ill, and the sisters managed with good cheer and optimism, even a sense of humor at their efforts. In a weak voice she told them how to make corn bread and turnip and potato soup, and what they cooked turned out fairly well. Of course, as they assured Mammy, it wasn't nearly as good as hers. They were delighted when Mammy took a turn for the better and a couple of days later almost suddenly got her strength back, declaring that while they had all tried hard, it was time she took over the cooking. But her return to work promised no improvement in the diminishing food supply.

Late one afternoon a little Negro boy who could not have been more than eight years old appeared at the back door. He was a total stranger. The boy was covered with dirt from head to foot—not the filth of months of unattended accumulation, but the grime of days on the road without respite.

"Ma'am, ah be lookin' fo' uh place whar ah kin stay an' wuk fo' mah keep. Ah'se good wukuh," he said seriously, hope reflected in his dark eyes.

Violet smiled at him and asked, "Where did you come from?"

"Frum de big town dey call Clumbya."

"From Columbia? My goodness, how did you get here?"

"Awalkin'."

"You walked all this way? How long did it take you?" asked an astonished Violet.

"Free nigh's."

"Three nights! Where did you sleep?"

"One nigh' in de straw pile in uh field, an' one time in uh barn dat wuz mostlee burn' down, and de udder time ou' in de grass."

What a courageous little boy, Violet thought, and then asked, "Weren't you afraid?"

"Yassum, ah wuz kinduh afeared, Ma'am, bu' las' nigh' ah dream dat ah come ta uh booful ladee, an' she tek me in an' lemme wuk fo' mah keep."

He no doubt said that to all the ladies where he may have stopped...but no, he probably hasn't seen anyone since he left Columbia. So many along the way were burned out and have gone to stay with friends and relatives elsewhere. And there certainly are no horses or carriages on the road these days. She asked, "Where are your mother and the folks where you used to live?"

"Dey gone, dey done gone, an' ah ain't seed nawbudy ah kno' sense de big fah. De whole hous' done burn' down, an' ebbertin' an' ebberbudy gone."

Violet's heart went out to the little Negro. Their own home in Columbia had burned to the ground, and, except for the main house at Fair Oaks, the Yankees had stolen or burned down everything else. At least she had her children and her sisters and Mammy. But this little fellow had no one—and nothing but the ragged clothes on his back. *He'll be one more mouth to feed, and our food is almost gone now.* She smiled tenderly at him, saying, "Well, I'm glad that you found me. I do need somebody to help us. You can help in the garden...you can carry water for us out in the field...and you can keep wood on the fires in the kitchen...and you can help around the house...what is your name?"

"Mah name be Joshua, Ma'am, buh ebberbudy call me Josh, sometime Li'l Josh."

"All right, Little Josh, Mammy will get you cleaned up and try to find some clean clothes. She'll find you a good place to sleep in the basement."

"Oh, tank ya, tank ya, Ma'am. Ah be so gladta mek mah home heah wif yo'. Ah wuk hard fo' ya, Ma'am. Jes' ya wait an' see." His eyes sparkled with joy and his wide smile indicated his happiness at having found a home with such a kind and beautiful lady.

"Now come with me, Josh, my boy, I'll take you to Mammy. After you get cleaned up, I'll introduce you to the rest of the family. I live with my two sisters who will be pleased to have additional help with the chores. And my two children will be delighted to have someone else to play with them.

Little Josh was so happy at finding a place to live that he radiated good cheer all around him. He never complained, and was so anxious to help that quickly he became a great favorite of everyone. But he developed a special attachment for Violet. Everywhere that Violet went, Josh was sure to go. Whether to the kitchen, to the nursery, or to the fields, he followed everywhere. Violet began calling him her "little shadow." She soon appreciated that having him on hand to do chores, to run errands, and to deliver messages was saving her many footsteps.

Josh brought in wood for the fires in the kitchen stove and carried out garbage, placing it on the garden or burying it at some distance from the house since they had no hogs or chickens to consume it. If Violet were near he would help Mammy with the cooking by bringing her water and ingredients. He carried water for all the sisters when they were in the fields or garden, and for the bathing room and the bedroom pitchers, and for Mammy's tubs for washing dishes and clothes. He watered flowers inside and outside the house. He was clever at making little toys or playthings for Bonnie Anne and J.J., and he would rock their cradles or play with them whenever he had the chance, and he lavished a kind of attention on Old Dan that the dog had not enjoyed since the departure of the Major. The children and Old Dan adored him.

Violet noticed a special keenness of mind in the boy and an unusual ability to learn quickly and to retain what he learned. She began to instruct him in reading and writing, and she was greatly pleased with his progress. His memory was so sharp that sometimes she could not tell whether he was actually reading a story or was just reciting it from memory after hearing her read it to him. He began to read primary stories from the McGuffey readers to Bonnie Anne.

After one walk with her to the neighboring Cherry Vale and Glenmerry plantations, he could be trusted to deliver messages to, or trade with, or borrow items from the Friersons and the Thompsons. He never tarried along the way, making the round-trip as fast as the sisters.

He was so glad simply to be alive with a place to eat and sleep, that nearly everything else was an added pleasure. A growing sense of humor and security even led to the playing of practical jokes, though he heeded firm warnings against false cries of 'De Yankees acomin'!"

There never was any boredom for his busy hands and feet and his lively imagination. He never seemed to tire, though of course he did, and he never seemed to be disappointed, though at times he was. Violet wondered if perhaps he were older than he looked, but then she decided not. Probably in his circumstances additional years would have brought a certain cynicism, and longer training would have dulled his natural curiosity.

If I can just keep him going, keep him on the right track, let him learn as much as he can, she thought, *he will be of greater and greater help around the house, but more than that, he will be a great influence on my own children..and maybe when he's grown, on others of his race.* She could hardly wait to introduce him to Brent. She knew that Brent would recognize the spark that lay within Josh and would help to nourish this spark.

Chapter 14

Scrounging for Food

1865

As spring broke into summer, the days became longer and hotter. Drought set in. The ground hardened, and as the hoeing became more difficult it became more important.

Violet made the daily rounds of feeding the children, hoeing the cotton and corn, bathing the children and tucking them into bed, and found little time for reading except a bit on Sundays. There was no time for conversation except at meal time, no chance for visiting nor entertaining. Life had become a struggle just to exist, but she was determined to keep going—for the sake of those for whom she now felt responsible, as well as for her own sake. She still had received no word from Brent, and as the days passed she became increasingly anxious about his safety. Something was not right or he would have come home. Of that she was certain.

Charlotte was growing in maturity. She was depressed by the continued work demands that seldom left time for oneself, but she rarely complained. She was not distraught, and her faith in the future and concern for others kept her at her work. Her sense of humor that so often had lifted the spirits of the others in the past, seemed to have deserted her. Indeed she seldom smiled these days—except when Leland Thompson stopped by for a visit with the girls.

Susan had lost her sparkle. She had become melancholy. She no longer complained much, but that was more a sign of her feeling of helplessness and defeat than of an improvement in attitude. She played with Bonnie Anne and J.J., not as a source of delight as in the past, but more out of a sense of obligation or compulsion. She cared for Old Dan with the same indifference. Little Josh was the only one that could make her laugh—and that was infrequent.

This time of year generally was referred to as the awkward season—the season between the exhaustion of food supplies from the previous year's crops and the maturity of this year's. But this year the situation was critical. The little flour, corn meal, and ham that Potter's men had left them had just run out. So, too, the last of the wheat flour that the Frierson's had given them when Aunt Sheba died was gone.

Violet knew that immediate action was needed. At a meager supper of only thin turnip soup—shadow soup they called it—she said to her sisters, "Our food situation is serious. There is still some seed corn back in the Storm Cellar. Tomorrow I'll go get some. We'll have Mammy make some lye from the kitchen ashes so we can make big hominy out of some of it. We'll grind some of it for corn meal and parch the rest to eat directly."

"What's parch? What kind of corn is that?" Susan asked.

"Oh, Susan, you've had parched corn when you were little. We used to sit in front of the fireplace and eat it on cold evenings. We've not had it for a long time.

You just put it in a skillet with a little grease and set the skillet on the stove. It goes 'bang, bang' and swells up, and you put salt on it, and it is quite good, except it's a bit tough to chew. When Indian warriors would go on a long trip, all they would carry for their rations would be pouches of parched corn. Frontiersmen like George Rogers Clark and William Clark and Meriwether Lewis carried bags of parched corn on them when they went exploring."

Charlotte perked up. "Sounds good. I wish we had some right now. I always seem to be hungry these days. It may be unladylike, but my stomach growls all the time, and I can't help it."

Ignoring her sister's observation, Violet said, "Charlotte, maybe you can scrounge in the old garden for potatoes and Irish potatoes and turnips. There always are some of those left in the ground from last year."

"Forget the turnips," Susan said.

"We'll take anything we can get," said Violet. "Susan, you can gather the greens."

"Greens? Where are there any greens?"

"All over the lawn. I'm not talking about collards or turnip greens—I'm talking about dandelion greens."

"Dandelions!"

"Of course. Look at that yard. There are dandelions all over the place. At the base of each flower is a tuft of greens. That's what we want." grinned Violet.

Charlotte spoke up. "Susan, you may not know it, but Mrs. Manning had dandelion greens in the salad she served us. Mama even had Mammy boil some for us a couple of times, and Daddy used to have some dandelion wine around here some place."

"I thought Mrs. Manning's salad was delicious," commented Violet with a smile of remembrance, but then her countenance showed concern as she went on, "The children haven't had any milk since we were there, and they should be drinking it every day. They are growing so fast. I don't know what to do about that, but I've got to figure out something—and soon."

As the others nodded their agreement, Violet, looking out the window, said, "Look how terrible the lawn looks. Daddy always had it looking so beautiful. Now we have no mower. Even if we did, we have no horses to draw it. Maybe one of these days we can find a scythe and some sickles, but right now we've got to find food. We can't worry about the lawn right now." She rubbed her temples as if to ease the worry away.

After a little time with the children the next morning, Violet left them in Mammy's care, and each of the sisters went on her quest. Little Josh, as usual, went with Violet.

Arriving at the Storm Cellar in the woods, Violet reassured herself of the presence of a fairly good quantity of seed corn, and some pumpkin seed and sunflower seed as well. Now the question was, how much could she carry? She decided that she and Little Josh would make an Indian travois, similar to the one John Frierson had made to carry Aunt Sheba and the cedar chest up to the cemetery. Only this one need not be so large and thus would not be so heavy.

Finding some slender but sturdy tree limbs on the ground, she and Little Josh pulled off the twigs, and then with pieces of rope and twine off the sacks in the Storm Cellar they tied cross pieces on the limbs. To these she tied two sacks of corn and sacks of pumpkin and sunflower seed. Then taking an end of one of the poles in each hand, and with Little Josh pushing, she dragged the load slowly back to the house.

By noon all came in with a report of some success. Mammy was happy to see some additional food supplies. During the afternoon they all took turns grinding corn with mortar and pestle. Mammy fixed a good supper of sweet potatoes and dandelion greens—with wild onions that Susan had found—and corn bread, and the next morning for breakfast she served fried mush and even some wild honey that she had taken upon herself to find.

A repeat of the previous day's activities doubled the food supplies. Then Mammy set about making her lye hominy.

Violet still thought they needed some kind of meat. Then it struck her, why not fish? The Yankees had stolen all her father's fishing gear, but the next morning she searched the drawers in the office and finally found a couple of loose fish hooks, but nothing more. Then she found some spools of heavy thread. She didn't have to call Little Josh; he was already beside her. Optimistically she picked up two pails for the fish she was sure they'd catch, a kitchen knife, and a jar for the fish worms. They stopped at an uncultivated area of the garden where they were able to dig up several fish worms, and on they went. Near the creek they found a young sapling that would serve well as a pole. They cut off the thin limbs and pulled off the twigs, and Violet attached the thread and hook. She carefully showed Little Josh how to bait the hook so that he could do it from then on.

They found a grassy spot on the bank to sit, and Violet threw out the line. The water was low, and the fish not likely to be plentiful, but it was worth a try. Her patience and efforts were rewarded after several minutes by a nibble. Quickly she landed a medium-sized catfish. Unaware of the special care necessary in taking a catfish from the hook in order to avoid being horned, Violet drew back a bloody hand in her first effort. She carefully examined the fish and then tried again with success. She dropped the fish in a pail that Little Josh had filled with water. While he baited the hook, she rinsed her hand in the creek, and then threw out the line again.

It was pleasant sitting there beside the running water. *This is a far more enjoyable way of going after food than digging in the garden,* she thought. Lulled by the soft sounds of the water and the breeze playing through the leaves on the trees, Violet allowed her thoughts to wander in daydreams. She noticed a piece of a log floating down the stream, and she imagined that it was a ship carrying Brent back to her. She imagined the dragon flies and butterflies were magic flying machines with which to explore exotic places.

Another hour brought two more catfish. Then she decided to transfer her efforts to the pond. There she caught a dozen white perch in a short time. Finally an especially heavy weight bent her pole. *This really must be a big one,* she thought. It turned out to be a turtle, the hook caught in its mouth. Little Josh removed the hook, and she gladly took the turtle along. It would make flavorful soup—a change from potato or turnip soup.

When they arrived back at the house with a full pail, everyone crowded around to look at the fish and the turtle and exclaim about their next meal. What good fortune! Meat, at last, and how clever Violet and Little Josh were to catch so many. Mammy filled a tub with water where the fish could be kept alive until they were needed. First for the kitchen was the turtle—meat that night and soup from the broth for the next day. On the third night, Mammy cooked five perch. She had scaled the fish, taken out the bones, rolled the meat in corn meal, and fried it to a golden brown. It was delicious. At the first bite, each of the sisters moaned with delight.

"Charlotte...Susan, do you remember when Mammy and Aunt Sheba went to Columbia with Mother and left Evelina to prepare our dinner, and we had dog fish..."

"Oh, that was awful!" interrupted Charlotte, shuddering at the memory of the taste of Evelina's fish.

"Even I remember that sickening fish. It made me throw up!" exclaimed Susan. "But what was wrong with it? Why did that taste so terrible and this so delicious?"

"Poor Evelina, she felt so badly about that fish, but she didn't know what was wrong. When Mammy came back and we told her what happened, she just put her hands on her hips and laughed and laughed..."

Mammy had heard the girls talking about Evelina's fish, and entered the room chuckling at the thought. "Now, Miz Violet, ah tole ya whut wuz wrong wif dat fish, an' de nex' time de Majuh brough' mo' fish, ah mek sure dat Ev'lina kno' whut ta do frum now on. She jes' ain't nebber cook'd no carp befo'."

"Yes," acknowledged Violet. "I remember what you said. Evelina didn't know that you have to take out the insides very carefully. Daddy used to say you had to be careful to take out the mud vein of a carp, and apparently that's what Evelina had left in."

"Well, Mammy, I sure am glad that you know what to do with carp. I'll have two more, please."

"Ho, ho," chuckled Charlotte, looking at the empty platter. "Dream on, Susan."

Why, Charlotte's sense of humor is back. It's amazing what a full stomach can do, thought Violet. She looked at Mammy and said, "Mammy, do remember to be careful when you clean the catfish. It hurt my hand when I tried to take it off the fish hook."

"Yassam," replied Mammy. "ah kno' dat fish stickya iffen ya ain't keerful an' hit gotta have de skin pull'd off. Hit ain't like de udder fish we git." Then she looked at Violet's hand and said, "Miz Violet, did ya put dat oinmen' on dat place? Ya gotta be keerful of fish hurts."

Violet told her that she had gone upstairs after getting home, washed the fish odor off of her hands, and applied the ointment, and she was sure it would be all right. She didn't even feel it any more. Mammy nodded her head in satisfaction and returned to the kitchen, carrying plates.

Violet had made the fishing expedition sound so enjoyable that the other sisters demanded a turn at it. Some days later they all decided to go along and make a picnic of it—with corn bread and cold fish meat for dinner. Little Josh served as the hook-baiter, and the fish taker-offer for everyone. He was not kept very busy at those tasks, but still there was enough fish for another week. They sang songs, picked wild flowers for the house, played hide and seek with Bonnie Anne and Josh, and could not remember when last they had such an enjoyable day.

Before returning to the house, they went along the meadows to some sassafras trees and picked a batch of young shoots and roots to use for sassafras tea. Their cache of regular tea had run out several weeks before. Along the edge of an old back garden they found some pie plant, or rhubarb, now big enough to be edible. *Thank goodness for the vegetables that come up each year on their own like this pie plant and the asparagus and the strawberries,* thought Violet.

All these days the sisters continued to be busy in the garden, in the fields, in the kitchen, in the nursery, with the housework, but mostly scrounging for food. They were reduced almost to the status of wild birds and animals that spend nearly all their time and most of their energy just in searching for food and caring for their young.

Although the scavenger hunts and fishing had improved the food supply substantially, Violet still worried about nourishment for her children. They had not had any milk for such a long time, except for those two days at the Mannings. She saw no prospect for getting any. None of the near neighbors had a cow, so far as she knew. And she had no way to get into town on any regular basis. Even so, she had no money.

Sitting at dinner with her sisters on one of their regular food gathering days, Violet once more was looking out the window at the overgrown front lawn. "I wish we could find some way to trim the lawn," she said.

"Well, I could try hacking with a sickle instead of digging dandelion greens—if we had a sickle," Susan responded, with a total lack of enthusiasm.

"But, Violet, don't you think that would be a waste of time unless we could eat the brush and grass," Charlotte put in a bit sarcastically.

"Wait, maybe we can. Charlotte, I think you're on to something though you may not know it...another one of your great ideas!"

"Oh? What on earth are you talking about? Do you think we can digest grass like cows? Not unless we have another stomach or two and can chew our cud." She shook her head at the very thought.

"But Charlotte...Susan," Violet said, looking at each sister. "What we need is a goat, a nanny goat that can clear the brush, trim the grass, and provide milk for the children. The goat is the poor man's cow—its milk is richer than cow's milk, and just what the kids need!"

"Sure what the kids need," Charlotte laughed, "the baby goats!"

"I'd like to have some baby goats," said Susan, taking her sister literally.

"No, really," Violet insisted, "this is just what Bonnie Anne and J.J. need."

"Sounds good," Charlotte said, "but how can we buy a goat? With what? Violet, you know we don't have any money."

Violet quickly responded, "I think Mr. Ellison up at Stateburg did have some goats, and John Frierson said Potter's raiders did not harm his plantation in the way they did others. I think I'll go up there and see what I can find."

Charlotte persisted. "Violet, I agree, we do need a goat, but we can't buy a goat without money. You know Potter's scavengers stole all our money, our jewelry—all our valuables—and that damned Farley stole all the cotton we had hidden in the woods."

Violet pushed her chair back from the table and walked over to the window without saying anything. Charlotte and Susan looked at one another with raised eyebrows. Violet turned around and slowly raised her left hand. She spoke softly, but with determination, "The only material thing of any value that I have left is my gold wedding ring. I'll use that."

The other two gasped. "Oh, no, you can't do that, Violet!" both Charlotte and Susan said, almost in unison.

"But what else can I do? Of course I hate to have to lose it...of course it's sentimental value is greater to me than its material value, but the health of the children is more valuable than any ring, or anything else, and I'm certain that Brent would agree with me."

"Of course," they assented.

"And I'm not going to lose any more time. The children have been too long without milk. Little Josh could use some milk, too. I'm going to walk up to the Ellisons'—you know their place, just beyond Stateburg. I'll go this afternoon."

Shortly, with Little Josh in tow, Violet was on her way. The sun was hot, and she was grateful for the sunbonnet shielding her head. Little Josh wore an old cap that Christopher had worn when his age. Eventually, they arrived at the Ellisons' general store.

"Wale, good affernoon, Miz Violet," Henry Ellison greeted her. "Hits been uh long time since ah las' see ya. Ah hope ebberbudy be well at yo' house."

"Good afternoon, Mr. Ellison. Yes, it's been a long time, but we have only our feet for transportation these days. We're all right. You heard about Daddy being killed at Cheraw?"

"Yassum, Miz Violet. Ah sho' sorree 'bout dat. De Majuh, he be a mightee fine genulman, mightee fine genulman. Ah sho' sorree." Henry Ellison was a tall man, and he looked down on Violet with sympathy in his eyes.

"Thank you."

"Whut kin ah do fo' ya, Miz Violet?"

"Mr. Ellison, I'm trying to find a nanny goat so the children can have milk. I thought you might have one that I might buy. Did the Yankees leave you with any...I hope?"

"Well, Ma'am, dere be some up dere on de plantation. Mah bruddah, William, he dere. Go on up an' see 'im. Tell 'im ah send ya'." He smiled, wiping the perspiration from his black face with a bandanna handkerchief.

"Thank you, I will." She bade him good-bye and left.

It was not long to the Ellisons' plantation. Immediately William Ellison came out to greet her. She repeated her request about a nanny goat and mentioned that his brother had sent her on to the plantation.

William thought for a moment and then, with a big smile, said, "Yassum, dere be one good nanny up dere, jes' fresh. Come an' see. Hit ain't fah."

Violet and Little Josh followed him out to a meadow where half a dozen goats were grazing. "Heah, righ' chere, dis uh good one," he said as they came upon a tan and gray, short-haired nanny goat. "Dis uh good one. She give ya lotta milk fo' yo' babies. She jes' whut ya need."

"How much milk does she give?"

"Ah gits 'bout two quarts in de mornin' an' mebbe uh quart an' haf in de evenin'."

"How long will she give that much milk?"

"Hits 'bout six munts."

"That sounds good. She's what we need very much. Now, about the price?"

"Oh, ah don' kno', de price go up an' down so much nowuhdays, whut ya' athinkin',?" he hedged.

"Mr. Ellison, I know nothing about the price of goats, except it should be much less than a cow. Do you have any cows?"

"Only one now, dey all go off wif de Yankees fo' dere food."

"Yes, well now, the Yankees stole everything from us—all our cows and horses and hogs and chickens. They also stole all our valuables, our money, our jewelry—everything. The only thing I have left of value is my gold wedding ring." She took off the ring, and her heart missed a beat as she realized that this was the first time she had taken it off since Brent put it on her finger at their wedding.

Taking the ring in his hand, William Ellison said, "Dis uh bootiful ring, and hit be mo' dan de goat. Ah give ya de goat an' credit at de sto' fo' some tings ya need."

Tears came to Violet's eyes at the integrity of this man. She said simply, "Thank you very much. You are an honest man, indeed." She noticed that Little Josh was taking all this in.

"Ya stop at de sto' now?"

"Do you have any sugar? Any flour?"

"Don' have much uf eenyting ta eat, but dey be some sugah dere an' uh li'l flour."

"Oh good. I'll get some sugar and flour, and anything else I'll wait until I have more time. Little Josh and I have to get home before dark, and we can carry just so much."

"Dis be Li'l Josh?" he asked, looking at the boy kindly.

"Yes, he's come to live with us. I couldn't get along without him. He can do anything."

Little Josh beamed at the man and said proudly, "Yassuh, ah kin do ebberting, an' Miz Violet, she teech meh ta read."

"Wale now, ya mus' be uh smar' boy iffen ya kin do dat, Josh. Dat migh'tee nice uv Miz Violet ta do dat."

"Yassuh."

William put a lead collar and line on the nanny goat and then walked with Violet and Little Josh to the store. Josh held the goat's line while Violet went into the store. With the excitement of special discoveries, she picked up the five-pound sacks of sugar and wheat flour, bade Little Josh to come along with the goat, and headed for home.

"Miz Violet! Miz Violet!" called William Ellison. "Hol' on. Ah gots ta go down de road uh bit, an' yo and de boy be welcom' ta ride uh spell. Ah git de wagon in back. Jes' wait." He disappeared behind the store, and in a couple of minutes appeared driving two horses pulling a wagon. He pulled up beside Violet and Little Josh, hopped down, and helped Violet up on the seat. He lifted the goat into the back of the wagon, and then Little Josh, saying, "Now boy, yo' hold onta dat line an' don' leb dat goat git outta de wagin."

"Yassuh," said Little Josh, happy to be riding instead of walking.

About a mile from Fair Oaks, Ellison said, "Miz Violet, hit ain't fah ta yo' house. Ah migh' as well tek ya all de way. Ain't no truble t'all. Glad ta hep uh neighbuh."

When they arrived at the house, it was well past supper time. Everyone came out to say hello to William Ellison and to see the nanny goat. They were thrilled to find the two sacks of sugar and flour in the wagon. Mammy nodded her head at Ellison, picked up both sacks, one under each arm, and marched straight to the kitchen. She felt she was holding treasure.

The children were enchanted with the goat—as was Susan—which Little Josh was holding proudly.

"Mr. Ellison, we'd be pleased if you could stay for supper. We don't have much to offer, but you are welcome to join us." said Violet.

"Tank ya, Ma'am, but ah'se gotta git on mah way. Ah be seein' ya later." He could tell by their thinness, as well as their eagerness in getting the small sacks of sugar and flour, that they were having lean-pickings. They needed the little that they had for themselves.

After he left, Violet got some rope that Frierson had left and staked out the goat on the front lawn. She looked at Susan and said, "Susan, the goat will be your job. Milk her in the morning and in the evening, and move her stake every day so she can mow the whole lawn after a time. And listen, you must be careful to keep her out of reach of the shrubs and flowers because she will eat everything in sight."

"But, Violet, I don't know how to milk a goat."

"Neither do I, Susan, but we can try. We've seen cows being milked before in the barn."

Little Josh took hold of Violet's arm. "Miz Violet, ah kin teech ya. Ah milk'd uh cow befo'—de folks ah live wif 'n Clumbya had uh fahm 'n de countree, an' 'Lijuh lemme milk de cow fo' 'im."

"Josh, are you serious? Susan, run to the kitchen and get a large jar."

Susan returned in a flash, and the three sisters, along with Bonnie Anne and J.J. watched in fascination as Little Josh set the jar under the goat and, placing his hands on a teat, proceeded to draw milk.

"Ooooh, look at it squirt out!" exclaimed Bonnie Anne.

Little Josh stopped milking and looked up proudly. Then, imitating Violet's teaching voice, he said, "Now, Miz Susan, ah sho' ya, an' den Miz Violet, an' den Miz Charlotte. Now sit down, Miz Susan, an' grab hol' dis tit, mekin' yo' finguhs do dis." He demonstrated the procedure to each girl carefully. By the time he finished, all could milk the goat somewhat.

Supper that evening was a cheerful one—catfish, lye hominy, dandelion greens, corn bread, and milk. Bonnie Anne and J.J. were delighted when they received their white, sweet, nourishing milk in their colorful small weaning cups.

Later that evening Mammy took a little of the milk, a little of the sugar, and sassafras flavoring to make a small plate of fudge. It was a special treat for everyone.

Chapter 15

A Starvation Party

1865

One evening a couple of weeks later, the three sisters were sitting on the front porch, munching on sunflower seeds and parched corn. They had not been having much time to relax and just chat, but this evening they were taking the time. They would be going up to bed shortly before dark while they could still see their way around the house. Their supply of illuminating oil had been long exhausted. The stock of candles, stored in the cool basement, had given out a few weeks ago, and they were now reduced to using lightwood resin-rich slivers of pine as a substitute for candles. The pine slivers, however, burned much faster than did the candles, and they tried to use them only when absolutely necessary. So their schedule was usually early to bed and early to rise to take advantage of the daylight hours.

They were admiring the job of clearing and cutting the grass that Nanny had been doing on the front lawn, and they were enjoying the beauty and perfume of the gardenias, roses, and honeysuckle blossoms. It was the fourth of July, but nobody took any notice.

Violet broke a period of silence. "We certainly have not been having much of a social life here these days, so seldom do we see anybody. Nobody has any carriages, and I guess everyone is as busy as we are just trying to survive day by day."

"No, we don't see anyone these days," Charlotte agreed. "It's terrible that so many of the young men had to die in the War, and the women are all having to scrounge so hard for sustenance, just like us."

"Yes," sighed Violet in a low tone.

"I wonder why Leland hasn't been back to visit us," added Charlotte, a frown on her face.

Violet gave no reply to Charlotte's comment, but continued with what was on her mind. "I've been thinking that perhaps we should have a party." She turned to look at her sisters.

"A party! That's wonderful! I'm always in favor of a party, and heaven knows we haven't had one for—for ever so long," exclaimed an excited Susan.

"But Violet," asked Charlotte, incredulously, "Where are we going to find any men?"

"I wasn't thinking of men. I was thinking more of a hen party—just women. There are several neighbors who are now widows, and others whose men are not yet back from the War, and some are alone while their husbands are off on either a business project or trying to get a restart elsewhere. And then there are some who have never married—whose fiances were killed, or who were never asked in the first place, or who have grown up during the War."

"Like Charlotte and me," interjected Susan, smiling.

"Well, yes."

"But what on earth can we offer for refreshments—carp and boiled dandelion greens?" inquired the ever-practical Charlotte, her eyes twinkling.

Violet smiled. "You may think you jest, Charlotte, but that may be part of it. Nobody has anything just now. We all have to scrounge for everything. So what we'll have is a Starvation Party."

"Now *you* jest," returned Charlotte.

"Well, the starvation part would be nothing new," said Susan ironically.

Violet continued, "Here's what we can do. You see we would have each guest bring some concoction, made only from ingredients found on her own place. Then everyone could share recipes for all the different kinds of foods that they've been having to prepare these days. Maybe we can get some ideas for a little variety. Well, what do you think?"

"I like the idea," Susan answered enthusiastically.

"That could be fun," Charlotte conceded. "But how do we get the word to them, and how do they get here? Scarcely anyone has a horse or buggy or wagon—the Ellison brothers are the only ones that I know who has any kind of transportation."

"We walk to them with the invitations, and then they walk to the party here."

"Oh, there you are," Susan said, "and I suppose I will be designated the one to have the honor of delivering all the invitations! I should have known there's a catch to it."

Violet smiled at her younger sister with amusement, "Susan, we'll divide the invitations up, and each of us will take some to deliver."

"Oh," was all a somewhat disconcerted Susan could manage. Her pink cheeks reflected her embarrassment.

"I'll write the invitations—if I can find any ink around here. You can take three or four, Susan, and Charlotte and I will take the same, and Little Josh can deliver some, too."

"That sounds fair to me," Susan agreed, "but when shall we have the party? I hope we choose a day when it won't be raining."

Violet replied quickly, "If I thought we could choose a rainy day I'd have it tomorrow, to break this drought. Unfortunately, that's something over which we have no control. Now, what do you say, today is Tuesday; we'll get the invitations ready tomorrow, and deliver them on Thursday. We'll have the party on the following Wednesday which will be the twelfth of July. That's about the beginning of lay-by time for us, when the cotton is too big to be hoed any more and not yet ready for picking until September or October. Of course we don't know how many of them are planting cotton this year, but it's still too soon for there to be much yield from whatever gardens they may have."

"It might be fun," Charlotte repeated. "Whom shall we invite?"

"Well, let's think about that," answered Violet, noting the waning of twilight. She rose from her chair. "We'd better get to our rooms in time to wash up before it's completely dark. Tomorrow, after our morning chores, let's meet at the dining table and make out our list together."

That afternoon, Violet went into the office to write the invitations. Frustrated in her hunt for ink, she did find some old lead pencils and some faded note paper. Taking these in hand she applied her skillful penmanship:

Mrs. St. Julian Ravenel
Acton Plantation

Dear Mrs. Ravenal:

Charlotte, Susan, and I cordially invite you to have dinner with us and other ladies of this area at Fair Oaks on Wednesday, the 12th of July, at noon.

Please understand that this is to be a "Starvation" potluck dinner, where each guest will bring a dish of any kind, made of ingredients found on her own place. Then we shall share recipes that we have developed to gain some sustenance during these difficult days.

Unfortunately, the Yankees either broke or stole most of our dinnerware silver, and other eating utensils, and we must ask our guests to bring a plate and eating utensils, along with the food.

Please reply by the bearer whether or not you will be able to attend.

Respectfully,
Violet Storm Sutler

Violet prepared similar notes for the others on her list. By the time she had finished, her wrist was aching from the unaccustomed exercise of small muscles, but she felt a sense of accomplishment.

The day of the Starvation Party was all the sisters had hoped for—clear skies, a slight breeze, and not too hot. In the large, formal dining room, they had placed on the oval table one of their mother's white linen tablecloths, decorated with a cut-out, embroidered pattern through which the cherry wood could be seen. Matching napkins lay at each place. Fortunately the tablecloth and napkins had been stored in a chest in the attic where the Yankees had not ventured. The girls had gathered a variety of fresh flowers, and Violet had created an attractive centerpiece of mixed flowers.

The ladies began arriving at eleven o'clock in the morning. After their long walks some wanted to rest a bit before the dinner; others wanted to have time to get their food warmed up after the walk. They all wore broad-brimmed hats to keep the sun off their heads and to shield their faces. Although in the spirit of a party they wore their finest, such apparel in most cases consisted of mixed outfits, somewhat faded from age and use. They all wore gloves, as was proper, but a small hole or two could be seen in most. They carried their contribution to the dinner in covered baskets, some of which were made of woven strips of the white oak tree, sweet grass palmetto, and pine straw; others were made of woven corn and sugar cane husks. In these baskets were also a plate or bowl and one or more eating utensils. One guest had only a small wooden bowl overlooked by the raiders who had almost totally stolen everything. Her man servant had carved forks for them to use from a small limb with twigs at the end.

The guests were all in good cheer and looking forward to this social event which was the first in many a month. They were eagerly anticipating hearing news of those in the area, as well as what the others might know about the affairs and future of South Carolina and the South in general.

Violet had anticipated a variety of creative concoctions, and she was not disappointed. In addition to the house offerings of chunks of salted boiled fish in goat cheese sauce and sassafras tea, the guests contributed boiled quail eggs; a pudding of corn meal and dried whortleberries sweetened with sorghum; stewed pie plant, roasted green apples, also sweetened with sorghum; a dish containing a mixture of boiled dandelion greens, cowslips, and burdock; hominy with chopped wild onions, split pea and potato soup flavored with mint; rice muffins without yeast; asparagus spears with strawberry sauce; potato pudding; "artificial oysters" of corn and flour; mulberries, cider jelly; a salad of dandelion greens with bits of hearts of cattails as substitute for cucumbers, and three kinds of coffee: from dried beans, dried apples, and sorghum; from dried okra seeds; and from ripe acorns.

As the ladies sat down to their special dinner, a din of conversation arose. At first, groups of two or three all around the table developed separate and competing conversations. The rising volume of the voices reflected the enjoyment they were having in the chance to visit after such a long interval. They exchanged bits of personal news, comments, and gossip. Gradually they began to turn their attention to one speaker at a time.

Violet: I'm glad that most of us have been able to survive Potter's raids even though he left us nothing to work with.

Mrs. Frierson: Have you all heard how Violet held off the Yankee raiders with an empty musket until the officers came and saved this house for a headquarters?

Mrs. Murray: No! How courageous! Tell us about it, Violet.

Violet: That was all there was to it. Fortunately, I was able to hold a group of them at bay until an officer rode up and said they were making their headquarters here.

Susan: Violet is just being modest. She faced them all—like a tiger, er, tigress.

Violet: I just wish I could have stopped the soldiers from carrying off Evelina. She was so frightened. And of course earlier the soldiers took Aaron and Uncle Job and Aunt Beulah with them, prodding them with their guns to keep them moving—like cattle or something. There was nothing I could do then.

Miss Watie: A cousin of mine, Mrs. Rees, had a similar experience over at Midway House. She and her children were living there with our old aunt, Mrs. Bentham. When Potter's raiders approached, my cousin and her children fled over to our place, but our aunt stayed there alone and defied them. She saved the house from burning. A few Confederate soldiers came up from somewhere and then the raiders went on. Auntie stood out on the porch and bravely ordered the last Negro soldier to leave the premises. Now my cousin and her children are safely back there, thank goodness.

Mrs. Burkett: Did you hear what they did in Sumter: It was mostly that regiment of Negroes from Massachusetts. They tore up the Court House even though it was being used as a hospital. They burned lots of the other public buildings, all the hundreds of bales of cotton, and lots of houses.

Mrs. A. Blair: I'm surprised as many escaped injury as did in Sumter, but did you hear what happened to old Robert Bee? Drunken soldiers came into his house and hanged him from the rafters of his attic while they violated his daughter in front of his eyes and then tortured him until he died.

Several Ladies: Oh, no, that's awful!...How dreadful!...Shocking!

Mrs. Burkett: And did you hear about poor Fannie McKagen, the doctor's wife? Late that Sunday evening a pair of those Yankee looters came running into her house. They found the children's nurse asleep on a couch, and one ran over and stuck the barrel of his musket right into her mouth. The children were simply horrified and went running around screaming until he withdrew. But that was not all. Then that same soldier went over to Mrs. McKagen who, though ill, had been attracted by the screams of the children, and he asked her if any member of her family had fought that day at Dingle's Mill, outside Sumter. She replied directly, "Yes, my husband." Then she was so anxious for news of her husband that she described him and asked the soldier if he might have seen him. The Yankee laughed and said, "Oh, yes, I saw him all right. He was lying on his belly, and I stuck my bayonet through him and rolled him over." She practically fainted in shock. The next day she received a note from her husband saying that he was all right. But it was too much. A couple of days later she died...and left all those children.

Mrs. A. Blair: Yes, wasn't that terrible? If you ask me, that Yankee soldier killed her as surely as if he had stuck his bayonet through her.

Mrs. Bradley: And is that the kind of people we are going to have ruling over us now, a bunch of Northern barbarians?

Mrs. Bradford: I understand that ole Potter missed twenty-seven bales of seed cotton at Moore Hill and a storage house half full of gunpowder—and these not a hundred yards off King's Highway where the main part of his army was marching down.

Violet: His raiders didn't miss much here. Took nearly all our food, drove off all our animals and wagons and carriages, dug up the valuables and household items that we had buried in the garden, and they burned the cotton in the storehouse and our outbuildings. Only a few of the slave cabins still stand—and they were completely looted. They did miss forty-eight bales that we had hidden in the woods. We were so excited about that, but then that scalawag Farley came along and stole it in the name of the United States Treasury.

Mrs. Burkett: I understand that they seized a lot of cotton with the claim that it had belonged to the Confederate Government.

Violet: Listen everyone, Miss Constance Simons...

Miss Simons: Connie.

Violet: Connie Simons, who has just recently arrived, is planning to reopen the school at Edge Hill this fall.

Several: Wonderful!...What good news!...At last.

Charlotte: Although we attended school in Columbia, all of our family enjoyed some years at Edge Hill.

Violet: Yes, indeed.

Mrs. Pinckney: I guess a lot of us remember school days there—the Sumters, the Rutledges, the Waties, the Andersons...

Miss Watie: Ah, those were great days, indeed.

Mrs. Anderson: Well, it certainly is a different world, isn't it? Our old civilization is gone, carried away on the winds of war, and there's no use pining for it.

Violet: Nonsense. Southern civilization is not gone. Of course there have been and will be lots of changes, but we cannot forget our history and our values. Those as well as the external pressures and our own will and industry will determine our future.

Mrs. Prescott: I hope we can salvage something out of this, but I'm sure I don't know how.

Violet: I wonder if we are going to be able to get back on our feet soon, or are the Yankees going to be so vindictive and vengeful that they won't let us recover?

Mrs. Burkett: That is the question that must concern us all. I'm afraid the assassination of Lincoln will make things more difficult, much more difficult for us.

Mrs. Ravenal: You know there have been attempts in many places in the South to express condolences. I hear from Charleston that they had a huge meeting of that kind at the Hibernian Hall there. They say that even Confederate soldiers in Northern prisoner of war camps expressed sympathy. Of course no one knows whether this will do any good in helping Northern understanding of our feelings. There seem to be so many rabid politicians up there.

Mrs. Prescott: *So* true, alas.

Mrs. Ravenal: You know the Northern newspapers said that Jefferson Davis cheered when he heard the news of the assassination of Lincoln. But to the contrary, I heard from the man who was holding a horse for a cavalry major when Jefferson Davis arrived in Charlotte from Greensboro, that when Davis stepped down from his horse, he was handed a paper by this major. It was a report of Lincoln's assassination. Davis simply turned away and said softly. "Oh, the pity of it all." Then he handed the paper to another gentleman and said, "Here are sad tidings." They said that Mrs. Davis was then at the Armistead Burt house at Abbeville, and when she heard the news she burst into tears.

Violet: Mrs. Ravenal, have you heard from Mary Chesnut since the raids?

Mrs. Ravenal: I did hear that their Mulberry plantation had been partially destroyed. She said the house was all smashed up on one side but intact on the other. The General had come and stopped the destruction when he found it occupied by Mary Whitaker and her ninety-year old mother whom the Chesnuts had left in charge. And the raiders carried away sacks of books and papers—which were strewn all over the place. They said somebody had found one of their letters as far away as Vance Ferry. Now why would anyone want to steal those?

Mrs. Burkett: Why Vance Ferry is halfway to Charleston!

Mrs. Ravenal: And Mary Chesnut wrote about a friend of hers by the name of Mary Kirkland who, with her three children and mother, were taunted mercilessly. Yankee soldiers came storming into their house and ordered them to stand against a wall. Their Mammy and Lizzie came and stood by them, and the Yankee soldiers reviled them for standing up for their 'cruel masters'. They kept those women and children standing against the wall for four hours while they ransacked the house. Finally Mary's mother just fainted dead away. Mary Kirkland ran to her side and turned on the Yankees and shouted, "Leave this room, you wretches. Do you mean to kill my mother? She is ill. I must put her to bed." And they all slunk out of the house like weasels.

Susan: That sounds like our Violet!

Mrs. Frierson: It does, indeed.

Mrs. Pinckney: Not all the darkies were that loyal. I've heard that in some instances the maids ran up and put on their mistresses' dresses and paraded around like they owned the places, and then went off with the Yankees.

Mrs. Ravenal: A friend, Mrs. Adger, in Camden was watching a Yankee soldier accost a young woman on the front porch of one of the big houses. Then suddenly the soldier slapped the young woman. Mrs. Adger prayed that God would strike him dead. In departing, the soldier fell down the steps, and his revolver went off and killed him.

Susan: Serves him right!

Mrs. Bradford: Violet, have you had any word of your husband yet?

Violet: No, not yet. I had hoped he would be here by now, but since he is in the Navy it is hard telling where he might have been when the War ended. I look for him any day now.

Mrs. Pinckney: You all know Mrs. Brownfield of Woodville. She was born in Brazil while her father was in the diplomatic service. She says there is a lot of sympathy for the Confederacy in foreign countries.

Mrs. Burgess: I haven't heard much news lately, but some say that Andrew Johnson has softened a bit and may carry out Lincoln's policies of moderation.

Mrs. Frierson: Yes, my husband reports that Johnson's proclamation of a few weeks ago is a hopeful sign. He is offering pardons to everyone, provided they take an oath of allegiance, except those who held civil offices in the Confederate government, and those who own property valued at over twenty thousand dollars—and even these can be pardoned by special petition.

Violet: I wonder whether property will be valued at what the Yankee tax assessors claim it is worth or at what the Scalawags and Carpetbaggers are willing to pay for it.

Miss B. Blair: But what is going to happen to the darkies? I can't help but worry about their future.

Violet: I hope most of them will come back to the plantations, though there are no signs of this happening here yet. Still, I expect many of ours to be back in time. I fear most will not find happiness and security out in the world on their own.

Mrs. Bradford: I wish they could get to work and turn out like the Ellisons. I must say, you have to hand it to that family.

Mrs. Burgess: Yes, the Ellisons are proud folks, highly respected by all who know them, and none of them has turned into a brass ankle, trying to pass over.

Violet: And we must never forget that they supported the Confederacy throughout, helping every way they could, except, of course, they could not join the army.

It was now two-thirty. The time had passed quickly as they ate and chatted. They complimented each other on what they had brought and shared their recipes. Mammy and Little Josh had cleared the table, enjoyed what was left of the banquet, and had cleaned the dishes, bowls, and utensils the ladies were to take back with them.

The guests were discussing what time they should begin their return trips when they heard the kitchen door slam and a voice call out, "Mammy! Mammy! Ah'se back ah las'! Whar Miz Violet 'n de udders?"

Just as Violet was rising from the table, Susan exclaimed excitedly, "Why, it's Evelina! Evelina's come home. Hurrah!"

Violet met Evelina at the dining room door and threw her arms around her young maidservant, and then pulled her into the room. Violet turned to the guests, and said, "You've all heard how Potter's soldiers kidnaped Evelina, dragging her away against her will. Now she's back. Isn't that wonderful!" She asked Susan to fetch another chair for Evelina, and said, "Now, Evelina, tell us what happened to you after we last saw you. We've been terribly worried about you."

"Yes, yes, tell us," asked the others. Mammy was standing in the doorway beaming with happiness that her young charge was safe and sound and back with them all.

"Evelina, it is so *good* to see you. Everyone has missed you so much," added Sarah Frierson, smiling at Evelina with pleasure.

Susan and Charlotte were hugging Evelina with delight. Violet had to ask them to return to their seats while Evelina related her adventures.

"Now start from the beginning," said Susan. "We want to hear everything that happened to you."

Evelina turned to look at Mammy and then at Violet. She replied, "No'm Miz Susan, yo don' wan' ta hear ebberting, bu' ah tells ya some." And she began her tale while all listened attentively. Gasps of dismay could be heard, interspersed with moments of shocked silence. Several of the ladies had to call for their smelling salts.

She related how the three soldiers had forced her to march along with them, and when she tried to escape, they tied her hands together and attached a rope with which they pulled her. "Lawdy, Miz Violet, ah ain't nebber bin treated like dat, jes' like a cow or hawg bein' pull'd along. When ah tripp'd, dey jes' yank'd de rope an' kep' pullin'."

She went on to tell how when they stopped to camp, they tied her to a tree out in the woods. They gave her a sip of water and a corn pone to eat, and then left her all by herself in the dark. Then later, when everything was quiet, the three soldiers who had taken her crept out to where she was tethered. "Ah ain't gwine tell ya whut dem Yankees do ta me, buh each one do hit ta me. Ah try ta figh' em off, buh dey jes' too strong fo' meh. When ah scream'd one of dem take off uh 'kerchief and stuff'd hit 'n mah mouf so ah mek no noise...Den dey tek off dere trousers...an'...ah can't tell no mo'..." And she burst into sobs.

Violet and the others told Evelina that she didn't have to tell more, but she regained control of herself and went on. She said that the next day the bummers resumed their march, moving diagonally across fields and roads toward Camden where they met the main army and set up camp. Again she was left in woods, tethered to a tree, and that night the episode was repeated. She heard the soldiers talking about how Sherman had already ransacked the town thoroughly, and Potter had given orders to leave the next day. The daily walking and experiences at night in the woods, coupled with fear of wild animals and the possibility of other roaming soldiers, took their toll on Evelina. She escaped the horror of her existence by sinking into an exhausted daze, unaware of the passage of time. She vaguely recalled the soldiers mentioning Stateburg, Manchester, and then St. Marks Episcopal Church. The mention of the latter revived her somewhat, for the Storm family had attended weddings and funerals there in years past, and she had usually accompanied the sisters as their maidservant. Memories burst upon her dull mind, forcing it into action again. She went on to say that that night, after they had finished with her, the soldiers fell into a drunken stupor. One fell almost at her feet. She waited quietly until she was certain they were not likely to awaken, and then carefully took a knife from the soldier's belt. Ever so quietly, taking care not to rustle the leaves on the ground, she cut the rope tied to the tree. She was unable to cut the rope binding her wrists, so she stuck both the knife and the end of the rope into her apron at the waist. With the stealth of wild animals in the woods, she slipped away. The skies were clear and the moon bright, so she could make her way fairly well without stumbling over fallen trees and bushes. She continued until daybreak where she saw the ruins of a chicken house by the woods. She forced herself to walk that much farther and sank in a corner of the dilapidated building, trembling with a chill though the night was warm.

"Oh, Evelina, how brave of you to make this escape." Violet said tenderly, with moist eyes.

Cries of "Yes...yes...you poor girl...so brave" burst forth. Mrs. Bradford and Miss Pauline Watie were fanning themselves with vigor.

"And then what happened?" prodded young Susan, whose innocence was such that some aspects of the full story were not clear to her.

"Well, Miz Susan, Miz Violet, ah wuz so skeer'd dem sojuhs come back dat ah stay 'n dat chick'n house fo' ah don' kno' how manee days. Ah eat berrees 'n chaw'd sassafra' roots 'n ah found a coup'l uh quail egs. Ah so hungree ah eat 'em jes' de way ah find dem. Ah git wader frum de spring nex' ta de burn'd down house. Den ah run back ta de chick'n house 'n hide some mo'."

After some days of near starvation, Evelina decided to venture forth again. She had sensed that the soldiers had traveled first north, and then south for a much longer time. She figured that the Storm plantation must be somewhere to the north. Her wrists were still bound, but this had not kept her from picking berries, digging for roots, or getting water from the spring. She saw no one along the way. She was feeling weak and somewhat faint from the exercise and insufficient food. The hot sun beamed down on her head. Finally she saw a partially burned house about five hundred feet off the road. She turned down the lane toward the house, forcing herself to continue. Just as she reached the house she fell to the ground in a faint.

She came to in the cooling shade of a large pecan tree. An elderly woman, in a tattered dress that once had seen fine days, was wiping Evelina's face with a wet cloth, and murmuring encouraging words. "You're all right now, Everything is all right. You're safe, poor thing...I saw you coming down the lane and then drop. My manservant, Fred, moved you to the shade of this tree."

At the sight of the man, Evelina shrunk with fright. She knew only too well what men could do.

The woman noticed her shrinking away, and in a soft, calm voice continued, "You need have no fear of Fred. He is as kind and loyal a person as can be. I wouldn't be here if Fred had not stayed to take care of me when the others left with Potter's army.

They helped Evelina into the partially destroyed house and laid her on a straw pallet in the corner of a room. There Evelina lay for three days, slowly regaining her strength as a result of the tender care of Mrs. Roberts and Fred.

Mrs. Roberts had heard of the Storms of Fair Oaks, and promised Evelina that they would find some way to help her get home. For now she had to get stronger. Which she did, basically being a healthy young woman. As she observed Fred and his compassionate care of his elderly mistress, she lost her fear of him. She was intelligent and knew that all men were not like those Yankee soldiers who abducted and used her. She remembered the goodness of Major Storm and Leo and Jarvis and Aaron. Fabian she had never cared for, but he was not a bad person. Up until now she had led a sheltered and protected life at the Storms. But no one...no one...had ever treated her as had the Yankee soldiers.

Mrs. Roberts had no means of transportation other than walking. Her cache of food, hidden in time by Fred, was not discovered by the bummers, and it was this plus the little her neighbors could spare that had sustained her and Fred. He had put in a small garden that was just now beginning to produce vegetables. Evelina had stayed with them, helping in the kitchen and the garden when her strength returned, but her heart longed for Fair Oaks. She told her hostess that she had to get back; they would all be worried about her. Besides, she was homesick.

So one morning the kind old lady and Fred placed a basket of food in her hands and wished her good luck and farewell. Mrs. Roberts wrote on a piece of paper Evelina's name and where she was going. She also wrote her own name on the paper, should there be any questions. Evelina set off down King's Highway.

She finished her tale by telling everyone, "So ah walk'd an' walk'd an' walk'd 'til ah come ta Manches'er. Den ah follow de track ta Stateburg. Den ah come down de road ta dese place. An' heah ah is, a' las'."

It was four o'clock. The guests should have left at least a half hour earlier, but no one, not even those who lived the farthest away, could leave until Evelina finished her story. They were happy that she had survived the ordeal and was home again. The kind ladies gathered up their dishes and utensils and put these in their baskets, put on their hats and gloves, kissed and hugged each other good-bye, and promised to have another Starvation Party in the near future. Sarah Frierson volunteered to have the next one at Cherry Vale. She had been somewhat more fortunate than the Storms and the others, with most of her dishes and china, and silverware and other eating utensils left intact. Of course, all the animals and carriages and wagons were gone, so, like all the others, they had no transportation other than their feet. They all accepted her invitation, promised new and exciting concoctions to eat. Being together had been the tonic they needed, and each left Fair Oaks in higher spirits than when she had arrived and with a more positive outlook.

Chapter 16

Farley Again?

1865

"Now, Mrs. Sutler, I don't want any trouble."

"You've already got it, and if you are here with another of your thieving schemes, you are going to have a lot more!"

Blake Farley had returned to Fair Oaks twenty weeks after making off with all the cotton they had hidden in the woods, and now he had quickly run into a broadside from the mistress of Fair Oaks plantation. This time the crafty Farley had brought along the new sheriff. They had found Violet at the back of the house on her way to the garden.

"Meet Sheriff Cecil Gary, here, Miz Storm."

Violet looked at the sheriff with suspicious eyes,. "How do you do, Sheriff. Where are you from?" *He reminds me of one of father's hunting dogs,* she thought, *right now I can't think of which one, but it'll come to me in a bit.*

The Sheriff's small dark eyes peered at her from underneath heavy lids. His prominent nose and large ears made his hawkish face seem even thinner. He was of average height and build. Somewhat nervously, for he had heard of Farley's last meeting with Violet, he ran his large bony hands through his thinning dark hair as he answered her. "Why, Sumter, Ma'am."

Violet came back quickly, "Oh, no, you're not. I asked, where are you from?"

"Oh, you mean where did I come from, why, I came down here from Ohio."

"I see, Ohio, all the way from Ohio. Of course," she said with a mocking smile. "I'm sure you're not here just to bring greetings. And we have no cotton left in the woods, as Mr. Farley can attest to." She felt that same sense of apprehension rising within her as when Farley had stopped by to ask about the cotton. Then she had jumped at conclusions, but she had learned her lesson well. She knew to be cautious this time.

Farley answered for the Sheriff, "Actually, we're here to carry out the instructions of General Saxton who is in charge of the Freedmen's Bureau in South Carolina–and he is carrying out the directive of the Federal Director of the Bureau, General Howard."

"What is the Freedmen's Bureau, pray tell," Violet asked, "and what is it that you really want?"

"It's a Bureau of the War Department..."

"What War Department?"

"In Washington. It was set up to assist the freed slaves in getting a start in their new situation."

"That sounds good. They should be doing something for them," Violet replied, "but what has that got to do with us? Except for Mammy, and Evelina who's just returned, all our slaves are gone—driven off by the soldiers or left on their own to follow Potter's army, and they've not come back, so you can go on and look elsewhere. You won't find any here."

"No, that's not it." Farley hesitated, his shifty eyes looking at the ground and everywhere else but into her eyes.

Violet observed his evasive behavior, recalling the last visit. *Dear God, be merciful. This weasel has something up his sleeve. What else can he do to us?* She braced herself for what was to come.

Farley continued. "You see, General Saxton's program is to provide each freed Negro with forty acres and a mule..."

Sheriff Gary cut in, "And to do that the Government is seizing certain plantations to be divided up into forty-acre farms."

Violet knew what would be next. She held herself in check, knowing that she had to keep her wits about her and think clearly. In a calm voice she said, "Don't tell me you have your eyes on this place."

The Sheriff went on, "Ma'am, it is my duty to inform you that the Government is seizing this plantation since the owner was a Confederate officer now absent."

"Of course he is absent, you damned fool," Violet exclaimed, "My father is dead, killed in battle by you damn Yankees!"

"So the Government falls heir to his lands," the Sheriff responded.

"My, God, how do you expect us to live?" asked Violet, unbelievingly.

With no trace of compassion, the Sheriff answered, "That's your problem, Ma'am. You people started this war; now you are going to have to live with the consequences."

*This isn't right! I've got to do something...Daddy...*the thought struck her. She said, "Hold on, you two. You said the *owner* is absent. Well, let me inform you most emphatically that the owner of this plantation—Fair Oaks plantation—is not absent. *I* am the owner, and I can prove it."

With a look of skepticism, Farley said, "You, Miz Storm? You the owner? Prove it."

"Stay here." Violet turned and hurried to the office where she took out Major Storm's will. She held it to her breast as she ran back outside. "Here," she said, holding up the will. "Here is the will. You can see my father left the plantation to me, Violet Storm Sutler. To me. *I* am the owner of this plantation, and I am not absent."

Without bothering to look at the document, the Sheriff asked, "Has this will been probated and your title recorded at the court house?"

Violet answered lamely, "Well, no, how could I?

"Forget it."

This can't be happening! she thought, anger rising within her. She cried, "You get off this place! Now! Right now!" She turned toward the house and screamed, "Charlotte, Charlotte, bring Daddy's carbine, quickly!"

Farley said hastily, "All right, all right, we are going, but you have just fifteen days to gather your things and clear out of here. Fifteen days, that's all. Understand?" He motioned to the Sheriff.

Susan, who had been taking all this in at a distance, quietly slipped away.

As the two men were turning to leave, Violet said in a cold, steady voice, "Listen to me, Mister Farley...Sheriff Gary...we're not going anywhere, and the freed slaves won't steal our cotton fields yet. Just you wait and see. Don't think you can run all over us and take everything we have. Now get out of here! Now! You get off this place, and if you don't want to get shot in the back, you'd better walk backward all the way down the lane!"

As the men disappeared around the corner of the house, to mount their horses which they had left at the front hitching gate, Violet muttered to herself, *I'll tell you one thing, Mister Farley and Sheriff Gary, first thing in the morning I am going to Sumter to see if I can head this thing off. There's bound to be a way and I'll find it.*

Susan was sitting on the side of the front porch quietly petting Nanny as the two men passed. Farley paused and in a patronizing tone said, "Hello, young lady, and who is your friend there?" Susan merely nodded as he passed on. Then she released the goat with a wave and a hard pat on its flank. Nanny turned and looked at Susan as though in acknowledgment, then turned back and lowered her head. With a sudden leap she raced toward Farley. In a flash she landed a resounding butt squarely on Farley's buttocks. Instantly he was sprawled face down on the ground.

Susan turned and ran into the house before he could recover. Violet and Charlotte had seen what had happened from the parlor front window and were convulsed with laughter at the sight of Farley getting his just due from Nanny.

When their laughter quieted, Charlotte turned to Violet, a worried look now upon her sweet face. "I saw what Nanny did, but what is this all about? I had just come down from upstairs when I looked out the window. What did Farley and the Sheriff want? Why were they here, Violet?"

Violet explained the substance of what had happened but tried to minimize it.

"Oh, no, Violet! Do we have to start packing our things, what little we have left from the Yankee raiders?" asked Susan, alarm causing her cheeks to flush.

Charlotte's first thoughts were for the crops. "You mean all that work we did to put in a little cotton and corn was for naught? Are they going to steal our cotton again?"

"Now listen, you two, we're not going anywhere," Violet reassured them, "and they won't try to steal our cotton yet; they're too lazy to pick it. But I'll tell you one thing: first thing in the morning I'm going to Sumter to see if I can put a stop to all this."

Early the next morning Violet lost no time in heading for Sumter. She was traveling alone for she had decided that the fourteen-mile round trip would be too much for Little Josh, and her sisters needed to be at their necessary work in the house and fields. She had put on her best shoes, though they were worn, and her prettiest dress, though it was frayed and faded, and what once had been a pretty straw hat with a broad, round brim. Carefully she had folded her father's will and placed it in her handbag. She thought about picking some fresh roses to put on the hat, but decided the sun and heat would dry them out before she even arrived in Sumter. Perhaps she could pick some wild flowers near the edge of the town. She picked up a pouch of parched corn and dried sunflower seeds from the kitchen, grabbed one of her father's old walking sticks, and about eight o'clock set out. Her anger fueled her determination, and her determination pushed her feet to a fast pace.

She needed to find someone to intercede on her behalf. She turned over in her mind the possibilities—Mr. Shelby, their friendly family lawyer, but he probably could not do much other than getting the will probated and recorded. Then she thought of young Frank Moses. He had been an army officer during the War and his father, Franklin I. Moses, Sr., had been an acquaintance of Major Storm's. Yes! That was it. She would go to Frank, Jr., and ask that he intercede for her.

I wonder what makes people like Farley be so mean, Violet thought as she continued her walk directly into the sun's rays. She pulled her hat brim down to shield her eyes. *Obviously he wants money, wants to enrich himself, but there must be more to it than that. He has always been a little man, in every sense, and now he thinks he sees an opportunity to gain some power. I wonder, what makes good people do good things? Are they, too, grasping for power, for a kind of control over those for whom they do favors? Does it make them feel good, always having someone beholden to them? The Carpetbaggers are coming down here now to gain influence and wealth at the expense of the downtrodden, but maybe also the charitable societies coming down from the North are doing the same thing. They, too, seem determined to stamp out the Southern civilization, but in a more "noble" way.*

Maybe that is just a part of human nature. Everybody wants to lord it over somebody—the man dominates the woman, the woman dominates the servants and the children, the children dominate their pets. Maybe that is why men find the army attractive—not only for the excitement of the ultimate contest, but to find a place to be domineering—the general lords it over the colonel, the colonel lords it over the major, the major over the captain, the captain over the lieutenant, the lieutenant over the ensign, the ensign over the sergeant, the sergeant over the private, and the private tries to control the enemy or any civilian that gets in the way. Even his gun gives him a sense of power, of being able to dominate people at a distance. Even the missionaries are trying to dominate the heathens in an attempt to extend some new religion over them.

And now we have the Carpetbaggers and the Scalawags to deal with.

Her thoughts turned to her own home. *Am I getting that way, trying to lord it over my sisters? I hope not. But we've got to have some kind of authority, some kind of structure to get anything done at all. At least I'll try to be more understanding and sympathetic than the Carpetbaggers and Scalawags are. I wonder, will there be any trouble when the men come home from the War and try to lord it over the women who have been running the plantations and offices and everything in their absence?*

Violet realized that she was approaching Sumter. She looked for wild flowers along the road and soon spied some black-eyed Susan and bluebells. She picked a few, removed her hat and tucked the flowers in the band. The effect was most attractive. She replaced the hat, and continued walking briskly, entered Sumter by way of North Main Street which, like all the other streets in town, was unpaved and dusty, bordered by rammed earth sidewalks and wooden curbs. She walked toward the center of town, near the intersection of Main and Liberty. Evidences of Potter's raid were still all around. Several houses showed marks of repair. Late summer roses were in bloom everywhere—no wonder they called Sumter the "Town of Roses"—and often these climbing roses masked the scars of fire and destruction. Workers, white and black alike, were busy at rebuilding or repairing houses and public buildings. Scores of other Negroes filled the downtown streets to no apparent purpose.

Blue-uniformed soldiers on the streets were constant reminders that the area was under military occupation. She learned that they belonged to a Massachusetts regiment, with headquarters in the Court House. It was clear that the local inhabitants were resentful, but their manners were correct. Sometimes they were even friendly toward the occupying forces, and there was no sign of friction on this day.

Violet noticed the work being done on the Town Hall and the jail which had been burned, on the Court House which had been severely damaged even though it was being used as a hospital, on the printing plant of the newspaper, *The Watchman,* and on several shops. Looking down a couple of blocks to the south, Violet could see the ruins of the railway station and several warehouses, wrecked railway cars and locomotives, and still, dark areas where hundreds of bales of cotton had burned.

It was almost eleven o'clock. On inquiry she learned that Frank Moses, Jr., had an office with his father and soon located it. She found Frank, Jr., very gracious. He was rather tall and slender. His dark wavy hair was parted on the side and trimmed neatly around the neck. He was clean shaven except for a luxuriant black moustache that gave the impression that somehow his bow tie had leaped from his throat to his upper lip, to be replaced at the lower level by a neat string tie. His sharp, brown eyes seemed to reflect a keen intellect with a hint of craftiness. His dark suit was immaculate.

Moses greeted her with a pleasant, resonant voice, affecting to know her, though he had only heard of her. His eyes indicated that he indeed would like to know her well...very well. He had long heard of the beauty of the eldest Storm daughter, and he now could vouch that all that he had heard was true. He smiled and pulled out a chair for her.

Violet explained that she had come to see him because of the friendly relationship of their fathers in the past. He listened sympathetically as she explained her situation, his eyes moving over her slender frame, taking in all of Violet's assets. Violet, usually perceptive of others' behaviors and reactions, was fatigued from her long walk with the sun beating down on her, apprehensive about discussing her problems with a stranger, and worried about what might happen to the plantation, and Moses' scrutiny went unnoticed.

When she had finished, he smiled at her and said, "Well, Mrs. Sutler, I'll look into it, and I'll be glad to do what I can to help."

"How refreshing to hear someone speak as you do," Violet smiled in return, her lovely eyes glowing with relief.

"Of course I cannot guarantee anything," he concluded, "but rest assured that I shall do what I can." *What a lovely lamb she is,* he thought, *and probably by now a widow.*

With a sigh of relief Violet took her departure and went around to see Victor Shelby who agreed to take care of having Alexander Storm's will probated and recorded. After that she stopped by the post office, not daring to hope that finally a message from Brent was waiting. There were only two brief letters from Grandmama Lee and Isabel Sutler, with both ladies expressing their concerns for the girls and children during these difficult times. *I know I should write them more often to reassure them that we are surviving these days as well as can be expected, but there is so much to do all the time. I never seem to catch up, and at night I am so tired I fall right to sleep.* She promised herself that she would do better.

Violet returned home with a lighter heart than when she had left. By the time she reached Fair Oaks, she was tired, near exhaustion, from the long walk to Sumter and back, but this was eased by a feeling that the trip had been worthwhile. As she soaked her feet in a tub of warm water that Mammy had heated for her, Violet filled her sisters in on the events of the trip and told them that she truly believed that Frank Moses would somehow help them.

"Oh, Violet," breathed Charlotte, with relief, "What would we do without you?"

"It's simple. We couldn't!" said Susan, giving her oldest sister a kiss on the cheek.

Fifteen days came and went with no further word from the Freedmen's Bureau or anyone else. Violet felt a sense of gratitude toward Frank Moses. When next in Sumter, she would certainly go to his office and thank him on behalf of all of them.

Chapter 17

Tournament of Roses

1865

It had been a long, hot summer, and when autumn came it still was hot. Frequent hoeing and sprinkling had brought good results to the vegetable garden. The corn and cotton had suffered more from the drought, but still there was enough to reward the hard work that had gone into cultivation. Fresh vegetables and roasting ears had been providing welcome additions to the summer cuisine. Now it was time for the harvest. With the additional help of Evelina and Little Josh, it took them only one day in late September to pick twelve bushels of corn. When they had finished filling the last basket, they all sat down on the ground to rest a few minutes before carrying the baskets to store in one of the unburned slave cabins.

Violet took a handkerchief from an apron pocket and wiped the perspiration and dust from her face. She retied her sunbonnet, her brow puckered in thought, and then directed, "We'll take about three bushels to the house to shell so we can grind part of it into corn meal, and to have the other for hominy and parched corn. The rest we'll store in one of the slave cabins to save for animal feed, if we ever get any animals."

"That sounds good," said Charlotte, nodding in agreement.

Susan looked at Violet with a smile. "Sister, dear, I have to admit that I have actually learned to like parched corn. It's not so bad after all."

"I, too, and it isn't" said Charlotte. Everyone laughed together.

How wonderful that we can sit here, tired and hot, but sharing humor, in a way laughing at our predicament. Our lives are so greatly changed from only a year go. Who would have thought then that we would be hungry all the time and working like farm animals and harvesting our own corn and sitting on the ground like this, just like the darkies, and joking about eating parched corn. Mama always said that laughter was the great healer and up-lifter of spirits. I guess if we can help each other to keep our sense of humor we'll likely come through these difficult times all right. Well, that is, if we can keep the Scalawags and Carpetbaggers from running all over us.

Their last work with the cotton had been in topping it late in August. Now, during the first ten days of October it was time to pick the cotton. Violet, Charlotte, and Susan, along with Evelina and Little Josh, put on shoulder bags and went to work. Again they used a vacant slave cabin in which to store the cotton they picked.

With no cotton gin and no bailing facilities on the plantation, and no transportation to get the cotton to market, Violet turned to what she was sure was the best source for all of these—the Ellisons. This required another walk to Stateburg. This time she and Little Josh found both of the brothers at their general store.

"You know we lost our cotton gin and bailer and all our wagons in Potter's raid," she explained to the two men.

They nodded their understanding, motioning her to sit down in one of the rockers on the front porch of the store. Little Josh sat on the steps and leaned against the railing post where he could see everyone.

The expression in William's eyes conveyed his sympathy. "Yas, Miz Violet, we heered whut dem Yankees do ta ya place. We sho' sorree, Ma'am," he said.

"We sho' is, Miz Violet," echoed Henry. The two brothers settled in chairs by Violet.

Violet continued, "As soon as possible I want to get another of your gins. But for now, we have grown just a little cotton by hand, and I wonder if I could arrange for you to come and get it, gin it, and carry it to market for us...for a fee, of course."

William answered with alacrity, "Sho' nuff, we glad ta do dat fo' ya, Miz Violet."

"How much would it cost?" she asked.

"How much cott'n ya'll git?" asked Henry.

"I'm not sure, but we had about ten acres," Violet responded.

The brothers looked at each other, and then William offered, "We come an' git ya cott'n an' haul hit, an' gin an' ball hit, an' den carry hit ta de Sumtuh mark't, fo' two cent uh pound. Dat fair?"

Violet wasn't sure what percentage that might be, but it sounded good to her. "Oh, yes, thank you," she replied, "and can you do it this week?"

"Yassum, we be dere 'n two day." Both men shook hands with Violet, and then William looked at Josh. He turned toward Violet and remarked, "Yo' Li'l Josh be righ' nice li'l boy."

"He is indeed. Josh is so much help to all of us. He's such a good little boy and a cheerful worker. And so smart, too." Little Josh beamed with pride and his face broke into a wide smile.

"Ah kno' dere be lossa work ah yo' house, buh ah sho' hope ya still got time ta hep 'im wif his readin' an' larnin', Miz Violet," said William Ellison. "Ah gotta feelin' dis boy kin mek sometin' uf hesef."

"Don't worry. I still try to have lessons several times a week, as well as give him some time of his own to practice. He gets that in by reading to the children, and that's a help to me, too. He's so sharp he seems to pick up things on his own before I even teach them. I can hardly wait for my husband, Brent, to meet him. He'll be teaching him about business, I expect."

Both William and Ellison broke into broad smiles on hearing of Josh's progress. They offered them a "part-way" lift which Violet graciously accepted again.

"Jes' uh minut, Miz Violet, den ussan go." William disappeared into the store and returned with a stick of hard candy for Little Josh, who accepted it with alacrity.

The Ellisons were prompt in their services. After all the cotton had been ginned and bailed, Violet and Little Josh rode with William Ellison on the last wagon to the market in Sumter. William had taken a liking to Little Josh and the two carried on a conversation all the way to town. It turned out that Violet had a total of five bales of ginned cotton, weighing 450 pounds each. She was pleased that it brought twelve cents a pound. This meant that after paying William and Henry Ellison the forty-five dollars due them, she had two hundred and twenty-five dollars. It was the first money she had had since Columbia, and she was determined to put it to good use.

But first William Ellison had a surprise for her. Flashing that big grin of his, he reached into his pocket and pulled out Violet's wedding ring that she had given him in exchange for the goat and a few store purchases. "Miz Violet, ah dun save dis, cause ah tink ya wan' ta buy hit bek w'en ya kin. Whut ya tink?" He held the ring out to her in the palm of his hand.

She practically hugged him. She exclaimed excitedly, "Oh, yes, thank you! How much do I owe you for it?" She slipped the ring on her fourth finger and gazed at it happily.

He smiled at his surprise and her joy. "De goat an' de provisions dat ya git come ta 'bout sebben dollar ah rec'on."

She paid him promptly, thanking him profusely again, told him good-bye, and left with Little Josh to make her purchases. As she walked along she could not help but sneak glances at the ring on her finger. *Yes, there is some justice in this world, and good people still exist, too. Now if Brent would just get home.* She shook her head to clear her thoughts. She had much yet to do.

Her first stop was at the livery. She wanted to buy two horses—a horse strictly for riding and a good, strong horse to pull a wagon or plow, and which might double as a riding horse. Several horses recently returned from war service were for sale. Violet went around examining each horse that looked fairly suitable. Her father had instructed her years ago on picking out a horse, and she knew what she was about. She looked in each horse's mouth, counting its teeth and observing their condition. She noted the appearance of the horse's coat to determine whether it was healthy and glowing or dull and straggly, and of its eyes to see if they were clear and alert. She ran her hands down the legs feeling the muscles and examined the frogs and hoofs. She took note as to whether the horse was steady or shied away at a clap of the hands. Finally, she chose a gray ex-cavalry horse that reminded her of her father's Fred. There were no side-saddles available, but with the horse came a McClellan military saddle. *Well, I guess I can don an old pair of Christopher's pants and ride like the men,* she thought. *Mammy will really have a fit at that; she'll say it isn't proper, but it can't be helped. I bet it's a lot more fun than riding side-saddle and keeping one leg up all the time. I'll soon find out. Oh, it'll be such fun to ride over the plantation again, as father and I used to do.*

To pull the wagon or plow, Violet purchased a strong, sturdy bay which had been a former artillery horse. The two horses, including the military saddle that came with the gray horse, cost a hundred dollars. For another sixty dollars she got a good one-horse spring wagon and a set of harness. It was with a feeling of sudden release and elation that Violet hitched the artillery horse to the wagon and tied the gray horse to the back of the wagon. She told Little Josh to climb aboard, which he did with great agility and enthusiasm, so excited was he with their new purchases and the fact they could *ride* home instead of *walking*. Violet clicked her tongue, shook the reins, said *"Giddiup!"*, and they drove off down the street.

Next they stopped for groceries, and Violet spent eleven dollars for ham, bacon, a small beef roast, coffee, tea, wheat flour, baking powder, yeast, sugar, salt, eggs, candles, a box of matches—and could not resist splurging on a box of French chocolates. Little Josh helped load these items, and then they were off again on their shopping. Violet bought a couple of chicken coops, and a dozen hens and a rooster, all for seven dollars. The final stop was at the stockyards where for nineteen dollars she rescued a healthy Guernsey milk cow from possible slaughter and tied her to the back of the wagon.

As they drove out of Sumter, Little Josh turned to Violet and said, "Lawdy, Ma'am, ah can't 'membuh when ah seed so much stuff. We sho' gonna eat like rich folks now, ain't we?" His thoughts turned to supper, and he asked, "Whut we gonna eat tanigh'?"

Violet just laughed. She was full of elation and delight that all their hard work had paid off at last.

When Violet and Little Josh drove up the lane of Fair Oaks, Charlotte and Susan came running out excitedly to meet them.

"Good heavens! Where did you get all that?" Charlotte cried, as she and Susan ran all around the wagon, moving items on top to see items concealed beneath, and patting the horses and the cow. They couldn't believe what they were seeing.

"This is what all our hard work with the cotton brought for us," answered Violet, laughing at the behavior of her sisters. She turned to Susan, "Do you think you can milk a cow as well as a goat? You really have become an expert with Nanny."

Susan answered with some hesitation, "Oh...I don't know about that...she just looks so...so *big* down there compared to little Nanny."

"Well then, we'll just put Evelina in charge of the cow."

Mammy and Evelina had emerged from the house just in time to hear of Evelina's new assignment. They hurried over to the wagon and examined all the wondrous contents contained therein, looked at the horses and then the cow. Mammy shook her head and kept repeating, "Mmm, mmm, mmm! Jes' see whut Miz Violet done brung home, mmm, mmm!" She called to Little Josh, "C'mon, boy, hep meh wif dese tings." She picked up as much as she could carry and took off for the kitchen, with Little Josh close behind, his arms full. Evelina looked up at Violet, waiting for instructions as what to do with the new cow.

"Evelina, you take the cow—What shall we call her. We'll have to give her a..."

"Buttercup. Let's call her Buttercup," suggested Susan, "and I hope we get lots and lots of butter from her."

"I like that. How about Buttercup, Violet?" asked Charlotte.

"Then Buttercup she'll be," agreed Violet. "Evelina, take Buttercup over there to the barnyard and tie her with a long rope. We'll have to fix up some fences later. She'll have to be milked this evening and then every morning and evening. Do you think you can manage this all right? Susan will continue taking care of Nanny."

"Yassum, Miz Violet, ah tek good keer uf dis cow. Ta tell da truf, ah bin missin' cow milk. Ah kno' hit's 'portant fo' de chillen ta git de milk, an' ah ain't ha' much, buh de goat milk, hit jes' don' be de same ta meh. Hit taste mo' sweet. Ah sho' likes de cheese tho'."

"Yes, there is a difference in taste. I guess it depends on what you are used to. I've heard, though, that goat's milk is easier to digest than cow's milk. At any rate, it's been good for the children. Bonnie Anne and J.J. certainly like Nanny's milk, but I wonder if they'll notice the difference when Nanny dries up and they have to drink Buttercup's milk. Anyway, there should be enough milk now for all of us."

"When de goat dry up? When dat happ'n, Miz Violet?"

"About the first of December, I think." Little Josh was back at her side looking up to see if she had any instructions for him. She did. "Josh, untie the gray horse from the back of the wagon, and then take him over and tie him to a post in the west pasture, over there. Now we've got to name the two horses. I've got a suggestion for the gray horse. He's an ex-cavalry horse. When I say cavalry, who do you think of?"

"Jeb Stuart!" chimed Charlotte and Susan in unison.

"You've got it! How about Jeb, a most worthy name for this horse."

"Agreed," they answered together.

"Now, let's think of a name for the bay horse. He's strong and sturdy, and handles beautifully..."

"How about Bella?" suggested Susan, always quick with her answers.

"Ah, Bella, how I miss my beautiful mare, I just hope the dammed Yankee who took her can recognize a treasure of a horse and takes good care of my beauty." Violet's eyes misted as she thought of her horse, now lost, but she pushed the memory to the back of her mind and returned to the matter at hand. "Susan, that's a fine name, but there's one thing wrong with using that one for this particular horse."

"What's that?"

"He's a stallion."

"Oops!"

"Then why not call him Beau?" Charlotte said.

"Yes," Violet came back, "how about Beauregard, a fitting name for a hard-working war horse, and we'll just call him Beau for short."

"Agreed," said the other two. This time Charlotte went on to add, "I don't think that other Confederate hard working war horse, General Beauregard, would mind a bit."

By this time Mammy was back for more groceries. Susan helped her carry the remaining grocery items to the kitchen. Little Josh carried the saddle to the back porch and then fetched a bucket of water for Beau, still harnessed to the wagon and nibbling the grass at his feet. Evelina returned from securing Buttercup, and she, Violet, and Charlotte took the chickens over to the vicinity of the ruined chicken house.

"Tomorrow we'll have to fix a chicken pen, and we'll try to repair some fences.

When they had finished putting things away, Susan pleaded for a ride on the wagon. Except for the walks to deliver invitations for their Starvation Party, neither Charlotte nor Susan had been off the place since their return from the Milford House after Potter's second raid, and that was six months ago. Violet had been only twice to Stateburg and today was only her second trip to Sumter.

"Come on," Violet called, "we'll take a short ride. We don't want to wear Beau out the first day." She sent Evelina to get the children.

Charlotte climbed into the seat beside Violet, and Susan, after lifting Bonnie Anne and J.J. into the wagon, made herself comfortable in the back, resting her back against a sideboard. Noticing Little Josh and Evelina standing back, but looking longingly at the wagon, Violet called for both to climb in. In a flash they were in and sitting across from Susan and the children, resting their backs against the other sideboard. They were all grinning with anticipation.

As if sensing their enjoyment of this special outing, Beau trotted down the lane at a brisk pace.

As they rode along Violet related her experiences with the Ellisons and the details of her trip to Sumter, buying the horses and wagon, groceries, and chickens. "And then William Ellison said to me, 'I have a surprise for you, Miss Violet.'–and what do you think that surprise was–Josh! don't you say a word now! Notice anything?"

"Nothing but your hand flapping about. Is something wrong with your wrist? Go on and tell us what Ellison's surprise was." called Susan, still impatient to know what the great mystery was all about.

"It's right before your eyes if you would only look."

"Right before our eyes?" asked Charlotte, noting Violet's hand still waving. Then the setting sun seemed to flash on something. She exclaimed enthusiastically, "Your ring! Your wedding ring! You've got it back. Look, Susan. Oh, Violet, I'm so happy for you!"

"Oh, that's the surprise. How wonderful! Tell us about it," said a thrilled Susan.

"Well, he just kept it until I had the money to buy it back. He said he knew I would want it back. He figured the goat and food items amounted to seven dollars, so that's what I paid him, and now my wedding ring is back where it belongs–on my finger. Oh, what a day this has been!"

"You can say that again," said Susan happily.

Violet continued, "Now I have a suggestion for two hard working sisters."

"What's that?" they asked.

"Well, after all my purchases I have twenty-one dollars left. I thought we could each take six dollars for spending money, and then give Mammy and Evelina each a dollar, and Little Josh twenty-five cents. Tomorrow we need to fix places for the animals, but how about our going into Sumter on Saturday and go shopping?"

"Wonderful!" exclaimed a thrilled Susan. "I'll look at dress fabrics first thing!"

"My six dollars seem like a fortune to me," smiled Charlotte. "I want to savor this and think awhile. I believe I'll just look around a bit at first."

When they returned from their ride, Mammy had a feast ready for them for supper–the beef roast, milk gravy, mashed Irish potatoes, wheat biscuits, greens, and sweet potato pie. Violet showed her the wedding ring on her finger and related how William Ellison had kept it for her until she could buy it back. With a wide grin, Mammy said, "Massuh Brent sho' be glad fo' dat." When she and Evelina heard that they would have a dollar to spend in town, they clapped their hands in delight and went back into the kitchen where they huddled, speculating on what they might purchase. But Evelina could be heard saying to Mammy, "Mammy, ya go ta town dis time. Ah stay wif chillen, an' ah go mebbe nex' time. Ah jes' soon not see any mo'Yankee soljuhs."

Saturday was a day of celebration. They were in Sumter by nine o'clock. Leaving the horse and wagon at the livery, they walked along the crowded streets to do some window shopping. Mammy saw some church acquaintances and crossed to chat with them. She agreed to meet the sisters back at the livery after shopping.

Susan lost no time in buying material for a new dress, and she did not neglect to get a pattern, needles, and thread. Charlotte bought a wide-brimmed hat, with flowers around the crown, and gloves, and Violet bought some badly needed shoes and some ink. For the children, she purchased fabric for new outfits. Josh bought a wooden top and string, a sling-shot, and a stick of licorice. They went to the post office for mail and again found letters waiting for them from Grandmama Lee in Virginia and Brent's mother in Charleston, asking for additional news of their welfare. Still there was no letter or telegram from Brent. They picked up newspapers.

In several places they saw notices of a tournament scheduled to be held at the fairgrounds two weeks hence, and they'd better cut short their shopping and save what was left of their money for the tournament. When they returned to the stable, Mammy was waiting for them. She had purchased fabric for a new apron, and thread. She had also gotten a new head wrap and a stick of candy. Violet paid the livery fee, and they all took off for Fair Oaks in high spirits.

During the week, Violet got used to riding Jeb. She had put on a pair of Christopher's old trousers and soon found the military saddle much more practical, and actually more fun. She found herself riding all over the plantation, racing across the meadows, trotting around the pond, and walking through the woods. Jeb was an intelligent horse and quickly learned his mistress' touch and voice commands. Soon horse and rider seemed to react as one. Occasionally Charlotte or Susan would slip on a pair of their brother's old trousers and would ride Beau bareback to join Violet for a walk about the place. Sometimes Little Josh would climb on Jeb and ride behind Violet. Then his job was to slide off the horse and open the few remaining gates not destroyed by the Yankees. After Violet had ridden through, Little Josh would climb back up behind her on Jeb.

Mammy realized she couldn't do anything about the girls riding like that, but found it all disturbing. She just felt it wasn't fitting for the girls to dress like men and ride that way, but she admitted they enjoyed it, and so she said nothing. For that matter, the girls had been working in the fields like men. These times were hard on Mammy in more ways than one.

On Thursday, the 19th, a spectacle of nature interrupted their work. Although it was a clear day, all the world became dark a little before noon. It was a near total eclipse of the sun. The chickens went to roost, the cow bawled for milking, and

Mammy came running to inquire if the world was coming to an end. Charlotte and Susan joined Violet on the front lawn.

"What is it?" asked Susan in wonder.

"An eclipse of the sun," Violet explained. "Now don't you look right at it, even if it is dark; if you do, it will hurt your eyes."

After a brief pause Violet continued, "Yes, it is an eclipse. I suppose they'll be saying that it symbolizes the eclipse of the Confederacy." After another pause, she went on thoughtfully. "But you know something? People who talk about the 'eclipse of the Confederacy' seem to forget that after an eclipse of the sun, the sun again shines as brightly as ever."

Within a few minutes the sun began to brighten. The rooster crowed to signal dawn, and all resumed their activities excited about their experience.

Saturday, the 28th, was a day of October weather at its best. The sisters took parasols out of the porcelain container by the door and called good-bye to Mammy. Evelina and Little Josh, going along to help, were neat and clean and happy to be going. With a basket of ham sandwiches, apples, and musk melon, they set out at nine o'clock. Mammy stayed behind to look after the children and to do the milking.

Beau, apparently happy at not having to be pulling a heavy artillery gun, trotted most of the way without any urging. When they arrived at the fairgrounds, crowds of people were pouring in.

Soon they were renewing many old acquaintances and making new ones. It was a festive occasion. Bands were playing, flags and pennants flying, hawkers selling souvenirs and refreshments. As it became time for the tournament itself to begin, they found good places on the first row among the spectators.

Thirty knights dressed in brightly colored suits of armor made of wood or canvas, and covered with splendid tunics and mounted on beautiful horses, paraded by. Each knight wore a plumed helmet and held up a long wooden lance. As the parade ended, a knight on a beautiful black horse with a silver saddle rode right up to Violet. He gazed at her with dark brown eyes. He removed his helmet to reveal a head of black hair and mustache, and a handsome face. She recognized him as a long-time friend of Brent's.

"Ma'am, I am Sir Charles Rhett," he said in a deep, musical voice. "May I crown you Queen of Love and Beauty after I have disposed of all of my rivals?"

Startled, Violet smiled feebly. Before she could reply he turned his horse and rode away.

"Well, I declare!" gasped Charlotte.

"I know he's an old friend of Brent's but I don't think Brent would like that, Violet. So now what are you going to do?" inquired Susan loyally.

"Nothing. What can I do now? The knight's gone. He gave me no opportunity to reply. I can only hope he gets defeated—and early." said Violet lamely.

Soon the contest began. In each round two knights would come out, one at each end of the field, turn and face each other in lanes several yards apart. Near the center of the course, a row of five poles with an arm on each from which a wooden ring was suspended, stood in a row parallel to the course. A knight would receive a point for each ring that he caught on his lance and an additional two points for being the first to reach the opposite end of the course. Here was great showmanship—the gallant horses galloping by, the skill of the contestants in spearing the rings, the roar of the crowd urging them on, the cheers of greeting their successes. Here for a couple of hours the fancy of colorful Medieval combat replaced the more immediate memories of violent, ruthless real war.

Violet and her sisters thoroughly enjoyed the whole contest. Sir Charles Rhett survived until the next-to-last round, but Violet was greatly relieved that he was not the champion who received a large blanket of roses and had the honor of crowning the Queen of Love and Beauty.

After a picnic supper Violet and her sisters walked over to the pavilion for the grand ball. When the dancing started, they all joined in the Virginia Reel. When the numbers turned to waltzes, Charlotte and Susan were glad to accept partners, but Violet withdrew at that point. However, that did not diminish the invitations that came her way. First in line was Charles Rhett. Tactfully, Violet declined his invitations to dance and his requests to call on her in the future, explaining that she was a married woman who expected her husband home from the Navy. He said he surely hoped Brent would be home soon and that Brent was lucky to have a woman like Violet waiting for him.

Frank Moses, Jr., dropped by to give his greetings. Violet turned to him with a sweet smile and said, "Oh, I've been wanting to thank you for helping on that matter of saving our plantation from the land grabbers. We're so grateful to you for your help."

"Oh, that, think nothing of it," he replied, his eyes taking in every bit of her lovely figure. Before she could ask any questions as to what he had done, he bowed and continued on his way, rather hastily she thought.

Leland Thompson came over. He explained that they had lost their plantation to mortgage foreclosure and back taxes, and he and his father had moved to Columbia where both were employed in an office at the cotton mill. Violet declined his invitation to dance, but suggested discreetly that Charlotte seemed to be in the mood for dancing. She watched as he crossed over to Charlotte, gave a light bow, and invited her to dance. Charlotte's face lit with an expression of instant joy. She accepted readily.

Between dances Charlotte and Susan rejoined Violet and witnessed the string of young men who came by to see Violet—some old acquaintances, some bringing along a father or relative to make an introduction. Violet was flattered by the attention but felt a little uncomfortable all the same.

Charlotte and Susan would have been happy to stay another two hours, but neither protested when Violet said that she thought it was time to go home. They left about 8:30. Violet had worried a little about how Beau would handle at night, but he gave no trouble at all. After a full day of excitement, food, noise, and adventure, Little Josh was soon asleep, and Evelina followed shortly. The three sisters talked quietly, reliving the day. They were home before ten o'clock, with a better sense of good feeling than they had had in months. For just a little while at least they had been back in their old world. Perhaps something of it was still here.

Chapter 18

Retrenchment

1865

By late November Violet was worrying again about securing enough food to get through the winter. But then came a bigger blow. Sheriff Cecil Gary delivered a notice that a tax bill of nearly four hundred dollars was overdue, and land would be sold if not paid within thirty days.

"Charlotte, I don't like the idea of going into debt," Violet said to her sister one morning as they gathered clothes for the laundry. "I hate it, but I'm afraid it cannot be avoided. We've just got to pay these taxes. We've got to have food for the winter, and we've got to get some kind of shelter up for the animals before the severe weather arrives."

"But, Violet, what can we do? What collateral do we have? Your wedding ring won't get us all of that," worried Charlotte.

"I'll go into town tomorrow and see Mr. Montgomery at the bank. Perhaps I can put up some of our land for collateral."

Clifford Montgomery, agent of the Bank of the State of South Carolina, peered through his round, wire-rimmed spectacles at Violet. His dark eyes were questioning each expression, and his hand ran over his gray hair and down his matching goatee to punctuate his own comments. His whole demeanor discouraged Violet before she even made her request.

Violet took a deep breath and squared her shoulders. Her large violet-blue eyes looked right back at his dark peering eyes. "Mr. Montgomery, much as I hate to do it, I'm just going to have to take out a mortgage on our Fair Oaks plantation in order to pay the taxes and make it through the winter."

"Well, Mrs. Sutler," he began slowly, "with land values being what they are and the unsettled nature of the economy, we are discouraging expansion of loans on land. You know your father already had a mortgage on your place, and it is still outstanding."

"He did? How could that be? Daddy never went into debt but for very short terms, and he was doing very well with the plantation." asked a surprised Violet.

"That may be, but nevertheless, he did take out a mortgage for what to him was a very good reason."

"How much is it?"

He leaned back in his leather chair, moved a few papers on his desk, and then answered, "With interest it's a thousand dollars."

"A thousand dollars!" Violet exclaimed in astonishment. "How could that be?"

"Well, the price of goods he had to buy went very high during the War, and the cotton was left sitting on the wharves at Charleston, with no way to get it out. And then he put a good deal in Confederate war bonds."

"Oh, of course, Confederate war bonds. Well, just let me cash those."

"They are ten-year bonds. They're not due until 1873."

"Oh, well, Mr. Montgomery, I'll just take the present cash value of the bonds. I need the money now."

He leaned forward and put his elbows on the desk, folding his hands together. "Mrs. Sutler, although our own legislature has not acted on this yet, the Federal Government has decreed that the Confederate war debt must be repudiated, so I'm afraid those bonds have no cash value."

"No cash value! Then what can I do?" Violet asked, horrified at what he was telling her.

"You have a good-sized plantation. Maybe you could sell a piece of it to meet your immediate needs, with the consent of the mortgage holder, of course."

Violet paused a moment in thought, then inquired, "Maybe we could sell the four hundred acres on the other side of the woods. Will you consent to that?"

Again he settled back in his chair, and he looked away as he answered "Oh, I'm afraid the bank no longer holds the mortgage. You see, we have sold it."

Violet stared incredulously. "Sold it? To whom?"

"To Mr. Farley."

"Farley? Not Blake Farley!"

"Why yes, Mr. Blake Farley."

"That no-good renegade and scalawag? How could you?"

He ignored her retort and went on, "Mr. Farley might be willing to deal with you."

"I would not be willing to deal with him if I could help it."

Again he ignored her retort and continued, "Another thing that you might do, as some other plantation owners are doing, is to divide the rest of your land into little farms and rent each one to a freed slave or to a poor white. Let them have a cottage on the place, furnish them the seed, and let them work it for a share of the crop."

Violet was astonished that he could suggest such a thing. As she rose to leave, she flung out, "I guess we know where you stand, Mr. Montgomery, sir. You're sounding just like the Yankees' Freedmen's Bureau!" She walked out of the room without a glance backwards.

Violet knew she had no other choice. Fighting an inner fury, she forced herself to walk over to Farley's store. She found Blake Farley in his office in the rear. He rose to his feet, a questioning look on his face, as she entered the room.

"What can I do for you, Mrs. Sutler?" he inquired.

She went straight to the point. "I understand that you own the mortgage on Fair Oaks, and I would like to see about selling some of the land to cover that and other expenses."

He licked his lips; his eyes flickered. He had a slight twitch in his left eye as though winking at his conscience. "Oh, so you want to sell Fair Oaks?" he asked.

"No, no, just a little piece of it. There are 440 acres on the other side of the woods. It's what we call The Old Place. It's separated from the rest of the property by the woods, and I'm thinking of selling it."

"Yes, I know the place. I'll tell you what I'll do. I'll give you seven, no...six and a half dollars an acre for it."

Why, you thieving Scalawag, you must think me stupid, she thought. *Just because you hoodwinked me once, you think you can again.* Aloud, she said in a calm voice, "Come now, surely you can do better than that. You know it's worth five or six times that, Mr. Farley."

"Well, take it or leave it. There's lots of land available now–lots of sheriff's sales and lots of mortgage foreclosures, and I take what I can get at the best price."

Violet hesitated, and then asked, "What do you plan to do with the land after you get it?"

"Now, Mrs. Sutler, you know the Yankees have been promising the ex-slaves that each could have forty acres and a mule. Well, I'm going to rent them twenty acres and a mule. I'll divide those 440 acres of yours into twenty little farms of twenty acres, keeping the old house and a few acres for myself. Then I'll put a little cabin and a little shed on each farm for the ex-slaves, and I'll rent the farms–with a plough and a hoe and a horse or mule–and give them some cotton seed, and let those ex-slaves work it for a one-fourth share of the crop." He couldn't help but smile at his own ingenuity.

"Why couldn't I do that myself?" Violet asked. "No use turning it over to you."

"Sure you could, but where are you going to get the horses and mules? How are you going to build cabins and barns? Where are you going to get your cotton seed? More to the immediate point, how are you going to pay off your mortgage, and how are you going to pay your taxes? Think about that, Mrs. Sutler." Again he grinned at his own cleverness and rubbed his hands together.

"Well what makes you so high and mighty, Mr. Farley? Where are you getting all your money–other than going around seizing other people's cotton?"

Farley's beady eyes twitched as he answered, "In the first place, I cashed in all of my Confederate war bonds right after Gettysburg, and I sold everything I could, and then I converted everything into good Yankee notes. Anyone could see that the Cause was lost by Gettysburg."

"Why you scoundrel; you damned traitor!"

"Traitor? You're the rebel. I'm a patriot, and I get along just fine with those Northern capitalists who are coming down all over."

Violet shot back, "Yes, Northern capitalists who come to the South to take everything from the widows and orphans, and you are helping them do it. You are all a bunch of vultures!"

With a dry, triumphant chuckle, Farley said, "I think you've said all that once before, Mrs. Sutler, and it didn't do you a bit of good. Now, do you want to sell your north four hundred or not? If you don't do something, I'll soon have all of Fair Oaks, just as soon as you default on your mortgage or don't pay your taxes."

Violet capitulated. "I don't like it, but I guess I'll have to do it. I'll be back shortly with a deed and bill of sale. You have the money ready."

"I'll wait for you here." He thought to himself that here was a smart and feisty woman. He admired a woman with spunk. And now he had the upper hand with Mrs. Sutler.

With sadness and disappointment, Violet made her way over to the office of Victor Shelby, long-time family lawyer and friend. Shelby was the one person above all others that she could trust, and he had a certain positive spirit that extended to all those about him. She had not seen him since the day she gave him her father's will to be probated. Rising from his roll-top desk as Violet entered his office, he greeted her with a smile that radiated kindness and good will. He invited her to a Bank of England chair near his swivel chair, returned to his seat, and faced her. He was wearing pince nez glasses, attached on one side to a black ribbon from his ear. A fringe of graying, reddish hair surrounded his bald head, and no facial hair obscured the chiseled features and friendly expression of his face.

Quickly Violet explained her business. He said little while she told of her financial needs and her decision to sell The Old Place.

"But I must confess I hate to do business with that Blake Farley. Not only did he seize our cotton in the name of the U.S. Treasury, he tried to take over the whole plantation. He said they were seizing it for the Freedmen's Bureau. I tell you, Mr. Shelby, I don't know what I would have done if it had not been for young Frank Moses. If he had not interceded to stop the seizure, I don't know where we would be right now."

"You say Frank Moses?"

"Yes, Frank, Jr."

"Did he tell you that he interceded?"

"Well, not knowing what to do, I went and asked for his help, and he assured me that he would do whatever he could to stop the seizure. And then I heard nothing more from them—no seizure."

"When did you say that was?"

"Oh, about the second week in September, I guess, when I came to see you about Daddy's will."

"Wait a minute, Violet. Let me show you something." Shelby went back to a table and pulled out a paper. "Look at this," he said. It was a War Department circular dated September 12 directing that no further lands were to be confiscated, and that those previously confiscated from pardoned Confederates should be restored. "This came straight from President Andrew Johnson," Shelby explained. He was actually overruling General Howard and General Saxton, and I doubt very much if Frank Moses, Jr., had any influence with the President."

"Well, for goodness sakes," exclaimed Violet. "And to think that when I thanked him at the Tournament Ball he didn't have the honesty to say one word about this."

"By the way," Shelby went on, "did you get a receipt for that cotton that they picked up?"

"Yes, why do you ask?"

"Hold on to it. We may be able to do something about that one of these days."

"That sounds promising. I'll keep it in a safe place, you may be sure."

Shelby then leaned over close to her and assuming an air of confidentiality, said in a low voice, "And do you know who is really behind all these deals and shenanigans of Farley?"

"Who?"

"Frank Moses, Jr., that's who."

"Well, I'll be damned," gasped Violet, and then blushing, she said to this long-time friend, "Oh, I beg your pardon, Mr. Shelby."

Shelby just smiled fondly at Violet and advised, "I think you had better go ahead with your sale. It'll give you a chance to get restarted, pending the return of your husband. Any word from Brent yet?"

"Not yet. I'm assuming he has been at sea somewhere. I still keep looking, and hoping, every day."

"All right, you sign these papers and take them to Farley. I'll take care of things at the Court House. And, Violet, do stop in next time you are in town. Bring Charlotte and Susan with you. I haven't seen them for a long time, and I fear your father would consider me remiss. Of course, considering the times, I think he'd probably understand."

"I'm sure he would, Mr. Shelby." smiled Violet. She thanked him for his advice and help, gave him a hug, and was on her way.

Back in Farley's office she presented the papers and asked for payment. Farley gave her his personal check for $1,860. "This represents six and a half dollars an acre, or $2,860 less the one thousand dollars for the mortgage," he said.

This time Violet knew to be cautious of the shrewd Farley. "Yes, thank you. I'll give you the deed after you walk down to the bank with me and they accept your check as a deposit to my account."

Protesting, Farley grabbed his coat and hat and went along with her. At the bank the clerk had to call Mr. Clifford Montgomery who said it would be all right, and the deal was closed.

Violet stopped at the Court house to pay the three hundred dollar tax bill. She picked up Little Josh and the horse and wagon at the livery and drove home, emotionally tired from her endeavors. Her mind was whirling with ideas. All the way home she was planning how she might put the money to use to restore Fair Oaks and make the plantation productive again.

"We have to figure a way to get some laborers back out here," Violet said to Charlotte over a cup of morning coffee in the informal dining room.

"Have you given up on our slaves coming back, Violet? Surely some will. I just know Leo and Jarvis will, and probably Aaron, and I bet soon some of the workers will come back."

"No, I haven't, not altogether. I'm sure they have been scattered all over and put to work at various places. Some may just be malingering, depending on handouts, but I feel sure that most of them will find their way back here eventually. The last thing that Leo said to me was that he'd be back with others. I know he will if he's able to.

He promised Daddy to look after us and the place, and Leo takes his responsibilities seriously as you know."

"But in the meantime?"

"I've been thinking of going to Sumter and seeing if I can hire some of the Negroes on the streets there, or maybe we should even try to get some Chinese coolies."

"Do you think the Chinese really would work?"

"They do at lots of places. I've heard that they are using them in great numbers out west. Anyway, we must get started building the barns, the mills, and the other outbuildings if we are ever going to get this plantation going again the way it should."

"That'll take money."

"Yes, it will. We'll use what's left from the sale of The Old Place."

"But, Violet, think a minute. Don't you think we should use that for food and necessities, at least until Brent gets back? That amount should last three years, if necessary, shouldn't it? We don't ever want to have to scrounge for food again as we did this past year. I know I don't. And I'm confident that Susan would agree with me. Frankly, we came close to starving, and that was a frightening experience, one I'll never forget as long as I live."

Violet understood her sister's feelings. The year had been hard on all of them, and none of them would ever forget the pangs of hunger they had felt. She said gently but firmly, "Charlotte, I'm not thinking about just eating for three years. I'm thinking about really living for a dozen or twenty years. When Brent comes home I want things to be running as much and as well as we can make it. We don't want merely to drift along for a few years; we want to make things happen at Fair Oaks, to improve the place as much as we can." She stopped as another thought came to her, which she shared with her sister. "Mama and Daddy and Christopher loved Fair Oaks. They would never want us to leave it the way it is now. No, they would encourage us to take the chance. You know they would."

"All right, that did it, Violet. They would, and you have convinced me, but how do we start?"

"I'll go to see Victor Shelby again and ask if he has any suggestions for engaging some workers."

"But, Violet, I thought you were going to say Frank Moses," teased Charlotte.

"Ha!" retorted Violet.

Mr. Shelby's suggestion was for her to see about some of the construction crews then working in Sumter, get someone between jobs to get things started, and then bring in some regular workers to finish up and get planting started, maybe on a share basis. He warned her about picking up freed slaves from the streets, saying that was a bit risky, and she had to keep in mind that there were only women at Fair Oaks, other than Little Josh.

Violet found a John Jones who would be able to have a crew work for the next ninety days, when he would have to be going to Columbia. He would bring his men out in wagons each morning from Sumter. He asked that they be furnished their noon meal. He said he would bring a mechanic, two carpenters, two brick masons, and ten laborers, together with horses and wagons, working five days a week, weather permitting, at a total cost of twenty dollars a day.

Winter was coming, and the weather was likely to be unsettled, but Violet was determined to push ahead.

Jones and his full crew arrived, ready for work on Monday morning, December 4. After repairing and reconstructing the partially burned down outside kitchen and refurbishing it so that Mammy and Evelina could prepare the noon dinners there, purchasing tin cups and plates and eating utensils to be used by the laborers, and restoring the overseer's house where Jones made his headquarters, the first priority was rebuilding the sawmill. While laborers brought logs from the woods by horses and wagons, the mechanic was able to recover the saws and rig the waterwheel, and in another day he and a couple of the workers had the sawmill working even while other workers continued work on the building. The new sawmill was essentially like the old, except that there was provision for later installation of a steam engine.

Next, with beams and boards coming from the sawmill, work began on the carriage house. It was designed with four box stalls for riding and driving horses, tack and harness room, feed room, space for a carriage and a buggy, and several stalls and carriage space for visitors. Initially it would be home for Buttercup, as well as for Jeb and Beau until the barn could be built. A small box stall there would be the permanent home for the goat, Nanny. The roof lines of the carriage house, except for a cupola in the center, paralleled those of the east wing of the big house.

Each day of work brought additional obvious advances in building. After the carriage house came the chicken house which took only a couple of days, and then the big cow barn. It included a dozen new stanchions and mangers, where cows could be held steady for milking, a large hayloft, feed room, and storage areas. Upon completion, it would provide shelter not only for additional cows, but for horses and mules until their barns could be completed.

Meanwhile, the brick masons were working on new brick necessaries, located discreetly behind low mounds, and on walkways to the outhouses, a brick floor for the central area of the carriage house, and a new milk house.

Directly under Violet's supervision, they dug an excavation for the milk house that would allow the brick walls to be mostly below ground level. A concrete trough, about waist high, ran along the wall on three sides to carry a continuous flow of cold spring water for cooling the milk. A brick floor had room for tables and presses for cheese and wooden churns for butter.

Violet decided to add a small brick ice house. Even though there were not always hard freezes in winter, in years when there were freezes, ice could be cut from the pond and stream, and then stored under straw in the ice house for use in summer. A small, concrete-lined fish pond provided a place to keep fish alive until needed for the kitchen. A smoke house was built on the other side of the ice house.

After the cow barn was mostly finished, Violet asked Jones to continue with frames and roofs only, to be completed later, for a horse barn that would have stalls and corn crib and oat bin to store feed, to accommodate a dozen horses, another barn for twenty mules, and sheds for wagons and implements. Finally they added a small tool shed near the carriage house.

By the end of February the project was essentially completed. New quarters for workers, a grist mill, cotton gin, cotton bailer, storage house, corn cribs, all would come later.

Coats of white paint on the new carriage house and the new cow barn brought a bright aspect to the whole scene. The new buildings seemed like monuments to a rebirth of hope.

The final touch was the mounting of the weather vane atop the cupola on the carriage house. Violet had found the old weather vane—a bronze gamecock perched on an arrow. She cleaned and refurbished it and had it mounted so that it would be non-circulating. It would always point south.

Chapter 19

Faith and Doubt

1866

It was a Sunday afternoon early in January 1866. Now and then just a suggestion of a snow flurry drifted down from a gray sky. The three sisters of Fair Oaks were sitting before a low, glowing fire in the library. They were taking advantage of a rare opportunity to return to some of their favorite readings and to explore other books that they had been able to save from Potter's raiders. Little Josh was sitting quietly, practicing his letters and reading some stories that Violet had made up, using words he could read. She had hand printed these stories for him and sewn the pages into a book. This had taken some time, but she knew she'd likely be using them with the children when they were older. For now, the children were taking their afternoon naps. Mammy was resting in her room, and Evelina was busy in the kitchen.

Suddenly they heard a knock at the front door. As Evelina came out of the kitchen to answer the door, Susan scooted to the front parlor window for a look. She ran back with a report that it looked like Father Roberts of Holy Cross Church. Immediately, Violet's and Charlotte's hands went to their hair to smooth soft ringlets that might have strayed and then down their bodices and skirts in an attempt to smooth out any wrinkles in their dresses. Susan started toward the stairway, saying quickly, "I'm sure the children will be waking from their nap about now. I'll go up and look after them. See you later." She was up the stairs in a flash.

Charlotte rose and looked at Violet. "I think I'll go up, too. Susan may need my help and, besides, I have to do some things in my room." And she was up the stairs and out of sight.

Somewhat provoked at the behavior of her sisters, Violet was about to call out for them to come back, but it was too late. Already Evelina was at the library door with the rector.

With her habitual cordiality and graciousness, Violet greeted their visitor. "Good afternoon, Father Roberts, it's nice to see you again. Give your hat and coat to Evelina and come in and have a chair by the fire." She asked Evelina to bring some tea, and leading her guest into the library, continued, "I guess you must have had a cold drive, Father. We even saw some snow flakes a bit earlier. Susan was saying she wished we could have a real snow like they do up north."

As they each took a wing chair by the fire, the rector smiled and said, "Ah, this is wonderful. Yes, it's a bit nippy outside, but I must confess that I do not agree with young Susan on snow. It's cold enough without that." He rubbed his hands as he glanced about the room. "Where is that lovely young girl? And Charlotte? I do hope they are well." He looked through the door into the parlor as if expecting the two to enter. *Those rascal sisters of mine. What an awkward situation! I ought to go up and drag them down right now,* thought Violet. Instead she smiled sweetly at the Father and answered, "They are working upstairs. I'm sure that as soon as they hear you are calling they'll be right down to chat with you." *Oh, my, goodness, now I've just told a fib. And to a minister. Oh, those rascals. I'll get them for this, but good!*

"Violet, I am so glad to see you again. I did not see you at church this morning."

"No, I was not there."

"In fact, it's been a while since I've seen you."

"Yes."

"Charlotte and Susan seem to attend now and then."

"Yes, they do, Father." To herself she thought, *But I'm sure that it's as much to get out of the house as to worship.*

"Are you all right?" he asked. His gentle face reflected his concern.

"Yes, I'm all right."

Her blue eyes looked steadily into his worried gray eyes.

He paused and then said gently, "Violet, I have known you since you were a little girl. Your mother and father and all of you have meant a great deal to me. Violet, do you know that you are in violation of the law?"

She at first was surprised, then dismayed. "Oh, my goodness! Is that what you have come to tell me? What other scheme have the Yankees hatched to plunder us? Father, I know that you've not gone over to the Scalawags, bearing news of new demands from the Yankees. I don't understand."

With distress at such an idea he replied, "Oh, no, Violet, you know not."

"Then what on earth do you mean, that I am in violation of the law?" she inquired in wonder.

Still speaking in a gentle tone he asked, "Well, Violet, my dear, just how long has it been since you have been in church?"

"Oh, Father, I don't know...almost a year, I guess...most of which we had no transportation...but what has that got to do with it?"

"Why, Violet, don't you know that in South Carolina the law requires all adults who are able to do so to attend church?"

"Oh, my goodness!" she repeated, and wrinkling her forehead in thought she said slowly, "Come to think of it...I guess I have heard of it, but I never gave it any attention. You know, Father, that such a law is ridiculous...ridiculous."

"Actually I think there is at least one *Yankee* state, Vermont, that has such a law."

"Well, that makes it even more ridiculous," Violet replied firmly. "What are they going to do, put me in jail and then have you visit me there to save my soul?"

Father Roberts laughed heartily, and said, "Oh, I trust that won't be necessary. To tell you the truth, I don't believe in such a law either."

Evelina brought in a tray with tea and biscuits. Violet poured as the rector went on. "However, I *am* interested in encouraging attendance among our parishioners, and I am concerned that something may be keeping you away. I've known you a long time, Violet, and if you need help of any kind I wish you'd let me know." He looked at her with compassion.

He's such a good man, thought Violet. *I must be honest with him.* She responded, "It's nothing that you or any of the congregation have done, Father, or for that matter, failed to do. It's just that I'm afraid church has lost much of its meaning for me."

"How is that?" he asked kindly.

"Well, Father...many people think that the church is filled with hypocrites...and I'm afraid if I were there I would only add to their number." She paused a moment, thinking. The priest waited patiently. Violet opened her heart and, her voice full of emotion, asked, "How can I go and give thanks and praise a God who allows devils like Sherman and Potter to ravage our homelands and leave women and children to starve? You know all the things that have happened, Father, you know what's happened. You've said plenty of prayers over those dying of starvation or heartbreak over the loss of their loved ones, their homes, all that they had."

He sighed deeply and nodded, "But strength of character may be measured in terms of going through adversity and coping with it."

Violet went right on with what she had to say, "How can I praise a God who takes my mother and my father in their prime of life...and takes my brother before he ever has a chance for any life of his own...and my own children, look at the kind of world they have...and what kind of God would keep a wife and husband apart so long and the wife not know how her husband is, where he is, or even if he is still alive!" Her voice broke, and she stopped to gain control.

In answer, Roberts replied, "But you see, this world has been brought about by supposedly intelligent men in exercise of free will. We are not puppets on a string. We have been given intelligence and feelings, and we are supposed to use those."

"Yes, but in a way I feel as though I have been riding a log on a heavy sea without any means of control–rising to great heights on the crests of the waves, and then dropped to the bottom of the troughs, rolling over and over all the time. There was the loss of mother–and then some hope of victory early in the war; then the loss of my brother–then South Carolina being spared from invasion and our nice Christmas together a year ago; then the coming of Sherman and the burning of Columbia–then our feeling of relief when Sherman by-passed this area; then my father's death; and the shock of Potter's raid–then our relief that that was over; and then Potter's return–then relief that we had been spared–and then a certain elation that we had a store of cotton with which to get a new start; then having it stolen by that Scalawag Farley for the Yankees, and then trying to scratch out enough from the ground for bare existence, and having to sell The Old Place to pay the mortgage and taxes and start rebuilding; and now who knows what to expect next from the vindictive Yankees." She had to catch her breath.

Father Roberts broke in, "But whole nations have their ups and downs, don't they? Periods of peace and periods of war; periods of prosperity and periods of depression; years of plenty and years of famine; victory and defeat. Do you have Lord Clarendon's *History of the Rebellion*?"

"Oh, I think so, though I haven't read it. I think I remember Father speaking of it," answered Violet, rising to look for the book. After a brief search she came up with the multivolume history of the English civil war of the seventeenth century. She pointed it out to the rector who pulled out a particular volume, and finding his place, read:

In war, the confidence...which a victorious army contracts...and the dejection of spirit which a subdued party undergoes...is not at an end when the war is determined, but hath its effects very long after; and the tenderness of nature and the integrity of manners which are driven away...by war are not quickly recovered: but instead thereof a roughness, jealousy and distrust introduced that makes conversation unpleasant and uneasy, and the weeds which grow up...can hardly be pulled up...without a long and unsuspected peace.

He stopped and looked at Violet inquiringly, interested in her reaction to what he had just read.

"Yes, I am afraid that may be describing our situation." she assented.

Father Roberts nodded. "I remember reading somewhere of an old theological book whose contents were listed as, 'Chapter I, Hell; Chapter II, Hell Continued.' I fear we are in Chapter II now."

"It surely appears that way."

"Well, now, what do you think the purpose of life is?" he asked.

"Aristotle says it's happiness, but did he ever see a war?"

"Well, he tutored Alexander the Great, didn't he?"

"Well...I guess life is what you make of it. I don't see that there is any purpose except what you make your own purpose."

"Have you been reading Kierkegaard?"

My goodness, with these questions he's beginning to remind me of Daddy. She answered, "No, I don't think I've ever heard of him. Who is he?"

"He was a Danish theologian, died about ten years ago. He was critical of systematized, institutional religion. He emphasized a more personal commitment. But then, doesn't God have an essential role?" He was leading her, asking such questions deliberately.

"Frankly, that's what bothers me. Remember in the *Medea* of Euripides, how Medea was asked, 'Country, wealth, husband, children, all are gone; and now what remains?' And she answered, 'Medea remains.' And...well, I rely on Violet...myself...me, and I'll teach my children that they have got to be tough-minded and self-reliant.

"Your concern for your children shows that you are no Medea."

"No, I hope not."

"But I do commend your sense of self-reliance. That always must be an essential part of it."

"Yes, but there is so much over which one has no control, and there is no evidence that God, if there is a God, cares."

"God demonstrates caring in many mysterious ways. You and your sisters *have* come through this ordeal. You have and are meeting the challenge placed before you. You have suffered, yes; you have worried, yes, but you have coped and, I can say, conquered your adversity. This is not to say the adversity is over, of course. We have yet to see what lies ahead of us, but I am confident you will succeed."

"But Father, it always seems strange to me how people suffer some great disaster, some catastrophe, and then praise God and give thanks that it wasn't worse. If he were so caring, why did he allow the storm or earthquake or fire in the first place?"

"But Violet, think what a completely chaotic world this would be if God suspended the laws of nature at the whim of every individual who might plead for it."

She continued, "Father, I'll tell you something that bothers me more and more, and that is the absence of my husband. I have kept up a front of hope all along, and it was sincere, but now I must confess my hope is fading. Frankly, I am frightened. There are moments when I fear that Brent is not coming back."

"Where was he supposed to be?"

"In the Navy, but we have heard nothing since he left. Not I. Not his mother. Not anyone. I know that he might be at sea and that it would take time to get home after the War. I guess all along I have felt, as Tennyson put it, 'He seems so near, and yet so far.' But now, everyone I know is home from the War or has been killed and will never be home again. It has been eight months since Johnston surrendered to Sherman and still no word—no word from Brent, no word about him from his parents in Charleston, no word from the government, no word from *anybody*.

"Perhaps he is on what Robert Browning called, 'Some unsuspected isle in far-off seas.' Violet, unless you hear to the contrary, you must have hope, you must believe he will be home."

"Yes, that is possible...he may be off in far-off seas...I've told myself that so many times before."

"Remember Gibbon's statement in his *Decline and Fall of the Roman Empire*, 'The winds and waves are always on the side of the ablest navigators."

"Yes, I am confident of that."

"Violet, my dear, we must keep faith—faith, hope, and love."

"Faith in what? All I feel is doubt, Father."

"You know, doubt is an essential part of faith."

"What a strange statement. How is that?" *He does remind me of Daddy, and of Mama, too, in some ways. She was always talking about faith and hope.*

"Without doubt there is no room for faith. Remember the account in the Bible how the man cried out to Jesus, 'I believe, help thou mine unbelief'?"

"Yes, I do recall that. I remember my mother reading that to us."

"Faith does not mean putting aside your intelligence; it means going beyond it. Faith goes beyond the knowable and even the reasonable."

"Then isn't it just the imagination?"

"Oh, it's much more than that. You mentioned Tennyson. Do you have his poems?"

"Yes, indeed."

"I think I can remember from his poem called *In Memorium*: 'There lives more faith in honest doubt, Believe me, than in half the creeds.' And how about Robert Browning?"

"Oh, yes, he and Elizabeth Barrett Browning are two of my favorites." She thought of the nights in years past when she lay in bed and could faintly hear her mother and father reading the love poems of these two poets to one another.

The rector looked up and said, "You already have demonstrated a deep faith right here, Violet.

"I have? How?"

"Didn't I notice some new buildings, a carriage house and a big barn?" he asked with a sparkle in his eyes.

"Yes, you did. We've been busy around here lately."

"Isn't that an indication of faith in the future?" He enjoyed talking with intelligent young women, and Violet was one of his favorites. All too many young ladies seemed to think they had to conceal their brightness.

"I suppose it is some hope, or just necessity if we are going to live."

"Now just think, DeLesseps would not now be digging a canal across the Isthmus of Suez if he did not have faith that he could do it, would he?"

She grinned and said, "No, I suppose not."

"And Cyrus Field would not now be completing the transatlantic cable if he had not had faith that it could be done, would he?"

Again she grinned, and again she assented, "No, I suppose not."

"And the Central Pacific and Union Pacific Railroads would not now be pushing to make a transcontinental connection if several people had not had faith that they could do it, would they?"

"But Father, their faith is in themselves. They all have faith that they can do something. I don't see that God has anything to do with it except put obstacles in their way."

With a chuckle he went on, "Well, Violet, listen to this cry of helplessness from the 22nd Psalm." He pulled a small Bible from his inside pocket, turned to a marked page, and read:

My God, my God, why hast thou forsaken me? Why art thou so far from helping me, and from the words of my roaring?

O my God, I cry in the daytime, but thou hearest not; and in the night season, and am not silent...

But I am a worm, and no man, a reproach of men, and despised of the people.

All they that see me laugh me to scorn: they shoot out the lip, they shake the head, saying.

He trusted in the Lord that he would deliver him; let him deliver him, seeing he delighted in him.

- - - - -

Be not far from me; for trouble is near; for there is none to help.

"That's for me, all right," Violet interrupted, "but I remember one of the Proverbs that says, 'Hope deferred maketh the heart sick.' Father, do you really believe that prayer makes any difference?"

"Of course, don't you?"

"Why should I? I have prayed and prayed that Brent is all right and will soon be home, but I have had no word from him. When I pray for fair weather to plant the crops, it rains. When I pray for rain for the crops to grow, we have a drought."

Father Roberts came back, "As I said before, I don't think we look to prayer to change acts of nature, for that would result in total chaos. You may want rain, and another may want more sun."

Violet responded, "Well, I can't think of anything where prayer has done any good—I haven't heard whether Brent is alive or dead, and look at the War, look at what we have been through. Father, I used to pray—a lot—for my mother and father, my brother and sisters, Brent, our children, our soldiers, the Confederacy; now I don't pray at all, and I cannot see that it has made one bit of difference."

Accepting a refill of tea, the Reverend countered, "You know, prayer is not simply a wish list of things we want, a list of things that we ask for, and then just sit back and wait to be filled. I think of prayer more as an obligation, a commitment." He sipped his tea slowly as he waited for her comment.

"How do you mean that?"

"Simply that in offering a prayer we are obliging ourselves to do everything in our power to make that prayer come true. It is no good praying for something for which we are not willing to exert ourselves fully."

She pondered that and found what he had to say intriguing. "No, I suppose not," she conceded.

"When we pray Bless Aunt Martha or somebody, that is not the end of it. That is only the beginning. Then we must do our best to do something that Aunt Martha really will count among her blessings. It means nothing to pray for peace or prosperity or good health unless we then do everything we can, in whatever way we can, to help bring these things about."

Violet broke into a big, relieved smile. Her eyes seemed to reflect a new light as she said, "Father, that *is* a different way of looking at prayer, and it does make sense to me. Yes, it makes a great deal of sense."

"I think one of the greatest examples of the unselfish prayer is the prayer of St. Francis. Do you know it?" he asked.

"I've heard it in church, of course," she blushed and looked quickly at him as she added, "and I think Daddy or Mama used to read it sometimes in the evenings before we went to bed, but to be honest, I don't really remember much about it."

"It goes like this:

Lord, make me an instrument of Thy peace.
Where there is hatred, let me sow love.
Where there is injury, pardon.
Where there is doubt, faith.
Where there is despair, hope.
Where there is darkness, light.
Where there is sadness, joy.

O Divine Master, grant that I may not so much
Seek to be consoled, as to console;
To be understood, as to understand;
To be loved, as to love.
For it is in giving that we receive;
It is in pardoning that we are pardoned,
And it is in dying that we are born to Eternal Life.

Violet realized that she had bowed her head and followed Father Roberts in prayer. Her heart felt as though it had been released of a heavy weight.

Chapter 20

Black Codes

1866

The cold days of January—unusually cold for South Carolina—threatened to become even colder as the stack of firewood dwindled. Violet decided it was time to put the wood-cutting squad into action. They assembled out near the woodshed attached to the restored outside kitchen. Each had put on several layers of clothing for extra warmth.

Violet began delegating the assignments. "Susan, you and Little Josh hitch Beau to the spring wagon and haul ends of logs and scrap from the sawmill to me right here. If any needs to be split, I'll do that, and Charlotte, you and Evelina can carry it to the inside kitchen until the bin is full. We'll store the rest here in the woodshed."

"Yassum, Miz Violet," grinned Susan, delighted that she would get to drive the horse and wagon.

Little Josh, his eyes sparkling at the humor, repeated, "Yassum, Miz Violet" He danced alongside Susan as they went to hitch up Beau to the wagon.

As soon as the two returned with a load of wood, Violet began splitting it. She wore old gloves to give her hands some protection, but actually the callouses on her hands provided more protection from blisters as she wielded a hard-hitting axe that sent pieces of wood flying in all directions.

Susan jumped down from the wagon and asked, "Violet, let me split some."

"Sure, go right ahead," Violet said as she handed over the axe. She and Charlotte had taken on the chore of chopping wood in the past, but she thought now was a good time for Susan to take on this task, too.

Susan leaned a half log against a log on the ground and held it in place with her foot as she started to raise the axe. Violet grabbed her arm, shouting, "Stop! Susan, you silly girl, you'll cut your foot off—that is, if you hit where you are aiming."

"Oh, Violet, for goodness sake, I wasn't aiming at my foot. I was going to split it just beside my foot," said Susan, looking a bit exasperated.

"Susan, that's dangerous. *Always* keep your foot away from the log."

Susan tried a couple of swings that only took a sliver off the side, and she decided that she and Josh should go back for another load. Violet, relieved, agreed that that would be a good idea. She returned to her vigorous swings of the axe.

Suddenly she heard a deep voice behind her calling, "Miz Violet, lemme do dat fo' ya. Dat ain't no wuk y'all oughta be doin'."

She turned around to see Leo walking toward her at a fast pace.

"Leo!" she cried as she ran and threw her arms around him. She gave him a quick hug and than stepped back to look at him. "Oh, Leo, it's *so* good to see you. We've all missed you so much...Leo, you have come home to stay, haven't you? You won't leave us again?"

"Miz Violet, ah is heah ta stay, as long as ya lemme. Ah would uf bin heah befo' now iffen dose Yankees dinnah mek meh stay wif dem so long. Come see whut ah brung ya." He led her around to the side of the house. There it looked like the retinue of Potter's army coming up the lane—scores of black men, women, and children. Some of the older ones were pushing carts filled with belongings, tattered blankets, and children. Some were walking empty-handed, some leading donkeys with children on their backs.

Violet could scarcely believe what she was seeing. She turned to Leo, gratitude showing in her now sparkling eyes, moist with tears, "Oh, Leo, this is wonderful. Is everybody there?"

"No Ma'am, not ebberbudy. Most be comin', an' dey be udders who wanta come an' wuk heah iffen ya let 'em. Dey ain't got no whar ta go, Miz Violet. Dey ain't got no udder folk." He looked at her, his thick eyebrows raised in question.

"Of course, Leo, bring them all in. Most of the old cabins were ruined by the Yankees, but some of the buildings are usable. First, put those with little children in them. We have a new cow barn and carriage house, but not much else, and the rest can live in them until we can get more houses built. Go ahead and get them into shelter and then come back here. You can move into your old house there, with a few others. But come back as soon as you can and tell me everything that happened to you since you've been gone...and...oh, Leo, it's so good to see you again and to know you've come to no harm."

"Yassum, ah be bek righ' way—and doncha be choppin' no mo' wood, Miz Violet, ah come bek an' do hit, an' ah git some udders ta hep me wif de wood."

"Thank you, Leo. I'll be waiting for you in the house kitchen. I'll go tell everybody that you've come home."

"Yassum." He disappeared around the house, but was back in the kitchen a few minutes later. Mammy and Evelina and Charlotte all greeted him with love and delight in their voices. Then they noticed that he was holding the arm of an attractive young woman, tall, with a wiry build. Violet could tell that in spite of her leanness she possessed strength and energy, and Violet could discern intelligence behind her bright eyes.

"Miz Violet, Miz Charlotte, ebberbudy, dis mah wife, dis Rachel," he said proudly with a wide smile. "Dis mah wife, dis Rachel," he repeated. The young woman smiled at them somewhat apprehensively as if unsure of her acceptance, but she held her head up with pride and dignity.

Everyone smiled at her in a friendly way. Violet greeted her warmly, "Hello, Rachel. Welcome to Fair Oaks. We are so glad Leo has found such a lovely wife."

Rachel returned the smile and said with relief, "Howdy, Miz Violet, Miz Charlotte, ah glad ta be heah."

Susan and Little Josh burst in, full of curiosity. They had seen Leo leading a strange woman into the kitchen. Upon hearing that Leo was married, Susan let out a whoop, and said, "That's wonderful, Leo! You've always taken care of everyone; now you have somebody to take care of you!" Leo laughed heartily at that. Rachel's eyes glowed in amusement.

"Leo," asked Violet, "where did you find this fine young woman?"

"Charleston, whar de Yankees hav' ussans wukin'."

Rachel volunteered, "Ah wuz uh househol' servan' at uh plantation befo' Gen'l Shermun done burn'd hit down, an' all de udder folk done go wif Gen'l Shermun."

"Well, we're glad to have you here with us at Fair Oaks," smiled Violet. She could hear the wood being split, over by the woodshed. *Leo has already got some men working on the wood. Goodness, but it's wonderful to have him back taking charge,* she thought. She turned to Leo and asked, "But where have you been all this time? What took you so long to get back to Fair Oaks?"

"Ah neber wanta leave, Miz Violet," he answered. "Ah follow'd uh bunch uv our folk all de way ter Charleston, an' den de Yankees mek ussan wuk on de street an' road an' jail an' railroad an' ebberting. Dey say ussan free ter go anytime, bu' dey keep ussan in uh soljuh house, an' dinna wan' ussan ta leave. Buh ussan getuhway an' heah ussan be."

"Well, we are so glad, so very glad. You know you are free now. You can leave anytime you want to, but we all hope you will stay, Leo, and be our overseer again. Frankly, we really need you."

"Yassum, ah wanta be dat," he smiled. "Ya an' de Massuh an' yo' mudder an' all uv ya treat meh good all de time. Dis mah home. De Yankees, dey say 'Ya is free, ya is free. Ya don' hafta go bek ta de plantation.' Buh Miz Violet, ah say ah be free when ah be whar ah wanta be, an' ah wanta be righ'chere a' Fair Oaks wif all uv ya."

"Yes, Leo, you *are* free, and we are glad you want to be here. By the way, have you seen Jarvis and Aaron? What about Aunt Beulah and Uncle Job and Fabian–did you see them anywhere? We've been worried about them."

"Yassum, dey all heah. Dey hepin' ou'side, buh dey be comin' in soon. Some of dem wuz at udder plantation, buh when ah see dem an' tell dem dat ah comin' heah, dey wanna come too."

Upon hearing this news, sighs of relief filled the room. Susan and Evelina clapped their hands in delight. Violet exclaimed, "That's wonderful! Tell them to come to the house when they can. Jarvis and Aunt Beulah and Uncle Job and Aaron can have their old rooms in the house, and Fabian can stay in the carriage house with some of the others."

"Yassum."

"And now, Leo, perhaps you had better go ahead and see about getting everybody into shelter. Tomorrow morning early I'll come over to your house, and we'll talk about what needs to be done and then plan the work schedules. And Rachel, welcome again. We're so glad you'll be with us here." Violet smiled graciously at the young woman, trying to make her feel comfortable and welcome.

Leo and his new wife said good-bye to everyone and went out of the kitchen, but those inside could hear Rachel saying to Leo as they went down the steps, "Dat Miz Violet, she sho nice ladee. Dey all be nice peepul. Ah gwine be happee heah, Leo, ah kno' dat."

They heard Leo's reply, "Yas, Rachel, ah tol' ya dey nice peepul. Dey famly folk."

Then they heard him call out to someone, "Dey mightee happee ya be heah. Dey waitin' fo' y'all."

Just then Aaron burst through the door, followed by Jarvis, Aunt Beulah, Uncle Job, and then Fabian who stayed back a little from the others. "Howdy, Miz Violet...Charlotte...Susan! Howdy Mammy! Howdy Evelina! We back now. We home a' las'!

"Lawdamercy!" gasped Mammy. "De Lawd be praised!" She held out her arms to all. The room was full of sounds of joy and greetings and even tears. When things quieted down, Violet said, "You've all got to tell us what has happened to you. Jarvis, where did you disappear to that day at Milford Plantation when you were forced to leave?"

Jarvis related how Potter's soldiers had made him go with them all the way to Charleston. Along the way he had to help carry equipment and stores, set up tents, pack up, and many other chores. And then in Charleston he had to work a long time there for the soldiers. Then one day they said he was free. He ran into Aaron shortly after that, and then two days later they ran into Fabian and some other men who were just walking around the town doing nothing.

Fabian broke in, "Yassum, dey say dey ain't nebuh gwine ta wuk no mo'. Buh ah say, 'Look a' de jay bird, he free. Ya see 'im hop roun' and roun', an' he gwine die sho' nuff if he don' hop roun' an' pick up de worum. Ah no bedda dan de jay bird. Ah gotta pick up mah worum or die. So ah migh' as well come home–pick up mah worum righ'chere wif y'all a' home."

"Dat righ'," said Jarvis. "Den ussan see Leo, an' he say y'all be needin' hep, dat he worried 'bout de young Mizzes, dat he promise de Massuh he tek care ebbuhbodee, an' he say hit time ta go home now. So ussans all star' mekin' our way back. Dat whar we saw Beulah and Job a' one of de plantations on de way. Den ussan met udders 'long de way home. Leo tell dem all dat hit time ta go home, an' he tell udders dey can come, too. So heah we be, an' ah sho' glad." He took a big sigh of relief and added, "An' ah ain't nebuh gwine leave heah no mo'. No suhree, *no* mo'."

"You know you all can stay at Fair Oaks for as long as you want," replied Violet warmly, her eyes moist with happiness.

"Indeed, yes," added Charlotte.

"Forever! We don't ever want you to leave again," chimed in Susan.

Violet told Beulah and Job that they could move back into their room in the basement, and Jarvis and Aaron to their rooms on the top floor above the Major's room. She told Fabian that he could bunk out with the others in the carriage house, but in time he would have a small room for himself there. He was visibly moved, for he recalled his gleeful departure from the plantation. He had learned that things did not always turn out to be what one might be led to think. The jay bird lesson was one that he would never forget.

The next morning Violet was in the office early to make notes of what she wanted done to get organized for plowing and planting–to have a productive season at last. She had given this a great deal of thought in days past, and her mind had been busy most of the night, so it did not take long for her to get her ideas jotted down on paper.

By the time she arrived at the overseer's house, Rachel had the place cleaned up. She had found a table and some chairs, but not much else in the way of furniture other than the old cord bed in the bedroom. A warm fire was burning in the fireplace.

As Violet began to relate her plans to get the plantation moving again, Rachel started to leave the room. Violet sensed that she had a sharp mind and likely a good memory, so Violet called her back. "You come and listen, too, Rachel. You can help Leo remember what has to be done. Now first of all, we must get houses for everybody. We've got to build them quickly. Leo, do you have some mechanics and some carpenters in the group?"

"Yassum, dere some good ones."

"Good. We've restored the sawmill down on the creek. Let's get a mechanic and two or three operators to work right away on it...and get some men to cutting timber in the woods...and have two men hitch the horse to the spring wagon and haul timber to the sawmill and haul boards and beams to the places we are building the houses."

"Yassum," replied Leo, listening intently.

"We'll take a walk after a while and put stakes in the ground where we want the houses to be. I want each house to have two rooms—a bedroom and a kitchen-sitting room, a loft where children can sleep, and a covered porch on the front. At each site leave extra boards so that those who are to live there can make benches, tables, and bedsteads that will do for the time being."

"Yassum."

"Each house must have a well or a ditch from a spring or the creek to have water, each must have a little garden plot, and each must have its own necessary—built away from the water source. Family units will live in these houses, Leo."

"Yassum, dat be good."

"Get your best carpenter to be in charge. He will be the foreman. Then get some other carpenters to work on the houses, but I want the people who are going to live in each house to work on building it, too."

"Dat be good." He thought that she was certainly the Major's daughter, the way her mind worked. Rachel was concentrating on every word, and even began taking notes. She nodded her agreement with all that Violet was saying.

"We must get this done quickly. Later we'll see about paint and plaster." She paused in thought, then continued, "As you have seen, most of the cabins were burned by the Yankees, but there are some that are usable or can be restored quickly, and we probably can use some lumber from the others. We probably will need about fifteen new houses. At least that many, I should think, depending on the families. I guess we'll have to have some barracks and some kind of a dining hall for the single ones. Leo, how many are there, not counting the house servants?"

"Ah tink dere be 'bout uh hundred or mo' people." he estimated.

"Well, after the houses and the barracks are built, I would like a special building to be built at this end of the village, near the pond. It should be as big as four houses and will be a church for all the workers and their families, a place where they can have services on Sundays and prayer meetings at other times, and during the week it will be a school for the children. On weekends the workers can use it for singing and dancing and the like."

"Oh, dat be good fo' ebberbudy," Rachel volunteered, pleased with what Violet was saying.

"We'll build some rooms at one end where the man who will be the teacher and preacher can live, and in the big room we'll build desks and benches."

Violet had told him so much that Leo was anxious to get started at once, but Violet restrained him to hear the rest of her plans. "Next," she went on, "we'll finish the horse barn and the mule barn and the wagon shed and build a new blacksmith shop. As soon as I get some animals, after that, we'll start plowing and then planting."

"Law, Miz Violet, ya sho' hab bin tinkin' uh lot. Ya jes' like de Massuh." He grinned. He could tell already that in a short time things were going to be better for everyone.

A short time later, Violet walked with Leo and Rachel over to the grove on the other side of the creek and the pond that would be the site of the village. Incorporating the usable old cabins within their plan, they laid out village streets, with houses to be ranged on either side. Leo drove stakes to indicate specific locations, and marked out a quarter-acre garden plot for each house.

Now with the workers back, Violet looked forward with some confidence toward getting the plantation back into full production. She knew she had to get hold of some money. She knew that she had to get the animals and the implements and the seeds to make production possible, and she needed lots of foodstuffs to feed everyone, as well as dishes, utensils, and pots and pans. Some of the workers needed clothes desperately. As Violet considered the situation, she concluded that the only thing to do to get the money essential for all those things was to put a lien on the crops. This meant another trip to Sumter since the food they had in store would soon be consumed with so many mouths to feed.

Early on a Wednesday morning in February, she asked Fabian to hitch Beau to the spring wagon, and she and Little Josh set off for town. She thought that it might be well first to call on their family friend, Victor Shelby. She always trusted him and always valued his advice. Explaining her situation to him, she told him that she planned to put a lien on the crops.

"How much money do you figure you need?" the old gentleman asked in his usual friendly manner.

"I think I'll need three thousand, five hundred dollars to get what I really need."

"How much cotton are you planning to put in?"

"Six hundred acres."

"Well, that should be enough potential for that amount of lien."

"I suppose I have to go again to that Clifford Mongomery to apply to the Bank of South Carolina. I wish there were someone else."

"I understand your feelings, but I'm afraid that is your only source, unless you can go to Columbia," he said kindly.

"I don't think going to Columbia would be practical." she replied slowly.

"No, no. You can get it from Montgomery, I am confident, though he is charging interest at 1.5 percent a month."

"What? Mr. Shelby, did you say 1.5 percent a month?"

"I fear so," he said sympathetically.

"Isn't that awfully high?" she asked, stunned at the interest rate.

"Yes, it's practically usury, but, Violet, that's the only source here. And after all, it is for only eight or nine months, so the total should be manageable. Anyway, you surely don't want to sell any more acreage."

"No, certainly not," she said emphatically. She frowned at the thought of such an idea.

Shelby went on, "And you have a big advantage now, with your workers back on the plantation. Having all those field hands back at work will give credence for your anticipation of a high return on your crops."

"Yes, I think so."

Shelby paused a moment, looked out the window thoughtfully, then turned to look directly at Violet. "There is one thing...tell me, Violet, have you entered into a contract with these workers?"

"I told them that I would furnish housing, basic food, work clothes, tools, and use of the work animals, and that at the end of the year one-third of the money from the sale of the crops would be divided among all the workers according to the number of days of work each had contributed. Of course, Leo, my overseer, and the foremen would get more."

"That seems fair enough, but did you put it into a written contract and have everybody sign it?" he asked.

"No, Mr. Shelby, how could I do that? They can't read or write."

"Well, Violet, you need to write it out, read the entire contract to them, have each make his mark, an X, and have someone–you, Charlotte, Susan–write each one's name beside his mark."

"All right, I can do that, but is this really necessary?" she asked. She knew in her heart that he would not have mentioned it had this not been so.

"Yes, and there are several other conditions that are supposed to be included. Violet, don't you know about the black code adopted by the legislature in its special session in September?"

"The black code? No, I'm afraid I missed that. What else do I have to know—and do?"

"Well, first of all you should know some of the general provisions of the law. It defines a person of color as anyone who is more than one-eighth Negro. They are guaranteed certain rights: Regulations about slavery are no longer in effect, colored persons are allowed to acquire property, to sue and be sued in a court, and their persons and property are protected under the law. They can enter into marriage contracts, and their children were given legitimate status. Plantation owners cannot evict them before next January 1."

"That all seems reasonable enough," observed Violet.

"Yes, but on the other hand, Violet, the law contains a number of restrictions intended to keep the Negro in his place. Inter-marriage between the races is prohibited."

"That's not really much of a restriction, is it?"

"Not really, I guess, except it may reinforce a sense of inferiority."

"What else?"

"A colored person must have a special license to practice any trade or profession, on his own account, except farming or being a servant."

On hearing this, she leaned forward and asked in a worried tone, "What about being a mechanic or a carpenter on the plantation?"

"No, no, that would not be on his own account, and that would be a part of your farming operations."

She relaxed a bit and asked, "Anything else?"

"Yes. Any colored person coming in from another state or country must post bond to guarantee his good behavior, and any colored person is liable to suffer the death penalty if found guilty of willful homicide, assault upon a white woman, impersonating the husband of a white woman for immoral purposes, raising an insurrection, stealing a horse or a mule or baled cotton, or if guilty of house-breaking. For other crimes, colored persons may be confined at hard labor, whipped, or transported. They are not allowed to sell farm produce without a written permit, they may not serve in the militia, and they may not possess any weapon other than a fowling piece."

Violet looked pensive. She said slowly, "Do you think all those provisions are wise?"

Shelby shook his head vigorously. "On the contrary. For some reason that wholly escapes me, our legislators thought that this would restore order and thus help pave the way for our restoration into the Union, but I'm afraid it is more likely to have the opposite effect. A Federal Congress that has been demanding equality for blacks is not likely to look upon this with favor."

"No, I guess not. But what else do I need to know?"

"Colored workers are supposed to work from sun up to sun down, with reasonable time out for meals, they must be quiet at night, and must not leave the premises nor receive visitors without specific permission. They may be discharged from your employment for cause and their wages forfeited. The master may whip servants, moderately, under eighteen years of age, but you have to have the authority of a court to whip those above that age."

Violet exclaimed with emotion, "Mr. Shelby, you know that slaves were *never* whipped at Fair Oaks. We've always had a policy—like Mr. Davis's—of not whipping *any* of them for *any* reason. I have no intention of doing anything like that."

"Yes, yes, I recall your father's comments on that subject," he said hastily, taking some papers from his desk and examining them for a few minutes. Then he cleared his voice and continued, "General Saxton of the Freedmen's Bureau has prepared a model contract for the employment of agricultural workers. Now, Violet, you must put into writing their wages and periods of service..."

"Does that mean year to year?"

"Probably—and they cannot be required to do unreasonable tasks, and cannot be required to work on Sundays or at night, and they must be provided adequate food."

Violet asked Shelby to repeat the points that ought to be included in the written contract so that she could take notes. That done, Shelby went on to say, "Just a few weeks ago planters of this area held a meeting here in Sumter to agree on other items to include in uniform labor contracts, so that they would all act together."

"What do I need to know about that?" *Will all this never end? Yet I need to be aware of all this. I've got to learn to be cautious and prepared. I'll never be caught again by any Scalawag. Thank God for dear Mr. Shelby.*

Shelby scratched his head, settled back in his chair to be more comfortable, picked up his notes, and answered, "A lot, Violet. According to this agreement, Negro workers should keep no poultry, dogs, firearms, or whiskey; they must agree to be careful in the treatment of animals and with tools, and pay for any damage that they cause to these, and they must keep their living quarters clean. A work day is determined by tasks to be completed in a day: hoeing cotton, half an acre; splitting rails, 125 to 150; cutting grain, three to six acres, and so on. If work is not defined by the task, then the minimum work day is ten hours. If a worker is voluntarily absent, he will be fined two dollars a day; if he misses work involuntarily, he is fined fifty cents. If a worker is absent more than once without permission, he may be dismissed, and he forfeits his share of the crops. In return for their labor, each worker should have one-fourth of an acre of ground for personal use, should have the privilege of collecting firewood, and should be entitled to one-third of the net proceeds of the ginned cotton, though you may deduct from this the cost of food provided." He took a deep breath.

"Good heavens! Do you think all those things should be included?" asked Violet in wonder.

"Well, I suspect some people, especially the Yankees, may think some parts are too strict, but it probably would be well to go along with the other planters at this point, Violet," he replied.

"Surely that's all?"

"One more thing, Violet. You are supposed to register these labor contracts with the Freedmen's Bureau, and, of course for this they will expect a fee."

"Of course they would." She sighed as she asked, "How much?"

"Twenty-five to fifty cents for each worker."

"Oh, no! Another expense...and so much. It just isn't fair."

"I fear there's a great deal that's not fair these days, my dear." He straightened the papers on his desk and went on, "Violet, you probably ought to have a copy for the bank for your loan. The fact that you have labor present and at work will be a big factor in the approval of the loan."

"Yes, I can see that you are right. You always give me such good advice, Mr. Shelby, and I thank you so much for your time—and your caring. Now, what do I owe you for all this?"

"Not a thing, Violet, nothing at all for a little advice to a good friend. I'm glad to see you. When you have your contracts signed, bring a copy to me and I'll see that it is registered at the Freedman's Bureau for you." He smiled fondly at his young friend. Someone had to look after the Major's girls.

"Yes, I shall, and thank you so much, Mr. Shelby. What a friend you are!"

Taking her leave, Violet lost no time in getting to the bank to see Clifford Montgomery. When she explained that the field hands were back at work and she planned to put in six hundred acres of cotton, plus hay and corn, he was completely cooperative in authorizing an advance of $3,500 for a lien on the cotton crop. Indeed he seemed rather pleased at the prospect of putting Violet in his debt again. He did say that he would need a copy of the labor contract, and that the loan would be ready for her when she returned in a week.

She spent the rest of the day making the rounds for a whole series of major purchases, to be paid for and picked up next week—first to the Curtis Carriage and Buggy Shops at the corner of Main and Dingle streets, the old wagon makers, for two-horse box wagons, which would be suitable for carrying loose grain, loose cotton or bags of cotton after picking, and provisions, and two flat-bed wagons with hay ladders, suitable for carrying hay, unthreshed wheat, or bales of cotton, and all would be useful for carrying workers to and from the fields. The wagons had extra double-trees that could be used whenever it might be necessary to hitch four mules or horses to pull a load. And she made a good deal for a new red-wheeled buggy.

Then she went on to pick out twelve mules, six draft horses, a driving horse, another riding horse, and, to keep the mule population stable, she bought two brood mares and a jackass. Then she arranged for adding five more cows, three sows and a male hog, two dozen hens, a dozen geese, and a dozen ducks and a drake. Finally, she arranged for cotton seed, hay seed, and seed corn. She picked up some food provisions and returned home at dusk.

The next day Violet, as mistress of Fair Oaks, had Leo assemble all the workers outside the caretaker's house for the signing of the labor contracts. Charlotte and Susan came along to help.

Speaking in a strong voice, Violet addressed the group, "I want to welcome our old friends and workers back to Fair Oaks, and I want to extend a special welcome to the newcomers. It is wonderful to have you here. You know that you are free, but if you choose to stay here, you must obey certain rules. I shall keep a record of each day's work, and at the end of the year, one-third of the money from the sale of the crops will be divided among all of you according to how many days you have worked. You will get food and work clothes and your houses, and each house may have a garden. Is this acceptable to you? Do you all agree with these conditions?"

Heads nodded in assent as they shouted happily, "Yassum! Yassum!"

She explained that she would read to them the entire agreement, and if they agreed they should come up in turn and make a cross mark on the paper. Then Miss Charlotte or Miss Susan would write each one's name by his or her mark. She explained that they each had to make their mark on three separate sheets so that she would have three copies of the agreement. They formed two lines and waited with good humor for each one's turn to make a mark three times. In a little over an hour and a half, all had signed as instructed, and names were beside each mark.

A week later Violet had Leo and Jason, the chief animal husbandman, assemble a group of mule-skinners and other animal handlers to go with her on the spring wagon back to Sumter to pick up her purchases. She was careful to take two copies of the labor contract—one for Mr. Shelby to file with the Freedmen's Bureau, and one for Clifford Montgomery at the bank. The third copy was secure in her father's office safe.

The return journey from Sumter looked like a circus parade—four mules hitched to each of the two hay wagons loaded with hogs, chickens, geese, and ducks. Two mules were led at the back of each wagon, plus the jackass following one. Four horses were hitched to one box wagon and two to the other, with the two brood mares led by one. The five cows were tied in line behind the other. The box wagons were carrying full loads of bacon, ham, salt pork, salt beef, flour, lard, coffee beans, and molasses, a hand-operated corn sheller, a corn grinder, a coffee grinder, and assorted pots and pans, tin plates and cups, and eating utensils. Violet, with Little Josh at her side, led the parade in her new buggy, with Beau in the harness. Jason, driving the spring wagon, and Fabian, mounted on the new riding horse, brought up the rear.

Now we're getting somewhere, thought Violet happily as they rolled along, *at last things are really looking good for all of us. Oh, I can hardly wait to get the plantation back in full production! Daddy and Mama would be so pleased. At last I feel sure we're going to be all right again. Father Roberts said we needed faith, and I know the future will be brighter, I just know it. Now all I need is for Brent to come home.*

Chapter 21

The Freedmen's Bureau

1866

After six weeks of feverish activity, the building of houses for workers' quarters was near enough completion to allow families to move into the new houses and single workers into the barracks. Work continued toward completion of the barns and other buildings and toward the building of what would become the village school and church. But now it was time to begin plowing and planting.

Violet called Leo into her office to discuss her plans. "Nearly all the land, except what little we could till by hand, has been lying fallow for a year, so all crops should do well," she said to him.

"Yas Miz Violet, dat righ'."

"Now I think we should have three fields of cotton—that must be first. We can use the middle north field, the one the Major used to call Number Two, and the next one, the northeast corner, Number Three, and the one just south of that, the southeast corner that comes down to the road, Number Four."

Leo nodded his understanding as he agreed, "Dey be fine fo' de cott'n. Whut 'bout de cawn?"

"Number Six, at the southwest corner, will be in corn. Leo, I wish we could have some wheat, but it's too late for that now, isn't it?"

"Yassum, gotta plan' de wheat 'n Novembuh. Too late now, Miz Violet."

"Well, let's put oats in Number One-B, you know, the part on this side of the creek, and then on the other side `of the creek, One-A, we'll put in hay. The oats and hay will provide food for the animals."

"Yassum, dey gotta haf food ta ea', too." He was thinking that Miss Violet was one smart woman. He figured she must have been studying the Major's books to know all this.

"Now, Leo, we must organize our workers to get all the work done. I want us to choose several good foremen—what you used to call "slave-drivers". It's not easy to try to be everywhere at once supervising all the workers."

He grinned and again nodded his head in understanding and agreement. Violet's business-like attitude reminded him of her father. Leo was proud of the way she was taking on the role of the mistress of the plantation. Of course he had worked the plantation for many years, but she was now the Missus, and a mighty fine one at that.

Violet went on, "Jason will continue to be foreman for the animals, that is, the chief animal husbandman. That will be to supervise the milking of the cows, the gathering of eggs, the feeding of the hogs—everything."

"Yassum, he good wif horse an' mule an' cow an' all. He kno' jes' whut ta do wif dem."

"Now, Leo, we need a foreman for cotton, one for corn, one for oats and hay, one for the gardens and orchards, and one for machinery to supervise the operation of the sawmill, and when we get them in, the cotton gin and press, the hay bailer, the threshing machine and grist mill, and to keep all the plows and harrows and reapers and everything in good repair. We'll also need someone for construction and upkeep of the buildings–I hope by the end of the summer we can paint the big house. And we'll need a blacksmith to shoe the horses and mules and repair harness and everything. That's seven men, in addition to Jason."

"Ah git dem." He liked the idea of this kind of division of labor and responsibility.

Violet glanced briefly at some notes on her desk, and added, "And you will assign the daily workers to each foreman as needed, more to one and then more to another according to the work that has to be done. The foreman in charge of buildings will continue, but only with a few workers while we are putting in the crops. Then, as needed, workers will help with buildings and with fences. Later, I want white board fences around the meadows and around the house lawns...and post-and-rail fences all around the farm...and stake-and-rider split rail fences around the edge of the rest of the plantation...but all of the fences can be done later."

"Ah unnerstan', buh fust we start wif de cott'n, yas?"

"Yes, Leo. Begin plowing the cotton fields right away. Then wait a couple of weeks, then plow the furrows about four feet apart and plant the seed."

"Yassum, Miz Violet, ya kno' ah kno' dat. Doncha worree none. Ah git de cott'n 'n fo' ya, jes' like ah do fo' de Massuh. Den w'en de leaf on de oak tree be big as uh squirrel ear, ah git de cawn plant'd."

Violet smiled. That was one of her father's sayings. "That's right, about the first week in May. The oats and hay may go in just before that, but I'll be talking with you every day or so on what is to be done." She picked up her pen to make some notes, dipped it in the inkwell, and asked, "Now, about the foremen. Who knows the most about cotton and can keep people working?"

"Oh, dat be Henry, he bin heah long time, an' alway wuk de cotton. He kno' whut ta do."

"All right, good. And for the corn?"

"Dat hasta be Izayuh, I tink."

"Isaiah, all right...I'm putting all these down on paper..."

Leo volunteered other suggestions: "An' ah tink Avery fo' de hay an' oats, and later, de wheat. Fabyun already de gardner. Ah tink Amos fo' de 'chinery. He kno' all 'bout de mill an' ebberting."

"And Enoch has been supervising the construction, hasn't he? What about him as foreman of building?"

"Yassum, he do good fo' dat."

"Do we have anybody now who can do the work of a blacksmith?"

"Yassum, dat be Zeke, one uf de new men."

Violet sat up straight in her chair and stretched a bit. "Good. Now, Leo, this afternoon let's ride over in the spring wagon and see each of the foremen to tell them their duties. Then we'll take Henry over to look at the fields where we plan to put the cotton. Later we'll take the other foremen over to look at their fields."

Leo had to express his admiration, "Ya kno', Miz Violet, ya 'splain tings eben bedda dan de Majuh ah tink. And Miz Violet, ma'am, ebberbudy wuk lot bedda w'en dey kno' zactly whut dey 'spos'd ta do."

"I'm sure that's right, Leo, and we must make sure that everyone knows what is expected."

Plowing began the next day.

One afternoon two weeks later, as Violet was returning on horseback from an inspection of the work in progress, she found Sheriff Cecil Gary waiting for her near the back door of the office. *Now why is he here again?* she wondered, keeping her face composed as she dismounted and walked over toward him.

"Good afternoon, ma'am," he greeted her, "I'm Sheriff Gary."

As if I could ever forget your face! she thought to herself, and said politely, but coolly, "Yes, I remember you. Won't you come into the office?"

He followed her into the office and took a chair as she indicated. She sat in her desk chair and looked him straight in the eyes. "Now, Sheriff Gary, what brings you here?" she inquired.

He evaded her direct gaze. He looked at the floor and then finally at her. "Well, I tell you, ma'am, we have had complaints that you are in effect reinstating slavery here at Fair Oaks."

She stared at him in amazement. This was the last thing she expected to hear. She asked in shocked tones, "What? What on earth do you mean by that?"

"Well, I understand the darkies are not allowed to leave the premises without permission, they are not allowed to work for anyone else, they are not getting paid for their work, and so on. I ask you, how is that different from slavery?"

Violet repressed her anger with difficulty. In a calm voice she answered, "I'll tell you one big difference. After the first of January I can discharge any of them who has not been doing good work. I could not do that with the slaves."

"No, I suppose not." he replied reluctantly.

"And anyway, don't you know I have labor contracts with them filed with the Freedmen's Bureau—at fifty cents a head?"

"Yes, I know. That's where I read it."

"Then you must know that is the same agreement used by nearly all the planters in Sumter District." *He must think me a fool,* she thought. *I wonder who's behind this.*

"Maybe so—"

"Then why are you picking on me?"

"Because I am making inquiries only where there has been a complaint."

"A complaint? By whom? I am sure you have heard no complaints from any of my workers."

He shook his head. "No, but from a neighbor."

"A neighbor? Who?" She couldn't imagine any of her friends doing such a thing.

Reluctantly he answered, "Well, since you ask, it was Mr. Farley."

"Farley! That damned Scalawag again? What does he want? He's already got some of my property that I had to sell. What gain does he see in all of this?"

"Probably worried about competition, ma'am."

"Well, I'll thank you to clear out of here now and let us alone. You tell that damned Farley if ever I see him over this way again, I'll shoot him. Tell him that."

"Yes, ma'am, I don't mean you no harm, ma'am. Just tryin' to do my duty as sheriff," he said lamely as he rose to take his leave. "I'm obliged to investigate all such complaints."

Violet followed him to the door. Suddenly a thought occurred to her. She asked, "Sheriff Gary, isn't the Freedmen's Bureau supposed to provide food for freed slaves?"

"Yes, ma'am, where the slaves have no other resources."

"Well, Sheriff, about a hundred returned here a little over two months ago, and I am running out of food to feed them. I can tell you that most of them are living better here than when they were out on the streets wandering around, or at various other farms and plantations."

"Probably so," the Sheriff conceded, "I suggest that you apply to the Freedmen's Bureau for food supplies for them." He took his leave, feeling a bit chagrined at having had to investigate Farley's complaint about Mrs. Sutler, whose spunk he couldn't help but admire.

Two days later Violet, with Little Josh sitting happily at her side, drove the spring wagon into Sumter to pay a visit to the Freedmen's Bureau. Leaving Little Josh to tend the horse, she strode into the headquarters in the Court House. She did not look forward to what she had to do, and her pride was hurting. This showed in her demeanor as she demanded to know who was in charge.

A clerk responded, "Captain Pace is in charge here, ma'am, Captain Samuel Pace."

A tall, well-built officer came up to the front counter and with courtesy identified himself as Captain Pace. Violet skipped the pleasantries and went straight to the point. "Captain, over a hundred freed slaves arrived on my plantation a few weeks ago, and I am out of food for them. I am wondering if you can help."

"Where is your place?" he asked attentively.

"Fair Oaks Plantation, about seven miles west of here, on this side of Stateburg."

"Yes, ma'am, I believe we already have been helping some folks near there, on farms owned by a Mr. Farley."

"Oh, Farley. Well, I'll tell you we are getting desperate."

"I'm sorry, but we are really short of provisions now, and I'm not sure what we can do."

But apparently you've got enough to help Farley on several farms, she thought in disgust and anger. Her eyes flashed as she asked, "What do you mean you don't know what you can do? What do you think I can do? You damned Yankees stole our food and burned our buildings, and you set these people free to roam around and stop working, so it ought to be up to you to feed them. We had no workers and so no production for the last year, and I'm telling you, you had better do something!"

"Oh, I don't know about that," the Captain retorted sharply. "What kind of quantities are you talking about?"

"Our basic daily allowance used to be a quart of corn meal and a half pound of salt pork or other meat for each person, supplemented by potatoes, Irish potatoes, field peas, syrup, rice, and so on. That means a barrel of corn meal and fifty pounds of meat plus those other things for a day."

"That's a great deal."

"Of course it is. That's the problem. Tell me, just what is the Freedmen's Bureau supposed to do?"

"It's intended to provide sustenance and to set up education and training to help the freed slaves adjust to getting along as free people," he explained.

"Captain, isn't this the first time the Federal Government ever has had a big welfare program to relieve poverty?"

"Yes...I suppose it is," he answered thoughtfully.

"I'm sure something of this nature is essential just now, though as much as we need it, I hope it won't become permanent—make the black folks wards of the Government, make them a permanent welfare class. You already have lots of them believing that the Government will take care of them and they don't ever have to work any more."

"No, no, that certainly is not the intention. That is why education has to be an important part of the program."

"Well, I hope so, but wherever did the idiotic idea come from to give to each Negro forty acres and a mule and make him a little independent farmer?"

"I think that came from General Saxton, our state director for South Carolina."

"Can you imagine how they could exist that way, even if you could take land away from the rightful owners and give it to them?" she asked sarcastically.

"Well...I suppose...they could do as well as our pioneer farmers."

"Oh, yes, yes, some chance! Captain, have you ever seen a Negro farmer up North?"

"Well...no...I don't know that I have."

"And yet you come down here and tell us how to run things for them! Now...how about those foodstores?"

"I'll see if I can get something for you." He wrote out a slip and gave it to her. "Take this down to our warehouse, down by the depot, and they'll see what they can find."

"Thank you," she said abruptly and walked out. *Oh, how I hate to be beholden to a Yankee,* she thought, *but we've got to have the food.*

At the warehouse the sergeant in charge took her slip and had a couple of workers load four barrels of corn meal and a hundred pounds of salt pork in the spring wagon.

Alarmed at the small supply, Violet said to the sergeant, "That's won't last any time. May I return for another load tomorrow or the next day?"

"That's all there is, ma'am, that's all for now. Sorry, ma'am. Just following orders."

A week later Violet headed back toward the Sumter Freedmen's Bureau. More in desperation than in hope, she had drivers bring both of the box wagons this time while she drove the spring wagon. As they entered the town she decided to make a stop to see Victor Shelby.

He greeted her with his usual cordial good cheer and kindly manner. As she explained her situation he said, "I should think that it would be possible to do better than that. What did you say to the Captain?"

"I gave him a piece of my mind, I can tell you. You know those Yankees turned the darkies loose on the streets and left us with no way to grow anything to support them. And, anyhow, it hurts my pride to have to beg something of the Yankees," she answered honestly.

"I understand your feelings, Violet, but let me give you a bit of advice. You may do better with those people by turning on a little of your Southern charm."

"My Southern charm!"

"Of course. Don't you remember the Biblical proverb, 'A soft answer turneth away wrath; but grievous words stir up anger.'?" he asked with a smile.

Violet paused thoughtfully and said, "I think I know what you are trying to tell me. Daddy used to say something kind of like that. He used to say, 'You can catch more flies with honey than with vinegar."

"Exactly."

Violet's eyes sparkled. She turned her back to Shelby, then with an exaggerated sweep of skirts she turned to face him, tilted her head enchantingly, flashed a wide smile causing her cheek to dimple, sank to a deep curtsey, and as she rose she said in a soft, syrupy voice, "Why, thank you so much for your welcome advice, dear Mister Shelby."

He broke into laughter and said, "That's it! Now be on your way...and good luck!" Violet turned and sped away, laughing at her own behavior. *So help me, I'm going to follow Shelby's advice and try a soft voice and a little honey.*

Once more confronting Captain Pace at the Freedmen's Bureau, she smiled sweetly, added a measure of syrup to her Carolina accent, affected a flutter of her long dark eyelashes over her sparkling blue eyes, and informed him that they were all really quite desperate for more food, and please couldn't he give them just a bit more help?

She left Sumter with all three heavy wagons fully loaded with sufficient provisions to last for weeks.

Chapter 22

The Carolina Central

1866

"How do you do, ma'am, are you the Widow Storm?" a strange red-haired man inquired as Violet opened the front door to his knock one morning the first week of April. In addition to his hair, his wiry red beard and side burns accented his florid complexion, and his small hazel eyes peered at her from beneath drooping lids that almost made slits of his eyes. Between these rose a long, hawk-like nose.

What an unpleasant looking man... Widow Storm, indeed, thought Violet, as she replied coldly and firmly, "I am Mrs. Brent Sutler. What do you want?"

The man's speech immediately betrayed his Yankee origins, and Violet thought at once, *Here's a damned Northern Carpetbagger, and he certainly cannot be up to any good. I'd better be on guard.*

"Ma'am, are you the owner of this plantation?"

"I am, indeed," and then she repeated suspiciously, "What do you want?"

The man smiled, showing stained teeth, and went on to say politely, "Ma'am, my name is Caleb Duprey. I represent the Carolina Central Railroad. We are building a new railroad that will be coming through this way, and I would like to discuss with you the question of obtaining right-of-way along your property."

Violet's first thought was that this was another Yankee scheme to get land and to make money off the poverty-stricken South. Her impulse was to throw him out without a hearing. Then she thought of Victor Shelby's advice and her father's saying, "You catch more flies with honey than with vinegar." Forcing an appearance of hospitality she invited him in and led him back to the office.

"What do you have in mind, Mr. Duprey?" she asked sweetly.

"Let me show you," he said as he unrolled a map on the corner table. "You see this new line will run from the Georgetown harbor, here," he explained as he pointed to the place with his finger, "northwest to China Grove, west to Kingstree, northwest to Sumter, then through Providence, here, just northwest of your place, on northeastward to Camden, and thence southwest to Columbia."

"I see," Violet said, carefully examining the map, "will there be a place here where we can ship out products?"

"Yes, there will be a siding there at Providence."

"And where do you want to put it through here? Show me on the map."

"You see the closest route, and that is what we always prefer, would be straight through your plantation on the diagonal from the northwest corner to the southeast corner." Again she repressed a shout of defiance. She took a deep breath. Fluttering her eyelashes and in her syrupy accent, said, "Oh, Mr. Duprey, surely you would not want to come straight through our place." *Dear God, how I hate to have to do this, but there's a lot at stake here, and I've got to deal with this man carefully.*

Visibly disarmed, he replied, "Oh, no no, I was thinking we could come along the western edge of your property, then, coming southeast, cross the road, and then curve a little more in an easterly direction to Summit."

"Oh, good, Mr. Duprey, and how is the work progressing? When do you expect to be coming here?" she asked sweetly.

"We've been working on this since last summer. The sections from Georgetown to Kingstree at one end, and from Columbia to Camden at the other are mostly finished. Now as soon as we get the right-of-way settled, we'll have a crew of a hundred men working from Camden toward Sumter, and another working from Sumter toward Camden, and the same thing, a crew working in each direction between Sumter and Kingstree. If all goes well trains should be running by the end of the summer. That's why I am anxious to complete arrangements for the right-of-way through here as quickly as possible."

"What would be the terms, Mr. Duprey?"

"It would be a ninety-nine year lease for ten dollars an acre." He noticed that the sheen on her dark waves reflected glints of sunlight filtering through the window. He'd bet that hair would be soft to the touch.

Noticing the look in his eyes, she nevertheless kept the tartness from her voice as she replied, "But Mr. Duprey, that's not much."

"No, but it won't involve much land. A forty-foot right-of-way along your border of about two and a third miles, including your woods, would be close to eleven acres, for which you will receive a hundred and ten dollars."

As Violet leaned over the table to look more intently at the map, Duprey's eyes fell to her bodice. He moved more closely and allowed his hand to touch hers. She pulled her hand away, still examining the map. He came closer again, placed his hands on her two upper arms, and turned her toward him. He thought he had never seen such gorgeous eyes and skin. He began to tremble.

"Ma'am, if you will...uh...cooperate with me, I probably can make that a hundred and fifty dollars," he gasped, desire flooding his whole body. He wanted to take her right there on the floor.

She stepped back with such force that his hands fell from her arms. Stunned at his familiar behavior, she asked in a tight voice, "What do your mean, cooperate?"

"Well, now, you being a widow and all, I was hoping we could become friends, you know." Realizing now that the sweet hospitality, the "honey" approach, was creating additional problems that she had not foreseen, she dropped that in favor of a more cautious attitude. "Why, Mr. Duprey, I'm sure I have no idea what you mean," she said, keeping her distance from him.

He peered at her through his slitted eyes, now glazed with desire, "Oh, come now, honey, of course you do. I'm just looking for a little friendliness from a beautiful and charming southern belle." Before she could move away he quickly stepped forward and grasped both of her shoulders firmly. She could feel his hot breath on her face.

The stench made her want to retch as she shouted with disgust, "Let go of me you damned vulture! Take your hands off me!"

He continued to keep hold of her as he said admiringly, "Now I like a beautiful woman with some fire in her. Yes, ma'am, it makes a man feel like a man...now, I know you want to cooperate. I know you can use the extra money. So just don't give me any more trouble."

Just then, having heard Violet shouting, Mammy and Evelina and Susan burst into the room.

"Anyting wrong, Miz Violet?" Mammy asked, taking in the situation immediately. She glared at Duprey who dropped his hands immediately.

Violet answered, "Oh, no, Mammy, Mr. Duprey is just leaving." Turning back to the visitor she said in an ice cold voice, "I would not sign your lease for a thousand dollars, or a hundred thousand. Now you get out of here and off this land. And you'd better hope my husband never hears of your actions."

He looked at Mammy, then Evelina and Susan, and lastly at Violet. All he said was, "But I have got to have this right-of-way."

"If you think you're going to put your damned railroad across my property, you've got another think acomin'!" she snapped back.

"Oh, I'll get it. Haven't you ever heard of eminent domain?" he sneered. With that Duprey grabbed his map off the table, rolled it quickly, stomped out the back door, climbed into his buggy, and was gone.

Two days later Duprey was back, this time in the company of Sheriff Gary and with a team of surveyors. Violet went out to meet them in the front yard.

"What are you doing here?" she demanded angrily.

"We are here to survey the right-of-way," answered Duprey, "and I am sure it will please you to know that we are bringing it in right through your corn field, through the meadow, and across your front yard, right about here, about half way down to the road."

"Why, you can't do that!" she cried, shocked at the news.

"Oh, yes, we can...show her, Sheriff," answered Duprey, his eyes glinting with power.

The Sheriff rather self-consciously handed her a piece of paper. The State was seizing the land for the right-of-way by the power of eminent domain, for which she would be compensated. The Sheriff handed her a check for $110. The State then would lease the land to the railroad company.

Violet turned and ran around to the back of the house, calling for Fabian to hitch Beau to the buggy. She wanted him to drive her to town to see Mr. Shelby, to see if he could do something to stop this invasion. *It's another Yankee invasion,* she thought, *but surely this one can be stopped. There must be some way.*

As always Shelby was sympathetic, his kindly old eyes looking at her with genuine concern for her welfare. It pained him to have to say, "Violet, my dear, I am very sorry, but I'm afraid the Carpetbaggers have us on this one. The State does have a power of eminent domain by which it can seize private property for public purposes. I would say the only thing to do now is go deposit your check and try to make the best of it. Perhaps later, when our state and local governments are more in order, we can make some kind of adjustment."

"So there is nothing that can be done," she said disheartened, sick at the thought of the tracks cutting across beautiful Fair Oaks, knowing that the noise and soot from the engine and cars would ruin the tranquillity of the place, and aware that a sharp eye would have to be kept on the children and the animals...some kind of protective fence would need to be built. She sat quietly, thinking. Shelby did not interrupt her thoughts. Then she said, "Mr. Shelby, I should report something else."

"What is that? Nothing as bad as this, I hope."

"I'm afraid your honey and charm approach does not always work the way intended."

Puzzled, he asked, "How is that?"

"It worked fine with Captain Pace at the Freedmen's Bureau. I came away with enough supplies for the rest of the season."

"I'm glad to hear that," he smiled, with a twinkle in his eyes, and then he added, "I told you so."

"But it didn't in this case."

"What do you mean? Explain."

"When that Carpetbagger Duprey came out about laying the railroad tracks, I wanted to throw him off the place. Instead, I used the southern charm—which he misinterpreted. Frankly, he tried to take advantage of me. It was a shocking and most unpleasant experience, I must say."

Shelby's astonishment and then dismay was evident. "Oh, I am sorry, so sorry!" He paused while he cleaned his pince-nez glasses, and then he added, "But I'll bet he didn't get very far."

"Certainly not! But that is the reason he is back now with this plan to put the railroad right through the front of our property instead of along the edge and on the other side of the road as he originally intended."

"I see," Shelby said, "but you know, I said that maybe later, when our government is in order it may be possible to make some adjustments."

"Yes."

"Well, that may come sooner than we had feared—I mean the restoration of our State government out from under military rule."

Violet's spirits lifted a little at that news. "Oh, what have you heard?"

"We have received word that on April 2nd President Andrew Johnson issued a proclamation stating that the rebellion was at an end, that in South Carolina and the other Southern states, let's see here, it says 'the law can be sustained and enforced by the proper civil authority.' That means that he is putting an end to military government here."

Violet's face lighted with a huge smile. "The end of Yankee military government? The end of military occupation? Oh, Mr. Shelby, that is good news indeed...that's just wonderful!"

"Yes, it is, Violet. Of course it will take a little time...it will be gradual...but General Sickles already has started reducing the number of Yankee soldiers here, and he already has abolished all military taxes."

"Oh, Mr. Shelby, that news almost makes me forget the grievance that brought me here. Maybe this will let us do something about that, too." She left him with hope in her heart for the future of South Carolina, indeed of the South as a whole.

Chapter 23

Another Proposal

1866

Within a couple of weeks advance railroad workers were on the scene, clearing and grading in preparation for the laying of track. An important accompaniment was the stringing of a telegraph line along the right-of-way, spoiling to a degree the expansive view from the house. Each time she looked out the front windows, Violet could feel the anger rising in her. She and her sisters now seldom sat on the front porch in the cool evenings to chat or read. The children were kept either in the house or in the back. Evelina had been told to always keep careful watch of them as they became accustomed to staying away from the front yard. Susan also helped Evelina with this responsibility when the latter was called upon to help Mammy in the kitchen. As for the Carpetbagger superintendent, Cecil Duprey, Violet saw no more of him—which was to her liking.

Meanwhile the spring planting and gardening and the continuation of construction all were moving ahead on schedule. With her new money from the railroad, Violet contracted with the Ellisons to put in one of their cotton gins, and she added a press for bailing cotton and a storehouse for storing it. In addition, she was able to arrange for restoration of the grist mill and for installing a threshing machine beside it. She also ordered a new hay bailer.

Her prize purchase for household work was a new washing machine. It was an oblong tub in which a wooden cradle was fitted that would swish the clothes back and forth through the water as one pushed the cross handle back and forth. Rubber hoses allowed the water to be drained and fresh water to be drawn in—so that hot soapy water could be exchanged for cool rinse water. On one end of the machine was a mechanical wringer, operated by turning a crank with one hand while guiding the clothes with the other.

Visiting with the newcomers among the workers, Violet and Charlotte found a middle aged woman named Hattie to take charge of washing and ironing and most sewing. Hattie still would have to iron in the old way—putting several irons on the top of the laundry stove to get hot and then attaching a wooden handle to each in turn to iron a garment or two while returning the iron just used to the stove for reheating. Rachel, Leo's wife, would supervise the restored outside kitchen used to prepare food for the other servants not eating in the big house, and she would have charge of the milk house.

The return of the workers—and the arrival of new ones—made it possible to add some help to the household staff. Finding a capable young woman named Ellie to help Mammy in the house inside kitchen, where food was prepared for those living in the big house, Violet decided to let Evelina be the head nursemaid, with a young helper. This would give Susan more freedom, too. The little ones were growing so fast, new clothes needed to be stitched, and the girl could help Hattie and Evelina with this task. And with the railroad workers out front and maybe soon the trains roaring across the front lawn, it was even more necessary for a close watch to be kept on the children. Aunt Beulah took over as the head housekeeper, with a couple of young assistants, while Uncle Job served as house man to help Jarvis and Aaron.

Everyone understood his or her responsibility and each took pride in doing well. They also understood that they would give and receive help to and from the others as necessary.

All this allowed Charlotte and Susan more time to pursue their own interests, though Charlotte took responsibility for supervising the household staff, and Susan was charged with supervising child care whenever Violet could not give it her personal attention.

Violet encouraged Charlotte and Susan to ride the new horse, which they named Feather, around the plantation and even to drive the new buggy on their own into town for shopping or just for amusement. The three sisters returned to their reading and playing the piano and singing several evenings a week. Life was taking on a normality that had not been experienced for a long, long time. They had adjusted to a life without their mother, father, and brother, although the loss would always be with them. They had heard nothing from Brent, but still believed he would be home when he could. From time to time when picking up the mail in Sumter, Violet received thoughtful letters from Brent's mother in Charleston. These were full of love and longing to see them all, especially her young grandchildren. She was unable to travel at the present time but hoped they could all arrange a visit with her. She was well aware of the difficulties that existed. She continued to assure Violet that Brent would be home when he could, and that they all must continue praying for his safe return. Violet, in return, sent her letters of news and reassurance.

Persuaded that it might be well to return to attending church on Sundays, as much to encourage Charlotte and Susan and to set an example for the children as for her own spiritual refreshment, Violet began driving with her sisters and the children to Holy Cross with some regularity. Father Roberts now had retired, but they quickly made friends with the new rector, Dr. Robert Wilson, and his wife.

May Day in 1866 was all that it should be—a clear, warm day, with flowers and tree blossoms in bloom everywhere and birds singing more loudly than ever. The rest of the week was May Day extended. On Sunday afternoon as the three sisters were relaxing in the library, Leland Thompson came by. All jumped up to greet him, and each gave him a friendly, neighborly hug.

"Are you moving back to your old place?" Charlotte asked, her eyes full of hope. She had heard that he and his father had bought back part of Glenmerry Plantation.

"Oh, no, Charlotte, my dear, just back there for a few days to settle things and see if there is anything that I can salvage."

"So, how are things going at the cotton mill?" Violet inquired.

"Very well. We are very busy, and the pay is good, and both Father and I are getting along quite well now."

"And what about Columbia?" Violet continued, "any more progress on rebuilding since we saw you in October at the tournament?"

"Oh, yes, lots of the old buildings are now restored, and lots of new ones have been built. It is about to be a very beautiful city again, I am pleased to report."

"I'm glad," said Violet with a smile. "I'm getting anxious to see it again. I've missed it. We all used to spend so much time there in years past, and, of course, that is where Brent and I were married and we spent most of our time together."

After everyone had enjoyed a cup of tea, and while Charlotte and Susan were upstairs getting the children so that he might see them, Leland asked Violet if he could see the rose garden. They went outside, and Leland looked around with admiration for her efforts. The garden seemed to explode with bright colors of red and yellow and white and pink nestled among green leaves. "How beautifully you make things grow, and what a change from when last I was here. You've got it looking almost like your mother used to have it. I remember when we were growing up how I would come out here to wander around and see the latest of her efforts."

"Yes, thank you, Leland. Somehow this has been kind of a memorial to Mama. Of course I couldn't do anything until our workers returned. Now, thank goodness, we can give more attention to such things as this garden and the house, too."

"I'm glad that life is a bit easier for all of you these days, but there is something special about you and Fair Oaks, Violet. There are other plantations between here and Columbia where the former slaves have returned, but the plantations certainly do not look like Fair Oaks. You've earned the admiration of everyone in this area, and indeed, your reputation has spread all the way to Columbia."

Violet broke into a big smile reflecting her pleasure, "Why thank you, Leland, you are kind to say that, but, of course, everyone here has worked very hard at getting the plantation producing again."

"Violet..." he said hesitatingly.

"Yes, Leland?"

"Violet, while I was away in the War I was thinking about you all the time. I am sorry for you that Brent did not come back...very sorry...but now, now since that is the situation...may I have your permission to call on you?" he asked, hopefully.

She sighed, then answered softly but firmly, "Leland, I am sure that Brent *will* be coming back one day, and in his absence I don't think it would be proper for you even to be thinking about calling. But I want you to know that I—and Charlotte and Susan—will always treasure your friendship."

Acting as though he had heard nothing that Violet had just said, he grabbed her by both shoulders as he blurted out, "Violet, Violet, I think I have loved you since we were children and used to play together. I never could think of anyone but you. Won't you at least let me call on you?"

She stepped back quickly, shaking off his hands. She replied in a sterner voice, "Now, Leland, please remember that I am a married woman. I ask you to respect that. You are creating an embarrassing situation."

"But, Violet—," he said longingly, lost in her blue-violet eyes which were now shooting off sparks.

"Leland, when we were growing up, I always thought of you as being a nice boy, fun to play with, and later after we grew up, a fine young gentleman and a loyal friend. Please do not do anything to spoil that." Her eyes showed her displeasure.

Still ignoring her words he stepped forward and put his arms around her tightly and gasped, "Violet, my love," as he tried to kiss her.

In anger her right hand flew to his chin, forcing his head back as she jerked away from his grasp. Then with her left hand she planted a resounding slap to his cheek. "What's the matter with you, Leland!" she shouted in fury. "Has the War robbed you of all your gentlemanly manners? Do you now think it all right to take advantage of a married woman?"

Stepping back and rubbing his cheek he was transformed in that instant from an aggressive bulldog to a whimpering mongrel. "Oh Violet, I'm sorry...I'm truly sorry...Please forgive me," he managed to say lamely. "I always did hope, especially when Brent did not return. Now, Violet, I feel awful, awful," he said plaintively, hoping for a bit of sympathy.

The sympathy was not forthcoming.

"I am sorry. I do apologize," he repeated sincerely. "I truly never meant any disrespect...I guess I had better be going now...I guess my presence will not be welcomed at Fair Oaks any longer," he said sadly, starting to walk away, his head bowed.

Violet took pity on him. She put her hand on his shoulder to reassure him and said, "Oh, Leland, you can still come around as a friend. Your family and mine have always been friends. I know you will not ever let this happen again. Let's just forget this and let the matter be closed."

"Oh, thank you, Violet. I do want to be your friend—and Charlotte's and Susan's, and Brent's if he comes back," he said, his face flush with shame.

She walked him back to the house and into the center hall. The children came bounding down the stairs, Charlotte and Susan close behind. He forced a quick smile at the two sisters, and chatted with the children for a few minutes, then said he had to be returning.

"So soon?" asked Charlotte, unable to hide her disappointment.

"Please stay, stay for supper," pleaded Susan.

Leland declined the invitation, saying that he needed to get back to Glenmerry. He no longer was in the mood for socializing. He said good-bye to Charlotte and Susan on the front porch. The children asked to walk part of the way down the lane with him, so they and Violet accompanied him for a hundred yards.

They stopped to say their good-byes, and Violet suddenly asked, "Leland, haven't you heard the old chantey, 'O tell me pretty maiden, are there any more at home like you?'"

He thought a moment and replied, "I think so, why?"

"Leland, haven't you ever noticed Charlotte?"

He turned and looked back at Charlotte who was still standing on the porch, watching them. She was waving good-bye again. Suddenly it struck him like a bolt of lightning. There he saw the Violet he had known before the War, and this one was unattached. He waved back vigorously. With a big grin, he said to Violet, "Yes, I just noticed Charlotte...I see what you mean...I'll be back soon!" He walked jauntily on down the lane whistling the old chantey.

Chapter 24

Homecoming

1866

"Violet! Violet! Violet!" Susan was screaming from upstairs.

Running into the hall and starting up the stairway, Violet called, "What is it, Susan? What's happened?" *Dear, God, let the children be all right!*

Susan met her halfway down the stairs. "Oh, Violet! I'm not sure, but it looks like Brent! He's coming up the lane!"

Violet turned and raced down the stairs and out the front door, stopping on the porch. "It is! It is!" she shouted as she dashed from the porch and on down the lane, her arms spread out in welcome.

When he saw her he waved and let out a rebel yell, threw down his canvas seaman's bag, and broke into a run. She leaped into his arms and he swung her all the way around. In his repeated kisses she felt the assurance of an old love and the thrill of a new lover. *Oh, dear God, thank you, thank you! Brent's home, safe and sound, home at last!*

When his kisses finally gave her time to catch her breath, Violet said, "Oh, Brent, Brent, I've missed you so. I've been so worried about you, but somehow I knew you were all right.Oh, Brent, darling!" and she melted in his arms again for another round of kisses and endearments.

Finally, he held her away to look at her again, his eyes devouring her. The sparkle in his sea blue eyes reflected his happiness at seeing her. He said tenderly, "Violet, my precious love, you are even more beautiful than the picture I've always carried in my mind and heart. And, my love, you could not possibly have missed me as I have missed—and longed—for you." His hands stroked her soft dark curls and tenderly followed the curved lines of her cheeks. A dark scraggly beard covered his face but could not hide a certain drawn look of fatigue. The beard and his fatigue made him look older than his twenty-nine years. He wore a rather tattered, almost threadbare blue uniform, with officer's double-breasted coat, and a visored cap covering his thick, dark hair, but at six-feet tall with an athletic lean physique, somehow he made even the worn uniform look good.

As they turned to walk up the lane, arms around each other, Violet asked, "What kind of a uniform is that? What are you doing wearing that damned Yankee blue? I thought our sailors had uniforms of steel gray."

"So we did, but everyone soon traded them for blues. I guess every navy in the world wears blue now." He paused a moment and then added, "That is, all the navies wear blue except the Russians. They wear dull green."

"And I see you are wearing Neptune buttons instead of CS," she remarked.

He answered in a bitter tone, "We were told that we did not dare to wear Confederate buttons when we got back to this country."

She said sadly, "I know, everybody around here has had to take off the Confederate buttons if they wear their old uniforms." Then she asked in the old teasing manner that he recalled with fondness, "But what about your epaulets? Surely you were a commodore or something?"

He replied, "Ha, I only got as far as first lieutenant, which was just fine for me. I did have a white star, right here," he said, pointing to his shoulder, "but we don't dare wear those either. Anyway, *civilian* outranks all those people, and that's what I am now."

Susan had run out to the garden to tell Charlotte, who was picking fresh flowers for the table, and to the kitchen to tell Mammy the wonderful news, and the three burst out the door just as Violet and Brent reached the porch. They all greeted Brent with joyful hugs. A few moments later Jarvis, Aaron, Aunt Beulah, and Uncle Job were on the porch greeting him with enthusiasm and relief that he had returned safely to them. Brent hugged everyone again and joined in their laughs of delight. Violet introduced Brent to Hattie and Ellie who had followed the others out to the porch. Just then Little Josh came running out, a huge smile on his face and his big eyes shining.

Violet placed her hand on Little Josh's shoulder and introduced him to the man he had heard about for so long but never seen. "Brent, this is Josh, Little Josh. He wandered out from Columbia after the fire and has been my little shadow, actually my right-hand man—he helps with everything."

With a smile Brent extended his hand and said, "Greetings, young man, I am glad to make your acquaintance."

Little Josh looked up at Brent and shook his hand, saying with pride, "Howdy Massuh. We sho' 'nuff glad ya bek home a' las'."

Brent turned to Violet then and said with a twinkle in his eyes, "I understand we have a son. Where is he? And where is my little Bonnie Anne? Where are the children?"

Before Violet could answer, Susan called out, "They're upstairs, with Evelina. I didn't have time to run up and tell Evelina."

Brent grabbed Violet's hand and they ran up the stairs, with everyone following, except Aaron who had gone down the lane to pick up Brent's canvas sea bag that he had dropped on the way. He knew he would be Brent's man from now on and serve him just as he had served the Major.

When they reached the nursery Brent knelt down and hugged each child in turn, then he picked them both up, one on either arm. He kissed their cheeks. and said, "Why Bonnie Anne, what a big girl you are now and how pretty you are!" He was amazed at how much she looked like Violet. To J.J. he said, "Hello little son, this is the best welcome home surprise I could have. What a fine boy you are!" It still astonished him that he had a son. He had not even known of J.J.'s existence until his mother had informed him when he stopped in Charleston on the way home. He kissed both children again and set them down gently, then he greeted Evelina with a hug, saying, "Well, Evelina, you've grown into a woman since I last saw you."

Evelina beamed with pleasure and curtsied, saying, "Yassuh, Massuh Brent, ah grow'd up now, an' ah takin' care uv de li'l ones fo' Miz Violet...and ya, too. Hit sho' nice ya bek. Ebberbudy sho' miss ya an' wurree 'bout ya."

Bonnie Anne pulled at his pants leg, seeking the attention of this tall man who was her Daddy, and they exchanged a series of one-line questions and answers. Then Brent picked up J.J. who began a torrent of baby talk. When he stopped for a breath, Brent asked, "Well, young man, when you grow up, are you going to be a sailor or a planter?" Suddenly a look of astonishment came over Brent's face. Handing the baby to Violet, Brent said, "Apparently he is going to be a planter; already he knows the principles of irrigation."

Violet laughed, "With this quantity of water, I'd say he'd have to be a sailor." Then laughing again, she handed J.J. over to Evelina who had observed what was happening and had grabbed a towel and a fresh diaper.

The servants returned to what they had been doing, chatting happily with one another about the young Master's return. Violet asked Job to go tell Fabian and Leo the good news, and then she and Brent, carrying Bonnie Anne, and Charlotte and Susan went down to the informal dining room to enjoy a glass of fresh lemonade. It was a Sunday afternoon, the first Sunday of June, and the three sisters were glad that they were still in their "church-going" dresses. Violet was wearing a full-skirted dress of the same color as her eyes. Narrow white lace edged the heart-shaped neckline and the edges of her sleeves, and a fresh pink rose nestled at the dip of the heart neckline. A sash of the same dress material nipped her small waist. Brent thought he had never seen anyone lovelier. He could scarcely take his eyes off her.

Charlotte was wearing a dress of light green material, with a navy blue collar and bands around her sleeves, and a matching navy blue sash around her waist. Susan wore a flowered pink dress of light material with a white lace collar and cuffs, and her hair was caught up in a ribbon made of matching material. Little Bonnie Anne's dress had been changed upon arriving home, and she now wore a slate gray dress covered by a white child's apron.

As they sat at the table, Brent and Violet holding hands, their questions tumbled out, one after the other. "Where have you been?" (Violet)..."How did you get here? (Susan)..."Why didn't we hear from you?" (Violet)..."What took so long for you to get home?" (Charlotte)..."Have you seen your mother and father?" (Violet)..."How is your sister, Phoebe?" (Charlotte)... "Your brother, Bruce?" (Charlotte)..."Have you been getting enough to eat?" (Violet)..."Did you get seasick on the boat?" (Susan).

Taking advantage of a brief pause, Susan repeated, "How did you get here?"

Brent was amused at all the questions flying at him too quickly to be answered. "Hey, slow down. One at a time, if you don't mind. Well, Susan, Thursday afternoon I took the shoo-fly from Charleston to Orangeburg—"

"What's the shoo-fly?" Susan broke in to ask.

"Oh, that's a passenger coach hooked on to a freight train, and I can tell you this was a pretty rickety one. The track from Orangeburg still has some breaks in it, so I took the stage, actually a spring wagon drawn by three horses, to Kingston. That took most of Saturday. Then this morning I got a train to Sumter and hitched a ride with some people who were driving a carriage to Stateburg, and they let me out right in front of the lane. I just walked up the lane and here I am."

"How is your family in Charleston? Your mother has been so good about writing me. I know she has had some health problems." Violet said.

"Yes, Mother's health is not very good, but I can tell you she was pretty excited in telling me about our son. They are both proud of what you've been doing at Fair Oaks...and they told me about the Major being killed in battle. Darling, I'm so sorry I wasn't here to be with you all at that time. He was truly a giant of a man in many ways, and I loved and respected him. I shall miss him greatly, as, of course, you do."

No one said anything for a short while. Violet broke the silence as she sighed, "Yes we do, so much, all the time...so much has happened...but you haven't told us how your father is."

"Father is still pretty depressed about the war damage. Did Mother tell you that he lost all his ships except a couple of old sailing vessels?" he asked Violet.

"I only knew that he had lost some ships. No doubt she did not want to add to my worries. But how is Phoebe?" Violet thought Phoebe a bit of an old maid, but she liked her.

"Oh, Phoebe's well enough. I think she is doing a lot to help Mother and Father these days. And Bruce, well, he is out west, working on the Union Pacific Railroad."

"But where have you been all this time, Brent? What took you so long to get home?" Charlotte wanted to know.

"I have been all the way around the world on the Confederate cruiser, *Shenandoah.–*"

"Around the world!" broke in Susan again, in amazement at the idea.

"Susan, hush, be patient. Let him tell us where he's been!" exclaimed Violet.

Brent continued, "Yes, around the world. We were in the North Pacific when we heard that the War was over, and that was not until June, a year ago. Then we headed for England where we hauled down our Confederate flag. They say it was the last of the Confederate flags to be lowered. It was a heart-rending moment, I must say. Tears were in all our eyes, even though we considered ourselves to be tough sailors."

Now Violet interrupted him. "But, Brent, couldn't you have come on home directly from there?"

Brent shook his head. "To tell you the truth, we heard that the Yankees had branded us pirates, and it would not be safe to return for a few months at least. In fact that is one reason we headed for England when we learned that the War was over. Then it became difficult to find passage home. We had no money for passage, so I had to wait until I could sign on as a deck hand on a ship sailing from Liverpool to New York, and then after a time in New York, I was able to work passage on a coastwise vessel to Charleston."

"But, Brent, why didn't I hear from you all this time?" asked Violet. This was something that had tormented her for a long time.

He looked surprised. "You mean you didn't?"

"You mean we should have?"

"Well, of course, Violet. I sent a telegram from New York—took about all the money I had left."

"Oh," she said in a small voice. She thought a moment and then asked, "Where did you send it to?"

"To the town house, in Columbia, at the corner of Sumter and Taylor Streets."

Violet gasped, "Oh, Brent, Sherman burned the Columbia house! No wonder I never received the telegram."

"Burned the Columbia house!" he exclaimed, dismayed at the news. He and Violet had spent many a happy day there, and while away he had fantasized about being back there with his lovely wife again.

"Yes, and now I'm afraid even the lot has been seized for taxes."

"Oh, no," responded Brent, "well, I had heard that Sherman had gone through Columbia, but somehow it never had occurred to me that the house would be gone. I have happy memories of that house."

"But, what about letters? Surely in all this time there could have been letters," persisted Violet. She didn't want to appear critical, especially when he just got home, but she had to know.

"And so there were. I did not dare write while the War was on—when we were preparing for a secret voyage. Then, of course, there was no chance during all those months that we were at sea. Then when we got back to England I did write you, Violet, half a dozen times, both to you and Mother. But then, I sent them to Columbia, too. Two or three did arrive for Mother in Charleston, but they were months late, and she and Phoebe were away at Aunt Nell's most of that time, and I'm afraid Father let them get buried under a bunch of other stuff. They only found them the other day when I insisted on a thorough search. Mother couldn't understand why she hadn't heard anything from me. If I'd only known about the Columbia house—but then, of course, I couldn't hear from you. What a mix-up!" He looked at Violet tenderly, his love for her showing in his eyes and voice, "You know I couldn't be away from you, Violet, without writing you as often as I was able to do so."

Violet's voice broke as she said, "Oh, Brent, you can imagine how worried we were after all this time, especially since the War has been over for more than a year, and all the other men from around here are either home or were killed in the War and are never coming home."

He put his arm around her and pulled her close to him. "Violet, my love, I truly am sorry about that, but do you know that in some ways my situation was even worse. I heard nothing from you and knew that I never could as long as I was away. That was a terrible thing to have to live with, missing you so much, as I did."

Violet smiled at him through a mist of emotional tears, "Anyway, we are glad that you are finally here, my husband, and I can't describe how wonderful it is to have you home, to know you are safe and sound, to talk to you, to have your arm around me like this—though I must say that scraggly beard does make you look like General Sherman."

Charlotte and Susan had been listening quietly, knowing that the conversation going on was between husband and wife, but now they broke out into laughter at

Violet's comment on Brent's beard. Susan, as usual, could not resist teasing. She said coyly, "I see what Violet means, but, Brent, I promise I won't call you by that name!" Brent just threw her a sharp look and said nothing.

Violet, noting the look, turned to Susan and said, "Susan, see if you can find Aunt Beulah and Aaron and send them in here."

Beulah appeared before Susan was even out of the room.

"Aunt Beulah," said Violet, glancing at Brent, "I think Master Brent might like a bath."

Beulah beamed, "Miz Violet, de wadda already hot 'n de bavin' room. Ah figur'd Massuh Brent gwine wanna tek uh baf affer his trip."

Brent smiled gratefully at the woman who had kept house for Violet and him in Columbia. "Thank you, Aunt Beulah." He looked at the others and said, "Why don't you all give me a few minutes to clean up." He left to go upstairs.

Violet followed after him, saying, "Brent, you remember Father's manservant, Aaron—"

"Yassum, ya wan' meh, Miz Violet?" called out Aaron who just then appeared with Susan in the upstairs hall.

"Aaron, help Master Brent find some clothes...Brent, would you mind putting on Father's smoking jacket?"

"Of course not, I would be honored. I'm afraid what I brought in my canvas sea bag isn't much better than what I'm wearing."

"Dat righ', Massuh Brent," agreed Aaron, who had unpacked Brent's bag, "buh ah keep Massuh Storm coat 'n ebberting nice 'n clean 'n ah brush 'em ebberdey 'n ya 'bout a' tall he be, tho' ya thinner, buh ah tink mebbee ya wear sum uf dem. Whutcha tink, Miz Violet? De young massuh need sum cloves bad ah tink." He looked questioning at Miss Violet, hoping that he had not stepped out of line in making this suggestion, but Master Brent surely did need some decent clothes to wear, a gentleman like him.

"Well, Aaron, of course that's up to Master Brent, but I'm sure he is welcome to anything of Father's that he wants to wear. I'm glad you have taken such good care of them."

"Well, thank you both...I can see there are two people who want to take good care of me," smiled Brent as he disappeared into the bathing room.

Violet turned and asked Aunt Beulah to make up the master bedroom in the best way she could. Now that Brent was home, they would be sleeping in the large, comfortable room that Alexander and Rosemary Storm had formerly occupied. From now on, Violet's room would be used as an extra guest room.

Violet went down and asked Mammy and Ellie to prepare tea and biscuits to be ready to serve in the library as soon as Brent came down, and then to prepare a special supper to be served in the big dining room at six o'clock.

When Brent stepped into the library a little over an hour after his taking leave, all three sisters and tea were waiting. The children were still taking their naps after their delay by Brent's arrival.

Brent had gone through a transformation. Now his face was completely clean-shaven, except for his neatly trimmed moustache. His dark hair was well-groomed, falling in deep waves across his head, and he had on a burgundy satin smoking jacket with a shawl collar and tasseled belt. The jacket fell to just below his knees, and he wore a white shirt with the detachable collar removed and gray trousers with a stripe down the side. He presented a striking appearance.

The sisters gasped in appreciation. Violet approvingly called out, "No more General Sherman there. Who is this handsome man? Oh, fortunate is the woman who can call him husband!" She held out her arms to him.

He grinned, crossed over to kiss her and give her a loving hug, and then took a rocking chair next to her as she began to pour tea.

Charlotte spoke up, "It will be wonderful to have a man in the house again."

Brent responded, "For me, it will be wonderful to have some women around again." He laughed heartily.

With a peevish grin, Susan said, "Oh, I know about you sailors—a girl in every port, right?"

Brent answered, "Actually we had pretty slim pickings in the North Pacific. I kept trying to tell the captain that we should stay in the South Seas hunting for Yankees, down around Tahiti, for instance, but he paid no attention; insisted that we keep looking for Yankee whalers in the cold, cold waters of the North Pacific. And I can assure you, little sister, Susan, there were no women in that quarter of the globe—we didn't even sight a mermaid." He paused, and then said, "There could be no lovelier women than the three right here with me. I am honored, indeed. Susan and Charlotte, you both have grown into lovely young women—the prettiest I've ever seen—other than my wife, of course." He raised his tea cup as if in a toast. After a pause, he said, "Speaking of Tahiti, would you excuse me just for a moment?" He stepped out into the hall and returned quickly with three folded cloth items. One was figured in deep purple and blue; he handed this to Violet. A second was of royal blue and light blue; he handed it to Charlotte. The third, all yellow, was for Susan.

As they unfolded the items, all asked together, "Oh, these are beautiful, but what are they?"

"These are Tahitian wraparound garments," Brent explained, "and they are called *pareos.*"

Each wrapped the garment around herself and expressed delight.

Violet just could not avoid noting, "Oh, so you did go down to Tahiti after all."

Brent quickly responded, "Oh, we stopped there on the way north, only for a couple of days to take on food and water, and in the process of exchange we were able to pick up a few souvenirs."

"Well, they are beautiful, and thank you, Brent. Not only that, but it is nice to know that you were thinking of us when you were way out there."

"Darling, you were never out of my thoughts or dreams," smiled Brent.

"Thank you," said Charlotte, wrapping the *pareo* around her again.

Just then Jarvis came in to announce that supper would be served in fifteen minutes.

After Jarvis and Job had served the supper of baked ham, roast beef, corn pudding, asparagus, string beans, candied apples, and Irish potatoes, the animated conversation resumed. At one point Violet commented, "Well, we surely can use another hand around here, I can tell you."

"I'll be happy to do anything I can, but you know I'm not much good at hoeing cotton," smiled Brent, in especially good humor with all the delicious food being served.

Violet answered, "Come on now, after all those lines and shrouds you have been pulling, you surely can pull a plow as well as I can."

Brent looked up and said, "You forget; I was an officer...but what's all this about pulling a plow?"

Susan volunteered, "Brent, she's not jesting. I was the driver and Violet and Charlotte were the mules."

Charlotte broke in. "We really did plow the field—and the garden. It was the only way we could get food. It was the only way we could plant cotton. It was the only way we could survive. It was awful and I hated it. We all hated it, but there was nothing else we could do."

"My God!" Brent exclaimed in disbelief, and then, turning to Violet, he asked, "is this true?"

Violet explained, "Brent, I'm not sure you understand what conditions were like here at home. We had no mules, no horses, no oxen, no cows—the Yankees either killed or stole everything, so there was nothing to do but to pull the plow ourselves if we were to have even a tiny bit of cotton and corn and something to eat to keep body and soul together."

Brent's face betrayed his consternation at the women having to do such work. "But what happened? Sherman didn't come through here, did he?"

"You've heard about Sherman's march through Georgia and through the Carolinas, haven't you?"

"Oh, yes, they were fully reported in England—we were horrified—but what about here, here at the plantation?"

Violet grimaced in recollection as she responded, "The Yankees burned all the outbuildings except some of the slave cabins. Luckily the house was used as a headquarters and so was spared the same fate. Brent, the reason that our outbuildings look so good is because they are all new, built with loans and the labor of our returned slaves."

"What Yankees, not Sherman?"

"No," Violet went on, "it was a lesser Yankee general by the name of Potter who fancied himself a Sherman. He brought a force—blacks and whites—up from the coast and came through Sumter and Manchester and here, and on to Camden. It was a completely inexcusable raid in practically the last week of the War. After Lee's surrender, Potter went up to Camden and then turned around and came back, though fortunately he missed Fair Oaks that time. John and Sarah Frierson came over in their wagon and insisted that we ride with them to take refuge at Governor Manning's house, Milford—which we did—Charlotte and Susan, Mammy and Aunt Sheba and

Jarvis, the children and me. The Yankees had kidnaped Evelina and forced Aaron and Aunt Beulah and Uncle Job to go off with them. The other slaves had all taken off to follow Potter's army. And then at Milford the Yankees took Jarvis away."

"And Leo? I can't imagine him leaving the plantation."

"Leo left to try to find our slaves and bring them back to Fair Oaks, but then, being so big and strong and smart, the Yankees used him as labor for their needs, so it was a long time before he could return—but return he did, not only with many of our freed slaves, but others, too. Evelina had finally escaped from her captors and eventually made her way back on her own."

"Amazing...but...it strikes me that I haven't seen Aunt Sheba anywhere..."

"No, Brent, she's no longer with us. She died and is buried back near the woods in the old cemetery."

"I'll miss that old woman, though lazy she was always ready to do what I asked."

"Yes, she was part of the family. We miss her, too, especially Mammy."

Just then Mammy brought in the dessert of strawberry shortcake, and it was difficult to tell whether her eyes or Brent's shone more brightly. Brent made a point of saying, "Mammy, it was a great supper from beginning to end, especially at the end."

Mammy beamed with pleasure.

"And Mammy...I've just heard about Aunt Sheba. I'm sorry."

"Tank ya, Massuh Brent, ah kno' ya be, buh doncha worree none, she wif de Lawd an' ain't sick no mo', an' Miz Violet an' de udders give her uh mightee fancee funer'l." She left the room thinking how wonderful it was to have Master Brent home again. Miz Violet had been needing her man back for a mighty long time.

Susan spoke up, "Well, I can say I'm really glad that now we have something to eat besides turnips and dandelion greens."

Violet changed the subject. "Don't you think we should have a dinner party to welcome our man home?" she asked, looking at her sisters.

Susan, as usual, jumped in before Charlotte could reply. She agreed enthusiastically, "Oh, yes, yes, when?"

But Charlotte had her say. "Yes, Violet, what a marvelous idea. Let's have it as soon as possible."

Violet answered pensively, counting off the days in her mind, "Well...I wonder if we could make it this coming Saturday?" She turned to Brent and asked, "Is that all right with you, dear?"

Brent smiled, amused at the sisters' excitement over a dinner party. "Oh, sure, of course, I'm always for a good meal, and it really would be good to see some of the folks from around here again. Sounds like a fine idea, the sooner the better. Saturday's fine."

"Whom shall we invite?" asked Charlotte.

"We'll need to make a list," said Violet as she got up for paper and pencil. Returning to her place, she continued, "First of all the Friersons, of course, and..."

Susan, casting a side-wise glance at Charlotte, said in her patented sing-song, "Oh, and Leland Thompson."

"And his daddy," Violet went on, writing down the names, "and I think it would be nice to have Mr. and Mrs. Shelby from Sumter; what do you think, Brent?"

"Sounds good to me," he agreed. "How about Frank Moses and Blake Farley?"

Instant silence and shock filled the room. Perplexed, Brent looked first at one face and then the other.

Violet caught her breath and retorted vehemently, "Oh, no! No, Brent, not those damned Scalawags!"

Noting the anger underlined with anguish in his wife's voice, Brent asked, "Why? Violet, what's happened? Tell me."

"Oh, Brent, you've been away too long. Moses and Farley are in cahoots with the Yankee Carpetbaggers to plunder us worse than Sherman and Potter. They tricked us and stole what little cotton we had hidden and the Yankees didn't burn, and tried to seize the plantation on the pretense that the owner was absent, and then when they found out that Daddy had made me the owner in his will but it hadn't been probated, they said they could take it, and Moses pretended to help, but he lied, it was his doing. And they made the taxes so high I had to sell The Old Place to Farley to save the rest of the plantation, and then I had to borrow money to feed the returned slaves and rebuild and buy seed and equipment, and Moses' banker charges outlandish interest...Mr. Shelby called it nigh usury..and, oh, Brent, I don't ever want to see those horrible men again."

Brent was appalled at what Violet had just told him. He replied emphatically, "Certainly not. I withdraw the suggestion." Then he went on to suggest, "How about young Doctor Will Anderson over at Stateburg? I know he hasn't gone over."

"Oh, no. He has a good war record and a good medical record. And maybe Scott Carson. He was in Daddy's regiment and they now live in Sumter." She jotted down the names and went on, "There is one other couple I would like to have, though they may be too far away..."

"Who?" asked Charlotte.

"The Mannings, Governor and Mrs. Manning." She turned to Brent, explaining, "Brent, you remember he was Governor before the War. Then he did some outstanding political service for the War effort, and last year he was elected U.S. senator...and we are indebted to them for taking us in during Potter's raid."

"Sounds interesting, and I do recall the Major speaking of him every now and then, and even going down there to play chess."

"Yes, he and Daddy were good friends, and, of course, the Mannings would visit here when Mother was alive."

"How about my old buddy, Charles Rhett?" asked Brent.

"Oh, I heard John Frierson say he was down in Georgia for a couple of months." Violet laid down her pencil and picked up the list of dinner guests. She looked around the table, saying "All right, that does it. Susan, tomorrow I'll have Fabian drive you to deliver invitations to the Friersons, Andersons, Carsons, and Shelbys. And while in Sumter you can send a telegram to Leland Thompson and his father. Aaron can ride Jeb down to Milford to carry an invitation to the Mannings."

Brent interrupted. "Jeb? What happened to Bella, and the Major's horse, Old Fred?"

"Oh, Brent, remember I told you the Yankees stole all the animals. We were left with none, absolutely none. After a long time we finally got Jeb for riding and Beau for the wagon."

He nodded his understanding. "Good names, Jeb and Beau, good Confederate names. I like that. I guess there's a lot of new stuff I've got to learn around here."

Susan agreed, "Yes, Brent, but I'll help you." Then she said to Violet, "I'll be glad for the ride and to go into Sumter again." She looked at Brent again. "Hey, Brent, what's the highest rank in the Navy?"

"Oh, the U.S. Navy had some admirals, but generally speaking, our highest was flag officer or commodore."

"Oh, commodore..then you shall be a commodore—Commodore Sutler."

"Oh, Susan, don't you dare call me that."

"Yes, Commodore Sutler?" she persisted in a teasing manner.

Ignoring her teasing, he looked around, "Do you all mind if I smoke?"

With a smile Violet answered, "No, not if it's not too strong. After all, tobacco means money in many parts of the South, and, after all, you *are* wearing your smoking jacket, aren't you? Anyway, I don't like the custom of having the ladies withdraw while the gentlemen have their smokes and continue the interesting conversation."

"Which in this case would mean that I would be talking to myself," Brent laughed. He pulled a small cloth bag from his pocket and a small pack of thin paper. Then he took a piece of the paper, about three inches long by an inch wide in his left hand. Holding it with his middle finger and thumb, he used his index finger to form the paper into a kind of trough. With his right hand he sprinkled tobacco from the little bag into the paper fold. When this was filled, he put down the bag, evenly spread the tobacco in the paper, moistened the length of one edge of the paper with his tongue and rolled the paper around to form a cylinder about the diameter of a lead pencil. Then he twisted one end slightly. He lit the open end by a candle on the table and put the other end in his mouth and drew. The outer end glowed, and then he blew smoke from his mouth.

The three sisters had watched all this with complete fascination. When he finished, Violet demanded, "Brent, what on earth is *that*?"

Brent took another puff and then answered, "Well, my dear, this is not a cigar, but—"

"No, I can see that."

"But a seegar-*ette*, a cigarette."

"Where in the world did you pick up a thing like that?"

"I think the Turks started it, and British and French soldiers and sailors picked it up from them during the Crimean War ten years ago. Some men already have been using it in this country, but we got used to it in England."

"Well, I must say, Brent, it doesn't smell as bad as cigars," said Charlotte.

"Thank goodness for that," added Susan, sniffing noisily to dramatize the situation.

Violet was thinking. She brushed a stray lock from her forehead and asked slowly, "Brent, do you think these things will become popular in this country?"

He nodded. "My guess is, cigarettes will become far more popular than cigars within a few years."

"Won't that mean a big new market for tobacco?" she asked.

"I should think so."

"Then next year we plant some tobacco!" she exclaimed, excited at the idea.

As they rose from the dining table, a soft sound of music came drifting in. Stepping out on the back porch, they saw Leo and his young wife approaching, and at a distance beyond them was a double column of a large group of Negroes walking along as they hummed an old spiritual. They were coming to greet Master Brent.

Brent raced out to greet Leo and to meet his wife, Rachel, and to greet Fabian and some of the other old-time workers. After this he withdrew back to the porch to join Violet and the others as the singers gathered around. With great melody, harmony, and rhythm, they sang half a dozen songs—*Camptown Races; Swing Low, Sweet Chariot; Old Folks at Home,* and ending with *In the evening/By the moonlight/You can hear dem darkies singin'..."*

Just then the giant orange ball of the rising moon appeared in the eastern sky, though the sun was just setting in the west. Brent ran down to greet all the singers, shaking hands and thanking each individually. A choke in his voice gave evidence of the sincerity of his expression.

When Brent rejoined the others on the porch, Violet and Brent said goodnight to Charlotte and Susan, and hand in hand went upstairs to the nursery. Evelina already had the children in their little beds, though it was evident that they were too excited to fall asleep yet. Brent only added to their excitement when he pulled from his pocket a little oyster-shell necklace for Bonnie Anne and a small carved Indian canoe for J.J.

"I went out and found this canoe in Charleston when I heard that we had another hand on board," he whispered to Violet.

The children settled down as Violet and Brent took turns reading to them. When Brent put the book down, thinking both children were asleep, Bonnie Anne opened her eyes and said, "Oh, Mommy, sing about blow the wind of the sea."

Before Violet could respond, Brent was singing:

Blow the man down bullies,
Blow the man down,
To me way, ay, blow the man down,
Oh, blow the man down, bullies,
blow the man down,
Give me some time to blow
the man down.

J.J. giggled. Bonnie Anne laughed and said, "Oh, Daddy, that's not the one."

Violet said softly to Brent, "I guess about every night for the whole last year I've been singing Tennyson's *Lullaby* to them." She began singing softly:

Sweet and low, sweet and low,
Wind of the western sea,
Low, low, breathe and blow,
Wind of the western sea!
Over the rolling waters go,
Come from the dying moon, and blow,
Blow him again to me;
While my little one, while my pretty one,
sleeps.
Sleep and rest, sleep and rest,
Father will come to thee soon;
Rest, rest, on mother's breast,
Father will come to thee soon;
Father will come to his babe in the nest,
Silver sails all out of the west,
Under the silver moon;
Sleep, my little one, sleep, my pretty one,
sleep.

"Oh, Mommy," whispered Bonnie Anne, "you said 'Daddy will come to me soon, and he did, he did, just like you said he would."

Violet said to Brent, "You know, whenever I sang that I always thought I should be singing about the *eastern* sea, but you really were in the western sea, weren't you?"

Brent kissed Violet, then leaned over and kissed each of the children, and rose with tears in his eyes, too moved to speak. He followed Violet into the master bedroom and glanced around.. The beautiful old oversized mahogany tester bed was covered with a canopy of white woven lace that matched the underskirt of the bed. A beautiful coverlet of lavender and blue flowers on a white background covered the bed. Violet had had Hattie work on this whenever she had the time, in preparation for Brent's return. A mahogany blanket chest sat at the foot of the bed. Small cherry side tables were on either side of the bed, each with a kerosene lantern sitting on it. Draperies with valances matching the coverlet framed the windows and white lace curtains. Two large, comfortable rocking chairs with a cherry table between, angled toward the fireplace. Brent noticed that Violet had had Mammy place a bottle of scuppernong, two wine glasses, and some cheese and crackers on the table, alongside the lantern. A small vase containing blue and white flowers also sat on the table.

"The room is beautiful, Violet, and I can see that you have fixed it up so that it truly is *our* room decorated in *our* colors." She smiled with pleasure that he liked their room. He put his arms around her and said tenderly, "To tell you the truth, I used to think of you and getting back to you all the time when I was out to sea, a thousand miles from nowhere. You probably were interfering with my performance of duty."

She laughed at that. "I'm glad I didn't cause you to get shot or something."

He went on, now stroking her hair that she had taken down. "On the contrary, those thoughts were my links to home and something to make what we were doing seem worthwhile."

Violet smiled and reached up and took his hand from her hair, kissed the palm, then said, "Every time I saw a log floating on a stream I would think of your ship. Every time I saw the moon I would wonder if you were seeing it too. Sometimes I would actually talk to you in the moonlight."

Brent poured them each a half glass of wine and handed Violet's to her. They each took a sip and sat down in the rocking chairs. Brent continued, "Whenever we were riding out a squall or a violent storm I would think of my *Violet Storm,* and in the afterglow of a brilliant sunset, I would notice the range of color from red to violet, and then I would always think of my *Violet.*" Violet set her glass on the table and reached out for his hand.

Holding hands, they sat quietly for a few minutes, thinking their own thoughts. Violet got up and went to her dresser where she took a piece of paper from a drawer, then from the bookshelf beside the fireplace she picked out a small book. Returning to her chair she opened the folded paper as she explained, "Last summer we had a Starvation Party here—a number of women of the area, each bringing only some food from her own place. One of them was Harriett Ravenal of Acton plantation who is a friend of Mary Chesnut of Camden, and she gave me this little paragraph that Mary Chesnut had written—and oh, incidentally, Daddy and I had tea with the Chesnuts in Columbia before the arrival of Sherman—but this is what she wrote:

> *There are nights here with the moonlight, cold and ghastly and the whip-poor-wills and the screech owls alone disturbing the silence when I could tear my hair and cry aloud for all that is past and gone. I was sick at heart.*

"Often I felt that sense of loneliness at night, when all was quiet but the night birds. And, Brent, I have cried aloud for all that is past and gone. Yet I cannot believe that all is gone; I cannot believe that all of the Old South has been destroyed, has been blown away, can you?"

"No, my Love, I never felt that when I was away, because I never had a sense that we were losing the War. I was surprised by what I saw in Charleston, and on the train as I came here—but still, rebuilding is going on everywhere, and you don't rebuild on nothing." He lifted her hand to his lips and kissed the back of it.

She turned her hand upward so that he could kiss the palm, but continued the conversation. "What I hope for is the best of our old world, and the best of the new, but who can tell what will happen?"

Brent poured another glass of scuppernong for each of them. He placed a bit of cheese on a biscuit and placed it in her mouth and then handed the wine glass to her. She set the glass down, placed some cheese on a biscuit and placed it in his mouth, then she picked up her glass. They chewed their food, sipped their wine, considering what they had been talking about. One of the things Brent had missed was the conversations that he and Violet had in the evenings before going to bed.

Violet took another sip of her scuppernong and opened her book. "I've not had much time to read during the last two years. but whenever I could, before going to bed, I would read a little poetry or something. This is Shelley, and here are some verses I would read often, listen:

The desire of the moth for the star,
Of the night for the morrow,
The devotion to something afar
From the sphere of our sorrow.

"That's from his poem called *One World Is Too Often Profaned.* But, a little more hopefully, here are some lines from *The Indian Serenade:*

I arise from dreams of thee
In the first sweet sleep of night
When the winds are breathing low,
And the stars are shining bright.

Brent was leaning back in his chair, eyes closed, a smile on his lips. As Violet finished reading he reached into his pocket and pulled out a little box which he handed to her, saying, "Here is something special for you, something more to let you know how much I was thinking of you."

She looked at the little box in surprise at the unexpected gift. "Oh, Brent, what is it? she asked as she opened the box. Then she saw it nesting on layers of silk—a large iridescent black pearl. Violet gasped at the beauty of the gem. "My goodness! It's beautiful, so beautiful...Brent, is this a black pearl from Tahiti?"

"It certainly is," he confirmed, pleased at her reaction.

She held it up to the light of the lamp. Turning it over and over she could see that it was dark gray with just a touch of green. "Oh, Brent, it's lovely! I've never had anything so wonderful, and I love you, too!"

"For you, my Darling, and I love you—with all my heart and soul."

"Oh, Brent, I know you do. This must have been worth a fortune in London. I've heard of Tahitian black pearls, but I've never seen one, and I certainly never dreamed I'd have one...but when you were in England without any negotiable currency, it must have been a very great temptation for you to sell it."

"Never, my Darling, I love you too much for that, and this pearl was to be yours, and only yours." He said, rising from his chair.

Almost simultaneously, she rose as she said, "It is so beautiful, but I treasure it most because it represents your love. And I love you with all *my* heart and soul."

Brent blew out the table lamp. Moonlight, flooding through the windows, gave enough light for them to see the furnishings of the room and to see each other. Taking

Violet's hand, Brent led her to an open window. The nearly full moon, now high in the sky, bathed the whole landscape in its cool, white light. Side by side, they looked out across the fields. The distant call of a whippoorwill, and then of a screech owl, fell on their ears. Violet took hold tightly of Brent's arm, and said, "Listen, listen, those are no longer the sounds of loneliness."

From a little farther away they heard a strange, rather high-pitched *caw.* "Listen, do you hear that?" Brent asked softly.

"Yes, what is it?"

"I think it is a yellow-crowned night heron. It doesn't get up this way very often—is usually around the marshes and rivers. James Audubon said it is one of the handsomest species of its tribe. And do you know what he called it?"

"No, what?"

"The *violet night queen.* That's what it is. And it is saluting *my* Violet Night Queen."

Violet's laugh was soft as velvet. Moonlight put a sparkle in her eyes.

He kissed her deeply, then lifted her in his strong arms and carried her over to the bed where he gently laid her down. He lay beside her and kissed her again...and again...and again.

Chapter 25

CSS Shenandoah
1866

Leland Thompson and his father, Andrew, were the first to arrive, about noon on Saturday, for the dinner party to celebrate Brent's homecoming.. The other guests arrived during the next half hour. As each pulled around the circle to the front of the house, Fabian and his helpers met them and took the horses and buggies to the carriage house. Jarvis opened the front door as each couple approached. Aunt Beulah and Hattie showed each couple to a guest room upstairs where they could leave hats and cloaks, could freshen up, and later could find a place to rest if they wished.

Gradually the ladies drifted into the parlor to join Violet where Ellie served them lemonade. Their conversation wandered from stories of survival during the last year to comments on reports of the latest fashions from Paris.

Brent led the gentlemen into the library where Jarvis had mint juleps waiting for them. Their conversation began with the weather—too wet early, too dry now—then turned to markets briefly but quickly moved into war stories. Will Anderson, a fairly heavy-set man in his mid-thirties, with light, thin reddish hair and neatly trimmed beard and moustache to match, called to everyone's attention that Scott Carson had served as captain of the Old Edge Hill Company in Hampton's Legion.

Brent turned to Carson and said, "My wife's father, Major Storm, served with Hampton's Legion in the last months of the War. I understand that you knew him."

Carson, a man of medium build, with blond hair and moustache, also in his mid or late thirties and with a military bearing, answered, "Oh, yes, Major Storm was a fine man. Too bad what happened at Cheraw—and only two or three weeks before the War was all over." He shook his head in sympathy.

"Speaking of Hampton," Will Anderson rejoined, "I heard from my father that shortly after the battle of Sharpsburg that General Lee offered to my uncle, General Richard Anderson, the position of General Stuart who had been killed at Yellow Tavern. But my uncle said that he would much prefer to remain with his old division. Lee, with great understanding, merely bowed, and my uncle turned and walked away, but then he turned around and came back and said to Lee, 'Why not Wade Hampton?' And I guess that began the rise of General Wade Hampton who thus far had been neglected because he was not a West Pointer."

"That surely was a wise move on Lee's part, and I think we all should be grateful to your uncle," John Manning said. "Frankly, I don't think we have heard the end of Hampton yet. He does an outstanding job in everything that he undertakes."

"He does, indeed," Victor Shelby agreed.

"I keep wondering if there could have been anything else that we might have done so that the War might have been different," Leland Thompson mused.

"We used to discuss that a lot after we learned the details in London. We probably should have given up after Gettysburg and Vicksburg," replied Brent. Then he asked somberly, "Why is it that in almost every war nations keep on fighting long after defeat has become inevitable? If it was not obvious before, it should have been obvious to everyone that the South had no chance to win after those battles in 1863. Yet we kept right on fighting. It was after Gettysburg that we suffered all those terrible casualties in the Wilderness, Spotsylvania, and Cold Harbor. It was after Vicksburg that Sherman brought his destruction to our homeland. Why did we let ourselves in for all that?"

Manning answered, "I suppose they were hoping for war weariness in the North, that then the North would agree to something better than unconditional surrender."

"Does that ever work?" asked Brent. "Have you ever heard of a nation that was winning giving up on account of war weariness?"

Manning pursed his lips in thought. "Well...you might say that Great Britain gave up on that account in the Revolution. Surely no one would say that they had been completely defeated on the battlefield."

"No, that's right," Brent conceded, "but there was one great difference–the colonists had the open and substantial support of France."

"Yes, that's true," Victor Shelby joined in, "but I suppose that was another consideration for us. One reason we kept on was in some continuing hope that the French or the British, or both, would intervene on behalf of the Confederacy."

"If you ask me, we went about this whole war in the wrong way," said Brent.

"How's that?" Will Anderson asked for the group, as all gave close attention.

"Well, if Jefferson Davis and Robert E. Lee had gone to Annapolis instead of West Point, the War might have turned out differently."

"How?" Scott Carson asked.

"Perhaps they would have thought more in terms of a maritime strategy instead of relying on big armies. Look...," Brent said as he walked over to a map on the wall. "The Confederacy is practically surrounded by protected waterways. You see the Potomac River along the northern border of Virginia; then it's only a short way to the big Ohio that forms the northern border of Kentucky all the way to the Mississippi. Follow the Mississippi all the way to the Gulf, and then there is an inner-coastal waterway where river boats can operate, all along the Gulf coast, and around Florida, all the way up to Virginia. Now what the South needed to do was to control all those waterways for our own movements and to deny them to the Yankees. The other thing we had to do was to build and man a fleet that could break the blockade and challenge the Yankee Navy at critical points on the Confederate coast."

Shelby objected, "But we had no shipbuilding facilities, no big factories and mines and everything."

Brent went on, "Somehow we found resources to field big armies. We should have used the army only for defense. You know it takes two or three times as many men to attack as to defend. Crossing over into Maryland at Sharpsburg, and later invading Pennsylvania, makes no sense. We should have remained on the defensive. We should have built and purchased from abroad gunboats to control the rivers and ships to keep the sea open. Then we could have maintained an effective defense indefinitely. And for the South successful defense meant victory; it could have meant independence for the Confederacy."

Just then Jarvis appeared at the door to announce that dinner was served. Everyone moved into the dining room to find assigned places at the big table. Violet and Brent sat at opposite ends of the long table, facing one another. Gov. Manning sat on her right, then beside him was Mary Anderson, then Leland, with Charlotte to his right, then Edith Carson, Victor Shelby, and Sarah Frierson at Brent's left. Mrs. Manning was seated on Brent's right, then Will Anderson, Andrew Thompson, Susan, Scott Carson, Virginia Shelby, and John Frierson on Violet's left.

The meal began with light corn chowder soup, followed by fresh trout laced with lemon juice, then the main course consisting of roast stuffed pig with baked apples, slices of roast beef with horseradish sauce and watercress, steamed asparagus, small buttered carrots, string beans cooked with tiny new potatoes, rice, corn, fresh garden peas with mint, Mammy's wonderful jumbo biscuits, tea and lemonade, and for their dessert the guests had their choice of one or more of the following: pecan pie, strawberries and cream, or sugared pound cake laced with scuppernong.

Violet was conscious of having to use pewter knives and forks instead of sterling silver, and earthenware plates, small bowls, and cups and saucers, instead of English bone china, and plain, thick glasses instead of cut crystal goblets, but she made no apology and carried through the whole affair in style. She was grateful that her mother's embroidered white tablecloth and large napkins had remain unscathed on the upper shelf of the linen closet. These could not help but add a touch of graciousness to the meal being served by Jarvis, Job, and Little Josh, all attired in their finest dark outfits with white shirts.

At a lull in the side conversations that had been going on around the table, Sarah Frierson spoke up, "Violet, has your vagabond sailor explained his whereabouts during his long absence?"

As all eyes turned toward Brent, he took on an uncharacteristically self-conscious look, hesitating to say anything.

"Come on, Commodore," Susan piped up, prompting him teasingly.

That only made matters worse for Brent's ease.

"When did you ship out?" asked Scott Carson, as a start.

"First, let me ask you all a question," responded Brent. "Can anyone tell me which was the first ship of war to fly the Confederate flag on the high seas?"

There was a pause. Then Manning answered tentatively, "Wasn't it the *Sumter*?"

"Yes, it was, and it was a steamship with screw, though it was only a small ship of five hundred tons," replied Brent.

"Don't tell me you were on the *Sumter*!" exclaimed Scott Carson.

"No, the Yankees got her cornered at Gibraltar after she had captured eighteen enemy vessels, and she was sold there in '62, but then did become a blockade runner for a while. But I did encounter several members of her crew."

"Where?" asked Carson with interest.

"Sometime later, in England." Now Brent was warming to his subject. A certain gleam came to his eyes as he went on. "To get back to the beginning I shipped out of Charleston, with several others, on a blockade runner called the *Atlanta,* bound for Liverpool. Our instructions were to report to the Confederate naval agent there, Captain James Dunwody Bulloch. He would assign us to a ship when one became available.

"As it turned out, we made it to Liverpool all right, but Bulloch said it would be some time until a ship would be available. Then he sent us to France, said there might be something going out of LeHavre or Cherbourg soon. There we met up with Lieutenant Waddell, James Waddell, who was waiting for a command. Actually we were at Cherbourg on June 19, 1864—"

Violet broke in to exclaim, "When the *Alabama* was sunk? I was so afraid that you might have been on the *Alabama.*"

"Yes, we were a part of the audience that watched the whole battle with the Yankee *Kearsarge.* It was a sad sight. But shortly after that we went with Waddell back to England, back to Liverpool, to report again to Captain Bulloch. This time he said that he was negotiating for a new vessel, and we should stand by to man her. Several weeks went by without further word. Then on the eighth of October we boarded a fast steamer called the *Laurel* that Bulloch had purchased to be a private blockade runner, so Waddell said. I found myself in the company of Waddell and seventeen other Confederate officers, and guess what, most of them had served on the *Sumter.* Some were survivors from the *Alabama.*"

"Then were you headed for home on that blockade runner? Couldn't you make it?" asked Will Anderson.

"That's what I thought," Brent went on, "but it turned out differently. Actually we were headed for Madeira—"

"Ah, and that great wine," Victor Shelby put in, "Ben Franklin said that when he died he wanted to be pickled in Madeira." They all laughed heartily at that.

"But where is Madeira?" Virginia Shelby wanted to know, and added jokingly, "I want to keep Victor away from there." Everyone laughed again.

"A group of islands belonging to Portugal, in the Atlantic, about three hundred and sixty miles off North Africa," explained Brent as he continued with his story. "There we anchored amidst some small outer islands and received a boat that came over from a larger ship alongside us. It was a lieutenant of the Confederate Navy. He reported to Waddell that the *Sea King* was ready for transfer. Then we discovered, or at least I discovered, that we were carrying six guns and their equipment. These were hauled over to boats and put aboard the other ship, and our complement of nineteen officers went along. There we went through the ceremony of commissioning the ship in the Confederate Navy and rechristened her the *Shenandoah.*

"Oh!" several listeners gasped.

Brent went on, "The crew of the former *Sea King,* from all different nationalities, had been told that they were bound for Bombay. Only twenty-three of the 120 seaman agreed to remain when they found out that they were to serve on a Confederate cruiser instead. And you know something? Two of the crew were

Negroes from the South. One jumped ship in Australia, but the other, a fellah by the name of Edward Weeks, stayed with us all the way, all the way back to Liverpool."

"Yes, yes, that's very interesting," Susan said impatiently, "but now get on with the action. Did you have many battles?"

Deliberately, Brent continued in the same vein, "What a beautiful ship she was! She was built in Glasgow only the year before, a full-rigged sailing ship of 1,160 tons, with rolling topsails but also with powerful steam engines that would develop 850 horsepower, and with screw that could be raised and funnel that could be lowered when sailing under canvas alone. Her frame, beams, and masts were of iron, but her decks and sides and bottom were covered with East India teakwood. The space between decks was seven and a half feet, and there were big air ports, so quarters for the men were good.

"We had so few men that at first Captain Waddell hesitated to set out, but the younger officers, and especially those from the *Alabama* insisted that we not risk going back to Europe. Waddell explained that our objective was the New Bedford whaling fleet which would be in the Pacific, but then he agreed to go. We all shed our jackets and pitched in so we could get going."

"A few days later, during a storm that was at least half a gale we captured the bark *Delphine.* After we had fired a shot across her bow her captain came over in a boat with the ship's papers. He said that his wife was on board, but she was nervous and of delicate health, and she had become so hysterical from our cannon shots that moving her from the bark through the heavy sea surely would result in her death. Our Captain was so moved that he sent our ship's surgeon, Lieutenant Whittle, over to the bark to tend to the distraught lady. The surgeon returned shortly with a tall young lady as healthy and vigorous and well-built as any you ever have seen out of Yankee land. It soon became clear that she was as domineering too. The poor husband, a sea captain, was a victim of continuous henpecking. Anyway, we took all the crew and all the valuables from the bark and set her on fire. Immediately the 'sick' woman turned her wrath and her charm on our captain. Waddell observed, 'a refractory lady can be controlled by quiet courtesy, but no flattery.' Anyway he was able to retain command of his ship. She began demanding the return of various items from the bark, including several books. We gave the books back to her—all except one. That was *Uncle Tom's Cabin* which we threw overboard, straight to Davy Jones's locker." Everyone laughed again at that and nodded their heads in agreement.

"From Melbourne we sailed in an easterly direction almost as far as New Zealand, and then followed a zig-zag course, first northward, and then northeastward to Tahiti in the Society Islands—"

"Oh," interrupted Susan in a teasing voice and with a quick glance at Violet, "I'm surprised you didn't stop in Tahiti for good—all those half-dressed dancers!"

"Yes, I agree, that might have been a good idea," said Brent with a smile, "but you know, as I remember it Melville put it in Moby Dick something like this: 'In the soul of man lies one insular Tahiti, full of peace and joy, but surrounded by all the horrors of a half-known life.' We sailed all the way through the Bering Strait a short distance into the Arctic Ocean. It was June, but I tell you the ice was heavy. We turned back southward through the Aleutian Islands, then southeastward. We saw nothing until we met an English bark, the *Baracouta*, near the Tropic of Cancer, on August 2nd. She was thirteen days out of San Francisco and bound for Liverpool. Her captain gave us the news that Lee had surrendered to Grant, and Johnston had surrendered to Sherman, and the War was over. We could scarcely believe it. We had had no sense of impending disaster.

"Now what to do? Waddell figured that it might not be safe to head back for the Confederate States. Instead, he decided to head for Liverpool. We went southeastward all the way through the North Pacific, continued southeastward through the South Pacific, rounded Cape Horn, and up through the Atlantic. We used only the sails until as we approached the Azores we sighted a ship that looked like a Federal cruiser. During the night we lowered the screw and piled on the coal while we made a hundred-mile detour. On November 5th, with our Confederate flag still flying—I guess it was the only one to go all the way around the world—we steamed into the harbor at Liverpool. We had not rated the chronometers since Melbourne, but our navigator found the way straight to our destination."

"Good Lord, what an adventure," Mary Anderson said, "but tell me, Brent, what did you eat all that time?"

"Mostly salt pork, some salt beef, and fish," he answered, "but whenever we could we got fresh fruit—good in the South Pacific, nothing in the Atlantic, because we were not risking any stops on the way back. You know it's important to get fruits or vegetables to prevent scurvy. Since the end of the last century the British Navy has decreed the issue of lime juice to all the men. That's the reason we call English sailors 'Limeys."

"What happened to the *Shenandoah*?" asked Carson.

"Waddell reported to the British foreign minister who directed us to turn ourselves over to a British captain. They asked us our nationality, and we all said, 'Southron.' The U.S. minister to England demanded that our ship be turned over to the American consul in Liverpool to be offered for sale to the highest bidder." Brent paused a moment, and then added with a sigh, "And so the great *Shenandoah* was sold to the Sultan of Zanzibar for something over a hundred thousand dollars."

Sensing her husband's chagrin at the fate of his *Shenandoah*, Violet spoke up, "My, what a long voyage. Now let's all take about a fifteen minute recess, and then we'll reassemble in the parlor for coffee. I never did care for the old custom of leaving all the interesting conversation to the men with their cigars."

"Violet, I wholeheartedly agree with you!" said Sarah. The men looked a bit surprised but were too polite to comment on this deviation from the usual procedures.

As everyone started to scatter, Brent introduced several of the men to his cigarettes. Within only a short time everyone had found a chair in the parlor, and all had received coffee.

Scott Carson resumed the conversation, "Brent, how much of an impact do you think all the Confederate cruisers had on the Yankees?"

Brent drew on his cigarette before answering, "Oh, they cost the Yankees millions—in direct losses, increases in insurance premiums, delays in getting goods, and so on, I can assure you of that. But in crippling their war effort? Near zero. Of course all the efforts of all the armies and the navy came to naught in the end. Frankly, I don't think commerce raiding is the way to fight a naval war."

"What else could we have done?" asked Governor Manning.

"The most unwise thing of all was Jefferson Davis' unofficial embargo of cotton. He actually was helping Lincoln's blockade. What we should have done was to ship out to Europe all the cotton we possibly could, before the blockade became fully effective. That could have given us millions of dollars—some say as much as two billion dollars—to buy ships and arms and everything. It could even have provided the basis for supporting Confederate currency and bonds. It could have rescued the Confederacy financially."

"Why do you think they put an embargo on cotton?" inquired Victor Shelby.

John Frierson volunteered to answer. "The assumption was that the British and French economies would suffer so much by the loss of their main source of cotton for their textile mills that they would be moved to recognize and assist the Confederacy in order to recover their source of cotton."

"Yes, that was it," Brent agreed, "but it should have been clear to anybody that that would not work; they would be risking war with the United States. Our best bet was to sell all the cotton to them that we could get out, to finance our War effort. I tell you, we should have gathered all our strength and bought and built a lot more ships, to keep at least some of the ports—Charleston, Mobile, New Orleans—open at least a part of the time so we could continue to get our cotton out to Europe and bring in the munitions and other things that we needed."

"Were we ever strong enough to do that?" asked Victor.

"If we had brought in all our cruisers—the *Alabama,* the *Florida,* the *Georgia,* the *Tallahassee,* the *Sumter,* the *Shenandoah,* and other vessels—instead of scattering them all over the world—and if we could have gotten out the Laird rams and several more like them, who knows what they might have been able to do?" answered Brent.

"What are Laird rams?" Virginia Shelby wanted to know.

"They were built by the Laird people in England and were ships with very sturdy frames and a heavy bow with sharp prongs with which to cripple or destroy a ship by crashing into it," explained Brent.

Violet noted, "You mean like the Romans fought naval battles?"

"Exactly. Napoleon III invited the Confederacy to obtain some ships in France; then, after we had contracted for two heavy, ironclad battleships and four corvettes, and when they were about ready, he reneged and wouldn't allow them to be delivered. They could have swept the wooden blockading ships from the sea. If we could have concentrated just some of those ships off our main ports, or even one or two of the ports, and used some clever maneuvering, they might have done some good. If we had sent our cotton out instead of holding it and later the Yankees confiscating it—we could have had many more ships."

"But we could never have matched the Yankees," Will protested.

"No, and in the American Revolutionary War, the French never could match the British naval power, but it was the victory of DeGrasse over the British fleet in their battle off the Virginia capes that paved the way for Yorktown."

"Yes, I see what you mean, Brent," responded Will.

Turning toward John Manning who was seated near the center of the room opposite, Violet changed the subject, "Governor, or I guess I should say 'Senator' now even though we always think of you as Governor, do you think the Yankee military occupation really has ended?"

Manning hesitated, and then answered somewhat reluctantly, "Well, Violet, I'm afraid that perhaps, as Tennyson said, 'The worst is yet to come."

"Oh, dear, why do you say that?" asked Violet apprehensively.

"Your addressing me just now as 'Senator' reflects a part of it. Yes, I have been elected senator by the General Assembly, but in Washington they will not allow me to take my seat."

"What!" several exclaimed in surprise.

"Why not? What is the trouble?" asked Sarah.

Manning sighed and responded, "I'm afraid the Federal Congress is going to make more and more demands before admitting us."

"Like what?" asked Virginia.

"Like granting the vote to the darkies."

Violet put in, "Why should the darkies vote when women, whether black or white, are not allowed to vote?"

Sarah agreed, "Indeed! Violet has a point."

Violet went on, "I really don't object to having black men vote—if they make sure they can read so they know what they're doing."

"That's the thing," said John Frierson, "if we don't have that assurance, then the Negroes are simply going to be marshaled by the Scalawags and the Carpetbaggers to vote the way they tell them to."

Brent observed, "Isn't that a game two can play? Can't the Democrats also bargain for Negro votes?"

"Of course," Frierson came back, "and that could prove to be very costly for everyone."

John Manning spoke up, "You know the whole thing is highly hypocritical. Only six Northern states allow unrestricted Negro suffrage, and twenty-six—*twenty-six states*—deny the Negro a vote altogether. Isn't that something? And now they are putting on the pressure to force all Southern states to allow the Negroes to vote when most of them don't allow it themselves!"

"One point we should remember," Victor Shelby said, "if they enfranchise the Negro, that means that they can no longer count him as only three-fifths for representation. In other words, the representation of the Southern states in the U.S. House of Representatives will be increased by a ratio of two-fifths of their Negro population. The Northerners won't like that."

"That's a good point," said Andrew Thompson.

John Manning reiterated, "But if the so-called reconstruction is renewed and prolonged, with this and other demands, indeed I am afraid that the worst is yet to come."

"God forbid!" exclaimed Charlotte.

Violet said, "Oh, dear, with our workers back and our crops in, and now with Brent back, I was having high hopes that we were well on the way to recovery."

Victor Shelby responded, "We can hope for the best, but we must be prepared for the worst..."

"Hear, hear!" several exclaimed.

He continued, "Looking ahead a little, who do we have who can take the lead in restoring civil government in this state?"

John Frierson answered promptly, "What do you think of Wade Hampton?"

"I was rather hoping he would be elected Governor this time," Mary Anderson declared.

Frierson said, "He would have been, but as you know, he was afraid that as a former Confederate lieutenant general his election at this time might be an aggravation for the Yankees."

Violet testified, "Daddy thought a good deal of General Hampton—thought he was a great planter, a great military leader, a great person." Charlotte and Susan nodded their agreement.

John Manning nodded and said, "As you know, I may be biased through his sister, my first wife, of years ago, God rest her soul, but I agree that Hampton is a remarkable person. He could be our Moses, to lead our people out of the bondage of reconstruction to the promised land of liberation."

"I agree, though I'm not sure 'Moses' is the name we want to use in Sumter District," ventured Charlotte.

"Indeed not!" Violet said emphatically, looking at Brent.

"The question is," said the elder Thompson, "whether anybody ever can lead us back into anything like full recovery."

Violet remarked thoughtfully, "Looking back to ancient history, remember there was a great Greek war between North and South, the Peloponnesian War, only that time the South, led by Sparta, won. They occupied Athens and imposed a Spartan-sponsored oligarchy. But within a decade Athens was free of Spartan dictation and had made a full recovery. In fact, historians say that Athens was then more truly the 'school of Hellas' than she ever had been before her defeat."

"An inspiring example," Mary put forth.

Violet asked her guests, "Well now, we've been sitting for quite a while. Would you all like a few minutes to walk around the gardens, or have a look around the house, or freshen up a bit?"

"Violet, do you still play the piano?" asked Virginia.

"A little. I've not had much free time to practice."

"I think we all would like to hear you play some tunes."

"All right then, in a little while, after we've taken a brief respite." Violet rose to signal that all who wished should feel free to leave the room.

After an interval of twenty minutes or so, Violet sat down at the piano and began playing some of her favorite melodies from Chopin and Beethoven. This was all that it took to draw everyone back to the parlor. Violet persuaded Charlotte and Susan to join in with their violin and flute. After several rounds of enthusiastic applause to this music, Violet suddenly called out, "Now all, let's sing!"

Will walked straight up to the piano and asked, "Do you know *Sailing, Sailing*?"

"No, Will, but if you'll lead I'll be glad to chord." She improvised an introduction and he waved his arms for everyone to join him as he began singing:

Sailing, sailing, over the bounding main;
For many a stormy wind shall blow
Ere Brent comes home again!
Sailing, sailing, over the bounding main;
For many a stormy wind shall blow
Ere Brent comes home again!

Everyone cheered loudly.

Will called for Brent to come up and give some of his favorites. With some coaxing out of his reluctance, Brent walked up to the piano, amidst loud cheers from the group and, without piano accompaniment, sang out in his rich, baritone voice:

Oh, blow the man down, bullies blow the man down!
To me way ay, blow the man down,
Oh, blow the man down bullies, blow the man down,
Give me some time to blow the man down.

He called out for everyone to join in the chorus, then sang on:

As I was a-walking down Paradise Street
Everybody!—*To me way, ay, blow the man down;*
A pretty young damsel I chanced for to meet,

(All):Give *me some time to blow the man down.*
'Tis larboard and starboard and jump to the call,
(All): *To me way, ay, blow the man down;*
Confederate cruisers can win over all,
(All): *Give me some time to blow the man down.*

Brent said an all-time favorite of his was *Aura Lee*. Everyone cheered. Violet said, yes, she could play that one. Will stood beside Brent, and together they took the lead as all joined in with:

As the bluebird in the spring 'neath the willow tree,
Sat and piped I heard him sing, sing of Aura Lee.
Aura Lee, Aura Lee, maid with golden hair.
Sunshine came along with thee, and swallows in the air.

Then without saying anything, Violet began playing *Dixie.* They all stood and sang, slowly, full of emotion. Tears fell down the cheeks of a few. Then came a couple of verses of *The Bonnie Blue Flag.* Finally, Brent set out on his own with:

Oh, Shenandoah, I long to hear you,
Way-hay, you rolling river!
Oh, Shenandoah, I long to hear you,
Ha, ha, we're bound away, 'cross the wide Missouri.

Book Two

South Wind

Chapter 26

At Loose Ends

1866

Over the next three or four weeks Brent had a chance to recover his 'land legs'—playing with the children in the yard, taking walks alone to the orchard or over to the workers' village, talking with Leo, visiting with friends, having conversations with Charlotte and Susan, hours of sharing with Violet.

But after a little while the euphoria of homecoming began to give way to a certain awkwardness and self-consciousness for everyone. Violet could not quite fathom it, but she sensed that somehow Brent had changed. They always had gotten along well during the time they had had together before he joined the navy. They always enjoyed each other's company, seldom had a disagreement, always had adjusted quickly and easily to change, but now each little decision seemed to grow into a major one, every situation a new crisis. Answers became shorter and words at times a little sharper.

It took some doing, but Violet persuaded Brent to go along with her and her sisters to church on the first Sunday in July. He enjoyed meeting people there, and his deportment was above reproach, but it was clear that he did not enjoy the service itself very much. He went through the prayers and recited the creed in a desultory manner. She appreciated Dr. Wilson's sermon on Hope, though Brent seemed to be daydreaming through most of it.

One evening later that week, after giving the children their supper and playing with them for a while, Violet and Brent walked out to the east garden in search of fresh air and time just to be together away from all the others.

"Violet, you've been doing a great job with the plantation and the children and everything," Brent said with sincerity and admiration in his voice.

"Oh, Brent, I have had to grow up in a hurry after Daddy died and the Yankees came down and times were so hard for us all. I've always loved Fair Oaks, as you know. Even when I was young, I used to dream of helping to manage it, much as Mama used to help Daddy. Then, after Mama died, Daddy began teaching me things and relying on me just as he had on Mama. Oh, not as much, of course, but I was learning quickly. Thank goodness for that, for what Daddy taught me helped us through the difficult road back to recovery."

"Well, you've done a lot, and it hasn't been easy. Folks around here and in Sumter are always talking about how you've been bringing the place back."

"I hoped I could really be in charge of managing the plantation when I was in my fifties—but to have full responsibility in my twenties—no, never! But I tell you, much more of this and I'll feel I'm sixty already!"

Brent looked out toward the front. His eyes raked over the area back and forth. In disbelief he exclaimed, "My Lord! They're actually beginning to clear for the railroad, right across the front lawn. Those poles are bad enough, but a railroad!

Violet, I've been wondering, why right out there? Why isn't it out along the road or over on the other side of the plantation?"

Violet glanced at Brent and then looked away. "Well...at first they were going to put it along the edge of the property...but then they changed it to here, across the front lawn."

"I couldn't believe that actually they were going to put a railroad across the yard. I can see now they're serious, but do you have any idea why they changed the route?" he asked.

In a small voice Violet answered, "Yes, Brent, I know why."

"Well, why? Why couldn't you get them to put it over where it belongs?" he asked, somewhat testily.

In a stronger voice, she answered, "The price was too high."

"What do you mean, too high? How high?"

"I'm certain you would consider the price too high—as I did, Brent."

"Well, Violet, my dear, will you please explain."

"Brent...the man...said he would put it at the edge of the property if I would be cooperative and grant him certain favors."

"Favors? What kind of favors?" An ugly suspicion was forming in his mind.

"You know, Brent...personal favors."

"*Personal* favors!" The realization of what she meant exploded upon his mind. In a cold, yet livid voice, he asked, "Who is he?"

Violet had never seen such an expression on Brent's face. Shivers ran down her spine. She had known he would be upset when the day came that she would tell him, but she had never expected such cold fury. "A man by the name of Duprey, Caleb Duprey, a Carpetbagger from Massachusetts, working out of Columbia for the Yankees."

Now his anger burst forth as he roared, "Why that son of a bitch! That lousy Yankee bastard! It's bad enough that they care nothing about leaving our women and children to starve and to fend for themselves, but they have no qualms about trying to take advantage of our wives! They're filthy beasts, that's what they are, but we'll have our day..." He took Violet in his arms, holding her closely, as he succeeded, with an effort, to control his anger. He knew that the experience had been a difficult one for Violet, and he did not want to upset her more. He wanted to protect her from ever having again to endure such an insult. He stroked her soft hair as he asked in a calm voice, "Violet, my love, when did they do all this?"

With her head leaning against his strong shoulder, relieved that it was all out now, and that he seemed to be his own self again, she answered, "They started clearing the day after he got the right of way by eminent domain a couple of months ago, and they started over there on the other side. They marked the way across the lawn, and other men put up those poles. Then they didn't come back here until today. I guess they were working this morning while you were over at the workers' village. When they didn't return, I just hoped they'd changed their minds. I should have known better, of course," she ended bitterly.

"Well I'll be damned," was his only comment. He kissed her tenderly and with his arm around her, they walked slowly back to the house. He listened intently and sympathetically as Violet related the event in more detail.

Early the next morning, as she had done several times since Brent's return home, Violet asked him to ride with her for an inspection of plantation activities. These rides reminded her of when she and her father used to "take a ride around the circle." They went out to the carriage house where Violet mounted Jeb and Brent climbed up on Feather.

Glancing at Violet, Brent said, "I've been wanting to tell you how well you do on that saddle. I suppose a lot of the women had to learn to ride like men when they couldn't get side saddles. Some might call this progress."

"This is a McClellan military saddle, and I can tell you, it sure beats the old side saddle we ladies used in the past."

"I'll bet."

"I've often thought to myself that it would make more sense for men to ride side saddle instead of women anyway."

He laughed and said, "You have a point there!"

She joined in his laughter and rode off at a fast pace to take the lead. At the cow barn, the cows still had their heads in the stanchions while Negro girls milked them. Outside, men were bringing up hay to go into the hay mow. They brought up a wagon filled with hay and hooked in a special hay fork that Amos had rigged up. Rope and pulleys, with a horse on the opposite end of the barn, pulled the hay up to the loft.

"You can see that this is clover hay, first cutting," Violet explained. "We've got to be careful not to store it when too green–might not be good for the cows and might even start a fire–and we don't want it too dry and dusty, that wouldn't be good either."

"No," was Brent's only comment.

They rode out to the corn field and along the edge for a spell. Violet showed some disappointment as she said, "Not growing like it should."

"No," was all Brent said.

At the threshing shed, oats were being threshed, and part of the grain was going to the horse and mule barns and part was going to the grist mill where it was being ground.

"Oats for the horses and mules, porridge for us," smiled Violet in satisfaction at what she was observing.

Brent looked around at what was going on, but said nothing.

They rode quickly through the workers' village, where quarters seemed to be neat and clean. Some painters were painting the cottages white, and a couple of carpenters were working in the church and school building.

"Things seem to be moving right along here," she noted.

Brent merely nodded.

They rode on out to the cotton fields where groups of men and women, along with a few youngsters, were industriously hoeing, singing while they worked. Just as in the old days the workers were moving across the field in line, hoeing side by side to the rhythm of their singing, *"Nobudy kno' de troub'l ah see'd..."—"Ah be climbin' Jacob's ladder..."—"Ah tek de wing uf de mornin'."* Seeing Leo, Violet shouted, "Good work, Leo!" and Brent called out, "The field's looking fine." Leo waved his thanks, a huge grin on his face and then returned to his work.

"He's a good man, Leo is. This plantation couldn't be run without him, that's for sure." said Violet, gratefully.

"Likely not," replied Brent.

As they rode back toward the house, Brent again complimented Violet on how well the plantation was running, what a good job of managing she and Leo were doing, and how all the workers seemed in good humor and good spirits. It was clear that he was favorably impressed with Violet's work, yet there seemed to be a trace of misgivings in his attitude that perturbed and confused her.

After dinner Brent joined Violet in the office where she had gone to go over some figures. When he entered the room she looked up and welcomed him with a smile.

"Well, Violet," he said, taking a seat in one of the big comfortable chairs across from the desk, "work on the plantation seems to be going very well, very well indeed."

Laying her pen down, she answered, "Yes, the workers are doing well. I'm glad you're pleased with things around here, Brent."

Then abruptly Brent asked, "How soon are we going to Columbia?"

"My goodness, I've not been to Columbia for at least a year and a half. I didn't want to see it while it was in ruins, but now it might be fun to go in. Were you thinking of going in for a day or for a weekend? Maybe I could do a little shopping, get a new hat or something...Yes, it'd be fun to be with you in Columbia again!" She looked at him with anticipation.

He stroked his chin for a moment and then said slowly, "No...no, that's not exactly what I meant, Violet. I was thinking, well, when are we going to move back to Columbia again?"

Violet paused in ill-concealed shock. Leave Fair Oaks? It had never occurred to her that Brent was considering such a move, especially since the management was her responsibility now. When she could catch her breath, she exclaimed with emotion, "Brent, I can't leave here. Besides there's no place in Columbia to move to. You know our town house is gone...and anyway, Daddy willed it to Charlotte...and besides...the Carpetbaggers and Scalawags confiscated the lot for taxes. Fair Oaks is the only home we have!"

"Oh, damn, those Yankees. Well, Violet, then we'll find another lot. There must be plenty that those scavengers are wanting to sell, and we'll build our own house—just the way we want it."

"Oh, Brent, do be practical. Where on earth would we get the money to do that?" Alarm began to spread through her.

"Couldn't you sell this place? It must be worth at least twenty-five thousand. Think what a house you could get for that and still have plenty to get our business restarted, and I'll get it back to you a dozen times. And of course, Charlotte and Susan and Mammy and the other house servants would come with us."

The very suggestion of selling Fair Oaks had sent her blood racing. Violet felt as though the top of her head would fly off. She choked with emotion as she exclaimed with vehemence, "What! *Sell Fair Oaks?* How *could* you even suggest such a thing? You mean *now*—now that I've been able to hold on to it all without any help, and *now*, when the field hands are back putting it into production, and we can make some money, *now* you want to let it go? And do you really think the Carpetbaggers or Scalawags would pay us any kind of a fair price for the place? And do you really think their prices on lots in Columbia won't be sky high to any Southerner? Don't you think we have a responsibility to all those workers who came here and are helping us to truly make this a profitable working plantation? Oh, Brent, how could you even think of such a thing!" The words had tumbled out so fast that she had to stop for breath.

"Violet, I'm afraid our world is gone, has come crumbling down all around us," he said in a defeated tone as he sighed deeply.

"Fiddlesticks, Brent Sutler! Does Fair Oaks look like it's crumbling down? And now the military occupation seems to be coming to an end." She looked at him searchingly and continued, "No, indeed not, our world is *not* gone!"

"Violet, my dear, I've got to be doing something, whether it's resurrecting our old world or building a new one. Right now I have the feeling of being at loose ends. I'm not used to that. I'm used to *doing* things. Can't you understand?"

"Brent, you'll be building a new world, but *our* world has not gone either. The new one will be an improvement and expansion of the old. A new world cannot be something completely disconnected with the past."

He was silent for a minute, thinking of what she had just said. Then he went on to explain, "I suppose that part of this feeling I have is because I don't know anything about farming—all I know is merchandising and shipping, and of course, sailing. I've always been a city boy, you know."

"Well, Brent, I reckon I can run the plantation and make a go of it...and surely, you wouldn't have me give up Fair Oaks after all these years. My whole life has been bent toward saving it. Besides, you could be such a big help here. You could, Brent," she said hopefully.

Brent shook his head. "You don't need me here. You and Leo have this place humming now." He paused, his eyes brooding, and then said with feeling, "Violet, I just can't hang around here doing nothing."

"That's not the situation at all. The women have had to take all kinds of responsibilities during the War—in offices, in factories, on plantations, but that does not relieve you of your responsibilities now." Her voice sounded sharp, even to her ears.

His voice was sharp in return. "Well, what do you want me to do? Do you want me to be another of your slave drivers to go around and see that the corn is being plowed correctly?"

"You can do better than that." *Can we really be talking to one another like this, Brent and me?* she thought. *What's happening to us?*

He asked in a sarcastic tone, "Oh, I might be first mate? I don't think I could be first mate with a woman as captain of the ship. Better to go get a ship of my own. You know, my dear, I'm used to giving orders more than taking them."

"Well, Brent, let's don't scuttle this ship in the process. Give me a hand here."

But he went on heatedly, "Violet, I'll tell you one thing. No wife of mine is going to be running a farm or any other business as far as I am concerned."

Angrily Violet flashed back, "I don't know what other wives you may have in mind, but this one certainly is. Who do you think were running things while all the men were off to war? The women left behind, that's who! Now I suppose you expect us all to sit and take up our needlepoint again!"

"Maybe I should go back to sea for awhile," Brent retorted.

"If that's what you want, to run away from your responsibilities here, then by all means, go!" she flung at him.

Without further words, but in troubled thought, Brent got up and slowly left the room. He walked around to the front porch where Charlotte happened to be sitting in a rocking chair.

Looking up and noting his expression, she asked, "Brent, is something wrong?"

He took a chair beside her and with a forced grin that quickly vanished, he answered, "No...no, nothing's wrong."

Charlotte had heard raised voices coming from the office. She asked, "Brent, is there anything wrong between you and Violet?"

"No, no, nothing like that. I guess it's just that I feel a little out of place, at loose ends.

"That would be only natural. You've been away a long time, involved in war and everything. It'll take a little time to get used to things around here." she reassured him.

"It's more than that, Charlotte. You know there is a big difference between coming home as a conquering hero, and returning as a *conquered* hero."

"But from what you've told us of the *Shenandoah* you should be very proud. Think of all those victories—with never a defeat!"

He sighed, "No, never a defeat, except in the War itself. That was the story of the Confederacy from the beginning—winning battles but losing the War all the way through."

"Still, the loss was not of your doing. You had nothing to do with it." she pointed out.

Again he sighed, "But all the efforts, all our victories at sea were to no purpose—completely futile, and now I'm afraid that I'm feeling futile about everything."

Charlotte gave a look that resembled the Violet of old. "Now you've got to pitch in and help get things here in the South started again."

"How can I do that? Our world is gone." His voice reflected his frustration.

"Violet doesn't think so, and neither do I."

"I must say that you all have done well in getting the plantation in operation again, but don't you see? That's part of it. You all don't need me around here. I'm just a fifth wheel. Somehow I've got to get my own ship."

Brent went around to the carriage house and asked Aaron to hitch a horse and buggy to take him to the station. He went into the house and returned a few minutes later with his navy cap on his head and his sea bag in his hands.

Violet came running out. When she saw his bag, she cried, "Oh, Brent, Brent! What are you doing? Where are you going?" She felt her heart leap to her throat.

He only said, "I've got to see what I can find." He gave her a peck on the cheek, climbed into the buggy, and told Aaron to get going.

Charlotte came out and walked with Violet around to the front as the buggy disappeared down the lane. They sat on the porch and kept looking long after there was anything to see, each hoping they would see the buggy coming back up the lane, with Brent having changed his mind.

After a short while, Violet turned to Charlotte and said sorrowfully, "I think he must be going to sea...and I will not see him again until God knows when."

"Now, Violet, you know he's going to Columbia–not to sea again," Charlotte said, hoping to reassure her sister.

"Well, maybe, but I can't understand what has gotten into him. He seemed so happy to be home again...but then...lately...I've noticed he's become kind of sullen...testy. We had a real argument in the office earlier." The plaintive tone of her voice accentuated the sadness in her eyes.

"Oh, Violet, don't you know what's bothering Brent?"

"I'm not sure I do. What do you think?"

"I'll tell you what I think. Brent wasn't prepared for a woman, his wife, to be running a plantation and doing very well without his help. He feels useless. He's also suffering the effects of fighting for a Lost Cause. His male pride has been hurt."

"Dear God, Charlotte, I hope he doesn't think I don't understand him, don't appreciate him, don't admire his service in the Confederate Navy and all that he's done."

"He needs more than just talk. He needs to *do* something, to be active like he used to be when he worked in Columbia. You see, *you* already are managing the plantation successfully."

Violet paused thoughtfully, digesting what her sister had just said. Then with determination she said, "Well, I love that man. He's the father of our children, and I'm *not* going to let him get away. I'll swallow my pride and go right into Columbia and find him. I'll head him off...I'll explain that I *do* understand."

Charlotte frowned and responded tactfully, "Violet, of course you probably know better than I, but I would say, don't do it. Let him have a little time to think, give him his head, so to speak. My guess is, he'll come back, and it will be much better if he comes back by his own volition."

Violet thought a moment and then smiled,. "Charlotte, you've grown up in a hurry through all this...you just may be right...thank you. Yes, I think you may be right. I'll wait."

Chapter 27

Division of Labor

1866

Violet had only two weeks to wait. Late one afternoon, in another futile effort to find a cool breeze, Violet and her sisters were sitting on the front veranda rocking and fanning themselves. They glanced down the lane and saw Brent walking toward the house. There was no rush out to meet him this time. Susan started to rise from her chair, but Violet reached over and held her arm, and Susan sank down.

"Violet! It's Brent come home!" said Susan excitedly.

"I know," answered Violet calmly in a low voice.

"Susan, wait," put in Charlotte, understanding what Violet was about.

They waited. As he came nearer he appeared to be downcast, almost sullen. There was no excitement, no hurrying in his steps to be with his family again.

They did get up to greet him when he came up the steps. He gave the requisite hug and kiss to each and exchanged hellos. Charlotte gave a beckoning signal to Susan, and the two went into the house and left Brent and Violet alone.

Brent took a chair beside Violet and braced himself for a torrent of invective. Instead, Violet reached over and took his hand, saying sweetly, "Brent, it's good to see you, good to have you back. We missed you."

For a moment Brent was so surprised at the unanticipated reception that he could say nothing. Then he smiled lamely, and said, "I'm afraid I didn't have much success in Columbia...a few contacts, but not much."

"I'm sorry," she answered, sincerely.

The sincerity in her voice did not go unnoticed by Brent. He went on, "But Violet, one very important thing I found out while I was away–it's no good without you. You are too much a part of me, my Love."

"Yes, I know what you mean. I feel such an emptiness when you are not here–as though part of me is missing...I feel incomplete."

Brent got up from his chair and began to pace back and forth across the front of the porch. After a few moments he stopped pacing and looked at Violet. He said thoughtfully, "I suppose you still are not willing to move back to Columbia."

"Oh, Brent, I want to be wherever you are, you know that, but don't you see if we don't make a go of Fair Oaks we won't have anything. Maybe if we can just get a good start here then in two or three years we can do as Mama and Daddy used to do, spend the winters in Columbia and the summers at Fair Oaks."

"Well, maybe, I don't know...I couldn't get much business done out here. I need to contact customers, follow the markets." He stood quietly for a couple of minutes, gazing out across the front lawn. Suddenly he spun around, and with a look of discovery and excitement on his face he exclaimed, "I've got it, I've got it! Violet, I've got it!"

Puzzled, yet relieved to see the bright look of excitement and anticipation on Brent's countenance, Violet asked, "What on earth are you talking about?"

Brent pointed out to the front lawn. "Look! You see that telegraph line out there?"

Violet looked out over the lawn, dismay on her face at the sight. "Yes, and it still makes me angry every time I look at that line."

"Well, my Love, be angry no longer. The Yankees branded me a pirate. Now I'm going to pirate a little off that Carpetbagger telegraph line!"

"What do you mean?"

"I'm going to tap into that line so I can learn the movement of market prices," he answered with a big smile.

"But Brent, can you do that?"

"Of course I can, and I know the Morse telegraph too."

"I mean, is it legal?" she asked.

With a glint in his eyes he answered, "As long as I don't get caught."

"But how can you send telegraph messages without somebody finding out?" The warmth of his excitement was spreading to her, and she began fanning herself briskly.

"Oh, I won't send anything from here, just be quiet and listen. Then I'll go into Sumter to send telegrams when necessary. Later I'll see if I can work out a deal to lease the use of a line for just five or ten minutes a day."

"My goodness, Brent, do you think it'll work?" she asked, almost breathlessly.

Pleased at Violet's interest in his idea, he answered, "Of course, and don't you see, my Love, *this* will make it possible to do business here–at Fair Oaks. I'll have to go into the city now and then, of course, but mostly I can conduct business right here at the plantation." He paused and then, his eyes twinkling, he added in a business like tone, "That is, if you will lease me a corner of your office for my office space."

"Oh, Brent, you silly goose, of course we can share the office."

"The first principle of business is to buy cheap and sell dear; the second principle is to get the information first so that you can do that," he informed Violet.

"How do we get started?"

"Well, Ma'am, I need a business loan. Can you lend me a little capital?"

"What do you have in mind?"

"Fifty dollars would do it, I should think."

"Oh, my goodness, that's a lot of money...but, of course you can have it, Brent."

"Good, then I'll be off to Columbia in the morning, but my Darling, I'll be right back, back tomorrow evening."

Susan, peeking from behind a bush at the corner of the house, saw Brent put his arm around Violet and lead her into the house for supper. She almost let out a whoop of joy, but clapped her hand over her mouth and turned and ran to the back steps where she rejoined Charlotte who was sitting there reading a book. When Mammy came to announce supper, Susan appeared so engrossed in reading that she didn't hear the first call. Charlotte took the book from her hands, saying, "You're just sitting there with a huge grin on your face, my dear little sister. In fact, you look like the goose who's just laid a golden egg. What's going on here?"

When Susan had told her what she had just seen, Charlotte just nodded knowingly. "Now, you know, Susan, that married folks need to be alone to work things out. They can't always be having others hanging around. This is your lesson for today...and remember, married people need privacy, so I'd better not hear of you eavesdropping and peeking at them again!" "Yassum, big sister," replied Susan, in mock meekness. The two girls entered the house laughing heartily.

The next evening Brent returned from Columbia with a coil of copper wire, some glass insulators, a telegraph key, and sounder. "I'm ready for business," he reported to Violet as they all sat around the supper table. "I made arrangements with a young fellow to look after things on the other end. He's a fellow by the name of Cedric Johnson. I made his acquaintance during my previous sojourn in the capital city."

"Who is he? Are you certain you can trust him, Brent?" Violet asked. At supper the evening before Brent had shared his plans with Charlotte and Susan, and he had stressed the necessity of keeping what he was doing a secret. He had warned them not to tell anyone, *anyone* about his work with the telegraph.

Brent frowned and said thoughtfully, "I'm pretty sure he can be trusted. I'm usually a good judge of character. He *is* a South Carolinian and not some Carpetbagger. He used to live in Orange—came to Columbia to find work. He served in the Quartermaster's Department during the War, so he knows a little about handling goods. I asked around about him and thought about it all carefully before broaching the deal. I'm confident he can be trusted."

"What kind of deal did you make?" Violet asked.

"Well, he has a little stall at the City Market, and he'll buy and sell for me on the side on a percentage basis."

"That sounds reasonable," remarked Violet.

Early the next morning Brent was out working on his line. He posted Little Josh to act as lookout, to report if he saw anyone coming. Little Josh had taken to Brent just as he had to Violet, and his greatest enjoyment was doing something to help either of those two. His second was helping to look out for and playing with their children. He took his guard assignment seriously, and consistently checked all directions with his keen eyes.

Brent found a pole fairly hidden by trees, where his connection would not be obvious, and with some effort managed to climb the pole. He held himself in place with straps from an old horse harness and hammered in a spike to hold an insulator. With the insulator in place he twisted his wire around the telegraph wire, wrapped it around the insulator, and descended the pole. He brought the wire to insulators on the trunks of a series of trees and finally through the northeast back window of the office. He put a lamp table beside the window and wired his telegraph key and sounder to sit on the table.

Violet watched while Brent played with his new toy all afternoon. Little Josh had stayed for a short while, but left to help Susan pick flowers for the house. Brent sat through long sets of instructions for the railroad workers—mainly, about construction and property. Then he beamed as some messages came through giving price quotations from the New York and New Orleans commodity markets, quotations that were being relayed from Charleston to Columbia.

Violet was impressed. As Brent was getting ready to close down, she said, "Brent, I have a proposition."

"Wonderful, my lovely wife, I'm interested. Upstairs?" he jokingly replied, raising his eyebrows and glancing upward with his eyes.

"Oh, Brent, stop that, I'm serious. Listen, I've been thinking about something while you were working away at that telegraph line. Why don't we become full partners and set up this office for joint operations?"

"Excellent idea. What arrangement do you propose?" He grinned at her.

"Well, why not let me continue to manage Fair Oaks, and you be vice president in charge of purchasing and marketing–"

"Now you're beginning to talk my language," he said, still grinning.

"And you run your business–what shall we call it?"

"The Sutler Mercantile Company?"

"The Sutler Mercantile Company, and I'll be vice president in charge of records and correspondence."

"Great," he responded without even a thought, "and what are the financial arrangements, the chief keeps all?"

"No...now hear me through...I was thinking of the net profits in each year, in each enterprise, you get one-third, I get one-third, and one-third goes into a common account that we want to use for common purposes–like new furniture, or someday a lot and house in Columbia, education of the children, and so on. Wouldn't that be fair?" she suggested.

"Seems quite equitable to me."

"I'll ask Carter to get right to work on some furnishings for the office. How about a big double desk, where we can sit facing each other?" she asked delightedly, her mind already busy on rearranging the office to suit the needs of both.

"Good idea. Don't forget to allow for some pigeon holes and space for papers, a table for the telegraph–and so on."

"Yes, I can see we'll need those. I'll talk to Carter first thing after breakfast tomorrow. He's been training an apprentice who seems to be quite good, and between the two of them it should not take long to have what we need." She paused and looked at Brent, her eyes sparkling. "Oh, Brent, this is going to be wonderful, working together like this, helping one another."

He leaned down to give her a hearty kiss, which she returned with equal enthusiasm. He took her elbow and guided her toward the door, saying, "Now, my Lady, do you by any chance have another proposition to proffer?"

Within a week the office was set up as Violet and Brent had envisioned it. Most important was an improvised desk to be used until Carter had finished the new one. For the present he had removed the roll top from the Major's old desk that already was in the office. He and his apprentice, Jonah, brought up a discarded desk from the basement and removed the roll top from it, and then placed them back to back with a side of each against the south wall, as Violet indicated. For a smooth cover, Brent ordered a sheet of canvas-backed linoleum from Columbia. Carter trimmed it to exact size and carefully tacked it to the two desks to make a single, smooth surface.

Each side of the combined desk had a Bank of England chair on rollers, and beside each was an armless Windsor chair. On the wall beside each of the desk chairs was a bank of pigeon-holes—alphabetically marked, with several additional slots still unmarked. On the wall between the banks of pigeon holes, and above the desks, bookshelves held several important though infrequently used reference books. In front of the fireplace in the east wall—the wall adjacent to the laundry room—were a pair of rocking chairs with a lamp table between them and a tea table in front. Behind Brent's side of the desk, in the southeast corner of the room was the heavy iron-and-steel safe. In the northeast corner, between the window and the wall, was a small square table on which rested the telegraph key and sounder. Two ladder-back chairs sat at two sides of the table.

In the northwest corner between the hall door and window, Violet placed a long, rectangular table to be used for unsorted, incoming mail and papers. On the end of the table, nearest the hall door, she placed a box for the outgoing mail. On the wall behind Violet's side of the desk, were bookshelves holding numerous books and magazines relating to agriculture and commerce. A small table in that corner held the chessboard and chess set on which Violet had played so many matches with her father and with Brent. Her father's carbine rested in a rack over the fireplace.

Violet was thrilled to have a part in these new joint enterprises. She prepared a ledger book and journal for "Sutler Mercantile" similar to those she kept for the plantation, and she prepared another book as a register of correspondence. In the journal she would enter whatever telegraphic messages Brent indicated and would record quotations of commodity prices from the newspapers.

Almost immediately Brent's mercantile business began to pick up, though the crops were suffering from drought and insects. The fourth hoeing of the cotton ended about the last of July, but under the circumstances Violet decided that there should be another hoeing from the first to the middle of August.

The days of mid-August were frightfully hot. The sun poured down relentlessly with the fierce, scorching heat of the dog days. It was steaming in the swamps, baking in the sandhills, and broiling in the cotton fields. Fabian and Little Josh made almost continuous rounds in driving Beau and the spring wagon with jugs of cool water out to the workers in the fields.

With September came the harvest—first the second cutting of hay and the cutting of the new crop of clover grown in the oat field. Most of this cutting was bailed for market. Then came the corn. The corn crop had done poorly, and all of it would be needed on the plantation—some shucked and stored for the horses and mules, some shucked and shelled and cracked for the poultry, and some shucked and shelled and ground for the kitchens. October was for cotton picking, ginning, bailing, and hauling to market. The newly installed Ellison gin was working smoothly. Some improvement in the weather, and the extra hoeing, had brought the total cotton yield up to 225 pounds to the acre, or a total of three hundred bales.

All the wagons, each carrying five or six bales, joined the long lines at the cotton market in Sumter where the cotton was bringing ten cents a pound. But Brent found that by hauling it to Manchester and hiring boats to carry it down Beach Creek and Shanks Creek and the Wateree and Santee Rivers, he could pay the transportation costs to Charleston and clear an extra two cents a pound. He had found an old boatman still willing to operate "match boats"—boats made to nestle so that they could be returned as one craft without having to pay tolls at the locks. These boats, propelled by long poles with metal point and a hook above the point for catching snags and limbs, could carry 125 bales of cotton.

"I'm proud you've found a better way to market," Violet said one afternoon as they sat at their office desks reviewing matters. "That single move, to use boats, netted us an additional nine hundred dollars."

Brent smiled and answered, "Yes, I'm glad for that, but we can do better once we get our communication system fully operational. And the railroad, I hate to see that damned railroad going across our front lawn, but when it gets into operation it should give us a big advantage in shipping out cotton. I wonder why they haven't done much work on it."

"I've heard that 'they' said it would be operating by the end of summer, but they've done nothing since they put up the telegraph. I don't know why, but I've not been sorry. I worry about the children and all."

"They've spent more effort at selling stocks and bonds than at laying track, but I suspect they may get started building again pretty soon just so they can qualify for more money from the state." He frowned as he continued, "I worry about the children, too. We're just going to have to make sure that they understand they are not to go anywhere near the tracks, and we've got to have someone watching them—always. I don't know what else we can do, do you?"

"No, that's just about it," she agreed.

Even as the cotton picking was ending, Violet, in November, gave orders to Leo to plow one of the two-hundred acre cotton fields and to sow winter wheat.

Christmas that year, as always was a time of nostalgia and sadness and gladness, but it did have special meaning, and the gladness exceeded the sadness for this was Brent's first Christmas with the family in four years.

The big event of Christmas was the payment of all the workers for their share in the year's crops. Violet had kept careful records of everyone's days of work and of the income from the crops. All of the corn—about eight bushels to the acre—and the oats remained on the plantation. The two hundred bales of cotton sold at Sumter brought $9,000, and the hundred bales shipped to Charleston brought another $5,400. One-third of the hay was stored, but the remainder of two hundred tons brought a surprising forty dollars a ton, for another $8,000. This brought the total from the cash crops to $22,400. Retaining $1,400 for additional cost of food for the workers, $21,000 remained, of which one-third or $7,000 was to be divided among the workers.

This meant that an average share for a full-time worker would be $70. Leo, of course, would get two shares, the foremen would get a share and a half, as would the chief for the household servants. Young workers would get half-shares, and several workers would have deductions on account of absence.

When Violet handed out the money to each worker on Christmas afternoon, they began singing and dancing and running around in circles. They never had seen that much money before in their lives. Some declared this another "day o' jubilo," and immediately ran off to town to spend it as fast as they could.

The following week was a continuous holiday. Violet told Leo that he could use a couple of the wagons to carry workers and their families to and from Sumter, but many did not want to wait for that and they took off on foot.

By the end of the week most of them had returned to their cottages, but they had been on a spending spree. They were wearing new clothes, and they bought all kinds of things for their cabins. Leo reported that about a dozen of them had left for good—some were paying fifty dollars an acre for land to have their own little farms. Nearly all had exhausted all their funds—a year's earnings in five days. But not all—Rachel had seen to it that Leo spent prudently, and she saved all of her own earnings. Mammy did not want to go anywhere just now, though she did have Evelina and Ellie buy a few things for her. Jarvis proudly replaced the silver watch that Potter's raiders had stolen from him, but he held on to most of his earnings, as did Aaron and Fabian, Aunt Beulah and Uncle Job, and Hattie.

One problem of all this was that hardly enough workers remained in place to look after the animals during these days. Leo and Rachel themselves, as well as Fabian and Aaron, had to take turns at milking and feeding until the workers got back to their places. Leo, never a complainer, had said to Violet in disgust, "Miz Violet, sumpin' gotta be done 'bout dese peop'l gwine off an' not takin' 'sponsbilitee fo' dis place. Ya bin so good ta ebberbudy. Lawdy, dey like chilluns. Ussan ain't nebber had no trub'l like dis durin' Chrismus week w'en de Major livin' an' dere alway hep 'roun heah. Ah tink all dis monee done gone ta dere head. Ain't no 'cuse fo' dis kind uf buhavior." Mammy and Evelina and Rachel had all made similar comments to Violet.

On Saturday, Violet and Brent went in to Sumter to the bank to pay off the crop lien and make a deposit and to do a little shopping of their own. Before returning home they stopped in to see Victor Shelby.

He greeted them with a hearty, "Well, hello, how is everything with you all?"

"We've had a very good year, especially with Brent back," Violet answered with a wide smile that showed off her white, even teeth and brought the hint of a dimple to her cheek. She extended her hand in greeting.

"Yes, Commodore," Shelby said, with a twinkle in his eyes, "have you readjusted to the life of a landlubber?" He shook hands with Brent.

In answer Brent grinned and answered, "Almost, Victor, almost."

"We've just finished our first year with all the workers back, and we were able to pay them seventy dollars a share," Violet told Shelby, with pride evident in her voice.

Shelby brought his hands together in a clap and exclaimed with genuine pleasure, "That is splendid, yes, splendid, indeed. I thought that must be the case when so many of your workers poured into Sumter to spend their earnings. I must say you've done much better than some of the others have been doing." He glanced at Violet.

"How? What do you mean?" she asked.

"Well, Violet, you...of course...know Blake Farley, on your Old Place—"

"Oh, lordy, now what has that Scalawag done?"

Shelby grinned derisively. "Well, you know he divided the place up into twenty acre farms and rented each to a freed slave and family. He insisted that they grow nothing but cotton. Then he required all of them to buy their seed and supplies at his store on credit—against a lien on the crops. His arrangement was for them to get one-half of their crops, but they also had to pay one-half of the expenses. After they had paid their bills at Farley's store, seven of them ended up with total earnings of $4.51 to $8.15 for their year's work. The other thirteen ended up in the hole, still owing amounts that varied from two dollars to seventy-five dollars."

"Sounds like Farley. Still, I can't help but feel sorry for his workers," remarked Violet.

"And there are lots of other Scalawags doing the same thing—certainly an embarrassment to the true Southerner, the true South Carolinian. People such as Farley are a blight on our good state."

A thoughtful look appeared on Brent's face and he said, "My dear, that may be a fertile source to replace some of our workers."

"Ha, you may be right," Violet agreed, a glitter in her eyes. She looked at Shelby quickly.

He held up his hand, palm out, declaring, "I have heard nothing, nothing at all."

On returning to Fair Oaks, Violet and Brent immediately went to see Leo in his house. Violet asked, "Leo, do you know any of the freed slaves who are working on our Old Place for Mr. Farley?"

"Yassum, Miz Violet, ah kno' some, an' dey ain't happee. Dey wuk hard buh dey ain't got no monee fo' dere hard wuk. Dey heah 'bout ussan gittin' so much fo' ya heah. Dey glad fo' ussan, buh dey ain't happee wif Massuh Farlee, no ma'am, an' dere be udders at udder place whar dey wuk twentee acre fo' de ownuh, an' dey dinnah mek nothin' fo' de whole y'ar. Tan't righ'."

"Leo," Brent put in, "do you suppose you could have Henry and Avery walk over there—be very careful that Mr. Farley is not there—and ask them if they would like to come and work at Fair Oaks, to take the place of the ones who left?"

Leo's eyes lit up. "Ah sho' nuf will, Massuh Brent, jes' leave ebbertin' ta meh. Ain't nobudy gwine heah nuttin' 'bout dis an' we is gwine git some mo' wukers fo' our plantayshun." He broke into a huge smile.

By Monday, eight families had moved into vacated cottages. Late that afternoon a couple of those who had left returned, and Leo let them stay, but he announced that if any others returned it was too late, and they could apply to Mr. Farley. Leo knew the plantation grapevine would spread the news and that next year the workers would think twice before leaving.

It was New Year's Eve. Festivities at Fair Oaks were minimal, and Violet and Brent were glad to get up to their bedroom shortly after midnight. He sat in his rocking chair and pulled Violet onto his lap.

"It's been a wonderful year in spite of everything," he said.

"Oh, Brent, it has, mainly because you're back. I missed you all the time, but it was especially bad at Christmas. And the children were growing so fast, and I knew you were having to miss priceless moments with them. But now you're back—back to stay. And it's just wonderful that we can work as partners, as a team. And, oh, Brent, my sweetheart, I do love you so much," she whispered, her melodious voice taking on a husky timbre.

"My beautiful wife, I love you more each day," he said softly, kissing the tip of her nose and then her eyes, and then he added, "or, as the French would say, 'Je t'aime mas que hier, mais moins que demain."

"What a wonderful saying, and that's exactly how I feel about you. And without you, when you're away, I feel incomplete." Her fingers lightly moved across his cheeks, his chin, resting a moment on his mouth.

"I know what you mean if it's anything like the way I feel," he said, kissing each small ear.

"Yes," she went on, "it takes both to make a good partnership—a good marriage—in fact it takes both to make one whole, or as we might put it, 'one plus one equals one."

"That's it exactly! One plus one equals one," he said, and then after a brief pause he added, "and two less one equals none."

"Two less one equals none," she repeated softly, as he kissed her again, this time deeply and with intense emotion.

Chapter 28

Reoccupation

1867-1868

"Anything interesting?" Violet asked as Brent walked into the plantation office on returning from his ride into Sumter to pick up the mail and newspapers.

It was a bleak day in early January. Brent tossed the mail on the table, took off his felt hat and his great coat and took a rocking chair in front of the fireplace. Holding out his hands toward the fire, he answered, "No, not much, except a letter from Victor Shelby...there, on top of everything."

Violet took the envelope and tore it open. Her eyes darted quickly down the single sheet. "Oh, Brent!" she exclaimed delightedly, "Shelby thinks we can recover for the cotton that that damned Farley stole!"

"That is good news, isn't it? How much cotton did he take? You told me, but I've forgotten." he asked, rubbing his chilled hands together.

"We had hidden forty-eight bales in the woods. Farley claimed it was cotton hidden by agents of the Confederate government in an effort to save something to prolong the War, and he was seizing it for the U.S. Treasury. When I told him that it was put there by us, not by any agents, he asked for proof that it was ours. Of course I had no proof other than our word—which he wasn't about to accept," she explained indignantly.

"What a scoundrel! I wonder how much he kept for himself."

"Victor Shelby says that the courts have ruled that those seizures of private property were not legal and the owners should be compensated."

"Violet, I don't suppose you insisted on getting a receipt showing the amount of cotton he was seizing?"

"Oh, Brent, of course I did. I remembered that Daddy always made sure to have a written receipt when doing business with buyers. I think that I should go right into Sumter tomorrow and take Shelby my receipt."

"I'll go with you," he said.

Early the next day Aaron hitched Beau to the buggy, and Brent took the reins. The morning was clear and crisp and sunny, but Violet felt the chill of the January air and sat close to Brent, drawing warmth from his body. She was excited about the possibility of being reimbursed for the cotton. The arbitrary seizure had been irritating her like a persistent pebble in her shoe ever since that day.

At Shelby's office Brent secured the horse at the hitching post, and he and Violet entered the office. When his secretary informed Shelby that the Sutlers were waiting to see him, he hastened into the outer office to greet them cordially and invite them into his private office. Violet told him they had received his letter about the cotton seizures and had brought him the receipt for the cotton taken. When Violet showed Shelby her receipt, a scowl appeared on his face as he read it. "I already have made inquiries of Blake Farley," he told them, "and he shows only twenty-four bales turned over to the U.S. Government. Your receipt shows forty-eight bales taken from Fair Oaks."

"That scoundrel!" Brent exclaimed heatedly, "he stole twenty-four bales for himself and still got his big percentage from the Government."

Shelby replied in his usual calm manner, "Well, we'll see about that. There will be no problem in recovering from the Government for the twenty-four bales. If Farley doesn't fork over we'll sue him, and in addition to that we'll threaten him with a criminal charge of grand larceny."

"Good!" Violet and Brent answered at once. Violet went on to add, "Let's do it."

"Leave everything to me. I think we can settle it without going to court. If you will sign a power of attorney for me for this purpose, I'll get the refunds and deposit them to your account."

"Gladly," Violet answered, as she moved to sign, "and make the deposit less your fee. What will that be?"

"Does ten percent seem fair?"

"Very fair, and we appreciate all you've done for us."

"You know I'm always glad to do what I can to help you. It's the least I can do for my old friend, the Major." A kindly smile lit up his face as he concluded, "Your refund, less the fee, should amount to $1,944. I'll send a note to you when it's settled."

As they drove home Violet hugged Brent's arm and said happily, "Well, that's a welcome windfall, isn't it? I had tried to put all that out of my mind, figuring it was a total loss, but I'll have to admit that it's been eating at me."

"Indeed it is a welcome munificence, my Love, and now...may I make a suggestion?" he asked, glancing sideways at her.

She caught his glance and answered teasingly, "Oh, you have figured out how to spend it already, I suppose?"

"Yes, you're right. I have." He grinned at her.

"What do you have in mind?"

"I suggest that we order some steam engines. Two small ones for the present grist mill and an additional mill, in the same building, and one large one for the cotton gin and one for the saw mill. Then we could carry on those activities whenever needed, with a much higher rate of production."

"Sounds interesting; go on."

"Now you have one of the big fields in wheat, don't you??"

"That's right."

"Well, with steam power and additional capacity, we could grind most of the wheat, and sell flour at a much higher price–instead of the wheat. And if the corn turns out better, sell some corn meal. And with the cotton ginned more rapidly, we could take advantage of early season prices. I can order some Wood and Mann engines from New York through Charleston."

"Do it."

They grinned at one another. Brent leaned over to give her a kiss, saying, "I knew you would like my suggestion." She said nothing, returning his kiss.

They rode along in silence for a few minutes, each thinking their own thoughts. Then Violet said, "Brent, there's another thing we need to talk about. I think we should change the way we pay our workers."

"What do you mean?" he asked, somewhat surprised at her statement.

"Well, I've given this a lot of thought. You know how the workers went on a spree after being paid at Christmas—most of them spent their whole year's earnings in a week, some even in less than a week. Now they have nothing for the rest of the year."

"You're right about that. What do you have in mind?"

A strong breeze caught her bonnet. As she secured it more tightly, she answered, "Well, now that we have a little money ahead, I think it would be better to pay them once a month—say at a rate of a quarter of a dollar a day for the regular workers, and then at Christmas give them a bonus based on their additional share of the earnings. What do you think?"

"Sounds good, but then won't there be little sprees every month—and some may fail to show up for work until their money is all spent."

"Probably, but we'll reduce their next month's pay by the number of days they lose—and double it as a penalty."

"May work, may not. I'm not sure many of them think that far ahead. Maybe they'll learn to. Maybe in the long run it'll help them to plan ahead." He shook the reins and clicked at Beau to pick up the pace a bit.

"Maybe, and, Brent, it will be better than their having no money to spend all the rest of the year."

He nodded his accord as Beau moved forward in a steady trot toward home.

Brent spent much of his time in the next few weeks at monitoring his telegraph receiver. He mentioned one day that he should have a couple of other people familiar with the telegraph so they could monitor when he was away.

"I already have determined to learn the Morse Code," Violet declared. "Did you have anybody else in mind?"

"Good, I'm sure you can do it, my Love," Brent replied. He paused in thought, and then went on, "Often a bright kid can learn it more quickly than anybody else."

"You're thinking of Little Josh? I'm certain he can learn it."

Surely enough, Josh picked up the code very quickly. Soon Brent had taught him to send as well as receive with great dexterity. Susan asked to learn, but while proficient, the novelty soon wore off, and she did not maintain the interest and enthusiasm that Little Josh did for the telegraph.

By mid February gangs of railroad workers had returned to their task of laying track across the front lawn. Again there were promises that "trains will be running by fall."

At the same time Violet was moving ahead with spring planting. This year she would put cotton in the field at the southwest corner, number six, and in number two, the north middle. Wheat already was in number three at the northeast corner, and number four would be for hay and oats—one-half for two cuttings of hay, the other half for oats to be followed by clover. Since corn was bringing such a low price she decided to plant only one hundred acres in field number one-A, north of the creek. She held to her determination to plant tobacco which would go into the hundred acres of one-B, south of the creek.

"Are you sure tobacco will grow here?" Brent asked as she prepared to leave the office one morning to see Leo.

"Of course, they used to grow lots of tobacco around here." she answered with confidence.

"They did? Why did they stop?"

"More money in cotton, I suppose."

"Well, Violet, my Love, what makes you think that situation has changed?"

"Cotton is down, and you said yourself that your new cigarettes are going to create a whole new market."

"Yes, but are you sure you know what you are doing?"

"Of course, Brent Sutler, you leave the planting to me." She smiled to soften her retort.

"All right, of course, but tell me, how much are you planting?"

"A hundred acres."

"Sounds like an ambitious start. How much will that yield?"

"Oh, how should I know...I've no experience with tobacco, but I tell you, I'm going to find out," she replied with determination.

"He laughed at her boldness, and said teasingly, "I thought you didn't like cigars and chewing tobacco."

She wrinkled her nose in distaste. "I don't. I think they are disgusting habits, but I won't mind selling tobacco at a good price—I'm banking on your cigarettes."

"Oh, is that it, well, I'll oblige you by smoking as many as I can," he said with a grin.

"Not near me, I hope!" she returned quickly, wrinkling her nose again.

He laughed and said, "Why you two-faced little operator...but I do think you look mighty cute when you do that with your nose." He leaned over to kiss the tip of her nose.

She pushed him away with a giggle. "Oh, get on out, you silly goose. I'm going over to see Leo."

Violet went straightaway to find Leo at the overseer's house. "Leo, I want to plant tobacco in the northwest field south of the creek, the hundred acres where we had oats last year."

"Terbaccuh? Yassum, Miz Violet, iffen dat whutcha wan'," he said, a bit reluctantly.

"Which of our men knows most about growing tobacco?"

"Miz Violet, dere ain't nobudy ah kno' dat kno' 'bout growin' terbaccuh. Dey all ain't kno' nuttin' 'bout terbaccuh, an' ta tell ya de truf, ah ain't kno' nuttin' nebbuh 'bout wukin' terbaccuh."

"Well, Leo, we're going to plant tobacco next to the corn, and we'll work it like corn so let Isaiah be in charge of the tobacco."

"Yassum, he do good. De seed, ya git hit?"

"No, but I'll get it this week. I just wanted you to be thinking about this."

"Yassum, ah be tinkin' 'bout hit all," the good man answered.

Brent said that he needed to go to Columbia early the next day, and he would try to find tobacco seed in the capital city. His quest was successful, and he returned with a large bag of seeds.

The next morning Violet sent for Isaiah to meet with her and Leo. "Plant the tobacco about the way you do the corn—a few of these little seeds spread along the furrow, and make the rows about three and a half feet apart, about like the corn. Then when it comes up, hoe it several times to keep the weeds out."

"Yassum, Miz Violet, buh ah dunno' iffen dis grow heah, buh we try, we try. Ah ain't nebbuh wuk wif terbaccuh buhfo' buh ah do meh bes' fo ya, Miz Violet. Ya kno' dat," Isaiah said, as Leo nodded his assurance even though a questioning look appeared on his brow.

When Violet returned to the office, Brent was waiting for her. As she sat down in her desk chair, he took his, opposite. Then, with a kind of smirky grin on his face, he said, "I thought that you would like to know that I have sold your tobacco crop."

She looked at him in astonishment, "What? Sold it? Why you silly goose you know it's not even planted yet."

"No, but you see I am dealing in futures, selling short, or as the English say, 'selling forward'."

"What on earth are you talking about?"

"I sold it in Liverpool for delivery next April—"

Violet broke into a laugh. "I was almost beginning to take you seriously, but you know even your cigarettes cannot come up and ripen in one month."

"Oh, but I am serious," Brent came back. "I'm talking about delivery in April 1868, and I got fifteen cents a pound for good quality lemon-yellow leaf."

"Next April? Why not this September? You know it doesn't take tobacco any longer to grow than corn."

Brent looked at Violet quizzically, one eyebrow lifted, before asking, "Haven't you heard about curing?"

"Curing? Oh, yes, of course, tobacco has to be cured," she answered with a knowing manner.

"And are you planning to use the flue-curing, or fire-curing, or air-curing method?" he asked deliberately.

Violet frowned, and then laughed. "Oh, Brent, how should I know? What kind did you sell?"

"Flue-cured tobacco."

"Good," she sighed in relief, "that's what I was planning to do."

"Where?"

"Where?"

"Where are you going to cure it?" he persisted.

"In the flues, I guess," she laughed. "Oh, Brent, I guess I have a lot to learn about tobacco."

He went on, ignoring her comment, "Well, Violet, my Love, we had better build one or two log barns with kilns at the side and long sheet-iron flues to carry the heat all through the barn without letting the smoke touch the tobacco."

"Right. We'll build those this summer during lay-by time." She looked at him hard for a moment, impressed with what he knew about tobacco—and she was supposed to be the planter in the family. "Brent, tell me, how is it that you know all this about tobacco?"

"I don't know. Just picked up bits of information over the years in my travels, I guess, listening to planters and buyers and shippers, reading about it here and there, seeing it growing in Virginia and North Carolina when I was up there years ago on errands for my Father on shipping business."

"Well, I'm impressed with my husband."

He took a mock bow, saying in deep tones, "Why, thank ye, milady!"

On Monday afternoon, the fourth of March, Ramey arrived from Cherry Vale Plantation with an invitation for Violet and Brent to have supper with the Friersons the next evening. "This is short notice," wrote Sarah, "but we are hoping to have a chance to review some of the serious political developments that are taking place." Violet sent a brief note of acceptance back with the messenger.

Brent and Violet left for Cherry Vale about five o'clock the next afternoon. They drove the half mile toward Stateburg and then turned left into the Frierson's lane. Violet had always admired the beautiful old house of white clapboard, with gently sloping roof, gables at either end, with a pair of broad brick chimneys at the back, and a gabled portico with four plain Doric columns at the front. Ramey greeted them at the door and took their wraps. They passed through the large central hall, and entered the west parlor where they found young Dr. Will Anderson and his wife, Mary, had already arrived and had been served hot cider to help warm them up. Sarah and John welcomed Violet and Brent with enthusiasm and bade them take a seat near the crackling fire. Sarah rang a small silver bell, and soon Ellen, her house maid, appeared at the door with two more mugs of hot cider.

"How wonderful, just what we need to take the chill away. I declare, the wind has certainly picked up since this morning," said Violet, gratefully taking one of the mugs and holding it with both hands.

Just as the mugs were emptied, Ramey announced that supper was served, and the six moved into the dining room. It was papered with a pattern of blue and yellow flowers entwined among green leaves, which, though faded, brought a graciousness and charm and brightness to the room. The velvet fabric of the dining chairs and window draperies picked up the same blue of the paper. A white linen tablecloth, embroidered with blue and yellow flowers along a thin vine of green leaves, covered the table. Matching napkins lay at each place. A centerpiece of green magnolia leaves and dried blue and yellow flowers set in a silver bowl graced the table. The tablecloth, napkins, and silver bowl, had been hidden in the swamp and had escaped the hands of the looting Yankee marauders.

As soon as everyone had been served, John Frierson spoke gravely of recent developments. "I'm afraid that John Manning was right about 'the worst is yet to come'," he said, looking around the table with a worried look on his face.

"What do you mean?" Will Anderson asked, apprehensively.

"Have you seen the Columbia Sunday paper? Not content with the so-called reconstruction that Johnson has approved, the Federal Congress has taken upon itself to prescribe its own conditions of reconstruction," John Frierson informed his guests.

"What have they done?" asked Brent.

"On Saturday they passed over Johnson's veto the so-called Reconstruction Act. This treats the South in effect as conquered provinces and wipes out all we have done up to now toward reconstruction. They are dividing the Southern States into five military districts, each under command of a Yankee major general who will be a virtual dictator for his area. North and South Carolina are to form District 2."

"Zounds!" Brent exclaimed. "Isn't that unconstitutional? The President has declared that the so-called insurrection is over, so there is no reason, no pretense, for military occupation."

"That means more Blue Bellies will be coming in just when we thought we were about to get rid of their army of occupation," said Violet, her eyes flashing in anger. "What else? More taxes?"

John answered with a sigh, "I'm sure that will come. All the states are supposed to hold elections for state conventions to form new constitutions. Negroes must be allowed to vote in these elections, while any whites who ever held any office—national, state, or local—under the United States and then served the Confederacy, will not be allowed to vote."

Will heaved a big sigh. "I can see where that is heading," he said.

John went on, "And they are requiring the states to adopt new constitutions that guarantee Negro suffrage and disfranchise former Confederate leaders. Then the new legislatures elected under that constitution have to ratify the pending Fourteenth Amendment to the Federal Constitution—which also will prohibit former office holders from holding office. If the legislature ratifies that amendment, then Congress will *consider* admitting the state's representatives to Congress. Until then, the state governments are merely provisional, under the authority of the generals."

"That's *awful*!" exclaimed Mary Anderson, shocked at what John Frierson had just told them. Her anxious look moved from one to the other in dismay.

Violet frowned and said in a dry tone, "It certainly is, Mary, and I can imagine what kind of legislature we shall get under those arrangements. We can all rest assured of higher and higher taxes."

"Is there anything we can do?" Brent asked.

John sighed again and shook his head as he answered, "My advice will be to do nothing so far as a new constitution is concerned—better to go along with our present so-called provisional government rather than exchange it for one dominated by Carpetbaggers and Scalawags with the Negroes as their pawns."

"I should say so," agreed Will.

"And one more thing," John went on, "we need to have some public meetings so that people can be informed about the situation. One already is scheduled for tomorrow at the Sumter Courthouse to consider the dire financial condition of the district. I hope you all can be there." He looked at his guests in inquiry.

"Are women included?" asked Violet.

"Yes, indeed, from now on ladies always will be included in public political meetings, even though they can't vote. Would you and Brent like to ride in with Sarah and me?"

Violet and Brent exchanged glances and nods, and then Brent replied, "Of course, we should be glad to. Thank you."

Early the next afternoon when they arrived at the Courthouse a substantial crowd already was gathering. The sounds of agitated voices signaled the disgruntled attitude of those present.

A Mr. F.H. Kennedy called the meeting to order. John Frierson led off as the first of half a dozen speakers to address the crowd. At the end the group adopted a series of resolutions and appointed a committee of two to prepare and publish an address. Their preamble said, "Our county is groaning under a load of affliction and distress unparalleled in its history, involving not only political oppression and difficulty, social disruption and disorganization of our industrial system, but stern, absolute, and pressing want of bread."

"Things are worse around here than I thought," Violet commented to Brent on their way out.

"It certainly looks that way," Brent replied. "You know, my dear, we are much better off than most of the folks around here."

Overhearing Violet and Brent, John Frierson added gloomily, "And I'm afraid they will not be getting any better for a while."

As the people of South Carolina and the other Southern states did nothing toward electing constitutional conventions as the Federal Congress had decreed, the Radicals took steps to force action. Over another presidential veto the Congress passed a Second Reconstruction Act on March 23rd. This directed the commanding general in each district to initiate proceedings for the registration of voters, the election of conventions and the adoption of new state constitutions.

Violet and Brent joined the Friersons for another meeting in Sumter one night in late April. This was a different kind of meeting. The principal speaker was General Robert Scott, head of the Freedman's Bureau in the state, and the audience was mixed, black and white. The purpose was to inform the blacks of their rights and to reassure the whites. Both Franklin Moses, senior, and junior, and a couple of other white spokesmen followed with remarks after General Scott had finished, and then three Negro preachers spoke.

The Sutlers and the Friersons found little reassurance in the whole affair.

Violet found more hope in a meeting sponsored by the Freedmen's Bureau a couple of weeks later. She and Brent were in town shopping when they happened to hear about the meeting.

"Brent, let's go," Violet said, looking at her husband.

"I think this is for the darkies, not people like us," Brent responded.

"Yes, I know, but it might be interesting to hear what they are being told."

"Oh, all right."

Truly enough, it was mostly a gathering of darkies—the recently freed slaves—that filled the court room. The speaker was an eloquent black woman from the North, Frances Ellen Watkins Harper, and she had an emphasis little heard in these circles up to now.

"Labor, work, must be your watchwords," she declared. "Now you must learn how the government works, and you must be a part of it. You must know what you are doing when you vote."

After each comment there would be a scattering of "Yassum, Yassum," and "A-men," and "Praise de Lawd," as though in a church revival meeting.

The speaker went on, "You must be careful not to use the ballot in the wrong way, vote for the people who will do the most good, don't just vote for somebody because somebody told you to. I would advise you to join the Republican Party; it is to them that you owe your freedom. But don't trust them too far. Most politicians are working only for themselves.

"And let me tell you something else. I don't care about equality of the races. And nobody should try to force equality by laws. Things like that have a way of regulating themselves. Equality will come in time.

"And the Northern states should not be making the Southern states allow Negroes to vote as long as the Northern states themselves do not allow it."

As Violet and Brent slipped out of the meeting, Violet said, "Sounded pretty good for a Northerner and a black and a woman, didn't it?"

Brent smiled and agreed, "It sounded pretty good for anybody, except for one thing."

"What was that?"

"That part about joining the Radical Republican Party. That will be their undoing."

By the end of June the early harvest was underway—the first cutting of hay, then the wheat, then the oats. Brent had the new steam engines in place, and he and Violet went out to check on the operation.

For the harvesting of the wheat and oats, a primitive McCormick reaper drawn by a team of mules cut about six acres a day. Teams of men and women followed the reaper to tie the sheaves with light wire and to stack them into shocks. At the same time, twenty men were at work with scythes and cradles. Also followed by men and women to tie the sheaves and stack the shocks, each man with scythe could cut an acre a day. Thus in eight days it was possible to cut and shock the two hundred acres of wheat and then in another four days to harvest the oats in similar fashion.

The grist mills were of the upright type, with an upper stone held in place by plaster and a lower bound by a metal band. The very quiet, smoothly functioning steam engines, burning charcoal, were providing steady and continuous power, though water power still could be used when the water was up. Each mill could turn out about five hundred pounds of flour a day.

With August, the tobacco curing barns were going up, and the church-school building in the workers' village was coming into use.

Inquiring of the Ellisons for recommendations after Sunday services at Holy Cross, Violet found a Negro freedman—one who had been free since before the War—in Sumter by the name of Elijah Jackson who had had good experience both in preaching and teaching. As soon as he saw the village at Fair Oaks he agreed to come, and he and his wife, Esther, moved into the quarters at the end of the church-school building.

Violet emphasized to him the need for all men to learn to read if they were going to be responsible voters, but the long-range purpose would be instruction of children, boys and girls alike, and looking after pre-school children while their mothers worked in the fields. Violet assigned some teen-age girls to help with this. In addition, Elijah was glad to conduct Sunday services and Wednesday evening prayer meetings for all who wished to attend.

One morning about mid-August, Violet asked Brent to ride out with her for a look at the fields. She was not her usual talkative self as she rode straight out to the tobacco field. "Will you look at that!" she exclaimed, pointing.

"Look at what?" he asked, glancing up and down the field.

"Nothing, that's what it is. Look at that tobacco."

In some rows the plants were thick, but small; in some spots the plants had grown very tall, but the leaves were very small. In many rows there was little or nothing at all.

With a bit of a smirk which Brent instantly tried to conceal, he said, "Well, my Love, it's going to take some doing to get five thousand pounds of lemon-yellow, flue-cured leaves out of that, isn't it?"

"Oh, Brent, what can we do?" she asked. The plaintive tone of her voice reflected the disappointment in her eyes.

Her voice softened his heart, but he could not keep from saying, "Oh, it isn't due until April. You have plenty of time to cut and cure."

"Sure, and nothing to cut. Oh, Brent, I know the relative advantage of barn manure, Charleston phosphate, and Peruvian guano, and I know how to plant and top and hoe and pick cotton, but I guess I don't know about tobacco. Not a thing, obviously. Oh, damn your cigarettes anyhow!"

It was all Brent could do to keep from taking her in his arms when she was like this. She was so capable and so determined, so willing to take a chance, to try something new. Instead he said, "Well, don't worry for now, prices are in our favor."

"What do you mean, in our favor? Prices are going down."

"Precisely, my Love. That may not be good for the cotton, but it may save our exchequers on the tobacco deal." He smiled at her knowingly.

"Oh, fiddlesticks, Brent, how can that be? What on earth are you talking about?"

"Check with me again later. We'll see." And he would say no more.

One evening after supper a couple of weeks later, Brent and Violet joined Charlotte and Susan on the front porch. Brent was carrying a copy of the latest issue of the *Sumter News.* As he took a rocking chair he said, "Well, I see they have completed voter registration, so now I guess the Carpetbaggers and Scalawags should be happy. In Sumter District we have registered 3,288 Negroes and 1,191 whites."

"Did they let you register, Commodore?" asked Susan. "After all, you were in the Confederate navy."

"Yes, they let me register because I never had held any office or been in the army or navy before the War."

"Good!" said Charlotte emphatically.

Brent went on, "And the ratio is about the same in the rest of the state, about two to one."

"But Brent, you know that the Carpetbaggers and Scalawags will manipulate the black voters," said Violet bitterly.

"How do they do that?" asked Charlotte curiously.

Brent explained, "Well, for one thing, they are turning the Freedmen's Bureau into a political instrument. Oh, yes, the Freedmen's Bureau has done some good in its relief and educational work, but now they are using it for political pressure, telling the Negroes that they must vote right if they expect help to keep coming."

"How can we fight that?" Violet asked.

Suddenly in an obviously agitated attitude, Leo came trotting up on his horse. He dismounted and walked up the front steps. "Miz Violet, Massuh Brent, ah beg ya pawd'n—"

Sensing something wrong, Violet rose and asked him, "Leo, what is it? What's happened?"

"Ah come ta tell ya dere be uh man, uh strange man, down a' de church-school, an' he git all de folks dere, an' he be tellin' dem tings ya should kno' 'bout."

Brent leaped from his chair, "Come on, we'd better get down there!" He called for Aaron to follow.

Violet ran after him as he raced to the carriage house, and, with Aaron's help, he quickly put bridles and saddles on Jeb and Feather. By the time Violet caught up with him the horses were ready. She jumped up on Jeb, paying no attention to her skirts. Brent mounted Feather, and they galloped out across the barnyards, across the bridge over the creek, and over to the workers' village. As they approached the church-school building they dismounted and walked up quietly so that they could hear what was going on.

Standing near an open window they could hear someone shouting, "Now you must swear to follow the principles of the Union League, 'cause if you don't you will have to go to court for lying, and then go to the penitentiary, and if you don't keep your oath, it will be reported to the President of the United States, and he will put you back in slavery!"

"It's the damned Union League," Brent whispered to Violet. Then without another word he burst in the door and shouted, "That's enough! Enough! *You* are the one who is lying! Yes, *you* are the liar! Now you get on out of here, before I arrest you for trespassing on private property. And don't let me ever see your face on this plantation again!" He shook his fist at the interloper and watched as the man, along with a companion, slunk out the door and vanished into the darkness. Brent turned to the gathering and realized they were showing signs of panic.

Violet clapped her hands to get their attention as Brent lit another lamp to bring more light into the large room. He held up his hands for a moment, and then said, "Now listen, folks, listen, everything will be all right...but don't be paying any attention to what strangers come and tell you. Just listen to Reverend Jackson and Leo and your foremen. You are free to vote how you want when the time comes, and nobody is going to do anything to you. Now get back to your singing and finish your service, and after that, go on back to your homes. Put what you heard from that fellow out of your minds." He looked at Violet, waiting for her to add her own note of reassurance.

She spoke calmly, as he had, trying to restore tranquility. "There is no need for anyone to be afraid. Everything is all right, and those men are gone. We will not let them—or anyone—hurt you. You know you are safe at Fair Oaks, and respected here. You are free and can vote and you don't need anyone telling you how to vote." She paused and then added, "Now, I'd love to hear you sing one of my favorites, *Swing Low, Sweet Chariot.*" A voice rose from the back, and then another, with the volume increasing as the workers joined in the song.

Violet found Elijah Jackson and took him aside to ask what had happened. He explained in an embarrassed manner, "Dem two men come heah, one black, one white, an' dey say dey wan' ta talk ta all de black folks."

"But Elijah, you shouldn't allow strangers to come in the church like that."

"No ma'am, ah know an' ah told dem dey can't come heah an' make speeches wifout permission from de massuh or de missus, buh one man took my arm and hold me while de udda start talking. Ah see Amos and ah nod and waive at him ta go tell Leo. Ah sorry, Miz Violet, dis won't happ'n agin."

"Good. You did the right thing by having Amos find Leo. Now, tell me, what did that stranger say to you all?"

Reverend Jackson scratched his head in thought and then told her what he recalled. "He say dat he represen' de Union League, dat all de field hands kin jine and hep support de Union. Den he mek uh bunch uf strange sound an' said dat de four sacred words be Lincoln, Liberty, Loyal, an' League, an' dat ebberbudy should 'member dose sacred words, an' alway vote fo' de Union 'Publican Pawty."

Other strange and irritating sounds were coming over the landscape before the end of September—the puffing of steam, the clanging of bells, the clinkity-clank of iron wheels on iron rails, the long whistles of locomotives. The trains were now running on the Carolina Central across Fair Oaks front lawn. Violet worried about danger to the children and smut on clothing, the fresh washing, and on the white house. She longed for the days of tranquility and quietness, with only the sounds of the birds singing, the occasional mooing of the cattle and neighing of the horses, and distant singing voices of the workers.

Brent looked into the use of the siding at Providence for shipping out products from the plantation. However, the newly gained advantage in transportation was more than offset by the bad weather and insects that reduced production, and by a sharp drop in prices, so that total income was only about half that of the last year. This meant that the workers would not get much of a bonus at Christmas time, but with their six dollars and a quarter a month and a little extra for Christmas, they would be contented.

Brent reported to Violet in late October that the Federal military authorities—the army of occupation—had confiscated $8,797 that had been raised for the remounting of Hampton's cavalry as a South Carolina militia unit.

"Damn!" he exclaimed, "we've got to have some kind of protection around here or people are going to start running wild."

The November election for the state constitutional convention resulted in a delegation of two white men, Frank Moses, Jr., and T.J. Coghlan, and two octoroons, Sam Lee and the Rev. W.E. Johnson. All together the convention would be made up of seventy-six blacks and forty-eight white men. Less than half of the white men were natives of South Carolina.

After the constitutional convention assembled in Charleston in mid-January 1868, Violet and Brent followed with misgivings and anxiety the newspaper accounts of the proceedings. They also were following with some anxiety developments in Washington.

"What are they up to?" she asked as she and Brent sat in the library before a warm fire one evening late in February. They were reviewing the Sumter and Columbia newspapers.

"Do you mean the Vindictives in the U.S. Congress or the upstarts in our constitutional convention?"

"Both, I guess, but what—"

Brent interrupted, "Oh, oh, what have we here?" He glanced up with a worried look.

"What is it?"

"Well, they've voted an impeachment resolution against Andrew Johnson."

"Impeachment? Does that mean he is out?"

"No, not yet. It has to go to the Senate for trial, but it probably won't take them long to finish the job."

"But I thought that failed. Wasn't it voted down several weeks ago?"

"Yes, in December, but they don't give up."

"What is the charge?"

"They haven't even come up with any articles of impeachment yet. They vote first and then look for a supposed reason."

"But what has led them to this point?"

"Their main complaint is that Johnson ignored their Tenure of Office Act in attempting to dismiss Stanton as Secretary of War without their consent."

"You mean a President cannot dismiss a member of his own cabinet without the consent of the Senate?"

"That's what they are saying. But the real reason is that they want to control the so-called Reconstruction. Talk about a tyrannical oligarchy, here it is. The House Judiciary Committee was very frank about it." Brent paused and then went on to say, "They gave no evidence at that time to 'high crimes and misdemeanors' as stated in the Constitution. Instead they said that the impeachment refers 'not so much to moral conduct as to official relations.' Some of them even claim that Johnson had a hand in the assassination of Lincoln."

"Why that's incredible. If they put Johnson out, who becomes President?"

"None other than the chief of the Radicals, Ben Wade, who is president of the Senate in the absence of a Vice-President."

Violet helped herself to more cheese and crackers, took a bite, and then commented, "I don't know if I can stand any more of that kind of news, but what is going on at the Charleston convention with respect to a new state constitution?"

"Oh, I suspect some of the things they want to put in the constitution will be unexceptionable enough," he murmured.

"Yes, apparently some good parts on education," agreed Violet, "and I think it's probably a good thing to make the districts counties and give more power to local officials."

"I suppose so, but don't you see what the main feature is, Violet?"

"What?"

"Negro suffrage. They are determined to grant the vote to all the ex-slaves, whether or not they have any education, and even whether or not they can read and write."

"Yes, I see that's coming, but isn't that because the Yankees are requiring it?"

"Yes, I suppose that's part of it, but don't you see, my Love, the Radical Republicans, the Carpetbaggers and Scalawags, are counting on manipulating the Negro vote to put themselves in control of the state and to perpetuate themselves in office," he answered disgustedly.

"Oh, dear God," Violet exclaimed softly.

After a few moments of silence, Violet looked up from her paper and asked, "Did you see this?"

"See what?"

"Why there's a resolution in the constitutional convention to the effect that nobody should be called 'nigger,' or 'Negro,' or 'Yankee' introduced by one of our white delegates from Sumter, T.J. Coghlan."

"Ha, I guess some blacks don't like to be called 'nigger,' though I never have quite understood why."

"I suppose it's just a diminutive from Negro. Our Southern accent no doubt tends to make that sound like Negrah, or Niggrah, but is not intended to be disrespectful." She hesitated and then added, "Though I suspect there may be some, the po' buckaroos maybe, who may change it to nigger in a nasty way. But you know, Brent, I've often heard them call each other that."

"Yes, I, too, but as far as calling them 'Negro' is concerned, I've never heard any of them object to that."

"Of course not, after all, 'Negro' is simply the Spanish and Portuguese word for black."

"Of course, so that's understandable, but then...when it comes to 'Yankee'...I can certainly understand why nobody would want to be called that."

"Ugh! Not after all they've done!" she exclaimed, making a face.

Brent laughed and said, "I guess we'll just have to be careful always to call them 'Damnyankees'."

Chapter 29

Railroad Dangers

1878

The bluebirds and the robins, the meadow larks and the mockingbirds were welcoming the first day of spring. It was a day like the first day of spring is supposed to be, blue sky with a trace of haze, a light breeze, and pleasantly warm.

The sun was high as Violet rode toward the house from an inspection of the fields. Noticing someone riding up the lane, she continued around to the front of the house to greet Leland Thompson.

"Hello, Leland, what brings you to these parts?" she asked, stopping her horse and giving him her hand in greeting.

He let go of the reins with his right hand, doffed his hat, then took her hand for a moment. With a wide smile, he replied, "Morning, Miss Violet, is Miss Charlotte about?"

Violet smiled in return, pleased at the direction of his interest. She answered, "She and Susan have gone down to the creek. They should be back soon. Come on up and wait."

They rode to the hitching posts and dismounted. Leland tied his horse beside Jeb and followed Violet up to the porch where they sat down in a pair of rocking chairs.

Leland went on to explain. "We are buying back about half of our old place, going to divide it into small farms and rent them to individual farmers." He gave a quick glance in the direction of the creek.

They paused in their conversation as an approaching train, coming from Sumter, made it difficult for them to hear anything else. All they could do was sit and watch the train. It gave a long whistle as it crossed the lane in front of them. A fast passenger train, it was quickly out of sight.

Suddenly, with a roar of the sounds of wood cracking on wood and horse hooves on gravel amidst a cloud of dust, a team of horses pulling a box wagon came roaring around the corner of the house and into the lane. With the wagon swerving from one side of the lane to the other, the galloping horses rushed pell-mell toward the road.

"It's a runaway!" Violet cried out in alarm.

"My God, it's Charlotte!" shouted Leland as he bounded to his horse, quickly untied the loose knot, jumped on his horse, and took out in pursuit. Violet ran to her horse and followed several lengths behind.

Crossing the railroad tracks, the wagon bounced into the air but kept on going without any reduction in speed. At the road the horses turned left toward Sumter, nearly overturning the wagon, and sped out of sight. When Violet turned into the road she could see nothing ahead but dust. The runaway and Leland had disappeared around a right curve in the road. Violet urged Jeb to full speed. As she rounded the curve she was relieved to see that the runaway horses had stopped, but her apprehension about Charlotte grew with each step. As she came closer she could see what had happened here. The horses had been running at such high speed that they could not negotiate the curve fully. Drifting out to the left shoulder of the road, they had encountered a large tree. One horse went to the right of the tree, the other to the left. That had brought a sudden halt to the wagon.

Jumping down from her horse, Violet ran up to the wagon. There she saw Leland on his knees in the grass, holding Charlotte's head tenderly and speaking endearing words of reassurance. As Violet came up he turned his head toward her. His face was covered with dust, and the skin beneath the dust was of the same color. Charlotte was trying to force a smile, though her face, too, was ashen.

"Is she all right?" Violet called out.

"I think so. When the wagon hit the tree she was thrown out onto the grass here." Gently he brushed her hair back from her face. She opened her eyes and looked up at him, startled at first, but questioning as soon as she recognized Leland.

"Charlotte, oh, Charlotte, are you all right? Can you talk?" asked a worried Violet.

Between short gasps of a panting breath, Charlotte managed to answer, "I...think so. I think so. Let's see." She sat up slowly. Her dress was torn at the left shoulder, baring soft white skin that was slightly scraped.

Leland helped her to her feet. Holding his arm firmly and leaning against him for support, she tentatively put her weight first on one foot and then on the other. "Yes, yes, thank goodness, I think I'm all right. Just shaken up a bit. I don't hurt anywhere."

"I expect you'll feel a few aches tomorrow though. You really flew out of that wagon fast," said Leland, as he put his arm around her to steady her and smiled tenderly at her.

They stood quietly for a few moments to give Charlotte a chance to catch her breath. Then Violet asked, "Oh, Charlotte, what in the world happened? And where is Susan?"

"We...Susan and I...were walking back toward the house from the creek when Fabian drove up with this wagon and asked if we wanted to ride. He was delivering flour and corn meal. He had finished at the workers' village and was coming up to make deliveries at the kitchens. This was his last stop, and he asked me if I would hold the reins while he carried the flour and meal in. The horses shied at the first sound of that train, and then when they heard that long, loud whistle, they just bolted—"

"But Susan! What happened to Susan?" interrupted Violet.

"Oh, she jumped out the instant the horses took off. And then they broke the reins, and there was nothing I could do but hold on to the seat for dear life. They were going so fast! And I was bouncing all about. I just shut my eyes and held on as tightly as I could and prayed and prayed they would come to a halt."

"Well, they certainly did when they came to that tree, an abrupt halt—and so did you, my dear," smiled Leland, wiping the dust from his face with a white linen handkerchief.

"Even if the reins had not broken, you probably could not have done anything," Violet said. "When a horse runs away he just becomes wild. Those blasted noisy trains!"

"I was hoping I could catch their bridle," explained Leland, "but I was not gaining very much. Then I saw them run into that tree. My heart stopped when I saw Charlotte going right up in the air and then landing in the grass. I was frightened that she might have broken her neck." He paused, and then said softly, as much to himself as to the other two, "I found myself saying a prayer or two."

"I must confess I was calling on the Lord's help as I raced behind you, Leland, but Charlotte, how did all that feel—flying through the air and landing in the grass?"

"Violet, I don't remember. I don't remember a flight through the air at all. At one instant I was sitting on the wagon seat, and in the next instant I was looking up at Leland."

Leland looked at Violet and asked, "What do we do now?"

"I'll get Charlotte back to the house so she can change her dress and maybe rest a bit. Would you mind waiting here with the horses and wagon? I'll get Fabian and Jason and a couple of the others to come down here in the spring wagon to lead these horses back and to get the box wagon rolling again. You come on back to the house then, and we'll all have a cool glass of tea."

"Of course I don't mind. I'll be glad to stay." He walked over to the wagon and examined it, then he said, "I think the wagon is all right, but the tongue went right into that tree. That spared the wagon itself. And some of the harness is broken." He turned to Charlotte and, with concern in his voice, asked, "My dear, do you feel steady enough to ride my horse back to the house?"

Charlotte's blue eyes reflected her feelings as she looked at him. "Oh, yes, Leland, and thank you, thank you for coming to my rescue."

Leland grinned and helped her mount his horse, then waved them off with his hat. His eyes followed them until they disappeared around the curve in the road.

As Violet and Charlotte neared the entrance to the lane, Susan was running down to meet them. Breathlessly she cried, "Oh, Charlotte, Charlotte, are you all right?"

"Yes, little sister, I'm just fine, but it was a wild ride and I had a great flight through the air."

"Weren't you scared?" asked Susan.

"Indeed I was, scared to death. I hope I never go through anything like that ever again!" Charlotte declared emphatically.

Violet told Susan to jump up behind her on Jeb. In one leap Susan was on the horse and asking Charlotte, "How did you get them stopped?"

"It wasn't I who got the horses stopped. They went too wide in rounding a curve in the road. Then they came upon a tree and could not decide which side to go on, so one went on one side and one on the other. I can tell you that stopped them, and suddenly. Only I didn't stop until I tumbled into the grass."

Susan gave a nervous laugh, glad that she had jumped in time to miss all that. She followed Charlotte into the house so she could help her out of her torn dress. She told her that she had to start at the beginning and tell *everything* that happened. "Wait 'til Mammy hears about your wild ride, Charlotte, she'll have a fit for sure."

"I suppose she'll always think of us as her little chicks," Charlotte replied, smiling at the thought.

Violet was on the porch when Leland returned. After a refreshing glass of tea, he rose from his rocking chair and said that he had to leave. "I guess Charlotte is still resting, but I'll be back as soon as I'm able to do so." He hesitated a moment, then took a deep breath and words tumbled out as he said, "Violet, I never realized how deeply I feel for Charlotte until I saw her in that runaway. Of course you would want to help anybody in those circumstances, but this was rather special. When I saw her hurtling through the air my heart leaped to my throat as surely as if it had been I who was flying through the air. My knees were complete jelly as I ran up to see if she were badly hurt—"

"We all appreciate your help, Leland," Violet said gratefully.

"Violet, I just never realized how deeply I feel for her." He shook his head in wonder.

"Why don't you tell her that, not me, and if you're asking for my permission, as head of the family, to come calling on her, you have it with my blessing." She was delighted with this turn of events, and she knew Brent would be pleased, too.

"I shall, oh, Violet, I shall declare my feelings, the next time I am here," he promised as he mounted his horse and rode away at a jaunty pace.

Neither runaways nor anything else could deter Violet from her spring planting. On Monday morning she was going over her plans in the plantation office while Brent sat opposite at the big desk, hatching some plans of his own.

"How do you think cotton will do this year, Brent?" she asked.

"Do you mean growing or selling?"

"Both, but God only knows what the weather will be."

"True enough, but actually I think prices will be up this year."

"Good, we'll go back to six hundred acres, fields two, three, and four. And in field six we'll have a hundred acres of corn and a hundred acres of wheat and then a hundred acres of hay for two cuttings, and in field 1-A, a hundred acres of oats and then hay, and, Brent, here comes the big question." She laid her pencil down and leaned back in her chair.

Brent looked up with that teasing, smirky grin of his and said, "Oh, my dear, what about tobacco?"

"Well, what about it? Do you want me to go out and lose another seventy-five hundred? I'll admit I made some horrid mistakes last time. Isn't that enough?" She picked up her pencil and began doodling on a piece of paper, waiting for his answer that was not long in coming. He had never chided her about the tobacco loss.

"Oh, I don't know, that wasn't a total loss. I've been intending to talk to you about this."

"That figures, but...what do you mean, 'wasn't a total loss'?"

He grinned again as he answered, "Well, my dear, we are shipping the required fifty thousand pounds on schedule."

"Brent, what on earth are you talking about?"

"That the tobacco is on the way." He darted a teasing glance at her. He loved to keep her in suspense at times like this. She looked so beautiful when she got exasperated.

"Oh, Brent, do stop poking fun at me. What have you done?"

"Well, my dear, I bought the required amount of good North Carolina tobacco at nine cents a pound, and so am filling the order as contracted at fifteen cents. So instead of losing it all, we are making six cents a pound, which should come to about three thousand dollars." He laughed aloud at the expression that came over Violet's face when she heard his news.

She was at first astonished, then excited, for her ignorance about growing tobacco and the loss had weighed heavily on her mind. "Oh, Brent," she laughed, "that's wonderful! Not as good as cotton, of course, but it's marvelous you saved us from a horrible loss." She paused in thought and then went on, "But don't you think we've had our lesson?"

He gave her that teasing grin again. "Oh, I don't know. Study these. You may do better next time." He tossed some papers to her. They were reports on tobacco culture from the State Agricultural and Mechanical Society of South Carolina.

For a while she examined the papers, then she said, "As the proverb says, 'a wise man will hear,...fools despise wisdom and instruction.' Thanks, Brent, thank you very much. And Brent, tell me, can you sell forward, or whatever it is, again?"

"Well, the tobacco people prefer not to buy that way. They like to see the tobacco in the warehouse and then bid on it. We should ship it to a warehouse in Charleston."

"Oh. Can you sell forward on cotton?"

"Yes, you can, people do it all the time. In fact the world prices for cotton and wheat are set in Liverpool."

She looked at him in admiration of his knowledge of pricing. "How can they do that?" she asked.

"By the bids that come in. It's the free market at its peak."

"Let me see here, where did we go wrong?" She studied one of the papers awhile. "Oh, in the first place we must plant the tobacco seeds in beds—carefully fertilized and watered, carefully tending, thinned, and covered with cheesecloth for protection. Then we must put the field in tilth, with hills about three feet apart, and, when the plants are big enough to handle, wait for a good rain and transplant them carefully to the hills. If dry weather returns, we must wait for another rain for further transplanting. Then we keep plowing and hoeing until the lay-by." She paused to read some more, and then continued. "When the plants begin to bud at the top, we must top them, then when suckers appear at the junction of leaf and stalk, we are supposed to pull them off, and we must watch for worms and pull them off. And when the plants begin to turn yellow, that is the time to begin cutting and curing." And she had tried to grow tobacco like corn! Well, she'd often heard her Daddy say 'Live and learn,' and heaven knows, she was living and learning about tobacco now.

"Now you are seeing how to do it. But you aren't through, there's more to be done." cautioned Brent.

"Oh, yes, I know, and I'll study this much more thoroughly and go on to study curing—flue-curing as you would have it," she assured him.

"Good. Now there is one more thing, if I may make a suggestion."

"Of course, Mr. Vice President, what is it?"

"Well, it is better to cultivate tobacco in small plots rather than in the great fields like cotton or corn. Instead of having a big gang of workers spend so many hours each day, assign each one a row or an area to be responsible for, and when he gets his part done, he is finished for the day. And you need to develop some real experts at the topping, but pull in everyone for the suckering and worming. What do you think?"

"Yes, that's a good idea. In fact, I think I'll do that everywhere possible on the plantation; I mean assign stints of work for a day instead of so many hours—like hoeing an acre row of cotton or corn, or cutting an acre of wheat, or whatever, and then when they have finished their stint they can have the rest of the day for their own gardens, looking after their kids, and so on. Pay will be at the same rate, with Christmas bonus according to total earnings and total days of work."

"Sounds good," Brent concurred.

Saturday afternoon Violet and Charlotte were working with Aunt Beulah on some redecorating in the main dining room. Violet had asked Susan to go with Fabian to see about some additional planting in the garden—where Little Josh was riding the plow horse for Fabian. Evelina and Ellie were playing with Bonnie Anne and J.J. out on the lawn. Brent had ridden into town for the mail and newspapers.

A rattling of the windows caused Violet to glance out a front window. To her surprise and wonder she saw Susan in full flight, running down the lane as fast as her legs would carry her, arms pumping, her long blonde hair flying in the wind. A glance to the right revealed that a freight train, perhaps half a mile away, was approaching the meadow at full speed.

Violet ran out on the front porch. Quickly looking back and forth she saw Bonnie Anne playing with her doll in the middle of the railroad track, twenty or thirty yards to the left of where the track crossed the lane. *Dear God! My little girl is on the railroad track, and that train is speeding straight toward her!*

Violet started running down the lane, screaming at the top of her voice, "Bonnie! Bonnie!" She could see Susan reach the track and turn toward Bonnie Anne as the train crossed the meadow and entered the lawn area, its whistle blowing. Bonnie Anne looked up and, seeing Susan, began running toward her with outstretched hands. She dropped the doll and stopped to pick it up. *Hurry, hurry, don't stop, run!* shrieked Violet's mind to her child. Holding her doll tightly, little Bonnie Anne continued her run toward Susan as Susan raced toward her at top speed. The locomotive was within a few feet, closing behind Susan. It appeared that Susan and the locomotive reached the child at the same time. As the train roared by they went out of sight.

Violet almost collapsed, but she continued running. The train began to slow, and gradually came to a halt. Violet ran around the caboose and up toward where she had seen Susan and Bonnie Anne. She almost collapsed again, this time from relief when she saw them get up from a small ditch alongside the track. Susan was laughing and crying and soaking wet with perspiration. Bonnie Anne, her doll still in her arms, was laughing, too young to understand her close call with death.

"Oh, thank God, thank God! And thank you Susan!" exclaimed Violet, tears of happiness running down her cheeks.

Just then the locomotive engineer walked up and introduced himself. "I was driving this train," he said, "and I want to tell you that was the bravest act I have seen in my twenty years with various railroads. This young lady is certainly full of courage—and she sure can run fast. Thank God she didn't trip on the ties or anything."

"Oh, she is brave, she saved my little girl," sighed Violet, still weak from the experience.

"When I saw the lassies on the track I applied the brakes immediately, but I knew it was impossible to stop before reaching them. I braced myself for that familiar crunching sound when we hit an animal or something. They went out of my sight when the head of the engine reached them. Then I looked out my side window and saw them rolling down the embankment. At first I couldn't be sure whether they had jumped in time or whether the engine had struck them and pushed them in that direction. Then a closer look assured me that they seemed to be all right, thank goodness. Praise be the Lord!" He looked up to the sky as if in prayer.

Susan spoke up, "Mr.—?"

"O'Neal, Luke O'Neal, ma'am."

"Mr. O'Neal, probably your slowing down just a tiny bit allowed us just enough time to roll out of the way. I wasn't sure we could make it. I could hear the roar of those wheels and feel the heat of the locomotive on my back."

"Well, my young lassie, I am going to recommend you for a medal. Such heroism should be acknowledged. Now what is your name, my brave lassie?" He took a small notebook and pencil from his pocket and wrote down Susan's name and address, along with the date and a few notes. He also recorded Violet and Bonnie Anne's names. Then he took his leave. He climbed into the cab and waved to the three as the train pulled away.

When Brent returned home that night and Violet told him what had happened on the railroad tracks, his face took on a dark flush and fire lit up his eyes. Without a further word he strode rapidly out to the tool shed, picked up a sledgehammer, and, without breaking stride, walked rapidly down to the railroad track. A series of fierce blows with the sledgehammer loosened several rails, and he pounded them over to one side.

When he returned to the house, Violet asked, "Brent, what were you doing out there? What have you done?"

"Done? I've done a Sherman on that damned railroad."

"Good, that serves them right," she agreed and then added, "but Brent, what will happen when a train comes along?"

"It'll jump the track."

"But Brent, somebody might get hurt."

"Serve them right."

"Not if it's some innocent passengers. There might be a little girl like Bonnie Anne or a little boy like J.J. on the train."

Without another word, Brent went out and lit two kerosene lanterns and planted one on either side of the break. That done, he returned to thank and praise Susan for her heroism.

"Any time, Commodore," she said with an obviously pleased smile.

"Well, I hope you do get a medal. You certainly deserve one for what you did." He gave her a brotherly hug.

Later, as they prepared for bed, Violet and Brent exchanged glances when they heard a train approaching. When they heard the train come to a halt and then begin backing up, they exchanged grins of satisfaction.

Early on Monday morning Caleb Duprey and Sheriff Gary were at the back door. Uncle Jarvis announced their presence to Brent and Violet who were having breakfast with Charlotte and Susan and the children.

Violet got up and started to go to meet them, but Brent restrained her. "Jarvis, show the gentlemen into the office and tell them to wait until we have finished our breakfast. If they've not eaten, tell them they are welcome to join us at our table, but I suspect they have already eaten."

"Yassuh, Massuh Brent." Jarvis left the room to take care of the guests.

Brent took his good time to finish as he took second helpings of sausage, eggs, grits, and corn cakes. Then both he and Violet excused themselves from the table and went into the office.

Violet introduced Brent who then asked, "Gentlemen, what can we do for you?"

Duprey gave the Sheriff a sly look and then responded, "We are here to seek amends for destruction of railroad property here."

"Why Mr. Duprey, what can you be talking about? Some damage to our railroads by your damn Yankee Potter that has not yet been repaired?" asked Brent.

"We're not talking about any war damage. We're talking about some deliberate destruction to our rails on Saturday night," answered Duprey, rather heatedly.

"That is remarkable, Mr. Duprey." Brent turned to Violet and asked in a serious tone, "Mrs. Sutler, have you seen anybody destroying railroads since Potter?"

"Why no, I haven't seen anything like that, Mr. Sutler," she answered in the same tone.

"Let's stop the charade," demanded Duprey. "We know there was a near accident here, and we know you probably were taking revenge, Mr. Sutler."

"You're damned right, you Carpetbagger son of a bitch," Brent blurted out angrily. "There was no reason for you to put that damned track there, right across our front lawn. Within a single week your trains have caused a runaway that almost killed our sister, and now you almost killed another sister and our little daughter, and if you don't get out of here I'll be tying you to the track!"

"Now hold on," Duprey said. "I'm sorry about the accidents, and we want to be reasonable."

Scratching his head, the Sheriff spoke up, "Destruction of property can lead to a jail sentence or a fine or both, Mr. Sutler."

"Oh, you damned Scalawag, you only help them to prey on the people of South Carolina!" retorted Brent disgustedly.

"I only do my duty," protested the Sheriff, still scratching his head.

"Mr. Sutler, here is what we are prepared to do," stated Duprey. "We have taken into account that you did put lights out as a warning so there would be no train accident. Now, you may pay for the damage, which we estimate at a hundred and twenty dollars, or you may work it out on the railroad at two dollars a day, or we can turn it over to the Sheriff here, and you can spend thirty days in jail. Now, which is it?"

Brent thought a few moments and then asked, "If I work for the railroad where would that be?"

"Right in this section," Duprey answered drily. "You can live at home, and the handcar will pick you up each morning to join the section gang for maintenance work on the track and right-of-way."

Brent shrugged his shoulders as he said, "All right, I'll do it. I've always wanted to work on a railroad." He followed the visitors out the door as though to assure himself that they really were leaving.

As Duprey went down the porch steps he cast an apprehensive glance toward Nanny, peacefully grazing on the back lawn, and he hastily shied away.

Chapter 30

Deconstruction

1868

Brent Sutler completed his first day of service on the railroad in time to take Violet into Sumter for a Democratic Party rally. The appeal had gone out, "Fellow citizens of Sumter District, arouse from your lethargy. Think of your wives and children. Let the love of them stimulate you to action!"

John Frierson was chairman of the meeting. Altamont Moses, a farmer in Sumter County and no kin of Frank Moses, Jr., was secretary, and Clifford Montgomery, chairman of the nominating committee. A series of speakers denounced the new state constitution that was about to be submitted and warned against enfranchising the freed slaves before they could read or write. Then the meeting chose John Frierson and six other men to be delegates to the state Democratic convention that would meet in Columbia this week to make nominations for state offices and for Congress and to choose delegates to a national convention.

"I'm afraid they're just going through the motions for nothing," Brent said as they drove homeward in the near darkness. The April evening was clear with a slight breeze, and a quarter moon was well above the horizon.

"Oh, Brent, why do you say that?" asked Violet with concern.

He signaled the horse to pick up a faster pace and then he answered with disgust, "You can see how the Radicals are going to control the Negro vote while denying the vote to ex-Confederates, and there is just no way to stop them until we can change that."

"I fear you're right," she responded in a worried voice.

A week later came reports of a Republican meeting in Sumter that attracted Negroes counted in thousands. When the new constitution was submitted to the voters later that month, it was approved by a vote of 70,758 to 27,228.

By the end of the month Brent had completed his term of service on the railroad. Then it turned out that he had performed so well that the railroad wanted him to stay on as section foreman.

"What do you think of that? Section foreman! And here I've been practically a prisoner working for them," Brent said to Violet when they met in the office after breakfast.

"Well, congratulations! They recognize a smart man when they have one." She smiled, proud of the success of Brent's "tour of penance" that had been enforced upon him. She paused and then asked half in jest, "What about the pay. Is it good?"

"Three dollars a day."

"Are you considering the offer?"

"As a matter of fact, I am."

"Three dollars a day is not much...and what would this do to your—our—mercantile business?" She liked their present arrangement of working together. She had missed him at the office these past sixty days while he was working off his sentence on the railroad, and she had been counting the days until his time was up. There seemed to be so many things she wanted to discuss with him during the day and not have to wait until the children were asleep and Charlotte and Susan had gone to bed, and they were in their own bedroom, alone at last. There were better things to do then than lie in bed and talk about business.

He knew what was going through her mind, so he hastened to answer, "Ah, but that is only for working half days, five days a week, but Violet, there is something maybe even more important." His voice rose in excitement as he continued, "Access to the telegraph line, openly, for sending as well as receiving, and a pass for my wife and family to travel anywhere on the Carolina Central—that is, between Charleston and Columbia."

"Oh, that does sound good. *Half* a day, and access to the telegraph line...and free travel on the railroad."

"Yes, with that and with other connections I should be able to make, it should be a great advantage for our buying and merchandising. So you see, my Love, this will be of great benefit to our business."

She had been quick to understand what this would mean. "Yes, I can see the advantages...but there's one thing—"

"What's that? What's worrying you, Violet?"

"Will that Carpetbagger...that Duprey be your supervisor?"

He shook his head. "No, thank God. It's another Carpetbagger from Ohio by the name of John Fraser, but he seems pretty reasonable, as far as Carpetbaggers go."

She breathed a sigh of relief and said, "Well, Brent, I have to admit that it sounds like you've made a very satisfactory arrangement."

"Yes, I think so, and I plan to take full advantage of it, full advantage of it, believe me."

In fact Brent lost no time in getting into action. His first move was to put the telegraph connection in a proper way, with poles across the yard, and he got batteries to boost his sending equipment. He went into Columbia one day and arranged for the lease of a warehouse near the railroad station. There he set up Cedric Johnson in a little office, to which he ran another telegraph connection. Then he went to Charleston and arranged to set up a telegraph in his father's warehouse.

On his return from the Charleston trip, on Wednesday, May 27th, Brent reported briefly to Violet, and then after supper he and the three sisters retired to the library for a game of whist. By the draw he and Susan were partners, and immediately they began to win. During a pause between rounds Brent remarked, "Well, ladies, I understand that old Johnson had a very close call in his impeachment trial."

"Oh, Brent, what happened?" asked Violet.

"The Radical Senate failed to convict him by just one vote in their final vote yesterday."

"What was the vote?"

"It was thirty-five for conviction, that is, for removing him from office, and only nineteen in his favor."

"You mean thirty-five Senators voted to remove Johnson as president? How could you say he won?" asked Susan, not understanding.

Brent smiled at her fondly. "Because it requires a two-thirds vote for conviction, that is, they had to have thirty-six out of the fifty-four votes, and they got thirty-five—after all kinds of pressure on the seven Republicans who refused to go along with the Radicals."

Thunderstorms and politics filled many of the days of late spring and early summer that year. In March, South Carolina, together with five other states, had been granted readmission into the union to be effective when they ratified the Fourteenth Amendment. State and local elections came in June, with the Radical Republicans winning almost everywhere, since Carpetbaggers and Negroes could vote, but ex-Confederate soldiers and officials who had had any previous government connection could not. General Scott, who had been serving as director of the Freedman's Bureau in the state, was elected Governor, and the Carpetbagger—Scalawag—Negro legislature met in special session early in July.

At the end of July, Brent and Violet, along with the Andersons and Shelbys, were invited to dine with the Friersons. After dinner at Cherry Vale, John Frierson related briefly his experiences at the State Democratic Convention. His conclusion was pessimistic. "It was some comfort to see all the delegates there who were thinking about the same way on the so-called Reconstruction, but there was a general climate of futility."

"Which has been more than borne out in the elections and everything else," said Will Anderson sarcastically.

Victor Shelby added, "Yes, and now that South Carolina has theoretically been readmitted to the Union under the outlandish conditions demanded by the vindictive Federal Congress, and General Canby has turned over his authority to the elected civil authorities, things are bound to get worse."

"Oh, no! Is that true?" asked Violet apprehensively.

John Frierson turned to Violet and nodded. "No question about it, Violet. First of all look at what is now Sumter County."

"Don't you think it a good step to have counties with our own elected officials and authority to tax and to borrow and appropriate money?" asked Violet.

"Yes, theoretically it could be a very good step in the long run, but look at the results of the recent election," answered John. "We got for our first board of county commissioners three men—not one of whom is a native of the county or even the state—one a captain of the Freedmen's Bureau, one a captain of the local garrison who comes from Massachusetts, and an Irishman from County Cork who came to Sumter from Boston in 1865."

"Dear Lord, what should our attitude be toward these people and toward the continuing occupation forces?" asked Virginia, looking around the table at the others with anguish on her face.

Mary Anderson responded quickly, "How about passive resistance, non-cooperation?"

"I'm not sure that would be wise," said Victor thoughtfully, stroking his chin. "I think it may be better to adopt a completely friendly attitude toward the Yankee soldiers. You know it is not their wish to be here, and you know they would rather be at home, and if we antagonize them we are more likely to make matters worse."

"And on that score, don't forget that those Yankee soldiers have good dollars to spend," added Brent shrewdly. "They can be a boost to the local economy. Goodness knows we need it."

Victor Shelby chimed in, "That's right, you know how badly we need those dollars in view of the fact that the town of Sumter has been driven to printing its own scrip just to carry on local business."

Sarah refilled everyone's coffee cup. John turned to Violet and said, "Violet, how was your cotton yield last fall?"

"Considerably down from the year before, unfortunately."

"How do you account for that?"

"Mostly drought and insects, I guess. I thought we'd get more."

"Ah yes, but there may have been another factor, Violet," he went on.

"Well, John, what might that be?" she asked curiously.

"It's what you might call 'moonlight requisitioning'."

Incredulous, Brent spoke up, "Moonlight requisitioning? You mean stealing cotton out of the fields?"

"Yes. They move into the fields at night," answered John.

Victor cleared his throat self-consciously and said, "Violet, I probably should have said something earlier, but I didn't have enough to go on. I still probably could not prove it, but I am persuaded that Blake Farley had his tenants going out at night and picking cotton in your and other people's fields, and turning it in as their own crops. Then he was taking it in for ginning and selling it at a good profit. Some of Farley's tenants had not been able to get a bale of cotton out of the little plots they were cultivating, but now they were turning in two to three bales."

"Why that scoundrel, that blasted thief!" exclaimed Violet in disgust.

"But what is worse," Victor went on, "the blacks have seen what can be done, so they are taking it upon themselves to venture out on their own at night and pick what they can in neighboring fields."

"Where do they sell it?" asked Will.

"Oh, there are several storekeepers around who are willing to buy seed cotton at a favorable price, with no questions asked."

"How do we stop that?" Brent asked.

"Good question," Will mumbled.

"Maybe we need some of Nathan Bedford Forrest's night riders," suggested Brent, "to scare the darkies out of the fields and scare their buyers out of buying stolen goods."

There was a hushed silence.

John Frierson broke in with a comment that something was going to have to be done to curb the rising waves of crime in general.

Heads nodded in agreement. Victor said, "You are certainly right about that. Look at what is happening. At the November term of the Sumter district court, just last November, the term held for the trial of Negro suspects, the jurors were dismissed for the lack of any cases. Now, this year, hardly a week goes by without a report of a Negro crime."

"I can vouch for that," Will put in, "Three Negroes were caught robbing Childs' smokehouse at Stateburg; two others were jailed for stealing cattle from James Booth; and up near Bradford Springs they carried away all of Joe Bossard's bacon, sugar, coffee, and corn from his barn."

"And isn't it frightening how there have been Negro riots in Washington, D.C.?" interjected Sarah, wiping her forehead with a lace handkerchief. All this talk of increased crime was making her warm.

"Oh, yes, I read about that, too. Dreadful," agreed Mary, fanning herself briskly.

"According to the *Daily Phoenix*, a Negro mob ransacked the home of a conservative judge there," Sarah continued. "They murdered a soldier—cut his artery with a razor—mobs threw rocks and bricks through restaurant windows, broke windows, and looted stores. Many of the blacks were carrying muskets, clubs, and pistols, but the paper said their favorite weapon was the razor. They say that one thing that inflamed the mobs was a lie by the former Secretary of the Senate to the effect that two regiments of Lee's rebel troops were in the city with hostile intent against the colored people."

"That's the worst kind of news," said Violet heatedly. "I have always been confident that the former slaves and the former slave holders could adjust amicably to their new situations, but this sort of thing is going to make it much, much more difficult."

"I, too," nodded Victor. "And interestingly enough the Negroes themselves are getting worried about the crime. A dozen of them on the Mechanicsville Plantation signed an appeal to the colored people of the county for law and order."

"Obviously something is going to have to be done about it," put in Brent.

Violet asked, "But don't you think a large part of the problem is that so many people, blacks and whites, are in dire straits and are hunting for food?"

"Undoubtedly," agreed John, "But you know this year the Freedmen's Bureau has been giving out large quantities of rations, including allowances for the whites, though General Scott has been insisting on taking liens on the crops for such advances, so next year they may be as bad off as ever." He frowned at such a thought and then heaved a big sigh, shaking his head.

"Yes, but don't you think his being assistant commissioner of the Freedmen's Bureau is what allowed him to command lots of the Negro vote in the election for Governor?" asked Mary.

"A wise observation, Mary. No doubt about it," John answered, "so now you see, we have a newly elected Governor who also never was in South Carolina before the War. In fact, he first arrived in Charleston as a prisoner of war. He was colonel of a regiment of Ohio volunteers. Later he was made a brevet major general, and in January two years ago he was made assistant commissioner of the Freedmen's Bureau for this state. His record there has been mixed—benevolent to some extent, but also weak. Heaven knows what he'll do as governor of our state."

Will Anderson spoke up, "But what about the legislature? That is what scares me."

"It should. Look at its makeup and look at what they have done during their first month in office," John rejoined. "Altogether there are eighty-four blacks or mulattoes, and forty-nine Radical Carpetbaggers and Scalawags. That leaves only seven white conservatives in the Senate and sixteen in the House. And most of them are not even taxpayers. But you can bet your bottom dollar they will be levying plenty of taxes on us before they are through."

"I dare say," responded Will.

"You may be sure of that," agreed Brent.

"I see how prominent our Frank Moses, Jr., is becoming in Negro politics. You see how he got elected to the legislature," commented Virginia.

"More amazing," added Mary Anderson, "I understand that Frank senior has turned Republican and has his eyes on the new state Supreme Court."

"Already this legislature has given us indications of what we can expect," continued John. "When they opened their special session this month they met in Janney's Hall in Columbia, and they have their eyes on elaborate furnishings for the State House, I can assure you. I understand they are replacing the old, reliable five-dollar clocks with six-hundred dollar ones, putting in six-hundred dollar mirrors to replace the four-dollar looking glasses, replacing two-dollar window curtains with new ones that will cost a thousand dollars, fourteen-dollar brass cuspidors to replace the forty-cent spittoons, and on and on. And members are given all kinds of special privileges, including free use of Western Union Telegraph."

Now Brent pricked up his ears. "Looks like there is a fortune to be made in the legislature," he said with a wry grin.

"Or stolen," Violet added.

"And then their first major legislative act, a requirement for getting South Carolina back into the Union, was ratification of the Fourteenth Amendment to the Federal Constitution," John informed the group.

"You say a requirement for getting back into the Union?" inquired Violet.

"Yes," John reiterated.

Violet smiled and said mischievously, "Why didn't we just refuse to ratify, and then we could have what we wanted all along—separation from the Union!"

"Violet, Alabama did refuse to ratify...but it does no good," explained John. "You see, we are being treated as conquered provinces. They say the Confederate States committed suicide; they remain U.S. territory, but not as full states until they have met the stipulations that the Congress laid down."

"This is plain tyranny," murmured Violet angrily.

Victor Shelby had been following closely. His face reddened as he spoke up, "That adoption of the Fourteenth Amendment was the most ridiculous thing I have ever heard of, completely illegal, completely unconstitutional, and never even really ratified!"

Violet looked at him in astonishment. "You mean an amendment to the constitution itself can be unconstitutional?"

"Yes, the Constitution prescribes how an amendment is to be adopted, and that was not done. Frankly, ladies and gentlemen, right there is the loss of all we fought for in the War."

"What do you mean, Victor?" asked Will.

"I mean that I always had held out a little hope that when the Northern people saw how seriously we took states rights, that we were willing to fight and die for them, that they might ease up a little on Federal control and domination. But this amendment puts an end to any hope of restricting Federal domination. You see in all of the first ten amendments, in the so-called 'Bill of Rights,' it always was assumed that it applied just to the Federal Government. For instance, it says in the First Amendment, 'Congress shall make no law respecting an establishment of religion' and so on. But now this new amendment says, 'No *State* shall make or enforce any law which shall abridge the privileges and immunities of citizens of the United States,' and 'no *State* shall deprive any person of life, liberty or property without due process of law, nor deny any person...equal protection of the law.' And I tell you, that section is full of mischief. By all kinds of unforeseen interpretations of those clauses, all the states may be little more than conquered provinces in years to come.

"And that is not all," Victor continued, "another section of the amendment deprives the Southern States of their leadership. Now they have put into the Constitution that nobody can hold any office, civil or military, Federal or state, who ever previously held such an office and then engaged in insurrection or gave aid and comfort to the enemies, though Congress by a two-thirds vote of each House may remove such disability. You know up to now the President has been granting pardons–Johnson has granted them by the thousand. Now Congress reserves this to themselves. People used to fear that a strong President might become a dictator, but I tell you what we are facing now is a tyranny of Congress."

"If you ask me, this is not *reconstruction*, but *deconstruction*," Violet interposed, lifting her small chin in an act of defiance of what she was hearing.

"That it is," agreed Mary, vigorously fanning herself.

Violet came back, "It looks like what Shakespeare might call 'the ill wind which blows no man to good.'."

"Well, we have an old saying," Brent volunteered, "a calm sea never makes a skillful sailor'."

"If we get through all these ill winds we should have lots of skillful sailors," responded Will gloomily.

"But I thought you said this amendment was unconstitutional," Violet protested.

"And so it is, Violet, but this Radical and Vindictive Congress pays attention to the Constitution only when it suits its purpose. Its main purpose now seems to be to punish the South. They are not interested in reconciliation, but in vengeance. Look what they have done here. They proposed the Fourteenth Amendment two years ago because some were concerned that their so-called Civil Rights Act might be declared unconstitutional. Within less than a year after the amendment had been submitted to the states, and twelve of the thirty-seven state legislatures, including all the Southern states except Tennessee, had rejected it. That meant it had been defeated, because three-fourths of the states, or at least twenty-eight, were needed for approval.

"But of course that was not the end of it. Congress took over the so-called reconstruction and stipulated that the seceded states had to ratify the Fourteenth Amendment in order to be readmitted. Now, if they were out of the Union, how could they be counted among the three-fourths needed for ratification? And in any case you can't coerce a state into ratifying an amendment. That would be totally illegal, but you see they used the coercion anyway. Without the forced ratifications of the seceded states, the amendment would not have been adopted. Six carpetbag governments, including ours, now ratified the amendment. Those who had voted yes were included in the Union for counting purposes while those not voting yes remained outside, and were not counted. During all of this the legislatures of two northern states, Ohio, and New Jersey, rescinded their votes in favor of ratification, but Congress would not recognize their change in votes."

"In other words," concluded John Frierson, "if a state earlier had voted yes, but now changed that to no, that was not recognized, but the six Southern states who earlier voted no, and now, through their Carpetbag legislature, voted yes, were counted as having ratified."

"Precisely."

"Well I'll be damned," Brent exclaimed, without any apology to the ladies for his language.

Chapter 31

Night Riders

1868

"Well, it appears that old Grant is sure to win the election this year and be the next U.S. President," Brent remarked as he and Violet and Charlotte and Susan sat down for supper one evening in late October. They had stayed longer than originally planned in Sumter that afternoon and were eating later than usual. The little ones had already been fed. Evelina had taken the children upstairs to bathe and get them ready for bed.

"I suppose so," Violet said with reluctance.

"Brent, will it make any difference; that is, for us here in the South?"asked Charlotte.

He leaned back in his chair a moment and then answered thoughtfully. "Likely not. He probably will be a more willing tool of the Radicals in Congress, but they have been doing anything they want to over the opposition of Johnson anyway."

After the servants had returned to the kitchen, Violet said, "Politically, I don't see how it could get much worse."

Just then Ellie entered carrying a large platter, with Mammy close behind carrying a large silver fork. As Ellie stopped at each place at the table, Mammy served succulent slices of roasted pork that Jarvis had cut in the kitchen. He was now following Mammy, serving the vegetables—stewed tomatoes, fried squash with onions and seasoned with basil, thin slices of beets sprinkled with ginger and sugar. Ellie took the platter to the kitchen and returned with a basket of hot, buttered, baking-powder biscuits and a small dish of wild honey. Mammy returned with a pitcher of cooled tea to refill the glasses.

"Though I must say," Violet continued, "our food situation here at Fair Oaks has gotten better."

Brent nodded. "Thank goodness for that, but as I've stated before, unfortunately that can't be said for many others in this area."

"Yes, alas."

There was a brief pause. Brent glanced around the table at the disheartened faces. He decided everyone needed a lifting of spirits, so he ventured, "You all have heard about George Washington and the cherry tree. Now I see in the Columbia *Phoenix* an account of Ulysses Grant and the pear tree."

"How did that go?" asked Susan, always ready for a bit of humor.

"Well, when Ulysses was a little boy his father gave him a hatchet. The boy was so delighted that he went about chopping everything in sight. After a week of this it happened that he cut down one of his father's favorite pear trees. When his father discovered this he went to the boy and said, 'Ulysses, who cut down my favorite pear tree?'

'Father, I cannot tell a lie,' replied Ulysses, 'Ben Johnson cut it down with his hatchet.'

As he spanked the boy, the old gentleman said, 'My dear son, I would rather have you tell a thousand lies than lose so fine a tree.'

"Ha! I'll believe that," laughed Violet.

"Oh, Commodore!" giggled Susan, rolling her eyes in mock dismay.

Brent turned to a more serious note. "It appears that moonlight stealing of cotton from the fields is beginning again."

Violet's eyes widened with consternation. "What have you heard?"

"Well, a band of night riders burned Robertson's store and threatened to burn Neason's if he didn't stop buying seed cotton from Negroes."

"What has seed cotton got to do with it?" asked Charlotte.

Brent smiled at her and answered, "If the cotton is being brought in loose and unginned, you can be pretty sure that it's been stolen."

"But Brent," asked Violet, "who has been burning the stores and threatening the owners?"

"Oh, I guess it's the Ku Klux Klan."

"Brent, what in the world is the Ku Klux Klan?" asked Susan.

Just then Mammy and Ellie entered to remove the plates. Brent waited to reply until they had returned to the kitchen. "It's a secret society devoted to maintaining a semblance of order, and in some areas it operates to intimidate the Negroes away from the polling places in elections."

Susan was persistent. "How does it operate?"

"Groups of men dressed in white robes and masks, with peaked caps, ride over the countryside on horses with muffled hoofs—"

"How do that do they? Muffle the hoofs?" interrupted the inquisitive Susan.

"They use rubber pads secured with leather straps."

"Well why do they dress up like that and ride around with muffled hoofs?"

Brent smiled, amused by Susan's usual curiosity. "They don't want to be recognized, and they present those ghostly appearances to frighten the Negroes."

"It sounds kind of mean to me...Are you a member, Brent?"

Brent shook his finger at her, saying, "Susan, my little inquisitor, you are not supposed to ask that—of anybody. Actually, there isn't much Klan activity around here. General Nathan Bedford Forrest started it in Tennessee, and now it has spread all over the South. In Louisiana they started a similar group called the Knights of the White Camellia, and in Mississippi, the Knights of the White Rose, and there are others."

Conversation paused as Mammy and Ellie came in with generous slices of pumpkin pie topped with whipped cream. The pause continued as those at the table devoured the delicious dessert.

Charlotte finished first and asked, "Brent, is there any violence?"

Brent swallowed his last bite with relish, laid his fork on the plate, and answered, "Well, yes, Charlotte, there has been in some places. They act as vigilantes—where carpetbagger governments don't enforce the law—and they execute rapists and murderers. In some places they have even dragged culprits from their jail cells—knowing they would likely be released soon—and held trials of their own, and carried out the executions."

"But, Brent, that's terrible—to take the law into their own hands!" Violet protested.

"It's also terrible to allow all that crime to go on without being punished," retorted Brent.

Charlotte was worried. "I haven't heard of anything like that around here," she said.

"No, not so far. Not much Ku Klux Klan activity around here apart from what I've said. They sometimes burn fiery crosses in front of people's houses or stores to indicate their disapproval of something."

"Well, I think it all sounds exciting," remarked the quixotic Susan.

Violet gave Susan a sharp look, and then went on, "But to get back to the stealing of cotton, what on earth can we do about that? We have bumper crops and bumper prices this year, and I don't want to lose any of it, not any of it."

"We may have to post some guards until the picking is finished," responded Brent.

Susan spoke up, "Look everybody, I've got a wonderful idea. Why don't we form our own little Ku Klux Klan and have a Halloween party in the cotton field and scare those thieves away? It'd be fun!"

"Oh, Susan, don't be ridiculous," reprimanded Violet.

"Hold on a minute," Brent said with a glint in his eyes, "maybe Susan has something there." He turned to his young sister-in-law and asked, "Go on, Susan, what do you have in mind?"

Susan laughed. She cocked her head to one side for a moment, looked saucily at the other three, and answered, "Well, all of us, I mean Brent and us three girls, and maybe Leo, we could all dress up in white sheets and hide in the field, and when they come to steal the cotton, we could rise up and scare them away."

"You know, Susan, that just might work—if we knew when they were coming," Brent granted.

Ever practical, Charlotte ventured, "We could hardly go out in a cotton field and hide every night for the rest of the month."

Brent nodded in agreement. "That's true, but maybe we can arrange for some spies—have Leo send a couple of men to work on the far side of the woods, near what are now the Farley farms, and see if they hear anything from those people. If we do it right, I'll bet we wouldn't have to do it more than once. The word will get around pretty fast. Have you heard about the giant that is stalking the countryside?"

"No, what is it?" asked Susan, her eyes sparkling with excitement.

"Why, it was reported in the *Sumter News* last spring. They say the giant is thirty-feet tall and walks along the roads at night. He wears an iron chain from which is suspended a blacksmith's anvil and sledgehammers, and as he walks along he makes strange noises, and he picks up rails from the fences to scratch his head. The Negroes call him the King of the Ku Klux."

"Oh, Brent," exclaimed Susan, "we could make a giant, a thirty-foot scarecrow, with sheets on poles!"

"Hah, maybe we could at that," Brent agreed, running his hand through the dark wave in his hair. Then his even, white teeth flashed as he broke into a laugh and added, "Even if we make it only fifteen feet tall they would think it was thirty."

"And maybe we could light some jack-o-lanterns for some more scariness," Susan added.

Now Susan's excitement began to infect Violet and Charlotte. All agreed that it could be done, would be a lot of fun, and no doubt would put a stop to the stealing of cotton from their field. They began discussing how they would go about this adventure, tossing ideas back and forth to one another.

"All right," Brent concluded after a while. "Here's what we'll do. Susan and Charlotte will put on sheets and hide deep in the field. Violet and I will also be covered with sheets, but we'll ride horses to come up behind the cotton stealers, and we'll light half a dozen jack-o-lanterns along the edge of the field. We'll mount a fifteen-foot giant scarecrow at some distance down in the field. The most likely field, of course, is number four, as the road runs past it. Tomorrow I'll see Leo and Henry about getting a couple of trustworthy spies out, but now hear this everyone—we must not...we absolutely must *not* tell anybody else what we are doing. Is that understood?" Heads nodded, and he continued, "Now you girls need to get all the old sheets you can find, make pairs of eye holes in six of them, get some more just to throw over the backs of the horses—never mind masks for them. And we'll need some more sheets for the giant scarecrow, and I'll cut some saplings for our giant."

It was just two days later when Leo came in with a report that a raid on a cotton field could be expected that night by a group of Farley's tenants. He spoke to Violet and Brent in the office.

"Which way do you think they'll come, Leo?" inquired Brent.

"Ah tink dey come down de railroad track ta near de road, an' den along de road ta our field number fo'." he answered.

"What time do you think they will arrive at the field?"

"Dey leave dere place jes' 'bout dark, Massuh Brent."

"All right, good work, Leo, now don't tell anybody...*anybody*...but as I've told you, we are planning a little surprise to scare them away. We won't hurt anybody." Brent explained the plan for frightening the cotton stealers.

When Brent had finished, Leo laughed heartily, and with a gleam in his eyes said, "Massuh Brent, ah tink dey be comin' no mo' affer dat!" Then he broke into laughter again. The stealing of the cotton had perturbed Leo greatly, for he was the overseer and responsible for the production of the crops. He took pride in his work and that of his helpers. He was all for the plan and knew it would work. He asked Brent if he could take part, and said Henry could help too, and maybe Fabian ought to go along to drive the spring wagon and to hold the horses. Leo wanted to be down with Susan and Charlotte, and since he was so large, he would make an even more threatening specter. Leo broke into a huge smile when Brent said he had never even considered not having him take part. And, as foreman of the cotton fields, Henry should be included, and Fabian can tend the horses, but he warned Leo again, of the necessity for confidentiality.

"Doncha worree none, Massuh Brent, dat Henry, he good man, an' he say dat w'en dey steal his cott'n dat don' look good fo' him, he be de fo'man of de cott'n fields, an' he mad at dem niggers dat rob ussan. He ain't say nuttin' t'all."

Everyone went into furious activity to complete preparations for the evening's foray. They had Fabian bring the spring wagon into the carriage house where Brent and the girls loaded sheets and poles and candles and a half dozen pumpkins Susan and Charlotte had carved into jack-o-lanterns. Susan tossed a bucket in the back of the wagon before Fabian covered everything with a large piece of canvas.

"What's the bucket for?" asked Brent, lifting his eyebrows in question. The use of a bucket had not been mentioned in the planning.

"For water in case somebody faints," she answered. "They're going to be awfully frightened when they see these ghosts coming at them." She giggled in anticipation.

Shortly after sunset, Fabian hitched Beau to the spring wagon and saddled Jeb and Feather, but kept them all in the carriage house until the night riders arrived. Well aware of Fabian's loyalty, Brent had told him about the plan and asked if he would drive the wagon. Fabian had accepted with eager alacrity. Jarvis, too, had been told, although he would not take part. He had gone over to the carriage house, and he and Fabian were whispering and joking about what was going to happen when those cotton stealers saw those ghostly spirits. At one point they laughed so loudly, slapping their thighs so hard, Violet could hear them from the house. Ellie and Hattie looked at each other, wondering what was going on. Violet decided she had better slip over to the carriage house.

"Jarvis! Fabian! Shush! We could hear you laughing all the way from the house. You know we can't let anyone get suspicious about something unusual going on. It'll spoil everything if we don't keep all this a secret."

Immediately Jarvis and Fabian were crestfallen; they had not realized their voices could be heard. They apologized profusely; even their apologies were in whispers. They promised to keep quiet, and Violet knew the good men would keep their word. She went back to the house to wait for Brent.

Just as darkness was falling, Brent, on Feather, led the way out. Charlotte and Susan, with Fabian at the reins, followed in the spring wagon. Violet, on Jeb, brought up the rear. They took the road toward Sumter and quietly moved the quarter mile down the road to the bridge over Long Branch.

There the approach to the old ford beside the bridge gave a gradual access to the creek.

They went down under the bridge to prepare. Leo and Henry were waiting for them. While Fabian stayed with the horses to keep them quiet, the others silently took the poles and sheets and other trappings for their giant scarecrow and carried them up the bank, through the gate, and a hundred yards or so into the field. There they wrapped sheets around the poles and put a rope around the neck of the scarecrow. Susan had shaped pillows to look like an anvil and hammers, and these were suspended from the rope. They put a make-shift large hat on the head and set the scarecrow up between the rows of cotton. Then they all returned to the creek to get the jack-o-lanterns and spread them atop the east fence. Henry would light the candles later.

With those props in place, the conspirators returned to put on their costumes. Brent reviewed the directions in a low voice. "Don't anyone talk when we get there," he cautioned. "It never would do to let them know there are women out there." He glanced at Susan.

"Not a word," Susan assured him.

"Now, Charlotte, you and Susan go up and hide, one on each side of the giant. Leo, you go on up with them. Lay low until the intruders approach and then suddenly jump up. After they have passed into the field, Henry will slip up and light the jack-o-lanterns, then he'll crouch down between the rows. After the pumpkins are lighted, Violet will mount her horse and hold mine and stay under the bridge until the culprits have gone into the field. I'll keep watch. Then Violet and I will go up on the left, opposite the jack-o-lanterns. That way we'll be herding the intruders back toward the road."

The women helped Brent, Leo, and Henry put on their sheets, and then, giggling in anticipation, they donned their own. Fabian would remain with the horses and wagon where sheets and props would be quickly returned and concealed by the canvas. Susan told him to fill the bucket with water and keep it handy just in case it was needed. Then she and Charlotte and Leo went up to the field and found their places. There they crouched down out of sight between the cotton plants. A three-quarter moon magnified the eerie spectacle of the cotton field and the specters among the plants. Now and then a jagged cloud glided across the moon, making jagged shadows across the field and causing the bursting bolls of cotton to blink like a thousand ghostly eyes.

The conspirators did not have long to wait. Less than an hour after the darkness had become as complete as it would be so long as the moon was up, Brent could make out figures coming down the road. Soon they were passing over the bridge, and then they turned through the gate. Brent gave three short calls of the hoot owl, the signal that the intruders were seen and Henry was to light the pumpkin faces. There appeared to be eight men.

Brent slipped back to Violet waiting under the bridge on her horse. He mounted his horse, and he and Violet moved at a walking gait to the road and waited. Only moments later, a series of wild cries rose from the cotton fields. Brent and Violet rode quickly up to their stations in the field. They could see men running helter skelter. They had seen the ghosts. The interlopers ran for the nearest fence until they realized waiting for them was a whole row of fiery heads glaring at them. They fell over each other as they turned around to run the other way. Now the mounted ghosts came up in that direction. After some minutes of wild thrashing around they ran toward the road, scrambled over the fence, and then ran screaming at full speed up the road until they were out of sight. All but two, that is. One had become entangled in brambles beside the road.

While Violet continued to ride as a ghost up and down the road, Brent returned quickly to the bridge, threw off his sheets, and came riding up to inquire what was going on. He found the man writhing in the bushes.

"Please, Massuh, please, we see de giant, de King uf de Ku Klux, an' many hants in de field...please hep me git outta chere and git goin' from dis place!"

"What are you doing here?" Brent demanded authoritatively.

"Lawdy, Massuh, nuttin', nuttin', we jes' come walkin' by, an' den all dese hants see ussan and dey come affer ussan, an' we run fas' as we can ta git from heah." The man was sobbing from fright, his eyes mammoth in his head.

"If you don't tell me what you were doing here, I'll leave you to the ghosts!"

Violet, still the ghost, rode up within view. Seeing her, the man let out a scream. "Oh, no, no, Massuh, I be pickin' de cott'n—"

"Why you thief, don't you know you can go to jail for that?"

The man's sobbing became louder. "Oh, no, no, suh, I jes' do whut Massuh Farley say. Don' tek meh ta jail, Massuh." Between the ghosts and the prospect of being put in jail, the poor man was becoming almost hysterical.

Brent got down and helped the miserable one out of his brambles, told him to get going and never come back. Brent was confident that he and his partners would spread the word about what had happened in the cotton field at Fair Oaks.

Just as the man sped out of sight, Susan came running up, crying, "Brent, Brent!"

"Yes? What is it, Susan? What's happened?"

"One of them fainted dead away when he saw the giant, either that or he dropped dead from fright."

"I'll go take a look at your casualty. You and Violet and Charlotte get the pumpkins and put them and your sheets back into the spring wagon. Tell Leo and Henry to dismantle the giant as quickly as they can and put the sheets and poles in the wagon. Be sure to tell Fabian to cover everything in the wagon with the canvas." He got the bucket of water and went up into the field to where Susan had pointed.

A few minutes later, Brent and a black man, drenched with water, came walking out of the field. Brent was holding the man's arm tightly. Violet walked up to take a look at the man.

"Do you recognize this damned thief?" Brent asked between clenched teeth.

"Indeed I do." She glared at the man as she explained, "He is one of our own workers. He's one of those we hired away from Farley to replace those older hands who had not returned to the plantation."

The man was looking all around, not paying any attention to Brent and Violet or to the conversation. "Whar de ghosts? Whar de ghosts? Whar de big giant?" he kept asking in a quivering voice.

"They're gone" answered Brent sternly, "but they'll be back if anyone—*anyone*—tries to steal cotton or anything else again at this plantation—"

Violet broke in and asked angrily, "Ben, why would you do such a thing, stealing the cotton from us? Aren't you well taken care of here at Fair Oaks? Haven't we always been good to you?"

The man looked at her, guilt in his eyes. "Yassum, ya be mightee nice ta meh, ta ebberbudy heah, buh w'en ah come heah ta wuk, Massuh Farley say he give meh extra money iffen ah hep him, an' he say he hepin' yall pick yo cott'n dis yeah, an' ussans is ta hep wif dat, an' we git mo' money." He looked first at Violet, then at Brent to see how well his lame excuse was received.

He had not long to find out. He knew he was fired when Violet said harshly, "Well, Ben, Leo and Henry will walk you back to your house. Tomorrow morning early, you must take your things, and nothing but your own things, and leave. Do you understand?"

"Yassum, yassum, Miz Violet."

Brent had been holding the man's arm during all this, but now released him. "And you go right back to Blake Farley and tell him that you no longer work here, and you are now back in his care. And if you don't do that, and if you steal any more, you will go straight to jail. Understand?"

Brent called Leo and Henry to come over and get the man. They had been standing back out of sight and had heard Ben's confession. Both were furious but controlled their anger at this traitor to Fair Oaks. Leo and Henry each grabbed an arm and led the man off at a fast pace, neither saying a word.

Brent and Violet joined the two girls and Fabian at the bridge where the latter had the wagon waiting. Charlotte and Susan climbed up on the wagon and rode home in high spirits, laughing and going over again and again the details of their little escapade. They were confident there would be no further stealing of their cotton.

Chapter 32

Valleys of Fear

1868

During mid-morning two days later Violet was in the office reviewing her crop records. It was with a sense of accomplishment and satisfaction that she noted that it appeared that this year's cotton crop would be the best ever. Rotation of crops and greater quantities of guano and phosphates had paid dividends. With the additional advantage of fair weather, the yield so far was running at three hundred to three hundred twenty pounds to the acre. And the price that Brent had been able to get was running to seventeen and eighteen cents a pound. In addition, the cotton seed was being reclaimed as never before—for oil, for animal feed, for fertilizer.

The grist mill was running continuously, turning out flour and corn meal for sale as well as for the kitchens and for making mash and bran and shorts for the animals. Yields of both wheat and oats were up. The surplus hay was bringing as much as the cotton. Even the tobacco had turned out well this year. At least the yield was nearly six hundred pounds an acre, though the cash would not come in until curing had been completed, and sale could not come before the next spring and summer.

Now she hoped that she could get another, improved McCormick reaper and other tools and machinery, and she could begin to replace the silver and china and other items that had been lost in Potter's raid. She hoped to have the big house painted again.

The one financial drain that she worried about was the rising taxes—they would be $420 this year, but promised to be much more in the future. In addition there were higher prices for the things that had to be purchased for the workers and for the household. While the plantation now was making a fair profit, she never could forget the thousands it took to run it.

A knock at the office door interrupted Violet's thoughts about plantation business. It was Sarah Frierson. Glad to see her neighbor, Violet invited her to come to the informal dining room for coffee and cakes.

Quickly it was evident that Sarah had stopped by less for coffee than for a report on what had happened night before last.

"What are you talking about?" asked Violet in response to the inquiries.

"Why that commotion that was going on up and down the road and apparently in your cotton field!" Sarah wanted to know.

Violet set down her cup, threw back her head, and laughed with glee. "Only a few ghosts were around there. Nothing to worry about."

"Well, I guess there must have been," Sarah said tartly, not seeing the humor in all this. "I tell you our workers are so agitated and nervous that we can hardly get any work out of them. They are scared to death, scared of something, I don't know what."

Violet controlled her smile and replied sweetly, "So were ours, though we have been able to reassure them and settle them down."

After some urging Violet finally explained what had happened on that ghostly night.

Violet laughed at the memory of that night and poured another cup of coffee for each of them. "Susan deserves most of the credit for the idea, I must confess. But the bigger problem remains. I worry about how Negro crime has been rising, and how it is bound to lead to greater animosity between whites and blacks." Now she sighed.

Sarah nodded her agreement. "I sense that too, and I'm afraid the Carpetbagger governments are not to be relied upon to give us much protection. John says that they are even moving to enroll a Negro militia. Can you imagine that?"

"The worst of it now is a growing feeling of lack of safety," said Violet as she offered another small cake to her guest. "I used to walk or ride alone all around the plantation, or into Sumter, and even to Columbia, without any feeling of fear at all. Even during the War, when my father was away and no other man was here, I had no sense of fear at all. We girls felt perfectly safe. During the last of the War and right afterwards when we had no horses, I walked to Sumter and to Stateburg, and all around here, too, without any thought of being afraid."

"I know, I know," Sarah agreed. She took another bite of the tasty minted cake. When she had swallowed the last morsel, she continued in a melancholy voice, "But you know the Northerners really do not care that we have become prisoners of the fear that they have fomented. They don't care if we are raped. They don't care if we no longer feel safe in walking alone about our own land or along the country roads or in town."

"Well, you know the so-called Reconstruction Acts set loose this dread—fears of servile revolt, dread of plunder and murder," declared Violet.

"And the Carpetbagger governments that the Yankees have foisted on us."

"And the worst of this, in the long run, is the development of a kind of racial prejudice that never existed before, a prejudice based on fear," said Violet with a sigh.

What I'm afraid of is that all those Yankee missionaries and teachers who are coming down here all assume the inferiority of the Negro and therefore think the Negroes must have their unending tutelage. You know you can kill a people with kindness, by developing in them a permanent state of dependency where they never will be able to get along without Freedmen's Bureaus and churches and benevolent societies to look after them."

"That certainly is a danger, all right. I have not thought of it quite that way, but I believe you are right."

"And have you noticed the Northern attitude toward Negroes? Northerners are not comfortable in their midst. They don't mingle with them. They don't even like to touch them or shake hands with them," noted Violet.

"Quite true. Rather hypocritical I would say."

"Yes, and you might say that, in a way, Southerners have a high regard for Negroes as individuals but fear them in the aggregate, while Northerners speak highly of them in the aggregate, or in the abstract, but despise them—look down on them with contempt—as individuals."

"I never quite thought of it that way, Violet, but you are absolutely right. But now we encounter a certain arrogance. Why, when you are walking down the streets of Sumter, groups of Negroes are likely to come swaggering along and force you off the sidewalk. Some of them have lost all sense of good manners," alleged Sarah indignantly.

"Yes," agreed Violet, "and talk about arrogance, did you hear what a bunch of the Negroes did at one of the little churches in the valley?"

"No, what?" asked Sarah, taking her needlework from her bag. Doing needlework always calmed her when she was disturbed or angry, and it kept her hands busy while helping to clear her head.

"Why, the pastor had just finished reading the text for his sermon when in came a whole group of darkies. They marched right down the aisle to the front, singing and shouting."

"Well, my goodness! Then what happened?"

"The pastor simply lifted his hands, pronounced the benediction, and dismissed the congregation," answered Violet.

"Well, of course at Holy Cross there never has been any need for that kind of entrance. The slaves always were welcome—"

"True, as long as they sat in the back, Sarah."

"Yes, but freed Negroes could sit with the congregation anywhere. Look how long the Ellisons have had their own pew."

"Yes, you're right," agreed Violet, and then she continued thoughtfully, "Of course another reason for the growing prejudice is simply economic competition." She smoothed the folds in the skirts of her blue dress that accentuated the blue of her eyes.

"How do you mean?"

"I mean competition for jobs, especially the po' buckras. They always have harbored a hostility toward Negroes, and now it is becoming much worse."

Sarah laid her needlework on her lap and looked at Violet with a solemn face. "I fear that is an attitude that will not soon go away, alas."

Violet toyed with the lace edging her sleeve as she said with some sadness, "I guess there is always some tendency toward prejudice between any groups that are very different, whether race or religion or historical culture."

"Oh, I suppose so," Sarah agreed, picking up her needlework again.

Violet went on, "You know the Greeks called all non-Greeks 'barbarians,' and considered themselves superior. And look at the Chinese. There is great prejudice against the Chinese coolies in California and those working on the western railroads...but then look at China itself—they are notoriously prejudiced against any outsiders."

"It's hard to say where all this is going to lead to. For now I had better get old Betsy to lead my buggy home, and get caught up with projects waiting for me there."

About nine o'clock in the evening, a week after Sarah's visit, Violet was at her desk while Little Josh worked at the telegraph in the far corner. A low growl from old Dan lying beside her feet startled Violet. She looked up just in time to see someone standing outside in the dark, looking in the window at her. She expected Brent home from a business trip to Columbia in about an hour. The train would let Brent off in front of the house.

Glancing toward the window without turning her head from her books, she saw a shadowy figure move away. Instantly she jumped from her chair, ran to the fireplace, took down her father's carbine from its rack, ran back to Brent's side of the desk, and dropped to her knees behind the desk chair and the outer corner of the desk.

Suddenly the back door burst open. With a furious bark Old Dan leaped toward the door, with Little Josh right behind him, as two unkempt Negro men sprang into the room. They deftly stepped aside as the dog and boy lunged through the open doorway; then they slammed the door shut. One of the intruders, nearly six feet tall, was wearing a tattered coat, a filthy shirt, and worn, baggy pantaloons. He was bareheaded. The other, similarly dressed except that he was wearing a slouch felt hat, was half a foot shorter. Their manner and their speech suggested that they had been into somebody's whiskey.

"Gib ussan de money from yo' safe!" the big one shouted.

"Yassum, yo' do dat," the little one echoed as both edged closer.

"Get out, you varmints!" Violet shouted, without any noticeable effect on the two men.

Quickly she raised the carbine above the desk and fired. The bullet missed. Instead it splintered the molding above the door.

Before she could even think about recocking the repeater in her hands, they were upon her. The big one grabbed the weapon, twisted it from her hands, and handed it to his partner. Then he dragged her to her feet and to the center of the room.

While the little man held the gun on her, the big one grabbed her dress at the collar and ripped it off down to her waist.

Violet did not scream, but she kicked like a mule and clawed like a tiger. She kicked her assailant in the shins and kneed him in the groin. She scratched his face until blood ran down in a series of stripes on his cheeks. This only seemed to excite him all the more. His wild eyes flashed in expectancy, and his lips curled as his panting alcoholic breath brought her to nausea. She continued to fight him off while the other man stood and watched with glee and excitement, cheering his partner on.

Just as Violet thought she could no longer summon any strength, Leo, called by Little Josh and aroused to swift action by the barking of Dan and the sound of the gunshot, ran into the room. He took in the situation in an instant. He grabbed the carbine from the smaller intruder's hands, threw it to the other side of the room, and then with one blow knocked the man to the floor. Violet's assailant turned just in time to catch a full blow on the jaw that felled him like a tree struck by lightning. Leo jumped to lift each one in turn to his feet and banged their heads together like a pair of crashing cymbals.

The big overseer did not even notice that reinforcements were arriving. Mammy with a rolling pin, and Ellie with an iron frying pan, came running in through the hall door. Charlotte and Susan, carrying a log hook and shovel from a fireplace, were not far behind, while Jarvis came running down the hall with a poker.

When the culprits hit the floor for the second time, Leo shouted to them to get up and get out, and he offered some assistance with the toe of his boot.

"Git on outta chere, ya damn'd nigguhs," he shouted, "git on, an' doncha nebuh come dis way agin or ah kill ya—ya heah, ah kill ya—git on now, git on, ya give ussan all uh bad name, yo' damn'd nigguhs!" They took off as if the devil himself was after them, as old Dan, barking fiercely, continued the pursuit.

Leo put his arm reassuringly around Violet who was crying softly. She could feel the strength of his will and the strength of his confidence restoring her own strength. "Doncha cry, Miz Violet. Ebbertin' all righ'. Ya safe. Dem niggahs go now an' dey ain't be back no mo'. Dey afear'd uh meh."

"Oh, Leo, thank God you came when you did. I was so tired, so tired of fighting that man, and I don't think I could have fought him off one minute longer. Oh, Leo, thank you, thank you. I'm sure you saved my life." And then she looked away as she added, "You saved more than that, Leo."

Leo grinned at her with a kind of nonchalance that suggested that this was only in his line of duty and nothing special at all. After all, he was the overseer, the top man, at Fair Oaks. And the Major had entrusted his three daughters to his care. He had only done what he was supposed to do, take care of Miss Violet.

Rachel came running in the back door to see if Leo was all right. Little Josh was right behind her. As soon as Little Josh had closed the door there was a persistent scratching on it. Susan opened the door, and the old collie came trotting in with fragments of pantaloons in his teeth.

Violet, lifting her dress to her shoulders and grateful her camisole had held together, was already a model of recomposure. She reassured everyone that she was all right and Leo had arrived just in time and taken care of everything. Charlotte's hands were trembling as she helped Violet tuck the dress in the straps of her camisole.

As soon as Mammy assured herself that her "baby" was really all right, she departed to the kitchen with Ellie to bring hot tea and biscuits for everyone.

Brent arrived about the time Mammy and Ellie came in with the tray. He saw Violet's dress and the faces of the others and knew something was wrong. When Violet told him what had happened, a look of outrage came over his face. Without another word, he put on his revolver and ran to the carriage house. Within minutes he could be heard galloping down the lane.

Within half an hour Brent was back. He reported that he had gone a couple of miles in each direction and had fired several shots into the air, but had seen nothing. "Have any of you seen these culprits around here before?" he asked, looking at first one, then the other.

"Naw suh, dey ain't be here befo', Massuh Brent," Leo answered first.

Charlotte and Susan shook their heads.

"Naw suh, Massuh Brent, ah ain't nebbuh see dem befo'," said Jarvis.

"They were complete strangers," said Violet, a shiver running down her back at the thought of what might have happened had Leo not arrived when he did. "We can't even blame Blake Farley for this one."

"I'm afraid this is another one of the disadvantages of having that damned railroad so close," said Brent. "Those damned bums were probably some of those who steal a ride on a freight train out of Columbia to some promising site in the country, carry on their nefarious activities, and then hop another train back or on to another destination."

Violet was alarmed. "Goodness, Brent, I hope that doesn't become a habit around here."

"I don't think it will," he reassured her. "When they get a rough handling such as Leo gave them, the word gets around, and they all are likely to avoid such a place."

"Well, I hope you all can get a good night's sleep. I'm not sure I can but I'll try." Violet turned to Leo and smiled. "Thank you, Leo, thank you. I don't know what else to say."

"Dat be 'nuf, Miz Violet. Now doncha worree no mo'," he said, taking Rachel's arm and guiding her to the door.

Brent followed Leo and Rachel to the door. He placed his hand on Leo's shoulder and said in an emotion-laden voice, "Leo, you know I thank you from the bottom of my heart, too. Thank God, you heard the shot."

"Dat be aw righ', Massuh Brent, suh," smiled Leo. He and Rachel disappeared through the door to return to their own quarters. Jarvis and Little Josh went downstairs to their rooms.

Violet was glad for the strong grip of Brent's hand as they followed Charlotte and Susan up the stairs.

Changing into their robes, Brent said in a low, but calm voice, "Darling, I'm terribly sorry about what happened tonight. Thank God you are all right. It scares the living daylight out of me to think what might have happened had Leo not heard the shot." He put his arms around her and held her close.

"Brent, I was never afraid before. During the War and since, I never had any fear of walking alone around the plantation, in the woods, anywhere. When I had to walk alone to get to Stateburg or Sumter, I never felt any fear, any worry concerning my safety. And when we went around to invite the ladies for our Starvation Party, I felt no fear for me or for Charlotte or Susan, and the ladies felt no fear in walking the country roads alone to get here."

"Yes, I understand that. This used to be an honorable country; people respected one another; people cared about one another; people had manners and respected the property of others."

Violet continued, "Then with all the things happening under the Yankee occupation and all the reports about Negro crime, I began to sense a growing fear in spite of myself. I hated it, but there was nothing I could do about it," confessed Violet sadly.

"Violet, my love, I can understand that, too. Everybody has a right to feel some fear these days." He smiled at her, his deep love for his wife showing in his eyes, his touch.

Violet looked up at her tall husband and confided, "I thought I had reached the point of absolute terror when those intruders broke in tonight." She shivered at the thought.

Brent felt her shiver. He stroked her lovely, soft hair, and pulled her close to him. God, how he loved this woman!

She looked up at him with her beautiful blue eyes, still moist with tears, "Brent, I feel safe with you, protected by your love."

He kissed her tenderly, and then kissed her again. He loved this woman so much, so very much. He said, somewhat sternly, "My darling Violet, we still must take no chances." God! If anything happened to Violet!

"You are right, Brent, we must take no chances, but we must do our best to carry on business as usual. If we're always taking counsel of our fears, then the Radicals and the outlaws have won. Then they have destroyed us in a way that the War never could."

Brent tenderly kissed her. He gently and lovingly pulled off her robe and led her to their bed. He needed to reassure her fears, and he felt a deep need to fill her with his love, his tenderness, his strength, his protectiveness, his need for her.

Chapter 33

A Garden Wedding

1869

Encouraged by the high crop yields and the good prices of 1868, Violet determined to do even better in the following year. Her first concern was to improve the yield of cotton. She had been faithful in the rotation of crops, and she had made good use of Peruvian guano and Charleston phosphates fertilizers. Now a bulletin from the South Carolina Agricultural and Mechanical Society caught her attention. It carried a report on the use of an oak leaves and hickory ash compost, together with stable manure and cotton seeds for a more useful fertilizer.

Early in January she explained the new approach to Leo and to Henry, and gave out instructions to get all hands to work on this as soon as possible. They hauled hundreds of wagon loads of oak leaves from the lawns and from the woods to build big compost piles all along the near edge of field number 6, the one directly west of the house and the meadows, which would be the first field of cotton this year. Then they hauled loads of scrapings from all the kitchens—the main house kitchen, the outside kitchen, the overseer's kitchen, and the kitchens of the workers' village—and from the abattoir, and spread these over the leaves. All this took until the middle of February. Then, waiting for some good rains to make the piles thoroughly wet, the workers spread cotton seed and stable manure over it. After that came loads of unleached oak and hickory ashes and several barrels of lime.

Then in March came the plowing. Even as Grant, in his inaugural address, was spreading chaff of hollow words over Washington, they were spreading fertilizer over the Number 6 field at Fair Oaks—about two hundred bushels of the compost plus one 167-pound sack of Peruvian guano per acre. There was enough of the compost only for the one field. They began planting, with drills, the first week in April. In the field that had received the compost they put the rows five feet apart. Those in the other fields again were four feet apart.

After the cotton came the oats planting and then the hay and the corn. The wheat already had been planted in November.

It promised to be a good crop year. Violet and Leo and Henry were eagerly awaiting the results of their compost experiment in field Number 6.

Just in time for Violet's and Brent's wedding anniversary, Carter and Jarvis brought in a beautiful partners desk that they had made to replace the makeshift desk that had been in use the last three years. It was a single unit, but over-size, with drawers and compartments and kneehole on each side. It was made of burnished black walnut, with a work surface of wine red leather with hand-tooled edging, and with brass drawer handles.

This spring Leland Thompson seemed to be showing greater concern for Glenmerry Plantation's tenant farmers than ever before. Taking advantage of the trains running from Columbia, he was coming out two or three times a week to check on things, and he always made it a point to come by Fair Oaks and call on Charlotte in the afternoon.

She was always alert to hoofs galloping up the lane, and as soon as she could determine the rider was Leland, she would race down the lane, with Old Dan by her side, to greet him with enthusiasm. He would stop his horse and dismount, and the two would walk slowly back up the lane chatting, while the horse and dog tagged along behind. They would go up to sit on the porch where Violet and Susan would join them for lemonade and idle gossip for a short while. Charlotte and Leland would usually take their leave and go out to the flower garden to sit and chat. Before they left, Violet would often invite Leland to stay for supper and take the late train back to Columbia. Noticing that he almost never refused, she had told Charlotte privately that it must be Mammy's cooking. Charlotte had just smiled sweetly and nodded her head saying, "No doubt that's true, Violet."

Often Charlotte and Leland would return to the garden after supper to sit and chat until dusk fell. At first Susan would accompany Charlotte and Leland to the garden, but inevitably Charlotte would ask Susan, "Don't you have something to do in the house, Susan? I think Violet needs you now." In time, Susan realized that Charlotte wanted to be alone with Leland, so when the time came for them to retreat to the garden, she wisely found other things to occupy her.

Then early one evening, shortly after supper, Leland made it a point to encourage Susan to go along with Charlotte to the garden while he tarried behind. Finding Violet and Brent in the library he asked if he could speak privately with them. After clearing his throat several times, he declared in a voice filled with emotion, "Miss Violet...Brent...I want to ask for Miss Charlotte's hand in marriage, and I hope that you will have no objection. In spite of all the Carpetbaggers and Scalawags and blacks running things in Columbia, Father and I have been able to do fairly well financially at the cotton mill. That, together with what I must admit is a modest income from our farms, I think should be enough to permit us a good start. At first we'll live with Father in Columbia, but I hope that soon we'll be able to have our own house there."

Violet and Brent both broke into huge smiles. Violet said, "Of course we have no objection. You are a good man, you are doing well, and Charlotte is a wonderful girl."

"And I second those sentiments completely," said Brent, extending his hand. "You and Charlotte will make a fine pair. I congratulate you on your choice."

Leland gave a deep sigh of relief and wiped his forehead. He shook hands with Violet and then Brent again, turned and dashed off toward the garden.

Within a few minutes Susan entered and said, "Leland said you wanted to see me."

"Yes, we do, Susan, why don't you sit down and have another glass of lemonade." Violet signaled Brent, looking at him demurely through her long eyelashes.

"Uh, yes, Susan.," said Brent. "Have you read any good books lately?"

"Huh?"

"Susan, just sit here and be patient for a little while," ordered Violet.

An hour later, just as a three-quarter moon was rising above the large magnolia tree by the window, Charlotte and Leland entered the room, hand in hand. Charlotte's face was flushed.

"We have news for you," announced Charlotte, her eyes shining.

"What in the world has happened now?" asked Brent, trying to keep a serious expression on his face.

With a nervous giggle, Charlotte answered, "Leland has asked me to marry him."

Susan jumped up, clapping her hands with excitement. "What was your answer, Charlotte?" she asked in a teasing manner.

Charlotte's response was to hold out her left hand for everyone to see a sparkling diamond on her third finger. There were hugs and congratulations all around.

Before anyone else could ask a question, Susan inquired, "When is the wedding? When? And where? Where will you be married?"

Charlotte laughed at her younger sister's stream of questions. "Leland and I have been talking about that. If it's agreeable with you all we are thinking of Saturday, May 15th—"

"At Holy Cross?" interrupted Violet.

"We were hoping that the wedding could be right here, in our beautiful flower garden. Leland and I have spent so many hours talking and reading to one another there," Charlotte answered, looking at Leland demurely. He was nodding his head and grinning from ear to ear.

"Wonderful!" Violet exclaimed. "The flowers will be lovely then, and that is one time this farmer will pray that it does not rain.;"

Susan pulled at Charlotte's arm. "Do I get to be in the wedding?"

"Of course, I was hoping you would agree to be my bridesmaid."

"Oh, that's wonderful!" Susan exclaimed, and then added, "Of course I'll have to have a new dress!"

"We'll all have new dresses," said Violet, laughing.

"And my Father will serve as my best man," added Leland.

"And do I get a new suit for this wedding?" asked Brent, mocking Susan's voice.

"Oh, Brent, you silly! Brent, will you give me away?"

"I would consider it a great honor," responded Brent solemnly.

Charlotte continued, "And of course, Violet, you'll be my matron of honor, and we want Bonnie Anne to be our little flower girl and little J.J. to be our ring bearer. They'll be so cute, won't they?"

"They will indeed," replied Violet, "and I can see that you and Leland have given a great deal of thought to this wedding. I'm glad you want it to be such a family affair."

"Ah, Violet," said Leland, "we wouldn't have it any other way." He looked at Charlotte with eyes full of devotion. The days of his crush on Violet obviously were gone from his mind forever. They talked on for another half an hour, making plans for the wedding. Then Brent said, "It's about time for the train. I'll get a lantern to flag it down, and I'll have Fabian return your horse to the farm." He left the room and was only gone a few minutes. He motioned to Violet and Susan to come on along with him. Leland took Charlotte's hand and the two followed behind, whispering to one another, giggling every now and then. They did not have long to wait for the train. Brent stood in the middle of the track and began swinging the lantern to and fro. The engineer brought the train to a slow stop. Leland kissed Charlotte good-bye and waved to the others as he climbed the steps, and then blew a kiss with his fingertips to Charlotte who now seemed close to tears at the separation. Brent waved the lantern again, signaling the engineer it was safe to move on.

They walked back to the house, talking excitedly about the wedding. Charlotte soon had forgotten her tears at the departure of her loved one, and was caught up in the plans.

"I've got to tell Mammy and Evelina and Jarvis and Aaron right away," said Charlotte, and she took off in the direction of the kitchen.

"Don't forget Hattie and Alma. We'll certainly be needing their help!" Violet called after her.

Susan, wanting to record the events of this day in her diary, said good-night to Violet and Brent and went up to her room.

Brent led Violet into the office and shut the door. From habit they each took their desk chair and faced one another. He turned to her and said, "As I understand it, according to the Major's will, Charlotte was supposed to get the town house and lot."

Violet smiled helplessly, "Yes, what a shame she doesn't have that—"

Brent interrupted her, "Of course, the house was burned by Sherman's men, and the land was sold for taxes, right?"

"Yes, unfortunately."

"When was that done?" he asked.

"Well, they sold it before I knew what was going on. As I understand it from the papers we finally received, I think it was the end of May, two years ago."

"Well, Violet, my love, I have heard that now the owner can recover property sold for taxes, at the original selling price and payment of back taxes, plus a penalty of fifty percent, if it is done within two years."

"Oh, Brent, is there a chance we can get that back? What a marvelous wedding present it would make for Charlotte and Leland!" She was elated at the idea.

"I'll see what I can do. There's no time to lose."

"Take the money out of our joint account."

"Of course."

"And do you suppose that we might add something to give them a start toward rebuilding the house?" she asked hopefully.

"Of course. What about a thousand dollars?"

"Indeed, yes. Oh, Brent, you're wonderful!" She jumped up from her chair and rounded the double desk. She swirled his chair around, threw her arms around his neck, sat down in his lap, and gave him a lingering kiss, expressing her love and joy and appreciation of his understanding and caring.

A week later the three sisters were on the train for Columbia to shop for dress material and other essential items for the wedding. Hattie had given them the estimated yardage for each dress and J.J.'s little suit, plus a list of trimmings, buttons, and other such items.

"I'm excited just for a chance to see Columbia after all these years. It's hard to realize that I've not been back since the burning. I wonder what it'll look like now," commented Violet. She had missed Columbia during this time but the scarred city of burned buildings and the stifling smell of smoke and smoldering embers had remained in her memory. She still occasionally had nightmares reliving that night and the following day.

"It's been longer than that for us," said Charlotte.

"Oh, yes, and I've been hoping for such a chance," said Susan.

"It's hard to believe that I am actually going to have a wedding dress," said Charlotte happily, "for I had almost resigned myself to being an old maid...in fact, I *am* already an old maid!"

Susan chimed in, "Yes, I guess you are, Charlotte. As a matter of fact, I'm almost an old maid myself."

Violet countered with a grin, "Oh, come now, you two, you know there weren't any eligible men around all during the War, so there was no chance for a woman to marry as young as they used to."

"Yes, Violet, but the War ended four years ago," rejoined Charlotte, "and I'm already *twenty-three* years old!"

"Charlotte's right. As I said, I'm just about an old maid myself," repeated Susan, and imitating Charlotte's voice, she added, "after all, I'm *nineteen*."

Violet came back, "Listen you two, to tell you the truth, I don't think those young marriages were often wise. You will be a lot better prepared to accept your responsibilities than those girls of seventeen or eighteen in the old days."

"Well, I don't care, I'll be twenty years old in July," Susan sighed at the thought of her advancing age.

Violet laughed. "Oh, fiddlesticks! You're both just too silly."

The train stopped briefly in Camden at nine o'clock, and half an hour later pulled into Columbia. The Carolina Central station was on the northwest side, adjacent to the station of the Charlotte, Columbia, and Augusta railroad. This was on the opposite side of town from the station they had used when they used to take the train from Columbia to Sumter. Brent, who had gone in the previous day to take care of some business, met them at the station with a two-seated, one-horse carriage from the livery.

First he drove them half a block up the tracks to see his warehouse. Violet swelled with pride as she read on the front of the building the words, *Sutler Mercantile Company*. Here they met Cedric Johnson and a couple of part-time workers. They returned to their carriage and Brent turned the horses into Taylor Street and headed downtown. At the corner of Sumter they paused. Here was the site of their old town house. The lot was grown up in high grass and weeds which hid to some extent, the charred remains that were still there. Charlotte and Susan burst into tears, remembering their happy days there. Even though Violet knew what to expect, a lump filled her throat and tears came to her eyes. With no attempt to ease the situation with further words, they drove on silently. Brent drove them to the office of the railroad in the National Bank Building on Main Street. The ladies felt the roughness of the ride. Years of neglect had allowed the streets to become beds of mud and potholes. They noticed that sidewalks too remained unpaved except for flagstones in front of the hotels and public buildings.

Arriving at the bank building, Brent gave firm instructions to be back at the building promptly at three o'clock. He impressed upon them that they were not to be late. Brent climbed out of the carriage, and Violet took over the reins. They said good-bye to Brent and assured him they would be back on time.

"Before we do our shopping, we just have to take a quick look around the city," said Violet. The others nodded their agreement, wondering what other unhappy sights they would encounter.

They took a circuitous route northward and westward, past the old site of the waterworks, now Sidney Park, across the Greenville and Columbia Railroad toward the penitentiary and the new waterworks, southward on Huger Street to Gervais eastward back across the tracks to Lincoln, south on Lincoln to Devine, and then eastward toward the College. Almost each new block brought surprise, sometimes of wonder and admiration, sometimes of shock and dismay. Indeed, Columbia was a city of contrasts. Many beautiful new buildings had arisen—shops, public buildings, churches—but also the scars of the great fire remained in many places throughout. In the outer areas, they saw one-room shacks that were homes to hundreds of freed slaves, and others where po' buckras dwelt. In some of the side streets, garbage filled the gutters and walkways. In others, there was no garbage. Evidently the people there did not have enough food to generate garbage. Shiftless blacks wearing rags and gunny sacks moped along or just stood or sat on the curbs waiting for handouts. Many children, even on this cool day, were running around naked. It was difficult to know whether the heavy stench hanging in the air was to be attributed more to the putrefying garbage, or to the hogs that were eating it, or to the unwashed people walking and sitting around it.

"And *this* is what they call *freedom*?" exclaimed Violet.

"For goodness sakes, wouldn't these people be better off working on the plantations?" asked Charlotte, holding her handkerchief to her nose.

"If you ask me, they were better off as slaves. At least they had something to eat and a place to sleep and clothes to wear," added Susan, looking around with disgust.

Charlotte repeated, "I wonder why they aren't back working on the plantations?"

"I suppose some of them really don't want to work," Violet said, "but you must remember, many of the plantations are no longer there. They were burned out or confiscated or the owners have had to leave and left their plantations to just run down. Many have been divided into small farms.

"Seems like the government ought to be seeing that at least these people have something to eat," said Charlotte with feeling.

"The Freedmen's Bureau helped for a while," replied Violet, "but now, obviously, they are not keeping up. The greatest irony is that the very people who ought to be helping them most—the black members of the state legislature—are simply tools of the

Carpetbaggers and Scalawags, and they are all more interested in plundering the state and lining their own pockets than in helping anybody."

Riding on down Devine Street they turned on Sumter and passed the U.S. Military barracks where the sight of Yankee soldiers at drill sent shivers down their backs.

Susan wrinkled her nose and said, "The sight of those damn Yankee soldiers makes me want to change the color of my new dress, even if the uniforms are a different shade of blue."

It was a relief when the carriage approached the College, though sadly the buildings were in a dismal state of disrepair, and the campus looked like a neglected garden overgrown by weeds. As they continued to the State House, they saw a company of colored soldiers in butternut uniforms parading across the grounds.

"Look there," said Violet, pointing, and then she added sarcastically, "those are our new 'protectors'; that's our new militia, another instrument for holding South Carolina hostage." Susan asked Violet if the State House was where she worked with the wounded during the War.

"No, that was in the old State House which the Yankees burned. This is the new one. Look carefully, Susan and Charlotte, and you will see pockmarks on the walls where the Yankee cannon balls struck them."

"Yes! I see them!" said Susan excitedly.

Even here litter was blowing all over the lawns. On the walks in the vicinity of the State House, groups of Negroes wearing fine Prince Albert frock coats and cutaways and high beaver hats, and carrying gilded walking sticks, strutted and swaggered along. Violet looked at them, scarcely concealing the disgust in her eyes. *What a contrast to the others we have just seen,* she thought, *surely they ought to care about their own people and help them more.*

Susan broke into her thoughts, asking impatiently, "Violet, *when* are we going to do our shopping?"

"Right now." She had seen enough. Violet drove directly to Gervais Street, tied the horse to a hitching post, and began looking for her favorite dry goods shop. Here again she had to adjust to changes. Her old shop no longer existed, but she found another down the street that appeared to be about as good.

Charlotte chose white faille for her dress, and sewn strings of pearl beads, satin ribbon, and lace for trim, and yards of lace for overskirt and a long veil. She selected light blue organdy for Susan's dress, and matching satin ribbon for trim. For Susan's underdress, she chose light blue faille. Violet picked out lilac taffeta and strings of matching beads to trim her dress. Bonnie Anne's dress would be a miniature version of Susan's. Little J.J. would wear a white linen outfit, short jacket and pants, with a pale blue shirt. They did not forget to purchase crinoline and new forms of webbing and binding.

The sales lady asked who would be making the dresses for the ladies. Violet told her that for this special occasion, they would be using an expert seamstress for the ladies' dresses. Their Fair Oaks seamstresses would make the children's outfits. The saleslady offered to recommend someone, but Violet said that her husband had already made an appointment for tomorrow morning, with someone highly recommended by some friends of his in town.

They left their purchases to be picked up in the latter part of the afternoon, and they left for a quick light lunch. Then they completed their shopping for slippers and large lace hats. The seamstress would add matching ribbons to the hats for Violet, Susan, and Bonnie Anne, and would form Charlotte's headpiece to which her veil would be attached. This latter would be decorated with pearls, and just before the wedding, with fresh white camellias. The two children would be wearing patent leather shoes.

They were barely on time to meet Brent. He was waiting for them on the walk. "Well, I'm glad you could make it. Did you get all finished?" he asked.

"We found beautiful fabrics and lace and trim, and tomorrow morning we'll be ready to see the seamstress," answered Violet with a smile, as Brent helped her down from the carriage. He helped Susan down, and as he took Charlotte's arm he said teasingly, "Ah, the lovely bride to be!"

Charlotte blushed, and exclaimed, "Oh, Brent, now you stop that, you hear?"

"Yes ma'am. Now come, ladies, come along with me." He took Violet's arm with his right hand and Susan's with his left as he led them up the stairway to the third floor. Charlotte followed along.

As they entered the outer office, a distinguished looking gentleman stepped out. Brent introduced him as John Fraser, now president of the railroad. He called for the other employees, half a dozen clerks, secretaries, and bookkeepers to come out and join him at the end of the room.

"Miss Susan Storm, will you come here," said Fraser, pointing to a place by him.

Susan looked around in bewilderment.

"Go on," whispered Brent, and he gave her a light shove in Fraser's direction.

Susan went over to stand by Fraser. He drew an oblong box from his pocket and opened it. Still holding it in his hand, he said, "I am pleased to present to a very special person for a special act this medal. At dire risk to her own life and complete disregard for her own safety, this young lady ran in front of a train, swept up her five-year-old niece, and jumped to safety. Without her action, the little girl, without doubt, would have been killed. Our locomotive engineer said that it was the bravest act of heroism that he had ever seen. The medal is inscribed as follows:

Presented by the South Carolina Railroads
To
Susan Phlox Storm
For Heroic Service
In Saving Life
March 30, 1867

Fraser slipped the deep blue ribbon over Susan's neck and shook her hand. For probably the first time in her life, Susan was speechless. Violet and Charlotte ran up to hug their younger sister. Brent gave her a hug and told her how proud he was of her.

Then everyone there had to shake Susan's hand and congratulate her and tell her what a courageous young woman she was. All she could muster was a husky thank you and "I'm completely flabbergasted."

After supper at the Columbia Hotel on Main Street at Taylor, where they were staying overnight, Brent said, "I think we all should take a ride to see some of the night life of the city. As they drove through the fashionable sections they were impressed at how strangely quiet were the fine houses, now repaired or rebuilt. Little merriment echoed through these parts. Driving back over to the vicinity of the barracks, they could see at once that this was where the action was. Here was the new society, black and white, ex-slaves, Carpetbaggers, Scalawags, and their ladies of all different hues. Dressed in their finery, they were parading around as a band played.

"This," explained Brent, "is what is known as the 'Gig Society', and you can be sure there's not much contact between this and the old Columbia society. And I can tell you that the women of Columbia have little to do with the wives and daughters of the Yankee soldiers, even the officers."

"I can't say I blame them," sniffed Susan disdainfully.

Friday the 14th, the day before the wedding, was filled with excitement and anticipation.

Fabian and a crew spent all day putting the finishing touches to their work in the garden. Flower beds were weeded, paths cleared, garden lawns clipped, and a wedding arch erected. This latter would have grape vines and flowers entwined through the lattice work. Hattie, with Alma's and Evelina's help, put last minute touches to the new gowns and undergarments, then pressed and hung them carefully from hooks placed high on the wall. The wide-brimmed hats were stuffed with white tissue paper and placed on flat chests.

In the afternoon, Father Wilson of Holy Cross arrived for last minute instructions and with his guidance, Violet organized the rehearsal. Everything fell into place, except it was difficult to get Bonnie Anne and J.J. to do exactly what they were supposed to do. They kept chasing after butterflies or picking flowers instead of standing still or marching when they were told to. Reverend Jackson and three of the workers who had formed a string quartet of three violins and a banjo, were there to practice the wedding music.

That evening after the children had been put to bed—not an easy job in view of their excitement about the wedding—Brent and the three sisters gathered in the library. Mammy brought in tea and left the room.

Brent rose from his chair and crossed over to Charlotte. He removed an envelope from his inside pocket and handed it to her, saying, "Here, with our love and best wishes, is our wedding gift to you." He bent over and kissed his future sister-in-law on the cheek.

When Charlotte opened the envelope and recognized the deed for the property in Columbia and the check for a thousand dollars, she jumped up and shrieked in delight. "Oh, my goodness, I never *dreamed* of anything like this. I thought that dream was gone forever! And so much money; how generous of you all. Oh, how can I ever thank you enough!" She burst into tears of happiness.

"Daddy wanted you to have that property, Charlotte, and I'm glad we were able to recover it in time for you, and we hope the money will be a start for you and Leland to rebuild the house," said Violet, with tears sparkling in her own eyes.

Susan rose and took from under her chair an object wrapped in white tissue paper. She handed it to Charlotte, saying, "I had a hard time keeping this secret and you out of the way when I was making it for you." It was a beautifully finished, heart-shaped pillow covered with white faille, scraps from Charlotte's wedding dress. The pillow was decorated with an embroidered spray of white silk roses and trimmed with narrow lace.

Charlotte flushed in delight as Susan asked, "Do you think this will be all right to hold the ring?" And then she ádded proudly, "I made it all by myself."

"Oh, Susan, it's lovely! Thank you so much. It's perfect." Charlotte hugged her younger sister with a special tenderness and kissed her on the cheek.

Just then a sound of running feet overhead distracted them. Violet stepped in the kitchen and asked Evelina to find out what was going on upstairs. She was back in a minute, whispering, "Miz Violet, Massuh Brent, ebberbudy, yo' gotta see dis!" And, with her finger on her lips to indicate silence, she motioned them to follow her.

Pausing near the top of the stairs, they saw J.J. wearing his father's silk hat that fell down over his ears so that his eyes could scarcely be seen. He also had on Brent's black cutaway that trailed behind him. Bonnie Anne was dressed in one of Violet's white petticoats, and her head was covered with a white silk handkerchief that she had secured with one of her mother's combs. They were doing wedding marches up and down the hall, and fussing about the right way to do it. The adults broke into gales of laughter. The children stopped immediately and, expecting reprimands, looked at their parents with guilt on their faces. But much to the children's relief, Violet and Brent just removed the dress-up clothes, and put them back to bed with a stern command to 'stay in bed and go to sleep'.

Saturday was the kind of day everyone had been praying for, sunny and just pleasantly warm. The air was sweetly scented with blooming flowers—gardenias, violets, lilacs, hyacinths, paper whites, roses, baby's breath, and honeysuckle. Beds of red and white azaleas and pink and white camellias brightened the borders, and rhododendrons, pink and violet, were centerpieces at the intersections of crosswalks. A hundred guests, mostly neighbors and friends from Holy Cross Church and Sumter occupied folding chairs arranged in rectangles on the cropped lawns on either side of the central garden walk. Brent's mother, father, and sister had arrived that morning and would remain over the weekend. The sisters' grandmother in Virginia, Catherine Victoria Lee, had planned to come for the wedding; however, that elderly lady had suffered an attack of pleurisy and had had to wire her regrets.

The ceremony began promptly at three o'clock and everything went precisely according to plan. On the arm of her brother-in-law, Brent, Charlotte marched down the aisle a pretty girl; on the arm of her husband, Leland, she returned a beautiful woman. The children performed their parts with unaccustomed seriousness. Bonnie Anne walked slowly down the walk, gracefully casting rose petals. J.J. followed proudly, holding on to the ring pillow tightly so as not to drop it. Leland had given Susan the ring and suggested that she take the precaution of tacking the ring lightly with thread to the pillow for security. This she had done, much to Violet's relief.

Guests mingled happily with their hosts and hostesses at the banquet and at the ball that followed. The quartet, old veteran musicians, sat in the balcony at the end of the big ballroom, and played waltzes, polkas, quadrilles, cotillions, and mazurkas.

Later, guests would argue over which of the Storm girls was most beautiful at the wedding–the blonde in light blue, the brunette in lavender, or the brownette in the white wedding dress.

Chapter 34

The Little Brown Jugs

1869

After the wedding Violet felt a lonesomeness for Charlotte that went far deeper than she ever imagined it would. The three sisters had become a close-knit family of mutual support in adjusting to the loss of their mother, and then their brother, Christopher, and then their father, in scratching out an existence with their bare hands, and in sharing the work of getting the plantation back into production. They had shared good times and bad, but now that close unit of family was broken up. Violet always knew that this day would come, and she hoped that it would, for Charlotte's sake. Yet, somehow she always hoped that it would be next year, not this.

Almost unconsciously to fill that void, Violet spent more time and attention to her children, not just playing with them, not just cuddling them, but instructing them. This took the form mostly of developing in them a sense of deportment and good manners, and of reading to them and singing to them. Violet enjoyed reading to them the stories that her mother used to read to her when she was a little girl, and singing the songs that she as a child used to sing with her mother and father.

Meanwhile Little Josh, now about twelve years old, was doing double duty in school as well as in chores. After helping Mammy in the kitchen with firewood and ashes, he would ride the horse for Fabian in plowing the garden when called upon, but mostly he would ride around the plantation with Violet to open and close gates and to take messages to foremen and workers when they were inside a building. Then Violet would drop him off to go to Reverend Jackson's school in the workers' village. In the afternoon Violet would give him further instruction in reading and writing, and then he would monitor the telegraph.

Sometimes Violet would take Bonnie Anne and J.J. to sing with her and Susan around the piano in the ballroom. Bonnie Anne's reactions to these sessions persuaded Violet that her little daughter, even at six, might be ready to begin piano lessons. A few days of instruction and practice convinced Violet that this was indeed true. Her little daughter caught on quickly and enjoyed learning to play.

J.J., at five, clearly was not ready for this. He showed his frustration by banging on the piano whenever he could get to it and sometimes would bang on the keys even while Bonnie Anne was having a lesson. When Violet stopped this with a stern reprimand and a light smack on the wrists to get him to remove his hands from the keyboard, he would react by hurling a blow directly at his sister.

Violet's immediate impulse was to give him a thrashing and send him upstairs under the care of Evelina, but she restrained herself. She wanted to be careful not to sour the young lad on music. Finally, she called Evelina to keep J.J. away from the piano, but to allow him to stay and listen if he would do so quietly. A few of his favorite toys kept him quietly occupied as he sat on the floor, and he seemed content with this arrangement, as he listened to Violet and his sister.

One afternoon after Bonnie Anne had finished her piano lesson and Evelina had taken both children upstairs for their naps, Violet stayed behind to do some piano practice of her own. As she was playing one of her favorite Chopin pieces, she noticed Little Josh looking through the window of the French door and listening intently. She invited him in and told him that he could sit beside her as she resumed her playing. Again he listened in complete concentration, beating time with his fingers. Presently she asked him if he would like to learn to play.

"Oh, yas, Miz Violet," he responded without a moment's hesitation.

She showed him the scale and had him play it. Then she demonstrated some little one-finger tunes, and he repeated each without a flaw. *Why, he has an ear for music and time, how wonderful! This is a talent we must do something with,* she thought.

She asked him if he would like to take lessons, to which he responded eagerly, "Oh, yas, Miz Violet, ah sho' would like dat." He agreed to come every day to learn and practice more piano. Soon he was picking up more tunes and playing with both hands. Violet would play something, with both hands, and he would follow by ear. He was doing all this without reading a note. Now Violet began to teach him to read the notes. That, too, came with surprising quickness. For his daily finger exercises Violet would put a cent coin on top of each hand, and if they still were there when he had completed the exercises, he could keep them as a reward for having held his wrists properly.

One afternoon Violet was coming down the stairs after putting the children to bed for a nap when she heard the piano. She slipped up to the ballroom door to listen. Little Josh was at the piano playing a one-finger piece that she never had heard before.

Walking in as he finished playing it for the second or third time, she asked, "Where did you learn that, Josh?"

"Oh, ah don't know, Miz Violet, it jes' came out."

"Well, that is very good. Wait a minute." Getting pencil and paper she said, "Play it again, Josh."

As he repeated the playing she wrote down the notes.

"That's excellent, Little Josh, now you have composed a piece of music," smiled Violet. "Tell me, have you thought of a name for it?"

"Well, Ma'am, while ah walk up heah, and ah hum dis tune, ah look up at de sky, an' ah see de moon."

"Yes."

"So ah wonduh iffen ah kin call hit 'Daytime Moon'; would dat be aw righ'?"

"Daytime Moon? Well, Josh, that's what we'll call it."

Little Josh beamed in satisfaction.

One day three weeks later Josh came in to play tunes on some new devices. First he played a fiddle made of cornstalks. Then he played a reed flute.

"Where did you get those?" asked Violet.

"Ah made 'em, Miz Violet."

"But where did you learn how to do that? The plantation children used to play these all the time, but I've not heard them for years. How did you learn?"

"Rev'rend Jackson sho' meh how," he explained with pride.

In another week he was back with another instrument. It was a violin that he had made from cypress shingles and horse-hair strings and a bass string of waxed twine.

"For goodness sakes," Violet exclaimed. "Did Reverend Jackson show you how to make that?"

"Oh, no, Miz Violet, ah do hit mahsef." Without any prompting he began playing the instrument.

"That's wonderful, Josh!" and she began to form in her mind ideas of how Josh's musical talent might be encouraged and developed.

During the next six weeks Violet was busy with hay and oats and wheat harvest, but she continued the lessons for Bonnie Anne and for Little Josh, but then she noticed that Josh was spending unusually long hours away from the house. When she inquired of his whereabouts during those periods, he explained that he was spending that time at Reverend Jackson's school, even though it was summer.

Then late one afternoon, Little Josh came to Violet when she was working in the office alone. "Miz Violet," he said with a sparkle in his eyes and a grin on his face.

She looked up from her work. "Yes, Little Josh?"

"Miz Violet, kin ya come down ta de school?"

"Down to the school? Now? Oh, I'm very busy just now, Josh."

That brought an immediate clouding over of the bright face that turned away. She could detect the trace of a tear in his eye. She knew that she had disappointed him for some reason. Her heart softened. Her work could wait.

"All right, Little Josh, I shall be happy to go to the school. You go tell Fabian to saddle Jeb and I'll meet you at the carriage house in a few minutes." At this he broke into a huge grin and his whole face lighted up with pleasure.

When they arrived at the church-school building, Little Josh slid off the horse and dashed inside. When Violet entered a few minutes later she saw a semicircle of six little black boys seated at the front of the room. The only other persons there were Reverend Jackson and his wife.

Little Josh jumped up, and at his direction, the group began playing with a wild assortment of instruments the song, *Little Brown Jug*. Three of the boys picked up brown jugs to blow in rhythm, while one played the melody on paper and comb, and one played a reed flute. Little Josh played his home-made violin, and then he broke into singing:

Ha, ha, ha, ya an' meh,
Li'l brown jug, how ah love de,
Ha, ha, ha, ya an' meh,
Li'l brown jug, how ah love de.

The group continued with special renditions of some Stephen Foster songs and a couple of spirituals. Violet was astounded. The melody, the harmony, the rhythm, were amazing.

Turning to Reverend Jackson, she asked, "Is this your doing?"

"Wale, ah hep 'em, buh hit's mostly Li'l Josh. Ah teach 'em de songs, buh Josh figure out de instruments, an' he train de others ta play 'em."

Little Josh beckoned for Violet to come up and meet his group and look at their instruments. Each boy had at least three instruments by his side and picked up whichever one might be called for at a given time at a given place.

"Dis be Robin," Little Josh said by way of introduction, "He play de spoon an' de gourd, an' dat washboard wif uh stick. He be 'leven year old." Robin drew his stick up and down the washboard several times to demonstrate the desired effect. Then he took the pair of tablespoons. Holding them back to back between the fingers of one hand, he hit them against the other hand and then up and down his leg for a clicking rhythm.

Violet grinned and said, "I see, he's a rhythm section."

"Yas, ma'am, buh so be Edward dere. He be ten. He play de water drums, de tin cup an' rocks an' de boards dat he clap tagedder." The water drums turned out to be four buckets that had been filled with water to a different level in each so as to give a different pitch, and covered with a tightly drawn piece of canvas. Edward gave a demonstration of his talents for Violet. Josh beamed proudly when Edward finished.

"An' Sanders, he be 'leven or twelve. He play de saw wif uh hammer an' he play hit wif uh bow, an' he play de flute, too."

"An' Hank, he be only nine, he play de cowbell, de elderberry whistle, an' de triangle." The whistle was a piece from an elderberry limb from which the soft center had been pushed out and holes made along the side. Now Hank showed Violet what he could do with these three instruments.

Little Josh continued, "Dat fine, Hank. Now Matthew heah, he be 'leven, he play de comb wrapp'd wif paper, bottles uf water dat we fill ta diff'ent marks ta mek de higher or lower note w'en he blow ovah dem. Matthew, he also rub de blocks uf wood ta mek uh speshul rhythm." Violet could see that the blocks of wood had been covered with sandpaper, and were rubbed together to make the sound. "Show Miz Violet whut ya kin do, boy," Little Josh said to Matthew.

When Matthew had demonstrated his instruments, Little Josh added, "An' we all play de jug, Miz Violet." She was soon to find out that in tone and rhythm the jug played the role of the bass violin.

Violet clapped her hands in appreciation. "This is wonderful! Are you going to play for all of the people here at church?"

"Yas, Ma'am, Rev'rend Jackson say we kin play nex' Sunday."

"Josh...Robin...Sanders...Hank...Matthew," she said, looking at each boy in turn. "I'm proud of each of you. Perhaps sometime later you will come and play for all of us at the big house. Will you do that?"

Little Josh answered for his group, "Oh, yas, Miz Violet, tank ya, Ma'am, we be dere, an' w'en we play dere ah play de piano iffen hit be all right wif ya."

Violet patted his shoulder fondly as she answered, "Of course you may play the piano. I'm looking forward to your performance. Is there anything else you need for your little orchestra?"

Before Little Josh could say anything Reverend Jackson spoke up, "Someday ah hope de boys kin have two real violins...an' uh banjo. Ah now Sanders kin larn ta play violin quickly an' uf course Li'l Josh be able ta play violin an' banjo—an' most anyting else. Dat boy has uh speshul gift, he has."

"I quite agree with you, Reverend Jackson," agreed Violet with enthusiasm and pride.

Sunday evening Violet persuaded Brent and Susan to go with her down to the church-school building. The place was filled with practically all the field hands and their families. The *Little Brown Jugs*, as Little Josh had named his small group, outdid themselves, and the audience cheered wildly after each piece. Soon everybody was joining in the singing.

Brent and Susan were altogether unprepared for this, so they were even more astonished than Violet had been. They knew Violet had been working with Little Josh on the piano, but they never thought beyond that. She grinned mischievously at them as they kept giving her glances of wonder and surprise and appreciation. After the service, back at the main house where they were discussing the *Little Brown Jugs'* performance and how talented were all the boys, it took no persuasion to induce Brent to pick up two violins and a banjo on his trip to Columbia the next week.

Brent and Susan were as enthusiastic as Violet about inviting the neighbors for a concert to be held on a Saturday, three weeks later. The *Little Brown Jugs* were excited to be holding a "real" recital in the ballroom of the big house.

Visitors and household servants gathered in the ballroom for the event. Even though the boys had had only a few weeks to familiarize themselves with the violins and banjo, they handled those instruments fairly well, but Little Josh stole the show with his piano playing. At one point he stepped up with his banjo and said, "Ah wanta dedicate dis one fo' one who always bin heppin' us." He broke into singing, *"Sweet*

Evelina, sweet Evelina, mah love fo' ya will nebbuh, nebbuh die..." All eyes turned toward Evelina who was beaming.

The guests enjoyed themselves immensely and heaped praises upon the *Little Brown Jugs,* and especially on Josh.

The recital brought invitations to play at church events and balls and parties all over this part of the county, and Fabian was kept busy hauling them around in a wagon. In time, all this led to an invitation to give a concert in Sumter.

Sponsored by the Freedmen's Bureau, a full crowd packed into the Court Room to hear the *Little Brown Jugs* on a Saturday night early in September. They were enthusiastically received, and with this, the little group had become easily the most popular band in the county.

Chapter 35

Sutler to the Legislature

1869

When Violet and Susan entered the bank in Sumter, Clifford Montgomery greeted them with an exaggerated cordiality. "Well, good-day, Mrs. Sutler, Miss Susan, how nice to see the two of you again." He told them he had been at the concert of The Little Brown Jugs, and he heaped praise on Josh for the performance of his little band, asking that Violet pass on his praise to Josh.

Violet said she would and then got right to the purpose of her visit to the bank. "Each year it takes more and more money for taxes," she complained as she prepared her withdrawal slip while the banker waited.

"Oh, yes," he answered, "it takes a lot to rebuild things in the State after all the War damage." He took the slip from Violet and looked at the amount of withdrawal.

"And even more for the Carpetbaggers' plunder, if you ask me," Violet came back.

Just then a young Yankee officer walked in. He was about six-feet tall, light complexioned, clean-shaven, and his blue uniform with black felt hat was neat and clean. His polished buttons reflected bits of sunlight that filtered through the windows. He waited his turn patiently to see the banker. As Clifford Montgomery handed the envelope of money to Violet, he introduced her and Susan to the young officer, saying, "Lieutenant Hudson, may I present Mrs. Brent Sutler and her sister, Miss Susan Storm?"

"How do you do?" Violet and Susan said politely, in unison.

The lieutenant smiled broadly, nodding to each lady, "Good morning, ma'am, good morning, ma'am." His eyes lingered on Susan for a moment.

"Lieutenant Hudson has arrived just recently on assignment with the Freedmen's Bureau," Montgomery informed them.

Just then Little Josh came up to the group, having deposited his parcels at the livery. The lieutenant smiled again, this time at Little Josh. "Isn't this the young man who led the band in the concert last Saturday evening?" he asked.

Little Josh beamed proudly, "Yassuh, ah de one."

"Well that was wonderful, just wonderful. I enjoyed every minute of your concert, little fellow." Turning toward Violet, he added, "I could not help but overhear that you were going to the Court House from here. That's where my headquarters are. May I have the honor of escorting you there?" He took a quick glance at Susan, and then looked back at Violet.

But before Violet could say, "You needn't bother," Susan blurted out, "Of course you may." Then she added demurely, her lashes lowered, "How kind of you, and thank you very much."

Violet glared at Susan, but she was caught in a bind. Her good breeding would not permit her to counter her sister in the presence of a stranger, and, most especially, a *Yankee* stranger. So the small group left the bank. Violet felt herself flush with humiliation at the thought of being seen in the company of a Yankee officer, but she noted with surprise and some trepidation that this did not seem to bother her sister in the least.

On the walk to the Court House the ladies learned that the lieutenant was from Indiana, that he had graduated from West Point, and earlier he had served as a private in the Union Army in northern Virginia. Violet felt a sense of relief when they finally reached the Courthouse and they were able to take their leave to go their own way to take care of Fair Oaks' taxes.

During the ride home Violet was unusually quiet. It was always depressing to pay taxes, and this time the amount was even greater than in the past. But she was even more depressed by the thought of having walked through the streets with a Yankee officer, and in the sight of everyone out that day. She was furious with her youngest sister for accepting his offer before she could decline.

On the other hand, Susan was more talkative than ever, even jubilant, and she filled the void left by Violet's silence with streams of small talk of her own, directed at Violet, at Little Josh, at no one in particular.

"Sutler to the legislature," Brent announced. "What do you think of that?" he asked as he sat down to a stack of papers on his side of the desk while Violet worked on her side. He had just returned from his morning's work on the railroad and she from her shopping trip to Sumter. She had settled down to work as soon as she got home, that always being an effective remedy to clear her mind of depressing thoughts and angry feelings.

She looked over at her handsome husband, wondering what he had on his mind, and queried, "Oh, Brent, what do you mean, 'Sutler to the legislature'?"

"Well, my love, don't you know what a sutler is?" he asked mischievously, enjoying this repartee with Violet.

"Of course, I know Brent Sutler."

"No, no, I'm talking about another sutler—the man who follows an army to sell all kinds of things to the soldiers that the army itself does not provide, such as extra fresh food, shaving soap, combs, paper and pencils, candy, tobacco, and the like."

"Oh. Well, yes, I've heard of such merchants, but what has that got to do with anything?"

Humor sparkled in his eyes. "Well, my dear, I, your beloved husband, Brent Sutler, am going to act as a sutler to our state legislature in Columbia. Now what do you think of that?"

"Do you mean that you're going to sell things to the state? Well, good luck!" she answered sarcastically, knowing the Carpetbaggers and Scalawags ran everything in the state.

"Not exactly. I mean I am going to sell things to the state for the legislators, that holy body of lawmakers we have sitting in our capitol."

"Oh, for the legislators. You mean the people who are serving as state senators and representatives? Those people."

"Exactly," nodded Brent.

"You'll need to explain this to me, Brent. I don't understand. What's so special about the legislators? Aren't they like everybody else? After all, they're in Columbia only a short time. The rest of the time they're at home. Can't they get their apples and tobacco and soap at the same stores as everybody else?" She gave a tug on the tapestry pull to summon Mammy or one of the kitchen servants to fetch two cups of coffee for her and Brent.

Brent grinned at his wife. He was enjoying this. "Oh, but our legislators have very special tastes. Those Carpetbaggers and Scalawags and ex-slaves want only the best. I heard about the kinds of things they were ordering, and I went around and persuaded them that I had access to the sources of the things that they wanted, including European markets, and I came away with a promise of a substantial order. Of course this will require a ten percent return fee to the leaders who are making the orders."

"Why, Brent!" she exclaimed with dismay, "do you mean that you must return ten percent of what they pay you to the men who place the orders?"

"That's it."

"But is that legal?"

In a mocking tone he answered, "Who am I to question the legality of our August legislators?"

"But that is a considerable bite out of your profit, Brent."

"Now don't you worry, I'll set the prices high enough to cover all that."

"What kinds of things are they ordering?" she wondered.

"Take a look at this list," Brent laughed as he tossed several sheets of paper on Violet's side of the desk. "In addition to a list of basic items needed, these are items for the members' refreshment room in the State House and for their offices. Look at what they've ordered."

Just then Mammy stuck her head in the door and looked at the two of them with a knowing look upon her kindly face. "Ah 'spect de two uv ya' be wantin' uh cup uv coffee. Ah bring hit righ' in soon now." She disappeared before Violet or Brent could answer.

"Just look at what they've ordered," repeated Brent, pointing to the list he had just handed her.

She looked in amazement as her eyes ran through the list:

> *Groceries and Delicacies:*
>
> *Best Westphalia hams, Bologna sausages, diamond hams, bacon strips, pineapples, Edam cheese. Switzer cheese, gilt edge butter, bacon sides, pickles, brandy cherries, brandy peaches, sardines, smoked salmon, canned salmon, canned oysters, canned lobsters, smoked beef tongues, smoked buffalo tongues, imported mushrooms, deviled ham, black tea, green tea, lemons, guava jelly, French chocolate, oranges*...and on to twenty-nine more items in this category.
>
> *Wines and Liquors:*
>
> *Six brands of Champagne: Heidsick, Green Seal, Vin Imperial, Verzenay, Moet, Chandon, and scuppernong, sparkling Moselle, Catawba, Madeira, blackberry wine, finest Otard-du-Puy brandy, finest French cognac, Baker cabinet rye, bourbon, Holland gin, Jamaica rum, imperial pale sherry, Chateau la Rose claret*...and twenty other kinds of beverages.
>
> *Cigars and Tobacco:* eleven kinds.
>
> *Furniture: finest walnut office chairs, office desks*...and forty-four other items of *chairs, lounges, and washstands, mirrors, sofas, mattresses, pillows.*
>
> A dozen kinds of "Furnishings" such as *tapestries, carpeting, curtains, mats, hassocks, oilcloths.*
>
> Two dozen items of dry-goods such as *damask, velvets, flannels, kid gloves, hosiery, tablecloths, shawls, ladies' hoods, bustles, chignons, garters, towels, sheeting, quilts, satchels, whale-bone, etc.*
>
> Seventeen kinds of crockery and glassware, Stock—*fine horses, mules, carriages, buggies, and harnesses.*

"Great Scot, Brent, surely you don't mean that all of this is being bought for the State House!" exclaimed Violet.

"Sure, and that's not nearly all. Here are four more lists for clothing, printing and stationery, and utensils and sundries. Glance over these." He threw the lists over to her desk, and went on, not waiting for her to finish skimming the lists. "And it all is to be billed as 'State House Supplies.' Of course you must understand that this is a kind of consolidated wish list I've made up from numerous requests, and quantities for most items are yet to be determined."

Violet quickly ran her pencil down the lists. "Brent, if you sold only one of each item and made only a dollar on each, do you realize how much that would be?"

"How much?"

"Three hundred and sixty-eight dollars!"

"But surely you can calculate more closely than that—a horse and buggy for a dollar each? A case of champagne for a dollar? A gold watch and chain for a dollar? Come on."

"Yes, that's what I mean. Only one of each item on these lists would run into thousands."

Brent shook his head, "But remember, this will be spread over time, and I shall have to share the orders with several other entrepreneurs, and who knows where it will end?"

Violet glanced down at a list she had picked up from her desk. Puzzled, she said, "Brent, I didn't know that there were any women in the legislature."

"Of course not." That sardonic grin of his appeared.

"Well then, what is all that diamond and gold jewelry and ladies satchels and dress goods and beds and mattresses, and everything for?" she asked in wonder.

"Oh, my dear, those things are for the legislators' wives and lady friends, and so on."

"Is that legal?" she asked again.

"I suppose it is if the legislature says it is. Who am I to question our noble legislators? You have to know what tune the devil is playing."

She rested her chin in her hands, thinking, and then asked, "Brent, could we order some of those things?"

"Why, Violet! You mean get in on the state graft?"

"Oh, no, Brent, not that, of course that's not what I mean. I just thought that when you ordered some of those things for the State House you could also order some for Fair Oaks, against our joint account. You know, silver and china to replace what we lost during the War. These days, items like that are so hard for us ordinary folk to get."

"Oh, sure, my dear. I'll do that. I'll be ordering in quantities and should be able to get some good prices." He paused to light a cigarette, and then went on, "Now I've got to break these lists down according to source—what I must telegraph Father to order from France and England and Belgium and the German states and so on, what to order from Charleston, and I'll send Cedric out to make inquiries around Columbia which I shall follow up. I can get fine, well-made buggies and carriages from the Curtis Carriage and Buggy Shop in Sumter, and I'll go to Camden in a day or two to look for some good horses."

Mammy appeared with a coffee pot and two cups and saucers. She poured the coffee, adding the amounts of cream and sugar that she knew each preferred, handed a cup and saucer and napkin to each, and then took her leave amid their thanks. They noted that she had left slices of apple pie on the tray for them to eat should they be hungry.

Violet took a sip of her coffee and then said, "Brent, if you bring in a fraction of the stuff on that list they are going to have to build a new wing on the State House to contain it."

"Or a whole new State House! And I'll need a bigger warehouse in Columbia." He took a deep puff on his cigarette and then drank his coffee down. He was silent for a short while before he said with sarcasm, "But, frankly, my love, I'm not sure all of this is going to end up at the State House."

"Yes, I know what you are saying. Now I understand why our taxes keep going up. *We* are actually paying for all of these luxury items for our honorable legislators and their *ladies*. We work like all get out, so they can have gold spittoons and silks and laces and fine china and fantastic food and wine that we cannot even dream of having or eating. Oh, Brent, it isn't fair!" she cried, her voice breaking.

He rose from his chair, crossed around to her desk and lifted her from her chair, holding her in his arms, her head on his shoulder. "No, my sweet love, it isn't, but remember, all this is bound to be temporary. In the meantime, we—you and I—will profit from their greed and immaturity and lack of integrity."

Over the next several days, Violet looked with interest as Brent prepared his lists and sent off a series of telegraph messages to his father, to Cedric, and to suppliers and manufacturers in Baltimore, Philadelphia, and New York.

While Brent began making frequent trips to Columbia, Susan found frequent reasons to be going into Sumter. Sometimes she took Evelina along and would go on the train, explaining that she had to pick up some dry goods, or other items that she just had to purchase. On another, she would volunteer to go with Fabian and Josh in the spring wagon to buy groceries and other items that Violet or Mammy or Hattie or Leo needed.

Now Brent was making almost daily trips to Columbia after arranging for some trade-off time in supervising the railroad section gangs. He would flag a morning train in front of the house and drop off there in the evening. During one period several weeks later, he remained in Columbia for three days. He let Violet know by telegraph that he would be returning on Friday evening. Although he gave no explanation, she knew his visit had to do with orders for the legislators, and that no mention of such could be made in a telegram.

When Violet heard the train stopping on that Friday evening, she ran down the lane to meet Brent. He greeted her with a big grin and a warm hug and a loving kiss.

"It's all fixed," he told her.

"You mean your State House sales?"

"Yes, I mean the first round, but this has been a good start, a very good start."

She took his arm as they began walking back to the house. "Oh, Brent, how did you do it? *What* did you do? Tell me about it—right now. I can't wait to hear!"

He laughed at her enthusiasm. "Now, Violet, my love, let's go back to the office, and then I'll explain. Not here. Just wait. Now, how have you and the children been? I missed all of you." He gave her another kiss.

She brought him up-to-date on the children's doings, and those of the household in general. Just as they reached the front porch Susan came out to greet Brent and inform them that Mammy had asked her to tell them that supper would be ready in an hour. Then the children piled out to welcome their daddy. Brent picked up both children at once, one on either arm, gave them each a big kiss, and asked them what they had been doing. They chatted a few minutes before Evelina appeared to take them in to wash up and have an early supper before the grown-ups ate, since the hour was late.

As Violet and Brent settled at their desks, Violet was all curiosity. "Now Brent, tell me about it—everything—but first tell me, what happened? How much did you make? You know I must record the company's financial situation in the ledger. Oh, Brent, hurry, I can't wait any longer to hear about this!"

"Well, darling, if you will but give me a chance, I shall." he said, amused. "Let's say that the total profit right now is double our total income from the cotton crop."

She caught her breath. All she could muster was "Brent!"

He went on, delighted with her reaction, "And, my dear, that is only the first phase, only the beginning—there is a lot more where that came from—a lot more all ready on order. How about that!" He was unable to conceal his own enthusiasm.

"Oh, Brent, tell me about it. Do tell!"

"To begin with, you must understand that I was up against a lot of competition. There were a dozen others bidding for major orders, and many others who were bidding on just an order or two."

"Obviously, you were able to beat the competition!" she said breathless from excitement.

"Mostly, on about everything but the printing contracts. They have that all tied up. Some of the legislators have formed their own printing company, and now they are awarding themselves the contracts for the state printing at unbelievable prices."

"How dishonorable! How can they do that?"

"Only by continuing to get reelected. If someone else ever comes in and discovers what they have been doing, they'll be candidates for jail. But you can see why they have to keep raising our taxes—to keep the money flowing to their pockets." Brent said disgustedly.

"That's disgraceful! But I don't see how they can keep getting away with this." She paused a moment and then went on to ask, "But, Brent, what about the other items?"

"We're in good shape on most, but let me tell you what happened."

"Please do!"

"First of all, through my earlier trading in the old days, and through my father, I had better access to sources of supply than did the others. I could get better quality at lower prices."

"I thought they would not be much interested in lower prices," she commented.

"Oh, but they are. That would allow them to get more of the luxuries that they crave. The only problem was that lower prices might lower the amount of pay-back that they received when figured as a percentage of the outlay. So, I let it be known that I was willing to pay them a fifteen percent fee, and in some cases, twenty percent, instead of the usual ten percent."

"I'll bet *that* was persuasive," she interjected sarcastically.

"They wanted the purchasing contracts to go to their friends and kinsmen, and especially to their political supporters."

"No doubt."

"But listen, the trouble was, most of them didn't know anything about merchandising, didn't know anything about good sources of supply, and they certainly didn't want to make public advertisements for bids—not for most of the stuff they had in mind."

"I should think not!" She couldn't keep the repugnance from her voice.

"Well, I didn't want to be greedy, so I said I would be content to bid for one-eighth of the order in each category."

"I guess that would be pretty big."

"Indeed, but that was not all. I quietly went around to each of the other major bidders and reported that I could help supply their requirements. Six of them jumped at the chance—so you see, in the long run I'll be getting all the profit, less the pay-back, on an eighth of the orders, and I'll be getting forty percent on most of the others."

Violet was impressed with her husband's business acumen, and she let him know her feelings. "Brent, you really do have a genius for trade, and I must say, you've been instrumental in our getting better prices for our cotton and hay and wheat and corn—"

"And tobacco?" he said with a smile. He was pleased at Violet's praise.

"Especially tobacco."

"But I may have spoken too soon in the comparing of the profit with income from the cotton?"

"Even better than last year's—we are getting twenty-one to twenty-two cents, and we are getting over three hundred fifty pounds to the acre, for six hundred acres," she said proudly.

In turn, he was impressed with her endeavors at the plantation. "Why, that's wonderful! How did you get that high yield, Violet?"

"Well, you know that the weather has been good this year, and we have been more effective in getting the worms, and you remember that compost we put on in the spring?"

"Oh, yes."

"Well, we didn't have enough of the compost for more than one field, but that certainly brought up the average."

"The cotton has not all been sold has it?"

"Oh, no, Brent, about half of it is yet to be picked and ginned and baled, and anyway," she went on impishly, trying to control a smile lurking at the corners of her mouth, "you know we don't sell it without word from the *Vice President* in charge of marketing."

"Naturally," he grinned. "Well, then good. Now, in spite of the good prices they are bound to be higher next spring and summer."

"You think so, Brent?"

"Yes, indeed I do, and here's what I suggest: I think it would be well to store the rest after it is baled, and I think it would be a good idea to put it in five hundred pound bales instead of the four or four-fifty pound bales that we've been doing."

"All right," she agreed, "and how about the tobacco? You know how well that went, now that Leo and Isaiah know just how it should be planted."

"Yes, actually that hundred acres of tobacco in last year's crop brought as much per acre when we sold it this summer as the cotton, and this year's tobacco crop—"

"For sale next year—" she added.

"For sale next year," he repeated, "and the tobacco crop was better both in yield and quality than last year's." He shook his head in wonder, and then continued, "You know, my love, I am truly proud of your accomplishments here at Fair Oaks. Tell me, now that you have mastered tobacco, have you ever thought of indigo?"

"Actually, I have. In the past, a number of plantations around here have done well with indigo, but I don't think it's for us."

"Why not?"

"In the first place, it's hard to grow, like tobacco, but more important, many think that indigo is harmful to the health of the workers, and anyway, the price is not good now."

"Sounds like three excellent reasons."

Violet smiled. "Brent, I do appreciate your judgment, and I really am proud of your business sense."

He took another puff of his cigarette, blowing the smoke in circles. Then he said thoughtfully, "You know something, Violet, I would say we make a splendid team—in more ways than one."

Chapter 36

A Yankee Proposal

1869-1870

"Violet," Susan said as they were finishing their supper alone one evening in mid-December. The children had been fed earlier, and Brent was staying overnight in Columbia for business purposes.

"Yes, Susan, what is it?" answered Violet, buttering her corn bread. She looked over at her sister who was sitting to her left.

"Well, I was wondering..." Susan hesitated.

"Yes? Wondering what?" Violet set down her corn bread and gave full attention to her sister. Susan was not often hesitant, and Violet sensed there was something serious on her mind.

"Well, I was just wondering if Charlotte and Leland will be here for Christmas."

"Why, of course, and they'll be bringing Leland's father, too, since there are no other relatives alive now for him to spend the holiday with, and actually, he's now part of our family through marriage." She gave Susan a penetrating look. "Why, do you have some reason to think otherwise?"

"Oh, no."

"Well, was there something else?" For some reason, Violet felt uneasy. Susan was behaving with uncharacteristic hesitancy.

"Well...yes...sort of..." Susan said in a small voice.

"Susan, for goodness sake, get to the point. What are you getting at?"

"Well...I was just wondering...would it be all right if I invited a guest for Christmas dinner?"

"A guest? Why, of course. Guests are always welcome at our house, and especially at Christmas time. Remember how Mama and Daddy used to include any neighbors or other friends who might be alone for one reason or another? That's just part of the Christmas spirit." Violet paused and looked at her sister fondly. "Are you thinking of anyone in particular? Maybe the Frierson's nephew?" Just this past month he had been down from North Carolina to visit his grandparents, and Violet had noticed him eyeing Susan with much interest.

"Well...yes...I was thinking of someone in particular...not him though." Susan answered, keeping her eyes focused only on her plate.

"Well, for goodness sake, who then?" Violet was beginning to become just a bit exasperated.

Susan cleared her throat, as much to give herself time as to strengthen her voice. "Well, Violet, do you remember that nice lieutenant we met in Sumter, Lieutenant Hudson? Gilbert Hudson?"

Before she could say anything else Violet exploded, "Zounds! *Not* that damn Yankee!"

Susan wouldn't look at her sister. She said meekly, "I was afraid you'd feel like that."

A sudden thought struck Violet. "Susan! Have you been seeing that rogue on your recent trips into Sumter—and without my or Brent's even knowing about it?"

"Well...sometimes."

"Only sometimes?"

"Well...most of the times I was in town." Susan admitted reluctantly.

"Oh, Susan, no wonder you've been so helpful and cooperative in doing errands in Sumter. Here I've been thinking you were just growing up and taking on more responsibility to help me."

"Violet, you know I'm glad to help with things here. I'm glad to do that."

Violet sighed deeply, trying to control her feelings and to think how best to handle this unexpected turn of events. "Susan, I'm afraid that having the lieutenant here for Christmas will throw a wet blanket over our whole holiday. Christmas is always a kind of sad time for us anyway, with Mama and Daddy and Christopher no longer with us."

For the first time Susan raised her eyes and looked directly at Violet. "Of course it is, but it should be a joyful time, too, and we ought to make it as joyful for others as we can. Christmas is a lonely time for those who are away from home. I was thinking that it would be thoughtful to invite a young man who is hundreds of miles from home to have Christmas dinner with a local family. No one should be alone at Christmas, Violet. You know Mama used to say that every year."

"Oh, Susan," Violet said sadly. She laid her napkin by her plate. She had lost her appetite for anything else. Mammy would fuss, but Violet didn't care. She couldn't believe what was happening.

Susan went on, now more like her old self, "If it had been possible, if the timing had been different, would it not have been nice if some Pennsylvanian family could have invited Christopher to Christmas dinner? You would want that, wouldn't you?"

Violet sighed again. "Oh, Susan, I doubt I would have wanted Christopher to have dinner with those people, not Yankees."

Susan's voice took on a coolness unlike her. "Well, if it can't be done...this is your place...and as long as I accept your shelter—" She folded her napkin and laid it on the table, pushing back her chair as if to rise.

Violet had never heard Susan speak like this. The coolness struck at her heart. She said quickly, "Now Susan, you know this is your home for as long as you want, and you know I—and Brent too—are indebted to you for so many things, and all your hard work here at Fair Oaks, and especially your rescue of Bonnie Anne from the train, and..."

Susan broke in, "Oh, no, Violet, please, please don't think I deserve anything in repayment for *anything...*"

"No, no. I'm just afraid I haven't taken enough into account your wishes, but you know how I feel about Yankees, what they did to us and our friends and neighbors and everyone in South Carolina, and what they are letting the Carpetbaggers and Scalawags and ex-slaves do to us now, with things so hard to come by and then at exorbitant prices, and the dreadfully high taxes..." She had to stop for breath.

"Don't we all? Feel that way, I mean. But I've been doing a lot of thinking, Violet, and I wonder if maybe we can feel about Yankees the way you say some feel toward the colored folks—have a high regard for them individually, but fear them or despise them in the aggregate."

"Maybe so." Violet smiled, and then capitulated, "All right, Susan, I suppose it won't hurt to invite the lieutenant this one time. Go ahead and invite him the next time you have an errand in Sumter—."

Susan jumped up from the table and went around to hug Violet. "Oh, thank you, thank you, Violet."

A frown flashed across Violet's face momentarily, and the smile disappeared as she added, "But I hope his visit here won't become a habit, Susan."

"I doubt that's possible; I think he'll be leaving the area in the spring."

At that Violet took a deep sigh of relief. *Well thank goodness for that!* she thought.

To the comfort of everyone, when Lieutenant Gilbert Hudson rode up the lane at Fair Oaks on Christmas morning, he was wearing mufti—gray great coat over his Prince Albert suit coat and trousers. A broad-brimmed gray felt hat sat jauntily on his light brown hair. On entering the house, he showed no sign of intimidation or lack of confidence in finding himself surrounded by "Rebs." And Brent Sutler respected him for that.

While Violet and Brent went to the overseer's house to make the annual bonus payments to the workers for their share in the crops beyond their regular wages, Susan took Lieutenant Hudson for a stroll around the gardens. The day was fairly warm for this time of the year, and just as Susan and her guest reached the far end of the south flower garden and were strolling along the arbored walk, a beam of sunlight filtered through the grapevines to light up the white petals of a single Christmas rose. The two sat on a wooden bench and admired the red and white bracts of the poinsettias along the sides of the brick walks of the garden. Fabian and his helpers took pride in the gardens of Fair Oaks, and all hedges and shrubs were neatly trimmed, and all walks kept weeded. In each of the four corners of the garden squares and within each center, ornamental topiaries of boxwood and small thick holly trees and crape myrtle trees sparked interest in and added color to the winter garden.

During dinner the conversation ranged from the Carpetbag government to high taxes, from the fun the children were having with their new Christmas toys to the delight and appreciation of the workers with their annual Christmas bonuses, and at last, the conversation turned to Lieutenant Hudson.

"I understand you are from Indiana," said Brent.

"Yes, sir, I was born in *southern* Indiana, Washington County," he replied, emphasizing the word 'southern.'

"Well I'm glad to hear it was *southern* Indiana," grinned Brent, always ready to appreciate a good joke.

"Oh yes, and you know *southern* Indiana was settled more from the South than from the east. The settlers came from Virginia, North Carolina, and South Carolina, through the Cumberland Gap and on into Kentucky, and then across the Ohio River."

"That *is* interesting," Violet conceded, "and did your folks come that way?"

"Well, Miss Violet," he said, in the way of Southerners, "my father came from North Carolina—Raleigh, North Carolina—though my mother came from Delaware."

"And where did you serve?" Leland asked, thinking of his own battles, and of the Major's, and of his best friend's, Christopher Storm's. When Charlotte had told him that Violet had permitted Susan to invite this Yankee lieutenant for Christmas dinner, Leland had had mixed feelings. In a way he knew it would open up new wounds, yet he knew the time had come when he had to put the past behind him. He was surprised at Susan, but he knew that she was younger and more impulsive than her sisters, and, he had to admit, the young man certainly seemed personable and respectful to the family. He glanced at his father who had had some stirring words to say about the Yankee lieutenant being invited to join the family for Christmas dinner; however, he observed that his father's stiffness had relaxed, and he seemed genuinely interested in what the young man was saying.

"I started out as a private in the 13th Indiana Volunteer Infantry. We went through Kentucky, then down the Valley in Virginia—"

"Not very pleasant, I guess," commented Susan.

He smiled at her as he answered, "No, lots of marching, lots of fighting, lots of casualties, but I was lucky."

"And, Lieutenant, where did you end up?" asked Brent politely.

"Fortunately, sir, I received an appointment to West Point and reported there the first of July, 1863."

"So you missed Gettysburg," Charlotte observed.

Charlotte is thinking about Christopher, Violet thought, *well, at least we know he's not the Yankee who killed Christopher.*

"Yes, luckily, but I did see a bit of action almost as soon as I arrived at West Point."

"What was that?" asked Brent.

"Well, it so happened that one company of cadets, which happened to be the one to which I had just been assigned, was sent to New York City to reinforce the troops dealing with the draft riots there."

Leaning forward with a look of great interest, Brent asked, "Tell us. What happened there?"

"Well, sir, the rioting went on for four days. Thousands of people poured into the streets from shops and factories and became a howling, mad mob. They fought the police and the militia, seized weapons from the Second Avenue Armory, disarmed soldiers in their barracks, set fire to buildings, looted buildings and robbed people everywhere, beat Negroes to death wherever they could find them, fired at random at anybody they thought might try to stop them."

"What a fascinating display of support for the Northern cause," Brent said sarcastically. "How did they ever get the riot stopped?"

"They had to send in heavy reinforcements. The Seventh Regiment of New York had to bear the brunt until reinforcements could arrive. Several units were rushed back from Gettysburg, the Governor mobilized additional militia, the city added police, naval forces came in, and of course our company from West Point."

"That's simply awful!" exclaimed Violet. "Were many people killed?"

"Ma'am, some say that a thousand were killed; most agree that there were at least five hundred killed."

"My goodness! So many!" gasped Susan.

Brent went on with his questioning of the young man. "You graduated from West Point after the War?"

"Yes, sir, in '67. I then served in Washington, D.C., for two years, and then here, with the Freedmen's Bureau," he answered with good humor.

Lieutenant Hudson retained his friendly disposition and courteous manners throughout his day at Fair Oaks, and everyone there treated him graciously. As he prepared to take his leave, he turned to Violet and Brent and asked with some trepidation, "Mrs. Violet, ma'am, Mr. Sutler, sir, may I have your permission to call on Miss Susan?"

Without even thinking, Violet answered impulsively, "Oh, you don't have to have my permission to see Susan." As soon as the words were out, she wanted to bite her tongue. Brent raised his dark eyebrows and gave her a questioning look, but it was too late, and she let it pass. Brent said nothing—until after the holiday, and the house guests had departed.

To the discomfiture of Violet, Susan resumed her fairly frequent visits into Sumter, always with Fabian and Little Josh or someone to serve as some kind of chaperon, but worse than that, Lieutenant Hudson began spending Sunday afternoons with Susan at Fair Oaks. Knowing that the young man would be leaving Sumter, Violet held her tongue and bided her time, thinking that shortly this source of irritation would be gone. She was always courteous to him and gracious in her conversation, but this was not an easy task in spite of the fact that he did seem to be a nice young man. It was just that he was another one of those Yankees.

One Sunday afternoon in early March, Lieutenant Hudson left Susan sitting alone in the garden and went to find Violet and Brent in the library at Fair Oaks.

Shifting from one foot to the other, he asked, "I wonder if I might have a word with the two of you, ma'am...sir?"

"Of course, Lieutenant Hudson, have a chair," answered Brent, motioning for the young man to sit down.

Violet could feel a surge of apprehension rising up the back of her neck. *Oh, dear God, don't let this be what I'm afraid it might be. Please, not that!* she prayed. "What is it, Lieutenant?" she almost whispered. She felt her husband's glance of concern in her direction.

"Well, ma'am...sir, you see, I am very much in love with Miss Susan. Now I know that she is old enough to take responsibility for her own actions, but I am also cognizant of the customs of the South, and I was hoping, ma'am...sir, that I might have your permission to speak to her, to ask for her hand in marriage." Then he added humbly, his voice choked with emotion, "I do love her very much," he repeated, "and I shall cherish her and take care of her always. You can count on that."

Violet immediately jumped to her feet, saying in an agitated tone, "I don't—"

But Brent, rising deliberately, interrupted Violet in a calm voice, "Well, Lieutenant, this comes as something of a surprise to us, and you do understand that there are many considerations to be taken into account—" He gave Violet a warning look.

"Yes, sir, but—"

"And we are sure that you would not mind allowing us a week or so to consider these matters..."

"No, no, of course not, sir, only I was hoping—"

"Then perhaps we can look forward to seeing you in a week or two."

"Oh, yes, sir, yes, sir, I shall be back next Sunday, if that is convenient, sir...ma'am." He bowed in Violet's direction. The Lieutenant, for the first time showing any indication of embarrassment, turned and strode out of the room.

"Well, I never!" gasped Violet, speechless. After a few moments of heavy silence, she went on, "Oh., Brent, I think we'd better have a word with our little sister, right away."

"What was that?" It was Susan. She came bubbling into the room asking what it could possibly be that Violet wanted to talk to her about.

"Oh, Susan, how could you?" was all that Violet could say at the moment.

Brent took a cigarette from the box by his chair and lighted it. He took a deep puff and exhaled. A stony look darkened his face.

But Susan was unaware of their reaction and went on, easily filling the void, "Oh, Violet...Brent...don't you think he's handsome? Isn't he wonderful? And Violet, I think he wants to ask me to marry him! Maybe I won't be an old maid after all! I really thought he was going to ask me this evening, but then he didn't quite bring himself to do it. Next time I'll help him along a little."

By the time Susan finished her enthusiastic prattle, Violet had somewhat regained her composure. She searched Brent's face for a sign of support, but saw nothing there but a controlled, blank stare. She turned to her sister and said in a breaking voice, "Oh, Susan, I just don't understand all this. Frankly, I just cannot imagine one of us marrying a Yankee, and a Yankee army officer at that! What on earth has gotten into you? Mama and Daddy would turn over in their graves—and think of Christopher!" *Surely this is just a nightmare, and I will soon wake up and find this is not really happening*, she thought.

With a noticeably declining exuberance, Susan responded, "Oh, but Violet, the War is over—"

"Not for South Carolina, it isn't," Violet shot back, "not with all those blue bellies on our streets and the Carpetbaggers and Scalawags and darkies running all our affairs—"

"But he's not like *them*!"

"Susan that would be consorting with the enemy!"

"Oh, Violet, you can't go on blaming boys like Gilbert for all the policies of those radical politicians in Washington. He didn't have anything to do with that and you know it. Anyhow, Gilbert will be leaving the Army in a few weeks."

"Then what?" Violet asked, "don't tell me you plan to move with him to some God-awful place like Indianapolis." Her heart ached at the thought of her baby sister living so far away from all the family, among strangers likely to be resentful of any Southerner, and certainly not understanding of Susan's southern manners and ways.

"No, he doesn't know anybody in Indianapolis. He has an offer from an uncle to go to Vicksburg to be a railroad engineer."

"Well, at least you'd be living in the South," Violet sighed. Then she asked, "Susan, do you mean he'll be driving those dreadful locomotives?"

"No, of course not, silly, I mean an engineer who *builds* railroads."

Brent broke in, conceding, "Well, at least that sounds hopeful." He clearly was impressed by this information.

"But surely, Violet, you don't think all Northerners are corruptible, and I'm certain Gilbert is not," Susan protested. "He's kind and good and honest and a man of integrity."

Violet continued, "But Susan, dear, those people are so different. They are lacking in the manners and decorum that we take for granted. Their culture is different. They don't appreciate art and literature the way we do. They are a nation of mechanics and factory workers; ours is a society of cultivation—cultivation of the land, cultivation of a sense of humor, cultivation of the arts, cultivation of social graces, and cultivation of the intellect."

"Oh, Violet, you are holding to stereotyped impressions of Northerners and Southerners that do not apply to many individuals on either side, least of all to Gilbert."

"Susan, how can you be so sure? You really have not had much experience dealing with men," quipped Brent, lighting another cigarette and taking a deep drag.

Susan tossed her blonde hair in frustration. She sighed and then answered with firmness, "Because I *know* him. I know how kind and considerate and thoughtful he is, and anyway, he is not so far removed from Southern culture. You must be forgetting that his father is from Raleigh, North Carolina. That at least makes him half southern. And his mother is from Delaware, and that's not so far north. In fact, it's a border state."

Violet ignored this and went on with what she had briefly touched upon earlier in the conversation. "Can you imagine what our father would think about one of his daughters' marrying a Yankee? Or our brother, Christopher? Or Mama?"

In anguish Susan cried, "Oh, Violet! That isn't fair. Daddy was a very understanding and considerate man. I think if he were here now, and if he knew Gilbert as I know him, Daddy would give us his blessing!"

"I doubt that," Violet objected, "and every time I see one of those blue uniforms I think of that scoundrel who attacked me in Columbia; I think of the hundreds I watched walk through the embers of Columbia; I think of those wretches that we held off at gunpoint to keep them from destroying Fair Oaks; I think of their running like locusts through our fields and barns, taking food out of the mouths of babies and mothers, and I think of the Yankees now occupying our country like barbarian conquerors." Her face was flushed with anger at these remembrances.

Listening to Violet, Susan began to hang her head. Tears were welling in her sad blue eyes, usually so bright with humor and the joy of living, as she thought of the many terrible things that had happened to them because of the Yankees.

Violet's heart softened, but she kept on pounding. "If you won't think of yourself, think of how you would humiliate us."

Susan's head snapped up. "Is that what worries you most?" she asked as a trace of anger began to replace her sadness.

Violet looked at Brent. "Well, what do *you* think, Brent?" she demanded. "Speak up, tell her how thoughtless she is being and what a mistake she would be making."

As the two women waited in silence for him to speak, Brent rolled another cigarette, lit it, and leaned his head back as he blew smoke toward the ceiling. Then, in measured words, he answered, "There is no one who has greater contempt for Yankees and Carpetbaggers than I, and I shall be in the forefront of every action we can take to get rid of the Carpetbag government, to get the federal government off our backs." He paused for another puff on his cigarette and then continued thoughtfully, "But I do have to admit some of the Carpetbaggers are not as bad as some of the others. Now you take that damned Duprey, for instance, and compare him with John Fraser, the one who presented Susan with her medal. Both work for the Carolina Central, but what a world of difference, wouldn't you say?"

Violet, calmer now, agreed, "Yes, I would have to grant that." Turning again to Susan, she said, "But Susan, you know there is one other very important aspect to all this. Are you sure that he loves you, really sure? Some time ago I learned that our Southern accent causes those Yankee jackanapes to practically swoon. Add a little moonlight and magnolia, and they go berserk. But that is not love; it's only blind romancing for the moment."

Susan nodded and said, "I know what you mean, Violet. The first visit I had with Gilbert in the hotel dining room, he just kept me talking endlessly, about anything. Then I discovered that he was not paying one bit of attention to anything I said. He admitted he just wanted to hear my Southern accent, but later he began to pay closer and closer attention to what I had to say. Oh, yes, the moonlight and magnolias have great influence, though we seldom saw any of that—but we found that we longed for each other whether in cold rain or warm sun."

"Brent, do you honestly think the marriage can really work out?" asked Violet, still worried and not yet convinced.

"No one can be sure about such things," he answered softly, "but we both know how capable Susan is and how determined she can be, and you know, we never can forget that we owe Susan for our little Bonnie Anne still being with us now."

This brought Violet to tears. She turned to her sister and said, "Susan, it's your life. I want what is best for you, but you have to decide that. I really was not meaning to put obstacles in your way. I just wanted to be sure that you are going into this thing with your eyes open. You do realize that you will have special problems, will encounter all kinds of special situations, some of which will be adverse to your happiness."

"Yes, I know, but I also know I can handle it. Honestly, I can, Violet."

Brent smiled and said in the teasing voice he so often used with Susan, "To avoid embarrassment to us, don't you think you could arrange to elope?"

Susan brushed away her tears and laughed, "Commodore, I'll take my whole inheritance of Confederate bonds and clear out of here as soon as possible."

He laughed in return, "And I'll furnish the ladder."

"Oh, for goodness sake, you two, that won't be necessary," said Violet, weakly joining in the laughter, "I'll be proud to be with you wherever you are, Susan, you know that."

Susan ran over and hugged her sister. Brent poured glasses of scuppernong for each.

A week later, Susan, with her fiancé close behind her, ran into the library to show the diamond engagement ring that Hudson had just slipped on her finger. The sparkle of the stone could not outdo the sparkle of happiness in her blue eyes. She held out her hand for Violet and Brent to see. They each gave Susan a big hug and loving kiss.

Violet smiled and said, "I assume, like Charlotte, you will want a garden wedding here at Fair Oaks."

"Oh, no," answered Susan with a grin, "Gilbert and I plan to be different. We want to go back to the old tradition of a church wedding. My wish is to have it at Holy Cross on May 7th. Is this all right with you all?"

"Of course. I think that's wonderful," Violet reassured her. Brent nodded his agreement, too, and shook hands with the young man after giving Susan another quick hug. Violet gave each a kiss on the cheek and welcomed Gilbert to the family. She noticed the shine in his eyes, too, and the loving look that came into his eyes each time they rested on Susan. *He does love her—very much—and after all, that is what is most important in a marriage. I know that his love will be there to support her whenever Susan needs it,* she thought, more relieved than she would have thought possible.

Chapter 37

A Special Anniversary

1870

Over the ensuing weeks Brent continued to work assiduously at filling the orders for the state legislature. As his profits spiraled he leased a second warehouse in Columbia, just across the tracks from the first one. He hired a young woman to work as clerk and secretary with Cedric, and he hired two ex-longshoremen and two black freedmen to work as goods handlers in the warehouses.

On the afternoon of April 8, when Violet met him as he descended from the train at Fair Oaks, she noticed an unusually bright glint in his eye and an involuntary grin on his lips. After their greeting she demanded, "What is it, Brent? What have you been up to now?"

"Oh, nothing, my Love, why do you ask?"

She recognized only too well that mischievous look. "Oh, Brent, you are acting a little strange—even for you. Now tell me, what's happened?"

But he only said, "Hey, before you distract me completely, I've got to get Fabian and Aaron to hitch up a box wagon and drive me over to the railroad siding at Providence." He gave her another quick kiss.

She pulled back, puzzled, and exclaimed, "To Providence? What on earth for? Can't that wait until later?" *Surely he hasn't forgotten this is our wedding anniversary,* she thought.

"No, my dear, it can't wait until later. I must go quickly." Without further explanation he called Aaron to get Fabian and the rig, and he said good-by to Violet, giving her a warm kiss, and in a few minutes they were off down the lane. Just like that. Violet watched until they were out of sight, still puzzled by Brent's strange behavior. She couldn't figure it out.

Within an hour they were back, and Aaron and Fabian were unloading eight barrels into the central hall.

Violet could stand the suspense no longer. "Brent, what in the world is all this, and where did it all come from? Why are you putting all these old barrels in our hall? What a mess!"

Brent broke into a wide grin of triumph and explained, "Here, let Jarvis bring his little crowbar and open them up."

"Brent Sutler, *why* are you bringing all that stuff in here?" Violet went on, "Is this some more of your orders for the legislature? Are your warehouses in Columbia full? Why here? *Answer* me!"

"You'll soon see. Be patient a few minutes more." He called for Susan and Aunt Beuluh and Uncle Job to help Jarvis and Aaron with the unpacking.

Jarvis opened the first barrel, and Violet became speechless. Her eyes grew bigger with each opening of a barrel—sterling silver from London, cutlery and plate from

Sheffield, Baccarat crystal from Lorraine and Daum crystal from Alsace, Wedgwood jasper and china from Staffordshire, English bone china from Cornwall, and Haviland and Limoges porcelain from Limoges.

Finally she cried, "Oh, Brent, Brent, this is wonderful. I can't believe I'm really seeing all these beautiful things." Tears of delight and happiness were falling down her cheeks and turning her eyes into sparkling sapphires.

Brent had been standing aside, watching with great pleasure and some triumph as Violet exclaimed over and examined the various items he had brought. Each cry of joy widened the smile on his face. After the last barrel was opened, and Violet had looked at its contents, he crossed over and took her in his arms. "Happy anniversary, my Darling."

"Oh, Brent, *my* Darling, thank you, thank you!"

"You're welcome, my Love, and see here, we have eight place settings of china and silver for Susan in honor of her forthcoming wedding...here..." He turned to Susan, holding up a plate for her to see the pattern. "How do you like this, Susan?"

Susan screamed in delight as she ran to give Brent a hug. "It's beautiful! I love it...oh, thank you, Brent."

He continued, "And we have eight settings as an additional wedding gift for Charlotte whenever we can get them to her."

Violet looked at her husband with love in her luminous eyes as she said, "Oh, Brent, how thoughtful you are. What a wonderful thing to do—for all of us."

Violet said nothing else about this being their wedding anniversary until she and Brent were alone in their bedroom that evening. He had looked at her inquisitively several times during dinner and afterwards as they chatted with the children, but said nothing.

After she had brushed her hair the requisite one hundred strokes, she slipped into a new lavender and light blue satin negligee and sat in a rocking chair beside Brent's. She cut some squares of cheese and poured some scuppernong into their glasses, as she still pondered the transactions that Brent had been making.

"Brent, how on earth did you do it?" she asked in wonder.

"As I said I would, added our own orders to those for the legislature and got good prices, bargain prices."

"This isn't going to get us into any trouble, will it?"

"Trouble?" he asked, flashing that mischievous grin of his. "Not us. Maybe some of those smart alecks in the legislature. You know, they really are amateur crooks."

"My goodness, what do you mean, Brent?"

"Well, when they sign invoices and vouchers they are for the actual items and the actual prices. Of course there may be a lot of skullduggery and concealed transactions going on that I know nothing about, but it seems that on the whole, if they are going to steal from the state they are going to do it honestly."

Violet laughed as Brent continued, "You see, when I submit my invoices, they are always for actual items and prices. You would think that they would be listing ladies' perfume and handbags and hosiery and so on as stationery or kerosene or something, but no, they put it down for what it is. That leaves us clean, but I'm thinking that someday someone is going to catch up with them."

"I certainly hope so."

He took a sip of scuppernong and a bit of cheese, then remarked, "But, oh, not until we have made our fortune for as much as we can."

Violet decided it was now time to change the subject to a more important matter. "Oh, Brent, that's enough of business for tonight. What time is it anyhow?"

"How should I know, and why do you ask?"

From the drawer of the little table between their chairs, she withdrew a small, square package which she handed to Brent, saying, "Happy anniversary, my Darling."

His eyes lighted up as he realized that Violet had remembered their anniversary after all. He opened the gift and gave an exclamation of delight as he saw a gold pocket watch. It was a Waltham with spring case. He pushed on the stem; it sprang open. He wound it—just to see the second-hand move. He opened the back of the case, and there he saw an engraving: *To Brent, April 8, 1870, with love from Violet.*

"Oh, Darling, this is marvelous," he said, "probably the best watch made, and the most beautiful I have ever seen!"

"Go ahead and set it."

"Well, I see by the mantle clock that it is after eleven. I'll just be sure to set it well before twelve, midnight."

"Why is that so important?"

"Otherwise we might be celebrating the fifth anniversary of Lee's surrender at Appomattox!"

"We certainly mustn't let that happen."

Then Brent withdrew from his robe pocket a little package that he handed to Violet. "Happy anniversary, Violet, happy eighth anniversary."

"More? Oh, Brent, there can't be more after all those things down stairs!" she exclaimed.

It was a gold necklace with a rectangular pendant. Inscribed on the pendant were the words, *Je t'aime plus qu' hier, moins que demain.* And on the back, *To Violet with love, Brent, 4/8/70.*

Now it was her turn to exclaim in delight. "Oh, my Darling, it's the loveliest thing I have ever seen." She repeated the message in English softly to herself, "I love you more today than yesterday and less than tomorrow.' Oh, thank you, thank you so very much. I shall treasure it always."

She refilled their wine glasses, and a little self-consciously took from her pocket a piece of folded notepaper. Coming closer to the lamp for better light, she said, "Listen, here is a poem I wrote for our anniversary," and she began to read:

Why do I love thee? Let me count the ways:
I love thee for thy quick mind, and all the beautiful thoughts,
Contained therein.
I so love thy noble heart, and the sensitivity,

Contained therein.
I love thy sense of honor, with sincere dedication,
That lies therein.
I love thy depths of passion, and thy heights of feeling,
That lie therein.
I love thy sweet tenderness, that gentles thy being,
Contained therein.
I love thy spiritual, overtones given our love,
Contained therein.
Thus, I do love thee, in so many ways.

"Wonderful!" whispered Brent in a husky voice, "Did you write that? Just for me?"

"Of course, Darling. I'm so glad you like it."

Then he took a piece of paper from his pocket and read:

To be with you is to reach the height,
Like flying so high on a starlit night.
We meet as others on earth below,
But soon our souls are set aglow
As we reach to heights unknown before,
And share in a sense the days of yore,
While rising beyond all previously known
To the summit of the best to which we've grown.

"Reach for the heights," is never in jest,
Reach always to find whatever is best.
Look to the end of the rolling sea,
To find what is best for you and me.
Sail on to the moon in our ecstasy,
Drift on to new worlds with a rhapsody.
Look on to the Venus as evening star,
Remembering I love all that you are.

"Why, Brent, that's lovely! Don't tell me that you wrote that!" Her feelings were reflected in her glistening eyes, reminding Brent of the lavender-blue sunsets over the rolling sea on hot nights.

"Of course, my Love."

"But when did you write it? You've been so very busy lately."

"Oh, during long nights at sea and long days on the railroad," he laughed.

"Well, it's wonderful," she declared.

He rose from his chair and, taking her hand, he drew her to her feet and kissed her with deep passion. He whispered tenderly, "You know, one plus one equals one."

"And two less one equals none," she answered before he sealed her lips with another kiss.

Chapter 38

Natchez vs. Robert E. Lee

1870

When wedding bells rang from the tower of the Church of the Holy Cross for Susan at one o'clock on Saturday afternoon, May 7, 1870, over a hundred relatives, friends, and neighbors were gathering for the ceremony scheduled for an hour later. The sisters' grandmother, Catherine Victoria Lee, now in better health, with her personal maid, Judy, had arrived a few days ago from her home near Williamsburg, Virginia. In all seriousness, that indomitable widow announced that the girls' late grandfather would never forgive her if she missed Susan's wedding too, and she certainly didn't want to be chastised when she rejoined him on her way to the Lord. Brent's mother and father and his sister had come up by train from Charleston the day before. Brent's brother, Bruce, was still working on the railroads in the west and was not expected to be present. The bridegroom's parents, Samuel and Martha Hudson, were there from Salem, Indiana. All had been warmly welcomed and given comfortable, refurbished chambers at Fair Oaks. Quarters for personal servants that the guests had brought with them were provided on the third floor and in the basement.

For her wedding, Susan wore the traditional white bridal gown with a long train and veil. Two layers of overskirts were swept around to the back, creating the latest style of a bustle effect, and were draped over a long full skirt worn over a smaller hoop than that of the past. Her gown was decorated with exquisite lace and tiny seed pearls sewn into rose patterns. Little shimmering lights seemed to bounce off the satin folds of the dress and the beaded pearls as Susan moved. The neckline was cut in the sweetheart style and edged with lace and pearls, with little puff sleeves at the shoulders. Gilbert had given her a gold chain and inscribed heart locket for a wedding gift and had insisted that she open her gift early so that it might be worn at their wedding. In turn, she had given him a gold watch chain with a tiny heart attached. Susan's lovely blonde hair was swept up and back, her curls cascading down the back, repeating the layered design of her skirts. Her train-length veil was held to her head by a tiara decorated with fine lace and tiny pearls as on her dress, but also fresh white roses matching those in her bouquet.

Susan had selected pink, her favorite color, for her three attendants who all wore the new fashioned dresses with bustles. Violet, the matron of honor, wore a dress with the taffeta bodice and first overskirt swag of deep pink. The bodice came down over her hips and ended in a rounded point in the front. The sleeves were dainty and puffed, the neckline modestly low, and the tight waist emphasized the smallness of Violet's waist. The second overskirt of tulle and lace, and of a lighter, more delicate shade of pink, was pulled back into a swag, and the full skirt under the first two overskirts, of the same light pink tulle and lace, went into a small train at the back.

Charlotte and Patricia Rutledge, Susan's long-time friend whom she had met at Edge Hill School, wore dresses styled exactly like that worn by Violet, except their taffeta bodices and skirts were all one same shade of soft pink. The three attendants wore chokers of tiny pearls and matching drop earrings. Their nosegays were made of pink camellias and white baby's breath surrounded by white lace, and with narrow pink ribbon streamers. Their hair was worn similar to Susan's, pulled up and back off their faces, with curls cascading down the back.

Leland and two of Gilbert's fellow lieutenants from the Sumter garrison attended the bridegroom. All the men in the wedding party wore dark gray Prince Albert frock coats and gray striped trousers, and wore dark gray ascot ties over their high collars and white starched shirts.

Brent gave the bride away and Bonnie Anne and J.J. were on duty again as flower girl and ring bearer. Much to Susan's delight, Charlotte had brought the exquisite pillow that Susan had made for her wedding, and which J.J. would again carry. This time it was Charlotte who lightly stitched the wedding ring to the pillow so that little J.J. would not accidentally drop it on the way down the aisle. Bonnie Anne's dress, less elaborate and with no bustle, was made entirely of light pink tulle and lace. Her long hair was pulled back and tied with narrow pink ribbon, with baby's breath blossoms tucked in the knot of ribbons. She carried pink rose petals in her basket to drop along the white aisle runner. J.J., having outgrown the little suit he had worn for Charlotte's wedding and now a year older, was dressed much like the groom's attendants, except that his trousers were tucked into gaiters, which were worn over black patent lace-up shoes.

Mammy, Evelina, Hattie, Ellie, Aunt Beulah, Rachel, Leo, Fabian, and other house servants and field foremen, all occupied pews adjacent to those of the family. The faithful servants, Jarvis, Aaron, Uncle Job, and Leo, dressed in frock coats, gray trousers, gray ascot ties, and white shirts, and so much a part of the family, proudly showed the guests to their seats. This latter had been a special request of Susan's, and did not go unnoticed by their Yankee guests, who had never been a part of such a special relationship, yet they recognized this as a gesture of appreciation and fondness for the individuals involved.

The church organist brought out the best in the great organ in the prelude of traditional music and the wedding march. Father Wilson read the ceremony in his own dignified way.

After the wedding, the wedding party and the guests gathered at Fair Oaks for a gala reception in the beautiful garden that Fabian and his helpers had labored over so lovingly for Susan's big day. Josh and the *Little Brown Jugs* provided the music at first. Then Rev. Jackson and his violinists played for the guests. For a while, Violet had been in a quandary about the reception music. She personally wanted Little Josh and his band to play, but the Rev. Jackson, who had played for Charlotte's reception, mentioned to Violet that he and his musicians were looking forward to repeating the performance. She finally decided the wisest and most diplomatic thing to do was to let both groups have the honor. Both Little Josh and Rev. Jackson seemed satisfied with her decision, the Rev. Jackson declaring with pride that, after all, he was the one who discovered Little Josh's talents—to which Violet made no comment, for certainly he was partially right.

After the bride and groom had cut and served the first pieces of the wedding cake, a very rich, unleavened fruitcake, they retreated to change their clothes for travel. Brent and Violet caught them on the way in and asked the young couple to come into the office for a few minutes. Without a word, Brent went directly to the safe and took out an envelope. "Here, Sue-girl," said Brent. "With the compliments of Violet and me, here is redemption for your Confederate war bonds that your father, the Major, willed to you. We hope that this will help you and Gilbert with a start toward your new home."

Susan burst into tears. Even Gilbert was close to tears at the generous gesture. He loved Susan with all his heart, and yet he was all too aware of the difference in the financial and social standing of the two families. He had been honest with Susan about salary expectations, but he knew that, in time, these would increase. Much to his relief, none of this seemed to faze Susan in the least. She told him that she loved him, period, and that they would work things out. She knew he could and would be able to take care of her—and that she didn't eat much anyhow.

As the guests threw rice after them, they ran down the lane to catch the late afternoon train for Columbia where they would spend their wedding night. They would leave the next day for their new home in Vicksburg, Mississippi, where Gilbert would be going to work as an engineer for the railroad.

The loneliness and sense of emptiness that Violet had felt after Charlotte's wedding was if anything redoubled after Susan's wedding and departure from Fair Oaks. The absence of Susan's bubbling personality, good humor, wit, and helpfulness seemed to leave empty echoes throughout the house. More than ever Violet devoted herself to the plantation and to her children who also were missing Susan, as was Little Josh, for Susan had paid so much attention to all of them, cared for them so lovingly, played with them so often, and teased and vexed them. Even Old Dan seemed to mope about for a week or so.

A month after the wedding Violet was happy to receive a long-awaited letter from her youngest sister. After describing their trip to Vicksburg, Susan went on to say,

> *We have found a small house, brick with iron grillwork galleries, on the corner of Walnut and Jackson Streets, on the bluff high above the Mississippi River. We do have a couple of guest rooms, and we hope that you and Brent and Bonnie Anne and J.J. can make use of them soon.*
>
> *The whole city is built among the Walnut Hills which rise about 260 feet above the river. It still bears the marks of war everywhere. The cupola on the courthouse is still full of holes from the cannon of the Yankee gunboats. Grant's siege in 1863 lasted forty-seven days. During that time they say three thousand civilian inhabitants lived in*

caves. They say that during that time people were paying $12 a pound for mule meat, $200 a barrel for flour, and $100 a gallon for rum! They printed newspapers on the back of wallpaper.

And the people here have been going through some of the same kinds of Reconstruction oppression as we in South Carolina. But at last Mississippi was admitted back into the Union just this last February. Before that they had a lot of turmoil.

Just as we had a new state constitution in South Carolina in 1868, they also did in Mississippi. Theirs was framed by a notorious "Black-and-Tan" convention of Radicals. They did not allow anybody to vote who even had <u>supported</u> the Confederacy. Still at the election which followed, the voters rejected the Radical constitution by a big majority, and the conservative Democrats even were able to elect the governor, about half of the legislature, and most of the Congressmen.

But the Black-and-Tan convention would not stand still for that. They appointed an investigating committee which claimed to find enough fraud to overturn the outcome of the election, so they declared that their constitution had been adopted and that the Radical Republican ticket had been elected. But the people would not take that either. Then Yankee soldiers forced the elected governor out and installed a general by the name of Aimes who ruled as military governor until they could install the Radical Republican James Alcorn.

Later Congress said that parts of the Constitution could be voted on separately; then the voters voted for it, but overwhelmingly rejected the parts against the ex-Confederates.

Gilbert already is hard at work, restoring and improving the Alabama and Vicksburg Valley Railroad.

We have put our membership in Christ Church, the Episcopal Church at the corner of Locust and Main Streets, only about five blocks from our house. The church is a beautiful English Gothic built about twenty-five years ago. Gilbert has been very broad-minded about this, since he comes from Presbyterian background.

And we are meeting many new friends at the church—and not of just the 'Gig' society, either, Commodore Brent!

Yes, there are Carpetbaggers and Scalawags who try to control the Negroes to run things here, but now I guess we may have a little more freedom than in South Carolina. Actually we have run across several "good Yankees" and lots of good old Southerners, of course.

I miss you all and hope you'll come for a visit soon. Love to you all and Mammy and Evelina, Jarvis and Aaron—and everyone. Kiss the children for me, and give Old Dan a hug.

Yours, Susan

That summer, crops at Fair Oaks promised to be the best since the War. For the wheat harvest at the end of June, Violet was especially proud of a new implement just obtained by her vice-president and purchasing agent, Brent Sutler. It was a new model McCormick reaper, this one drawn by three mules. And it was a self-binder, that is, the sheaves came out bound, so that crews of workers followed it only to shock the wheat, not to bind the sheaves. The reaper could cut and bind twelve acres a day. With the old reaper still able to do six acres a day, this meant that the work crews could be reduced by a third.

For his part, Brent was pleased to see an extension of the telegraph service. Now the newly-formed Southern and Atlantic Telegraph Company took over the line that ran along the Carolina Central Railroad, though the railroad retained its use of the line for dispatching trains, and Brent retained his right of access at Fair Oaks, at Columbia, and at Charleston.

Near the middle of July another long letter arrived from Susan. It was filled with a report of the great steamboat race on the Mississippi River between the *Natchez* and the *Robert E. Lee.* After supper that evening, Violet joined Brent who was sitting in a rocking chair on the front porch, smoking a cigarette.

"Have you heard about the steamboat race on the Mississippi?" she asked him.

"Only that they were having one. Why do you ask?" he replied, glancing at her with eyebrows raised in question.

"Oh, it was very exciting. Susan tells all about it and sends newspaper clippings."

"Well, tell me, who won?"

She laughed, wanting to keep him in suspense. "You just wait and see. Listen to what Susan says."

> *All that anybody has been talking about these days was the steamboat race between the* Natchez *and the* Robert E. Lee. *Gilbert found these specifications in one of the papers. I don't know very much about all this, but Brent (the Commodore!) may be interested:*
>
> *The* Robert E. Lee *was built in 1866. Its registered tonnage is 1,467. It is 300 feet long, with breadth of 44 feet and depth of 10 feet. Its paddle wheels are 36 x 16.5 feet, and its engine cylinders are 40 x 10 inches.*
>
> *The* Natchez *was built in 1869, has a registered tonnage of 1,547, and it is 301.5 feet long, with breadth of 42.5 feet and depth of 9.5 feet. Its paddle wheels are 42 x 16 feet, and its engine cylinders are 34 x 10 inches.*
>
> *Both of these vessels can carry 2,000 tons of cargo, but the best parts are the upper decks. They are built like palaces—big brass*

chandeliers, red-woolen covered floors, velvet curtains, big open red-carpeted staircases from the main deck up to the top. There are silver water coolers, wooden parquet decks, and outside on the main deck, a spittoon every six feet.

The Robert E. Lee *was built at New Albany, Indiana, on the Ohio River. They say that when the builders started painting the name on the side—in big letters on the wheel guards—the people made such an uproar that the builders towed it across the river to the friendlier locale of Louisville, Kentucky, to complete the painting of its name,* Robert E. Lee. *And I always thought that southern Indiana was more sympathetic toward the South!*

The Natchez *was built at Cincinnati, and people think it was built for the very purpose of beating the* Robert E. Lee.

From the time the boats left St. Mary's Market, New Orleans, at 5:20 p.m. on June 30th, crowds were gathering in front of the Western Union Telegraph Office to read the bulletins in the window. Thousands of people gathered at the river banks and levees all along the way. Two thousand excursionists were on other steamers to watch.

The newspapers reported that in the first mile the Robert E. Lee *was four minutes ahead, and twenty-five miles later the difference still was just four minutes. People were betting which boat would get to which place first, and by how much time. Someone in Louisville bet $15,000 that the* Robert E. Lee *would beat the* Natchez *to Vicksburg. Another man bet $40,000 on the* Natchez.

The Governor of Louisiana rushed from giving a commencement speech at Louisiana State University at Baton Rouge to board the Robert E. Lee *with only ten minutes to spare, to ride as far as Natchez, Mississippi. The* Robert E. Lee *was ten minutes ahead when they passed the city of Natchez.*

You can imagine the excitement here when we learned that the boats were approaching Vicksburg on Friday afternoon, July 1st. Many people ran down to the waterfront, but Gilbert and I joined the crowd on the bluff where we had a grand view up and down the river. Hundreds of men, women, and children were there. When the Robert E. Lee *came into sight about 5:20 in the afternoon, just twenty-four hours after leaving New Orleans, loud cheers went up, and then cannon began booming a salute. Excited men were running around betting how many minutes it would be until the* Natchez *appeared. Actually, it was just eighteen minutes behind the* Robert E. Lee, *and the crowd cheered it wildly, too.*

Farther up the river, as darkness fell, people lit great bonfires to welcome the boats. A news report from Memphis said that ten thousand people shouted in competition with the roar of artillery and

> *bursting of bombs when the* Robert E. Lee *came into sight there about 11:00 o'clock that night. The* Natchez *was an hour and a half behind.*
>
> *Another report said that both boats had had some trouble with their pumps. At Cairo, Illinois, where the Ohio River empties into the Mississippi, a thousand people from Louisville, Evansville, Paducah, and other places were on steamboats to watch the race. But it was at Cairo that the* Natchez *ran into trouble. Actually, both boats ran into dense fog and hit bottom in the shallow shoals, but the* Robert E. Lee *kept going, while the* Natchez *was delayed for five hours.*
>
> *Then came the wild celebration in St. Louis when the* Robert E. Lee *arrived at 11:33 in the morning on the Fourth of July, with a record for the whole trip from New Orleans of three days, 18 hours and 13 minutes. Now the* Natchez *was six and a half hours behind...*

"Sounds mighty exciting," responded Brent. "I'd like to have been there. Is that all of her letter?"

"There's just a little more," said Violet, as she resumed her reading of Susan's letter.

> *Gilbert won fifty dollars in bets on the* Robert E. Lee. *I don't much approve of wagering, but have to admit that did add to the excitement. For a while the losers refused to pay Gilbert—they said that the captain of the* Robert E. Lee *had taken an unfair advantage by arranging to have moving barges bring coal to him so that he would not have to stop to take on coal, and even at one place he had a fast steamer come alongside to deliver coal while he continued moving at a good speed. But my contention was, that if there had been no rule established against it, it should be applauded. I thought the whole idea was for a captain to use his ingenuity to gain an advantage. Frankly, I thought him terribly clever!*
>
> *The losers said also that the* Natchez *carried a full load of cargo and passengers, while the* Robert E. Lee *carried no cargo and only seventy-five selected passengers. I guess maybe Captain Leathers of the* Natchez *decided to make some good money in carrying cargo and passengers in the race, while Captain Cannon of the* Robert E. Lee *figured he could make more by betting on his own boat. Good thinking on his part, I would say.*
>
> *Anyway, it was an exciting boat race, and it thrilled thousands. How Gilbert and I wish you all could have been here and seen it with us. We do miss you all just so very much, and I must confess that in*

spite of all the excitement of the race, I am a bit homesick for Fair Oaks and everybody. Do give the children a kiss for us and a hug for everyone else. Come visit as soon as you can!

Yours, Susan

"Lordy, wasn't all that exciting!" exclaimed Violet, as she laid down the letter. "I really do wish we had been there to join in all that fun and suspense."

"I, too, but you know that this has been a busy time for us, Violet." Then he broke into a broad grin and laughed out loud.

Violet looked at him suspiciously. She knew her husband well. "What is it, Brent? Had you already heard of this race? There's something you've not told me, my dear husband."

Brent could scarcely contain himself. He was trying hard to suppress his laughter and high spirits, but managed to blurt out, "Heard about the outcome, but none of the details."

"All right, Brent Sutler, out with it. What about all this?" demanded Violet.

"Well, my Darling, I had a couple of hundred on the race," answered Brent nonchalantly.

"A couple of *hundred*! Do you mean dollars?" asked a stunned Violet.

"Yes, my Love, a couple of hundred dollars."

Violet found her voice. "Oh, Brent, you rascal! You mean you wagered all that? Why Brent Sutler you know you should not—"

He hastily interrupted—"with five men in Columbia..."

"Well at least they did not risk so much. Their wives will have to be only one-fifth as furious—"

"Two hundred with each of five men—"

"Brent! You mean a thousand all together?" she was nearly breathless.

"Sure. You see, Violet, I really thought the *Natchez* had a good chance of winning this one, and they did give good odds—"

Violet was horrified. "Brent, I just cannot believe that you bet on the *Natchez* instead of the *Robert E. Lee*!" She paused to catch her breath and then went on in an agitated voice, "Brent Sutler, do you mean that you lost a thousand dollars? *A thousand dollars*! Why you silly goose—"

He held up his hand as if to stop her, and still laughing, he went on, "No, no, Violet. I thought better of it. I stayed with the *Robert E. Lee* all the way through the betting, so you see, my sweet wife, we *won*—with two to one odds—two thousand dollars. I figured we could use a little venture capital."

Violet just looked at him. She didn't know whether to be angry at him or exult in their good fortune. She decided the latter was far better. She, too, broke into laughter, albeit a bit forced at first. "Oh, Brent Sutler, what am I going to do with you?"

He crossed around, lifted her from her chair, and kissed her soundly. "Ha!" he murmured huskily, and then he returned to his rocking chair beside her.

The temperature of the evening was comfortable on the porch. A slight breeze brought currents of perfumed air from flowers in bloom, and the songs of various birds created a medley of symphonic tunes—the low mournful *coo-ah, coo, coo, coo* of the Mourning Dove, the musical, somewhat melancholy trill of the Pine Warbler coupled with the clear-ringing, flirtatious *tawee-tawee-tee-o* of the Hooded Warbler, the whistled *peter-peter* of the Tufted Titmouse, and *chickadee-dee-dee-dee* of the Chickadee, whilst the Red-cockaded Woodpecker pecked time for the score generated by the others. Occasionally he would let out a rattling scold note as if to speed them on. Brent and Violet sat in companionable silence that was occasionally broken by comments and observations, as each read newspaper clippings of the race.

He broke the silence by commenting, "Did you realize that the bets on the race, including many on the other side of the Atlantic Ocean, ran into the millions?"

"Incredible! Will there be another race soon, do you think? Maybe next year?"

"Not like this one, Violet. This was an event of a lifetime."

"Brent..."

"Yes, my dear?"

"I was wondering—have you ever seen the Mississippi River?"

He nodded. "Only once, before the War, around New Orleans."

"Don't you think it would be fun to go to Vicksburg and visit Susan, and then take the *Robert E. Lee* to New Orleans?"

His smile was tender as he answered her question. "Indeed I do, my Darling, that would be most enjoyable and interesting."

She took a big sigh. "Well then, may we go this fall, after the cotton is in? Oh, Brent, may we? I would like that just so very much!" Her beautiful blue eyes pleaded for her.

He nodded again, smiling gently. He always found it hard to resist Violet when she looked at him like that, but there was a plan formulating in his mind, something that would take a large chunk out of the fall. He still had some loose ends to tighten up and did not want to mention his idea to Violet until he had worked out these few problems. So he just answered, "Not this fall, my Love, next year, maybe."

"Oh, Brent!" she came back in a sharp tone, not understanding and vexed that he didn't want to go this fall. "It seems like you're always saying 'next year' or 'later'!" Then, realizing how she must have sounded and knowing that he would have a logical reason for his decision, it was she who rose and walked over to his chair to kiss him. "I do understand this is a busy time for you, but it *is* disappointing to me. May I ask why?"

"Not now, later. Maybe next week."

She sighed in frustration. "See what I mean?"

Chapter 39

Seaward Bound Again

1870

One evening a few days later Violet walked into the library of Fair Oaks where she found Brent, sitting in a rocking chair in front of the fireless fireplace, Bonnie Anne in one arm and J.J. in the other, teaching the little ones to sing with him, *"Blow the man down—"*

"Brent Sutler, you've got salt water in your veins, and I don't think you're ever going to get it out," smiled Violet, her eyes twinkling with humor.

"Well, to tell you the truth, I am thinking of just one more little run at sea, down to the Caribbean, to help get us on our feet—and more," he said, glancing up at her with some trepidation as to her reaction to this news.

"So that was what you were getting at in wanting to postpone a trip down the Mississippi. I guess you would rather sail on the Caribbean than on the Mississippi," she said with a note of exasperation in her voice.

"Well there I'll be my own captain, and making a fortune, I hope. On the Mississippi I would just be a passenger under some other captain, and it would be costing me a fortune."

"But the Caribbean? What on earth are you talking about?"

"Now hear me out, Violet. There's going to be a war between France and Prussia. I think there is no doubt of it, and they are going to be wanting guns and ammunition and cotton."

Looking at him with her hands on her hips, Violet asked, "I don't understand. What has that got to do with us?"

"I've learned recently that there is a large cache of weapons hidden in underground storage near the old Palmetto Armory that Sherman's Yankees did not find."

"Really?"

"And, my dear, you know your good friend Franklin Moses, Junior—"

"That crooked scoundrel! Surely you are not counting on having any dealings with him!" she said. She was shocked at the very idea.

Brent went on in a calm voice, "As I was saying, you know he is state adjutant general as well as speaker of the house. He already has been diverting to his own pockets substantial sums appropriated for the purchase of new weapons for the militia. Now I am sure he would jump at the chance to realize a dollar or two for several thousand old weapons."

"For the state?" she asked with contempt.

"Of course for the state so long as he can get half for himself." He snickered at the thought of Moses' crooked dealings.

She stared at him incredulously. "Brent! Are you thinking of buying those weapons?"

"Well, yes," he nodded. "I was just thinking, a little voyage down to the West Indies with a cargo of guns and ammunition and cotton would be worth thousands, worth a fortune, Violet."

"Oh, no you don't, Brent Sutler, the last time you went to sea we didn't see you for three years. I don't want to ever go through such a separation from you again!" She could not hide her distress at the thought of Brent's taking another sea voyage.

"Oh, Violet, this is different. This is business, and it would be just this one time. I could make it there and back on an old sailing vessel in less than a month. I'd be gone no more than a month, my Darling, I promise."

"Sure, sure, just this one time. I know you well, Brent. If you fail, you'll have to go one more time to make up your losses, and if you succeed and make lots of money, you'll be saying how easy it was, and you should go one more time to make twice as much money." She was troubled by all this.

The children were getting restless with all this grown-up talk. They climbed down from Brent's lap, and Bonnie Anne asked, "Mommy, may we go to the playroom now?"

"Yes, yes, go find Evelina or Little Josh and ask them to go up there with you. I'll come read you a story later," Violet answered.

"Don't run up the stairs!" warned Brent as they ran into the hall.

Brent returned to the topic at hand, saying gently but firmly, "No, Violet, this war between France and Prussia is not going to last very long. Everyone thinks the French have superior weapons and forces, but I think old Louis Napoleon is going to be in for it this time. Now if the great Napoleon were still there in charge, he probably could pull it off with a great victory—but not this one. The French have plenty of arms and everything right now, but they won't after the Germans hit them."

Violet could not help but be intrigued by what Brent was telling her, but she still had a frown on her face as she said, "I still don't like it, your going away."

"Now, Darling, you know very well that I don't want to be away from you and the children, but this is a chance to make a fortune—a real fortune I tell you."

"How much of a fortune?"

Brent thought a moment, figuring up sums in his mind. The corners of his mouth curved into a wide smile. "What would you say to a hundred thousand dollars?"

Violet gasped in disbelief. She paused to catch her breath. At the thought of so much money she began to adopt a more positive attitude. "Just exactly what do you have in mind?"

He noted her deepening interest in the subject and continued with a tinge of excitement in his voice. "First, I'll need to run down to Charleston and see if my father has been able to recover an old ship that he could let me use—and see what the prospects might be for getting together a crew. Then, if I do get a ship, I need to hurry to Columbia to see Frank Moses and get my hands on those weapons. And I'll carry our remaining cotton and save the shipping charges to Europe. I'll try to get more cotton in Columbia, too. I would hope to be able to be ready for the voyage in a month or six weeks, and, as I said, Violet, the trip itself should take less than a month."

As usual, Violet's keen intelligence spiked her curiosity. "You said the West Indies. Why there? Why are you going to the West Indies?" She rose from her chair and crossed over to look at the globe on a small table by the bookcases.

"For good reason. There's a little island in the Lesser Antilles, in that part known as the Leeward islands, called St. Martin. It is half French and half Dutch. In case some Prussian ship or agent is concerned about contraband of war going to the French, I'll simply be on my way to the Dutch port. Then I can make my deal with some Frenchmen, slip around to the French side of St. Martin, and load it on to one of their ships bound for Bordeaux." He leaned back in his chair with a sigh of satisfaction at the prospect of this adventure.

"But why not take a steamer? Wouldn't that be faster?" Now Violet found herself completely caught up in the venture.

"Not much faster, and I don't think any steamers would be available at the price I have in mind," he responded with a grin, "and anyway I don't want to waste precious cargo space with machinery and coal."

The children came racing back into the room. "Sing to us some more, Daddy," Bonnie Anne insisted, climbing back on his lap. J.J. leaned against his other knee, looking up at his father in anticipation.

Brent laughed and sang again the strains of *Blow the man down,* and then paused long enough to say to Violet, "But I've got to move quickly to keep a jump ahead of that Napoleon. I must buy those arms before he declares war; then others will be getting ideas."

She nodded her understanding, "Yes, you're right about that, but Brent, what about your work with the railroad? Are you just going to let that go?"

"No, no, on the contrary, I am angling for a promotion."

"A promotion?" *What a man,* she thought, *he's full of surprises. Life is certainly never dull around here.*

"Yes, a promotion. I understand there's going to be an opening for superintendent of maintenance." He broke into a laugh as he went on, "You know how a promotion is less work for more pay. For now I'll be requesting a two-month's leave of absence. That should be no problem, for things are pretty slow there just now."

"Oh, Brent, that sounds good. I hope this all works out the way you want it to."

"I believe it will, but for now," he said as he lifted Bonnie Anne to the floor and rose, "it is time for these little ones to go *Sailing, Sailing* off to bed, I think. Come along children, we'll go up with you for a bedtime story."

The children ran into the hall, and, as he and Violet followed, Brent called after them, "Walk! Don't run up the stairs!" He turned to Violet and asked, "Where do they get all their energy? They seem to always run, never walk."

Violet took Brent's arm as they reached the stairwell, laughing as she replied, "From their father, I'm sure."

Violet was in the nursery reading to the children on Thursday evening, July 21st, when she heard Brent come bounding up the stairs two steps at a time. His broad smile as he burst into the room revealed that he must have had some success in arrangements for his voyage to the West Indies.

"We're in business!" he said gleefully. Then he paused long enough to kiss her and the children. His excitement was so contagious that Violet began to become infused with it. But that contagion carried with it a dread on her part, a dread of his being away for that long, a dread that something might happen to him, sailing down the Atlantic Ocean with war goods, sailing down the Atlantic in hurricane season.

But she only smiled and said, "Come on down and tell me all about it." She beckoned for Evelina to watch the children, and she and Brent went downstairs.

They stopped in the kitchen for a pot of coffee and then went into the office. Violet poured the coffee as they took their chairs on their respective sides of the large desk.

Brent started by saying, "I really had a close call on timing."

"How do you mean?"

"Haven't you picked up any news dispatches on the telegraph?"

She shook her head. "Sorry, I'm afraid I've not been monitoring that as I should."

"Well, I made the deal with Frank Moses, Jr., on Monday, and I learned from the Columbia paper yesterday that France had indeed declared war on Prussia on Tuesday, the 19th."

"Oh, my goodness, that was close. What did you get from that scoundrel, Moses?"

"Six thousand rifles, muskets, and carbines—"

"Six thousand?"

"Yes, six thousand—a number of them made right there at the arsenal, but never delivered to our troops, weapons turned in by the men when the War was over, Yankee weapons picked up on the battlefields, and, get this, Violet, a bunch of French rifles that arrived too late to be of any use to the Confederacy, and now I propose to sell them right back to the French! Ha!"

She laughed at that and said, "Ha! And did you get a good price?"

"I think so—three and a half dollars apiece," and then he added contemptuously, "of which I assume half will end up in the pocket of Frank Moses, Jr."

"No doubt, but that price does sound good." She paused as a thought struck her. A frown appeared upon her smooth forehead. "But wait, that means twenty-one thousand dollars. Brent, where on earth are we going to get that kind of money?"

He looked at Violet questioningly. "Well, partner, for a starter, we have the ten thousand in winnings from the *Robert E. Lee.*" And I was hoping we could invest our joint account, and my personal account, and then I'll borrow if necessary. After all, the two hundred bales of our cotton that I am going to sell down there should bring more than that."

"Well, yes, I suppose so...all right, go ahead. Do that." she agreed.

"Some of those rifles already are on the way to Charleston, and I am moving the others to the warehouse to ship as soon as cars are ready," he explained.

"What else?" she asked. She could tell by the tone of his voice that there was more.

"Fifty tons of ammunition."

She drew in her breath in one big gulp. "Brent! Won't that be dangerous?"

"No, not if it's handled carefully," he reassured her, "and I can assure you this will be the case as soon as the crew is aware that they are handling ammunition."

"Is there anything else?"

"Yes. I bought three hundred bales of cotton at eighteen cents in Columbia–got some of it right from under the cotton mill."

"Can you make anything on that?"

"I believe so, and of course I hope I can add a thousand bushels of our wheat."

Amazed at his organization and execution of plans, she asked, "Of course, but you seem mighty sure of getting all this out, so I assume you found a ship?"

He nodded. "Violet, that's the best part. Father has been reconditioning an old pre-war barquentine. And, oh, is she a beauty! Now called *Aura Lee*. She's freshly painted, wood of oak and teakwood. Beautiful lines. Will be ready for loading in about four weeks, and Father will let me use it for a low fee if I will carry about a hundred tons of general cargo for him for transshipment to Europe and South America, and if I will stop and pick some things up for him at Charlotte Amalie in the Danish West Indies."

"That seems fair enough, and it's awfully kind of him to help us out like this."

"Indeed, it is. He's very interested in all this."

"Did you have a chance to do anything about a crew, Brent?"

At this he appeared slightly frustrated. "Only a beginning, but that will be no problem. When I put out the word that I will pay sixty dollars for each seaman for a month's cruise to the West Indies, they'll be lining up to sign on. Father said he would handle that and would have a good crew on board when we were ready to sail."

What an adventure! thought Violet. She asked hopefully, "Oh, Brent, it sounds so exciting! May I come along with you?"

He hated to disappoint her. In some ways it would be a lot of fun to have her along, but he answered in a gentle tone, "My dear, I don't think that would be a good idea this time, but I will promise you this. Some day, when things quiet down, I would love to sail the *Aura Lee* to Europe with you and the kids on board."

Violet sighed with disappointment, although his answer was not unexpected. "I'll remember that and remind you of it at a later date," she said, smiling at him in understanding. She knew he did not want to endanger her–and there was definitely an element of danger in this voyage.

"But I want you and the children to come to Charleston and see us off...and maybe be there to greet us when we return," he went on.

"Oh, yes, that would be wonderful. Let's plan on it."

"Certainly. My parents would be glad to have you all stay with them for as long as you like." He paused and looked over at her, a question in his eyes as he asked, "I was wondering...how would you feel about my taking Little Josh along as my cabin boy?"

She hesitated a moment, thinking about his request. "Oh, I don't know how I could get along without him—and I would hate for him to miss his music practice—and we would miss his cheerful disposition around here...but...what a great experience this would be for him...and he would be a trustworthy helper. You know you can always count on him...what does a cabin boy do anyhow?"

Brent knew Violet would not deny Little Josh this opportunity for a different kind of education and experience. "The cabin boy keeps the officers' quarters clean and neat, serves the captain's table, run errands, and so on." he explained. "And as you say, I can always count on him. He'll be of great help to me in many ways."

"Then of course he should go. What about Aaron? Do you plan to take him, too?"

"Yes, I thought I would take him as an orderly. He will continue to care after my clothing, do laundry, do odd chores as needed. He's already told me he wants to come along."

"All right, it would be a great experience for both Little Josh and Aaron. Plan on taking them with you. As a matter of fact, now that I think about it, it will be a comfort to know that you have those two looking after you."

He grinned at her and just said, "Thanks, my Love. I know you'll miss them...along with your husband, of course."

On a Sunday afternoon in August, while Violet and Brent were relaxing on the front porch from the preparations for the voyage, John Frierson and Will Anderson drove up the lane. Exchanging pleasantries quickly, they gave the impression that they were on a serious mission.

Taking a chair beside Brent, John went directly to the point. "Brent," he said, clearing his voice, "some of us in this part of the county have been meeting on several occasions, and we have come to the conclusion that we would like for you to be a candidate for the State Senate."

"Well, I don't know about that," was all that Brent could manage to say in his state of complete surprise at this request.

Will, who had taken the chair on the other side of Violet, put in, "Brent, we've just got to do what we can to relieve us from the plunder of this state legislature."

"I'll agree to that," Brent responded, "but I don't see what I could do to help that situation."

"It's not just you," John explained, "we must work all over the state to change the complexion of the legislature. Every county organization must do what they can. And with you as the conservative Democratic candidate, we think there is a chance to make a gain here in Sumter County." He looked inquiringly at Brent.

"Oh, I'm interested in that all right, but I never thought of myself as getting involved in politics," protested Brent modestly.

"We all have to do everything we can if ever we are to get out from under the oppression of the Carpetbag government," persisted John.

"Then I take it your objective is to get rid of the Carpetbag government," said Brent.

"Precisely," John agreed.

"But that will take more than just electing a few Democratic Senators," Brent rejoined.

"Of course," Will said, "as soon as we can we must muster a majority in each house of the legislature, but we have to start somewhere."

"And perhaps even more important, we must elect a governor," added John.

Brent asked with interest, "Have you anyone in particular in mind?"

"Yes," answered John, "Wade Hampton."

"Oh, I'm for that," Violet volunteered. "He's an exceptionally capable and personable man."

"If all the women had your attitude, I wish women had the vote," said Will with a smile.

Violet replied ironically, "They do in Wyoming Territory—voted in last December."

"No doubt it will come here one day, too, Violet," Will said kindly, "but for now, we must depend on the votes of the men."

"Brent," interjected John, "we know that you get along with the Negroes, and we think that you might be able to get enough of their votes that, when added to the votes of the native whites, you would have an excellent chance of being elected. More important, we think that once you are elected you can be a force for moderation and integrity in the legislature. Brent, we really need you to do this."

Brent was still hesitant. After a pause for cigarettes all around, he said reluctantly, "Oh, I don't know, John. One big problem is that I'm planning an expedition to the West Indies, and I'll be away four to six weeks right in the midst of your campaign."

"That will be all right. Good experience to be out of the country for a while, less time to get into trouble. We'll organize meetings while you're away, and when you get back you'll still have a month to wrap things up when it counts most."

"Well, I want to do what I can to help, of course, but let me think about it for a day or two," answered Brent. "We always like to sleep on it when making an important decision."

"Yes, that's what we do," Violet added, "but you may be assured that we want to do what we can to help liberate our state."

"Fair enough," John said as he, and then Will, rose and shook hands with Brent and Violet.

"I'll stop by your place not later than Wednesday to give you our decision," promised Brent.

"That's fine," said John cheerfully, "see you then, and good-bye to you both."

After the visitors had gone, Brent turned to Violet and asked, "Well, my Love, what do you think of this idea?" as they walked into the office.

Violet was proud of Brent's reputation and stature and that others had thought that he was one who had the capabilities to help free South Carolina from its chains. So she answered, "I say, go for it. Why not? It will no doubt be quite exciting, and I know you can do it, Brent...Yes, I agree with them, you are the one."

"Well," said Brent thoughtfully, pleased that Violet would be behind him if he decided on this route, "I wouldn't mind, though I'm not sure how it might affect our business deals with the legislature." He drummed his fingers on the desk in thought.

"That is a thought," agreed Violet, "but maybe it is just possible that it would give you better connections."

"I doubt that, Violet, not unless I play ball with the Carpetbaggers and Scalawags."

"Well," Violet encouraged him, "if your West Indies expedition does all that you think it will, maybe the sales to the legislature will be less important."

Brent stopped drumming his fingers and nodded in agreement, "Quite right. All right, if we feel the same way tomorrow morning, I'll ride over and tell John we'll do it...and, Violet, thanks for your support on this. We'll be in this together, you know."

"I know."

The next morning, Brent rode over to Cherry Vale and told John Frierson that he would be willing to make the race for the Senate.

A telegraphic message from Brent's father on Friday, August 26th, reported that *Aura Lee* should be ready to set sail by September 3rd. Brent acknowledged the message and replied that he and the family would plan to arrive on the afternoon train on Thursday, the first.

When they arrived at the Charleston station about four o'clock that afternoon, James Sutler was there with a two-horse carriage for the family members and Evelina, and a one-horse gig for Aaron and Little Josh and the baggage. The elder Sutler was a few inches shorter than his son and several pounds heavier. His hair was graying and thinning. He sported a moustache and muttonchop burnsides that matched his hair, and he wore a gray suit and a dark derby. He greeted everyone cordially, giving his grandchildren special hugs. His man, Jacob, helped Aaron and Little Josh load all the baggage into the gig, and they made ready to follow the others in the carriage.

"We'll take a turn by the moorings so you all can catch a glimpse of the *Aura Lee*," Brent's father announced as they started out. He drove generally southward on Concord Street, along a railroad spur to Charlotte Street. Turning left, eastward, across the tracks he pointed out his warehouses, and then straight ahead they saw a trim ship tied up at a quay on the Cooper River.

"There she is!" he called out enthusiastically, pointing to the *Aura Lee*. The three masts were bare, and the sleek lines of the hull were evident. Men were hurrying to and fro loading barrels aboard.

James Sutler turned the horses about, recrossed the tracks and continued on to the corner of Charlotte and East Bay Street where he pulled up at a large house, turned right, and drove through the driveway entrance. The posts of the elaborate cypress and wrought-iron gate were topped with carved pineapple welcome symbols. Except for the driveway entrances and a back gate, the double lot was surrounded entirely by a six-foot brick wall, one side of which was completely covered by vines of lilac-tinted wisteria.

"Here we are at the old place," he said nostalgically, as they drove into a circular drive in front of the house, "took a right smart of fixing up after the War, but it's livable now."

"Oh, it looks beautiful," Violet remarked.

It was an old Charleston two-and-a-half story brick house, with dark gray slate roof, and full basement. A garden full of blooming flowers, tall trees, and brick walks, adjoined the left side of the house.

Brent hopped down and opened the gate to admit the carriage and gig. He had no more than opened it when his mother and his sister, Phoebe, were running out to greet them.

"Here we are, Isabelle, my dear," called James Sutler, "safe and sound."

Brent's mother, of French Huguenot descent, was slender and only slightly shorter than Violet. Her dark hair was peppered with streaks of gray, and her face, though pleasant in expression, reflected the signs of intense worry and the hardships of the difficult years of the War. But her grey eyes were shining with love and excitement at the arrival of her visitors. At the sight of the children her eyes shone like lights. She made over them extravagantly, and then showed them and Evelina to their rooms. She then led Violet and Brent to their guest room.

That evening over a supper of French onion soup, creole crayfish on rice, baked buttered acorn squash with cinnamon, green peas with mint, fried okra, sliced tomatoes, cucumbers, and onions with dressing, and yeast biscuits, the conversation quickly turned to plans for Brent's great adventure.

"I take it all our cargo has arrived in good shape," said Brent.

"Oh, yes, I think so, we'll look over the records in the morning, but you can be assured that the crates of rifles went in first, with ammunition in center, all those covered and surrounded by bales of cotton, then sacks of grain, then at one side my stuff, and near the galley, the food stores and water."

"Excellent," Brent responded, "and the crew?"

"We have signed all you asked for," his father answered, "and they seem a good lot."

With some lingering concern, Violet inquired, "Father Sutler, is there not some danger in trading with one side in a war?"

"Oh, there is always danger of interception by the other warring power," James Sutler acknowledged reluctantly.

"And what about violations of neutrality?" she persisted.

The elder Sutler sighed and went on in a gentle voice, "Of course we have to be careful about that. You know negotiations are underway right now between the United States and Great Britain on the so-called *Alabama* claims, the claims of the United States for damages on the grounds that Britain allowed her ports to be used for the fitting out of the *Alabama, Shenandoah,* and other Confederate cruisers."

Brent interjected, "Yes, but please remember that *Aura Lee* is a merchant vessel, not a war vessel. She is not going to the French Navy, and according to the Declaration of Paris of 1856, 'Free ships make free goods'; that is, all the goods on board a neutral ship are neutral, and in addition, a neutral has the right to trade with anybody, including belligerents."

James Sutler raised his hand to make another point, "Of course if there is an effective blockade you run that at your own risk, but the thing that concerns me is this: If a belligerent has reason to believe that you are carrying contraband of war; that is, arms and ammunition and so forth, he may stop you for search, and if he finds contraband, may seize it. In other words, if a Prussian man-of-war should overhaul you, he could search and seize your cargo if it is contraband destined for his enemy."

Brent protested, "But we shall be heading for the *Dutch* West Indies, St. Maarten, so he would have no recourse. And anyway, he would have no reason to suspect contraband."

"I hope not, my son," Brent's father responded dryly.

Brent's mother broke in to say that she hoped he knew what he was doing, and then she changed the conversation to local and family news.

The next morning everyone was excited about going down to see the ship.

Just before breakfast, Brent came down in new navy-blue uniform, with gold captain's stripes on the sleeves, and a soft blue cap with stiff visor.

"Whew!" Violet whistled. "How dashing you look in your uniform!"

"This is for show and negotiations," he laughed, "my work clothes will be my old Confederate uniforms–"

"Can you still get in them?"

"Sure, of course I had to have Hattie set the buttons over."

"Ha! That's no doubt due to Mammy's cooking all those pies and cakes you love to eat, but I thought you didn't dare wear Confederate buttons."

"Oh, they're all covered," he grinned.

"May Bonnie Anne and J.J. come along to the ship?" asked Violet. She knew the children would love such a visit.

"Of course," Brent answered. "Is everyone going?"

"Yes, all but your mother. Of course your father has been ready to go for an hour, and Phoebe wants to go, and I thought if the kids came along, Evelina could come, too, and keep an eye on them."

"All right, and tell Aaron and Little Josh to prepare to stay on board. They may as well start getting used to the ship. After the kids have had a good look around, Phoebe and Evelina can take them back to the house in the gig. I'll need to stay all day to check things out, and I hope you will stay and help, Violet."

"Of course," she answered.

At shipside, Brent's father introduced the officers of the ship's company who were present–John Hawkins, an experienced officer on the elder Sutler's ships, as mate; Owen Douglas, a veteran of the Confederate Navy, boatswain; Edward Jones from

Columbia, another Confederate Navy Veteran, boatswain's mate; Henry Young, another who had sailed for the elder Sutler, quartermaster; and a friend of his from the same service, Charles Caldwell, quartermaster's mate. Most of the crew were present, but remained on board.

"Isn't she a beauty" Brent said enthusiastically as he looked at the ship. As the other officers returned to their work and Brent's father walked over to his warehouse, Brent turned to Violet to recite the characteristics of the ship. "First of all you remember, she is a barquentine."

"What's that?" she asked.

"Well, you see she has three masts. When the sails are set you will see that she is ship-rigged, that is, square sails on the foremast, and fore-and-aft rigged, like a schooner on the mainmast and mizzenmast. That makes her efficient and easy to handle—sails can be raised and furled more quickly and easily; she can make good speed, and she can sail close into the wind."

As they walked up the gangplank, with Phoebe, Evelina, and the children, and Aaron and Little Josh following, Brent recited the ship's dimensions—along the main deck she was 120 feet long with beam of 32 feet, and the depth of the hold was 18 feet. Meeting them as they boarded, Mate Hawkins led them on a tour of the ship. First, aft to the quarterdeck, to the officers' quarters.

"Here is your cabin, Sir," Hawkins said to Brent, "and here is the place for your orderly and cabin boy. The others already have moved into their cabins, and here is the captain's mess." Brent called to Aaron and Little Josh, now bubbling with excitement, to stow their gear in their cabin and then follow as they toured the ship.

As they went out past the wheel, near the stern, Brent explained, "Here is the quartermaster's main responsibility—to be in charge of the helm and the binnacle, there, containing the compass and a lamp, beside the wheel. Their job is to keep the ship on course."

Walking forward they looked down a hatch where they could see many bales of cotton and hundreds of barrels and sacks in the hold. Forward of the foremast, they glanced at the crew's quarters in the forecastle where bunks lined the bulkheads and hammocks were swung along the gangways.

The women and children were most fascinated by the galley where the two cooks already were at work preparing meals for those on board. Food stores included a side of fresh beef, several hams, barrels of corn meal and wheat flour, and a barrel of apples, all from Fair Oaks. In addition there were several sacks of potatoes and beans, baskets of tomatoes, and several cartons of canned and dehydrated foods, including milk, that had come into use since the War, and three coops of chickens.

Bonnie Anne and J.J. broke out and began running up and down the decks, climbing the rigging, and leaning over the gunwales to look at the water below, until in answer to cries from Violet a couple of seamen caught them and took them in tow. Violet and Brent agreed that it was time for the little ones to go ashore. Phoebe and Evelina led the reluctant children off the ship to drive them home.

Brent led Violet to his cabin to check the roster of the crew and the ship's papers. "We have a small crew," he explained, "so the men will have to perform double duties. As you know, we have the six officers, or petty officers. Douglas, the boatswain—which is pronounced 'bos'n'—Douglas is kind of like a first sergeant in the army. He's responsible for the discipline of the crew, for weighing or lowering the anchor, and hoisting and lowering the sails. Jones, his assistant, is especially responsible for stowing the cargo. You've met the two cooks, and we have twenty-four seamen. With Little Josh and Aaron, that makes a total of thirty-four people on board."

"What is the capacity of the ship?" she asked.

"It's rated at three hundred tons."

"Does that mean it can carry three hundred tons of cargo?" she asked.

"Well, a ton is calculated at one hundred cubic feet," Brent explained, "and since thirty-five cubic feet of sea water weighs a ton, you can see that actually in weight she can carry over twice that amount." He paused to leaf through the papers. Pulling out a sheet, he said, "Here's our cargo. First of all, here's the main part, all the way down at the bottom are six thousand rifles, muskets, and carbines. About half of them are Palmetto muskets of 1863, mostly made by William Glaze and Company, in Columbia. The rest is a collection of rifles and muskets picked up from the battlefields, many from Union soldiers, and as I mentioned earlier, a number of which had been bought from the French in the first place. So the rifles, muskets, and carbines, with accouterments, are packed in boxes and make about forty-five tons, and then carefully stowed amidships are forty tons of ammunition. Covering all the munitions are two hundred bales of cotton from Fair Oaks, fifty tons, and three hundred bales from other sources, seventy-five tons. And we have thirty tons of wheat in sacks. Now all that comes to about two hundred and forty tons. The rest consists of various items that we are delivering for my father."

"That's very impressive," Violet said, "except I feel uneasy about all that ammunition."

"It'll be safe as long as no one is smoking around it, as I've said, unless somebody shoots at it and gets a lucky hit."

"Oh, Brent, with all your smoking—your smoking alone would be enough to endanger the whole ship, and who knows what the Prussians might do if they catch up with you."

"Now, Violet, my dear, don't you worry about that. We'll manage. Come on and let's see if we can find Jones and have a look below." He took her arm and they went out to the deck. He sent Aaron to find the bos'n's mate, Jones.

The orderly returned quickly with Jones. Violet followed them down the ladder into the hold. While Jones pointed out locations of items, Brent called them out to Violet who checked them off the list. Jones beamed when Brent commended him on the care with which the cargo had been stowed. When they got back up on deck, Brent's father was waiting for them.

"Brent," he said, "I have just seen a news bulletin over the telegraph that Napoleon and practically the whole French army have surrendered at Sedan. In fact, Napoleon was taken prisoner."

"My God!" Brent exclaimed, "Does that mean that the war is over and we are going to be stuck with all this stuff?"

"It kind of looks that way, doesn't it," the elder Sutler responded.

Violet broke in, "What do we do now? See if Moses will take all these guns back?"

Brent replied, "He won't do that unless he feels sure that he can sell them somewhere else at a higher price."

Thoughtfully James Sutler asked, "If either Jefferson Davis or Abraham Lincoln had been captured during our late War, would that have been the end of it?"

"I'm sure it would," Violet quickly answered.

"Oh, I don't know about that," protested Brent.

"Well, I think we had better wait a few days until we have some indication of whether the French are going to try to continue the war," said James Sutler. "There certainly is no point in sending all this down to the Indies if they are giving up entirely. On the other hand, if some new leaders arise, with a determination to continue to fight, they'll need arms more than ever since apparently they have lost so many."

Jones, who had been standing aside but listening to the conversation, came up to Brent and said, "Captain Sutler, sir, does all this mean that we will be delaying our departure?"

"Well, Jones, we're just going to have to wait and see," answered Brent.

"Oh, Captain, one other thing,..."

"Yes, Jones, what is it?"

"I was just wondering, sir, you see, my wife is expecting a baby and I wonder if there might be some way I could use the telegraph here to find out if anything has happened."

Violet broke in hastily, "Oh, Mr. Jones, surely you would not want to leave your wife now." Turning to Brent she said, "Brent, can't someone else be found to take his place?"

Before Brent could answer, Jones protested, "Oh, no, no, ma'am, I'm sure she'll be all right, 'cause her mother's with her, and you see, we'll be needing the money especially now with another mouth to feed."

Brent smiled and said, "Yes, Jones, I think something can be arranged. Here, take my cabin boy, Josh, along. Josh is an expert telegrapher, and he'll send a message to your wife for you. Go ahead and take him up to the warehouse office." Jones and Little Josh took off.

Just then Aaron came by to announce that dinner would be served at the captain's table in fifteen minutes and that there would be places for Mrs. Sutler and the elder Mr. Sutler.

Violet was impressed by the fare of beef stew, wheat biscuits, and fruit. During the meal, Brent and his father filled in the other officers on news of the French disaster. In their lively conversation, each seemed to have a different assessment of what it all meant. Brent explained that sailing would be delayed until they had some word about whether the French would continue fighting. He poured glasses of scuppernong all around from a leather decanter. Before they had finished eating, Jones and Little Josh returned from the warehouse. Jones immediately set about catching up on the food, and Little Josh helped clear the table as they finished. He would eat after all had cleared out.

"Did you get your message through all right, Mr. Jones?" asked Violet.

"Oh, yes, thank you, Mrs. Sutler," Jones replied.

"You say your wife is in Columbia?" continued Violet.

"Yes, ma'am."

"Where do you live in Columbia?" she asked.

"On Myrtle Street."

"Oh, Myrtle Street, and what is your house number there?"

"Well, uh, ma'am, it's upstairs at 642."

After the others had left the table, Violet said to Brent, "I was thinking it might be a nice gesture to send some flowers to Mrs. Jones."

"Yes, it would," he agreed, "but how do you propose to do this?"

"Why don't I telegraph Cedric to take a bouquet over to Mrs. Jones." She called to Little Josh, who had been gulping down his food. "Come on, Josh, go with me over to the warehouse. I want to send a telegram."

His little face broke into a happy smile. "Ah'se comin', Miz Violet," he said as he skipped over to her, always delighted to be by her side, especially now that he would be taking off on the ocean voyage with Master Brent.

Brent's father said that he would come along, too, and that he would go on home from the warehouse and send the carriage back to get Violet and Brent later.

Violet was able to get through to Cedric promptly, and then she and Little Josh returned to the ship. She sent Little Josh to help Aaron, and she rejoined Brent in looking over the ship's readiness.

Below the officer's quarters, on the quarterdeck, he showed her the armory. "Look," he said, "twenty-four Yankee Spencer repeating rifles. They carry seven rounds in the magazine in the stock. Confederate soldiers used to call them the 'seven-forked lightning.' They said the Yankees would load them on Sunday and fire them all week without reloading. And look at that, that little thirty-seven millimeter French brass cannon. It goes on a swivel up near the bow."

"But what if some German ship attacks you?" she asked worriedly.

"Well, we'll just have to count on these," Brent chuckled. "We don't have any big guns, but these can be mighty handy I can assure you.".

An hour later, they decided to return to the house. Violet said, "Let's stop by the telegraph office in the warehouse and see if Cedric was able to deliver the flowers to Mrs. Jones."

"Fine with me," answered Brent. "I'll wait here in the carriage. I need to go over a few things on the ship's papers."

Violet was able to reach Cedric quickly, but his response caught her by surprise. "NO SUCH ADDRESS AT 642 MYRTLE STREET. NUMBERS END AT 408.

INQUIRED AROUND NEIGHBORHOOD. UNABLE TO LOCATE ANY JONES FAMILY IN AREA."

How strange, thought Violet, *I'm certain that is the address Mr. Jones told me. The numbers on that street don't even go that high. Now the poor woman won't get the flowers to help her cheer up. But where could they live? If I happen to see Jones again, I must ask him for the address again.* "Make connections all right?" asked Brent absent-mindedly, his mind still focused on his papers, when Violet returned to the carriage.

"No problem with the connections, but Cedric said he could find no such address as the one that Jones gave me. Odd."

"What was that?" he asked as he looked up from his papers with sudden interest. "What did you say?"

"I said that Cedric was unable to find any such address as Jones gave; he couldn't even find any trace of any Jones family in the whole neighborhood."

"Well that *is* odd."

"That's what I said. Maybe we should we go back to the ship and find Jones so that I can get the correct address. I must have misunderstood him."

"No," answered Brent thoughtfully. He knew the accuracy of Violet's mind for figures and her ability to remember whatever she heard. "No, I don't think we should go back now. Let's not mention this to him or anyone else. It sounds as though something is rotten in the state of Denmark."

"What do you mean?"

"Right now I don't know, but it could mean trouble for the *Aura Lee*."

"Oh, Brent, I hope this doesn't mean danger!" she exclaimed, alarmed at what he was suggesting.

"Not if we keep alert." Noting the worried expression on Violet's face, he went on to say, "Now Violet, my Love, don't worry. Have confidence that I can take care of this and anything else that might come up."

She only nodded, her eyes averted. She resolved to do her best to follow his advice.

Violet and Brent and the children enjoyed the next few days visiting at the Sutler house. They went for walks down to the Battery, and through the areas of old picturesque houses, and friends stopped by for tea. On Sunday morning the whole family went to worship services at the French Huguenot church. They offered special prayers for a safe voyage for Brent and his crew. During this time Violet did not return to the ship.

On Monday, September 5th, James Sutler came in with the news that the French had formed a Government of National Defense to continue the war.

"This *is* good news," Brent said, with relief.

His mother, distraught over the news from France, was glad to hear that the effort would continue, and she was even glad that her son might be able to make some contribution to the French defense.

"I'm sorry about the French losses, but I must say, things could not have been better for our purposes. I think we had better plan to sail with the tide tomorrow evening." His eyes sought Violet's across the room.

Early the next morning Brent told all the family to be down at the dock by four o'clock that afternoon if they wanted to see the *Aura Lee* off. Then he had Jacob drive him quickly to the ship so that he could get the word to the crew and make final preparations for sailing.

On hearing that they would be departing that afternoon, Jones asked if he might make one last inquiry by telegraph about his wife.

"Of course," Brent responded, and he told Little Josh to go along again to send another message for Jones.

When Little Josh and Jones returned an hour later, Brent sent the boatswain's mate to report to Boatswain Douglas to help see that all the crew were instructed in their duties for casting off and getting underway. Then he called Little Josh to come with him into his cabin.

When they were in the cabin with the door closed, Brent asked, "Well, Josh, are you all ready to sail?"

"Yassuh, Massuh Brent, uh, ah mean Cap'n Sutler. Dis be a mighty fine trip fo' meh." Little Josh's eyes sparkled and his lips broke into a wide grin. He was full of excitement that finally they were going to sail.

"Tell me, Josh, did you have any trouble in sending the telegraph message for Mr. Jones?"

"Oh, nosuh. Ah send hit, an' righ' away an' de udduh people say dey git hit."

"I wonder, Josh, did you write down the message that you sent?"

"Yassuh, ah alway write down de message afore ah send hit, jes' like ya tell meh."

"Do you still have it?"

"Yassuh, ah tink hit be heah in mah pocket."

"May I see it?"

Little Josh pulled a crumpled piece of paper from his pocket and handed it to Brent who straightened out the paper and read the penciled marks:

To: EJR, State House
Aura Lee sails today for Dutch West Indies.

"Damn!" Brent muttered as he put the message in his pocket. *That EJR is probably a clerk or secretary to Frank Moses.* To Little Josh he merely said, "All right, that will be all. You may go now." The boy scampered away to see what Aaron was doing.

That afternoon, the whole family went down to the quay to see the *Aura Lee* off.

Brent came down to greet them and say his goodbyes. "If all goes well, we should be back in twenty-four to twenty-eight days, depending not only on the weather, but also on whether anyone tries to delay us, and how long it will take to make our deals and unload cargo."

"All right," said Violet, "we'll return to Fair Oaks tomorrow, but you can be sure we'll be back in Charleston in less than twenty-four days, and we'll be waiting right here to welcome you home."

Brent shook hands with his father, nodded good-bye to the servants standing by, kissed Violet, the children, his mother, and his sister, and then kissed Violet again, this time longer and more longingly. Then he turned quickly and strode up the gangplank where he turned to wave one last good-bye before going about the Captain's responsibilities for embarking.

Wives and sweethearts were there to bid adieu to their loved ones from whom they would be parted. It was an impressive sight when *Aura Lee* cast off, hoisted sail, and headed toward the sea.

Violet felt a strange sensation at finding herself one of the countless women who, through the ages, had gathered on the waterfront to watch their men "go down to the sea in ships" as the Psalmist said, "that do business in great waters."

Chapter 40

Contraband of War

1870

It was smooth sailing for the *Aura Lee* as she crossed Charleston harbor, passed between Fort Sumter and Fort Moultrie, and glided past the Isle of Palms into the open sea. Brent gave instructions for an easterly course under full sail. With sails set and a fresh breeze, all hands stood on deck to watch as the land receded to the stern, and rays of the setting sun colored the sails.

"This is where the Cooper River and the Ashley River join to form the Atlantic Ocean, as the people of Charleston put it," Brent said with a grin to John Hawkins who was standing beside him near the wheel.

"Indeed, indeed," the mate responded, "and it's a good time to be seeing it."

"Let's keep her on an easterly course until noon tomorrow," said Brent.

"Aye, aye, sir."

Just then the boatswain, Douglas, came over. He beamed as Brent commended him on the smartness of the crew in getting underway. Then Brent asked Hawkins and Douglas to meet with him in his cabin immediately after the evening mess.

Supper was late this evening on account of the hour of getting underway, but it was tasty. Brent rejected the tradition of a ship's captain's dining apart from the other officers. He regarded the mess as the best opportunity to communicate with the others and to entertain exchanges of views. Yet there was a certain awkwardness in this regard as he guarded his comments during the meal while all were present.

It still was daylight when the officers arose from the table, but dark enough to begin lighting the lamps. As the other officers went out to go about their duties, the mate and the boatswain, along with Little Josh, followed Brent to his cabin. Brent asked Little Josh to stand just outside and watch the door and to allow no one to enter without permission.

"I think we have a good crew, and they are working well as we get started," Brent began.

"Yes, they all seem to be good workers," agreed Douglas. Hawkins nodded his assent.

"As long as the weather and other conditions permit, we'll follow the regular schedule of watches for duty, four hours on, four hours off, except for the two-hour dogwatches at four o'clock to six o'clock and six to eight in the evening. Have you divided the officers and crew to stand watch?"

"Yes, sir, certainly," came the response from both men.

"Our routine for mess," Brent went on, "will be reveille at four bells, six o'clock; breakfast, six bells, seven o'clock; dinner at eight bells, noon; and supper at two bells in the first dogwatch, five o'clock."

"Aye, aye, sir."

"And Hawkins," Brent said as he unrolled a chart on the table and pointed with a cigar, "we'll maintain our easterly course to the 70th meridian, about here, to take advantage of this favorable westerly wind to get across the Gulf Stream. You know that runs about three knots in these waters, and that could slow us down."

"Quite right," agreed Hawkins.

"Then we'll turn south southeast," Brent continued as he traced the route with his cigar, "and pray we can get through the horse latitudes south of Bermuda, and then we should pick up the northeast trade wind as we turn southward to our destination."

"Right," agreed Hawkins again. "Captain, you sound as though you have sailed these waters before."

"Oh, a couple of times before the War, but during the War I was on the *Shenandoah* and we spent most of our time in the South Atlantic, the Indian Ocean, and the Pacific."

"The *Shenandoah!*" Douglas exclaimed. "What a voyage that must have been!"

"Greatest ship in the Confederate Navy, I always thought," said Hawkins, obviously impressed.

"Greatest ship of her kind in any navy," rejoined Brent. He offered each of the others cigarette papers and tobacco and rolled a cigarette of his own, and then continued, "Of course she had steam power, but she could make good speed under sail alone. But frankly, gentlemen, I'll take the old *Aura Lee* here, all sail."

"Aye," the others said in unison.

"But I did not call you in here just for all this. I'm afraid we have a real problem."

"What is that, Captain?" Hawkins asked as a look of uneasiness spread over his usually cheerful face.

"I'm worried about pirates," Brent answered.

"Pirates?" Douglas asked in disbelief. "I thought they had been swept from the seas."

"I hope so," Brent said, "but actually we may be in danger from two quarters. First, some Prussian man-of-war or privateer may want to seize our cargo as contraband of war, which it is, mostly. But in addition to that, I have reason to suspect that somebody may try to steal our cargo."

"How is that?" asked Hawkins.

"Frankly, I'm afraid that the bos'n's mate, Edward Jones, may have been in communication with somebody who covets our cargo. Now, I don't want to arouse his suspicions, so Douglas, go ahead and put him in charge of one watch, but Hawkins, let's make sure that Henry Young or his quartermaster's mate is on watch with Jones to keep an eye out for anything suspicious."

"Aye, sir, but I find it hard to imagine Jones as the culprit," Hawkins said reluctantly.

"Ever sail with him before? Know anything about his family or background?"

Hawkins shook his head and admitted, "Well, no, sir, I'm afraid not."

Brent went on, "Now, the most dangerous place for us to be overhauled would be in the horse latitudes. If we get becalmed there, and an unfriendly steamer comes up, we have had it. So, Hawkins, let's be very careful to make our speed and direction such that we can cross through the horse latitudes at night, and we'll run without any lights."

"Aye, aye, sir, we should be able to manage that," responded the first mate.

"Another advantage of this route," continued Brent, "is that it takes us well into the Sargasso Sea, that vast area of calm, warm water, filled with floating seaweed, and you know that many steamship captains are afraid to go in there for fear of getting their propellers fouled by the weeds. That is where we want to cross the horse latitudes—because a steamer is not likely to follow us there."

"Good point," agreed Hawkins.

Brent turned to his boatswain and said, "Now Douglas, we have twenty-four good Spencer rifles and a thirty-seven millimeter cannon in the armory. There are three keys to the racks, one for each of us—you, Hawkins, and me. Keep sharp control over those. Now, each day, I want you to put all the seamen through rifle marksmanship drill and find two good men to handle the cannon. Throw some empty boxes and crates overboard and have contests among teams of three or four men to see who can destroy the targets most quickly. And make note of those who are the best marksmen. Give the winners an extra round of rum or something."

Douglas's pleasant face beamed. "I'm sure they would like that, Captain. Exercise and contests are always good for the morale."

"But, now hear this," Brent cautioned, "You must see to it that Jones never gets his hands on any of these weapons, is that clear?"

"Aye, aye, sir."

"And gentlemen, this conversation is to be held in the strictest of confidence. What we have just talked about is for our ears only, is that also clear?"

"Aye, aye, sir," answered Hawkins and Douglas at the same time.

Fair weather continued the next day and the two days after. By now they were indeed in the extra-warm waters of the Sargasso Sea. Brown weeds were floating all around, though not as dense as Brent and Hawkins had expected. Brent called to Little Josh to bring a bucket of garbage from the galley. Brent went with the lad to the leeward side of the ship and told him to dump the garbage into the sea, and then walk along the ship toward the stern while he kept his eye on the place where he had thrown the garbage.

"Massuh Brent!" Little Josh shouted within just a few moments. "Ah see uh bunch uv sometin' dere," he exclaimed as he pointed to the water.

"What is it?" asked Brent, coming over to stand beside Josh and looking in the direction Josh was pointing.

Little Josh looked hard at the sea and then looked up at Brent anxiously, "Lawdy, Massuh Brent, is dey water snakes?"

"No, Josh, they are eels, fish that look like snakes; they're just like the ones we find in our rivers."

"Fish? Lawdy, Massuh Brent, is dey good ta eat?"

"Yes, and they will bite so hard on the bait on a line that you don't even have to have a fishhook to catch them."

"Yo' wait heah, Massuh Brent. Ah be bek soon." Josh took off toward the mess and returned shortly with the cooks. All three had lines with chunks of meat tied securely to the ends. Soon all of them were pulling in eels.

Brent thought he'd better mention, "Those eels aren't very good compared to the ones in our rivers, but they are all right if you are hungry." The cooks assured him that when they finished with the eels the fish would taste delicious. And that evening everyone declared they were.

On the fifth day the weather was too fine; the winds were dying down. A bright sun shone through openings in the clouds, and waves breaking against the bow were throwing up a spray through which the sun cast a partial rainbow over the water.

"Tonight is when we try to make it through the horse latitudes," Brent announced to the mate and the quartermaster as he stood by them near the wheel.

"How far across, do you reckon?" asked Hawkins.

"That's hard to say. Sometimes the calm may spread across a hundred miles or more; at other times it may be thirty or forty miles."

Quartermaster Young removed his cap and scratched his head, then replaced the cap as he inquired, "Sir, how can we move if there is no wind?"

Brent smiled at the young man. It was a good question for a sailor to ask. "We hope for a little breeze, but if there is none at all, we'll have to do our best with manpower. You know why they call this the 'horse latitudes', don't you?"

"Sir, I've always wondered, but didn't want to show my ignorance by asking," said Young.

Brent smiled again and said, "Well, they say that in earlier years when the Spanish and others were shipping horses to the Indies in large numbers, many of the horses died when the ships were becalmed for many days at times, and they ran out of water for the horses."

"Oh, my goodness, sir, I hope that doesn't happen to us and the *Aura Lee*," Young said somewhat nervously.

"We'll not let it happen," Brent assured the young sailor. Then he added, "And Young, make it a habit to ask if you wonder about anything. That's how we learn."

"Aye, aye, sir, I see what you mean. I'll do just that from now on," grinned Quartermaster Young.

By one bell in the first dogwatch, 4:30 p.m., the wind had almost stopped, and the sails on the foremast were beginning to flap. Brent called all the officers and petty officers to meet with him in the wardroom.

As soon as all were assembled, he announced, "We cannot risk being becalmed here indefinitely. We're going to work our way out of it. The glass has been falling steadily all day. That could mean that a tropical storm is out there somewhere to the east. It could hit us with a lot more wind than we want, but if we are lucky it will pass well to the south of us but will give enough wind around the edges to help us out of this calm. Now what we are going to do is try to pull ourselves up by our own bootstraps; we are going to pull ourselves out of here during the night. Douglas, lower all sails as soon as the wind has stopped completely. We don't want any resistance to our movement."

"Aye, aye, sir."

"Right now I want you to secure a long line to the canvas sea anchor and wind the line on the portside forward windlass. And I want you to secure another line of about the same length to the starboard forward windlass, and secure the other end to the stern of the launch."

"I don't understand, sir."

"Here's what we are going to do," Brent explained, "we'll lower the launch with eight oarsmen and a coxswain at the tiller. They will take the sea anchor on board and row out to the end of their lines. Then have four men on each windlass reel in the sea anchor and the launch. Of course this will bring the sea anchor and the boat back toward the ship, but it will also cause the ship to move forward toward them. Then when they have closed in to the ship, we repeat the exercise. While the oarsmen are rowing back out, the windlass men will have a chance for a little rest, and the oarsmen can rest a little while the windlass men work. Can we do that?"

"It just may work," Hawkins interjected.

"Aye, sir, we can do it," said Douglas.

"We may have to work at this all night," Brent warned them. "We are pretty short-handed for this sort of thing, so the petty officers will have to take turns at the windlass, and let the windlass men and oarsmen rotate with each other." He looked at the mate and went on, "Hawkins, you and I will take turns at manning the wheel."

"Aye, sir."

Immediately after supper, Brent put his plan into operation—sails down, sea anchor and launch out. With his spyglass he scanned the sea to the horizon in all directions. No vessel was in sight. As the evening nautical twilight faded into total darkness, he knew that he was out of sight of any possible predator. Only a gentle swell disturbed the otherwise calm surface of the sea, and the only light to be seen in any direction were the brief displays of phosphorescent ripples in the wake of the boat as it went in and out and in the wake of the ship itself.

After the second round of rowing out and pulling in, Brent calculated that the ship must be making about one and a half knots. If they could keep this up through the night, they should be twenty to twenty-five miles farther along their course by early morning. If necessary, they would continue in daylight through the next day.

When Brent went up to relieve Hawkins at the wheel at the end of the morning watch—eight o'clock—Hawkins reported, "By shooting the North Star I figure that we have indeed made a little over twenty-five miles during our self-pulling exercises. Who says a calm sea does not make a skillful sailor?"

"Excellent!" Brent exclaimed with a triumphant grin.

"But, sir, I think the men are about petered out."

"I can understand that."

"And look, Captain, the sea is becoming a little choppy—strangely, without any wind."

"There will be," responded Brent confidently, "and my guess is that the sea will be getting rougher, but we will pick up some wind—probably the benefit of what I thought might be a tropical storm. The storm, if that's what it is, probably has passed a distance to the south of us, but it has whipped up some choppy seas, and we'll probably get the benefit of some of its outer wind, and then very shortly we shall be in the northeast trade wind. Then we should make good time. Just now we'll hoist the sails on the mainmast and the mizzen mast, set on the port tack. Then for each watch we'll post only a helmsman and a lookout. Everyone else will be free just to sleep and eat. We'll resume regular watches with the first watch at eight bells tonight. Will you pass the word on all this?"

"Aye, aye, and I'm glad to hear it, Captain. If whatever is out there will give us this day, we should be all set for anything."

That arrangement continued until evening twilight, but then the sea became so rough that no one could either sleep or eat.

Brent took a quick walk around the deck and then to the wheel where Hawkins was standing.

"Looks like we may be in for a bit of a squall," said Hawkins.

"Yes, and more," replied Brent, "probably the effect of a hurricane down to the south. Anyway it promises to break our calm and give us some wind. We'd better slip on our oilskins and sou'westers."

Suddenly a full thunderstorm burst upon the area. Streaks of lightning leaped across the sky in nervous repetition. The thunder was heavy, the waves choppy, and the wind gusty.

Brent called out, "Trim the sails and cast out the sea anchor astern to help keep the bow into the wind." Spindrift and rain wasted over the sailors as they worked at the sheets.

"We're trying to keep the bow into the wind, but it's hard to find; it just keeps fishtailing," Hawkins called to Brent.

"That's all right, no danger, we'll ride it out," Brent returned.

Aaron and two of the sailors came running up, "Cap'n, Cap'n," Aaron screamed, "de ship's afire!"

"Look, captain," one of the young sailors shouted and pointed, "atop the mainmast!"

Brent looked up to the top of the mast to see a fuzzy ball of fire with wavering streaks shooting out in all directions.

Another young sailor came running up shouting, "My God, my God, look!"

Brent called out, "Relax, mates, that's St. Elmo's fire; it does no harm, just a sort of brush lightning that often appears at sea during stormy weather.

Almost as suddenly as it had struck the storm ended. The light disappeared over the mast. Swiftly moving clouds uncovered the stars above, but choppy waves and a fresh breeze remained. They had got through the calm more completely than anticipated in such a short time.

By the beginning of the first watch that night the *Aura Lee* had picked up the trade wind. Brent called for full sails and with the benefit of the strong, steady cross wind the ship was moving at ten knots.

Two days later at noon, Hawkins announced that they were crossing the Tropic of Cancer and soon would be changing course to due south.

Brent was gaining a feeling of confidence that they were going to make their destination without interference. But his new confidence was premature. As Brent relaxed on the deck after dinner, the lookout in the crow's-nest suddenly called out "Sail ho! On the port bow!"

Brent ran to the bow and put his spyglass in the direction indicated. Studying intently he could see a ship coming in the direction of the *Aura Lee*, and in addition to sails he could detect smoke. It was a steamer, and at the relative speeds of the two ships probably half an hour away.

Brent did not change course or attempt evasion. He notified Hawkins and Douglas to alert the crew. The boatswain put out an "all hands on deck" call.

As the ship came to within half a mile it ran up a flag. Brent identified it as Prussian. He ordered the U.S. flag run up. As the steamer rapidly closed the distance, Brent ordered a new tack to avoid a collision course. At that point the steamer fired a shot across the bow of *Aura Lee* and a loud voice came through a megaphone "Heave to! Prepare to receive a boarding party!"

Brent ordered the sea anchor out and the sails lowered. Then he called Hawkins and Douglas to join him near the helm.

"We'll show them every courtesy," he said, "but if they make trouble, we'll give them plenty when they leave."

"What do we do now?" asked Douglas.

"Nothing just now," Brent answered, "but I want us to be ready for fast action when the boarding party leaves. Get the men to their posts ready to man the lines and sheets to hoist the sails as rapidly as possible. As soon as the sails are set, have all seamen ready to pick up rifles if ordered to do so. Hawkins, set our course southwest, and then, as soon as we get some distance, put it in whatever tack will give us the greatest speed. But do none of these things until I give the word. Any questions?"

"No, sir," both answered.

"Good. Now, leave the talking to me."

"Aye, aye, sir," they replied.

Soon the boat from the other ship was alongside, and a couple of seamen gave a hand to the two officers and two men who came aboard while others of their party remained in the boat.

"I am Lieutenant Schmidt of the Prussian ship, *Bremerhaven*," the first boarding officer said in good English. "Please take me to your captain."

Brent stepped forward and introduced himself. "I am Captain Sutler, what do you wish?"

Approaching Brent to within close range, the visiting lieutenant said in a surly manner, "In the name of the King of Prussia I wish to search your ship for contraband of war."

"By what right?" Brent shot back.

"By the right of a belligerent to search any ship thought to be carrying contraband to his enemy. Prussia is at war with France, and I am instructed to search for contraband destined to France," he replied churlishly, stroking his goatee.

"We are bound for the West Indies. We shall not be going within three thousand miles of France," Brent informed him coldly.

The lieutenant smirked as he went on, "Oh, but the French have territories in the Indies, and for our purposes that is a part of France. May I see your manifest?"

Brent merely nodded and said, "Of course. Follow me."

He led the visitor to the captain's cabin, drew some papers from a wall chest and handed them to the officer who quickly glanced over the papers.

Lieutenant Schmidt said, "Mm, I see you list cotton and miscellaneous implements for the Dutch West Indies. Now Captain, you know that is not enough. What is the port of destination?"

"St. Eustatius," answered Brent tersely.

"Mm, and just what are the implements that you are carrying to the Dutch?"

"Go and see for yourself." Brent stepped out and called to Jones. "Ahoy there, Mr. Jones, will you escort the officer to the hold for an inspection of the cargo?"

Jones came forward eagerly. "Aye, aye, sir," he said and as he led the Lieutenant and his two men down the hatch Brent invited the other officer, a junior lieutenant, into the cabin.

"What is your home port?" Brent asked the young officer.

"Bremerhaven."

"Where is that?"

"Uh, near Bremen, sir."

"What is your home city?"

"Frankfurt."

"On the Oder or the Main?"

"Yes, on the Main, sir."

"Oh, yes, that is southeast of Berlin, isn't it?"

"Yes, sir."

Brent observed that the young man was beginning to shift from one foot to another somewhat nervously. Brent continued his questioning in a friendly manner. "And I suppose you have some of those famous Westphalia hams for your chow."

"Oh, yes, sir."

"Tell me, I forget where Westphalia is. I should know, because it is one of the main cities of Prussia, isn't it?"

"Oh, yes, sir, it's in West Prussia."

"You mean the old state of West Prussia?" asked Brent, his eyes narrowing just slightly.

"Yes, that's right."

Brent smiled and said, "Well, I'm glad to clear that up. Tell me, are you in the Prussian Navy, that is, is your ship a naval vessel?"

"Uh, well no, not exactly. I guess we are an auxiliary, a privateer."

Brent paused thoughtfully, and his eyes narrowing again, he asked, "May I see your letter of marque and reprisal?"

"Oh, sir, I don't know about those things; you'd have to ask the captain."

Brent's voice became cold. "Then what gives you the authority to board my ship?"

The young officer's face flushed as he answered lamely, "Well, sir, the laws of war, I guess."

"I see," said Brent, "and how many guns does your ship carry?"

"Oh, not many, I guess you can see them from here."

Brent stepped out for a further look. "All I see is one swivel gun fore and one aft," he muttered. He turned to the officer. "How many below decks?"

"Oh, sir, that is all; nothing below, you know, we're not a real warship."

The return of Lieutenant Schmidt and his two men interrupted the conversation.

"Captain," Schmidt said tersely, "I find that beneath all that cotton you do indeed have many boxes of weapons. We must escort you to a neutral port where you must transfer to us all your contraband; we seize it by the terms of the Declaration of Paris of 1856."

"As you wish, your highness," Brent replied sarcastically, "and I think no towline will be necessary; I'll send along my bos'n's mate, Mr. Jones, here, as hostage to guarantee our acquiescence." *Ha, it'll be nice to have that traitor off this ship,* he thought grimly.

"Excellent, and if you depart from our course, I must warn you, we shall open fire with our main guns." threatened the Lieutenant.

"I am very impressed," responded Brent in further sarcastic slur.

As the visitors turned to go over the side to return to their boat, Brent called out, "Mr. Hawkins! Mr. Douglas!"

The mate and the boatswain hurried aft and joined Brent in the privacy of his cabin. He closed the door. "Those are no Prussians," he muttered. "That so-called young lieutenant does not know one Frankfurt from the other, and he does not even know where Westphalia is or what it is. Those are damned pirates sent out by Scalawags to steal our cargo!"

Brent began speaking in fast staccato. "Hawkins, hoist all sails and get the ship underway. Then proceed with all possible speed on a course due south. As soon as any man can be spared from the rigging, send him to Douglas, and Douglas, remember you are to unlock the Spencers and issue one, with eighty rounds of ammunition to each man as quickly as they come to you from hoisting the sails. However, first give a rifle and ammunition to Caldwell and send him to the stern, and then to the best marksman among the seamen, and send him up to the crow's nest. When we give the word to fire, they are to rake the two swivel guns on that ship, fore and aft; their mission is to not allow anyone to fire those guns. Got that?"

"Aye, aye, sir," answered the two men. They were both breathing rapidly at the prospect of combat.

Brent continued, "Then, as each seaman gets his rifle and ammunition, send him immediately to positions along the gunwale where they can take that small boat under fire. Their mission is to sink that boat, not to kill the occupants. We want the occupants to be swimming around in the water a while so that their ship will lose time picking them up. Got that?" he asked again.

"Aye, aye, sir," the men repeated, nodding their understanding.

"Be sure to tell everybody to aim for the waterline on that boat. We must sink it quickly."

"Aye, aye, sir."

"Any questions, Hawkins?"

"No sir, I'll put Henry Young at the wheel as we get underway."

"Good, and Douglas, bring four rifles and plenty of ammunition here to the cabin. Give one to Young and one to Aaron, and Hawkins and I may want to fire a few rounds, and take one for yourself to show the men how to do it."

"Aye, aye, Captain," answered Douglas with an excited grin.

"All right, let's go!" ordered Brent. "Set sail and get underway. As soon as that boat is far enough out to be a good target, we'll open fire."

He turned to Little Josh who had been standing by his side. "Josh, you stay here by me to carry messages."

Even Brent was surprised at the speed at which the sails went up. Pulling in the sea anchor helped to get the *Aura Lee* underway.

Catching sight of the small boat as it separated from the ship, Brent shouted, "Open fire!" Already half a dozen men were along the gunwales, and they began rapid fire. Two men raced to the bow and quickly got the brass cannon into action. Water splashed up all along the waterline of the boat. Almost at once three or four of the oarsmen leaped over the side and began swimming to avoid the hail of bullets. At the same time, the special marksmen took the opposing ship's swivel guns under fire. No one dared venture close to those guns.

Within another fifteen minutes all twenty-four seamen, Aaron, the quartermaster's mate, and even the boatswain, the mate, and Brent himself were engaging in the fire. Soon Douglas had Aaron and two of the seamen cease their firing to devote themselves to carrying ammunition to the others.

Someone on the *Bremerhaven* was shouting through the megaphone, but the chatter of the rifles completely drowned out the voice. Brent could not be sure whether someone was shouting threats to him or was trying to give instructions to the boat.

In either case it was useless. As the *Aura Lee* gathered speed, its course passed to the starboard of the boat and actually came closer to the *Bremerhaven* as the ships faced roughly bow to bow.

Within another fifteen minutes all the crew of the small boat were in the water, and the thoroughly splintered boat was sinking. As the marksmen kept up their steady and accurate fire, the swivel guns on the *Bremerhaven* remained silent. Not a single shot either from cannon or small arms threatened the *Aura Lee*. She was sailing at six knots as she came closest to her adversary. Brent called out to Hawkins to pass within fifty yards of the other ship, and he called to Douglas to have the brass cannon and all riflemen, except the two firing at the swivel guns, to fire at the engine room and at the rudder of the enemy.

"Switch fires now and keep firing until we are out of range," Brent called out. Then he claimed the satisfaction of firing a few rounds himself into the *Bremerhaven's* engine room.

It took only six minutes for the *Aura Lee* to move out of effective range, but not before the *Bremerhaven* engine room had been riddled and the rudder had been splintered. Now the crippled ship launched two other boats to rescue those who had been in the sunken boat. That done, it would take a great deal of time before it could get its rudder repaired and turn about to give chase, and it surely would have no steam power for many hours.

When Brent gave the order to cease fire, rebel yells and excited shouts of triumph went up all over the ship. Little Josh, still standing by Brent to carry messages back and forth, clapped his hands with delight and let out a rebel yell of his own. Brent gave him a fond pat on the back and called all hands on deck to congratulate them on their skill and to thank them for their support. He promised a bonus for everyone at the end of the voyage. This announcement brought further cheers from everybody.

At the officer's mess that evening animated conversations continued on the success of the day's action.

"Did I hear you say that we are headed for St. Eustatius? And why?" wondered Hawkins.

Brent laughed. "Forget St. Eustatius," he answered, "I was hoping to lead those so-called Prussians, those damned Scalawags, to hurry on down there to wait for us while we stop, as planned, at St. Maarten. You know, during the Revolution, the Dutch island of St. Eustatius was a great entrepôt for the exchange of American produce for European munitions, and during the late war it performed a similar service for Confederate blockade runners."

Hawkins addressed his captain, "So what is our course to be now, sir?"

"Straight to St. Maarten, first to the Dutch port of Philipsburg, on the south side. I'll go ashore there, slip over to the French side and see what kind of deals I can make, and then, if all goes well, have you bring the ship around to the French port, Marigot," Brent replied. He glanced at each of the men in turn.

"But sir, why not go straight into the French port?" Hawkins inquired.

"Because we are carrying contraband, and there may be some real Germans around there. So we must be very careful."

Now in the strong, steady wind of the northeast trade, the *Aura Lee* made good time all the rest of that day and that night, and the next day and night, until just before noon on the 15th of September, she stood in the Philipsburg harbor and dropped anchor.

Warning Hawkins to keep a sharp lookout for saboteurs, Brent put on his new uniform and had six oarsmen and a coxswain row him to shore in a small boat. He left them at the pier to secure the boat under guard. He told them to alternate guards to give each a chance to explore the town, with eyes and ears open and mouths shut, and he would meet them there in five hours. He might be late, but they must not be late.

Finding a livery on the main street, Brent hired a horse and gig and drove directly to the north side of the island, to the French government house in Marigot. A clerk there led him to a purchasing agent. When Brent showed him a copy of his manifest the Frenchmen's small dark eyes swelled with excitement.

"Monsieur, you are a gift from heaven. We will give you a good price for all the weapons and cotton you have; we must have them quickly!"

"What is the situation now?" asked Brent.

"You knew about the disaster at Sedan?"

"Yes."

"Well, a new Government of National Defense is organizing a new army to carry on the war; they are reorganizing the Garde Mobile of half a million men and are mobilizing the *Garde Nationale* of another million and a half. If we can arm them adequately, we may yet defend France from the German invaders. What are you asking for your rifles and muskets?"

"What do you offer?" countered Brent.

"Fifteen dollars each in gold U.S. dollars," the Frenchman answered, looking at Brent steadily yet with a glint of hope in his eyes.

"I understand the Prussians are willing to buy them at twenty-five dollars just to keep them out of French hands."

"We'll give you fifteen dollars each in gold dollars and another eight dollars each in French merchandise at wholesale price from which you can earn even more profit in the United States."

"Agreed," smiled Brent, shaking hands with the purchasing agent.

Brent waited for clerks to draw up the papers. The French agent explained that a French ship already was waiting at the pier, and if the American would bring his ship to the same pier, opposite, French officials would inspect the goods, and the transfer of the cargo could be made quickly.

Elated, Brent drove back to Philipsburg and returned to the ship. From his seamen who had been making the rounds of the saloons and cafes, he learned that there were indeed Prussian agents around who were trying to discourage ships from going into Marigot.

Brent decided that in spite of being in strange waters he should make the run that night. He sent a small boat out in front to guide the ship away from obstacles, using covered lantern signals, and managed to have the *Aura Lee* in Marigot harbor before daylight. With the coming of dawn he moved on into the dock and tied up at the pier opposite the French ship that was bound for Bordeaux. Soon French officials came aboard the *Aura Lee*, and then a gang of stevedores and longshoremen arrived to unload and reload the cargo.

As this activity got underway Brent went ashore to find other buyers for the grain and for the miscellaneous items—woolen goods, mechanical devices, and other items that his father had sent.

After everything had been unloaded from the ship, Brent had the cargo handlers load the new cargo—French perfumes, laces, linen, silks, porcelain, crystal, china, brassware, champagne, French chocolates, and other items that he could use to fill some of his State House orders and others that he could sell in Charleston. All this allowed some time for the crew to visit the shops and cafes and bistros.

Brent himself took time to pick up a lavender and black negligee set and a blue silk dress with matching bonnet for Violet. He selected a French porcelain doll with long curls for Bonnie Anne and a hand-carved, colorful train for J.J. For Mammy and Evelina he purchased silk scarves, and for the other house servants and for Leo and his wife, Brent bought various small gifts that he knew would delight them. Finally, for his mother, he found an exquisite French lace shawl; for his sister, Phoebe, a brooch; and for his father a carved pipe.

Early on the 20th, the *Aura Lee* sailed for Charlotte Amalie on the Danish island of St. Thomas. As they sailed into the beautiful protected harbor that evening, Brent pointed out the castles of the pirates Bluebeard and of Blackbeard, standing like sentinels on the hills, to Little Josh and Young and Douglas, and others standing near him.

"Mean as they were," Brent told his listeners, "they were men of honor compared to those damned Scalawag pirates that tried to steal our cargo."

Heads nodded in assent. "A beautiful place," Quartermaster Young said. "I don't blame them for settling here. And have you ever seen such blue water in all your travels!"

"A beautiful place indeed" agreed Brent. Then he added, "This may soon belong to the United States."

"You mean this whole island?" asked Young in surprise.

"Yes," Brent answered as he surveyed the whole scene. "I understand a treaty already has been signed. The question is whether the U.S. Senate will ratify it. Some of those damned Yankee senators probably don't want to add any more southern territory to the Union."

The next morning Brent docked his ship and arranged to pick up cargo that his father had ordered—coffee beans and cocoa beans brought in from South America, and sugar, aloes, bananas, and oranges, and some fine furniture produced locally.

After a twenty-four hour stay, Brent announced that it was time to sail for home. "Our course will be generally northwest," he told Hawkins, "keeping to the north and northwest of Puerto Rico, Hispaniola, and Cuba, and then bearing northward through the Florida Straits, and keeping as closely northward as we can to Charleston."

"Aye, aye, sir, that's the best route," agreed Hawkins.

"Yes," Brent went on, "we should have good winds and currents most of the way. This time we'll not have to worry about bucking the Gulf Stream; we'll be riding on it. And we should not have to worry about calms in the horse latitudes. Even if there should be no wind at all there, the Gulf Stream will carry us through it, but in addition, we'll probably be close enough to land as we go northward to gain some benefit from the circulation of air between land and sea."

"Right you are, sir," said Hawkins, "should save a day or two this way."

The northeast trade wind indeed held strong and steady throughout the area. Boosted by the northwesterly Antilles current, the *Aura Lee* sailed through the Old Bahama Channel. As they skirted the Great Bahama Bank on the 25th, Brent encouraged the cooks, and any others who wished, to try their hands at fishing. Half a dozen fishermen had good luck in bringing in good numbers of the fish known as sailor's-choice, and which they enjoyed for supper that evening.

Moving into the Santaren Channel the next day, the *Aura Lee* crossed the Tropic of Cancer. Turning northward to the Florida Straits she entered the Gulf Stream. The deep blue waters clearly marked that stream which in this area flowed at its greatest velocity.

With satisfaction Brent walked up to Hawkins and remarked, "We should be able to fly through here. The Gulf Stream must be running at six knots, and with the trade wind blowing steadily abeam makes for good reaching, so that probably gives us another eight knots."

"At least," responded Hawkins as he secured his cap more tightly to keep from losing it in the stiff breeze, "we'll be doing ten knots through the water, but with the speed of the Gulf Stream current we'll be doing fifteen to sixteen knots with respect to the land."

"Looks good!"

On the afternoon of Thursday, September 29th, the *Aura Lee* entered Charleston Harbor. As she sailed up the Cooper River to her mooring, Brent, neatly dressed in his uniform, was on the quarterdeck at the port rail. He, and nearly everyone else on the ship, was looking down at the quay to see if anyone familiar might be there. He was not disappointed. There waving frantically were Violet and the two children. His father was standing beside her on one side, Phoebe on the other, and Evelina beside the children.

In this case the Captain was first off the ship. In turn he embraced Violet and the children and Evelina, and shook hands with his father and gave Phoebe a quick hug. Everyone started talking at once.

"Oh, Brent, it's so wonderful to have you back home, safe and sound. I worried so very much!"

"Tell us about the voyage."

"Daddy, did you bring me anything?"

"How are things with you? Any Prussian ships?"

"Any storms?"

"Daddy, were the waves big?"

At last Brent made himself heard as he asked, "I can't tell you how much it meant to look ashore and see you here, but how did you happen to be here exactly at the time we arrived?"

"Your father has been going down to the Battery every day at low tide to see if you were in sight." answered Violet, placing her arm in his and looking up into his handsome face, thankful he was at last beside her again.

Brent glanced down at her with a loving smile, squeezed her arm with his, and asked teasingly, "What if we had come in the night or at a different time?"

His father answered, "I figured you would come in with the tide, and not at night, either, and I figured that with my spyglass I could recognize the *Aura Lee* far enough out to get the others down here ahead of you. And that's exactly what happened. Son, I'm so glad you are back, and I can scarcely wait to hear all about the voyage, but for now, we know you have ship matters needing your attention, so we'll return to the house and await your arrival there."

Brent and his father helped the others into the carriage. They shook hands and the elder Sutler climbed into the carriage, and all took off amid waves and calls to Brent to hurry home as fast as he could.

Brent returned to his ship, and when the *Aura Lee* was secure and the stevedores and longshoremen had arrived, he invited the crew members to come to the warehouse for their pay. To their great delight he added the bonus that he had promised and which was more generous than they had imagined: one hundred dollars for each seaman and cook and orderly, and a hundred and twenty-five dollars for each officer. He also placed bonus money in envelopes to give to Aaron and Little Josh who had collected his baggage and were waiting for him in a hired carriage.

On Sunday everyone acceded again to the wishes of Brent's mother and went with her to the French Huguenot Church. On Monday, things were in order for an early departure to Fair Oaks. It happened that a passenger car was coupled at the rear of the freight train that was carrying their goods, so they went right along with it as far as Fair Oaks. There Mammy prepared a special supper for the returning travelers. She and Evelina, delighted with their gifts, wore their new French scarves around their throats throughout that evening.

As the children climbed over Brent, Violet reported, "You'll be interested to know that our daughter started to school the first of the month, as soon as we returned."

"Well, that's good news," Brent replied. Lifting Bonnie Anne to his knee he asked her, "Which school are you going to?"

"Edge Hill," the little girl answered.

"And do you like it?"

"Oh, yes. Miss Simons is our teacher, and she's very nice."

"What have you learned so far?"

"A,B,C,D,E,F,G."

That made Brent break into a big smile.

Now J.J. wanted recognition. "A,B,C,D,E,F,G," he echoed, sticking out his lower lip. "Why can't I go to school, too? It's not fair for her to go and not me."

"Now, J.J.," Violet admonished, "you know you'll start school next year. I've told you that."

J.J. was not satisfied. "I want to go now. I don't want to wait until next year," he argued, squirming around on Brent's other knee. "It's not fair," he repeated. "Bonnie Anne gets to do everything."

"Next year," Violet said firmly, "and now, young man, it is time for you to go to bed."

"Does Bonnie Anne have to go, too?"

"Of course," sighed Violet.

Afterwards, when the children were in their beds along with their new toys, and the house was quiet, Brent led Violet into their office and pulled out her desk chair for her. Then he crossed around to his and sat down, facing her.

With a gleeful smile he said, "My darling wife, I can see that you are chaffing at the bit, so let me give you the accounts for the Mercantile Company in this venture."

"Oh, Brent, you are so right. I've been so anxious to hear how that went that I could hardly contain myself. Did you make a quarter of a million or did you lose your—our—shirt?"

"Well, get your book out, and I'll run down the list." He paused to pull some papers from his pocket and gave her the data:

Rifles, muskets, and carbines, 6,000
Purchase price, $3.50 each; Sale price, $23. Net$117,000.
Ammunition, 40 tons
Purchase price, $10,000.; Sale price, $25,000. Net 15,000.
Cotton from Fair Oaks—

"Now this should go into the Fair Oaks account," Brent interjected.

"By all means!" Violet agreed, as he continued.

Cotton from Fair Oaks, 200 bales
Sale price, 24¢ a pound Net 24,000.
Cotton from other sources, 300 bales
Purchase price, 18¢ a pound; Sale price, 24¢ Net 9,000.
Wheat from Fair Oaks, 1,000 bushels
Sale price, 56¢ a bushel Net 560.

TOTAL: $165,560.

LESS: Crew's wages..1,950.
Foodstuffs ....800.
Bonuses ....3,250.
Lease for ship & equipment. ....10,000.
Stevedores 300.
-16,300.

NET TOTAL:.. $149,260.

"Added to that will be profit from our French goods." Brent opened some bags by his side. Withdrawing a handful of bills of various denominations, he tossed them in the air as he laughed gleefully. "Not bad for one short voyage, eh?"

She joined in his laughter. "No, Brent, not bad at all!" Then in a somber voice she went on to ask, "Darling, don't you think you should put all that money in the safe as quickly as you can?"

"Quite right, but I should reassure you that this is only a little of the residue. I put most of the cash in banks in Charleston before I even went back to the house. I don't trust those Scalawag banks in Columbia."

"No, and we certainly would not want to put our profits in that scoundrel Montgomery's bank in Sumter."

"Certainly not." He looked at her with a serious expression, but behind his sea blue eyes there lurked that playful sparkle of humor. "Indeed, yes, I'll put this money in the safe right away, but I've been thinking, my dear, we've done so well, why don't I try just one more run down there next month"

Violet jumped from her chair and ran around to Brent where she plopped down on his lap. "Oh, no, you don't, Brent Sutler, this will be quite enough! You said you'd make just one voyage, remember? Now don't be greedy–next time you may not be so lucky." She took his face between her two hands and kissed him long and hard, then leaned back with a happy smile. She knew he would not leave again.

Chapter 41

The Candidate

1870

Brent had no more returned to Fair Oaks than John Frierson was telling him that the county convention had indeed nominated him for the State Senate, and reminding him that there was no time to lose in getting started to canvass votes since the election was less than three weeks away. Brent begged for two days for business in Columbia—mostly to complete the selling of goods picked up on his voyage to the West Indies—with a promise to devote himself fully to the campaign thereafter.

Agreeing to that, Frierson worked with Violet to map out a schedule for Brent to cover the county with political rallies and speeches—and speeches by leading supporters from all walks of life.

Late one evening as Violet and Brent sat opposite each other in the office at Fair Oaks, Violet mentioned it to him.

"Brent, you know, you are not only highly respected, but well-liked by all the darkies on this plantation. Word of the kind of man you are is bound to have spread already through the Negro grapevine."

Smiling, and with a nod of his head, Brent responded, "Thank you, my dear, and you, too, are admired and well-liked by our workers." He paused, and then went on, "You may be right about the latter. I've noticed that whenever I'm in town or at another plantation, the blacks either speak or wave to me cordially."

"But Brent, don't you see, all the black men here will vote for you, no matter what the Carpetbaggers and Scalawags say. And as soon as those on other plantations get to know you better, and perhaps encouraged by their friends here, they will too."

"Well," he said somewhat modestly, "I don't know about that. I surely hope so."

"Oh, I'm sure of it, Brent. Instead of trying to exploit a wedge between whites and blacks, why not cultivate both?"

Brent paused to roll and light a cigarette as he thought about that. Then he said, "You know, you may have a point there, although I'm not quite sure how we'll go about it. Anyway, John Frierson and the others have arranged for me to appear at a series of meetings all over the county during the rest of this week and the first of next. I'll make those rounds, and then we'll see what we can do in this direction."

She smiled as she said, "Good! I know you'll be persuasive wherever you go, Brent."

Accompanied only by Aaron, Brent took to his horse and saddle and rode around the county like a Methodist circuit rider, but soon he was feeling more like Don Quixote, fighting windmills. At first he felt something like a sensitive war horse that shied from his own shadow, yet faced shellfire without flinching, but this was a new kind of warfare for him, and soon he was suffering from shell shock. He had been used to giving orders and having them obeyed, not to have his every word invite a verbal barrage of invective, innuendo, and falsehoods.

Now wherever he went it seemed that ugly whispering campaigns had preceded him. In the precincts where the old guard still held sway, he was made to appear to be a Scalawag himself, who had taken short cuts to profit at the state's expense. In the precincts dominated by Carpetbaggers, Scalawags, and Negroes, he was made to appear to be a white supremacy extremist interested only in feathering his own nest without any concerns for the welfare or rights of Negroes. His short, eloquent speeches and friendly handshaking gained him support, but could do little to neutralize the mudslinging of his opponent.

He returned home in an uncharacteristic state of discouragement and pessimism. In conversation with Violet over cheese and scuppernong in the library that night, he expressed doubt about letting himself in for such an experience. Violet remained undaunted. She believed fervently in restoring the government of South Carolina to "the people," and she still had faith that Brent was a man who could help bring this about.

She stroked his brow gently and then replenished his cheese and crackers and wine. She said thoughtfully, "Darling, I've been thinking, I guess we were somewhat naive about not splitting the white and black votes. Maybe it would be wiser to change our strategy. Now I believe we should devote ourselves to cultivating the Negro vote; we know you have the votes of the planters and the professional people, but they are not very numerous. And there is nothing we can do—or would want to do—to convince the Carpetbaggers and Scalawags. We just need to do a little missionary work among the blacks."

"And just how might we go about that?" he asked with interest.

She brushed a stray lock back off her face. Her smooth brow crinkled in thought. "First we'll spend some time with our own hands. You impress upon them what a fine person you truly are and can be trusted to handle the matters of our state, and I am going to teach them how to mark their ballots. Then we'll arrange to have Leo drive our black men—and women, too—around to as many other plantations and villages as possible and have them mingle with the black people there, persuade them how to vote, and teach them how to mark their ballots."

"Zounds! I think you've got something there!" Brent exclaimed as he sprang from his chair and began pacing around the room. Then he went on, "And I think we ought to give our workers a few days off with pay to do all this."

"Yes, I think we should," she agreed with enthusiasm.

"And some days off with pay to register themselves and other black voters."

"And a whole day with pay to vote."

"Especially to vote—and to get others to the polls to vote." By now Brent's confidence had returned, and he was excited about their change in strategy. He paused, and then added, "I guess I should put in a couple of thousand to the county Democratic fund."

"Why do you have to do that?"

"It costs money for posters and handbills and everything."

"What good will that do? So many of the folks, practically all the Blacks, can't read, and you'll be paying your own travel expenses."

"Sure, but that won't amount to much. The main thing is to have enough money to have enough Democratic ballots printed."

"Yes, of course," agreed Violet, "do be sure that we have plenty of ballots. I'll instruct the darkies how to vote, but how can they vote with all those scalawags standing around there browbeating or paying them to vote Republican?"

"Well, we'll have some observers there, too. Probably the best thing is to have our voters be sure to ask for both a Republican and a Democratic ballot. And remember, the Democratic ballot will be blue, and the Republican, pink."

"Yes, I'll remember, blue for Violet."

"That's it. Then tell the voters to be sure to circle my name on the blue ballot; anyway they mark it should count, but a circle around the name will be easier, and then tear up the pink ballot and stick it in their pocket and put the blue ballot in the ballot box. They should do those things as unobtrusively as possible so that maybe they can make it appear a little doubtful how they vote."

I'll do it, but, Brent, that doesn't seem quite fair to me. Shouldn't there be a way to vote in secret?"

"Of course there should, but what politician wants to be fair? Actually, some of the colonies of Australia have adopted the secret ballot. I heard about it while out there during the War. There, the government pays for the ballots, and all names from all parties appear on a single ballot. The voter marks it secretly in a special voting booth."

"That sounds like a great improvement to me," Violet declared.

"Probably is. I understand that now they are talking about adopting that system in England."

"Why don't we do it here? If you get into the legislature, will you vote for it?"

"Sure. I'll introduce a bill for it. But it will never get through our legislature."

"Why not?"

"My Dear, you don't think those Carpetbaggers and Scalawags are going to give up their means of controlling the votes, do you? I dare say this state will not have a secret ballot for years to come."

"But surely there will be when the Democrats get back into power"

"Oh, I doubt it, even then, but now we had better be giving our attention to the ballots that we have."

The next five days Brent and Violet spent several hours each evening with the black workers in their village—with groups in the school-church where Violet patiently instructed them how to find the name, *Brent Sutler*, on the ballot, and mark it.

They visited every worker's cabin and all the men in the barracks to explain to them the political issues and why they should vote for Massuh Brent. No one dissented on that. On the contrary, they became excited about visiting black workers on other plantations and villages to spread the word and show them how to vote. Even the women were anxious to go along and said they could talk and show how to mark ballots just as well as the men could, even though the women themselves could not vote.

When they were ready, Leo organized convoys of two to five wagons each day for a week to carry his workers around the neighboring plantations and farms and villages to do their work of education and persuasion. Brent had already gotten permission from the various owners for his workers to do this.

For his part, Brent returned to the speaking circuit. This all ended with a big meeting in the Sumter Court House on the Saturday afternoon before the election. A mixed audience had gathered—old and young, white and black, rich and poor, farmers and townsmen, men and women. Violet was there, on the front row.

After a few preliminaries, Brent took the podium. In measured, sonorous tones he began speaking:

> I am here today to enlist your support in a battle for the restoration of freedom to the people of this state and for the restoration of honesty and integrity in government.
>
> We have seen the savagery of man released—in the War and now in the so-called Reconstruction. In the War the savagery was rationalized to some extent. It was accompanied by devotion to a Cause, on both sides, I guess. We were fighting for freedom and independence, especially freedom from the economic exploitation of the South by the North, with their high tariffs, financial monopolies, and all the rest. And I guess the Yankees thought the Union was a Cause worth dying for.
>
> But now the savagery goes on only to appease guilty consciences of Northern hypocrites and tyrants and to satisfy their greed to gain at our expense, to profit from the misery of our people. I tell you the devil is loose in the land.
>
> A slogan of the American colonists on the eve of the Revolution was, No taxation without representation. Yet that is the yoke under which we now live. Now we have taxation and everything else without representation.
>
> And who are these people who come down here from the North to punish South Carolina for slavery and who promise all kinds of things to our Negro people just to use them to maintain their own stranglehold on the state? The only prosperity they are interested in is their own. Their own, not that of our state.
>
> Listen to what a famous Massachusetts author, John Greenleaf Whittier had to say in his book called *A Stranger in Lowell.* Lowell, you know, is in Massachusetts, and the author is commenting about the cotton mills there. I quote: "Every web which falls from these restless looms has a history more or less connected with sin and suffering, beginning with slavery and ending with overwork and premature death,"—end of quotation. And you know many of those

> doing slave labor in the Northern cotton mills are women and children. I say, let these Carpetbaggers go back North and do something about their slavery there!
>
> We have got to make our people safe in their homes, in their businesses, on their farms. Marauders and bandits are stealing our crops, robbing our stores, and burglarizing our homes. Before the Yankees came our women could walk along the country roads and the city streets in complete safety, with no feeling of fear. Now they are even being attacked in their own homes. A curtain of fear has descended over our whole land. We cannot depend on vigilantes like the Ku Klux Klan and the Knights of the Camellia to protect us. We must have honest sheriffs and honest constables and honest police, with full support of an honest county, town, and state government.

Brent went on for fifteen minutes or so and then opened himself to questions from the audience. The first one got his attention immediately.

"During your long absence at the end of the War, what was your wife up to, dallying with Carpetbaggers so she could get a railroad through your place so you all could have an advantage in shipping out cotton and—"

Before the man had finished his question Brent was at his throat. He grabbed the heckler's collar and lifted him right up from his chair and then set him down with such force that both the man and his chair toppled over backward.

Stepping back, Brent shouted vehemently, "If you make any more asinine insinuations like that about my wife I'll hide you good and proper, right here in front of everyone. Now you get on out of here before I lose my temper!" Amidst some cheers and claps for Brent, the man got up and slunk out with a sulky look on his face.

Brent's first impulse was to turn his back and walk out of the meeting, but, steeling himself against further abuse, he determined to stay on. "If anybody has a civil question, I'll return to the platform and try to answer it. As for that man's question, I will say only that the railroad tracks were placed across our front yard *precisely because my wife would* <u>not</u> *cooperate with the Carpetbaggers and Scalawags!* And I ask you, who in the world would *want* a noisy, dirty train passing through their front yard?"

Violet was practically in tears, but she called out to him, "Carry on, Mr. Sutler!"

There was a moment of awkward silence. Then the audience broke into applause. This gave Brent time and encouragement to regain his composure.

"Now do you have questions?" he asked calmly, looking about the meeting room, and flashing an encouraging smile to Violet.

A man near the center aisle raised his hand and asked, "Do you favor the vote for the Negroes?"

Brent answered promptly, "Of course I favor the vote for the Negroes, and I favor their civil rights, too, same rights as everybody else—but above all I favor education for them. I think that as a condition of voting a man should be able to read and write so he can think for himself. We have had enough of the selfish interests using illiterate Negro voters as pawns for their own selfish gain." There was loud applause at this.

A woman from the back ventured to ask, somewhat timidly, "Do you favor woman suffrage?"

"Yes, ma'am, I certainly do. I think that women should have the vote, provided, like anyone else, they can read and write. Already they have the vote in the Wyoming Territory, and I am confident that many of the states, including South Carolina I hope, soon will adopt it." This comment was followed by polite applause, more enthusiastically by the women in the audience, less so by the men.

A man near the center asked, "Did you favor ratification of the Fourteenth Amendment to the U.S. Constitution?"

"Certainly not—not with the provision that prohibits anyone who ever held a federal or state office and then served the Confederacy from holding any federal or state position again. It was not legally adopted, you know, and I think we should have had no part in it. They forced Southern states to approve it as a condition for readmission to the Union, and then counted them as being in the Union for this purpose, and they refused to accept reversal of votes in a couple of Northern states which, having approved it, then rejected it. But that is our Carpetbagger-Scalawag government for you." There was loud applause and stomping of feet.

Another asked, "Do you favor state support for the building of railroads?"

Brent nodded. "As you know, I am committed to railroads. I believe that the state should give its support in making rights of way available through eminent domain, and I think it is well for the state to guarantee long-term bonds, but it should not give direct financial assistance, and certainly not in the kind of graft that has been going on. More of the railroad effort in this state has gone into selling watered stock than in the laying of track. When the state guarantees bonds, it should see to it that the money goes into building railroads and not into the pockets of a bunch of Carpetbagger speculators." Again loud applause and stomping of feet broke forth.

Then came a less friendly question. "There have been stories that you obtained a bunch of weapons from the state for a dollar a piece and then sold them for a big profit. Is that true, Mr. Sutler?"

"Sir, I did the state a favor by taking a lot of surplus weapons off its hands for cash, and if you think the state got only a dollar a piece for them, I suggest that you look in the pockets of your honorable adjutant general and speaker of the house for the difference between that and three and a half times as much. Anything else?" This was followed by sustained applause.

Finally an older man in the back called out, "What is your main objective in running for the Senate?"

Brent smiled as he answered, "To be elected! But why do I want to be elected? To do what I can to get us out from under military occupation and to get relief from the exploitation by the Carpetbagger-Scalawag regime. To restore the government to the people of South Carolina." He paused a moment and then added, "Now I think it is time for us to adjourn, and I just want to thank you all for coming out and for being so patient."

The audience responded with loud applause and cheers.

Election day, Wednesday, October 19th, was gray and cool. Actually the polls would be open two days in some areas, but the days would still be gray and cool.

Leo was out early organizing his convoy of five wagons of black voters from Fair Oaks. Brent and Violet drove their buggy ahead of them. When they arrived at the polls at Edge Hill School, they almost overwhelmed the election officials. Shortly afterwards, wagons from other plantations and farms began to arrive, full of workers, ready to vote.

When those from Fair Oaks returned to the plantation, Brent gave to each of the voters their dollars for this and previous days off when they had visited other prospective voters. That done, Leo and the drivers continued with the wagons to other places to help carry black voters to the polls. All day long they continued their activities.

When the results became known on the following Friday, Brent had won election by a two-to-one majority. He would be joining the 49th General Assembly when it began its next session on the fourth Tuesday in November, the 22nd.

Chapter 42

The Senator

1870 - 1871

"Well, Senator, now what? What are our arrangements to be while you are in the Senate during the legislative session?" asked Violet as she and Brent sat in the library at Fair Oaks on the Sunday evening after the election.

"Frankly, I had not counted enough on being elected to have thought much about it. Surely you will not want to miss the show that they put on in the State House."

She knew he wanted her with him in Columbia, and for that matter, she wanted to be a part of all this with him, so she answered affirmatively, "You know I want to be there. What is the schedule for the session?"

"As I understand it, they meet for the opening of the Legislature on November 23rd. That's when I get sworn in, I guess."

"Well, I certainly do not intend to miss that!"

"And I want you to be there, my Darling. As for the regular schedule, they just meet for a month at this time. Then they recess for Christmas on December 23rd, and then resume in January, on the 5th, and probably adjourn about March 1st."

"Oh, dear...I don't like the idea of taking Bonnie Anne out of school after such a short time. And, Brent, where would we live in town?"

"In answer to your question of where we might live, I guess we could go back to the Columbia Hotel, good location, not far from the State house. Or, maybe you would rather arrange to stay with Charlotte and Leland in their new house."

"All of us?"

He raised his dark eyebrows and answered, "Why, yes, I should think so—you and I and the two kids and Evelina. Charlotte and Leland have sufficient room, don't they?"

"Well, yes, but after all they really still are newlyweds, and I hesitate to impose on them for that length of time." She looked at Brent impishly. A slight dimple darted in and out of her cheek as her lips curved in a tempting smile. "Surely you recall how we were after we were first married, how we needed to be *alone* together at times—"

He grinned in understanding, "And after I came back from the Navy...and as a matter of fact, we still do, don't we? Look, maybe we can look for a town house of our own. Yes, why not? After all, my term is for four years, and I still have to look after the Mercantile Company and do my chores for the railroad."

Violet clapped her hands in delight. "Oh, Brent, can we? It would be wonderful to have our own town house and spend the winters there like we used to in the old days before the War. And we could entertain, and oh, Brent, let's do!" Her liquid eyes shone with excitement.

He grinned again, moved as always by her effervescence and radiant beauty. "Then that's what we'll do. It should be possible for us to find a house for next year, but the question now is, what do we do for the present?"

"Why not book rooms at the hotel for the period before Christmas? I'll come along for just a few days, at least so I can be there for the swearing in, and I think the children and Evelina could come along. Bonnie Anne and J.J. should see their Daddy sworn in as a senator, even if they don't know what's going on—"

He interrupted with a laugh. "Ha, they'll have that in common with most of the members who don't know what's going on either!"

"I can take a few days to begin looking for a house, and then the children and I will come back here to Fair Oaks, and maybe you can come home on weekends."

"I should hope so!"

"And all this will give us some time to figure out what we are going to do after Christmas."

"Sounds good to me."

Early the next week a letter arrived from Charlotte that said in part, "I see by the paper that Brent was elected to the State Senate. Congratulations! Now we are hoping that you all will come and stay with us in our new house (at the old address!) during the session. We have plenty of room, and it would be such fun to be together again. Leland said to be sure to tell you that he thinks this is a fine idea, too."

Violet was attracted by the offer, but decided she should wait until their short visit for the opening of the legislative session when she would have a chance to visit Charlotte and talk with her a while. She and Brent were toying with the idea of building a house, rather than renting one, but this would mean a delay in moving into their own house in Columbia.

Brent and Violet decided that they would go into Columbia on Sunday afternoon, three days before the opening of the session and would return to Fair Oaks on Friday. This would give them time to begin initial inquiries with a couple of real estate brokers for either a house or lot, and also time to visit a bit with Charlotte and Leland. Brent sent a telegraph message to Cedric to meet their afternoon train with a carriage to take them to the Columbia Hotel. The next morning, Brent went over to the State house to check out the schedule and to meet with other arriving members, while Violet drove the carriage with the children and Evelina over to visit with Charlotte.

Charlotte was out the door to meet them as soon as they drove up. She called her house servant to take the horse and carriage around to the carriage house, and after enthusiastic embraces with everyone, she invited them all to come in. "Do you realize, my dearest sister, that it has been two months since we last were together?"

They had no more than settled into chairs in the parlor, with J.J. on her lap and little Bonnie Anne nestling beside her beloved aunt, than Charlotte was insisting that they should all have supper there. She had missed everyone so much, and how wonderful that they would see more of each other now that Brent was a senator.

"We miss you, too, Charlotte, you know that. Yes, we'll be in Columbia more now that Brent is a member of the Legislature—"

"But why didn't you plan to stay right here with us instead of the hotel?" demanded Charlotte.

"We didn't want to come in unannounced and impose on you," smiled Violet.

"Oh, fiddlesticks, that would be no imposition at all. How long will you be in the city, until the end of the session?"

"We'll all be going back to Fair Oaks on Friday. Then Brent will return Sunday afternoon and stay at the Columbia Hotel until the legislature's Christmas recess. We've not yet decided what to do when it reconvenes in January. As for supper, well, Charlotte, Brent and I plan to see a couple of real estate brokers about the possibility of finding a house to rent, and maybe a lot if we decide to build. But I don't see why we can't come back after that to have supper with you all and visit a little more. We could pick the children up at the hotel on the way over. They really do need to take a nap, you know."

"Well I do declare! I guess I have a few things to say about all that! First of all, you can leave the children and Evelina here for the day so I can visit with my niece and nephew. They can take their naps here. Then you and Brent come on back after you've completed your business; but as to that, why can't you, all of you, just stay here, with Leland and me, while the legislature is in session? Oh, Violet, it would be wonderful for us all to be together again!" Her voice broke on the last sentence. Her beseeching eyes filled with tears.

"Oh, Charlotte, you are so generous, so sweet, but we don't want to impose on you two. After all you've only been married a little over a year," said Violet, hesitatingly.

"Oh, fiddlesticks!"

Brent and Violet arrived at Charlotte's before Leland and his father, who was living with them, arrived home from the mill. The children hugged their parents and excitedly told them about their day's adventures with Aunt Charlotte. Just then Leland and his father walked in, pleased to see the Sutlers. Charlotte had sent word to them at the mill that they would be having guests for supper. The meal was delicious, and most of all it gave everyone the chance to visit together again. Charlotte was a gracious hostess, and Violet was proud of her younger sister's maturity. She noticed that Charlotte's cheeks were flushed, and she did not miss the silent messages that were exchanged between Charlotte and Leland. It was obvious that they were happy and well-suited to one another. Violet's heart was gladdened.

After supper, as the men made their way into the parlor and Evelina took the children upstairs to get their new toys, Charlotte motioned to Violet to follow her into the butler's pantry. As soon as the door swung closed and they were alone, she said, "Oh, Violet, I've got something exciting to tell you. Guess what?"

"What is it, Charlotte?"

Charlotte's face reddened as she answered with a proud smile, "Oh, Violet, I'm expecting!"

"Your complexion seems to have a wonderful glow, and I thought you were putting on a little weight around the middle," smiled Violet, as she gave her sister a hug. "Any idea when?"

"The doctor thinks probably in May."

"In May! That's a good time of the year to have a baby." Now Violet's eyes were moist at the thought of her sister having a child.

"And Violet..."

"Yes?"

"I was thinking it would be nice if you could be with me. There's no one else, you know. That's one reason I was so hoping that you all would stay with us if you are going to be in the city while Brent is in the legislative session." The beseeching look returned to her eyes.

"Oh, Charlotte, of course I want to be with you. We'll arrange it so we can stay with you when the legislature reconvenes in January. Then I can send Bonnie Anne to our old school." She hesitated and then continued, "But Charlotte, you know that you can have the baby at Fair Oaks, if you wish. Mammy would be delighted–"

"No, Violet," answered Charlotte gently, "You know how much I love Fair Oaks, but this is my home now, and I want to be with my husband. I wouldn't want to do that to Leland, he's so sweet and loving, and so thrilled about our having a baby. And he would be able to get away from the mill only on weekends. Then, there's his father, too. No, Violet, please understand, I want to have the child here."

Violet threw her arms around her sister, saying tenderly, "Of course I understand, Charlotte, and we'll make arrangements. I'm certain Brent will want to do this. I think he would much rather build than rent a house, and he'll be able to overlook the construction while we are with you."

"Oh, Violet, thank you, thank you. I'm so relieved...I...I'm just a bit scared, you know."

"That's only natural. I was, too. Every woman is."

Violet, the children and Evelina, and Charlotte took their seats in the gallery of the Senate chamber a little before noon. As she looked down, Violet could hardly believe her eyes. She knew that many of the legislators were black. She knew that Carpetbaggers, Scalawags, and Negroes controlled the legislature. But to see it with her own eyes carried a much greater impact. She immediately caught sight of Brent. Dressed neatly in a dark gray, Prince Albert coat and striped trousers, he stood out in the group. Around him were nineteen other white senators, and ten colored senators. Presiding was the first colored lieutenant governor, Alonzo J. Ransier–actually a light-skinned mulatto who was a native freedman before the War.

As Brent was escorted forward with the other newly elected senators for swearing in, Violet held up Bonnie Anne and Charlotte held up J.J. so that they could see. As soon as the ceremony was over, Brent joined them in the balcony while cursory business continued on the floor.

"I'm going to feel pretty lonely in this outfit," Brent said in a low voice.

"Why?" Violet asked. "Looks to me the whites outnumber the blacks down there."

"Sure, they outnumber them twenty to ten, but do you know how many of those whites are Radical Carpetbaggers and Scalawags?"

"How many?"

"Fourteen of them. Add them to the darkies and they have twenty-four Radical votes. One is an independent. That leaves only five regular Democrats–four besides me–or, as they are calling them this year, Reformers or members of the Fusionist ticket to avoid party labels.

"Oh, my, that is certainly one-sided. That's not good, is it?"

"And the House of Representatives is even worse. They have seventy-five colored and forty-nine white. Imagine that! A black majority of seventy-five to forty-nine...but then think of this–twenty-six of those whites are Radical Carpetbaggers and Scalawags, so that gives them a total of 101 Radicals, one independent, and just twenty-two regular Democrats."

"Brent, it becomes more remarkable all the time that you were elected at all. Is it possible that you can do *anything* in this setting?"

"Probably not, but we'll just have to keep chipping away until we can get more of our people elected. In the meantime, it still will be possible to play politics sometimes to drive a wedge between the blacks and their Carpetbagger and Scalawag tutors."

"We've already found out that we can do a little tutoring of our own," Violet responded with a smile.

Brent sighed deeply. "We had better do something, or God help the public treasury."

"And God help the taxpayers," added Violet.

Charlotte and Leland and his father came out to Fair Oaks for Christmas. As always the family missed those loved ones now departed who had been so much a part of this special season of the year, but time had eased their grief, and although quiet, the holiday was an enjoyable one for all. The workers were especially pleased to find that their annual supplemental payment was even greater than last year's.

With Brent's enthusiastic concurrence, Violet decided that Little Josh should go along with them to Columbia. He was now thirteen years old, tall and lanky for his age, and everyone began calling him Josh, rather than *Little* Josh which seemed incongruous now. If anything, his alert mind was even sharper. He worked the telegraph with an expertise that few men achieved. He read avidly all the books that Violet lent him, and then later discussed them with insight and understanding, applying the new knowledge to the world about him. His musical abilities were known throughout the county. And his devotion to Violet and Brent and the children had only grown with the years. He was thrilled to be going to Columbia with his "famly." Violet was determined to send him to study at the music school conducted by Ellen Brennan Carter, the famed former "Carolina Mocking Bird" and her husband.

Everyone left together on the train on Tuesday, the second day after New Year's. Leo as well as Mammy and the other servants were at the train to see them off. All assured Violet and Brent that Fair Oaks would be in good hands. All the servants and hands were immensely proud of Brent's having won the election and now being an important senator. Their successful efforts in the election had made them feel a part of the whole process. They felt that, in a way, they were going to Columbia, too, to make things better for all, especially those less fortunate than they.

Leland and Charlotte's house was similar to the old house that it replaced, brick and square. Its overall dimensions were smaller, though its liveable space was just as large. Leland's father occupied a bedroom off the parlor on the first floor. There were four bedrooms on the second floor. Charlotte and Leland were in the master bedroom. Bonnie Anne and J.J. shared a room, and Evelina had a room adjacent to them. Violet and Brent had the large guest room with a sitting alcove area. Josh had a room of his own in the third floor garret. Charlotte and Leland's two servants, Mercy and Lorenzo, a black married couple who had worked for Leland's father on their old plantation, had quarters in the basement, along with Liza, the housemaid who helped with the cleaning, washing, and cooking. Violet and Brent had brought along capable Hattie who would take care of their family's clothes and the cleaning of their rooms. She, too, occupied a room in the basement.,

The first thing Violet did the next day after moving in was to see about school for little Bonnie Anne. She was able to enter her in the elementary section of the Female Academy where Violet and her sisters had gone to school, and she entered Josh in the music school. There he would study voice with Ellen Brennan Carter and violin with Mr. Carter.

One day in early February, after the General Assembly had more or less settled into its routine, Brent suggested that Violet might like to spend a day at the State House and see the legislature in action. She was intrigued at the prospect.

As she sat in the Senate gallery, matters were relatively quiet. The colored lieutenant governor presided with some dignity and apparent fairness, though most of the members paid no attention either to him or to whomever of their colleagues happened to be making a speech. Their laughter and back-slapping and talking drowned out most of everything else. They only paused long enough, now and then, to cast a vote. *How rude they all are,* she thought, *and how can they possibly get anything done?*

Brent joined Violet for a few minutes and then suggested that they go over to the House of Representatives "where the real action is."

Although she had an idea of what to expect from the earlier visit and from conversations with Brent, she was not prepared for the bizarre spectacle that she looked down upon from the balcony of the House of Representatives.

"They never miss a meeting," remarked Brent. "They have the persistence of courthouse pigeons."

"And about the same concern for tidiness," Violet added.

Colored men—mulattoes, quadroons, octoroons, and of the darkest black—dominated the scene. Some, wearing glossy, threadbare black frock coats struck pompous attitudes. Some wore the rough, soiled clothing of the cotton fields. Some wore stub jackets and carefully pulled woolen scarves around their necks so that their lack of linen would not be evident. Many sat with their feet up on their desks or upon the velvet-covered chairs. Some were smoking long cigars. Some were chewing tobacco and spitting into gold-plated spittoons. The cracking of peanuts, raucous laughter, and talking filled the hall with competing, grating noises, while the Speaker rapped for order.

Brent nodded toward the rostrum. "You see who the speaker of the house is, don't you?"

"Oh, yes, I recognize our friend, that damned Frank Moses, Jr. How did he ever get there?"

"By being more corrupt than anyone else."

With the calls to order, members would drop briefly to their seats. The Speaker would recognize a member to have the floor, but he would be greeted by incongruous questions and guffaws, and soon would sit down to resume cracking peanuts, tossing the shells on the carpet, and smoking cigars. Within moments everyone was on his feet again, moving around to greet each other.

"Let's move back over to the Senate side," whispered Brent. "Maybe there is more business there."

When they returned to the Senate gallery they found a continuation of similar turmoil on the floor, but on a smaller scale.

At last one Negro orator was able to command a modicum of attention. Wearing a dark wool coat with braided piping, white vest, white shirt and black bow tie, his hair trimmed neatly and parted on the side, a full neatly trimmed mustache and small goatee, he presented a striking figure.

"That is Richard Harvey Cain," Brent explained. "Everybody calls him 'Daddy Cain.' He was born in Virginia, but then went north and became a preacher. He's lived in Iowa, Ohio, and New York. He left his church in Brooklyn in 1865 to come down here as a missionary."

"Sounds like a black Carpetbagger," Violet commented.

"Well, I guess he is, but he has taken it upon himself to try to protect the blacks from the white Carpetbaggers and Scalawags. He's editor of a paper called the *Missionary Record* which is the most influential Negro paper ever around here."

Now Cain boomed forth in a sonorous voice. He was presenting one of his strongest supporters, the black Senator Beverly Nash from Richland County.

Brent whispered to Violet, "Nash was a slave before the War, then he worked as a waiter in the Columbia Hotel. He pretty much taught himself to read and write a little."

Violet looked down as Nash rose to speak. He was charcoal black, of medium height, and with a round face that presented a pleasant countenance. His black coat, too large for him, hung loose, showing an abundance of white shirt spotlighted with a multicolored, flowing tie. He launched a speech in favor of social and economic equality for Negroes. He spoke in a flowery language that frequently included multisyllabic words that were ludicrously misplaced or misconstructed, but the others were listening. He was making his points to his followers.

Brent motioned Violet to listen.
The orator on the floor spoke on:

> Now my brudders, I tell ya, de man an' de land is free. De man an' de land is equal an' uninalienable. An' dey ain't nobudy dat kin deposit taxes on de man or de land wifout unequal misrepresentation.
>
> My brudders, don' follow no false prophets. Many o' dem are righchere, wearing white faces. Don' pay dem no nebbermind, irregardless uf whut dey say.
>
> I got arthurtitus in my knees. I got redoubt in my toe. I got new algae in my back and old plurissy in my chest. But I got no log in my eye, an' I kin see very well whut be goin' on 'round chere. Dey vote pre-eminence domain fo' de railroad. Dey vote guarantee uf de species for de bank. Dey vote protection money fo' reconvicted felonophones.
>
> No, my brudders, doncha follow no false prophets. Dey tek you straigh' through de lion's den an' inta de fiery furnace an' if we don' watch out, den we all be axphixicated.

Enthusiastic outbursts of applause and shouts of "Amen!" from the gallery as well as the floor interrupted the speaker. He continued:

> As Moses done led de chillun uf Israel outta de bondage in Egypt an' inta de land floatin' wif milk an' honey, now Father Abraham has done led de chillun uf Africa outta de bondage uf Carolina ta de free land uf po'k chops an' watermelon."

Again there was loud applause, shouts, and stomping of feet. All this encouraged Nash to rise to new heights of oratory:

> We mus' command undisrespect fo' all our people. We mus' mek law ta be sure dat freedom nebber be disunabridged, but dat alway all de chillun grow up disproportionate an' free ta do all dey can an' wantta do fo' all de people all de time, an' know dat when dey is sick, an' when dey is po', de givment tek care uf dem.
>
> De po' haf disinherited de earth an' we bless dem, fo' dey haf de mercy uf de land dat now be free an' equal!

As soon as Nash sat down, the turmoil resumed on the floor—members coming and going, back-slapping, laughter, the ostentatious puffing on cigars and spitting tobacco juice, the cracking of peanuts, boots up on desks and chairs.

Violet leaned toward Brent and ventured, "Sounds more like a Holy Roller camp meeting than anything else I can think of."

"As you can see, that is what it is much of the time," responded Brent sardonically, "but do you know that three-fourths of the colored members of this legislature were totally illiterate when they arrived here?"

"I don't see how it could be otherwise."

"The Union Club has been working with them to teach them to read and write, so that I guess about half of them now can sign their names, with some effort."

"And I suppose teaching them how to vote."

"Exactly, but some of them are fairly well-educated, like Daddy Cain there, and some are good speakers and good leaders, but most of them are totally ignorant; over half of them ex-slaves, straight out of the fields, and now there they sit, lording it over their former masters."

Violet still was studying the scene below her, but she remained alert to Brent's comments. "Of course," she said, "most of them never had any chance for education—wasn't even legal."

"True, but we must remember, being ignorant is not the same thing as being stupid, my dear."

"No, of course not!"

Brent went on, "Actually, I would say that most of the coloreds are more reliable and better citizens than most of the damned Scalawags."

"That doesn't surprise me."

"As you know, in general, the Scalawags here are almost totally renegades, turning on their own people for their own power and financial gain. They're forever trying to control the darkies for their own purposes. They have sold their souls to the devil."

"And I gather some of the colored leaders are aware of that," she said.

"Yes, they are, but it is hard for them to do anything about it, because too many of their followers are too well rewarded for their votes."

"What about the Carpetbaggers?"

"That's where most of the real leaders are. About two-thirds or more of them are Northern adventurers down here to exploit the miseries of the South, bent mostly on plunder. Maybe a third of them have something of a missionary spirit and actually are trying to do some good."

"How do you sort out the hypocrites from the well-intentioned?"

Brent answered in a low voice, "Well, frankly, it's not easy. I don't trust any of them any farther than I can see them." He paused for another look around and then said, "How about some lunch?"

"I'd like some, where?"

"In the members' barroom."

"Oh...where is that?"

"Down next to the office of the clerk of the Senate. Come on." He rose, and taking Violet by the arm, they went downstairs and found their way through the crowd to the barroom.

Violet held back in hesitation. "Am I allowed in there?" she asked.

"Of course, come on," smiled Brent as he took her arm again and guided her along. "This is for members and their guests, and you'll find as many women in there as men."

Quickly, as soon as they entered, Violet could see the truth of Brent's statement. Women of all shades of complexion and all kinds of dress were chatting with men companions of similar diversity. As they found a small table near a corner, she observed, "I guess you might call this the Solons' Saloon?"

"Exactly," laughed Brent, his eyes twinkling, "now, how about a glass of champagne?"

"My goodness! Champagne?"

"Of course, and how about some smoked beef, or some buffalo tongue, or ham?"

"Such choices! Well, ham always sounds good."

"Fine. Now you must understand," Brent chuckled, "we are not content with ordinary Carolina ham here, or even Virginia ham. No, here we have Westphalia ham—all the way from Germany."

"Oh, yes, Westphalia ham. I remember that on your lists. You helped provide this, didn't you?"

Now he laughed uproariously. "Of course, and also the champagne, and the Swiss cheese, and Danish cheese, and we'll finish with a little peach cobbler and some nuts."

Violet was hungry, and she had to admit that the refreshments were very good, but she could not help wondering about the cost of all these delicacies.

"Now you know, my dear, you don't have to worry about that. All this delicious food is provided by the taxpayers of South Carolina," said Brent.

Violet could detect a hint of bitterness in the tone of his voice. She said, "Somehow what you have just said gives me an uneasy feeling, and it seems to me the booze flows pretty freely in this place."

He nodded in disgust. "With all the guests, lobbyists, state officials, and so on that come in here, it takes the equivalent of a gallon of wines and spirits and a dozen fine cigars a day per member. At the taxpayers' expense, of course."

"Why Brent, that's awful!"

"All depends on how you look at it. I guess this is just an exaggerated form of the German ratzkellar where the city fathers gather in the cellar of the city hall to transact their real business over glasses of beer."

"But at the taxpayers expense?"

"Well, not necessarily, but you see how they have improved things here." Brent lowered his voice and whispered, "Don't look that way, but listen very carefully to what's going on at the table to your right and to the rear."

Both continued eating quietly. Again in a low whisper, Brent told Violet, "The man on the left is Tim Hurley, one of our legislators. The other man is one of his constituents. Now listen."

Barely audibly, the constituent at the other table was saying, "We are hoping to get a charter for this mine. It should bring into the state $160,000 or $170,000 right away."

Hurley could be heard to say, "Whut dis thing worth?"

"It has not been tried yet, of course, but we hope to make it profitable soon."

Hurley burst into laughter and replied, "Man, you is green. Green, green. I mean whut be you willing ta pay ta git dis thing through?"

"Pay? Why, I'm not willing to pay anything to get it through. You are supposed to be legislating for our people."

Hurley laughed again, this time more derisively, and the other man got up and walked out. Hurley went over to the bar for a refill of his drink.

Brent's eyes followed Hurley to the bar, then he looked at Violet and said with a smirk, "If anyone wants to get anything passed, it costs so much per vote."

"Brent! That's terrible! And *that's* the kind of government the Yankees have fastened on us!" exclaimed Violet with disgust.

As they were slowly sipping a final glass of champagne, Violet was startled when Brent suddenly jumped up and ran out the door. He returned in a few minutes with a young man in tow.

"Violet, you remember Mr. Jones," said Brent coolly, "and I'm sure you remember my wife, Mr. Jones."

The young man seemed nonplused, but managed to stammer, "Oh yes, how are you, Mrs. Sutler?"

Violet nodded, but at first she could not place the man.

"Violet, surely you remember Seaman Jones. He was the one whose wife was about to have a baby as we were preparing to sail from Charleston. Remember?"

"Oh, yes, of course. I sent some flowers to Mrs. Jones, but I never was able to find out whether she received them." Her eyes narrowed as she went on sweetly, "How are your wife and the baby? Tell me, was the baby a boy or a girl?" *Let's see what you say to that, you treacherous so and so.*

Jones began to fidget uncomfortably His face was beginning to flush.

Brent pulled out a chair, saying, "Here, have a chair. Have a glass of champagne with us." *You two-faced slime, you could have gotten the other sailors and me killed with your treachery.*

"Oh, I don't think I should, sir, I'm late in getting back to the office."

"Oh come on," Brent insisted as he practically forced Jones into the chair.

"You haven't told me about your wife and baby," continued Violet in an innocent tone.

"Uh...no, ma'am, I'm afraid there's been some mistake."

"Mistake?" asked Violet with mock incredulity.

"Uh...yes, ma'am," replied Jones, "you see, I was just trying to get a message to my girlfriend back here and was afraid that wouldn't sound urgent enough to get permission." Beads of perspiration were beginning to appear on his forehead.

"Oh, I see," said Violet in an artificial tone of sympathy.

"Yes, I see," echoed Brent. "Tell me, Jones, how did those Prussians treat you?"

"Pruss-Prussians, sir?" stammered the nervous young man.

"Yes, the Prussians, the ones that took you along as hostage. How did you get away from them and get back here?"

Jones took a red bandanna handkerchief from his pocket and wiped his forehead. "Uh...they sailed around a little while looking for contraband, and then brought me back right to Charleston."

It was all Brent could do to hide a snicker. "Wasn't that nice of them?"

"Uh...yes, sir, it certainly was, sir."

"Now Jones, what are you doing here? Where are you working?"

"I'm a clerk in the office of the Speaker of the House, sir."

"Oh, is that so?" Brent's brow furrowed as he looked Jones straight in the eye. "Well, Mr. Jones, you tell your boss, Mr. Franklin I. Moses, Junior, that if he ever tries any more shenanigans like that with me, I'll be after his scalp personally!"

"Yes, sir; yes, sir," blurted Jones as he hastily rose, overturning his chair. He scurried out the door.

Turning to Violet, Brent said, "I knew that Jones was a flunky for that damned Moses. I suspected it as soon as Cedric could not find his address."

"What a rascal, but speaking of your expedition, apparently it didn't do much good for the French. Didn't I see in the paper just a day or two ago that they had surrendered?"

"I'm afraid that's right. Paris held out under siege for four months, under terrible conditions, but finally capitulated on the 28th. However, it appears that some fighting is still going on, and some say there are signs of revolution."

"Are the Germans still there?"

"Oh yes, they'll stay until they are sure they've got all they want. You know ten days before the Armistice they proclaimed the new German Empire at Versailles."

"At Versailles? In France?"

"Yes, kind of rubbing it in, weren't they? The Prussian King, Wilhelm, or William I, is to be their new Caesar–their Kaiser."

"Is that good?"

"Probably good for Germany, bad for Europe." Brent paused, smiled at Violet, and asked, "Well, my dear wife, would you like to go out this evening for another glimpse of capital society?"

She grimaced. "Has it changed any since the last time you showed us?"

"Only in being even more bizarre."

"Well then, no, thank you. I think I have seen about enough of this rich life for one day. How about a quiet evening at home?"

"Frankly, my Love, I was hoping you would say that."

Chapter 43

Hypocrisy

1871

To celebrate the end of the legislative session the first week of March, Charlotte invited a couple of political leaders for dinner on Saturday evening. These were James and Mary Chesnut and Matt Butler and his wife, Margaret, of Edgefield. Violet was thrilled at the chance to see Mary Chesnut and General Butter again, and though she had not met his wife, she knew that he had been the unsuccessful Democratic-Reform candidate for lieutenant governor in the last election, and she was looking forward to their visit. Brent had met both James Chesnut and Matt Butler at political meetings, but he had yet to meet their wives.

The first course consisted of tender, succulent catfish, seasoned with lemon and a touch of turmeric, and was followed by juicy roast beef with mashed Irish potatoes, tender asparagus tips, succotash, yeast rolls, and freshly churned butter. When the dinner plates were removed, a salad of watercress topped with avocado slices flecked with mint prepared the palate for the desert of pear halves sauteed in butter and upon which melted chocolate had been dribbled.

"An absolutely delicious dinner, Mrs. Thompson. My compliments to you," sighed James Chesnut as he laid his linen napkin on the table and sat back in his chair.

"Yes, indeed, I can't recall when I've had such a palatable meal," declared Matt Butler, as his wife nodded in agreement.

"Beautifully prepared, Charlotte," added Mary Chesnut, "and I must comment on your dinner service—your china is absolutely beautiful. Where on earth did you find such a lovely pattern?"

Charlotte explained with some pride, "Oh, this was a wedding present from Violet and Brent—as was the crystal."

"Well then, perhaps I should commend them on their choice," smiled Mary, as Brent looked across at Violet and winked.

Violet turned to Mary and said, "I've never forgotten that tea we had with you just before Sherman came in."

"Nor have I, Violet." She paused as a sad look came upon her usually cheerful face. "So much has happened since then, hasn't it, and most of it bad."

Violet's fingers toyed with her napkin as she answered, thoughtfully, "Yes...but bad as things have been, I must say we are better off than immediately after the War. Now if only we could get the Carpetbaggers out of here."

Matt Butler spoke up, "We had our ups and downs during the War and since, but I must say I came out of the War pretty discouraged. I returned as a twenty-nine year old major general, with one leg gone, a wife and three children to support, seventy emancipated slaves to feed and clothe, a debt of fifteen thousand dollars, and a dollar and seventy-five cents in my pocket."

"But you have done very well for us under the circumstances," protested his wife.

"Indeed," agreed Charlotte as she added, "Why don't we take our coffee and after-dinner liqueur in the parlor." She rose and led the others into the large front room, now softly lit with gas lighted tapers. Lorenzo had laid a fire to take the chill off the room, and the darting flames threw out moving shadows across the floor. Hot coffee and warm cream were awaiting in the silver coffee service, along with a crystal decanter of liqueur, on the round table in front of the settee. After all were seated around the fire, Lorenzo served the coffee and liqueur according to choice, then quietly departed to help Mercy and Liza in the kitchen.

"Leland, I'm certainly sorry that Andrew, er, your father, couldn't be here tonight. I had some questions for him," said Matt Butler, sipping his liqueur.

"Yes, he hated to miss this evening with all of you, but there were some urgent matters out at the farm that needed his immediate attention. He did say to give you all his regards and apologies, and that he hoped to see you all soon. He does expect to be back day after tomorrow."

"How is business at the cotton mill?" inquired James Chesnut with interest.

"Doing right well," replied Leland. "They are still adding spindles down there; we've gained some from the reduction of competition from New England."

"The state may prosper again if we can get out from under Carpetbagger-Scalawag-Negro rule," Butler proffered.

"General Butler, I am sorry that you were not presiding over the Senate, as you should have been," said Violet. "I visited there one day and was not sure whether I was at a po' buckras' Holy Roller service or a Negro religious camp meeting or a circus."

Matt Butler rolled a cigarette and lit it, then grinned at Violet. "Well, better luck another time, I hope." He turned toward Brent and asked, "But Brent, how in the world did you manage to get elected? You are certainly a rarity in this legislature."

Brent laughed and replied, "Well, you know the Carpetbaggers and Scalawags are not the only ones who can cultivate the Negro voters."

Violet explained how they had worked with all the Negro voters at Fair Oaks, had taught them to read the name, *Brent Sutler*, and then used them as missionaries on other plantations and farms and in the villages.

"That's exactly what we're going to have to do all over the state," James Chesnut said. "Last year's census showed a population of over 415,000 Negroes to less than 290,000 whites."

"By which census?" Brent asked with a nod and a smirk.

"Last year's Federal census, why?" responded Chesnut.

"Wasn't that the most ridiculous thing you ever heard of?" Brent went on. "The previous General Assembly voted to have a state census, with all the expense that that entailed, in 1869, just a year before the Federal government's much more elaborate census. Everybody knows there is a Federal census every ten years, and there would be one in 1870."

"Why on earth would they do a thing like that?" asked Charlotte with wonder.

Brent gave a short, sarcastic laugh. "To develop some more plums for their followers—it was simply another raid on the treasury."

"It probably will cost them more and more to keep the darkies in line," added General Butler derisively.

"Well, there may be hope—some of the darkies are wising up to how they are being used," said Brent. "You take Daddy Cain, for instance, he knows that the Carpetbaggers and Scalawags are not really their friends and are just using the darkies to fill their own pockets."

"And just what were the major accomplishments of this session of our illustrious legislature?" asked James Chesnut.

"Several million dollars more of debt, mainly," answered Brent. His voice was glum. "But did you hear of the final acts?"

"What were they?"

Lorenzo had returned to refill coffee cups and liqueur glasses. Brent waited until he left the room before replying. "Well, the House of Representatives took a full day's recess for a horse race just a few days before adjournment."

"*What?*" several gasped.

"Yes, well, one of the Negro representatives, a man by the name of W.J. Whipper, was bragging about his new horse, and finally he challenged the Speaker of the House to a match horse race, and Moses accepted, with a bet of a thousand dollars. The whole house then took a recess to go out to the fairgrounds for the race. Well, Moses lost."

"Good!" exclaimed Violet as others nodded their agreement.

Brent held up his hand. "Ah, but wait. Three days later as the last item of business on the day of final adjournment, Whipper offered a motion that a gratuity of one thousand dollars be voted to the Speaker of the House, for the, quote, 'dignity and ability with which he has presided over its deliberations,' unquote. It passed by a big majority, and of course the Senate concurred. So you see, Mr. Moses was reimbursed for the loss of his bet."

"And Whipper made sure he got his money," added Violet.

"So, nobody lost—except the taxpayers," sighed Mary Chesnut.

"That's it," said Brent, nodding his dark head and causing a wave to fall upon his forehead. He ran his fingers through his hair forcing the wave back in place as he went on, disgust showing in his voice, "Another last minute act was to create the Sterling Funded debt. This is supposed to create a new debt of one million, two hundred thousand pounds sterling at six percent, to refund the old debt, but if you ask me, this would just add to it, and there's a lot of opposition."

"I should say there is a lot of opposition," agreed Butler. "There is some talk of organizing a taxpayers' convention to look into these matters."

Violet broke in, "A Charleston newspaper reported that for certain votes in the legislature one man was promised ten thousand dollars, another a thousand dollars, and that some sold their votes for gold watches, and one poor wretch sold out for twenty-one dollars."

Brent nodded again. With a sigh he said, "Every measure had its price. Do you know what the regular legislative costs were for this session? Over eight hundred thousand dollars—ten times what they ought to be. And nobody knows what the total state debt now is—maybe as much as sixteen million."

"All the more reason for a taxpayers' convention," said James Chesnut grimly.

"Are we ever going to get out from under all this?" asked Margaret Butler.

"Not until we get a new government," replied Chesnut.

Mary Chesnut spoke up. "I think the Carpetbag regime is bound to undo itself by its very excesses. Efforts to control a population by excessive repression nearly always fail. Look what Cromwell did to the Irish, but he could not destroy them. And in England, he went too far in trying to perpetuate himself and his son in power, and the result was the restoration of the monarchy. And look how Napoleon tried to repress the Spanish, but his harsh treatment only led them to rise up in revolt. That really was the beginning of his undoing."

"Let's hope you are right, Mary," said Charlotte.

"Now listen you all, our time is bound to come," said James Chesnut with encouragement, "but not until we can elect a governor and a legislature."

Brent turned toward him with interest. "General, do you think there's a chance in next year's election?"

"I doubt it by then," responded Chesnut promptly. "Grant will be running for a second term as president. He hasn't done anything except become the tool of the Radical vindictives in Congress, but he is still popular throughout the North, and he'll carry a lot of the Carpetbaggers with him. We'll probably have a better chance in '76 when they will have to come up with a new presidential candidate."

"Who is that likely to be?" asked Margaret Butler. Do you think it might be General Sherman?"

"Oh, dear God, I hope not!" exclaimed Violet vehemently.

"But what about a candidate for governor here?" asked James Chesnut.

Matt Butler spoke slowly and thoughtfully, "You know, there *is* one man who can reconcile the factions of the state and lead us out of the wilderness."

"Are you speaking of Wade Hampton?" asked Brent.

"Of course," answered Butler. "I began the War as a member of Hampton's Legion and have admired him ever since."

Leland rose to fetch the liqueur decanter to replenish the guest's glasses. He held up the coffee pot in query, but there were no takers, so fascinated were they with the turn of conversation. Leland refilled the liqueur glasses, placed the decanter on the table, and returned to his seat by Charlotte.

Chesnut spoke up again, "But you know that Hampton keeps saying he is not interested in running for office."

"But don't you see, James, that makes him all the more desirable as a candidate," put in Mary Chesnut. "Frankly, I think that maybe in another four years he *can* be persuaded."

Brent rose and crossed to stand by the fireplace, resting his arm on the mantel. "We have got to be thinking in the longer term," he commented reflectively.

"We do, indeed," agreed Chesnut and Butler together.

The conversation moved to lighter topics and after a short while, the guests took their departure. They all had enjoyed the stimulation of intellectual conversation and relaxing with trusted friends.

The next morning, after Leland had left for the mill and Charlotte had gone upstairs to change, Violet and Brent sat at the breakfast table enjoying another cup of coffee and each other's company.

"I think it's time to get our schedules in order, don't you?" asked Brent.

"Yes, we do. Brent, I really must get back to Fair Oaks. You know it's time to get the crops in."

"And I've got to see about moving some goods in and out of the warehouses, and I need to spend some time out inspecting and giving orders for maintenance on the railroad."

Violet paused to take a sip of coffee and then went on, "I think I should go back to Fair Oaks tomorrow, Brent, and stay for about a week to make sure things are going well. If it's all right with Charlotte, I thought maybe we could leave the children here so that they can continue with their schooling—"

"You know we would love to have the children stay here with us." Charlotte had overheard Violet's comment as she had reentered the room. She smiled and sat down at her place, pouring herself another cup of coffee and turning it almost beige with milk. "You know how much we enjoy them. You can leave them here *anytime.*"

Violet grinned her thanks. "I'll leave Evelina here to look after them, but I'll take Hattie home with me. Then I'll be back in a week, and I hope we can stay on—"

"Until at least May, I hope!" interrupted Charlotte, with a light blush on her face.

"Yes, until May."

Back at Fair Oaks, Violet was relieved and pleased to find that Leo had things going well with the animals and in getting ready for planting, and Mammy and Rachel and the house servants had kept everything there in good order. They had all fulfilled their promise to take good care of everything while Brent and Violet and the children were in Columbia, and they all beamed with pride as Violet praised them generously and thanked them for their efforts and hugged them all. They were disappointed not to see the children, but Violet reassured them that they would shortly be out of school and home again.

On her return to Leland and Charlotte's house the following Saturday, Violet was greeted by the children with cries of enthusiasm and excitement. They loved their Aunt Charlotte and Uncle Leland, and of course, their Daddy had been with them, but they were unaccustomed to Violet being away from them, and they had missed her very much. That evening, only Violet could bathe them and put on their nighties, and while Daddy could be there and listen to prayers, only their mother could read the bedtime story.

After Violet and Brent had kissed the children good-night and tiptoed from the room, Brent grabbed Violet and teasingly said, "Well! I guess I know where I stand around here, especially after you've been away! Now I want some attention."

She kissed him soundly, and then laughingly pushed him away, saying, "Oh, you silly goose, you." They went down the steps arm in arm and still laughing.

In the parlor, Leland was engrossed in a newspaper. Brent picked up another and sat down to get caught up on what was going on. Soon he was as engrossed as Leland.

Not wanting to disturb the men, Charlotte called Violet aside. "Violet," she said, "a Mrs. Smith came by yesterday. She and her husband and her sister are renting Mrs. Brevard's house over on Blanding and Bull Streets."

"Yes, I remember the place."

"They came down here from Massachusetts. Her husband came to work for the Freedman's Bureau, and now he is working for the state. Well, Mrs. Smith has two small children. I think she said they are about three and one. She was asking me if I knew any reliable nursemaid or somebody who might stay with the children on Monday afternoon when she and her sister have to do some errands downtown, and maybe all day Tuesday when they expect to be away for the day. I told her that I could not promise anything, but maybe my sister could help out. Do you think we could spare Evelina for those days?"

"Of course we can help a neighbor newcomer out. That will be no problem." replied Violet warmly.

"Oh, good. I'll have Lorenzo take her a note to expect you and Evelina on Monday about one o'clock."

Monday was a fair day of blue skies with only an occasional cloud and a slight breeze. Violet welcomed the chance to walk with Evelina the three blocks over to Mrs. Smith's house.

When Mrs. Smith opened the door, Violet could see that she was ready to go out. Violet introduced herself in a friendly and gracious way, and Mrs. Smith responded in kind and then introduced her sister who had followed her to the door.

"I was so glad when Mrs. Thompson sent over the note that said you might be able to help us out," said Mrs. Smith. She was dressed in a dark dress with high neck and long sleeves. A small white lace collar around her neck and edges of lace at the ends of the sleeves lightened the somber effect of her attire. On her left shoulder she wore a pin of light green and gray stones. Her sister's dress was almost identical except that it's color was gray, and she wore no decorative pin.

Violet smiled cordially and said, "Oh, Mrs. Smith, we're always glad to help a neighbor out." She laid her hand on Evelina's arm and continued, "This is Evelina, and I can guarantee she will give your children the best of care. I have counted on her for the last seven years. And while I don't want to be without her even for a day, if we can be of help to you, then we want to do it."

Evelina gave her gentle, sweet smile and a slight curtsey to Mrs. Smith, then, taking off her coat she started for the three-year-old boy who was sitting on a rocking horse in the parlor.

The women had been staring at Evelina as she removed her coat.

"Oh, no!" gasped Mrs. Smith, standing rigidly.

Evelina stopped and turned to look at her, a puzzled look upon her gentle black face.

Mrs. Smith turned to Violet. "Is *this* who you intended to look after my children?" she asked as a strange look of dismay spread across her face.

"Why, of course...of course. Evelina is exceptionally dependable and responsible and wonderful with children. I don't understand...is there some problem?"

Mrs. Smith stepped back. Raising the back of her hand to her mouth in a gesture of protest, she said in a low but firm voice, "Why, Mrs. Sutler, I can't have a nigger touching my babies—never!"

"*Never*!" echoed her sister.

Violet was taken completely aback. She paused for several moments in a charged silence. Evelina seemed rooted to her spot, shocked at what the woman had just said. At last Violet found her voice and exclaimed heatedly, "Why, Mrs. Smith, I have heard of and seen many examples of Yankee hypocrisy, but this beats them all!"

"Oh, Mrs. Sutler, I meant no harm."

"Of course you meant no harm. You people come down here preaching equality of the races, trying to tell us how to run our affairs, and this is the way you really think!"

Evelina suddenly burst into tears and ran to Violet who grasped her in a tender hug and held her closely. Looking over Evelina's shoulder at Mrs. Smith and her sister, Violet added, "They sometimes say that hypocrisy is ruining the church. Well, with examples like this I can see that hypocrisy is ruining the country. Don't you have any sense for people's feelings? It's clear you have no regard for black people as persons."

"Well, of course, but this is different," said Mrs. Smith lamely.

"Yes, it's different," Violet said bitterly, "only you will never understand it. Why don't you people go on back to Massachusetts and do something about *your* slavery—the children and women in your textile mills?"

She looked at Evelina and said in tender tones, "Come on, Evelina. I apologize for exposing you to such humiliation. Please forgive me. Forgive me. I had no idea those women were like that. Why, there's no one in the world who's better with children than you are." She turned Evelina to the door, and with her arm still around her shoulders, led her down the front stairs. "Oh, those damn, bigoted Yankee women!" muttered Violet angrily.

Evelina looked up at Violet, wiping the tears from her eyes. The wounded look upon her face tore at Violet's heart. She knew the hurt went straight to Evelina's soul.

"Miz Violet..."

"Yes, Evelina?"

"Ah loves you, Miz Violet."

"I love you, too, Evelina."

Charlotte was surprised to see Violet return with Evelina. She was about to say something when Violet shook her head, motioning her not to say anything. Then she sent Evelina up to check on the children. After Evelina was well out of sight and hearing, Violet took Charlotte into the parlor and in a low voice told her about their visit to the Smiths. Charlotte was appalled—furious at how Evelina had been treated and dismayed that it was she who had suggested they might help out.

"Oh, Violet, I'm so sorry. I didn't know. I never dreamed—." Tears welled up in her eyes.

"Of course you didn't, Charlotte, how could you?"

Over the next several weeks the two families settled into a more or less regular routine, going and coming from work, household chores, child care, enjoyable meals, and continuous visiting. On Sundays all of them regularly attended morning worship services at Trinity Episcopal Church. Violet did so as a kind of regularized regimen. She did sense twinges of nostalgia on those occasions—memories of old family participation here, of her wedding, of the people she had known in earlier years, but for her, attending church still was mostly a matter of going through the motions. That was just what one did on Sunday mornings, and it was something of a boost to the morale simply to get dressed up and get out of the house. It would not have taken much to persuade her to skip church on most Sundays. Still she kept on, and somehow she was glad that Brent went along without any protest, and somehow she felt it was important for the children to attend.

During April, Violet devoted herself to house hunting. She checked with real estate brokers, and looked at notices and advertisements. Then one morning she said to Charlotte, "How about taking me for a drive around the city just to explore a little."

"Sure. How about this afternoon?"

As they drove around the city, Violet was impressed at how much it had improved since Brent had shown her and Susan earlier. Many new houses had been built, and old ones renovated, but she saw nothing for sale that caught her eye.

Finally, just as they passed the Columbia Male Academy, driving west on Laurel Street, Violet called out, "Stop! Stop here a minute."

"Why?" asked Charlotte, looking around.

"Look at that place on the corner," said Violet as she pointed in the direction.

Charlotte looked in the direction indicated. She saw only a tumble-down house standing amidst tall grass and weeds, and overgrown with vines. She grimaced and chided, "Oh, sure, that has real possibilities. When do you want to move in?"

"Come on now, I'm serious. Let's have a look." Violet jumped down from the buggy.

Charlotte tied the horse to a hitching post and followed Violet through the broken gate. "Beautiful kitchen," said Charlotte, pointing to a mass of charred ruins. "How about the master bedroom up there? Do you plan to swing a hammock on these vines or something? And I must say, the house does have plenty of fresh air!"

"Oh, you silly gosling," laughed Violet. "Look at the necessary."

Charlotte joined in the laughter. "Oh, yes, delightful, isn't it?"

"No, no, my little sister. The point here is, this is a good lot—double size, across from the grounds of the Academy, catty-cornered across from the Hampton estate, and within four blocks of the Carolina Central Railroad and Brent's warehouses, and you see its total neglect means that it probably could be had at a good price. We would have to clean it out, get all the debris of the old house out, and then build a wholly new house on the site."

"Now *that* is beginning to make good sense," granted Charlotte, "and still it's only six blocks from me. That would be marvelous."

"I can hardly wait to show it to Brent. He'll see the possibilities and advantages," concluded Violet excitedly.

As soon as Brent came in late that afternoon Violet was telling him of her find. "Oh, Brent, I found a lot up at the corner of Laurel and Henderson that I think could be an ideal site for our town house. And Brent, it's only four blocks from the station and your warehouses!"

His dark eyebrows raised in question. "Oh, have you, my Love? What's on it now, and who owns it?"

"Only a bunch of ruins. Looks like it has not been touched since Sherman's fire. It used to be a part of the B.F. Taylor properties, but I don't know who owns it now."

He was immediately interested, as she knew he would be. "Well then, let's have a look at it."

They borrowed Charlotte's horse and buggy and drove up to the site. Brent's imagination matched Violet's in seeing the possibilities.

"I'll inquire tomorrow about the ownership," he promised.

When Brent came in the next afternoon, he greeted Violet with a big kiss and then pulled back to look at her with a broad smile that indicated good news about the lot. "Well, I found that that place had been put up in a sheriff's sale and can be had for payment of back taxes."

"Back taxes? How much? Oh, Brent, can we buy it, can we? Oh, Brent, hurry and tell me, I can't wait any longer."

A look of mock indecision came across his face as he answered off-handedly, "Oh, I don't know. Maybe we should think about it a few weeks, look around for other possibilities–."

"Oh, Brent! I've looked around, and looked and looked, and I tell you, this is *it.*" Worry was beginning to overtake her now.

"Have you considered that there may be a lot of noise from the railroad roundhouse and shops up there, and you didn't mention that it is only two blocks from the lunatic asylum, my dear."

"Oh, Brent, I was so hoping," she said plaintively.

Brent grinned suddenly. His eyes began twinkling. "Well, my dear, weep no more." He pulled something from his inside pocket and tossed a folded document onto the dining table.

"What's that, for heaven's sake?"

"That, my dearest wife, is the deed to the property you have in mind. Knowing you had your heart set on it, I just went ahead and bought it on the spot."

"Oh, Brent, you rascal, you *are* a wonderful husband! Oh, I love you!" She flung her arms around his neck and showered his face with kisses of gratitude.

Over the next several evenings, Violet and Brent—with plenty of free advice from Leland and Charlotte and from Leland's father, worked over drawing up rough plans for the kind of house they wanted. Their final product showed influences of Fair Oaks, the old Storm house in Columbia, the Sutler house in Charleston, and several ideas of their own—and of their friendly advisers.

Brent took the plans to a building contractor recommended by several business acquaintances, and within two weeks work began at clearing the lot and then digging the basement and laying the foundation. By the first of May work began on the house itself with a promise that it should be completed by the end of September.

By this time, too, Charlotte was anticipating the birth of her baby, and Brent was looking forward to the taxpayer's convention.

The convention came first. Brent was one of sixteen state senators among the delegates, representing thirty counties, that assembled on May 9th. It was a distinguished body that included four ex-governors, two ex-lieutenant governors, three ex-United States senators, five former congressmen, an ex-chancellor, an ex-secretary of the Confederate treasury, forty-three ex-members of the state House of Representatives, eleven generals, and five bankers. Governor Robert K. Scott was admitted to the floor to speak, and the Attorney General, D.H. Chamberlain, served as third vice-president.

Violet was impressed when Brent reported on the evening of the opening session who were present. "As you could guess, James Chesnut and Matt Butler were there, and so were John Manning, J.P. Richardson, Johnson Hagood, M.W. Gary, and W.H. Trescott. Chesnut said that it was the most outstanding body he ever had seen assembled in the state other than the secession convention of 1860!"

"Goodness!" Violet reacted. "I'm impressed, but can they do anything?"

"They can make lots of noise. General Butler introduced a resolution for the appointment of a committee to inquire of the Governor about the bonded indebtedness of the state, and to inquire whether state and county offices had unnecessarily expanded since the reorganization of 1868."

"What if they do find excessive debt and so on? What then?"

"Just by exposing fraud and ridiculous expenditures maybe they can begin to make some headway. They are concerned with the horrible condition of the state's finances and the constant spiraling of expenditures and taxes."

"I certainly hope they can do something about that, or all that we make in planting and business will soon be eaten up," commented Violet.

The convention lasted until May 12th. It concluded with an exposition of conditions that were even worse than had been expected.

Charlotte's baby was born on Monday, May 15th. It was a healthy, very vocal little boy whom they formally named Leland Alexander Thompson. He would be called Lee instead of Leland to avoid confusion. Charlotte liked the idea because that was also her mother's maiden name. Everyone was delighted with the new member of the family, and Bonnie Anne and J.J. were fascinated with the idea of a new baby.

Charlotte, young and basically healthy and strong, soon regained her energy and health and was up and about more quickly than many other young women her age. Violet claimed it was the years of hard work on the plantation during and immediately after the War that made Charlotte so strong. Brent insisted she had inherited it from her mother and father.

With Charlotte and little Lee in good health, and with the end of the school term approaching, Violet began to make plans for her family's return to Fair Oaks. She was itching to get back to the plantation.

She visited the Female Academy on the last day of school and was pleased to learn from the first-grade teacher that Bonnie Anne had done well in beginning to learn to read and write and spell, as well as do her numbers. Her reading of the primary texts was clear and even, and she showed that she understood what she had read. Her handwriting was clear and neat.

Two days later Violet went with Little Josh for his last day at the school of music. Ellen Brennan Carter assured Violet that Little Josh had done the best with his voice lessons of any of her pupils. He seemed to have perfect pitch. She further reported that her husband had been amazed at Little Josh's progress on the violin.

As she supervised the packing for their return to Fair Oaks, Violet reflected on the joys and the accomplishments of those few months in Columbia–the visits with Charlotte and her family and friends, being with Charlotte for the birth of little Lee, seeing Brent off to a good start in the state Senate, getting a new house started, and seeing Bonnie Anne and Josh do so well in their schools. Now she was anxious to get back to Fair Oaks. All those other things could enrich her life and enrich her soul, but it was at Fair Oaks that her heart and roots lay. It was where all things came together. She could scarcely wait to get home.

Chapter 44

A Close Call

1871

Little Josh came away from the music school filled with enthusiasm for all that he had learned. Now he was talking about melody and harmony and rhythm. Every new instrument that he had encountered had held a special fascination for him. He wanted to learn them all. He had learned what the brass and the woodwind and the percussion instruments would do, but most of all he had excelled at playing the violin and the piano and in singing. No one had to prompt him to practice; his motivation and love affair with music were sufficient.

Before leaving Columbia he approached Violet with a request for additional instruments for his *Little Brown Jugs* band. He seldom asked for anything, and Violet was so favorably disposed toward him that she would have granted any feasible request, but music was something she was especially anxious to encourage—no use making all that effort for music school if it was not going to be followed up. She believed that a talent such as Josh had should be nourished and supported. Violet agreed to take Little Josh to some musical instrument stores, but she also wanted Brent along for his sense of quality and eye for a good bargain. At first Little Josh wanted everything he saw, but only a few cautionary words from Violet brought him to reasonable limits. Mainly he wanted a cornet, a clarinet, and one of the new-type snare drums.

"Are you sure you have somebody to play all these?" asked Violet.

"Yas, Miz Violet, ah know Matthew kin larn the clarinet fast. Ah teach him good. An' Edward already be a good drummer. Ah ain't sure 'bout de cornet, buh we jes' hafta haf dat, eben if ah hafta play it mahsef."

While Violet and Little Josh were talking, Brent strolled around the store and found to his liking a new type of three-piston cornet from Germany, a modern clarinet from England, and a new type of thin snare drum, with wire brushes as well as drumsticks, from France. Quietly he was able to make a good deal for each of them. Then he guided Violet and Little Josh in the direction of the instruments he had chosen, and then, with a little nudge pointed Josh in the right directions until he himself leaped toward each one in turn with a muffled shout, "Oh yas, dis one!"

As soon as they arrived back at Fair Oaks and Little Josh had cleared with Violet his schedule of chores, he ran down to the workers' village to see Reverend Jackson to tell him what he had been doing in Columbia, and to gather the members of his *Little Brown Jugs* band and tell them about the new instruments. The next day Reverend Jackson came up to the house. He and Josh asked to see Violet in the office.

"Miz Violet," said Little Josh with excitement, "Reverend Jackson know uh boy who already know how ta play de cornet!"

"Yassum, Miz Violet," smiled Jackson, "dere be uh boy stayin' wif de Ellisons in Stateburg; he play de cornet whenebber he kin borrow one. He got no parents, an' ah think it be all righ' iffen he come ta work at Fair Oaks iffen ya kin use him."

"An' he kin play cornet wif de *Little Brown Jugs,*" added Little Josh.

"How old is he?" asked Violet.

"Ah don' righ'ly know, 'bout thirteen, ah guess," answered Jackson, scratching his head in thought.

Violet smiled at the two—the boy and the man, both caught in the web of anticipation and enthusiasm and their love of music. "Well, we do need some younger workers, and it would be good to have someone play the cornet, wouldn't it? Of course he can come to work and live here, if the Ellisons don't mind. Reverend Jackson, you see if you can arrange it. Find the boy a bed in the barracks and have him report to Leo for assignment to his duties—probably with the animals around the barns."

"Oh, thank ya, Miz Violet, thank ya!" beamed Little Josh. "Kin ah go wif Reverend Jackson and tek de spring wagon ta git him an' ta tek de horns an' drums down ta de church, please ma'am?"

"All right, go ahead, Little Josh."

Later that afternoon Violet was distracted from her books in the office by a distant sound of a horn. Going outside for a look, she saw Reverend Jackson and Little Josh driving up the lane in the spring wagon, with a boy sitting in the back blowing loud notes on the cornet—mostly just blasts of unrelated notes.

Pausing near the house, Little Josh shouted, "Dis be Thomas, Miz Violet!"

Violet waved and called, "Hello, Thomas, and welcome to Fair Oaks!"

As the wagon turned into the barnyard and went toward the creek, the sounds of the horn became more melodic and less harsh, and finally recognizable tunes were drifting across the fields.

One afternoon Violet, returning from a lone visit of inspection and drawn by the sounds of music coming from the church/school building, stopped to listen. She slipped in unobtrusively and gave her full attention to the boys. She was amazed by what she was hearing. The *Little Brown Jugs* were in full rehearsal. They were playing old, familiar tunes, but in a completely different, distinctive way—characterized by strong syncopation in the melody while maintaining the regular beat in the accompaniment. Then they began experimenting—each of the major instruments would take turns in improvisation while the others followed. Then they tried harmonizing two and even three separate melodies and came out with perfect counterpoint. When they took a break, Violet broke into a loud solo of applause.

Little Josh came running back to Violet. "Ya like, Miz Violet? Ya like?"

"Oh, Little Josh, indeed I do! Your music is wonderful! Keep practicing and keep experimenting to see what you can do."

Little Josh's whole face crinkled with a happy smile at what his beloved Miz Violet said about his band. Then he said, "Miz Violet, ya see how good Sanders be wif de violin an' wif de saw, an' see how quick Matthew larn de clarinet, an' still got his water bott'ls, an' don' ya think Edward be wonderful wif de new snare drum? An' Hank, he give up de cowbell an' de elderberry whist'l so he kin be specialty on de jug, an' Robin, he still play de washboard an' de spoons an' de gourds, an' Thomas, ya hear how good he play de cornet?"

Violet smiled as she said, "And don't forget yourself, Josh. You are doing very well with your violin and banjo." Then she looked at the whole group and told them that they were all making wonderful music, and that she was very proud of their hard work and their improvement. This brought beams of satisfaction to all their faces. White teeth showed in the youthful dark faces as the boys grinned at her compliments. They were all anxious to return to their instruments and show more, and Violet was willing to hear more—for another half hour.

One afternoon in mid-June, after a two-and-half day siege of unusually heavy rains, Violet had the children out on the lawn to get re-acquainted with the sunshine. Suddenly Little Josh came walking up, grinning, and with his hands behind his back. He said to Violet, "Ah haf a presen' for J.J."

"Why, Little Josh, how nice of you. What is it?"

"Hit's uh surprise, Miz Violet."

"Well, for goodness sakes, go ahead and give it to him."

By now little J.J. had run up with outstretched hands. "Oh, Little Josh, what do you have for me?"

"A sailboat, J.J."

"Oh, Josh, yes! Thank you, thank you, Little Josh."

"Jarvis whittl'd it for you. See it has a sail, like your father's ship ah was on, an' ya see it has a string on it so's you kin let it sail out an' pull it back in."

"Oh, goody, can we go down to the pond and sail it, Mama?"

"*May* we," corrected Violet.

"May we, Mama, please, please?"

"If Little Josh goes with you and you do not stray away from him."

"Oh, I won't, I won't, I promise. Let's go, Little Josh!" And the two boys took off in a trot.

"Take Dan with you!" called Violet, though the dog already was on the way to follow the boys across the meadow to the pond. She always felt more comfortable when the dog was with the children.

After several turns at sailing the boat and at skipping flat stones across the surface of the pond, J.J. sat down to rest for a while. Presently Reverend Jackson came along and called Josh aside. This gave J.J. a chance to do a little exploring on his own. His mother still treated him like a baby, he thought, but he knew he was big enough to do things by himself.

Picking up his boat, he walked over to the creek, now nearly out of its banks after the heavy rains and flowing with a fast, swirling current. This offered a more attractive and adventuresome situation for sailing. He ran down past the mills where he could be out of sight.

Kneeling at the bank, J.J. set his boat on the rapidly moving waters of the creek. Immediately the strong current swept the little boat out of his hands before he could find the end of the string. Without a thought, J.J. reached to get the boat, but in doing so he lost his balance and fell into the creek. The rapidly moving current began pushing him down the creek. He tried to stand but could not keep his footing. The swift waters seemed to suck him down to the bottom while at the same time, tossing him about. He flung his arms about and managed to get his head above the water. He began kicking his feet and moving his arms as his Daddy had taught him to do when learning to swim. He began screaming with fright, and old Dan raced up and down the bank in a continuous fit of nervous barking.

This brought Little Josh running with the speed of a frightened deer. Sensing almost instantly what had happened, Little Josh ran along the creek bank until he spotted J.J. who was now whirling over and over as he was being swept downstream. Josh ran until he could get well ahead of the hapless young boy, and then jumped straight into the water. He was surprised at the strength of the current, but he was able to make midstream in time to catch J.J. Then he did not try to buck the current but let it carry them until they reached a slight curve. There he was able to make it to the bank with J.J. The latter came out coughing and spitting up water, and crying with terror. Little Josh put his arms around him and comforted him with soothing words and soft strokes to his head. Soon little J.J. stopped crying, took a deep breath, and suddenly cried, "My boat! My boat! Oh, Little Josh, where is my new boat?" Then he began to cry again at the thought of having lost his new toy.

Little Josh went back for a quick look and shortly found the boat hung up on some tree roots close to the bank where he could retrieve it. He brought it back and handed it to J.J., saying tenderly, "Heah de boat, li'l J.J. Hit ain't lost. De sail need fixin', but ah do dat fo' ya later."

Violet was beside herself when J.J. told her what had happened. She wanted to spank J.J. for being so careless, so curious, not minding her order to stay with Josh, and she wanted to thrash Little Josh for taking his eyes off of J.J., but she was so relieved to have J.J. back safely, and so grateful to Little Josh for having rescued him, that she simply hugged them both and took them in the house for a change of clothing and a cup of hot chocolate in the kitchen dining room.

After quietly reviewing their adventures and listening to some light reprimands from Violet, J.J. suddenly asked, "Mommy, where do niggers come from?"

"J.J., we don't call them `niggers', Violet said with a frown.

"Why not?" J.J. asked. "Isn't that what they are? That's what some people in Columbia call the darkies. I heard them talking one day when you took me shopping with you.."

"Now listen to me, J.J. We don't call them niggers because they think we mean something bad, that we are insulting them when we call them that, and it hurts their feelings."

"Whatcha mean, Miz Violet?" Little Josh spoke up. "Ah hear nigguhs call other nigguhs `nigguh' all de time. Hit don't bother meh none."

Violet explained, "Yes, Little Josh, that's true, but they understand that they don't mean anything nasty when they say that."

"But Mommy, I don't mean anything nasty or bad when I call them that either," protested J.J. "You know I love Little Josh and Mammy and Evelina and Jarvis and everybody else." Little Josh's face broke into a wide, happy grin.

Violet looked at her young son and smiled gently. "I know you do, J.J., and they know it, too, but while Little Josh and Mammy and Evelina and Jarvis and Leo and Rachel know you well enough to know you don't mean that as an insult, some of the others may not. So probably it's best not to use that word at all.

Looking at Little Josh with a grin, J.J. asked, "Then what are we supposed to call them?"

"Well, they belong to the Negro race, so some call them Negroes; others call them colored people because of their dark skin. Some prefer to be called African-Americans, and I guess they don't mind being called darkies."

Little Josh broke into a wide smile showing his sparkling white teeth. "Miz Violet, ah don' care whut you call meh; ah know you mean it kindly." Violet put her arm across his shoulders and gave him a big hug. She bent down to kiss him upon his cheek.

J.J. persisted, "But where did niggers, I mean Negroes, people like Josh and Mammy and Evelina, come from, Mommy?

Violet explained, "Their ancestors came mostly from Africa. That's a big continent across the ocean, on the other side of the world. That's why we may call them African-Americans. You see, our ancestors came mostly from another continent called Europe."

J.J. was quiet a moment, thinking about what his mother had said, then he had another question for her. "What are slaves?"

"We no longer have slaves, but in this country many of the Negroes used to be slaves and that meant that they were obliged to stay and work for their masters. Now workers are paid, and they may leave anytime they want."

"Were all Negroes slaves then?"

"No, slaves were mostly in the South, but before the War Between the States, there were many Negroes who were not—I think my father said at least 100,000, and that's a goodly number. They were called freedmen. Some had regular jobs; some owned farms; and some even had plantations and owned slaves themselves—like the Ellisons in Stateburg. You know them, J.J."

"Ah know them, too," broke in Little Josh. "Dey nice peop'l. Dat whar Thomas come from ta play de cornet in de band."

"Mommy, you said workers may leave anytime now." He turned to Little Josh, his love in his eyes. "Little, Josh, you won't ever leave me, will you?"

"Li'l J.J., ah ain't nebbuh gwine leave ya, boy. Ah ain't nebbuh leave ya, no' Miz Violet, no' Massuh Brent, nawbudy, ya heah?" Then he asked Violet, "Is hit all righ' iffen ah go meet wif my band now, Miz Violet?"

After Little Josh had gone, J.J. turned to his mother and said, "Mommy, Little Josh was very brave to jump in the creek after me; I was scared that water was going to carry me away from everybody." His sweet little face became solemn at the remembrance of the raging current.

"Yes, Little Josh was certainly brave, and he's a very good boy. And he loves you very much, J.J. He risked his own life to save yours, I know."

Again J.J. was quiet for a few minutes, thinking. Then he asked, "Mommy, when is Little Josh's birthday? Can we have a surprise birthday party for him?"

"*May* we have a surprise birthday party—" corrected Violet patiently.

"Oh, Mommy, *may* we have a surprise birthday party for Josh? Oh, that would be such fun, please, please, Mommy?"

Violet looked into the beseeching blue eyes of her little son, and her heart melted. "Well, I'm not sure. Let me think. You see, J.J., he came here all alone, without any mommy or daddy, so we don't know when his birthday is—"

"Well then, why don't we just make up one for him?"

Violet laughed and ran her fingers through J.J.'s thick wavy hair, so like his father's, then she gave him a hug. "Why not? Sure we can. Here's what we will do. Next month after the first crops are in we'll have a birthday party for him right here in the house."

J.J. clapped his hands in delight. "Oh, goody, and we'll invite Bonnie Anne and Evelina—"

"Yes, and everyone else in the house with whom he works—"

"And don't forget Daddy!"

"Of course, Daddy, and we'll invite Reverend Jackson and Mrs. Jackson and Leo and Rachel and all the *Little Brown Jugs*."

"And can we—*may* we—have lots and lots of ice cream and cake?"

"We'll have ice cream if there's any ice left next month, but we'll see. Anyway, we'll have a great big birthday cake."

"And will it say *Happy Birthday, Little Josh* on it?"

"Of course."

J.J. was beside himself, dancing around in his excitement. "Oh, goody, oh, goody. Mommy, can I—*may* I—go tell him all about it?"

Oh, no, J.J., if it's going to be a surprise birthday party, then we can't tell him yet. We have to keep it a secret until then."

"I can keep a secret, Mommy. I want to surprise Little Josh." J.J. clapped his hand over his mouth.

Violet giggled at the sight of him holding his mouth closed. "Yes, J.J., we'll keep it a secret. Don't tell anyone yet, except maybe Daddy. And now—it's about time for you to eat supper.

Chapter 45

The Last Concert

1871

The next weeks dragged for J.J., and he thought each day that the surprise birthday party must be in just another day or two, but the weeks raced by for Violet. After the wheat and oats and the first cutting of hay were in, she turned to related business matters. One thing she decided to do was to change banks in Sumter.

A new bank—a branch of the Citizens' Savings Bank—had just opened in Sumter. Violet was sure that Major John William Dargan, the man in charge of the new bank, was more reliable—politically as well as financially—than Clifford Montgomery now was. With Brent's concurrence, she decided to transfer funds to the new bank in mid-July.

Meanwhile, Josh's *Little Brown Jugs* were continuing to gain in popularity. Every week or two they had an invitation to play for some family or church picnic, for a dance sponsored by some social organization, or for some special event such as a horse race or a tournament. Reverend Jackson acted as their manager and booking agent—always acting with the approval of Violet—and he usually drove the box wagon to carry the boys and their instruments to the sites of their performances. The boys had determined Violet would be their banker, in charge of the accumulating funds they were earning. They gave Reverend Jackson ten percent of their earnings which he used to purchase this or that for the church-school, and to help those who came to him in need.

Now in July, an invitation came for the *Little Brown Jugs* to give a concert in the park at Sumter on Saturday the 22nd. Violet decided that this would be a good time to go into Sumter to see about her banking business and to do some shopping for a number of household and personal needs. In addition, she and Brent, with the children, had decided that Sunday would be a good day to have Josh's surprise birthday party, and she wanted to buy some gifts and favors and decorating ribbons. This would also give her a chance to go to the concert. Brent had not wanted to miss the concert, but business had called him to Columbia for two days; however, he assured Violet and the children he would be home on the evening train Saturday. Not for anything would he miss Josh's party.

She asked Josh to go with her in the spring wagon while Reverend Jackson and his wife, Esther, drove the other boys and the instruments in the box wagon. Josh then could help with tending the wagon and with loading purchases into the wagon. She planned to buy the birthday things when Josh was tending the wagon and purchases.

Saturday was a hot day, but not unusually hot for South Carolina in July. Big, white, cumulus clouds floated across the sun from time to time, and a fresh breeze would keep the temperature in a bearable range. Violet left fairly early that morning with Josh. This enabled her to finish at the banks and to do most of her buying before noon. The concert was scheduled for two o'clock.

Arriving at the park about twelve-thirty, Violet tied the horse and got some lunch in plenty of time for Josh to join his band at the bandstand by one-thirty. A large crowd had gathered before the playing started. The band opened with *Little Brown Jug*, Josh's *Daytime Moon*, and *Aura Lee* in traditional style.

Josh stepped up with his banjo and announced that he was going to sing a special song, a tune that a little black boy, "younger than me," made up before the big War, and his master had written down the music and made up the words. Then he added, "I dedicate dis song ta meh music teachuh in Columbia who ebbubudy call de `Carolina Mocking Bird."

Strumming his banjo while all the others joined in accompaniment, Josh sang, starting with the chorus:

Lissen ta de mockin' bird,
Lissen ta de mockin' bird,
De mockin' bird is singin'
o'er her grave;
Lissen ta de mockin' bird,
Lissen ta de mockin' bird,
Still singin' where de
weepin' willows wave.

And then he sang a verse:

Ah! well ah yet remember,
Remember, remember,
Ah! well ah yet remember,
When we gathered in de
cott'n side by side
'Twas in de mild September,
September, September,
'Twas in de mild September,
An' de mockin' bird
be singing far an' wide.

And then he repeated the chorus.

Thunderous applause responded to this. Then the group repeated all those pieces in their new syncopated rhythm and improvisation. This brought howls of approval from the audience—whites, blacks, rich, poor—and additional streams of people came from all directions to keep swelling the size of the crowd.

Enthusiastic applause encouraged the players to new heights. Soon they began experimenting with sounds that they had not even rehearsed.

Oh, Susanna!, *Camptown Races*, and *Swanee River* treated in this manner brought the audience into full action—clapping of hands, some on the down beat, some on the weak beat, in time with the syncopation, then marching around and improvised dancing to the rhythm of the band. A specialty number brought out even greater acclaim—it was a playing of *Dixie,* and then repeating it with a harmonic blending of *Battle Hymn of the Republic* in counterpoint, and finally making a triple counterpoint with the additional blending of *Yankee Doodle.*

With his singing, Josh could bring tears to the audience's eyes or laughter to their lips. His greatest reward was in the obvious enjoyment of the listeners.

Each boy had a chance to exhibit his special talents in some kind of solo segment—mainly the violins, the cornet, the clarinet, and the banjo, but also the snare drum, the jugs, the washboard, the spoons, and all the rest. Each new number seemed to surpass its predecessor.

When the band closed its program, after an hour of the most intense performance, the audience would not allow it. They demanded another half hour of the same. When it finally did end, the members of the audience suddenly returned to their normal state, and felt a fatigue almost as great as that of the boys—none of whom showed any sign of weariness as long as they played or afterward while the enthusiastic comments of the people continued about them. The boys were still exhilarated above their weariness when they finally returned to their wagon.

Violet sensed all this, and she felt an uplift of spirit and a certain pride in what she had seen, and the talent that she had nurtured. After the concert she returned to her horse and wagon to wait for Little Josh.

The wait was longer than she had expected. After a half hour her patience had grown thin. When Little Josh finally appeared, looking a little sheepish, her first words were, "Little Josh, where in the world have you been?"

"Oh, Miz Violet, ah sorry."

"You know better than that, you know you were supposed to help me with some more shopping. I declare, this isn't like you at all."

"Ah sorry, Miz Violet, buh w'en de concert ended an' all de people come around, ah forgit, an' ah run back an'—"

"But Josh, you should not forget when you have work to do."

"No, Ma'am, ah jes' run back wif de boys and ah git on de wagon wif Reverend Jackson, and then ah 'member—"

But Violet was not listening. "Come on, Little Josh, we have a lot to do, and we must hurry to finish our shopping and get back home."

Violet turned to look at Little Josh who now sat quietly on the seat beside her. The face which had been so happy and enthusiastic on the bandstand now appeared sad and forlorn. She wanted to bite her tongue for what she had been saying. She realized that she had thrown cold water on the afterglow of what she knew was an outstanding performance.

She patted Little Josh on the knee and said, "Josh, it was a wonderful concert, and I am so proud of you and the other boys. I didn't mean to fuss at you; it's just that I still have so much to do this afternoon."

But the damage had been done, and the last thing she wanted to do was to discourage such talent as Josh had. And usually he was such a good boy. *Well,* she thought, *we'll make it up to him tomorrow with his surprise birthday party.*

Violet drove up South Main Street as far as Caldwell, and there stopped to buy some household supplies. She tied the horse to a hitching post and had Josh go in to help carry things out and put them in the wagon. When she came out she saw a crowd of people milling about, nearly a block away at the crossing of Main and Liberty Streets. Without even thinking, she started walking in the direction of the crowd, more as a matter of curiosity than anything else. Josh jumped off the wagon where he had placed some parcels and walked along beside her.

As she came closer she could see that there was pushing and shoving going on. Then she could hear shouts of insults and epithets. The crowd seemed to be hostile factions, mostly of po' buckras and Negroes.

Someone shouted, "The soldiers are acomin'!"

Looking up the street Violet could see a platoon of soldiers of the Yankee garrison, running from the direction of the Court House at double time, with rifles held high. A hundred yards from the crowd the soldiers stopped. A lieutenant shouted something to the crowd, and then something to his men. They aimed their rifles in the general direction of the crowd.

People screamed and tried to run away. They opened a direct path between the soldiers and where Violet was standing. Suddenly Josh, who had lagged behind looking around, ran up to Violet and threw his arms around her neck as if to protect her. She almost fell as she heard the crack of rifle fire. She felt Josh's arms loosen from around her neck. By reflex she threw her arms around Josh and felt his body go limp. They sank to the road together, she on her knees, he on his back. Gently she laid him on the sidewalk, her scarf under his head. Blood was flowing from the area of his heart.

"My God, he's been shot! A doctor! Someone get a doctor! Quickly!" she shouted to the people who gathered around. She stared down at the passive face. Briefly Josh opened his eyes and gave a feeble smile. Then he closed his eyes again. A tremor went through his body, and he was still.

"Josh, Josh," Violet called softly, but there was no response. Then in a louder, agonized voice she called, "Josh! Josh! Hang on. The doctor is coming.!" *Dear God this must be a nightmare. This can't be happening, it just can't be!* she cried inside to herself.

Still on her knees leaning over him, she stared at his face, searching for a ray of hope where there was none. She kept repeating, "Hang on, Josh, hang on, you're going to be all right. Do you hear me, Josh?"

But there was no answer, no movement of any kind, no sign that he heard her pleading.

A doctor arrived within a few minutes "I'm Doctor Hartley," he said. "May I help? He knelt down by Little Josh and examined him quickly, only to confirm the worst of Violet's fears.

She shook her head and held up her arms in supplication. "Get him to a hospital!"

But the doctor only shook his head. "It's no use, Mrs. Sutler," he said gently. "What do you want to do with him?"

Violet was dazed with shock and emotion. She felt as though she were standing outside herself and watching the scene from afar. Finally she managed to say, in a voice that did not seem her own, "I'll take him home, out to Fair Oaks, of course."

"Do you have a way?" he asked. "If not, I'll see what I can do."

"My wagon is down the street." She pointed down the street.

The doctor leaned down, took her arm, and lifted her to her feet. He turned to one of the bystanders. "Here, Bob, take Mrs. Sutler's arm and walk with her to wherever her wagon is, and then bring it here." He turned to Violet and said, "We'll be waiting for you here to put Josh in the wagon."

When Violet and the man called Bob returned with the wagon, the doctor and several men and women were waiting to help her. They had already wrapped Josh in a blanket that one of the women had fetched from somewhere. The men then gently lifted Josh to the bed of the spring wagon.

"Do you want anyone to ride back with you, Mrs. Sutler?" inquired the doctor kindly.

She shook her head, and still in a daze, was helped up to the seat. She took the reins that one of the men handed her and she urged the horse up the street, now almost deserted.

She was out of Sumter before the tears started streaming down her cheeks. All kinds of regrets and "what-ifs" competed for attention in her stunned and confused mind. Gone was a chance to reassure him after her sharp words that now she regretted with all her heart. Gone was the chance for his surprise birthday party that she and J.J. and the others had been looking forward to with such excitement. Gone was all that rich talent that offered so much enjoyment and inspiration. Most of all, gone was his ambition to make something of himself—to be a master musician, to be an outstanding leader of his people, to do so much for all people. Gone, gone, gone was the young boy whom she had taken in and come to love so much. Each thought of what now could never be brought new streams of tears. Each thought of regret at not being able to do for him all the things she wanted to do brought new waves of remorse.

She knew she had to pull herself together. She dreaded having to tell the children and the house servants, and Reverend Jackson, whom she would ask to take care of the arrangements, the *Little Brown Jugs,* and Leo and the others. She knew she had to help them through their own shock and sorrow. Everyone on the plantation would have off the day of the funeral. Thank heaven Brent was returning on the train this evening. She would be waiting for him when he got off. He would be heartbroken, but he would be ready to comfort everyone. But he, himself, would need comforting, too. He loved Josh as much as she did and was just as proud of Josh's accomplishments. But then, she didn't know anyone who didn't love Josh and was proud of him.

Old Dan came running to meet the wagon, and ran beside it barking a welcome to Violet. When Violet pulled up to the back door of the house, Mammy was there beaming with anticipation and pride. With a wide grin she said, "Miz Violet, we bin awaitin' fo' ya. We gotcha fav'rite supper ready. De Rev'rend Jackson say dat Li'l Josh an' de *Little Brown Jugs* haf uh wonderful concert taday!"

Violet climbed down from the wagon and held out her arms to Mammy, saying in a still, small voice, "Oh, Mammy!"

Years of experience with her "baby" told her something had happened. She crossed over quickly to Violet who put her arms around Mammy and laid her head on her shoulder. Mammy felt a chill run down her back. "What is it? What is it, mah honey chile?"

"Oh, Mammy, it's Josh, it's Little Josh."

Mammy's heart grew cold. "Whut 'bout Li'l Josh?" she asked with dread in her voice.

"Mammy, he's dead, hit by a bullet when the Yankee soldiers fired into the crowd. Come, here he is." Violet took Mammy around to the back of the wagon and pointed to the blanket in which Josh was covered.

"Oh, Lawdy, oh, Lawdy, how kin dat be? Li'l Josh, daid!" She buried her face in her apron, sobbing from deep sorrow. Then she lifted her head, fire shooting from her eyes, "Whar dem Yankee sojuhs, Miz Violet? Ah go kill dem mahsef! Dey got no righ' ta kill Li'l Josh! He a good boy, always good."

"Yes, Josh was always a good little boy, always ready to help others. Mammy, there's no way of telling which soldier fired the shot. There was a group of soldiers." She took a deep sigh, patted Mammy comfortingly on her shoulder, and went on, "Mammy, you and I have got to be strong for the others. What's happened is a terrible, terrible thing—an unjust thing, but it's done, and we can't change what has happened. Mammy, I'm going to take Josh's body on down to Reverend Jackson and ask him to make funeral arrangements. We'll bury Josh up in the back cemetery by your sister, Aunt Sheba." She paused a moment, and then asked, "Where are the children, Mammy?"

"Dey still nappin', Miz Violet, buh hit's mos' time fo' dem ta git up." She used her apron to wipe the streaming tears from her cheeks.

"Then I should go in right away and tell the others what happened. I'll tell the children later, or maybe Brent and I together will tell them this evening. Mammy, get everyone into the kitchen as quickly as you can. Use the bell pulls. Let's don't wake the children."

All were soon assembled, wondering what was going on. A look at Violet's and Mammy's solemn, sorrowful faces confirmed their worst fears that something dreadful had happened. Violet, keeping her emotions in check, quickly told them the circumstances of Little Josh's death. Moans of heartache rose from Hattie and Evelina and Aunt Beulah and the other women, while Jarvis and Aaron and Uncle Job stood silently, clenching and unclenching their hands, their faces like petrified wood. Violet impressed upon everyone the importance of acting as normally as possible around the children, and that they would be told later, after she had taken Josh's body over to Reverend Jackson's and probably after Master Brent was home.

She left the others comforting one another, and went out to the wagon. *I don't know if I have the strength to get through all this, to go through yet another funeral—and Little Josh's! He's never even had a chance to grow up, to become an adult.* But she knew she would; she had no other choice. She got back up on the spring wagon and drove slowly down to the workers' village. At the church/school building she stopped to see if she could find Reverend Jackson.

Before she could get down he was out to greet her and give her a hand down. He was smiling and laughing as he said, "Warn't dat uh wonerful concert, Miz Violet? Dint de boys do well! Ah hope Li'l Josh not be too late fo' ya. He wuz so excited an' he done forgit he come wif us an' wuz 'sposed ta hep ya." He looked over at he wagon and asked, "Whar be Li'l Josh? Ya leave him up at de big house?"

Violet took a deep breath. "No, I didn't, and yes, Reverend Jackson, it was a wonderful, wonderful concert, but for Josh it was the last concert."

Reverend Jackson looked puzzled. "Whutcha mean, Miz Violet, dat be de last concert? Josh got lotta concerts ahead uf him."

Violet shook her head, cleared her throat, took another deep breath, and said gently in an attempt to cushion the shock, "No, Reverend Jackson, that was Josh's last concert. He'll never play again. There was a shooting in town. Some of the Yankees soldiers fired into the crowd in an effort to disperse it. Little Josh jumped in front of me to protect me, and instead he was hit—killed by a bullet from one of the guns. Josh is dead, Reverend Jackson." Her voice broke at the end, and tears began sliding down her face.

"Daid? Li'l Josh daid?" Jackson repeated in disbelief, yet as he looked on Violet's stricken face he knew that what she had told him was true.

"Yes, Reverend Jackson, he's dead. He died saving my life. The Yankee soldiers were shooting into the crowd, and Little Josh jumped in front of me, only to get shot himself."

"Oh, Miz Violet, Ah be so sorry. Po' li'l Josh. He be so brave." A look of total loss and helplessness crossed Jackson's face. It was with great effort that he regained his composure, and he continued, a deep sadness in his voice, "Miz, Violet, whut ya want meh ta do?"

"I hope you will arrange to have the services for Little Josh here at the church/school. Afterward we will have the burial in the cemetery where Aunt Sheba and some of the others are buried."

"Yassum, w'en ya like de service?"

"I think Monday, yes, Monday at eleven o'clock. Do you think that will be all right?"

"Oh, yassum, dat be all righ'. Ah tek keer of ebbertin' fo' ya. Buh, Miz Violet, whar be he be now?"

"I have Josh here in the wagon, wrapped in a blanket. Will you get someone to take him into your church and lay him on a cot for tonight? Then have some of the women sit with him tonight. I'll come down at midnight to take my turn."

"Yassum, we mek hit nice fo' him an' ligh' candles fo' him. Ah git Esther ta arrange fo' women ta tek turns ta sit wif him. Do Leo an' Rachel know? Whut 'bou de coffin?"

"Thank you, Elijah. I'll ask Carter and Jonah to make a nice coffin for him and to bring it down tomorrow, and I'll bring some clothes for him...I'm going over to tell Leo and Rachel after I leave you."

"Doncha worry none, Miz Violet. Esther an' meh, we all tek care uf Li'l Josh. Now ah git some men ta hep carry Josh inta de church. Jes' wait uh minute. Hit don't tek long."

"Thank you, Elijah."

She waited only a few minutes until Jackson returned with some helpers, and they gently took Josh from the wagon and carried him into the little church, their faces set in stone by grief. Then Violet rode over to Leo and Rachel's to tell them what had happened to Josh and that the funeral service would be on Monday at eleven o'clock. She asked Leo to notify all workers of the time of the funeral and that there would be no work on that day, other than looking after the animals. Both Leo and Rachel, deeply saddened by the news, promised to help in every way that they could.

On the way back to the house Violet stopped by Carter's woodworking shop and, after telling him what had happened, she asked him to make a nice coffin. He promised that he and Jonah would work all night if necessary to make Josh's coffin.

At the house, Violet sent a telegraph message to Charlotte and Leland, and one to Susan and Gilbert, though she knew the latter two would not be able to get to the funeral service. Then she sought out Hattie and asked her to make a silk lining and coverlet for the coffin, and she promised that she, too, would work all night if necessary to do it. Violet said that she could sew while she took her turn sitting with Little Josh in the night, but Evelina and Aunt Beulah insisted that they be allowed to help Hattie with this task, and said that Violet had enough things to do without taking that on, too.

Mammy and Ellie had prepared a light tasty supper that hardly anyone ate, other than the children. Violet's stomach felt in knots, and it was all she could do to sip a little tea. Everyone moved about quietly, seldom talking, so afraid that he or she might break into tears. Violet realized that the children would be in bed by the time Brent's train arrived at nine o'clock, so after supper she took the children upstairs to tell them about Little Josh. She knew that at their young ages the facts should be kept short and simple.

When she told them, Bonnie Anne was downcast, but said little. J.J. at first could not understand.

"You mean Little Josh is dead and is never coming back?" he asked and then went on to add, "But he said he would never leave me...not you...not any of us!"

"J.J., he's dead. We won't be seeing him again. He's gone."

It took a few moments for this to sink in. Then he began crying and protesting loudly. Violet let him have his cry, and then when he had stopped she told them that they must be brave. Everyone needed to be brave at times like this.

J.J. suddenly remembered something. "But Mommy, he has to be here tomorrow. 'Member? Tomorrow's when we're going to have his surprise birthday party. He has to be here for that."

Violet realized that J.J. did not really understand the situation, so she tried again, "He's already gone, J.J., so he can't be here tomorrow—"

"But where did he go? Where is he right now?"

Violet sighed. "He's in heaven with God now."

"Oh." J.J. had to think about that a while.

"Mommy, do you mean he is with the angels now?" asked Bonnie Anne who had been listening intently.

"Well, yes, he is."

Now J.J. was excited. "Mommy, is Josh an angel now, a real angel, and can he fly around like angels do?"

"Well, I guess so, J.J." Violet didn't know what else to say.

"Mommy, I bet it's a lot of fun to be an angel. I bet Josh is happy doing all that. He wouldn't be scared. He was always helping me, remember? He even jumped in the creek to pull me out."

"Yes, Little Josh was a very good boy and a very brave boy. He probably saved your life, J.J., and you know something? He probably saved my life today. If he hadn't jumped in front of me, the bullet likely would have hit me."

"Oh, no, Mommy!" Both children cried out at once, horrified at the thought their mother might have been killed.

"Little Josh was always helping somebody," put in Bonnie Anne, thoughtfully.

"Yes he was—always ready to give a hand. But we can help like Little Josh. Any time someone needs help, we must help them, and in a way, we will be doing it for Little Josh as well as ourselves."

"Mommy, will Little Josh know?" asked J.J.

Violet smiled tenderly a him, and answered, "I'm sure he will, I'm sure he will know."

Violet was waiting in the buggy when the train came into sight and began tooting its whistle. She climbed down and stood at the stop, waiting with sorrow in her heart at what she must tell Brent. She had set the lantern down beside her, and the flickering shadows cast eerie shapes about the place. The train stopped, and Brent jumped off. The conductor handed him his two pieces of baggage which he set down when he reached Violet, so he could throw his arms around her and kiss her heartily. The kiss lasted only a moment, and Brent drew back and tried to see Violet's face in the light of the lantern.

"Violet, what's the matter? What's happened?"

"Oh, Brent, let's get into the buggy. I have something sad to tell you."

"The children?" he asked with abated breath.

"Bonnie Anne and J.J. are all right."

He let out his breath, threw the bags in the back, helped Violet into the buggy, and jumped in himself. He turned to her and said only, "Now tell me."

"Little Josh is dead. He was killed in Sumter today!"

"*What*? Josh? Little Josh? How?" He was stunned.

Violet told him all the events of the day, how Josh had tried to protect her, how she might be dead herself if he had not jumped in front of her, how she had brought him home and taken his body to Reverend Jackson. She told of her conversations with Mammy and the house servants, and all the others, and what arrangements were being made, and that she was going down to the church at midnight to sit with his body for a couple of hours.

Brent listened without a word. He had taken her in his arms when she began, to comfort her, but Violet felt the rigidity of his body and the intense anger that lay within him. She also sensed his deep feeling of loss.

"The children?" he asked in a husky voice.

"I've told them. I'm not sure they really understand death."

"God! They'll miss Josh! We all will. What a wonderful young lad." And then his voice turned cold and full of hate and scorn as he exclaimed, "Those damned careless soldiers, those Goddamn Yankees–There could have been no cause to fire into a crowd like that. They probably had instructions to fire into the air, and the soldier lost his head. I'll be making some inquiries into that, you may be sure, and as soon as I can!" His voice broke. He took out his handkerchief, wiped his eyes, and blew his nose. "And to think you might have been killed!"

They returned to the house in silence. Brent went upstairs to give the sleeping children a light kiss, then talked to the servants one by one, trying to spread comfort. Just before midnight Aaron saddled up the horses, and Brent rode with Violet down to the church\school building. He had decided to share her vigil. When they entered, they were impressed by how nicely Elijah and Esther Jackson and the others had laid out Josh on the cot, in the neat clothes that Violet had sent down, and with flowers and burning candles all around. After Violet and Brent had sat there quietly for two hours, two women from the nearby cabins came to take their places. In doing so, they seemed especially pleased that Massuh Brent and Miz Violet had taken a turn there.

Charlotte and Leland arrived on the early train the next morning. As soon as they were settled in the informal dining room for coffee, Violet explained what had happened to Little Josh.

"Oh, Violet," said Charlotte, "what a terrible, terrible thing to have happened to such a sweet, smart little boy. I remember so well all the things Josh used to do. He was your little shadow. Always did all he was told, and then went out looking for other ways to help."

"Yes, he always did that, but Charlotte, you should have heard how his music had improved–violin, banjo, piano–and his little band, the *Little Brown Jugs*, are absolutely marvelous." She paused and then added thankfully, "Oh, Charlotte, I'm so glad you and Leland came today."

"We were all so fond of him," said Leland. "He was someone really special to the whole family. Special in his own right, I might add."

Brent said sadly, "The little fellow had a way of getting under your skin, and I must agree on his great talents. He was the best telegraph operator that I know. During our voyage to the West Indies he was an excellent cabin boy. During those days at sea I was able to get to know him as never before. He never ceased to amaze me with his quick understanding, his sharp wit, and his never failing desire to help. Dear Lord, I'm certainly going to miss him around here." His voice broke with emotion.

Later, on that warm Sunday afternoon, after a light dinner in the informal dining room, all the family, including Bonnie Anne and J.J., went in the carriage for a visit to Josh. Violet and Brent took the hands of their children as they went in. Now Josh rested in a beautiful, polished oak coffin, with white satin lining and coverlet. A candle burned near each end of the coffin, and flowers filled the whole corner of the room. Violet choked back her tears and gave reassuring hugs to Bonnie Anne and J.J. After only a few moments they left to return to the house.

The children had been whispering to each other on the way back. Now J.J. spoke up, "Mommy, you said Little Josh was in heaven with God and the angels. Why is he lying there in that box sleeping?"

Brent and Violet looked at one another. Finally, Violet answered, "That's only his body in the coffin. His spirit is now with God and the angels."

"Why isn't his body in heaven?" asked little Bonnie Anne.

"What's `spirit'?" chimed in J.J.

Brent raised his eyebrows at Violet, waiting for her reply to these inquiries. His mouth twitched as he refrained from laughing at her predicament.

She tossed him a restraining glance, and tried to explain further in a way that the children could understand. "One's body doesn't go to heaven; it stays here. Josh is not really sleeping, for he is dead now. But within us all there is a part of God, a holy spirit, a special mind, a special being, and this is what leaves our bodies when we die and joins God in heaven."

"Oh." The children looked at one another again, still somewhat perplexed. Then Bonnie Anne turned to her father and asked, "Daddy, when I die will I see Grandmommy Rosemary and Granddaddy Alex and Uncle Chris in heaven?"

Now Brent tossed a glance at Violet. He grinned and replied, "I'm sure you will, I'm sure you will." Before the children could ask any more questions, he changed the subject and asked if they wanted to take a short ride on his horse with him when they got back to the house.

"Yes, yes!" they answered, their attention now on that new adventure.

Later that afternoon, as Violet and Brent and Charlotte and Leland sat on the front porch in subdued conversation, a military officer, dressed smartly in blue uniform and black felt hat, came riding up the lane. Dismounting, he introduced himself as Major Wessels, commandant of the U.S. garrison in Sumter. Approaching Violet, the Major said, "Ma'am, I just want to express my deep regret at what happened and to offer my condolences. I am terribly sorry."

Coolly, but properly, Violet offered her hand and said softly, "Thank you, Major," and then she turned away even more coolly.

Brent's voice was sharp as a hunter's knife. He asked, "Major, just how did this happen?"

"Sir, it was like this. We got word from the police that an ugly crowd was gathering in the middle of town, and there was a danger of violence. I sent a lieutenant and a platoon of riflemen as quickly as I could. Their orders were to disperse the mobs—to fire into the air if necessary, but not to hurt anyone."

"Was anyone else hurt?" asked Brent.

"I understand that three other Negroes were wounded, one fairly seriously, the others only slightly.

"Isn't that ironic," interjected Violet in a voice now grown firm, "you people supposedly are down here to protect the rights of the blacks, and look what happens!"

"Yes, and I regret that. I truly do, Ma'am. The lieutenant has received a severe reprimand and is being transferred out, but you know, Ma'am, if our men had not come up, a lot more people might have been killed and injured."

"Maybe so," Violet conceded, "but all I know is that this was one of the most talented boys we have ever seen. He had great prospects for a wonderful future. Are you aware that he jumped in front of me, to protect me, and if he had not done that, the bullet would have struck me instead of him?"

"No, Ma'am, I was not aware of that."

"This seems to be the story of our lives," Charlotte said dejectedly. "We get our hopes up, and then something comes along to strike them down. That has been so for the whole last ten years."

"That likely is the story of life in general, Charlotte," responded Violet, "only the War and the Occupation have given new impetus to the ups and downs of living in our times."

Major Wessels turned to Brent and asked, "Where is the boy? Do you have him here?"

"He's lying in the little church down in the workers' village," replied Brent with cold eyes.

"I wonder if I might go down and pay my respects."

Every inch the gentleman, Brent responded, "Of course. I'll show you the way. Bring your horse and follow me." He walked to the carriage house where he had Fabian put a saddle on his horse, and then led the major down to the little church.

When the major entered, the black people there looked up in surprise, but no one said anything. The major stepped to the coffin, put his hat over his heart, then backed away and departed without another word.

When Violet and the rest of the family, including the children, and the house servants arrived at the little church about fifteen minutes before eleven on Monday morning, the place already was crowded, except for chairs on the front row that had been reserved for them. Reverend Jackson was on the platform, near the pulpit, and the *Little Brown Jugs* were seated behind him. It seemed that all the plantation workers and their children were there. Some were standing at the back and along the walls. Others were outside, looking in the open windows. All were dressed in their Sunday finest.

In addition to these, the Reverend and Mrs. Wilson of Holy Cross Church were there, not to officiate, but simply to be with the family and friends. The Friersons from across the way had come; also the Andersons and the Ellisons from Stateburg, and the Shelbys from Sumter.

Promptly at eleven o'clock, Elijah Jackson stood up and led the *Little Brown Jugs* in a slow rendition of *Goin' Home,* as a prelude, and then he offered a prayer of hope and salvation. With the band accompanying, he led the whole congregation in the singing of the words of *Goin' Home*:

Goin' home, goin' home; Ah'm jes' goin' home,
Quiet like some still day; Ah'm jes' goin' home,
Hit ain't far, jes' close by, through an open do',
Done meh chores, cares laid by, gonna work no mo',
Mama's dere, spectin' me; dere, all de friends ah knew,
Ah'm jes' goin' home, never mo' ta roam.

Jackson stepped to the pulpit and began reading from The *Bible*, first from *Ecclesiastes*:

To everything there is a season, and a time to every purpose under the heaven:

A time to be born, and a time to die;
A time to plant, and a time to pluck up that which is planted,
A time to kill, and a time to heal;
A time to break down, and a time to build up;
A time to weep, and a time to laugh,
A time to mourn, and a time to dance.

Then from *St. John* he read:

Jesus said, Let not your heart be troubled: ye believe in God, believe also in me. In my Father's house are many mansions: if it were not so I would have told you. I go to prepare a place for you.

And then he read *The Twenty-third Psalm*: After that the Reverend Jackson gave a short sermon in which he outlined the things that Josh had done and his great promise for the future. He concluded with: "Dey ain't none uf us be perfect. We be all sinners, buh lemme tell ya dis boy, Joshua, wuz de nearest ta perfect uf anybudy ah ebber know'd. He wuk hard wifout complainin'; he study hard w'en udduh be restin'. An' he mek music dat mek ebberbudy happy who hear him. An' now he be fit ta mek music wif de angels. His greatest joy wuz in bringin' joy ta other people. May we all try ta do as well."

Shouts of "Amen!" punctuated the conclusion of the sermon.

Then Elijah Jackson turned and led the *Little Brown Jugs* in a slow, soulful arrangement of *Daytime Moon.* This brought tears to the eyes of nearly everyone. Then the *Little Brown Jugs* acted as pallbearers, with the help of Leo, Jarvis, Aaron, and Uncle Job, to carry the coffin out of the church. At the direction of Esther Jackson, the other children picked up the bouquets of flowers as they went out to join the procession.

The old spring wagon, polished to a glow by Fabian, and draped with black crepe by Mammy and Evelina, Hattie and Aunt Beulah, served as the hearse. The pallbearers carefully lifted the coffin up and slid it in the back of the wagon. Fabian, wearing a beaver top hat and frock coat, sat in the driver's seat.

The *Little Brown Jugs* returned to the church to get their instruments and then took their places behind the wagon hearse for the procession. Reverend Jackson took his place immediately behind the hearse and in front of the musicians. A group of children carried the flowers out and formed behind the band. Violet and Brent, Bonnie Anne and J.J., and Charlotte and Leland took their places behind the flower bearers. Mammy and her helper, Ellie, and Evelina, Jarvis, Uncle Job and Aunt Beulah, Hattie and her helper, Alma, and Leo and Rachel, and Esther Jackson followed, and all the others then fell in a long line for the walk to the burial ground.

The band began playing slowly, *Goin' Home.* That was the signal for the procession to start moving. The band continued to play most of the way—*Swing Low, Sweet Chariot,* and *Down by the Riverside*—and then began repeating the melodies. Soon the people began singing in strong, melodic, but mournful voices:

Goin' home, goin' home,
Ah'm jes' goin' home...

Then they sang:

Swing low sweet chariot,
    Comin' fo' ta carry meh home,
Swing low sweet chariot,
    Comin' fo' ta carry meh home.
Ah look obbuh Jordan an' whut do ah see,
    Uh band uf angels comin' after meh,
    Comin' fo' ta carry meh home...

At the grave site, Reverend Jackson pronounced a prayer over the coffin, and then the pallbearers—with their senior helpers—lowered it into the grave. The children with the flowers threw their bouquets in and all around the grave.

The procession then reformed, Reverend Jackson and the band again leading the way for the return march, while this time the wagon waited to bring up the rear. Now the little band began playing *Little Brown Jug,* and the people began clapping time. This was followed by *Oh, Susanna, Aura Lee, Blow the Man Down, Listen to the Mocking Bird,* and *Camptown Races.* By the time the procession arrived back at the village, the band was playing these pieces in their new syncopated beat, and the people were whirling round and round, clapping to the rhythm, and trying to keep up with their singing.

They were rejoicing in expressing a faith that Little Josh had gone to heaven and would be happy forever after.

Chapter 46

The Housewarming

1871

During the rest of that summer Violet threw herself more than ever into her work—giving more attention to the daily farming activities of the plantation, more attention to the operation of the house, and, above all, more personal attention to the children. From experience, she knew that keeping busy, along with the passing of time, eased one's grieving for a lost loved one. Even now she thought of Little Josh at least a dozen times each day, but that was better than the hundred times a day at first. She knew she would always miss him and think of him, and what he might have become, had that horrible accident never occurred.

Even though it was summer, she resumed piano instruction for Bonnie Anne, but more than that she worked with her in other ways—helped her make clothes for her dolls, took her alone on walks through the flower garden and through the orchard. Beyond that, Violet encouraged her eight-year-old daughter in many activities that plantation daughters had missed in earlier days. She allowed her to help Aunt Beulah in dusting the house; she let her help Mammy with little chores in the kitchen, from fetching ingredients to beating eggs; she let her go with Ellie to feed the chickens and gather eggs, and from Evelina she even learned to milk the goat.

Little Jonathan Jackson also received special attention. Now Violet began taking J.J. regularly on her inspection tours around the plantation. Now he was the one to ride on the horse behind her, as Little Josh had done, and to slide down to open and close gates and then hop back up. In addition, he helped bring wood in the kitchen, and he ran errands for everyone about. He, too, sometimes followed around for feeding the chickens, and he also liked to help feed the horses and mules and cows. Milking time fascinated him. Violet began teaching him piano, for which he showed an instant liking, and, indeed, promise that he possessed a talent in that direction.

It seems so strange, thought Violet, *that J.J. almost has become a surrogate for Josh. Strange that her own son should take the place of a Negro servant boy.* As she thought about it, she was sure that some of this had come unconsciously as a search to replace Josh, but she knew it was more than that. No one could replace Josh. On the other hand her devotion to Josh had taken nothing away from her own son. On the contrary, her regard for each had made her appreciate each boy all the more.

Briefly after the loss of Josh she had thought she would bring another black boy up to help her. The logical candidate was Thomas, whom Reverend Jackson had made the new leader of the *Little Brown Jugs*, but she could not do it. She could not just get another boy to take Josh's place. At the same time, she encouraged all the boys in the band to keep up their music and to keep the group going just as Josh would have, and each boy responded with feeling and accomplishment.

Violet and Brent decided that Aunt Beulah and Uncle Job should return to their old roles as custodians of the town house, and they would live there permanently as they had done in the former Columbia house. A bright and attractive young couple that Violet recruited from the workers' village, Cora and Raymond Martin, would go in to help out when the family was in town, usually from January to May. The two had been brought into the big house for special training by Aunt Beulah and Uncle Job so that their future duties would be familiar to them. Evelina, of course, always would be wherever the children were.

Hattie would take over Aunt Beulah's role as head housekeeper of Fair Oaks, and her sewing assistant, Alma, would be in charge of the sewing needs of the family. Alma would have an apprentice to help her, just as she had helped and learned from Hattie.

During this time Brent was able to give his attention to the mercantile business and to his duties with the railroad. He developed a routine of taking the morning train into Columbia and returning on the late afternoon train. A day or two each week he would get a couple of men to go with him by handcar over sections of the track to make close inspections.

Violet, too, was able to develop a routine for going into Columbia one day a week, usually Wednesday, to oversee construction of the town house. She would spend the morning at the site, and Brent would join her at noon. Over a basket picnic lunch they would discuss progress and any changes they decided should be made. Then she would spend a couple of hours visiting with Charlotte before returning to Fair Oaks.

As cotton-picking went into full swing at Fair Oaks, the first week in October, the builder announced that the town house was finished. A week later it was furnished, and Violet and Brent decided to take the children in and invite friends to join them for a housewarming to be held on the twenty-fifth.

Fortunately the crops this year were exceptionally good. The cotton yield was over three hundred pounds to the acre, well above the general average of 190 to 200 pounds. The price was good for the times—twenty-one cents a pound locally. Violet figured that the cost of production—the labor, seed, fertilizer, forage and care for the horses and mules, maintenance and repairs for the plows, the bailer, the wagons—amounted to not more than ten cents a pound. That meant a clear profit of $27,720 for the 440 acres of cotton alone. In addition, the other acres did almost as well, relatively, with the corn, wheat, and hay that went to market and for the previous year's tobacco crop.

On the 18th, Violet took Aunt Beulah and Uncle Job and Cora and Raymond with her to Columbia so that they could get acquainted with the house and make preparations for the housewarming a week later. Carter and Jonah also came along to hang the draperies, pictures and portraits, and to move any furniture that needed rearranging.

It was a bright, blue day of October when the train on which Violet and Brent and the children, with Evelina, were arriving, pulled into the Columbia station on the morning of the 23rd. Uncle Job was there to meet them with the carriage, and Raymond was waiting with the wagon in which he would load the trunks and valises brought from Fair Oaks. Uncle Job helped Raymond with the baggage and then climbed into the carriage to drive the family to their new town house. He drove along Laurel Street the three blocks to Henderson and then turned the corner on Henderson.

"Wait!" Violet called out to Uncle Job. She wanted to stop for a moment to have a special look at the house from where they were. Bonnie Anne and J.J. clapped their hands in excitement as they looked at the striking new house.

It was a two-and-a-half-story house, with red tile hip roof and a single, wide dormer in front, with three smaller dormers in the back. The outside of the top half of the walls was of white stucco—made of portland cement and sand and lime, and then painted white. The lower half was of dark red brick. All the upper windows and the walls under the eaves were trimmed in brick. The windows of the first story and the basement were trimmed with limestone. A large brick chimney rose from outside the wall on the left, and three internal chimneys rose above the roof lines. A porch with concrete floor and brick half-walls topped with limestone, and with its own tile roof with lines paralleling those of the main roof, extended most of the way across the front of the house. The porch looked out eastward toward the grounds of the Male Academy.

Violet asked J.J. to jump down and open the gate of the iron grill fence that surrounded the lot. He responded promptly, and Uncle Job drove into the circular driveway and up to the front steps. Charlotte came running out to greet them. Brent jumped out and, after helping Violet out of the carriage, led her up the steps and then, laughing, picked her up and carried her across the threshold where Aunt Beulah and Cora were waiting with happy, wide smiles.

Although Violet had been following the construction and the furnishing closely all the way, somehow now it seemed that she was seeing the house for the first time. At least she was seeing it differently.

Inside the door was an entry hall paved with slate, with a cloak room on either side. The hall opened to a broad, carpeted, open staircase that led straight up to the second floor. At the foot the stairs flared out in both directions. On the left of the entrance was a large parlor that extended the full length of the house. In the middle of the long wall opposite the entrance to the parlor was a big brick fireplace. On the near side, a wall from the point that the staircase reached the ceiling extended a short way to a rear entry hall and back door, and under the wide stairway there was another set of stairs that led down to the basement. A narrow servant's stairway at the back of the house led from the kitchen to the second floor.

Above the fireplace hung a large portrait of Brent and Violet, standing together and in formal dress, that Brent had commissioned to be painted the previous summer. In the picture, Violet was wearing a blue gown trimmed with lavender roses. The neckline was cut "off the shoulder", and she wore a necklace of amethyst stones and diamonds that Brent had given her on her birthday. Her pendant earrings matched her necklace. Brent's suit was of dark blue with navy satin trim. He had insisted on placing a lavender rose boutonniere in his lapel, and a lavender handkerchief in his pocket. The gifted painter had been able to bring forth in the painting the deep bond of feeling that existed between Violet and Brent, the humor that so often lay in Brent's eyes, Violet's gracious personality, and the intelligence and energy of both.

The dining room was furnished with a large mahogany Chippendale table. Twelve chairs of the same period were placed against the chair rails of the room. There was also a small informal family dining area in the warming kitchen beyond. In the cooking kitchen there was a small dining area for the servants.

Outside the basement entrance were the woodshed and coal bin. A brick walkway led to a white clapboard carriage house, big enough for two carriages and two horse stalls, a feed room and a tackle room.

Violet led the others up the picturesque front staircase as Bonnie Anne came bounding down and nearly fell, but Brent caught her and carried her right back up the stairs.

"Mommy, Mommy, I found my room. I just *love* it. It's so pretty!" laughed Bonnie Anne from over her Daddy's broad shoulder.

Balustrades of white balusters with dark oak rail connected with the tops of the stair rails and ran along either side of the stairwell to border a hall on each side upon which the second-story rooms opened. The room immediately ahead of the head of the stairs was Brent's special pride. It was the office and library. There were bookshelves all around the room, some even holding books already, and a double desk for Brent and Violet sat at the right wall. Opposite the desk, near the left wall, was a pair of leather-upholstered wing chairs with lamp stand and colorful kerosene lamp between them. Beneath the window directly opposite the door, looking out toward the railroad and the warehouses, was a table with a telegraph instrument. Brent had arranged with owners along the way to allow poles to be set up and had workers string a wire the two and a half blocks across the backs of lots to hook onto the telegraph in his warehouse office.

Along the north side were three bedrooms of about equal size. On the other side, the large master bedroom was on the southeast corner, overlooking both Henderson and Laurel Streets. Next to it was a fairly small child's bedroom, which would be J.J.'s.. Bonnie Anne was in one of the three bedrooms along the north side. For this room, Violet had selected wall paper with a white background and a pattern of small pink roses. Hattie had made a white lace canopy for the four poster bed, with matching dust ruffles. The coverlet was white quilted chambray with pink roses twined across it. Beside the bed was a doll cradle with Bonnie Anne's favorite doll lying in it. Violet had slipped this away from Fair Oaks and sent it up earlier so as to be something familiar waiting for her. J.J.'s room was decorated with cut-out tracings of red and blue toy soldiers marching around the upper part of the white walls, just under the cornice. On his small youth bed lay a white coverlet with a large colorful soldier in red and blue uniform stitched in the center. On a small table in the room stood J.J.'s collection of his favorite wooden toy soldiers that Violet had sent to Columbia earlier.

In the southwest corner, was a bathroom with hot and cold running water, and next to it were two water closets, one opening into the bathroom, the other opening to the hall. Between the water closets and J.J.'s bedroom was a stairway leading to the third floor. The main feature up there was a large playroom for the children and two additional bedrooms for servants' quarters.

By the time they had all finished looking over the house and moving into their rooms, Aunt Beulah and Cory had a light lunch ready in the dining room. After lunch, Brent had to get back to the warehouse, but Charlotte stayed for the rest of the afternoon to help in getting ready for the housewarming two days later.

Promptly at two o'clock on Wednesday afternoon, guests began arriving for the housewarming. They found waiting for them in the dining room a spread of Westphalia ham, smoked beef, buffalo tongue, Danish cheese, Normandy cheese, and French champagne. There was punch in a beautiful large cut crystal bowl, scuppernong, ale, varied fruits, nuts, biscuits, cakes, and candies. The children, in their finest dress, circled the table and looked with amazement and desire at all the refreshments. They had been cautioned about their manners by both their mother and their father, and they were on their best behavior for they did not wish to be banished to the playroom and thus miss all the excitement. Bonnie Anne remembered to curtsey and J.J. to bow when introduced to the guests.

In addition to Charlotte and Leland and Leland's father, Andrew, guests included the Rev. Peter Shand, in his thirty-eighth year as rector of Trinity Episcopal Church, his wife and their daughter, Mamie; General and Mrs. Wade Hampton; General and Mrs. M.C. (Matt) Butler; Brent's four Democratic colleagues in the State Senate and their wives; Cedric Johnson, Brent's faithful assistant at the Mercantile Company, and his wife, Julia; the secretaries and the warehouse workers from the company; John Fraser of the Carolina Central Railroad and his wife; the neighbors on either side of the house and the neighbors who had allowed Brent to put his telegraph line across their lots. The Chesnuts had been invited, but they were away.

Charlotte and Leland acted as tour guides to show people the house, with one or the other of the children, or both, usually tagging along to brag about their very own room now that they were "almost grown up."

After seeing the house and exclaiming over the various furnishings and appointments, the guests congregated in the large parlor, and in the dining room around the table. As with most parties of that day, the women tended to cluster about one another, discussing the latest in fashions and furnishings and their children's progress and schooling, while the men were intent on talking politics and business. But Violet and Margaret Butler joined a group of men in conversation around the punch bowl.

A little self-consciously, John Fraser was saying, "You know, I guess I'm one of your ill-famed carpetbaggers."

Laughing, Brent said, "Of course you are, you're from Ohio, aren't you?"

"Yes, yes, from Ohio."

"How did you happen to come here?" asked Father Shand.

"Well, I was working for the Baltimore and Ohio Railroad before the War, and during the War I served under General Haupt with the U.S. Military Railroad."

"I understand that the Wilmington, Columbia, and Augusta Railroad has completed its line through Sumter to Columbia," Matt Butler said, "Is that going to hurt the Carolina Central?"

"Oh, I don't think so, at least not much," answered John Fraser. Then, turning to Brent, he asked, "Brent, what is your opinion on this?"

"No, we still have the advantage of going through Camden," answered Brent. "The one that really is going to be hurt is the Wilmington and Manchester that goes by way of Manchester. The new line almost parallels that one, but takes a shorter route. I wouldn't be surprised to see that line dry up very shortly, and the whole town of Manchester with it. Now a town probably will grow up around their new station at Wedgefield plantation and leave Manchester high and dry."

"Brent's probably right about that," agreed Fraser.

"Well, I swan, I guess people had better watch their railroad investments hadn't they?" Matt Butler said a bit nervously.

"I would say they're all on shaky ground," Brent came back.

"Except for the Carolina Central," amended Fraser.

"Of course, with the possible exception of the Carolina Central," Brent said with a grin.

Changing to another topic, Andrew Thompson commented to the group in general, "Wasn't that some fire in Chicago last week?"

"Indeed it was," responded Fraser. "It burned for three days. Practically the whole city burned down. I saw a report that over 17,000 buildings were destroyed and the total damage is over two hundred million dollars."

"My God, did Sherman go through there?" Wade Hampton exclaimed with an air of mock amazement. "I wonder who he would have blamed this one on."

"They say a cow, a cow belonging to a Mrs. O'Leary, kicked over a kerosene lantern in the barn and started it," answered Fraser, shaking his head as if in disbelief.

"Well, you know something," Hampton went on, "our fire in Columbia surely was just as bad, block for block. Of course Chicago is a very big city, and that is what makes this such a disaster, but Columbia, though a small city, was almost totally destroyed at the center, and for people in the path of the flames, one was about as bad as the other."

"But something closer to home this past week was Grant's reimposition of martial law in nine of our counties. What do you make of that?" grumbled Brent angrily.

"Wholly unnecessary," Hampton responded quickly.

"How did it come about?" asked Brent.

Hampton paused long enough for a refill of punch all around, and then he explained, "Well, they're after the Ku Klux Klan. Last Thursday a week ago, I think it was, Grant issued a proclamation that since a condition of lawlessness and terror existed in those nine counties, he was ordering all combinations and conspiracies that are obstructing the law to disperse. Then just five days later, last Tuesday, Grant announced that the so-called insurgents had not dispersed, and he said they were in rebellion against the authority of the United States, and he was suspending the writ of habeas corpus. That means allowing arbitrary arrests in those counties. I guess Federal marshals already have arrested several hundred people."

"Those counties did not include Richland, here, or Sumter, did they?" interjected Violet, with a worried expression.

Hampton smiled at her. "No, the counties are all in the northern tier, in the up-country, but the intimidation is here all the same. Now, frankly, I hold no brief for the Klan. I think it's all a mistake, but you really can't blame them much with the kind of anarchy we have."

Violet ventured another inquiry, "If these are all northern counties, that means that the so-called insurgents are small farmers and po' buckras, doesn't it?"

Everyone nodded as she continued, "Which goes to show that it is not mainly the plantation owners that have been having so much trouble with the blacks."

Heads nodded again. Hampton smiled in agreement, "That's right, Violet."

"And you know something else," put in Brent, "the Yankees should be watching out for law and order in their own neck of the woods. Did you see about the Irish riots in New York a few weeks ago?"

"No, what happened?" asked Rev. Shand.

"Well, there was a big riot between Irish Catholics and Irish Protestants in New York City. Fifty or sixty people were killed and several hundred wounded."

At this point, Violet suggested that they all join the others in the parlor. She went to the new piano and played introductory bars of several songs and then invited everyone to join in singing, first, *There's No Place Like Home,* and then *My Old Kentucky Home,* substituting *Carolina* for Old Kentucky. Everyone joined with gusto in these and a whole series of songs, including for Brent's benefit, *Aura Lee.* Finally, all joined in *Bonnie Blue Flag,* and then the guests, slowly, in groups of two or three, departed with enthusiastic comments on the house and all its modern features and the lovely furnishings, and with thanks for the delicious refreshments and for such a wonderful time.

Chapter 47

A Christmas Reunion

1871

Charlotte, Leland, and Andrew Thompson lingered for a while after all the other housewarming guests had departed. They joined Violet and Brent by the fireplace in the parlor, while Aunt Beulah, with Cora and Raymond's help, collected the linen napkins and picked up the party goblets, cups, plates, and utensils. Evelina was with the children upstairs, giving them their baths. Uncle Job was out at the woodpile, gathering more wood for the fireplaces.

Charlotte settled back in a wing chair with a sigh of satisfaction. "Oh, Violet, it was a wonderful—a *wonderful*—party. Everyone seemed so congenial and to have such a good time. And everybody whom I showed around was really impressed with the furnishings and the layout of the house, and they all commented on the delicious refreshments."

"Yes, our guests did seem to enjoy themselves, and there certainly never seemed to be a lull in the conversations going on. As a matter of fact, I had a delightful time. How about you?" She looked at Brent with a happy smile that reflected the outcome of their party.

He returned the smile, saying, "And so you should, my Love, so you should. We do have a beautiful house, and you have made it so. I thoroughly enjoyed myself, too; it was a great party."

Leland and Andrew nodded their agreement. "Wonderful housewarming," they chimed in unison.

"And the food," Charlotte went on, "Violet, where in the world did you get all that wonderful gourmet food?"

Violet laughed softly and gave a wave in Brent's direction. He grinned and said, "That comes from developing sources for the tastes and whims of our distinguished legislators."

"I knew that they were eating at the public trough," said Leland, "but I had no idea it was this lavish."

"Leland, you should see the `Solons Saloon' in the State House. You wouldn't believe it," commented Violet with disdain.

Cora brought in tea as all continued to relax in front of the low fire. After everyone had been served, Violet remarked with a touch of sadness evident in her voice, "I wish Susan could have been here for our housewarming. I miss that little rascal with her teasing ways and impish humor."

"Oh, so do I," agreed Charlotte, "only she isn't so little anymore. Sometimes I find it hard to believe that our little sister is now a grown-up, married woman, just like us. It all seemed to happen so quickly."

Uncle Job came in to add wood to the low burning fire. Violet thanked him as he left, and then for a few minutes, everyone sipped tea in quiet contemplation. Violet broke the silence by commenting, "I wonder if we could coax her and Gilbert to come back for Christmas. Wouldn't that be wonderful!"

Heads nodded in unison again as Charlotte responded with excitement, "It's worth a try. Oh, let's do. You invite them, Violet, and then I'll write, too, telling them how much it would mean to all of us."

Violet went on with enthusiasm, "Why dón't we have an old-fashioned Christmas with *everyone* at Fair Oaks?" She turned toward her husband, "Oh, Brent, do you think your mother and father and Phoebe and Bruce could come?"

With an answering sparkle in his sea-blue eyes, he echoed, "It's worth a try, though Bruce is still out west. Charlotte, Leland, how about you two and little Lee? And Father Thompson, would there be any problem in your getting away from the mill for a few days at that time?"

"Oh, no, I don't think so. They usually shut down for a week at Christmas, and surely will again this year," answered Leland's father. He was very fond of his daughter-in-law's family, and had been close friends with his good neighbors, the Major and Rosemary Lee Storm. In earlier days he and Leland's mother had spent so much time over at Fair Oaks that he had felt as comfortable at the neighboring plantation as he did at his own Glenmerry. Of course, with the deaths of Rosemary and Alexander Storm, and Leland's mother, along with the War and its resultant hardships, and his and Leland's move to Columbia–his life had changed considerably. But the memories of earlier times at Fair Oaks lingered, and he always enjoyed returning there for short visits when he accompanied Charlotte and Leland or to the cottage still at Glenmerry. Indeed, he would look forward to spending Christmas at Fair Oaks.

"And maybe Grandmama Lee can make it this time," Violet continued. "It was wonderful seeing her when she came down for Susan's wedding, but there were so many people around, and so much going on, and she couldn't stay long afterwards because of her commitments to that charitable organization in Richmond, that I never felt I had enough of a visit with her. Maybe she can stay a few weeks, if not more, this visit."

"What a lady," murmured Brent, "a perfect example of a lovely, intelligent lady who has grown old with graciousness and dignity, and in spite of all the difficulties and deprivations and hardships that have occurred in her life she has kept that marvelous sense of propriety and gentle humor. As far as I am concerned, she can stay here for the rest of her life."

"Oh, I wish that were so," remarked Violet, "but I fear she is too much a part of Virginia to make such a move, much as she loves and misses us all. At least there are cousins up there, so she is not all alone."

"Let's see," said Charlotte thoughtfully, "she was here briefly for Susan's wedding, but before that, we hadn't seen her since, when was it, 1863?"

"Yes, I think that's so," replied Violet, slowly, "yes, it was the Christmas after Christopher was killed at Gettysburg, when we needed her so much. She stayed with us for three months, until she felt we had everything under control."

"At that time one could still travel between here and Virginia, even though the War was on," added Brent.

"All right, everybody, then that's it," concluded Violet. "We'll all have a Christmas reunion at Fair Oaks. I'll alert everyone by telegraph tomorrow before we return to the country. This way, they can put it on their calendars and begin making their plans now, and then I'll follow up right away with a letter."

Everyone began talking at once about all the things they should remember to do—the decorations, the tree, the Yule log, the wassail, extra riding horses (the Thompsons had two they'd send over from Glenmerry farm), and then they'd probably need an extra buggy or two, along with a carriage or two, but then, Aunt Beulah and Uncle Job would be closing the town house and coming to Fair Oaks for Christmas and they could drive the buggy with the two horses, one of which was a riding horse...and on and on went the preliminary planning.

Back at Fair Oaks, Violet resumed her attention to the completion of the gathering and marketing of the cotton crop. Brent resumed his commuting to Columbia, and the children resumed their attendance at Edge Hill School.

One member of the family, however, was slowing down noticeably—Old Dan, the faithful collie. He was barking his greetings in a more subdued manner; he was not seeing as well; his hearing was impaired; and he slept most of the day. Indeed, everyone had to watch out that they did not trip over him as he slept in the hall or in front of a door. For a while everyone thought that he was being contrary when he failed to come promptly at a call. Then Violet noticed that if she clapped her hands sharply he would come almost at once. Obviously he could not hear voices far away. There was a white clouding in his eyes. Violet feared that Old Dan might stray onto the railroad track and fail to hear or see an oncoming train. She worried about him not getting out of the way of the horses or the buggy or carriage.

Violet explained to Bonnie Anne and J.J. that Dan was indeed getting old and weak, and they must treat him gently. She explained that, like people, dogs die, too.

Then early in December the word came. Jason came walking rapidly up to the house and, finding Violet in the office, he said to her, "Miz Violet, de dog, Ole Dan be daid."

"Oh, Jason!" gasped Violet, tears rushing to her eyes, "where is he?"

"Out in de cow barn. Ole Dan jes' go out ta de cow barn an' lay down in de straw an' die. He know his time done come."

When Violet explained to the children about the dog, they were saddened and cried a little, but then right away J.J. said, "Mommy, we must have a funeral for him."

"And Bonnie Anne added quickly, "Oh, yes, yes, can we, Mommy?"

"*May* we—"

"May we, please Mommy?"

"Of course." She went into the office and sent off a wire to Brent in Columbia informing him of Old Dan's demise and that the children were planning a funeral late that afternoon. It would be his decision whether to take the earlier train.

Fabian dug a grave beyond the far side of the garden. Carter and Jonah put together a box and made a wooden marker with Dan's name on it. They put the box and marker in the wheelbarrow and laid Old Dan's body in the box, nailing the lid on tightly. Fabian brought the wheelbarrow up to the house.

Just then the train rolled to a stop, and Brent hopped off and strode over to join them. Violet flashed him a grateful smile as the children, not knowing about the wire, told him about Old Dan. He gave each a comforting hug and asked if he was in time for the funeral.

"Oh, yes, Daddy. We were just about to begin. C'mon," answered J.J.

Bonnie Anne and J.J. got in line behind Fabian pushing the wheelbarrow, with Violet, Brent, Evelina, Jarvis, Aaron, and Mammy following. As they all marched along to the grave, the children pretended to be playing musical instruments and making imitation sounds. Then they would sing, *Goin' Home*, and then pretend playing their instruments again.

When they reached the grave, Fabian and Jarvis lifted the box out of the wheelbarrow, laid it in the hole, and covered the grave. Then he put the wooden marker on the grave. Bonnie Anne and J.J. picked some colorful chrysanthemum flowers, which they strewed on top of the grave. With Bonnie Anne by his side, J.J. pretended to open a book and read, "Dear Lord, please take care of Dan. We miss him but we hope he is happy in heaven. Tell him to be a good dog, and we'll see him when we get up there. Amen."

"Amen," said Bonnie Anne.

"Amen," echoed everyone else.

As Violet followed the others back to the house, she felt a tug of sadness. *One more link with the past broken,* she thought. *Old Dan has been around since I was a young girl of fourteen. He was a great comfort to Mama, and a great favorite of Daddy's. Christopher played with him for hours on end. Dan shared with our family those happier days before the War. Now, he too is gone.*

The house had become a bustle of activity as everyone took part in the preparations for the Christmas season. Secret objects were being made for gifts and quickly hidden under the folds of a long skirt or apron or under a doll or behind a pillow cushion when the recipient appeared. Evelina was helping the children make pin cushions for their mother, and Violet was helping them make a razor holder for their father, and a hair ribbon flower for Evelina, and both Evelina and Violet were helping them make various gifts for the other servants. There were trips to Sumter and Stateburg and Columbia to purchase gifts. For Brent, Violet had had an artisan in Columbia design a pair of silver cuff links, engraving each with a tiny heart that surrounded his initials, and there she had also purchased a gold stickpin, with a sizeable diamond as the centerpiece, for his cravats.

The servants were as excited as the Storms at the prospect of all the "famly" being there for Christmas, and gaily joined in the tasks of decorating the beautiful old plantation house. As in the past, garlands of pine and spruce were draped along the curved stair rails, with highlights of holly berries, bright ribbon, boxwood, and magnolia leaves. Arrangements of boxwood, magnolia and holly leaves and berries were placed on mantels and tables, and small sprays and twigs of cedar and holly were placed over paintings and portraits and tucked into the upper corners of the two Flemish tapestries facing each other on either side of the hall. Creeping cedar was twined around the chains holding the candelabras and along the backs of the mantels. Rosemary Lee's ball of velvet ribbons and fruits was hung again from the eighteenth century brass chandelier over the dining table. Fresh candles were placed in all the candelabras and chandeliers and wall holders. A kissing ball, as usual, was hung from the brass end knob of the hall chandelier, and tucked here and there in the thick sprigs of boxwood were clusters of holly berries, mistletoe, and thin red ribbons.

Fabian and Leo and Aaron had found and cut a thick, ten-foot cedar near the woods and set it up in the back left corner of the parlor, where it waited to be trimmed after supper on Christmas Eve. Aaron and Jarvis had brought down the boxes containing treasured decorations made in the past, and set these beside the tree. After the tree was trimmed, presents for everyone would be placed under the tree.

The Nativity scene had been set out on the parlor hearth, just as Rosemary Lee Storm had done each year in the past, and Christopher's collection of horses and their stable were arranged on the side table. The girls had continued these traditions after the deaths of their mother from illness, and their brother at Gettysburg. Somehow, doing this helped ease the sense of loneliness at their loss that lingered and, indeed, would always be with them, as was the vacuum left by their father's death at Cheraw.

Amidst all the activity, Violet took time to practice Christmas carols on the piano, along with Handel's *Messiah* and Bach's *Christmas Oratoria,* and to write notes on and address Christmas cards to various friends and relatives whom she and Brent would not see during the Christmas season, and to help the children as needed, and she continued their music lessons. They were now at an age when the magic of Christmas could truly capture their imagination and creativity. They would choose dolls to be the Baby Jesus and Mary and Joseph, and the shepherds and wise men, and set up the Nativity scene, and act out the Christmas Story. When they tired of this game, J.J. would pretend he was Santa Claus, and Bonnie Anne would pretend to be Mrs. Santa, and they would put the dolls to bed and then bring them presents, or the dolls might become Santa's elves and he and Mrs. Santa would work on toys for the good little children down in South Carolina, especially the two at Fair Oaks.

Everyone had accepted with enthusiasm the invitation to spend Christmas at Fair Oaks, and each arrival brought new waves of excitement. First to arrive were Charlotte and Leland and baby Lee, with Liza, the housemaid, and Leland's father, Andrew, on the Friday afternoon train from Columbia. They had no sooner gotten settled in when a telegraphic message came in from Susan with the news that she and Gilbert would arrive at the Claremont station, near Stateburg, at three o'clock the next afternoon, Saturday.

Grandmother Catherine Victoria Lee arrived, with Judy, her companion and maid, on the morning train Saturday, having changed trains in Camden. In spite of her age, she arrived in high spirits and anticipation of being with her daughter's children and their families. Violet took her up to her room to freshen up a bit after the long trip, while Jarvis and Aaron were close behind with her bags—which J.J. and Bonnie Anne imagined to be full of presents for them. Leaving Judy to take care of the unpacking, Grandmama was soon back down for a cup of tea and to chat with Violet and Brent, and Charlotte and Leland, to coo over little Lee whom she insisted on holding on her lap, and to kiss and hug and ask questions of J.J. and Bonnie Anne, for whom she had brought special small gifts that they could open right away.

It was soon time for Violet and Brent and the children to dash down the lane to meet Brent's parents and sister, arriving from Charleston on the train. Aaron followed with the wagon in which to carry their baggage.

The elder Sutlers and Phoebe received a warm welcome from everyone, and Violet showed them their rooms. It was not long until Brent's family came down to the parlor to join the others in a cup of syllabub and to give more presents to the children, much to their delight. After that they all moved into the dining room where Mammy and Aunt Beulah and Ellie served a delicious dinner. Here they relaxed, enjoying just being together again.

Right after dinner, which had been served late to include the elder Sutlers, it was time to go to the Claremont Depot to meet Susan and Gilbert's train. So many wanted to go meet them that it was necessary to take the spring wagon, the two-seat carriage, and the buggy that Aunt Beulah and Uncle Job had brought down from Columbia. Fabian came along with Aaron to drive and help load baggage. Although Bonnie Anne and J.J. had not had their usual naps, they begged their parents to ride along and promised to go to bed early if only they would be permitted to go along and meet their beloved Aunt Susan and her nice husband, Uncle Gilbert. The elder Sutlers and Phoebe, and Grandmama Lee declared they would take advantage of this time to get some rest and catch up from their train rides.

So Violet and Brent, Charlotte and Leland, Andrew Thompson, and Bonnie Anne and J.J. arrived at the train depot in good time, actually fifteen minutes early, only to discover that the train was an hour late, so they went inside to the waiting room to escape the chill. The children were so excited, scampering here and there, that Violet had to admonish them several times. After about ten minutes though, they decided they would pretend they were on a trip and were on one of the new sleeping cars their father had told them about. They each lay down on a bench and pretended to be lying on a train bed.

"Close your eyes, J.J. You're 'sposed to be sleeping," ordered Bonnie Anne, as she closed hers.

Within minutes, the children were fast asleep, and Violet gave a sigh of relief. This was just what the children needed, and they would be in much better humor for the remainder of the day. They were sleeping so soundly that neither the arriving train whistle nor the rumble of the wheels awoke them. Violet shook them gently. As soon as she told them the train was there, they jumped up and raced to the door, with Brent taking off after them.

Susan and Gilbert were the first off the train, and everyone surrounded them, giving them kisses and hugs and fond greetings. Bonnie Anne was tugging Susan on one side of her coat, and J.J. was doing the same on the other. She gave both children a warm hug and a kiss, then Gilbert did the same.

"Oh, my goodness," said Susan, her eyes glistening with tears, "it's so *good* to be home again, and oh, how I've missed you all, and, my goodness, the children have grown since I last saw them."

"And, how we've missed you, little sister! Violet exclaimed, throwing her arms around Susan again.

"Oh, my, yes!" said Charlotte, throwing her arms around both her sisters.

They stood that way a moment, and then as the embrace was broken, Brent smiled and said, "We need to get all your baggage together before that train decides to depart."

This was done in short order, and Fabian and Aaron soon had everything loaded in the spring wagon.

Just as they reached the beginning of the lane leading to Fair Oaks, Susan remarked, with fatigue evident in her voice, "Do you know, I feel that I have spent most of my life on a train. Trouble was, every time we dozed off for a nap, we had to wake up and gather our belongings, and then scramble out to change trains. We started out Thursday morning, and here we are finally, on Saturday afternoon." But then as she caught sight of the splendid white house waiting for her at the end of the lane, her tiredness seemed to vanish, and she exclaimed with joy, "Oh, look, what a sight! How beautiful! Oh, it's wonderful to be home again! Brent, make the horses go faster—hurry!"

The next morning, Christmas Eve morning, all attended Holy Cross Church to thank God for His gift to the world, for peace, for this opportunity for everyone to gather together as one family at Fair Oaks, and for the health and improved fortunes of all of them. They greeted their various friends, and introduced their guests to those who had not yet met them. John and Sarah Frierson gave everyone a big hug and a welcoming smile. Violet had invited these two good friends to share Christmas dinner with them, and to stay until late evening to join in their special activities. They said hello to Will and Mary Anderson, and wished a friendly Happy Christmas to Henry Ellison and his two brothers, Henry and William, Jr. Archibald Martin, from what was formerly the handsome Midlands plantation, brought his new wife, Dorothy, over to introduce her to the Sutlers. Sarah had told Violet that she was a young widow whom Archibald had met in Stateburg and pursued a year before she finally agreed to marry him. Violet was glad to observe that the couple seemed to be happy and to have an easy relationship with each other. She knew that Archibald had had a difficult time financially after the Yankees had burned part of the house to the ground and had destroyed all the crops on the place, but like so many others, somewhere he found the strength to hang on, although he lost much of his land because of back taxes that he was unable to pay. He and Dorothy now lived in a modest farmhouse on the property, and Archibald worked in Sumter, commuting each day in his buggy.

Sitting in their pew in church, Violet gazed at the lovely sanctuary windows of Bavarian stained glass. While the choir sang a portion of Handel's *Messiah,* her thoughts went back to that time in 1864 to the last Christmas with their father before he was killed at Cheraw. She remembered sitting in church that Christmas Day, feeling empty in one way, yet full of anxiety and dread and fear for what might lie ahead. Then she had felt disillusioned with what was happening to the South in the War, and she still felt the loss of her mother and her brother keenly. At that time she was worried about Brent's safety and could not understand why she had not had any word of him. She had felt numb and unmoved by the beauty of the church, of the music, of the rector's words, of the celebration of the birth of Jesus Christ.

But now as the choir sang the *Hallelujah Chorus,* it came upon her that she was filled with the beauty of the music and of the lovely old church; she felt a thankfulness, coupled with exhilaration, that she and Brent and the children and all the others with them were there on this glorious morning to worship together. She realized that her old faith had broken through the walls of doubt that had so beset her before. She was filled with joy.

As if sensing this awakening of realization within Violet, Brent reached over and took her hand in his, giving her a loving smile, before returning his attention to the sermon. Violet recalled how back in 1864, her father had sensed her distress and had placed his hand firmly upon hers, his eyes questioning what she was thinking and feeling. But she had only smiled at him in return, not wanting to add her concerns and worries to his many. *Thank heavens at that time I didn't know that Daddy was planning on rejoining his regiment. I would have been even more devastated,* she thought. Then she thought of Little Josh, *Oh, I wish there were a way that I could do something for him.*

When they came out of the church, the sun was shining with all its light and glory. There was not a cloud in the blue sky. Birds could be heard singing in the distance. There was a slight breeze that rocked the tree limbs gently and ruffled the needles of the fir trees, but the temperature was comfortable, with no sharp chill to the air.

That evening, as was the tradition on Christmas Eve, oyster stew was served for supper. Some Charleston friends of Brent's had sent up three gallons of shucked oysters—so the stew was not thin, and there was plenty for all the family and guests and house servants, and also for Leo and the other supervisors' families. And, as always, as Mammy placed the tureen of oyster stew on the table, she said disdainfully, "Dis ain't, it jes' ain't gwine stick ta ya' stumach." Although Mammy went through this routine each year, Violet had observed that she devoured at least two bowls of the stew all by herself—and with relish.

Last year little Bonnie Anne had suddenly discovered the tastiness of oyster stew and wanted another helping, as she did this Christmas Eve. And now, this year, little J.J. decided that oyster stew wasn't as bad as he had thought, so there was no need for Ellie to scramble him a couple of eggs to eat instead of the stew.

After a dessert of mince pie, they all went into the parlor where Jarvis had set a stepladder by the tall tree. Aaron had brought from attic storage the box of candle holders and tree ornaments that they had cherished and collected throughout the years, even the War years when so little was available, and imaginations were truly stretched to create tree ornaments and presents.

Now that the Major was no longer with them, Brent had taken on the first task of placing the delicate porcelain Christmas angel on top of the tree. With everyone standing around watching, Violet handed him the angel. He climbed the stepladder and then carefully and patiently secured it to the tree amidst advice from the onlookers, "Just a little to the left."..."Now to the right."..."Make her stand up straighter."..."No, the other way."..."That's perfect."..."Don't touch it again, it's just right."..."Daddy couldn't do it better." Through it all Brent just grinned with good humor and followed the suggestions. He descended the ladder amidst the usual applause and exclamations of approval, and when down, gave a little bow which brought on more applause.

Everyone placed the ornaments on the tree, with Brent and Jarvis and Aaron placing those on the upper branches. There was always someone to give them advice on just where they should be hung.

Susan had to hang the ornament with the three little kittens with bells, and the one of Mary and her lamb, both of which were made by her mother and father especially for her when she was little. Violet tenderly hung the small, beaded purse with silver chain that had been her mother's. She stood back to look at how the red and green beads caught the lights. Her eyes became moist and a lump came to her throat. She recalled that during her last Christmas with her father he had handed the purse to her and asked her to place it on the tree where it could be seen by everyone. She remembered the moisture in his eyes when he unwrapped and handed it to her.

Charlotte hung the gold star she made as a little girl. And so it went, with exclamations of delight and discovery as they unwrapped the carved or cut-out ornaments, crocheted angels and stars and corn husk elves and little people.

The privilege of hanging the last ornament had become Mammy's after Aunt Sheba died, and this she did with great pride. For this important task, she had saved a tiny wooden bowl with a miniature rolling pin glued to the edge, that Jarvis had carved years ago.

Then, except for the children, they all secured the candle holders carefully to the branches. With so many helping, this did not take long, nor did inserting the short, slim white candles into the holders. After that, Brent, Violet, Jarvis, and Aaron remained in the parlor, while all the others filed into the library and closed the door. Brent lighted a long taper at the fire and then lit those held by Violet, Jarvis, and Aaron. Very quickly they lit all the candles on the tree and then put out all other candles in the room.

"We're ready!" called Brent, and everybody rushed back into the parlor that was now darkened except for the Christmas tree candles.

"Oh, it's heavenly!"..."Just look at that!"..."It's absolutely beautiful!"..."Oh, my, oh, my!" they exclaimed in awe.

In the light of the Christmas tree, and with a few of the other parlor candles relighted, Violet followed the tradition of serving silver cups containing eggnog from the large silver punch bowl that Brent had purchased to replace her mother's and that the Yankee marauders had stolen. The children joined in with plain eggnog—no brandy or rum added—and then Evelina took them upstairs to bathe and dress them for bed. Alma followed to help her with the children.

The host, hostess, and guests relaxed and chatted and enjoyed their Christmas drink while Mammy and Aunt Beulah and Ellie left to take care of the supper dishes. After serving seconds on eggnog, Hattie left to help the others in the kitchen. Jarvis and Uncle Job went out to fetch more logs for the fireplace.

In a little while, Violet crossed to the piano and sat down, and the others gathered around to sing Christmas carols. Music filled the room and, indeed, could be heard and enjoyed throughout the house. The children urged Evelina and Alma to hurry, so excited were they about getting back downstairs for the rest of the Christmas Eve doings.

Just as Jarvis and Uncle Job returned with the logs, the children came running down the steps and back into the parlor, J.J. rushing to his father and throwing his arms around his long legs, and Bonnie Anne climbing on the bench by her mother. They sang a couple of simple carols with the children, who then began begging to hang up their Christmas stockings, and then after that Daddy had to read the Christmas poem to them.

As in past years, the children hung their large needlepoint stockings decorated with colorful Christmas pictures on nails that Jarvis had previously driven under the mantel. Then it was little Lee's turn to have his tiny stocking hung. Carrying the baby in her left arm, Charlotte hung up his stocking between Bonnie Anne's and J.J.'s. "See, Santa will come to you, too, my little one. Just think, this is your very first Christmas!" Little Lee cooed softly as if in answer.

After that was done, and the children's efforts admired, everyone moved into the library where Brent sat in the Major's big leather side chair on the right of the glowing fireplace. J.J. climbed on his father's lap, while Bonnie Anne sat on the arm of the chair so she could see the pictures, too. Violet took the rocking chair, and the others found places as they could.

First, as Major Storm had always done, Brent read Clement Moore's *A Visit From St. Nicholas* and after that, from the large, old King James *Bible*, Violet read St. Luke's account of the birth of the Christ Child. By the time they had finished, both children were nodding with sleepiness. Violet set the *Bible* on the side table and rose, taking Bonnie Anne's hand and saying, "Time for bed now, honey."

Brent lifted J.J. in his arms, and, amid good-nights from everyone, Brent and Violet took the children upstairs to put them in their beds and kissed them goodnight.

Chapter 48

A Christmas to Remember

1871

Bonnie Anne and J.J. could be heard chattering and getting ready for a dash downstairs long before dawn on Christmas morning, but Violet had posted Evelina as a guard to keep them in their rooms until Violet gave the signal to allow them to come down. At seven o'clock Violet rang a cowbell and the race was on.

While Brent hurried ahead to be in position to rescue anyone who might fall, Bonnie Anne and J.J. ran down the stairs and into the parlor. Charlotte, carrying Lee, and Leland were right behind them, followed by Susan and Gilbert. The other guests were not far behind. There the children found Santa's gifts awaiting them in front of the fireplace. For Bonnie Anne there was a beautiful doll with porcelain head, long curls, and blue eyes, and wearing a gown of pink and white organdy; a doll bed with pillow and sheets and coverlet; and a rocking chair just the right size for her to sit in and rock her new doll. For J.J. there was a colorful, wooden train of seven cars—engine, coal storage, two passenger, one sleeping, one freight, and a caboose; a spinning top with string; and a ship, a replica of the *Shenandoah,* with canvas sails and thin ropes. The stockings were full of candies and nuts and big oranges and apples. The children dumped the contents out to see everything, and in the toe of each stocking they found a little present wrapped in white paper. Bonnie Anne's was a thin gold chain with a heart locket, and J.J.'s was a small, carved, wooden pony, with a mane and tail of brown wool. The children loved everything they had found.

Charlotte showed little Lee a new sugar-teat and a peppermint candy cane that Santa had put in his little stocking. The baby grabbed the sugar-teat, held it up as if to examine it, then stuck it in his mouth. He gurgled little sounds of pleasure as he sucked on it.

"Now, let's open all the presents!" said J.J.

"Yes, right now!" agreed Bonnie Anne.

"No, not now," said Violet. She reminded them that presents were not to be opened until after breakfast—breakfast for the whole family together in the dining room, and then, when everyone had finished, they would all come back into the parlor for the exchange of gifts. She knew that with the prospect of unwrapping their presents awaiting them after they had eaten, that at least they would consume one good meal that day. Otherwise they would be filling up on Santa's candies and nuts and other goodies all the rest of the day and would not want anything more substantial.

After everyone had found their places at the table and eaten, Violet led the way to the parlor.

Bonnie Anne and J.J. could scarcely contain themselves, so excited were they, but they *had* eaten a substantial breakfast. They wanted to give their present to their mother immediately.

Violet smiled and said, "Oh my goodness, I wasn't expecting anything. I didn't see my name on any package here. Where is it?"

The two children looked at each other and giggled. "We didn't put it under the tree. We had to hide it," explained J.J., "so you wouldn't know what it is. We couldn't 'xactly wrap it up in paper and tie it with a ribbon. Mommy, you're going to love it!" He clapped his hand over his mouth as if he were giving away a secret.

"J.J., hush!" Bonnie Anne said quickly. They signaled Evelina with a wave. Grinning broadly, she ran outside and returned with a basket which she set down at Violet's feet. The basket was covered with a red-checkered cloth.

"What a pretty basket," said Violet with a chuckle.

"Look in the basket, Mommy!" Bonnie Anne directed.

"Yes, hurry, Mommy. Look inside!" bubbled J.J.

Violet lifted the cloth. There, curled up within the basket lay a beautiful collie puppy. She lifted him up and set him on her lap. Stroking his head she said, "He is adorable, a beautiful little puppy. Thank you both so very, very much!" She looked at her children with a knowing grin and continued, "I trust that you two will have lots of fun with him, and I trust also that you will teach him not to soil the house."

She lifted him gently off her lap and took the risk of setting him on the floor. Immediately he ran to the Christmas tree and began tearing paper with his little paws and pulling at ribbons with his little teeth.

"I guess he's trying to find if there's a present under the tree for him," laughed James Sutler.

"He's precious," said Charlotte, laughing at the puppy's antics.

"Oh, I just love him to pieces," Susan chuckled.

Violet laughed, too. "He'll have all the presents in pieces if somebody doesn't hurry and stop him. Bonnie Anne, J.J., catch him!"

The two children and Brent gave chase. The puppy thought it was a new game of "Catch me if you can," and dodged here and there until finally Brent caught up with him. He handed the puppy to Evelina. "Here he is, Evelina, I think you had better take him outside while we open the presents."

Evelina returned the wiggling puppy to the basket but had to hold him with one hand to keep him from jumping out. Fortunately, he soon quieted down and curled up as if to take a nap.

"Where in the world did you find him?" asked Violet.

With a sheepish grin, Evelina explained, "De chillun keep sayin' dey wanta puppy now dat Ole Dan be gone, an' dey say dey wanta puppy fo' dere Mommy who need anudder dawg. Den dey say hit be uh good Christmas presen', an' when we drive bek from school we go outta de way ta see Henry Ellison, an' he find dis dawg fo' de chillun ta give ya. Ain't he one cute dawg, Miz Violet?" she concluded proudly.

"Well, he is certainly a beautiful and very special gift, and thank you," Violet said as she gave Bonnie Anne and J.J. each a hug. She looked at the others, and to everyone in general she added somewhat wryly, "I doubt if any of us is going to be able to outdo this."

Evelina left to take the puppy outside, and Charlotte positioned herself by the presents. Susan, Bonnie Anne, and J.J. acted as messengers to distribute the gifts as Charlotte read off the names. Soon everyone had a pile of presents beside them. Then, as was the custom, one person at a time opened one present while the others waited and admired the contents, and then another took a turn at opening a present. There were woolen gloves or mittens, hats, and scarves for everyone, including the house servants. Other presents included exquisitely painted fans; lace handkerchiefs and caps; silk flowers for the hair, lace gloves; and silver hat pins for the ladies. The men received such items as silver or bone letter openers; card boxes; cigarette rollers; shaving brushes, mugs, and strops; needlepoint cases for spectacles; and embroidered white linen handkerchiefs.

The children, of course, had presents from everyone. For Bonnie Anne: a baby doll that looked just like little Lee (given by Charlotte and Leland), with its own cradle (from Andrew Thompson), and extra clothes and diapers (sewn by Evelina, Hattie, and Alma); a toy stove with pots and pans and a china tea set (from her parents), and with tiny towels and hot pads (made by Mammy and Ellie); little wooden bowls and dishes (carved by Jarvis and Uncle Job), a cornhusk doll (made by Aaron and dressed by Aunt Beulah); a deep blue velvet coat with a white fur collar, with matching hat and muff (from James and Isabel Sutler); a pair of white gloves and two pairs of white woolen stockings (from Phoebe), and a light blue organdy dress with a skirt of tiers of ruffles, and a matching bow for her hair (from Grandmother Catherine). Bonnie Anne had two gifts from J.J.—a ring of thin, twisted silver, with tiny blue stones, that he and his mother had picked out together when in Columbia, and a French harp, or harmonica.

J.J.'s gifts included a wooden wagon with removable sides (from his parents), wooden toy soldiers (made by Jarvis and Uncle Job, and painted by Evelina and Aunt Beuluh), to add to his set, a large stuffed bear (from Charlotte and Leland), a hoop and stick (from Andrew Thompson), a box of his favorite sugar cookies (from Mammy and Ellie), a stuffed toy soldier doll (made by Hattie and Alma), some sugar cane strips to suck on (from Aaron), a blue woolen coat and cap (from grandparents Sutler), and blue gloves (from Phoebe); and a navy sailor suit with white collar (from Grandmother Catherine). His gift from his sister was two-fold: a Jew's harp that he had envied his little friends in Columbia for having, and that Violet had duly noted, and a beanshooter that she had picked up when she was out with Evelina one day.

As a gift to both children together, the Frierson's had commissioned Carter to make a small table and set of four chairs for their playroom. Bonnie Anne and J.J. promptly put the new Santa Claus doll in one chair and the stuffed bear in the other. They then sat down in the other two chairs and pretended to be having tea, much to the amusement of the onlookers.

Violet and Brent gave Andrew Thompson and James Sutler bright woolen, Scottish glengarries for festive occasions. Brent received four boxes of the tiny cigarillos, and as he unwrapped the fourth, he laughingly commented that this supply should last quite a while.

Grandmother Catherine Lee, with Judy's help, handed Violet, Charlotte, and Susan identical packages, and the three sisters opened them together. For each it was a print of a painting, each in a beautiful gilded frame, about two feet by three. "These are copies of an engraving by A.G. Campbell of W.D. Washington's painting, called 'Burial of Latané.'"their grandmother explained, "Do you know it?"

"Oh, it is beautiful, but what is the picture, Grandmama?" asked Violet.

"Violet, you remember how in June of 1862 during the campaign on the Virginia peninsula Jeb Stuart rode his twelve hundred cavalry all the way around McClellan's whole Yankee army? Well, the only Confederate killed on Stuart's raid was a Captain William Latané. His body was taken to a nearby plantation for burial. But the Yankees were there, and they would not allow a local clergyman to come on the place. So, the women living there conducted a funeral service themselves. You see there in the picture the attractive matron of the plantation preaching the service, and the other women gathered around the coffin, all in this beautiful garden. They are said to symbolize the spunk and enduring strength of Southern women—and I think that represents all three of you girls."

The sisters looked at their Grandmother in thanks as their eyes moistened from their emotion.

She continued, pointing at the picture, "And you see the black men assisting at the grave, showing the loyalty of the slaves, and the neatly dressed little girl, symbolizing hope for the future. The painting created something of a sensation when it was exhibited in Richmond."

Brent's mother handed a package to Violet, saying, "For you and Brent."

"Looks like a book," smiled Brent, who always tried to guess a present before it was unwrapped.

"I hope so," said Violet as she removed the wrapping paper. "Wasn't it Erasmus who said, 'When I get a little money, I buy books; and if any is left, I buy food and clothes.'" The present was a copy, in English translation, of Victor Hugo's *Les Miserables.* Violet held it up for all to see. "This is wonderful, and don't you think Victor Hugo is the best French writer of our time?"

Heads nodded as Brent answered, "I think he's the best anywhere. I've heard a lot about this book, and I'm anxious to read it."

Violet opened the book and caught sight of a quotation from Victor Hugo inscribed on the fly leaf. She read aloud for everyone to hear:

> *Will the future ever arrive?...Should we continue to look upwards? In the light we can see in the sky one of those which will presently be extinguished. The ideal is terrifying to behold, lost as it is in the depth, small, isolated, a pin-point, brilliant but threatened on all sides by the dark forces that surround it; nevertheless, no more in danger than a star in the jaws of clouds.*

Laying the book in her lap, Violet asked, "Doesn't that speak to us? I often wonder if this military occupation will ever end."

The usually cheerful Susan responded gloomily, "Since I was twelve years old I have known only war and occupation, though thankfully it has ended in Mississippi. Anyway, that is almost half of my life, at least it is more than half of my life that I can remember."

Violet handed Brent a box wrapped in colored paper and ribbons.

"Cigars?" he asked as he began to unwrap it. He stopped short as he recognized a beautiful, inlaid wood chessboard. "Violet! This is a beauty!" Then looking more closely, a look of wonder crossed his face. "But what is this—why the red line all the way around to set off the outer two rows?" He paused a moment and then asked, "Wait a minute, who did this?"

Smiling in anticipation, Violet answered, "Jarvis and Carter have been working on this for six months—Jarvis carving the figures; Carter, the board."

"Well, I regret to say, there's a big mistake here."

"How's that?"

"Well, look, I count ten squares by ten; don't you know it's supposed to be eight squares by eight?"

"Oh, is it?"

"Of course. Well, let's see what else we have here." Brent dug more deeply and uncovered several wood-carved figures, some painted in blue and some in gray.

"Now, Brent, look," said Violet, "this is a very special chess set."

"Yes, I can see the figures are those of the War Between the States...er," he paused, glancing over at Gilbert, "or some might say the Civil War. Very interesting."

By now everyone had gathered around Violet and Brent for a better look at his gift.

"Here," Violet brought from nowhere a little table just the size of the chessboard and put the board on it. Picking up a piece, she said, "Now, this is Jeff Davis, the President; he takes the place of the King in the old chess set. And look at this...this is Robert E. Lee; the general takes the place of the queen. And you see these battle-flag bearers, with the Confederate flag? The flags take the place of the bishops."

"Brent's interest was evident as he picked up a figure of a cavalryman and said, "Let me guess; these take the place of the knights."

"Right."

"And these riflemen take the place of the pawns."

"Yes, that's the infantry."

"But what are these cannon? Where do they go?"

Violet was delighted at Brent's curiosity and quick perception of the relationships of the figures. "Can't you see what's left? The cannon take the place of the castles, or rooks, or whatever you want to call them."

"But, honey, that still leaves us with a board that has too many squares," Brent said kindly, not wanting to hurt Violet's feelings.

Violet just smiled sweetly. "Look further, my dear."

Digging down beneath more paper, Brent came up with figures of gunboats.

"How do you like that?" Violet asked triumphantly. "You see, at last we recognize the navy in chess. Here you see these gray ones are like the *Virginia,* or *Merrimac,* and the blue ones are like the *Monitor.*"

Brent looked at Violet, his eyes sparkling with excitement. "Fantastic! What do they do?"

Violet handed him some folded papers. "Here, I've written down the rules, but I can say that the gunboats have to stay outside that red line that runs all around, and they can move in any direction in a straight line, and they may capture any piece on the third square away, in any direction."

"Fantastic!" repeated Brent. "I'm ready to play, so long as you let me have the gray side. Maybe I can blast those Yankees out of the water yet!"

"Ho, Brent!" chuckled Gilbert, "I'll take the blue side, but I don't know much about boats."

This brought a trickle of awkward but good-natured laughter from the others.

"Good! We'll play later," responded Violet, happy that Brent liked her gift for him.

"And I'll take on the winner," the elder Sutler spoke up.

"And I the loser, after you play," chortled Andrew Thompson.

"Later, we'll have a real tournament for anyone who wants to play," said Violet.

Just then J.J. reached up to grab a handful of figures, saying that he wanted to play with the toys since Daddy wasn't. Brent caught his arm quickly and said, "No, son, these aren't like your wooden soldiers or sister's dolls. This is a grown-up game, and you must not—ever—touch these wooden figures. We wouldn't want to lose or break any of the figures. Then we couldn't play this game any longer."

"But, Daddy, I won't lose or break them. I promise to take good care of them. I want to line them up with my old soldiers by the fireplace."

"I'm sorry, son, you must leave these alone. Surely with all the things that Santa Claus brought and all your other gifts there is plenty for you to play with, and, maybe later, when Jarvis has time, he can carve some flags and boats for you. But as for these, you must not touch, understand?" he said firmly.

"Yes, sir," replied J.J. meekly.

Now it was Brent's turn to go into action. He handed a ball of twine to each Bonnie Anne and J.J. "This present is from your mother and me. Now, you see how this twine leads out to the hall? First, get on your coats and hats, and then follow the twine to see where it leads to. Wind the twine into a ball as you go along."

Evelina, previously alerted, already was there with their coats and hats. Dancing with excitement, they put on their wraps and began following the string. J.J. soon gave up trying to wind the string and just bounded along its course out the back door, pulling the string up in small bunches. Bonnie Anne was close behind. When they got outside they looked up and saw Fabian and Aaron, each holding a fully saddled pony.

"Oh, Daddy! Oh, Mommy! A pony! Which is my pony?" cried Bonnie Anne who had stopped in surprise and delight.

J.J. said nothing. He just kept moving along his string and then, with Fabian's help, jumped up on the pony to which his string led. "This is mine!" he shouted to everyone.

Bonnie Anne saw that her string led to the other pony, and she quickly ran over to it, petting him lovingly. Aaron helped her up and into the saddle. "This is mine!" she shouted, copying her brother. "Oh, thank you, Daddy, thank you, Mommy!"

"Thank you, Daddy, thank you, Mommy!" echoed J.J. And then he added, "It's Christmas Day, and I'm going to name mine after one of Santa's reindeer!"

"Yes! Let's call them Donner and Blitzen," suggested Bonnie Anne. "I'll call mine Donner, and—"

"No! I want to call *my* pony Donner!" said J.J., suddenly becoming stubborn with his older sister.

"No, you can't, I thought of it first," said Bonnie Anne, shaking her head vehemently.

"But I thought of naming them after Santa's reindeer first!" argued J.J.

"No! *My* pony is named Donner," insisted Bonnie Anne.

Violet could see that she had better intervene before a real argument and possibly tears might blight their Christmas Day. "J.J., why don't you call your pony after another reindeer. What about Comet...or Cupid...or Vixen—"

J.J. felt he had to assert himself. "No! I'll call *my* pony, Blitzen!" And without realizing it, he had resolved the argument.

"Fine," she said weakly, "Blitzen it is." She felt Brent beside her, shaking with silent laughter. She shook her head and said resignedly, "Children!"

"Can be so much fun," finished Brent, now unable to control his laughter.

Everyone had followed the children out the back door and stood on the porch and watched them. They were all chuckling at the feuding, and at its resolution.

Fabian and Aaron led each of the ponies for several turns around the yard. Neither child wanted to dismount when their father called to them that they had ridden enough for now and to come back into the parlor. Reluctantly they told their ponies goodbye and promised to come back and ride them that afternoon.

After everyone had resettled in the parlor, Brent, with a twinkle in his eye, handed Violet one last box.

Filled with curiosity, she opened it to find a new, unused horseshoe. Puzzled, she asked, "For goodness sake, what am I supposed to do with this, wrap it around your neck?"

"Hold your horses," Brent laughed. "Put on your cape and come with me."

"Don't tell me there's another pony out there," she laughed.

"No, there's no pony out there. Just come along," he instructed her.

Violet followed Brent out the back door, and then they went on out to the carriage house. As Brent opened the door and they came to the first box stall, Violet glanced through the open upper half of the Dutch door. A beautiful sorrel horse threw up his head and softly whinnied, as if in greeting.

"Oh, Brent, what a *beautiful* horse! Is he mine?" she burst out, stroking the horse on his forehead. The horse softly whinnied again, acknowledging her attention.

"He's yours, my Darling, all yours, for a Merry Christmas."

Violet held out her hand. The horse nuzzled her palm and then threw up his head proudly. He lowered his head and allowed her to stroke his white-starred face again. His sorrel coat shone like Chinese silk. Its luxurious well-combed mane and tail were of slightly lighter shade than the coat, and glancing down, Violet could see that all four of his legs had white boots.

"Brent Sutler! What are you trying to do? To pass off a weak-legged horse on me?"

"What are you talking about?"

"With a mock frown on her face, Violet said, "Don't try to fool me. I know that old ditty–*one white foot, buy him; two white feet–try him; three white feet–trouble all your life; four white feet, give him to your wife.*"

"Oh, Honey, don't be ridiculous, but I must confess I used that argument to get the price way down. You know that's just nonsense, don't you?"

Violet laughed, "Of course. Oh, Brent, he's the most beautiful horse I've ever seen. He looks like a real thoroughbred–so sleek and supple. Tell me, do I ride him or drive him? Surely, he's for riding?"

"He's not a thoroughbred; he's a pacer. And you can ride him or drive him, but he is best as a racer, hitched to a sulky."

"To a sulky? He's a race horse?"

"Certainly, Darling, and he's all yours."

"Why, Brent Sutler, you got this horse as much for you as for me!"

"Well, I thought I might challenge Frank Moses to a race; bet I could make a thousand dollars in a hurry. And you needed a decent horse," he ended lamely.

"What? With my horse? Never! Ha, this is pretty good. My kids give me a puppy dog that they want, and my husband gives me a race horse that he wants!"

"I knew you would like him," Brent said.

Violet took a deep breath. After all, it was Christmas. She went on, "Please enlighten me, what is a pacer?"

"Honey, he's a horse that paces."

"Well, of course, a pacer horse paces. I know that, for goodness sake."

"Well...of course. Now you know a trotter moves his left front leg and right back leg forward together; he goes along on the diagonal. His left front and left hind legs are extended, far apart, while his two right legs are coming together."

"Yes, I've noticed that, Brent."

"Well, the pacer is a side-wheeler. He puts both left legs forward at the same time and then both right legs."

"Oh."

"Of course, and this gives him a rocking motion. If you are standing in front of him you can see he swings from side to side. When you ride him you will find it a very easy ride, like sitting in a rocking chair, doesn't have the jolt of a trot. In racing, he is usually faster than a trotter."

"I see."

"Yes, and when you ride him, let him pace, don't go into a gallop because he is not as good at that, and it may ruin him for pacing."

"I think you mean for racing."

"Of course, but really, Violet, you'll find it a delight to ride a pacer on your tours around the plantation. I know what I'm talking about, honey."

"I'm sure I will, and I'm sure you do," answered Violet, somewhat tartly. Then she opened up and threw her arms around her husband's neck. "Oh, Brent, this is a wonderful, beautiful horse, and I love him already. I really do. I just wish I could go for a ride right now, but I'll wait until this afternoon." She stopped to catch her breath and then asked in wonder, "But Brent, Darling, where did you find him? How did you get him here without my knowing about it? Oh, you *are* a rascal!"

"Honey, I got him in Camden and brought him in on the train last night with the children's ponies that we picked out. You knew about the ponies, of course, but I had to keep the horse a secret from you. Lordy, but I was afraid you'd want to come out to the stable last night to take another look at the ponies after they arrived. Thank heavens you were too busy with all our company and the Christmas Eve doings. Whew!" He wiped his forehead in mock dismay.

"Well I think you are wonderful. I know they have lots of good horses around Camden, and to tell the truth, it did cross my mind to come out and see the ponies, but then it was time to do the tree, and then we had to read to the children and get them to bed, and take care of our guests, and then Charlotte and Susan and I got to talking, and I never did get out."

"I'm glad of that!"

"What's his name?"

"That's for you to decide."

"Any suggestions?" asked Violet, her mind already at work on names.

"Well, the great progenitor of harness race horses was Messenger. What about that?"

"Mm, Messenger," she said thoughtfully. "Oh, I have it, how about the Greek god who was the messenger for the other gods, Hermes."

"Hermes...sounds good!"

"Or I could take the Roman equivalent, Mercury. How about that?"

"Sounds even better."

"No, on second thought I think I'll stick with Hermes."

"Of course."

She grabbed Brent's hand and said, "Come on, let's go back into the house."

Rejoining the others, Violet explained in excited detail all about her new pacing horse which she was sure Brent wanted to use as a racer. They wanted to go right out and see it, but Violet suggested that the few remaining presents be opened first.

The last gift to be unwrapped was Brent's present from the two children. They wanted to run out and see Mommy's new horse, but they also wanted to wait and watch Daddy open their present to him. They hadn't even been able to tell their mother what it was. The look on Brent's face was worth a thousand words as he held up for all to see—a new leather collar for the puppy. Amidst the howls of laughter, he commented, "Well, thank you both, very much. Now tell me, is this for me to put on the new puppy, or am I to wear it for your mother to lead me around with?"

"Oh, Brent!" giggled Violet. Now she understood why the kids wouldn't tell her what they were giving their father. The puppy had to be a surprise for her, so of course she couldn't know about the collar.

She suggested that everyone have a rest and freshen up. The Friersons were expected at one-thirty, and Christmas dinner would be served at two o'clock.

End pieces had been added to the dining table to increase its size. The children insisted that they be allowed to eat at their new table, so the small table and two chairs were brought in and set in a corner of the dining room. Violet was receptive to this suggestion because she knew that they were still too excited and full of sweets to eat very much, and they soon would want to return to the parlor to play with their toys, or go out to pet their ponies. This also provided more elbow room for the thirteen adults seated at the large table.

Eyes brightened in anticipation as Aunt Beuluh and Ellie brought in the first course of chilled grapefruit halves, sweetened with crushed cherry juice and raw sugar. This was a very special treat for the Sutlers and their guests, as they had not seen grapefruit for some years.

Charlotte took a spoonful of grapefruit, savoring the taste. She looked all around the dining room, and applauded the decorations. Looking at the centerpiece, she said, "It wouldn't be Christmas without that decorative little tree of apples and twigs of boxwood stuck in between the fruit, and where on earth did you find the pineapple sitting on top? Oh, I know, don't tell me, Brent got it for you."

Violet nodded, but before she could say anything Susan burst forth, "And it wouldn't be Christmas without Mama's ball of red and green velvet ribbons hanging from the chandelier."

"Yes," added Catherine Lee, "and don't forget that your mother's father gave her that beautiful brass chandelier after she and your father were married and she left Virginia to come live here in South Carolina. I'm sure your mother has told you that it was designed by a Williamsburg silversmith for the Lee family and had been in the family for over a hundred years. Your grandfather said he wanted Rosemary to have a piece of the family's and a piece of Virginia to take with her to her new home, so he had it taken down from our dining room on our plantation near Williamsburg. Frankly I thought it was a marvelous gesture."

"Yes, Grandmama," said Susan as she smiled lovingly at her grandmother. "Mama would mention this every Christmas when we decorated the house, and she unpacked that ball to hang from the chandelier. That story is now part of our tradition each year."

Jarvis and Aaron removed the grapefruit plates, as Aunt Beuluh and Ellie set small bowls of creamed broccoli and cheese broth at each place. A delicious aroma arose from the steaming soup. Again eyes brightened in anticipation.

Violet glanced over at the children, who were beginning to wiggle a bit, although they had been well-behaved and not interrupted the adults' conversation. She called to them, "What shall we name the little puppy?"

"Just call him Little Puppy," said Bonnie Anne matter of factly.

Violet's forehead creased with thought. "Well...that would be all right for now, Bonnie Anne, but we have to think how Little Puppy will sound when he gets big, and he *will* grow into a big dog, you know."

"Oh, I didn't think of that, Mommy," replied Bonnie Anne.

"How about William?" J.J. suggested.

"Oh, I don't know," hedged his mother.

"Well, then, Philip?"

"Do you think those names sound like a dog?" broke in Brent.

"No, I think a wolf sounds more like a dog," interjected Susan with a laugh. Then, affecting a serious attitude, she winked at Brent and said, "How about Commodore?"

Charlotte had to enter the foray. "Major might be a good name, Major Sutler, just like Daddy—Major Storm."

Violet wouldn't be left out. "I think he should have a promotion. Call him Colonel."

Nobody said anything for a moment, but all eyes turned to Brent as if seeing his affirmation. "Well, I'll tell you," he said, "he can represent both the army and the navy if you name him Captain—of course a captain in the navy is of much higher rank than a captain in the army."

"Captain's a good name," agreed Leland. Gilbert nodded his concurrence.

"No!" exclaimed the children together.

Bonnie Anne looked at J.J., and then said, "A king is the highest of all."

"Yes, and a king is the boss of everybody, and our puppy is the most beautiful and the smartest and the best dog in the whole world—" J.J. said.

"I thought he was *my* puppy. Didn't you give him to me for Christmas?" teased Violet, and she couldn't keep herself from adding, "I think I'll call him Queen."

"Mommy! You can't call him that!"

"Why not?"

Bonnie Anne and J.J. looked at one another again. J.J. explained patiently, "Mommy, queens are girls, and the puppy is a boy dog."

"Oh..." was all Violet could muster as everyone broke into guffaws of laughter.

When things had quieted down, the children who had been whispering to one another, turned toward their mother. Very seriously Bonnie Anne told Violet, "Mommy, we did give him to you for a Christmas present, and you chose the name of Queen, but because the little puppy is a boy he'll have to be called King."

"Well, how about this: in Latin, which was the language of the ancient Romans who were famous warriors, the word for king was Rex. How about that name, Rex?"

"Rex, for a king; that's good, Mommy," As he called the little dog, Bonnie Anne chimed in, too, "Here, Rex; here, Rex!" And the selection of a name for the new puppy was settled agreeably.

Jarvis and Aaron came in to remove the soup bowls. Uncle Job brought in a succulent looking roasted goose and set it on the table in front of Brent. Brent looked at the large goose and then gave a big sigh as Jarvis returned with a platter of sliced goose that Mammy had prepared in the kitchen. For this number of guests she had cooked two geese and had sliced one so that all could be served more quickly. Brent would slice the other for second helpings.

Everyone complimented the food, and one after the other sent messages to Mammy and the others, or commented personally on the delicious cuisine when they came into the room for one task or another.

For a few minutes all ate in silence, savoring the food. Then Isabel Sutler looked at Violet and asked, "Weren't the children thrilled with their ponies? I'm sure this will give both of them a chance to learn to be good riders."

Always a little listener to the conversation of grown-ups, J.J. spoke up, "Grandma, I already ride with Mommy to open the gates, and sometimes I ride the plow horse all by myself."

"Well then, you have a good start, J.J.," smiled Isabel.

Bonnie Anne had to be included. "Sometimes Daddy puts me up on old Jeb and lets me ride all by myself."

"Ah, he holds the reins, and Jeb just walks around and around while you sit on him," her brother had to explain, a bit derisively.

Violet could see that to avoid an argument she had better enter the discussion. In an encouraging tone she said, "Never mind, you both will soon be riding all by yourselves, now that you each have your own pony."

"Betcha I'll be a better rider and will ride faster than Bonnie Anne," J.J. taunted his sister.

"No, you won't either! I'm the oldest, and I'll be the best rider!" Bonnie Anne returned.

"*All right,* that enough!" called Brent. "I can see that you've eaten what you can. Now why don't you go back into the parlor and play with your Christmas things."

That was all they needed to escape to their toys. They were gone almost instantly, dropping their napkins on the way, which Ellie patiently picked up.

Just then, dessert was brought in—a huge, flaming, English plum pudding with rum sauce, served amidst oohs and aahs as Jarvis held it high above his head with one arm and circled the table three times for good luck. He set it upon the sideboard, and served the helpings as Aunt Beuluh sliced the pudding and Ellie poured more of the sauce over the slices. Aaron served the champagne.

Violet signaled Evelina to take the children up for their naps, and the conversation continued in a different vein.

Looking at Susan, Grandmama Lee inquired, "Susan, has the Yankee occupation ended for sure in Mississippi?"

"Yes, ma'am, I'm glad to say," answered Susan, "but Vicksburg still carries scars of the siege, and the state is a long way from total recovery."

Catherine Lee continued, "Even though the occupation continues here in South Carolina, it seems to me you all have been doing very well here on this beautiful plantation, and now you have your new town house."

"Yes, we have done all right," responded Brent, "but it is not every man who has a wife who can manage a plantation with a substantial annual profit."

"With the help of an expert assistant in buying and marketing," Violet broke in, "and I might add, what woman has a man who can make a good profit at being a sailor, as a merchant, as a railroad man, and as a politician."

"And I must say with the help of my outstanding first mate," added Brent, smiling fondly at Violet. He lifted his glass of champagne in her direction.

"What do you mean, *first* mate," Violet came back, "I hope first and *only* mate!" This brought more laughter around the table.

"I must say that we are thankful for cotton, too, "said Charlotte. "The mill is doing well, outdoing the New Englanders, if you ask me."

Susan spoke up, "And at least so far I have a husband who is doing well on the railroad." She gave Gilbert a big smile.

After assuring that everyone who wished it had tea or coffee, Violet remarked, "We all have been fortunate—"

"Thank goodness it is better than when we were pulling the plow and having our Starvation Party," announced Susan, frowning at the memory of those hard times.

Violet continued, "But you know there are many people in this state who are in a bad way—actually suffering."

"And there are going to be a lot more who are going to be suffering if we don't get out from under our Carpetbagger-Scalawag state government," added John Frierson.

"Yes, true, only the good Lord knows what we may still be in for," said Brent's father, worriedly turning his glass around and around in his hand.

Brent went on, "Goodness knows how long we'll be able to hold on to what we have regained so long as we have the continuing spiraling of the state debt and constant increases in taxes, and the intimidation of black militia, and the unchecked crime—marauders roaming country roads and attacking farms as well as city streets and businesses and homes."

Thoughtfully Violet spoke again, "I am thankful we can have a holiday together like this. In times like these I think it more important than ever that we try to hold on to some of the old values and traditions."

Andrew Thompson nodded his agreement. "Some people now are saying the old South is gone, gone beyond our reach. Some of them say, 'The old South is not what it used to be, and never was!'"

"Nonsense!" Violet shot back. "As Daddy used to say, without a past there can be no meaningful future."

"Of course not!" Leland promptly agreed.

"Some people can be awfully stupid—the old South gone, indeed!" put in Susan angrily.

Violet continued, "The occupation goes on and on, and as Victor Hugo said, we wonder if the future ever will come, so we have got to do our best to live a normal life now—to try to enjoy a festive occasion sometimes—to enjoy a concert, a play, a good book. We just can't put all those things aside indefinitely. In times like these you are driven all the more to enjoy the moment lest it be snatched away from you altogether."

Leland was tapping his fork lightly on his dessert plate as he thought. With an apparent depth of feeling he said, "Yes, yes, it's like during the War, in the Army. You felt that you had to make the most of every moment, for there might not be many more."

Gilbert broke in, "Yes, I know what you mean. When you received something special to eat, like a fruitcake from home at Christmas time, or a box of fudge or something, you would feel driven to share it with your buddies and eat it all at once so that we could enjoy it before it was too late, for tomorrow might never come. I might add that some of the men did not even save necessities for future days, and sometimes they were embarrassed to find themselves still alive several days later."

Violet responded, "I'm sure we never can know the intensity of the long-term, day-to-day stress in an army at war, but what you all say fits exactly what we all feel in a way now, in an interminable military occupation."

"And now there is even more foreboding prospects with what I would call a witch-hunt for conspirators against the occupation," Brent said, frowning at the thought. "People are being arrested by the thousand. Just in the last two months, since the first of November, over five hundred indictments have been returned by the Federal Grand Jury in Columbia. In the counties where they have suspended the *habeas corpus*, they don't even have to give a reason for arresting you. Federal marshals may come to your house at any time and drag you away just on some suspicion, or on someone's trumped-up charges."

At that point Violet adjourned the group. Always well organized and punctual, she liked to keep to close schedule. While the others rested or looked around the house or went out to the necessaries or read books in the library, and Charlotte nursed little Lee, Violet and Brent went over to the overseer's house to give Leo and Rachel their special Christmas gifts from the family and to make year-end payments and to give Christmas bonuses and presents to the gardeners, animal hands, and other close in workers. The household servants had received their presents and bonuses that morning.

This year, Violet decided to make the payments to the field hands down at the church/school building, near their quarters. This would give her a chance to try out her new horse and see how it felt to ride a pacer. Brent went along on Jeb.

The worker's payments—substantially larger than last year's—set off a spell of singing and dancing to the accompaniment of the *Little Brown Jugs.* The animals would need to be taken care of, but except for those chores, everyone would have Christmas week off as usual.

Violet and Brent returned to the house, with Brent cautioning Violet to keep Hermes pacing and not to let him break into a gallop. Just as Brent had said, she found riding the pacer a comfortable experience, and she literally fell in love with her new horse.

After a light supper in the dining room, everyone gathered in the parlor to hear Brent's reading of an abridgement of Dickens' *A Christmas Carol.* At seven-thirty, Mammy had Jarvis bring in a wassail bowl filled with hot spiced cider, a bowl of eggnog, and plates of left over English plum pudding and Carolina fruitcake.

At eight o'clock, there was a noise of people entering the outside door of the ballroom and a few minutes later Violet asked everyone to go into the ballroom. She sent Jarvis to fetch the house servants and Aaron out to get Leo and Rachel and Fabian to join them.

In the ballroom enough chairs had been set in rows to accommodate everyone—family, guests, and servants. Candles, sheltered by hurricane globes, along all the walls and a bright fire in the huge fireplace at the far end of the room gave a soft light that created a certain coziness in spite of the large size of the room. In the orchestra balcony, above the fireplace, sat the *Little Brown Jugs.*

As soon as everyone was in place, the boys, under the leadership of their cornetist, Thomas, began playing. They played a concert of their old favorites—*Little Brown Jug, Aura Lee, Listen to the Mocking Bird,* and *Oh, Susanna,* first in traditional rhythm, and then in their new syncopated rhythm with turns at individual improvisation. Everyone was enthusiastic at what they heard. The visitors who had not heard them before were spellbound in wonder at the talent of these boys.

After a half-hour or so of that special concert, Violet moved to the big square piano in the far corner of the room. With the *Little Brown Jugs* backing her up, she played a few Christmas carols. Then she paused. She asked Charlotte and Susan to come up front. Handing Charlotte a violin and Susan a flute, she asked them to join her for old times sake. They played *Greensleeves* as though they had been rehearsing it for a week—which they hadn't.

Then Violet asked everyone to sing as they and the *Little Brown Jugs* played softly a series of traditional Christmas carols—*What Child is This?* to the tune of *Greensleeves; O Come, All Ye Faithful* or *Adeste Fideles,* which Violet, Charlotte, and Susan sang in Latin; *Angels We Have Heard on High,* of which Isabel Sutler sang a verse in French; *Hark! The Herald Angels Sing,* and *Joy to the World.* The black folks led out with gusto as everyone joined in all known verses of their favorite Christmas spiritual, *Go Tell It on the Mountain.*

Finally Violet arose and said, "Now I want us to learn a beautiful new Christmas song. It's called *Silent Night, Holy Night.* It's not really new. It was written over fifty years ago, I guess, especially for a midnight mass on a Christmas Eve in a little village church near Salzburg, Austria. Then it was lost for some time, and only several years later was published in German. Some German folk singers are said to have introduced it in New York in the 1840's, but only recently it has become available to us in English. It was translated into English during the War by an Episcopal priest, the Reverend John Freeman Young. I think he is now the Episcopal bishop of Florida. Anyway, I found this in Columbia a few weeks ago and thought we would just have to learn it. I and my little elves have written copies of the words for everybody." Violet and the children passed the copies around.

It was evident that Violet had been rehearsing this one. Everyone nodded and smiled at the beautiful melody. It was an instant favorite.

Everyone joined in the singing with scarcely a flaw, and the *Little Brown Jugs* picked it up softly in the background. Then Violet explained, "Now we are going to do something special with the third verse. Bonnie Anne and J.J. have boxes of candles near the door at the back. They'll give everybody a candle. Take it, and your word sheet, and we'll all stand in a circle around the room—everybody. Jarvis and Aaron will snuff out all the room candles. Then I'll light a taper from the fireplace and with that, light the person's candle on either side of me. Then each person will pass the light on to the next while I go back to the piano and set my taper in a holder there.

Everyone did as Violet instructed. She continued playing *Silent Night* as the candle flames went around the room. When the circle was complete, she said, "Let's all sing the third verse, and then while we're singing it a second time, everybody move around counterclockwise, following Brent back there, to file out. When you reach the door, blow your candle out and return it to the box there, and go on out."

Everyone entered into the spirit of the occasion as they sang together by the light of their candles:

Silent Night! Holy night!
Son of God, love's pure light,
Radiant beams from Thy holy face,
With the dawn of redeeming grace,
Jesus, Lord, at Thy birth,
Jesus, Lord, at Thy birth.

Repeating the verse, they filed out, while Violet and the *Little Brown Jugs* continued playing softly until the last candle was out.

Chapter 49

Conspiracy Charges

1871-1872

The next afternoon in the library, Violet had two tables set up for cards and two for chess–the old chess set brought in from the office, and the new set she gave Brent for Christmas. Violet challenged Brent on the new set, and as everyone else watched she beat him quickly in two games, with checkmate in five moves in the first game and eight moves in the second. She had an advantage because she knew the rules and he did not. As soon as he got the hang of it he did better than hold his own. Then, while others went to the card tables, Violet took turns with each one to teach them the rules of her new version of chess.

At the card tables the favorite game was whist. Violet promised that on Friday they would have a round-robin tournament both at whist and at chess. Meanwhile everyone could be practicing. Phoebe surprised everybody with her skill at whist.

During a pause, Catherine Lee put down the book she was reading and asked Violet, "Have you seen a book called *Miss Ravenel's Conversion from Secession to Loyalty* written by an administrator in the Freedmen's Bureau by the name of John DeForest?"

"No, I don't believe I have," answered Violet, "sounds interesting–and also a little suspect."

"Well," Grandmama went on, "it's a novel that details, as the author puts it, the 'filthy, lecherous, half-civilized life' of the poor whites in the South."

Violet quickly responded, "Well, I am glad to see that someone is paying some attention to the po' buckras, and most of all by someone in the Freedman's Bureau. You know the po' buckras have a difficult time. As Daddy used to explain, they have nobody to guarantee food and a roof over their heads, nobody to look after them, or give them medical attention. And you know, they sense a competition with the blacks for land and for jobs. I'm afraid that is the source of a lot of the racial prejudice and tension nowadays."

"Quite right," agreed Violet's grandmother.

On Wednesday morning the men went rabbit hunting with indifferent success. To the chagrin of Brent and the others, Gilbert was most successful. All together they did bring in enough for Mammy to make Brunswick stew in the big iron kettle that hung in the kitchen fireplace.

On Thursday morning the men had greater success at hunting partridges, which Gilbert insisted were the same bird that they called the bobwhite quail in Indiana. Again Gilbert demonstrated his marksmanship and brought in about half of the bag. This time there were enough for a festive dinner featuring individual roasted partridges stuffed with cornbread.

On each afternoon Violet and Brent spent time with the children, teaching them how to ride their ponies, and playing with their new toys. Susan joined in playing the more physical games of Hide and Seek, and Who Has the Pebble, and Roll the Hoop—as she used to do when she still lived at Fair Oaks. When she wasn't with J.J. and his sister, she was holding or rocking and singing to little Lee.

Friday was the day for the round-robin whist and chess tournaments. Violet invited the Friersons to participate. John had business in Sumter that would not wait, but he did bring Sarah over, and she agreed to be Catherine Lee's partner in whist and to learn the new version of chess.

Violet had worked out intricate schedules so that each pair of whist partners would play all the others and each person would play all the others in chess. This meant that two people would be free at any given time to rest or have a bite to eat or whatever.

A cold, all-day rain had set in, but nobody cared. There were warm fires inside and everyone was excited about the games.

Play began at nine o'clock and continued all day, with a break for coffee at eleven, for dinner at one-thirty, for tea at four, and finishing just in time for supper at seven. The children spent much of the day at playing with their toys in the hall where they got plenty of attention from people coming and going from and to the library, and, of course Evelina was keeping an eye on them at all times.

Each pair of partners won some hands at whist, but Phoebe and her father emerged as undisputed champions.

With ten victories each at the new chess, Violet and Brent met for the final contest as the others gathered around. Their first game went for twenty minutes and ended in stalemate. They decided to let it go at that.

On Saturday afternoon, Susan and Gilbert had to leave, for Gilbert had to be back at work on the railroad at Vicksburg on Tuesday. Brent used his telegraph to schedule their return trip so that they could take the train to Columbia from in front of the house. Everyone, including the Friersons who had driven over for this occasion, accompanied them down the lane and to the tracks to see them off. All eyes were moist at the thought that it might be some time before Susan and Gilbert could return for another visit. Indeed, tears were streaming down the cheeks of the three sisters who had become so close through the years. Gilbert reassured everyone that they would be back just as soon as he could get the time off for another trip, and in the meantime, everybody was invited to come visit them in Mississippi. "My father always said, 'Turn about is fair play,' and it is, you know. We really want you to come visit us."

"Oh, yes, do!" sniffed Susan, giving everybody one last hug and then stepping up into the train to join Gilbert. They all waved vigorously until the train was out of sight.

At Fair Oaks they took only slight notice of New Year's. For some, it had become too much of a Negro holiday in celebration of emancipation; others never had paid much attention to it. No one stayed up past midnight on Sunday night to see in the year 1872. On that New Year's Monday, Brent's parents and Phoebe returned to Charleston, and Charlotte and Leland and baby Lee returned to Columbia.

Grandmama Lee agreed to stay on for a while to be with Violet and Brent and the children for a couple of weeks in their town house in Columbia, which she had not yet seen.

Uncle Job and Aunt Beulah drove back to Columbia on Tuesday. They took the new puppy, Rex, with them in the carriage. Violet and Brent, and the children and Catherine Lee, followed by train two days later to be there in good time for the resumption of the legislative session and for the school term.

Grandmama Lee was as enthusiastic about the beautifully appointed town house as she had been about the plantation. She went from room to room admiring the decorations and furnishings. Violet introduced her to Cora and Raymond Martin, explaining that they were the couple who helped Aunt Beulah and Uncle Job. Violet complimented the young couple on the care they had given the house during the absence of the family. They beamed with pleasure and thanked Violet for the generous gifts they had received for Christmas.

Catherine Lee settled down to enjoy her days in the neatly restored capital of South Carolina. She liked Columbia very much, although she was partial to Richmond, the capital of her own Virginia, but both cities had suffered much destruction during the War, from occupation and from fire. The people were much alike, resilient and strong, courteous and thoughtful of one another, and with a sense of appreciation for historic values and allusions and learning and culture—except for the Carpetbaggers and Scalawags, of course.

The Christmas cheer and calm were holding until late on Friday afternoon. Shortly after Brent had come in from his warehouse office and he had just taken a chair in the parlor to read the daily newspaper, a knock came at the door. When Uncle Job opened the door a strange man asked for "Mr. Sutler." Uncle Job invited him in and asked him to wait in the entry way while he notified Mr. Sutler that he had a guest.

Brent asked Job to show the man into the parlor. As the man entered the room, Brent rose from his chair and said cordially, "I'm Brent Sutler. What can I do for you?"

"I'm a United States Marshal, Mr. Sutler," the stranger informed him. "I'm afraid I must place you under arrest and ask you to come with me."

Violet, who had overheard the man, came running into the room. "What is this all about?" she demanded, going over to stand by Brent.

Brent remained calm although he was plainly annoyed. "On what charges?"

"For conspiracy to obstruct the execution of Federal laws in guaranteeing the civil rights of freedmen and for defrauding the Federal government."

"Sir, I have no idea of what you are talking about," protested Brent, "and I don't intend to go anywhere with you."

"You clear on out of our house and be about your own business!" Violet cried out.

In the background, Grandmama Lee, practically beside herself, was pacing the floor in continuous circles.

"Haven't you heard of legislative immunity?" asked Brent, still struggling to maintain his calmness.

"State legislative immunity has nothing to do with a Federal offense," replied the man haughtily.

"The hell it doesn't!" Brent shot back, now showing his anger.

"I'm afraid I must insist," the man said coldly. "Will it be with handcuffs or without?"

Brent turned to Violet. "Darling, don't worry," he reassured her, "I'll go down and see what this is all about, and you may be certain that I'll be home shortly." He looked at the man, his eyes steely with controlled anger. "I'll wear no handcuffs. You'll soon see that this is all a grievous mistake on your part."

Brent and the man were no more than out the door and down the steps when Violet called to Uncle Job to harness the horse and buggy. Taking Uncle Job with her, she rapidly took out after the carriage that carried her husband. She followed them to the Federal Court House where she jumped out and, leaving the horse in Uncle Job's care, ran into the building.

Finding Brent in a room bristling with activity, she asked, "What is it, Brent?"

"This is simply to be a hearing before the grand jury which will decide whether an indictment should be returned. They'll let me go if I can post two thousand dollars bond and promise to meet with the grand jury on Monday."

Without even answering, Violet scurried around to the clerk's office and posted the bond. Returning to Brent, she said, "Come on, Honey, we'll drive you home." Brent grabbed his hat and was relieved to get out of there.

As they drove home, Violet asked, "This is crazy, just crazy. What could they possibly bring up?"

"Violet, I have no idea, absolutely no idea at all. As you said, this is just crazy. It's probably another scheme of that damned Moses to weaken opposition in the legislature."

"Shouldn't we get a lawyer to handle your case on Monday? Do you want to telegraph Victor Shelby in Sumter?"

Brent shook his head, answering disgustedly, "The accused is not allowed to have a lawyer at a grand jury hearing, and the proceedings are strictly confidential, and no visitors."

"Oh, Brent, can't I be there? You know I have to be there with you."

"Afraid not, Darling. Not allowed."

On Monday morning Brent reported to the federal grand jury as directed. Other than the twenty-four man grand jury, about half black and half white, the judge, prosecutor, and marshal, the only persons present were Blake Farley and Edward Jones.

Addressing Brent, the judge, a Carpetbag appointee, said, "Mr. Sutler, you have been accused of conspiring to interfere with the civil rights of freedmen and you have been accused of defrauding the Federal government."

The prosecutor, a John Dickey, bore down on Brent and engaged him in an exchange that went as follows:

Prosecutor: Mr. Sutler, are you now or have you ever been a member of the Ku Klux Klan?
Brent: No, sir.
Prosecutor: Have you ever belonged to the so-called Order of the White Camellia?
Brent: No, sir.
Prosecutor: Do you belong to any organization that has for one of its purposes the influencing of Negro voters?
Brent: Yes, sir.
Prosecutor: And what is that?
Brent: The Democratic Party! But I'm afraid it has not been as effective in that regard as the so-called Republican Party.

Even the prosecutor and judge had to laugh briefly at this answer.

Prosecutor: Now, as to the first charge. Is it true that you attacked two Negroes with a deadly weapon on the Sumter-Stateburg road on the night of November 8, 1868?
Brent: No, it is not.
Prosecutor: Would you tell the court what happened?
Brent: I returned home from Columbia that night to find that my wife had been attacked by two Negro intruders, attacked right in our own house, and they had attempted to rob her; one had even torn her dress from her shoulders, and one can only speculate what he had in mind to do with her.
Prosecutor: Was she physically hurt?
Brent: Thank God, our overseer appeared before any further harm was done, and he threw the two men out of the house. No, she was not seriously hurt, that is, physically.
Prosecutor: Was anything stolen?
Brent: No, as I said, our black overseer heard her screaming and threw the men out before they could do anything else.
Prosecutor: And then what?
Brent: As soon as I got home and found out what happened, I rode out to try to apprehend them.
Prosecutor: And did you apprehend them?
Brent: No.
Prosecutor: Were you carrying a firearm?
Brent: Yes, a revolver.
Prosecutor: Did you fire it?
Brent: Yes, into the air.
Prosecutor: Why?

Brent: In the hope of adding to their fright to discourage their coming back.

Prosecutor: And now, what about the night of October 30, 1868. Did you and a group of co-conspirators attack and intimidate a group of Negroes on the Sumter-Stateburg road?

Brent (smiling sarcastically): It was no attack. It was more of a Halloween hig jinks

Prosecutor: What was the purpose?

Brent: To frighten thieves from stealing cotton out of our field.

Prosecutor: Stealing cotton?

Brent: Yes, stealing our cotton.

Prosecutor: Who were your co-conspirators in this activity?

Brent (smiling sarcastically): Co-conspirators?—My wife, her two younger sisters, our black overseer, black cotton foreman, and black driver.

Prosecutor: Exactly what did you do?

Brent: We all put on Halloween ghostly costumes, and set up Jack-o-Lanterns with lighted candles in them, to frighten the thieves out of the field.

Then the judge asked if Brent had any further comments or any questions.

"Yes, your Honor," he replied, "would you please ask Mr. Farley how he came about this so-called information."

Turning toward Blake Farley, the judge asked, "Well, Mr. Farley?"

"They were reported to me by some of my tenants," responded Farley rather lamely.

Brent quickly asked, "Judge, is that not hearsay evidence?"

"I'm afraid it is," answered the judge.

Brent spoke up again, "Your Honor, I think you ought to be investigating whether Mr. Farley has been involved in a conspiracy to steal cotton."

"That would be a state matter," the prosecutor said in an off-handed manner as he returned to the exchange with Brent.

Prosecutor: And now for the second charge. Did you purchase a lot of arms from the State of South Carolina in July 1870?

Brent: I did.

Prosecutor: Did you not realize that all those weapons were federal property?

Brent: Certainly not; they were the property of the state of South Carolina.

Prosecutor: I'm afraid not. When the armies of the United States entered Columbia, they confiscated all firearms.

Brent: But they never retrieved these.

Prosecutor: Makes no difference; *all* firearms were confiscated.

Brent: Then I suggest you check with the adjutant general of this state. All of my dealings were with the Honorable Frank Moses, Jr. Of course I had no idea that I was receiving stolen property.

Prosecutor:	We understand that you purchased a total of six thousand rifles and carbines at a price of $1.75 each. Is that true?
Brent:	It is not. I have receipts that show that I paid $3.50 a piece, or a total of twenty-one thousand dollars. If the state received any less than that, I suggest that you look in the pockets or in the bank accounts of the Honorable Frank Moses, Jr.

A brief silence followed that statement, then the judge again asked Brent if he had any further questions or comments.

"Yes," nodded Brent, "may I know what Mr. Edward Jones is doing here?"

The prosecutor answered, "He provided the information about the purchases and the prices of the weapons."

"Of course," Brent said dryly, "he is an employee of the Honorable Frank Moses, Jr., so this information actually is coming from Mr. Moses. Evidently he is trying to get more money in addition to the share of the legislature's appropriations for new arms for the militia that he already has siphoned off to his own account. And may I explain to you that Mr. Jones, in the pay of Mr. Moses, signed on as a member of my crew for the voyage to the West Indies where I resold the arms to the French. Claiming that his wife was about to have a baby he used my telegraph supposedly to inquire about her condition when in fact he was reporting to Moses' henchmen the time of our departure and our general route so that they could lie in wait and try to pirate the weapons back for Moses, who now realized that with the Franco-Prussian War in progress the weapons might fetch a substantially higher price from either or both of the warring parties. Mr. Edward Jones may be the father of one or more babies, as he claimed, but so far he does not have any wife at all."

Looking rather grim at this, the judge dismissed the two witnesses, asked a marshal to take Brent back to a waiting room, and told the grand jury to go into its deliberations. Less than half an hour later another marshal came back to inform Brent that the grand jury had found insufficient evidence for an indictment, and he was free to go.

On his return home, a worried Violet and Grandmama Lee greeted Brent as though he had been gone for weeks. When he recounted his experience, both women were furious though they were relieved that he had not been incarcerated.

"It's ridiculous, absolutely ridiculous," Catherine Lee kept repeating, as they went into the informal dining area for a cup of tea.

"That Moses and that Farley will stoop to anything for any supposed advantage," said Violet angrily.

"Yes, my Darling, and we're fortunate they didn't get very far this time," Brent commented with a smile, which quickly turned into a frown as he added, "No doubt they'll try something again at another time. I'll have to stay alert, that's for sure."

Quickly finishing her first cup of tea and pouring another, Violet went on apprehensively, "But, Brent, what kind of life is it when you have to live in constant dread that at any moment there may come a knock at the door and some stranger will haul you away for no reason?"

"True, but there is a ray of hope in all this," replied Brent as he finished his second cup, and poured both Grandmama Lee and himself another, along with heavy helpings of milk and sugar.

"What's that, I'd like to know," Violet asked.

"Well, you know a few days ago I told you that over five hundred people had been indicted during November and December?"

"Yes."

"I made a few inquiries. They all have gone to trial in the U.S. Circuit Court over the last several weeks, and a jury made up mostly of black men found only five of them guilty. Only five! Another fifty plead guilty, but that's all. That's all."

"But that *is* wonderful!" exclaimed Catherine Lee.

"Yes, well, I guess that is something," said Violet thoughtfully.

Brent went on, "You see, this means that some black men still are thinking for themselves, in spite of all the efforts of the Carpetbaggers and the Scalawags to manipulate them. I find this most encouraging."

"Yes, thank heavens!" sighed Violet.

Chapter 50

Blue Ridge Scrip

1872

The first order of business for the next week was to get the children back into school to complete the school year. Bonnie Anne, of course, would be returning to the Female Academy, and she looked forward to seeing her little friends that she had met there last year. Violet had assumed that J.J. would go to the Columbia Male Academy for which he would only have to walk across the street and up half a block. However, she had been hearing from Charlotte and others of a school run by a Mr. Barnwell that had a high reputation among all who knew it, and, with Brent's concurrence, she decided that J.J. should try that one. It was only a couple of blocks farther away, over by the Presbyterian Theological Seminary. On clear days, Evelina would walk with the children to school, and then meet them afternoons to walk home with them. On rainy or very chilly days, Uncle Job would take them in the carriage, with Evelina coming along to help keep an eye on them.

J.J. was a little disappointed not to be going to the more imposing academy, diagonally across the street from his house. Violet explained that he probably would be going there later, and that the Academy was mostly for older boys. Anyway, he was too excited to mind very much one way or the other. Last year he had envied his sister going off to school each day, and now that he was older, he would be doing that, too.

With everyone dressed warmly in woolen coats and hats and mittens, and rubber galoshes, Violet and Evelina set out with the children on this first day of school. Each of the pupils carried a dinner bucket that Aunt Beulah had made sure was well stocked. Their first stop was at Mr. Barnwell's school. As they approached the building which was located behind the schoolmaster's house, J.J. blurted out with some accuracy, "Look, Mommy, Mr. *Barn*well's school *looks* like a big barn." He and his sister began giggling.

"Now you two behave," admonished Violet, trying to keep from giggling herself. It did look very much like a barn.

Inside the main door, Charles H. Barnwell greeted them warmly. Then he explained, "Some of the older boys, in the upper classes, serve as monitors to help shepherd the younger lads. Here, Mrs. Sutler, let me introduce the monitor who will be working with your boy."

He called over a tall, slender, fifteen-year-old youth and said, "This is Tommy, or more properly, Thomas Woodrow Wilson. He is an excellent scholar and works well with the boys. His father is a professor at the Theological Seminary."

The Wilson boy had a serious countenance, but he broke into a friendly smile as he accepted Violet's hand, said hello to Evelina, and shook hands with both children. Looking at Bonnie Anne he said, "I wish we could have girl pupils here, too."

Bonnie Anne's blue eyes twinkled with delight, but she simply smiled and curtsied, as she had been taught to do.

With a reassuring smile and a wave, Violet, Evelina, and Bonnie Anne said good-bye to J.J. and went on back outside. J.J. was a little apprehensive about being left behind here, but young Wilson quickly dispelled that feeling as he led J.J. away to show him where to put his dinner bucket and his wraps in the cloakroom. Then he showed J.J. to his desk and gave him a book to look at. J.J. decided that he liked Tommy Wilson very much and maybe this school was going to be all right after all.

At the Female Academy, Bonnie Anne quickly felt the security of familiar surroundings, said good-bye to her mother and Evelina, and soon was chattering with old acquaintances before classes began. Violet could not help but feel a sense of nostalgia and regret that already her little girl was becoming more independent, yet at the same time she took pride in that healthy accomplishment.

Brent spent most of the days during these weeks at the State House, though he managed to spend time at his warehouse office and at the railroad office. His attendance at sessions of the Senate and at legislative committee meetings was excellent. He attended not because he thought he could influence legislation, but in order to keep himself informed. And there was plenty to keep informed about.

One afternoon late that January, Violet left the children in Evelina's care and took her grandmother over to see Charlotte and her family. Brent joined them there for supper. As they all sat around the dining table finishing their meal, Charlotte, more to make conversation than to open an in-depth inquiry, asked him, "Well, Brent, what's new at the legislature these days?"

"Nothing new, just more of the same," he said glumly.

"Meaning what?"

"Meaning more graft and fraud and corruption."

"Oh, how discouraging," said Charlotte, frowning.

"Sure, but it just keeps getting worse. Frankly, before I went to the Senate I had heard a lot about graft and fraud. Now I find that it is far worse than I ever imagined!"

Catherine Lee spoke up, "Couldn't anybody see all this coming and nip it in the bud? You know the old saying, `a stitch in time saves nine'."

Brent sighed and responded regretfully, "Sure, people could see it coming, but what could anyone do against these foreign invaders? It was just like when people knew Sherman was headed for Columbia, but nobody could do anything, not anything, about it."

"What is the latest in the long series of fraudulent activities?" inquired Leland.

Brent thought for a moment and answered, "Actually there have been so many that I hardly know where to begin. I guess one of the biggest just now has to do with the Greenville and Columbia Railroad. I'm not quite sure who all may be involved, but it seems that several of the Carpetbagger and Scalawag officials have formed what is being referred to in the corridors as the Railroad Ring. The ring leader undoubtedly is 'Honest John' Patterson."

"Honest John?" Catherine Lee repeated, naively, "At least it must be a relief that somebody over there is honest."

"No, Grandmother Lee," explained Brent with a smile. "He is called Honest John because he is as dishonest as the day is long. I would not trust him as far as J.J. could throw him."

"Oh, I do declare," was all Catherine Lee could say.

"Who is he, Brent? Where is he from?" asked Andrew Thompson.

"He's a Carpetbagger from Pennsylvania—served in the Pennsylvania legislature. His own brother-in-law is said to have called him a swindler and a cheat, though we should recognize that Honest John did contribute to the Confederate Cause."

"How is that?" asked Violet.

"By stealing the money of the soldiers of an Ohio regiment while he was serving as paymaster."

Catherine Lee gasped.

"But that's terrible!" exclaimed Charlotte.

"Brent, who else is in the ring?" asked Andrew Thompson.

"We can't be sure of who all, of course," Brent responded, "but apparently it includes George Waterman who, as you know, is Governor Scott's brother-in-law and his stalking horse in all this...and the mulatto secretary of state, Cardozo...the land commissioner, C. P. Leslie...Joseph Crews who is chairman of the House committee on railroads...and another representative, Timothy Hurley. You probably remember him, Violet, he was that one whom we overheard in the capitol barroom—the Solons' Saloon as you call it—who was trying to sell votes."

"Yes, I do remember him," nodded Violet.

"And there is a fellow by the name of H.J. Kimpton who serves as their agent in New York, and the Carpetbagger from Massachusetts, Daniel Henry Chamberlain, who is the attorney general."

"Sounds like you have a pretty good line-up," Violet said. "Do you have Pinkerton's working for you?"

"Well, I do have some pretty good eyes and ears in key places," admitted Brent.

"Sounds intriguing," remarked Violet, with an anticipatory grin. "What has this ring been doing?"

Brent lowered his voice before answering Violet. "Some of it is kind of juicy." He looked around to see if any servant was in the room. Still in a low voice that could be heard only by those at the table, Brent continued, "Well then, one of their moves was to get control of the Greenville and Columbia Railroad for a song, and then to cash in on its bonds, all with state support."

"How did they do that?" asked Leland.

"Last year Chamberlain got a bill through the legislature to authorize the sale of stock held by the state in that railroad. The bill was framed as an act to dispose of property belonging to the state that was not in actual use. People thought it was intended to dispose of surplus—granite, marble, and so forth, lying around the State House grounds. Instead, the members of the ring organized what they called a 'sinking fund commission' and proceeded to sell to themselves the state's railroad stock for $2.75 a share—for which the state had paid twenty dollars a share. In the aggregate this made a total difference of $374,000.

"Great Scot!" cried Violet.

"Shocking, absolutely shocking!" exclaimed Grandmother Lee.

"That was not all. That did not yet give them a controlling interest so they appointed ex-Governor Orr and J.P. Reed to go around and buy additional stock from private parties, without telling for whom they were buying it, and they were able to get this additional stock at $1.75 to $2.00 a share—for stock that was supposed to have a par value of $25.00. Now comes the most interesting part: They were not even going to pay these low prices with their own money. The state was going to pay for it. They were going to do it by selling state bonds, the proceeds of which were supposed to be reserved for state purposes!"

"Where did they sell the bonds, Brent?" asked Andrew Thompson.

"Everywhere they could, and at bargain prices of about fifty cents on the dollar. They even have agents in Europe, but the most lucrative bloc was just early this month in New York, so they say. According to my usually reliable sources, members of the ring enticed Governor Scott, who also is probably a member of the ring; anyway they enticed him to New York. They set him up in a room in the St. James hotel there. They brought in a stack of bonds which they could sell for fifty cents on the dollar, but the Governor apparently suffered some pangs of conscience and refused to sign."

"Well, thank goodness for that, anyway," Grandmother Lee declared.

"Oh, but that was not the end," Brent continued. "It is said that the other members of the ring prevailed upon a young lady by the name of Pauline Markham to call upon the Governor in his room—"

"Who is Pauline Markham?" Violet wanted to know.

"That just shows you have not been around," laughed Brent. "She is one of the most famous and beautiful show girls in New York."

"Show Girl? Shocking!" exclaimed Grandmother Lee.

"Yes, Grandmama," grinned Brent, "to be more precise, a burlesque dancer."

"Oh, I do declare, I do declare!" was all that gentle lady could muster.

"Well, to continue with my story, they sent in plenty of wine and spirits, and presumably Miss Markham turned on her wiles and charm. Soon, deliriously happy, the Governor signed and sealed the bonds while the luscious charmer counted and stacked them. For her efforts she got a commission on the bonds. I guess everybody ended up with about $20,000 apiece. Now, of course, they are out after more game."

Then Catherine Lee did speak up, "All this and all the troubles with the so-called reconstruction and the military occupation remind me of a passage of scripture, from Jeremiah, that goes, 'They have healed the wound of my people carelessly, saying 'Peace, peace, when there is no peace.'"

During the next several days Grandmama Lee added a bit of sparkle to the house on Henderson Street. She shamelessly spoiled the children, gently bossed the servants, and lovingly gave free advice to Violet and Brent. Her advice never came in an obnoxious way. Usually it was in the form of some kind of directional wisdom from the sayings of "Pa," or "Granddaddy," her long departed husband and Violet's grandfather—"To plow a straight furrow you must look straight ahead,"—"Trying to change human nature is as futile as trying to plow furrows in the sea,"—"A bright sun blinds one assuredly as does a dark night,"—"Hopelessness in prospects leads to helplessness in action."—"A noise too loud may dull the ability to hear any noise at all; a light too bright may dull the ability to see any light at all."—"Man cannot control the weather, but he can prepare for it."

At the end of the month when Grandmother Catherine Victoria Lee left for her own home in Richmond, Virginia, she left a void in the house that persisted for weeks. Helping to ease the sense of loss was her promise that she would spend next Christmas with all of them, and indeed, would try to come down in the summer to spend a month at Fair Oaks.

On the afternoon of February 5th, the Monday after Grandmama Lee's departure, Violet was in the town house office, monitoring the telegraph and preparing orders for seed and fertilizer for this year's spring planting. She heard the front door open and close with a bang, and the pounding of rapid footsteps. Brent came bounding into the room.

With that characteristic smirk on his face, he paused only long enough to give her a peck on the cheek before waving some papers in front of her and fairly shouting, "Look at this!"

"Brent! What in the world has gotten into you? What is it?"

"The railroad ring is outdoing themselves this time!"

"What are they up to now?" she asked, catching his excitement.

Taking his chair opposite, Brent caught his breath and explained, "Honest John Patterson persuaded some of the representatives to introduce a bill in the House on Saturday which would authorize the printing of a million eight hundred thousand dollars in scrip to retire about four million dollars in Blue Ridge Railroad bonds owned by the state!"

"Well, Brent, is that bad?"

"Total fleece."

"Is it on the up and up?"

"It's as crooked as a dog's hind leg."

Violet laughed. "Well, that's certainly crooked. Are you going to vote for it?"

"No, I don't have to vote for it, but that needn't stop me from taking advantage of it."

"Taking advantage of it? What's the Blue Ridge Railroad? I never heard of it. Where does it run to?"

"It doesn't run anywhere, really, just thirty-three miles, Anderson to Walhalla. Years ago it was organized to build a link around the southern end of the Blue Ridge Mountains to connect with lines in Georgia, Tennessee, and North Carolina, but that was all they were able to build before the War."

"It never went anywhere else?" she asked in wonder.

"Nowhere."

"So now are these men refinancing to start building more?"

"The plan is supposed to be to complete the hundred and ninety-five miles to Knoxville."

"Well, Brent, I don't understand. Wouldn't that be good?"

"Yes, Honey, it would if they did it. Another group organized and tried to get building started back in 1868 and 1869. There were lots of financial manipulations but they never could get solid enough financing to renew the building. But this Patterson ring now does not have any more intention of completing that railroad than they do of flying to Guinea. All they are interested in is milking it for more personal financial gain."

"But, Brent, how did they get in a position to do this?"

Brent lit one of his Christmas cigarillos, took a deep puff, leaned back, and said, "In this case the state owned a majority of the stock. Governor Scott was persuaded that it ought to be sold to a private corporation. So last July the sinking fund commission–the same one that disposed of the Greenville and Columbia stock–sold the stock to a private corporation."

"I see nothing wrong with that."

"Of course not, especially when the private corporation turns out to be Honest John Patterson and his associates, and they got 13,100 shares; now listen to this–at one dollar a share, one dollar!"

"What good would the stock be to them if there is no track?"

"It also gave them control of four million dollars worth of bonds guaranteed by the state."

"Oh, my! Are the bonds any good?"

Brent laughed softly and said, "Not really, because a contractor has a lien of two million dollars on them, and state securities have depreciated so much that they don't have much value at all. That is where this scrip comes in. What they really propose to do is just print money, and the state will give this scrip in return for the bonds that Patterson's company now holds."

"But the scrip won't be worth anything either, will it?" asked Violet.

"They are going to make out like it is worth something by stating in the law that it must be accepted for payment of taxes and all other bills due to the state, and they are going to levy an annual state-wide tax of three mills on the dollar to retire the scrip, supposedly over a period of four years."

"How is all of this going to be any advantage to you?"

"Frankly, I think the whole scheme is likely to be thrown out very shortly, if it gets through at all. Apparently this is too much even for our Carpetbag governor and his attorney general to stomach. It seems that they have pulled out of the railroad ring, and there are even some indications that the Governor will veto this bill if it passes."

"Will it pass?"

"Oh, it will pass all right, and then the more shaky it is, the better. I propose to relieve my colleagues of some of their scrip at big discounts and then use it to pay taxes."

"Sounds interesting if it can be done."

One afternoon a few weeks later, Violet met Brent as he came in the front door. Again he wore a bit of a smirk on his face, but he did take time to give her a proper kiss before taking off his coat.

Over tea in the parlor he explained the latest developments. "Sure enough, the Governor did veto the Blue Ridge scrip bill," Brent informed her.

"Well, I guess that's the end of that," said Violet. She didn't know whether she was glad or sad at this news.

Brent grinned. "No, not at all. We, or rather I should say *they* passed it over the Governor's veto, 84 to 18 in the House and 22 to 6 in the Senate."

"My goodness, how did they do that?"

"Oh, Patterson promised substantial payments in the new scrip to several wavering senators and representatives—several of whom always waiver until they can be assured of a payment. My informants tell me that he passed around promises of nearly fifty thousand dollars in scrip."

Violet frowned. "How disgusting!"

"Yes, very disgusting, but now we are going to have to work fast."

"What do you mean by that?"

He gave that special mischievous grin of his. "They say that Ed Gary, the state auditor, is planning to go to court to have the scrip declared illegal."

"Can he do that?"

"Of course. The Federal Constitution states very clearly that no state can coin money or emit bills of credit or make anything but gold or silver legal tender for payment of debts, and if that is not what they are doing I don't know what is."

Puzzled, she persisted, "So, now what?"

Again he flashed that mischievous grin. "Well, my Love, don't you see, I go around to these people who will be receiving all this scrip for their votes, and I'll emphasize the action of the state auditor, and I'll cite the Federal Constitution, and then offer to do them a big favor by taking this illegal scrip off their hands for about ten cents to the dollar, and then I'll rush around to pay all our taxes—"

Excited at the cleverness of his suggestion and the possibility of having their taxes all paid up, Violet exclaimed, "Darling, you are absolutely marvelous! How sharp you are! What a smart husband I have!" She flung her arms around him and kissed him thoroughly.

Pausing for breath, he was able to mutter, "Of course." And then he took advantage of the moment.

Brent was in a flurry of activity over the next two weeks. On a Tuesday evening after supper he said to Violet, "I must go out to Sumter tomorrow. Do you want to come along?"

"Of course," smiled Violet, "why don't I get off at Fair Oaks and check on things there, and then join you on the evening train to return?"

Shortly after they boarded the train the next morning and found seats, Brent took some folded papers from his pocket.

"What are those?" wondered Violet.

"Here, take a look," he replied, passing the papers to her.

"This says 'tax receipt."

"My dear, that is a receipt for the payment of all taxes for the year on our town house." Pointing to another of the papers she was holding, he continued, somewhat triumphantly, "And not only that, here is a tax credit that covers all taxes at present rates, for the next five years!"

"Why, Brent, that's fantastic! What are the other papers?" she asked hopefully, thinking of Fair Oaks.

"Same thing, covering the taxes and five-year tax credit for Charlotte and Leland's town house–and for our warehouses."

"Oh, why that's good news, indeed." She looked out the window at the passing scenery and thought that here, in early March, spring seemed to be already at hand. The blossoms on the trees and flowers should be bursting forth at Fair Oaks. After a few moments of silence, she turned back to Brent and asked, still hopefully, "Brent, why are you going to Sumter?"

So close were they that he often could read her thoughts, and he still enjoyed teasing her. So he just smiled and said nothing, his blue eyes twinkling.

She spoke up again. "Oh, Brent, Brent, do tell me now, are you going out there to pay taxes on Fair Oaks? Don't tease anymore."

He could resist those beseeching beautiful eyes no longer and gave her the answer he knew she was hoping to hear, "You guessed it, my dear."

"Oh, Brent! That's wonderful." After a short pause she went on to ask, for she knew her husband well, "Brent, are you doing all of this with that Blue Ridge scrip?"

He laughed with gusto. "Indeed! With Blue Ridge scrip that I have picked up for ten cents on the dollar–in the State House, in the banks, and on the streets."

"Oh, my goodness," she gulped.

"And I may have another little surprise before I'm finished, my Love."

"Oh, Brent, what? Do tell me now."

He laughed again. "That's my secret until I see if it works out. You'll just have to wait, Mrs. Sutler, dear."

"I can't imagine what it might be..."

It was time to signal for the train to stop at Fair Oaks, for which Brent was glad. He enjoyed Violet's company and conversation, but he knew she would persist in her efforts to get him to reveal his secret, and he wanted to keep her wondering a bit longer.

Violet sighed and gathered up her things with Brent's help. As she descended from the car she glanced around and sighed again, this time for another reason. "I know it's convenient for our travels, but, oh, Brent, I still hate this railroad going across our front lawn."

He kissed her goodbye, and smiled understandingly as he reassured her, "Try to keep your mind on the convenience of having it so close to the house." Then he kissed her again and jumped back on the train just as it began moving. They waved to one another until out of sight.

At Fair Oaks, Violet was glad for the chance to ride Hermes around the property for inspection. She was pleased with what she saw being done on the plantation, and she told Leo so, with enthusiasm. Plowing was well underway and all was ready for planting. The big house was neat and clean, and she told Mammy and Hattie and Jarvis how pleased she was with their work. She commended Fabian for the well-planned and growing gardens—both vegetable and flower, and the well-cared for look of the shrubbery and other landscaping around the house. They had all accepted the responsibility laid upon them when Violet and Brent and the children moved to Columbia for the session; indeed, they took pride in the trust given them by the owners of Fair Oaks. But then, they all agreed with Mammy who often repeated, "Fo' mercy sake, dis be our home, too, why wouldn't ussan tek care ub ebberting?"

When the evening train pulled to a stop on the front lawn, Brent hopped down to assist Violet on the train. He had found seats at just about the same place where they had sat that morning. She observed that he was wearing that self-satisfied, yet teasing smirk of his, so she knew that something was up.

"Haven't you had your quota of smirks for this week?" she demanded. "What do you have up your sleeve now?"

This moved him to hearty laughter as he handed her an envelope. "Here, take a look."

There, sure enough, she found a tax receipt and a five-year tax credit for Fair Oaks. Ignoring the few other passengers on board, she threw her arms around his neck and cried out happily, "Oh, Brent, this is wonderful! Now, even if those Carpetbaggers and Scalawags keep raising our taxes we ought to be able to keep ahead of them!" Tears of joy and relief filled her eyes. He put his arm around her and she laid her head on his shoulder as she told him how worried she had been over the amount of and sharp annual rise in Fair Oaks' taxes, and how relieved she was now. Then she informed him of the excellent care that Leo and Mammy and Hattie and Fabian and everyone was giving the plantation, and they needn't worry about it while they were in Columbia, and how much she enjoyed riding Hermes again on her inspection tour, which pleased Brent very much. Both relaxed after that, eyes closed for several miles. By the time they reached Camden, dusk was settling over the landscape, with just a trace of red and gold and lavender sunset in the west.

As the train gathered speed toward Columbia, Violet suddenly sat upright. "Brent," she said.

"Yes?" he murmured drowsily.

"Brent, is that all?"

"Is that all what?" he asked, without changing his relaxed position.

"Was there anything else besides the Fair Oaks taxes? You said you might have another surprise. You haven't told me what the secret is!"

Brent straightened up, took a cigarillo from his pocket, and in a mild tone said, "Think I'll go up to the smoker and have a smoke. Will you excuse me, Violet?"

"Oh, no you don't, Brent Sutler! Put that cigar right back in your pocket and answer me!"

Brent laughed softly, his sea blue eyes twinkling again as he said slowly, savoring what he was about to tell Violet, "Well, you know old Farley—"

"You mean that damned Scalawag Farley?"

He chuckled. "Yes, that damned Scalawag."

"Well, what about him? Anyway, what do I care what about him." She was beginning to feel just a touch of exasperation.

"Oh, I think you may care about this one, Violet."

"Oh, Brent, for goodness sake, come on, quit stalling. Now what is it? Tell me."

"All right, I'll tell you. I found out in Columbia that Farley has fallen into disfavor with his Carpetbagger cohorts, and he has fallen behind in his taxes and about everything else."

"And?"

"And in Sumter I confirmed what I had suspected. It has not been made public yet, but his title to your Old Place was about to be sold for back taxes."

"How did you find that out?"

"A fee of a few hundred in scrip to the clerk."

"You mean you bribed him?"

"Tisch, Tisch, Violet, how can you bribe anyone with a bunch of worthless paper?"

"Well, then what? Do go on, Brent!" She felt that surge of hope rising again. *Was it possible?*

"Well, I persuaded them to give me an option on the Old Place for the payment of all back taxes, with Blue Ridge scrip, of course, and with the same resources I paid this year's taxes and paid in for a five-year tax credit."

Violet was almost breathless with excitement, "Oh! Oh, my! You could bowl me over with a feather! Oh, Brent, this is the best of all, to get The Old Place back! Oh, Darling, thank you, thank you, what a wonderful husband you are!" She paused just a second to catch her breath and then exclaimed, "And I'm so glad to see old Farley being done in. He deserves to have this happen to him." She stopped again, looked at Brent, her heart reflected in her eyes, and added sweetly, "Oh, Darling, you just go on up to the smoker and smoke all the cigars you want!"

Brent threw his head back in laughter, delighted with the reception of his surprise for Violet. "I'll wait," he said.

Chapter 51

The Joshua School

1872

The last day of school that year happened to fall on the same day in May for both children. Violet and Brent attended the closing festivities, first at the Female Academy and then they and Bonnie Anne attended J.J.'s at Mr. Barnwell's school. After that, Brent gave each of the children a hug and left to return to his railroad office to meet a client for a dinner conference, and Violet and the two children began walking home.

As they set out, Violet felt a strange sense of emptiness. What was it? Why should she feel this way when both children had just completed a very successful year of school? She stopped in her tracks as the reason came to her with a jolt. Just a year ago she also was attending the last day of school with Little Josh. Now he was gone, and with him all the high hopes she had held for the little black boy.

J.J. tugged at her hand while Bonnie Anne looked up inquisitively, wondering why her mother had stopped so suddenly. "C'mon, Mama, I want to get home. I'm hungry." said J.J.

Violet smiled to let them know they had nothing to worry about and resumed walking, deep in thought. Again and again, as it had all year, that deep-felt feeling of the need to do something came flooding back. The empty desire to do something for Little Josh lay siege to her mind and her heart, and the principle that had been gradually forming in her mind all this year now began to become clear. *The only way to do something for someone who is now out of reach is to do something comparable for someone else.*

As she and the children walked past the Male Academy, she looked up at the building and the thought struck her, *Why not a special kind of school to discover and develop the talents of other black boys like Josh? And why not girls, too?*

Her pace quickened as she turned over the possibilities in her mind. *Might Brent be able to use his scrip to get a building? Would Victor Shelby and Major Dargan and John Frierson serve as trustees? The Reverend Jackson could be the headmaster, and his wife, Esther, could supervise room and board—but would Jackson be willing to turn over his responsibilities at the church/school on the plantation to his young assistant, Jesse Wallace? Jesse is certainly a capable young man. So is Flora, his wife. Oh, and why couldn't the Little Brown Jugs help teach music and serve as monitors at the school? But what about the financing? I know. I'll appeal to churches all over the county for financial support. Perhaps each church could choose and support one or two or maybe even three pupils of promise.*

By the time they reached home, the sense of emptiness had been replaced by feelings of expectation and excitement, but the two children were expressing exasperation at the failure of their mother to respond quickly and precisely to each of their numerous observations offered all along the way. She now turned all her attention to them as they ate their dinner and relived the school closing festivities and made plans of what they wanted to do now that they would have long days for play and riding their ponies over the plantation—and, as they glanced at their mother, reading, of course. One of the rules of the house was that every day, if possible, quiet time was set aside for reading, or being read to, and writing or drawing.

Brent came home late that afternoon, saying he had missed them all at dinner, but the meeting was worthwhile. The children hugged and kissed him and filled him in on their afternoon's activities. Violet waited for them to settle down and turn their attention elsewhere She picked up the box of cigarillos and held it open for Brent to take one. He gave her an inquiring glance, and then his eyes took on that characteristic teasing twinkle.

"Well, Violet, my Love, let's have it. I can see that you are bursting to tell me something, and I must confess I am wondering what it is." He lit his cigarillo, leaned back in his chair, and waited for Violet's answer.

She broached her idea for a special school dedicated to Little Josh. At first Brent seemed to brush it aside as just a whim, but he sensed Violet's deep commitment to the idea and noted that her face was flushed from excitement. As she went on explaining the concept of the school he found himself warming to the proposal. The idea certainly had merit, and her enthusiasm was contagious. Her eyes were wide and sparkling, her hair tumbling down in soft tendrils, and her complexion seemed to glow; he thought he had never seen her so beautiful.

A cloud seemed to pass over her face as, with just a slight tremble to her voice, she went on, "Brent, you know how the loss of Josh left such a terrible void, and I just keep thinking that there must be other children with talents like Josh's, if we could only find them and give them a chance."

Brent nodded, took a deep puff of his cigarillo, and then responded seriously, "I'm sure you are right, Violet, and maybe we can do something like what you suggest. Where might this school be located? Are you thinking of Sumter?"

Violet smiled, now certain that Brent would support her in this. "Yes, and there will be children around the countryside who need this help."

"Yes."

"Do you think we could find a suitable building in Sumter?"

Brent's forehead creased in thought. "Probably. All the remaining school buildings of the Freedmen's Bureau are being put up for sale, now that they are closing down operations and leaving the responsibility to the state."

Violet stood up, smoothed her skirt, and began pacing back and forth as if she needed action to give impetus to her thoughts. "I wonder if we could get the Freedmen's Bureau school in Sumter. What do you think? If we could, that would do quite well."

"Well, my dear, it wouldn't hurt to look into it, and I'll do just that as soon as I can."

"You know that's the building on the square bounded by Church Street, Live Oak, Brown, and Peach Street—you know, the old Sumter Inn."

Brent chuckled. "Yes, yes, I know. Somebody may already have a corner on it, but I'll see what I can find out. Now, tell me, how do you plan to organize this school?"

"Well, actually, I haven't thought very much beyond the idea that we ought to have a school," she answered a bit sheepishly.

Brent chuckled again and then suggested they go up to the office and think about it. Settling into their desk chairs, Violet and Brent each took pencil and paper to guide their thinking and make notes. Then Brent set down his pencil and poured another glass of scuppernong for each from the crystal decanter that sat on his desk and which Aunt Beulah always kept filled.

Brent handed Violet her glass, took a sip of his wine, and stated, "First of all, you will have to have a board of trustees or directors and get a state charter."

"Yes, I've thought of the first, but didn't know about the charter. You can help with that, can't you?"

Brent waited until he had lit another cigarillo, and then responded, "Sure, I can help with the charter. That should take only a few hundred dollars for the secretary of state. Now what about the directors?"

"Well, I was thinking of maybe Victor Shelby, the lawyer; Major John Dargan, the banker; and John Frierson, the planter. How does that mixture sound to you?"

"Sounds good," he answered, "and I have a feeling all three would be willing to do it, but Violet, you, too, will have to be on the board—as president I would assume."

Violet grinned.

Brent chortled and then snickered as he added, "Though I hope it won't cost as much to get you elected president of this board as it cost Honest John Patterson to get himself elected chairman of the Blue Ridge Railroad board." He took another puff of his cigarillo.

"Speaking of Blue Ridge, Brent, do you suppose you can use any more of your Blue Ridge scrip to get that building?"

"Mm, well, I don't know. It depends on whether it has been sold to some private party and on how quickly we can act; the legislature is about to outlaw the scrip, I think."

"Then we'd better move quickly. How much would the building cost in real money?"

"I believe the Freedman's Bureau schools in most of the towns have been going for about fifteen hundred dollars."

"We could manage that, couldn't we?"

"Oh, yes, we should be able to do that, especially if we use scrip. But, Violet, I'm sure you are aware that it is going to take a lot more money than that to run the school. Is it to be a boarding school or day school? Where are the funds coming from—I take it the pupils will not be asked to pay, if they are going to be poor blacks?"

"And maybe po' buckras. It'll be both a boarding school and day school...and well, I'm thinking of appealing to all the churches in Sumter and in the county and to the public in general. Maybe the churches will be willing to sponsor one or more children."

"Churches sound like a good source, though I have my doubts about how much support from the public will be coming for the education of blacks."

"Oh, Brent, do you think people won't be willing to support the school?"

"Honey, you know that a lot of them won't; in fact, my guess is that a good many will actually oppose it, will be openly hostile to the idea."

"Oh, no, I hope that won't be the case!"

"Better prepare yourself for that. Now let's move on. What about teachers?"

"Well, I'm thinking that our own Elijah Jackson might serve as headmaster, and Esther might be in charge of room and board. Jackson's young assistant, Jesse Wallace, and his wife, Flora, could take over the Jacksons' duties at Fair Oaks, and anyway, Elijah and Esther could be back at Fair Oaks in the summertime. Jackson and the *Little Brown Jugs* could teach music, and those boys could also serve as monitors, and I might give piano lessons myself and maybe teach a little literature, and I thought we could have our Carter and Jonah teach woodworking, and Fabian and Avery could teach the boys some of the rudiments of farming..." She paused to catch her breath.

"Is that all?" asked Brent, both amused and impressed.

"Oh, no, for the academic subjects I was thinking we could find a couple of teachers who have been working for the Freedman's Bureau, and maybe another one or two from the Episcopal Missionary Society, and maybe one or two others that we might find in Sumter or Columbia."

Brent sat quietly for a short time, as if weighing in his mind whether he should say something, and then in an earnest manner, he said, "Of course, Violet, you must make sure that our own children do not get shunted aside or neglected as a result of this mammoth undertaking of yours, worthy as it may be–."

"Now, Brent, you know I would never let that happen!" she exclaimed a bit indignantly, surprised that he felt it necessary to voice that caution.

"I'm sure you won't let that happen. I just think it is something about which we need to be careful." He felt it would be unwise to remind her of how she could get caught up in projects. She was an intelligent woman, and he had said enough.

In a couple of days the family returned to Fair Oaks for the summer. Indeed it had only been a week since their conversation about the school when Brent came into the office one afternoon with that special look of smug triumph on his face.

As soon as Violet saw him, she rose from her desk, hope rising in her breast, and demanded, "What is it?"

He took her by the shoulders and began twirling her around the office. "We got it!" he exclaimed gleefully. "We got it! We got the school building!"

Violet flung her arms around Brent's neck, crying out, "Oh, Brent, Brent, that's wonderful!" She planted a big kiss on his laughing mouth, then pulled back and looked up at him. "Tell me, how on earth did you manage it? I can't wait to hear."

Still laughing, he said, "Let me sit down and catch my breath, and then you'll hear it all."

Violet called to Ellie to bring lemonade to the office, and after each had taken a rocking chair in front of the unlighted fireplace, she insisted, "Now, tell me about it. I just cannot wait another minute."

"Don't you want to wait until Ellie has brought our lemonade, my Darling?" asked Brent teasingly.

"No, I do *not* want to wait until we have our lemonade, Brent Sutler, you rascal. Now, go on, start your tale."

"Well, I found out that Robert Sellers, that speculator, had bought the place from the Freedman's Bureau for fifteen hundred dollars. Obviously he was not going to do anything with the property other than try to turn it over for a quick and handsome profit. I also found that in Columbia people have been unloading their Blue Ridge scrip for practically nothing. The word is out that it will be completely worthless within a few weeks. Well, Violet, I picked up a bundle of scrip and then went to Mr. Sellers in Sumter and offered him three thousand in scrip. That sounded like a great deal to him, double what he paid for it, and he jumped at it, congratulating himself, I am sure, on making such a handsome profit."

"Oh, my goodness!"

"Then I rushed to the Court House and recorded the deed before he could change his mind, and since the property now was in my name, I thought it would be a good idea to get a tax assessment and pay taxes as far ahead as they would let me. My remaining scrip oiled the way with the country treasurer, and I paid our taxes for the building for the next ten years, even though as a chartered school it may be exempt from taxes later."

Violet clasped her hands in delight as she said, "Brent, that's wonderful! You are so clever! Now I can get into action to make the best possible use of your investment." She paused and then said softly, "Thank you, my darling husband, thank you for standing by me and helping me the way you do." The smile she turned upon him was so radiant that it seemed to brighten the entire room.

Assuring herself that the cultivation of the crops and the care of the animals were going well, Violet went into a flurry of activity for her school.

First she called on the Friersons at Cherry Vale and was relieved to find that John would be happy to serve as a director. A trip to Sumter brought similar responses from Victor Shelby and John Dargan. She arranged for an all-day meeting of the Board for Saturday, May 25.

In the intervening days she brought in a crew of workers from Fair Oaks to begin needed repairs and painting of the old building. She spent as much time on the site as she could, frequently bringing Bonnie Anne and J.J., with Evelina to keep an eye on them. J.J. in particular was fascinated with the work and changes to the building, and everyone enjoyed the picnic luncheons that Mammy and Ellie packed. While all this was going on, Violet continued to develop in her own mind the best use of the facility.

Although Brent insisted that he should not serve on the Board of Directors, he did agree to go along with Violet for the Saturday meeting. The group met at nine o'clock in a room near the main entrance of the building, one that Violet had set up to be her office and the Directors' room. The first order of business was to confirm the election of Violet as president of the board, which also carried the title of Rector of the School. John Frierson would serve as vice-president, Major Dargan as treasurer, and Victor Shelby as secretary. Shelby agreed to work with Brent to obtain a state charter. Violet briefly outlined her ideas: the school day would be from nine to three, and the basic academic subjects should be offered for half a day for each pupil, and the other half of the school day should be devoted to the development of special talents—music, art, woodworking, telegraph, typewriting, printing, domestic science, gardening, and farming. Then Violet led the group on a tour of the building.

What had been a large ballroom in the old inn, opposite the main entrance and across a broad hall, would be the assembly room; an alcove on the left side of that room would be the library, accessible to all who might be studying in the assembly room. Returning to the hall, Violet led the group to the right to the dining room and kitchen. Then, on the opposite side of the main entrance was an office for the headmaster. At the opposite end of the hall was a smaller ballroom which would be a recreation room. Along the hall was a series of meeting rooms that would become classrooms.

On the second floor what had been guest rooms of the inn (or classrooms for the Freedmen's Bureau school) would become practice rooms for piano and various other musical instruments, and studios for painting and sculpture.

The third floor would be the dormitory, fitted with bunks for four students to the room, and a solid wall between the boy and girl areas.

In the basement—only a half-story below ground level—would be shops for carpentry and woodworking, machine shops, a printing shop, typewriter room, garden room, and telegraph room. Here Brent volunteered to run a telegraph line from the telegraph room to a similar room in what had been a small barn out at the edge of the lot, so that pupils could send messages from one area to the other. Stables out by the street would accommodate the horses of the staff and those who might be driving children to the school, as well as the horses that some of the students would likely be riding to and from school.

Back in their meeting room, the Directors expressed enthusiasm for Violet's plans, and agreed with her that the school might take day students from Sumter and the surrounding areas, but others, living farther away, could be boarding students.

"I think for planning purposes we need to have an idea of numbers. How many pupils should we plan for, and at what ages?" asked John Dargan.

Violet replied readily, "With our facilities here we could handle about sixty boarding students and maybe, eventually, a hundred day students, but I would propose that we begin with, say, forty boarding students and forty day students, ranging in age from seven to fourteen. These all would be elementary pupils. After a few years I would hope we could expand to include four years of high school; at that point we might become an academy."

"That sounds reasonable," responded Dargan, "and I think it's a good idea to start small as everyone acquires experience and we see how the financing goes."

"I agree with that," said Shelby, "but tell me, would you divide the pupils into regular grades? I'm a bit confused on this, for I know that some of these children have had little or no education, in spite of the Freedman's Bureau, and many of those who attended their school really did not make a great deal of progress. And the same goes for the po' buckras' kids. How do you plan to handle all this?"

Violet sighed, "It's a problem, all right, and I've given this a lot of thought. Eventually, perhaps we'll be able to have grades according to levels of achievement, but at the outset I would divide the children into classes according to age—or estimated age—and further, according to whether any already could read and write. You see, we would be having children of different ages, but most of them would be beginning school, or at that level. At first I think they would be studying about the same things, though the instruction and the materials used would vary from classroom to classroom according to the age of the group. But then, I would expect the older pupils to begin making faster progress, and so we will need to have flexible grouping and regrouping. I don't want any pupil to be held back by a slower group, and at the same time, I would not want any pupil to be in a group that was achieving at a level above that pupil's capability."

Frierson spoke up, "Sounds reasonable, and I'm glad to hear the emphasis on academic subjects as well as the development of special talents. I assume that will include solid grounding in reading and writing and ciphering."

"Certainly," answered Violet, "and as soon as they have mastered those basics, they will move on to history, geography, astronomy, and literature, and everyone will receive some instruction in music and art, not just the specially talented who will do much additional work in those subjects."

Violet was a little surprised when Brent spoke up, "On the matter of ciphering and calculation, a thought has occurred to me."

She smiled, "Yes, Mr. Sutler, what is it?"

He couldn't help but grin at the formal tone of her voice. "Frankly, we have not even had a chance to discuss this at home," he said, looking at the other men who smiled with nods of understanding. "It is simply this. You know in Russia and in China and Japan they are able to do calculations very rapidly with the use of an abacus. I've just been wondering if it might be a good thing to teach all these kids to use the abacus."

Dargan spoke up almost at once, "That would be excellent if we could do it."

"But Brent," asked Violet, "are those things still in use? Could we get enough for all the pupils? Don't misunderstand, I'm open to the suggestion, and I like the idea, especially that the children could count and manipulate the balls or squares on rods, and then could actually *see* the results, and all that."

Brent nodded and answered, "Of course the use of the abacus in one form or another goes back to medieval and even ancient times. Then it became a lost art in Western Europe until Napoleon invaded Russia. His army brought some Russian abacuses back to France, and now they are all the rage over there. I am sure that I can get all we'll need from France—small ones for each pupil, and a large demonstration model in each classroom for the teacher to use in explaining how it is used in the various calculations."

"Who will teach it?"

"I'll be glad to show the teachers how to use the abacus, so that they will be able then to teach it to the pupils," volunteered Brent. "Frankly, I think I'd enjoy doing this."

All agreed that the abacus would be a great advantage for all pupils and that Brent should proceed with the procurement of these. Violet also asked that he see about acquiring small individual slates for each child, and a large one for each classroom, plus a good quantity of chalk, pencils, and paper.

After a light lunch in the dining room prepared by Ellie, the group returned to the meeting room. Most of the remaining discussion centered around the matter of getting teachers and matters of finance.

"What does it take to get a good teacher, Violet?" asked Dargan while jotting a few notes on his paper.

"I understand the going rate for teachers is about thirty-five dollars a month, and sixty dollars for a principal. I would like to retain the teachers for a full twelve months so that they could be improving their own knowledge and preparation for teaching during the summer and to be available to direct special activities from time to time."

"Mm, a novel idea, but I say one that is reasonable and sensible," Shelby commented as the others nodded their concurrences.

"Now what about finances?" persisted Dargan, still making notes on his paper.

Violet explained that they had a clear deed for the property which they would put at the disposal of the school and that the taxes had been paid for ten years in advance, so those two items would not be a drag on finances. She then went on to explain how she planned to visit all the churches in hopes of getting many of them to nominate and support one or several pupils each. Organizations and individuals also might be persuaded to sponsor pupils.

Dargan and Frierson agreed this was a good plan—time-consuming, but feasible. Shelby commended Violet on it, but warned that she might run into some public relations problems. He also cautioned her not to be disappointed if there were no enthusiasm from the po' buckras who had hard feelings about coloreds, and who likely would be especially vehement about a black headmaster at the school, no matter how capable the person might be.

Over the next several weeks Violet visited nearly every church in the county. Her own church, Holy Cross at Stateburg, gave enthusiastic support. The congregation agreed to support four pupils the first year, and to add another each succeeding year; William Ellison agreed to support another two on his own. Nearly all the Negro churches agreed to nominate and support at least one pupil. The white congregations, other than Holy Cross, were rather less enthusiastic, though it was clear before the summer was half over that the full quota of forty boarding students would be chosen and supported.

At a summer fair sponsored by the Sumter Monument Association—mainly to raise funds for a Confederate war memorial—Brent contrived to get himself on the list of speakers. A sizeable crowd gathered near the center of town for the occasion. Violet mingled with the crowd in anticipation as Brent mounted the platform to speak. Removing his broad-brimmed hat, but looking cool in his light frock coat in spite of the heat, he paid tribute to the soldiers and sailors of Sumter County who had given so much to defend their state and their way of life. Then he slipped in his special appeal:

"My fellow citizens I would like to invite your support for a very special project—it is a school for pupils of no means but with promising talents. Perhaps you remember Little Josh and the Little Brown Jugs whose music you probably heard on a number of occasions. Well, as you know, Little Josh was killed very near here. He died just as many of our young men died in battle. Now we are hoping to find many other youngsters who have talents such as he had and give them the chance to develop theirs that he never had.

"Is this a school for nigguhs?" someone shouted angrily.

"We are thinking in the first place of Negro children," Brent called back calmly, "but it will be open to black and white, boys and girls."

"All together?" another man shouted, waving a dirty straw hat in Brent's direction.

Drawing some notes from his pocket, Brent responded in a clear, firm voice, "The Constitution of this state, adopted in 1868, has many unfortunate features, but one of its strong points is to call for universal education, and it states, quote, `All schools supported in whole or in part by public funds shall be free and open to all the children and youths of the State, without regard to race or color.'

"And ladies and gentlemen, one of the leaders in the convention that adopted this constitution was a colored man named Francis L. Cardozo. Now you know that I disagree with him on many things, but he did show foresight in that convention when he said the following, and I quote, 'The most natural way of removing race distinctions would be to allow children, when five or six years of age, to mingle in school together. Under such training, prejudices will eventually die out.'

"Now, ladies and gentlemen," Brent went on, "you know that in the condition the state is in after seven years of Carpetbag government, it will not be able to put into effect a good system of universal education for a long time. But we can make our own beginning here and now by giving a special opportunity for children to develop into the most useful citizens. What could be a better tribute to those we honor today—those who gave their lives for South Carolina—than to take steps to assure a continuation of the sense of honor and the high civilization they died to protect? Any who can help support this effort, please make your contributions to the treasurer of the school, Major John W. Dargan at the Citizens Bank. I thank you each for your courtesy of hearing me out."

Polite applause and some sullen side remarks greeted the conclusion of Brent's speech. Already Violet was moving through the crowd seeking contributions in her very pleasant and disarming way. She found herself in something of an embarrassing competition with ladies who were collecting for the memorial monument, though most of them did not seem to mind. To her dismay a number of the men turned their backs on her, and some even hurled insults. Still she moved on. When it was all over the ladies had collected nearly eight hundred dollars for the monument, and Violet had collected a hundred sixty-five dollars for the school—which she immediately turned over to Major Dargan who gave her a receipt for the amount.

While the Sumter meeting had alienated some people, clearly it had convinced others. Within another two weeks the whole quota of day students had been enrolled. Now Violet's major task was to recruit the teachers, even as she kept thinking about educational policies.

Reverend Jackson was pleased and flattered to be asked to be the headmaster and that Esther would be working with him, and he was especially pleased that he would be able to bring the *Little Brown Jugs* along. Esther was almost beside herself with excitement. Violet was able to get a young white woman from Massachusetts through the Episcopal Missionary Society to be the first teacher. Her name was Edith Wilkins. She already had been teaching for the Missionary Society in Columbia, but now welcomed the chance to participate in this project. She had been teaching elementary pupils in all subjects, although she had a special interest in reading and literature. Then Violet was able to get two black women, Maggie Holt and Betty Martin, who had come down from the North to teach for the Freedman's Bureau, a white woman from Sumter, Maria Shanker, who had been a public school teacher, and John Winston, a young white man who had returned from a year's service in the Army during the War, had attended a year at the University, and had been working recently at a bookstore in Columbia. Violet decided that she could use part-time specialists for the work in music, art, telegraph, typewriting, and so on.

On the basis of her conversations with experienced teachers and lots of reading in the classics of education, Violet outlined a draft of a teachers' manual that she would go over with the teachers when they met together, and then, with the benefit of their comments and suggestions, she would prepare a more complete version for their guidance.

Calling on Quintilian and Rousseau and others, she wrote, "The first care of the teacher is to ascertain the ability and character of the pupil entrusted to her, and to exhibit good character on her part...Let the teacher adopt a parental attitude toward her pupils, and regard herself as the representative of those who have committed their children to their charge...Be strict, but not austere, genial but not too familiar...There will be no flogging or other corporal punishment...Let the pupil's punishment consist, insofar as possible, in the natural consequences of his own actions...However, continuous acts of misbehavior will be assigned demerits, and after a stated number of demerits, a pupil may be expelled in order to preserve the learning situation for the others."

Violet made further notations from Plato and Aristotle on subject matter, on the place of music in education, and on the need for physical exercise and recreation. From McGuffey's *First Eclectic Reader* she excerpted the "Suggestions to Teachers" that reading might be taught by the "Phonic Method," by the "Word Method," or by a combination of the two, and she indicated that the preference at the school would be the combination of the two, and always in a meaningful situation of context. Indeed, the pupils would be encouraged to draw on the context of what was being read to figure out unknown words. Then she added further statements from Quintilian on the importance of literature in education.

Other sections went into the use of the abacus in arithmetic, to the place of science and history and geography in the curriculum, and then into the whole idea of discovering and developing talent for special skills.

This was not all. Violet turned her attention, too, to the collection of dozens of books from private donors for the school library. These included such titles as *Tales of Mother Goose, Renowned History of Little Goody Two Shoes, Mother Goose's Melodies, Grimms' Popular Stories, East o' the Sun, West o' the Moon; Robinson Crusoe, Gulliver's Travels, Alice's Adventures in Wonderland, Hans Brinker or the Silver Skates, Sing a Song of Sixpence,* Hans Christian Andersen's *Fairy Tales,* Nathaniel Hawthorne's *A Wonder Book for Girls and Boys,* and Louisa Mae Alcott's *Little Women.* She had workers at Fair Oaks make canvas covers for a couple of the box wagons so that they could be used for transporting day pupils to and from school, and she gave attention to further improvements at the school building. She arranged for uniforms to be made for all pupils—cotton for fall and spring (light blue jumpers or pants, with white blouses or shirts), and woolen for winter (navy blue jumpers or pants and jackets, with white blouses or shirts). Brent provided the cloth; she designed the patterns, and then she prevailed on ladies' sewing circles all over the county and in Sumter to make the blouses, shirts, jumpers, and slacks. Knee length navy socks were purchased for both boys and girls, for the year round, and were worn with black leather shoes.

While this was going on she ordered textbooks to be available for all the pupils when they arrived—*McGuffey's Primer, First,* and *Second Readers*; the 1866 revision of Noah Webster's *Elementary Spelling Book*, with its explanations of sounds of the English language, accents, key to pronunciation, different kinds of type, as well as groupings of words according to their accents and syllables; Lindley Murray's *English Grammar.* In Columbia she was able to get some used textbooks left over from the War, notably, Charles E. Leverett's *Southern Confederacy Arithmetic* and Mrs. M.B. Moore's *Geographical Reader for the Dixie Children* that had been published during the War in Raleigh, North Carolina.

At last, on the second Monday in September, all was ready for the opening of *The Joshua School.* Boarding pupils arrived on Sunday, and all the others were there in time to join together in the assembly room at nine o'clock for the opening exercises. Here they were, sixty black children, (forty boys and twenty girls), and twenty white children (twelve boys and eight girls), all eager to learn.

The assembly room had been freshly painted. Each pupil had a desk, assigned to rows by class according to ages, in the big room. The Reverend Jackson stood at a podium on a low platform at the front of the room. The Ten Commandments, printed in large letters on two tablets, were posted on the wall behind the platform, though it was clear that few of the pupils could read them.

The headmaster introduced the teachers and the monitors, explained where classes would meet, who would have which monitor—one of the *Little Brown Jugs* who would lead each group at the appointed time. Then Jackson set the pattern for opening exercises that would prevail in about the same way for the rest of the year:

The singing of *My Country Tis of Thee* and of *Carolina,* the state song, A Biblical reading, from a Psalm this day, but on other days from Proverbs or one of the Prophets.

A short talk—this day one of Aesop's fables, and on other days either a fable or an explanation of one of the Ten Commandments.

Group singing of a couple of songs such as *Old Dog Tray,* and *Listen to the Mocking Bird,* for which the *Little Brown Jugs* provided the accompaniment.

Finally, the *Little Brown Jugs* did one of their specialty numbers, and then Thomas continued to play his cornet while the pupils marched behind their monitors to their classrooms, and other groups remained in the assembly room for what would become a study period.

Brent had done well in collecting supplies and equipment. In each classroom there were individual slates and a large blackboard, a demonstration model Russian abacus, and an individual abacus for each pupil. The telegraph equipment was in place, the shops were ready for use, musical instruments and art materials were in the studios, and the kitchen larder was well-stocked.

During one of Violet's visits to *The Joshua School,* Elijah had a special project for her. He led her to the recreation room where Esther had assembled a newly organized children's choir. Elijah directed them in several spirituals for Violet.

"That was wonderful!" she told the children. "Now would you like to learn a new song?"

"Oh, yassum, yassum, Miz Violet," several shouted.

"All right. I'll play the piano so you can hear the whole song and get a feel for the music. It's called *New Britain* from *Virginia Harmony.* We don't know where the tune came from; it may be based on a folk song from Africa. I'm sure you'll like it as much as I do." She played the melody through a couple of times, and then on the third play-through the children hummed along. Then she played it again.

She went on, "About a hundred years ago a man by the name of John Newton wrote an Episcopal hymn which this tune just fits. Actually John Newton was a kind of scoundrel, a wretch, in his early years, and he became captain of a slave ship. Later, he repented and became a good Christian and a minister in the Church of England. His hymn is called *Amazing Grace.*" Patiently, Violet repeated the words of the song, "Amazing Grace, how sweet the sound..." and then sang the words. Then she had everyone join in. After several repetitions the choir began singing harmony and soon were singing all four stanzas.

Elijah beamed in appreciation and with pride at his "chillun."

On the whole, Violet was pleased with the start of *The Joshua School.* She was pleased about the care with which the sponsors—churches, charitable organizations, individuals—had chosen the pupils that they sent. Already she could feel the thrill of achievement as her little boys and girls, most of them black, but some white, showed sparks of talent in their music lessons and real desire and achievement in learning their letters and numbers. No, she had not found anyone yet who could take Little Josh's place. She figured she never would, and it really was not fair to the others to expect it of them. There never would be another Josh, but she was sure there were others who would make contributions in their own way that would be the equivalent. She felt a deep sense of satisfaction that at last she was doing something to help make this so, and in a way, Little Josh was living on.

Book Three

Carolina Phoenix

Chapter 52

Repentance

1872

Late one morning—it was the second Wednesday in October—as Violet and Brent were working at their desks at Fair Oaks, a knock came at the outside door of the office.

"Who is it?" Violet whispered to Brent.

"Some black fellow out there whom I don't recognize," Brent answered softly as he got up and went to the door, signaling to Jarvis that he would get it.

"Senator Sutler?" the man asked, holding his somewhat dirty, slouch felt, work hat in his hands.

"Yes, what is it?" queried Brent, stepping across the threshold and facing the man.

"Well, suh, ah got uh message fer ya an' de Missus frum Massuh Farley," he said as he stuck his hand into the pocket of his overalls and handed the note to Brent.

Brent stepped aside and invited the stranger into the office to wait and then looked at the note.

"What is it?" asked Violet.

"Farley is asking if he might come and see us."

Violet glanced at the visitor warily and asked Brent, "Oh, my goodness, what are you going to tell him?"

"Just listen," said Brent, as he returned to his desk and began writing a note:

Dear Mr. Farley,

We never want to see you or any of your cohorts on this place again.

Sincerely, B. Sutler.

Folding the note he had just written, Brent handed it to the visitor and said, "Now, take this to Farley and tell him if I ever see him on this place I'll fill him full of buckshot. Is that clear?"

"Yassuh, yassuh, Massuh Sutler," the man said as he scrambled out of the office, onto the porch, and disappeared in a flash.

Brent rose and crossed over to close the door that the visitor had left open in his haste. "I wonder what Farley is up to," remarked Brent, returning to his chair.

"Maybe he has had a change of heart?" Violet suggested.

Brent shook his head. "That sorry wretch? Knowing Farley, that isn't likely."

"Well, maybe it wouldn't hurt to find out. Aren't you a little curious?"

"Well, maybe I was somewhat hasty, and yes, I wonder what he has up his sleeve now. Shall we tell him to ignore the first message and come on over?"

"Sure, why not, I can't help but wonder what he is up to."

Brent called in Aaron and asked him to carry a note to Mr. Farley over at The Old Place. It said that they would be glad to see him on Saturday afternoon. Brent decided not to mention the first note.

At the appointed time Blake Farley drove up in an old dilapidated buggy drawn by a scrawny nag to the back door of Fair Oaks. With hat in hand and head bowed, he approached the back door of the office. Brent invited him in and showed him to a chair near the fireplace. Violet and Brent took chairs in front of him.

Haltingly, Farley began to speak, "Miz Violet, Senator, I know I've done lots of things I should not have done. Now, I want to say that I'm sorry. I want to apologize for any inconvenience I have caused you and beg that we can make a new start. I hope you can forgive me and maybe help me get back on my feet."

"Why you son of a bitch!" exploded Brent. "You have more brass than a brass monkey!"

Violet's face flushed as she added, "You have your nerve coming around here asking for our help after all you have done—taking all of our reserve cotton and turning it over to the Yankees, and keeping half for yourself. You were taking food out of the mouths of women and children—and then stealing cotton right out of our fields. And taking Brent to court on false charges, scaring the family and me half to death! Why don't you go back to your damned Yankee Carpetbaggers and your fellow Scalawags and ask them to help you?"

Brent continued the barrage, "You damned Scalawag, you knew what you were doing, and you didn't give a damn about the results of your actions!"

Farley flinched and hung his head, not looking either Brent or Violet in the eyes. He replied lamely, "But I really meant you no harm; I was just trying to look out for myself. Like anybody else would do."

"And just what in hell were you trying to do at the grand jury?" Brent exclaimed. "Weren't you trying to get me sent to prison on those trumped-up charges?"

Now Farley looked directly at Violet, "I'm truly sorry about the cotton, Miz Violet," he replied, "but I was getting in desperate straits and that was the only way I saw out. And Senator, I am truly sorry about the grand jury, but they were making me do it."

Brent came back heatedly, "Nobody was holding a gun to your head. What do you mean, making you do it?"

Farley looked at the floor, then the ceiling, and then briefly at Brent, and said, "Senator, you are regarded as one of the opposition senators, and Mr. Moses and his friends were trying to consolidate their power, and if I didn't do their bidding in accusing you, they were going to seize all my land for claims of back taxes and seize my store and everything."

"Well, you picked a hell of a way of doing it," said Brent scornfully.

Farley leaned back, took a deep breath as though calling up reinforcements and said, "Miz Violet, Senator, we were all in a terrible fix after the War when the Yankees came in. I guess none of us knew how we were going to cope with the situation. Many people said that the old South was gone. Nothing would ever be the same. They said it would be futile to try to go back to the old days, that the best we could do was to make our peace with the new order of things. They said that even the great plantations never would be able to make it without slave labor, and that all these would be broken up into small parcels. I had very little land. I only had my store, and I never would be able to live on that if the Yankees and the freed Negroes shut me out."

"Some of us had to get along on less than that," interrupted Violet, "a lot less. There were days when the children and my sisters and the servants and I had to live practically on water flavored with dandelion greens, or dried turnips or wild onions or roots, or whatever we could find."

"Yassum, indeed times were hard," continued Farley, "and to cope with the terrible situation of the Reconstruction; some tried to adapt the old ways to meet new conditions, as you did. Some simply sold, or lost, what they had and moved away. Others tried to cooperate with the Yankee occupiers and make the best of a bad situation. That seemed the sensible way to me."

"Unfortunately that seemed the way to too many of our people with weak backbones," exclaimed Violet contemptuously.

"But, to me, it seemed the only way at the time," protested Farley, wiping his face with a red bandanna handkerchief. He was perspiring profusely although the temperature of the room was cool. He stuffed the handkerchief back in his pants pocket and continued attempting to justify his position. "As things got worse, and at the same time I saw new opportunities for gain, frankly, I cut some corners. Then one thing led to another, and I began playing both ends against the middle, and I'm afraid I got caught in the middle. Lost the land for taxes, which you got, and then lost my store and everything else, too." A deep sigh of self-pity escaped from his lips as he seemed to shrink back into his chair while removing the handkerchief from his pocket to wipe his face again. The swaggering, boasting, often leering Blake Farley had become a timid, nervous, pleading weed.

Brent offered Farley a cigarette paper which he refused by a shake of his head. Brent then rolled one for himself as he commented, "You know a stacked deck may destroy the dealer."

Farley sighed again and nodded in agreement. "Quite right, Senator, I'm afraid I've been on a slippery slide to nowhere."

Now Brent leaned back in his chair, and his sea-blue eyes drilled into Farley's brown ones as if to see what lay in the mind behind them. In a cool, steady voice, he asked quietly, "All right, Farley, let's have it. Just what do you want from us?"

Again with some hesitation, Farley leaned forward and explained shakily, "To tell you the truth, Senator, I'm at the end of my tether. I do appreciate you letting me stay on at the old farm until this year's crops are in, but I wonder if there may be some way we could work out a mortgage to let me buy back that piece of land you call The Old Place."

Violet and Brent exchanged glances, eyebrows arched in surprise. Violet turned toward Farley and asked contemptuously, "What guarantee do we have that your word is any better now than it has been in the past? How do we know that your intentions are any more honorable now than they were when you paid less than half price for that land in the first place at a time when we were desperate, or when you stole our cotton, or when you tried to have the Senator sent to jail?"

"Ma'am, all those things were because of threats and inducements from the Carpetbaggers and from Mr. Moses. It was all their fault, and now they have turned against me."

"Why?" asked Brent.

"Maybe because they thought I was trying to gain at their expense."

"Likely," muttered Brent.

"Well, were you?" Violet inquired.

Another deep sigh. "Well, yes, I was."

Brent flashed a smile and said, "At least that bit of honesty is a step forward."

Violet motioned to Brent and said to Farley, "Mr. Farley, will you excuse us for a few minutes?"

She led Brent across the hall to the library. Closing the door behind them, she turned to Brent and said, "What do you think? Is he any more trustworthy than ever? To tell you the truth, I would feel better if he just went away. At any rate, we just got The Old Place back; it belongs with the plantation property, and I have no intention of parting with it again if I can help it."

Brent threw the butt of his cigarette into the fireplace and turned toward Violet. "As for him being more trustworthy, I can't help but have my doubts, and if that's the way you feel, let's just tell him to go to hell."

Violet paused in thought as she paced slowly around the room. She stopped and looked at Brent. "Still, if there is such a thing as repentance and forgiveness, maybe he is a candidate for it."

"Maybe, but I'm not sure," Brent said doubtfully.

"Well, if Christianity means anything, and I must confess, sometimes I have had my doubts in the past, but now if it does mean anything, it means to substitute love for hate and to encourage repentance and forgiveness. We recite those words every Sunday in the prayers and collects, but those are just mere words if we cannot put them into practice. Maybe if we handle it right old Farley can be redeemed."

Brent couldn't help but grin as he asked, "How do you propose to do that?"

Looking into the glow of coals in the fireplace, Violet took Brent's hand in hers and began thinking aloud, "You know, I can see in a way what old Farley is getting at. How does one cope after four years of war and defeat and then an interminable military occupation—already seven and a half years with no end in sight? How does one cope with little resources and lots of fear and worry, living under the exploitation of alien masters?

"Yes, some move away to Mexico or the Far West to get a new start, and I think of your brother, Bruce. Some cut their country roots and move to the city to be a part of what becomes a more and more Yankified nation of factories and shopkeepers at the risk of civility and *belles lettres,* and I think of the Thompsons and my own sisters. Some try to hold on to the old values of our agrarian society and resist change; they become a part of a resistance movement against change and against the alien overlords, and I think of the Friersons, and some in the cities who keep trying to restore the old ways, like your father and mother. And some resort to a more active and even violent resistance, like the Ku Klux Klan. Some drift to the cities and become dependents of other people's charity, or wards of the state, and I think of those like some of the slaves who left and never came back to work on this or any other plantation. And I think of some of the others who have become pawns or unwitting tools of their alien masters.

"Then there are others who do all they can just to eke out an existence, who just live from hand to mouth, day to day, like many of the freed Negro workers and the po' buckras. And there are some who are resigned just to accepting things as they come, who live in their memories and hope for the best, and I think of Grandmama Lee. And I think of the youngsters, so full of potential and hope, only to be blocked out, or cut down, like Little Josh.

"But then, some try to cooperate with the alien masters and become collaborators with the enemy. They see no other way, and they become Scalawags, like Farley.

"But there are also those who are determined to hold to the best of the Old South, but who also adapt to the new conditions; try to make the most of fleeting opportunities, and look to the future with some hope, however remote that future may be. And Brent, that is us. That is Fair Oaks plantation, with its free labor and new machinery, and the Carolina Central Railroad, and the Mercantile business. That is us!"

"Whew!" exclaimed Brent, his hand brushing across his brow. "You've said a mouthful, but I must grant, you have laid it all out, and it makes a lot of sense."

Violet smiled at his reaction and went on, "And if someone who has chosen the way of collaboration and has come to bad straits, and now sees some hope in trying our way, maybe we can help save a soul–save him from the hell he has brought on himself."

Brent nodded and agreed, "Clearly Farley is in a fix."

Violet chuckled as she said, "It appears to me that he has been in more tight corners than a feather duster."

"Indeed," laughed Brent.

Violet let loose of Brent's hand and resumed walking around the room, her head bowed in thought. Finally she stopped and turned to Brent, asking, "Well, what do you think?"

He answered slowly, "You know, if we saw even a pirate who had fallen overboard and was drowning in the sea, we would toss him a line. I'm willing to take the risk if you are, but what do you have in mind?"

"Well, we certainly want to hold on to The Old Place, but what about having Farley be the manager over there? He could live in the house there; the tenant farmers could remain, but now we would provide the seed and fertilizer and supplies. By holding on to the land, we would retain control, and if Farley should step out of line we could expel him. What do you think?"

"That sounds reasonable."

Then Violet added thoughtfully, "And maybe, somehow, we could help him get his store back in Sumter. If he makes that go, and if he does well in managing the land, he should make out all right."

"Yes. Perhaps we could go on a note. What would you say might be his compensation for managing The Old Place?"

"Mm, I would say each tenant gets fifty percent of the proceeds of the crops on his land, and each also has a garden to grow his own food and has pens for chickens and pigs, so, Farley gets twenty-five percent, and we get twenty-five percent."

"How much do you reckon that would amount to, Violet?"

"Well, put in cotton and tobacco, it ought to make at least fifty dollars an acre. That would mean about five hundred dollars for each farmer, twenty-five hundred for Farley and twenty-five hundred for us, less our costs for seed and fertilizer."

"That sounds reasonable," said Brent. "Shall we go and put it to him?"

Farley was nervously pacing the floor when Violet and Brent returned. He tried to manage a smile, but looked pale and haggard.

They returned to their chairs. As Violet explained their proposal, color began to return to Farley's face, and a gleam of hope appeared in his eyes.

After Violet had completed her explanation of their proposal for Farley to manage The Old Place, Brent added, "And if you can arrange for a loan with the Citizen's Bank, I'll go on your note so you can get your store back."

By now Farley was on his feet, grasping first Violet's hand and then Brent's, spilling all over the place in gratitude. "You won't be sorry, you won't be sorry," Farley promised. "You can always count on me from now on, and I'll do my best for everybody to make money on The Old Place."

"We expect you to," said Brent, and then asked, "Aren't you going to the political rally tonight at the Court House?"

"Oh, no need of that; anyway, I don't want to come in sight of those Moses people any more."

"A wise decision," replied Brent.

"And, Senator, you can count on my vote at the next election; me and all my friends and our tenants."

"Well thanks, but you know I'll never be able to dispense the favors that Mr. Moses could—and you know he may be our next governor."

"Yes, Senator, I know all that, but he's not going to be doing me any more favors anyway, and I certainly am not going to be doing him any. No, siree. Right now I am crossing the River Jordan. From now on I am a Sutler Democrat."

"Good for you," smiled Brent, "a Sutler Democrat and a Wade Hampton Democrat, I hope."

"And a Wade Hampton Democrat," Farley said as he fairly trotted out of the room as though great weights had been lifted from his back.

Chapter 53

A Siege of Sickness

1872-1873

Joining Violet in the informal dining room on the following Thursday morning for their "second breakfast" of biscuits and coffee after the children had been sent off to school, Brent announced, "Well, it appears to be settled."

"What appears to be settled?" asked Violet as she put her cup down after another sip of coffee.

"Why, your old friend, Frank Moses, is going to be our next governor."

"Oh, damn! How do you know that now?"

"I've been listening to the telegraph reports. The votes are about half in, but Moses is leading two to one."

Violet sighed in resignation, asking, "Does it really make any difference?"

Brent shook his head. "Probably not, but we know how much Moses has been stealing, while we're not sure what Tomlinson might do."

"Yes, but why such a choice? Where did Tomlinson come from? How come the conservative Democrats did not put up anybody?"

"Just seemed futile."

Violet sighed again. "Doesn't seem we are making much headway against the rascals if our party doesn't even put up a candidate."

"No, I'm afraid we are not going to get anywhere until we can get Wade Hampton or someone like him to make the race."

"But what about Tomlinson?"

"Well, Reuben Tomlinson came down here from Pennsylvania as a missionary, and he was superintendent of education for the Freedman's Bureau, and then he was state auditor."

"I know, but I thought he was one of the Radicals, just like Moses."

"You're right, but at their convention in August, about a third of the delegates bolted in protest against the nomination of Moses, then they met separately and nominated Tomlinson to run against Moses."

"So even some of the Radicals were fed up with Moses?"

"Apparently, though some of them probably just wanted more plunder for themselves."

"How much do you figure Moses has stolen from the state so far?"

"Who knows? We do know that as adjutant and inspector general he spent a hundred and ten thousand dollars for which he gave no accounting, and as speaker of the House, where actual expenses were a little over a hundred and forty-three thousand dollars, he signed pay certificates for over a million dollars."

"Oh, my goodness!" exclaimed Violet in dismay. "And I remember seeing in the *Sumter News* a report from Beaufort that said Moses had sent two mules to the Negro state senator there for hauling campaign speakers around, and then the piece said that mules were too honest-looking for such work and said one was named Validating Bill and the other was named Certifi Kate, and their tails were shaved like the state treasury. Now I know what they were talking about."

"Ha, yes," Brent said, holding out his cup, "Hey, my coffee is getting cold; how about a refill?"

"It's not cold, it just seems that way when you get to thinking about Moses," grinned Violet picking up the coffee pot and pouring more in their cups.

Accepting his hot refill, Brent added, "And you know there was a move to impeach Governor Scott last year."

"Oh, yes, we talked about that at the time, remember?"

He went on, "And Scott spent forty-eight thousand dollars in the legislature to stop that action. I heard a third of that went to Moses!"

"But, Brent, if Moses is such a fraud and thief, why do they vote for him? Does Tomlinson have any such record?"

"No, I haven't heard anything to match Tomlinson with Moses on that score. As for the election, Moses probably spent a lot more, but then maybe a number of voters preferred a native South Carolinian, even if a Scalawag and a reprobate, to a Yankee Carpetbagger."

"Any idea of how the blacks voted?"

"Obviously they had to vote for Moses to give him a two-to-one margin, and from the locales that have reported, you can see that it was the mostly white counties of the up-country that gave the greater part of their votes to Tomlinson."

"Why would the blacks vote for Moses?"

"Several reasons. He's friendly to them; he can buy them more easily, and maybe lots of them also prefer a native South Carolinian to a Carpetbagger, difficult as that may be for the Yankees to understand." He buttered another biscuit, took a bite and a sip of coffee, and then went on, "I must say, there was a good deal of fireworks between the Radical factions, and that may give us some hope for the future. Did you hear about their rally in Sumter last Saturday night?"

"No, I didn't. Tell me, what happened?"

"Well, a crowd gathered at the Court House, and the Reverend Johnson began speaking from the balcony in favor of Moses, and then Sheriff Coghlan started shouting in opposition from the main floor. It was total chaos until Sam Lee managed to take the floor and introduce our distinguished black congressman, Robert Brown Elliott. We have to grant, Elliott is quite an orator, and he made an impassioned plea for Moses."

"I can imagine."

"Anyway, we're in for it now with a damned Moses administration to look forward to!"

Violet sighed again and said, "If you ask me, the whole state is sick—sick, sick, sick!"

The excitement of newness had not worn off for Violet in her work with *The Joshua School.* On the contrary, she found herself looking forward more and more to her visits to the school and working with the pupils and their teachers. But when she went in on Friday, October 25th, she felt a tug of uneasiness as she watched the opening exercises that morning. Frequent coughing from all quarters of the room interrupted the singing and the story-telling. As she looked around there seemed to be an unusual number of absences. Here was a kind of trouble that she had not anticipated.

When the pupils went to their classrooms, Violet approached the headmaster, "Elijah, aren't there more absences than usual today?"

"Oh, yassum, Mis' Violet," he answered, "de las' three days mo' an' mo' uf de chillin be takin' sick."

"What kind of sickness?"

"Oh, ya kno' how li'l chillin alway be gittin' sick wif colds, measles, chicken pox, an' ebberting."

"Oh, yes, that's true, but is this different?"

"Ah'm not sure, buh in de las' three days ten uf our boys an' girls heah have come down wif fevers, an' six uf our day students be absent, mostly ague, ah reckon."

Violet immediately went up to the sleeping rooms to check on the sick ones. She got a couple of the young black women who were helping with the cleaning, and she had them move all the sick children to a separate area and put them in beds, one to a room. She told the helpers that one of them must be there at all times, day and night, to look after the sick children.

Then she hurried to the stable to get Hermes and the buggy and drove quickly down Church Street to the office of Dr. John Hartley. She found the doctor seated at his roll top desk working out his schedule of calls. He rose to greet her cordially. He was a middle-aged man whose gray eyes almost matched his neatly combed gray hair and gray goatee. He had not seen her since he attended Little Josh on that fatal and unhappy concert day, but he had heard of her grief, and about the work she was doing with her school.

His eyes were gentle as he looked at her and asked, "Hello, Mrs. Sutler, what can I do for you?"

Extending her hand, Violet explained worriedly, "Oh, Doctor Hartley, up at the school, our new *Joshua School,* a number of the children are taking sick and need a doctor. Can you come?"

"What seems to be the nature of the illness?"

"Mostly chills and fever, and some look like they may have measles."

"Mm, lots of that going around. Of course you can expect that sort of thing in children. It's just a part of growing up."

"I know, but these seem uncommonly numerous and severe."

"Ah, yes—"

"And I was wondering if we could make an arrangement for you to come up every couple of days or so; perhaps on the basis of some kind of regular retainer." Then she repeated, "Can you come?"

The good doctor smiled. He excused himself and went to a back room. Moments later he returned with a tall, slender, clean-shaven, young man with light hair, who was putting on his frock coat as he walked into the room. "Violet, may I present Dr. Aldrich, Violet Sutler of Fair Oaks, the Senator's wife."

After their exchange of courtesies, Dr. Hartley said, "Dr. Aldrich here is joining me as a partner. Now we shall be glad to include your school on our daily rounds—one or the other of us will be there each day—"

"Oh, that's wonderful—"

"And there will be no fee. We appreciate what you are doing with that school, and let this be our contribution to your project."

Violet was almost overwhelmed at the doctor's response, and she had to blink quickly to keep the tears from her eyes. She was pleased to learn that Dr. Hartley knew what she was doing at the school and wanted to support it, and she was even more delighted in getting his promise of medical assistance on a regular basis.

Dr. Hartley smiled gently at Violet and asked, "Are you going back to the school now?"

Her blue-violet eyes still sparkling with the moisture of tears, she answered, "Why, yes, I am."

"I'll tell you what let's do. Give me time to get my rig, and Dr. Aldrich and I will follow you over there. You can show us around, introduce us to your staff, and we'll have a look at the patients. Then we'll know our way around for return visits."

On arrival at the school, Violet introduced the two doctors to Elijah and Esther Jackson, showed them the kitchen and classrooms, introduced them to the teachers, and then, with Esther Jackson accompanying them, showed them to the third floor area where Violet had put the sick children. The doctors decided that there were half a dozen cases of measles, and most of the others seemed to have a case of fairly mild influenza.

"Keep them separated," ordered Dr. Hartley, "and keep them in bed, warm. Feed them lots of chicken soup and all the fruit or juice you can provide. If it appears that they need it, give them a little castor oil. If you have trouble getting that down, try mixing it with honey or molasses."

"Yassuh, Doctor," said Esther, as Violet nodded her head. Violet looked to see if the two young women she had assigned to look after the children, and who were now standing to the side unobtrusively, watching the doctors, had heard the instructions. They had.

"And something else may be advisable," Dr. Hartley went on. "Get a jug of carbolic acid. Make a solution of that in water of about one part to twenty, and scrub everything they come in contact with—floors, bedsteads, chamber pots, cooking utensils, dishes, everything. We don't know just why this works, but we learned during the War that this is a powerful disinfectant and may prevent the spread of disease and infection. I would use this with all your pupils, not just the sick ones, to try to help prevent the spread of their illnesses."

"Indeed we shall do that," promised Violet.

Esther Jackson stayed behind to talk with the two young helpers, while Violet escorted the doctors down the steps and to the front door. There she thanked them for coming to look at the children and for their suggestions. They smiled and doffed their hats and assured her that one or the other would be back the next day to check on the sick children. Then they took their leave, and Violet went back upstairs to help Esther.

After Brent had taken the morning train for Columbia on Monday, Violet had Fabian saddle up Hermes so she could make her usual circuit of the plantation. It was a bright, sunny morning, and Violet looked forward to riding Hermes and chatting with the workers. To her dismay she found that there was a great deal of sickness among the children of the workers—and among the older folks, too. She stopped at every cottage in the workers' village. Wherever she found sickness, she comforted the ill and reassured the parents or others who might be there. Then she decided that more drastic measures were called for, like those taken at *The Joshua School.* She stopped at the church/school building to see Jesse and Flora Wallace, who had taken on these responsibilities when Elijah and Esther Jackson moved over to *The Joshua School* in Sumter. They were a bright young couple and had been trained well by the Jacksons, and Violet and Brent were pleased with their efforts.

Explaining her concern about the illness on the plantation, Violet said to Rev. Wallace, "Let's forget about school for a while; we'll turn this into an infirmary and bring the sick people here where you and the girls can watch over them."

"Yassum, we do that," responded Jesse Wallace quickly. "When we move them?"

"Right now. I'll have Leo get some men to move beds and everything in here, and when that is done, bring the sick children in, and then the older folks. We'll spread them out, not too close together, and don't let anybody else come in except the children's parents and the people who are bringing in things. And Flora, you can use your kitchen to feed them. We'll bring food and get some of the girls to help you. And I know Leo's wife, Rachel, will want to help."

Flora nodded eagerly, anxious to do what she could, "Yassum, Mis' Violet."

Violet rode up to Leo's to give instructions to him about moving things into the church/school building, and to Rachel who said she'd go right over to help the Reverend's wife. Then, without even stopping at the big house, Violet rode up to Stateburg to see their friend, Will Anderson, Jr., who had taken over his father's medical practice there. He promised to come by Fair Oaks that afternoon.

By the time the doctor arrived, the infirmary was well-organized, and all the patients were resting comfortably. Dr. Anderson moved to each one in turn, examining eyes, ears, nose, and throat, and looking at their skin, feeling foreheads for fever, and listening to lungs with his stethoscope. He made brief notations for each patient. When he had finished, he spoke with Violet. "It appears that you have six children with influenza, four with measles, and there are two that we should be most concerned about, the boy and the girl over there have nasty throats, and I'm afraid they have diphtheria—that can be very dangerous for young folks, and it is very contagious. Keep them down there at the far end, away from everybody else."

"And, Will, in town, at *The Joshua School*, the doctor said we should disinfect with carbolic acid solution. What do you think of that?"

Anderson nodded enthusiastically, "Excellent, by all means, scrub everything here with that. We are not sure why it works, but it does. Maybe it is one poison neutralizing other poisons. Or, some people now are suggesting that some kind of germs, tiny bacteria that can be seen only with the microscope, cause these diseases. I read a report just a few months ago that a fellow in France, a chemist by the name of Pasteur, has discovered that a disease of silk worms is caused by a certain bacterium. So perhaps carbolic acid simply kills certain kinds of those germs."

"Oh, my goodness, that's very interesting. What do you think, Will?"

"Well, I think there may be something to it."

"Could that have anything to do with the spread of contagious diseases?"

"It certainly could. Whether by poison air or germs, or what, we certainly can see that many diseases are contagious. In fact, that may have something to do with what we have here."

"What do you mean?" inquired Violet, fascinated with what Anderson was telling her.

"Well, Violet, the bringing of all those children from all parts of the county to your school may, simply by their contact with each other, be spreading these diseases around more extensively than usual."

"Oh, dear," gasped Violet, "should we not be bringing them together? Should we close the school, at least for a few months? Oh, Will, I don't know what to do."

"Oh, no, no, you know children get most of these diseases anyway; this probably just facilitates the spread so that they get them a little sooner. We cannot even be sure about that, and the steps you are taking to care for them, both here and in town, may help the sick to get through these diseases better than if left on their own."

Taking his leave, Will Anderson congratulated Violet on her work and promised to return to Fair Oaks every two days as might be necessary.

A few days later, Violet was startled when Evelina brought Bonnie Anne and J.J. down for their breakfast. Both children had red spots on their faces. She felt a chill come over her and she turned to Brent, her worry reflected in the tone of her voice. "Oh, Brent, look, look at the children. Do you think this might be smallpox? I remember that Mother had red blotches on her face."

Brent recognized her alarm, and he answered calmly and deliberately in a mild tone, "Oh, I don't think so."

Violet wasn't satisfied. "How can you be so sure? Do you think it's measles?"

"No, I'm pretty sure it's not measles. If you ask me, I would say chicken pox."

"Maybe so, but don't you think you should ride over and get Will Anderson?"

"Isn't he due here today?"

"Yes, he is, but not until this afternoon."

"It'll wait, Violet," he reassured her.

"Well, all right, if you say so."

Dr. Anderson confirmed Brent's diagnosis. "Nothing to worry about, really," he assured Violet. "They have a mild case of chicken pox. Keep them in, and quiet, and it should run its course in about a week."

"So they'll get a little holiday from school, I guess," said Violet, at which both children cheered enthusiastically.

As both Brent and Violet walked the doctor through the hall to the back door where he had parked his buggy, planning to ride on over to the workers' village after seeing Bonnie Anne and J.J., he said, "I might mention one other thing."

"What's that?" asked Brent.

Will Anderson cleared his throat before speaking. "Well, as you know, smallpox can be pretty devastating, and that is one disease we can do something about."

"You mean by inducing a so-called mild case by introducing matter from smallpox from somebody? I've read about that," remarked Violet.

"No, no, that was what they did back in the old days; that is what George Washington did with his troops during the Revolution. For several years now we have been able to accomplish the same thing with cowpox matter. Vaccination, we call it."

"From the Latin *vaccinus,* from cows?" smiled Violet.

"Precisely. Now, you see that gives immunity without having any smallpox, and the cowpox usually does nothing more than make a red and sore arm for a while."

"Do you recommend that?"

"Yes, I do."

"For children?" broke in Brent.

"For everybody above the age of about six."

Violet turned to Brent, "Sounds good?"

"By all means," he answered.

Violet now turned to Will Anderson and asked, "Could you do that for all our people here at Fair Oaks, and then maybe arrange with Dr. Hartley to vaccinate the pupils and staff at *The Joshua School*?"

Will Anderson nodded, obviously pleased his suggestion had been so readily accepted by the Sutlers. He answered with a smile, "Certainly, but it will take a few weeks to get the vaccine, and we should not give it to people who are sick."

"All right, in the meantime we'll work hard on getting those who are ill healthy again. Let's hope everyone can have the vaccination when it arrives."

But it was a season of serial diseases. During the next few weeks, several of the children in the church/school infirmary moved out while others moved in. The two diphtheria patients recovered sufficiently to return to their homes, but three others came in. Influenza was spreading among adults. At *The Joshua School* the situation was easing though continuing.

When the vaccine arrived, Will Anderson came out to Fair Oaks to vaccinate those who were healthy. Violet and Brent had explained it to the house servants and then they had gone over to Leo and Rachel's where they explained it to Jesse and Flora and all the foremen, and then they, in turn, spread out to explain it to the workers and their families.

Violet and Brent knew the servants and workers would likely be afraid, never having experienced anything like this before. The two discussed how they might allay the fears, and decided that Violet would be the first to be vaccinated at the main house, while the servants and children watched. Brent would wait, and Anderson would vaccinate him in the yard of the church/school, while the workers and their families watched. Most accepted the vaccination stolidly, except for some of the younger children who couldn't understand what was being done to them.

About the first of December, Bonnie Anne introduced a new element—mumps. Then a few days later J.J. came down with the same malady. They complained of aching jaws on both sides and were miserable and unsettled, but within ten days they seemed well, although somewhat lackadaisical, and Violet was wondering what would be next.

This also was the time for Brent to go into Columbia for the opening of the legislative session. With the children just over the mumps and not really themselves yet, Violet and Brent decided to delay the family's move to the town house until after Christmas. They would have scarcely gotten settled in before it would be time to return to Fair Oaks for the holidays, and they felt the children didn't need all the traveling back and forth in the cold weather.

Brent went on in to Columbia by himself, and when he returned late on Friday afternoon, the 13th, he joined Violet for hot chocolate in the library. She had just returned from the school in Sumter. Bonnie Anne and J.J. were still upstairs in the playroom, and both Brent and Violet welcomed some quiet time together.

Violet was anxious to tell Brent about the activities at school, but she was even more anxious to hear what had happened in the General Assembly. After Mammy had brought in the chocolate service, poured each a cup of the sweet concoction, she left the room to join Ellie in preparations for supper. Violet took a sip and then set down her cup. She turned to Brent and asked, with a twinkle in her eyes, "Well, what new sickness has the legislature contrived for the illfare of the state now?"

Anticipating Violet's reaction to what he was going to tell her, he broke into a chuckle before saying, "Well our greatest accomplishment this week was electing Honest John Patterson to the United States Senate."

Incredulous, Violet exclaimed, "Honest John, a United States Senator? How in the world did that come about? Brent, are you putting me on? Did you vote for him?"

Brent laughed with gusto. Then he answered, "No, my Love, I'm not putting you on, and no, I did not vote for him." In a teasing voice he went on, "My price would always be too high for him—but he found enough takers among the Radical Republicans."

"What happened? How on earth did he manage it? Oh, Brent I can scarcely believe this!"

"Believe it. He hired a suite of rooms over Fine's saloon, you know, it's right near the State House..."

"Yes, go on."

"Well, he turned those rooms into a house of free entertainment for the legislators. You know how those legislators, fresh out of the cotton fields and slave cabins, many wearing their old work clothes, would be susceptible to being influenced by the glamour of special entertainment, and especially by proffers of money made there."

"Is that true?"

"I have it from my reliable sources."

"How much money?"

"Well, some would sell their vote for one or two hundred dollars or some attractive gift; others cost several thousand. They say the whole thing cost him over forty thousand dollars."

"Oh, my goodness!"

"Oh, yes. I understand that he sent one of his agents to offer ten thousand dollars to Robert Elliott, one of the leading candidates against him, to withdraw. Anyway, he got away with it. Neither Elliott nor ex-Governor Scott could beat him after all that."

"Well, I declare!" exclaimed Violet. She poured each another cup of chocolate. The twinkle returned to her eyes. "Maybe there's a bright side after all. Maybe there will be some gain simply in getting him out of the state while Congress is in session."

"Ha, quite so," laughed Brent.

"But who are the princes of plunder that Moses has brought with him as he looks into the promised land?"

"I'm not sure who may be the greatest accomplices on that score, but it is interesting to note how many of his Negro friends are in the top administration. Of course you know the lieutenant governor, Howell Gleaves, is a mulatto, and Samuel Lee, a Negro from Aiken—not to be confused with our Sam Lee of Sumter—is speaker of the House, and Negroes in the administration include Henry Hayne, the secretary of state; Cardoza, the state treasurer, and H.W. Purvis, the adjutant general."

"All very interesting, and I fear things are going to get even worse before they get better," sighed Violet.

"No doubt."

Early Monday morning just before breakfast, as Brent was preparing to return to Columbia, he complained that he must have a bad tooth and said that he ought to do something about it as soon as he got back to the city.

"Oh, dear," said Violet sympathetically. "Which one?"

"Lower right jaw tooth; can't you see how it's swollen?"

Violet had to suppress a grin as she looked at him. "Looks to me like you have a bad jaw tooth on the lower left as well."

"You think so?" He winced as he ran his hand over his left jaw. "That's strange, isn't it?"

"Very. In fact it is so strange, my dear, that I would say you don't have a tooth problem at all. Brent, you've got the mumps!"

"Mumps! My, God, don't you know what that can mean for a man in my position?"

"I don't know about your position, but I know what it can mean for a man of your age; you'd better move very carefully so they don't go down on you."

"I know, if that's really what it is."

"Of course it is, and if they go down on a man it can be terrible."

"Yes, I know that...terrible," he muttered dejectedly, "so what do I do now?"

"Get back in bed, and stay very quiet, which I know will be very difficult for you, but you've got to do it, Brent."

"Oh, all right, but hadn't I better move into a guest room so that you won't be exposed?"

"Fiddlesticks, I had the mumps when I was seven years old. Now you get back in bed, and we'll bring your breakfast up to you, and I'll send Aaron to fetch Will Anderson so he can take a look at you." She took a fresh nightshirt out of the dresser drawer and handed it to Brent.

"Nothing that I have to chew, please," pleaded Brent as she left the room to go down stairs. He removed his shirt and pants and struggled into the nightshirt and back into the large bed. He closed his eyes and wondered what lay before him.

In just a short while, Jarvis, with Violet right behind him, brought in breakfast for Brent. The orange juice, poached egg with pieces of buttered toast in a glass, and a pot of coffee looked good to him, but clearly it was a major effort for him to eat it. Violet's heart ached for him as he labored to swallow. Finally, he laid down his fork in despair.

The swelling and the pain in Brent's jaws increased as the morning wore on. Will Anderson arrived about noon to take a look at his friend. He said there was little to do other than what they had done for the children—a little castor oil when necessary, the application of warm fomentations to the swollen and painful parts, taking soft food, and mainly rest. He said it was especially important that Brent, being an adult male, remain quietly in bed to avoid the danger of the mumps going down to infect the testicles.

By nightfall Brent could hardly sit up, and his countenance had taken on the grotesque appearance of an image in a curved mirror. He showed no improvement over the next three days, though he assured Violet that the mumps had not gone down. At last the pain eased, and slowly the swelling began to reduce, but Violet insisted that he remain in bed another three days in order to minimize the danger. In all, he was in bed for ten days. He followed all instructions religiously, and finally he was able to rejoin the legislature for a few days before it adjourned for Christmas, but it took several more weeks before his accustomed high energy level returned.

Celebration of Christmas was subdued that year, though there was a light snow, and the children thrilled at the sight of a rare white Christmas.

After New Year's Brent had to return to his Senate seat. Again he returned alone to Columbia. He had agreed with Violet that she and the children should remain at Fair Oaks a little longer in view of all the illness. Bonnie Anne and J.J. were now down with colds.

Bonnie Anne developed catarrh, with runny nose and yellowish discharge, and sore throat. Her forehead felt warm. *Dear God, don't let this be diphtheria! I've got to get Will Anderson here in a hurry.* To her relief, after examining Bonnie carefully, Will assured Violet that this was not diphtheria and that she should be all right within a week.

Then a serious chest cold set in. Violet tried to draw it out by applying mustard plasters to Bonnie Anne's chest and hanging onions around her neck. The little girl hated this treatment and resisted as much as she was able, but Violet persisted, knowing that it was necessary to help her daughter get well.

J.J. followed Bonnie Anne only by a few days in developing similar symptoms. Each now was confined to his and her own room. Violet spent much of every day and night with them. She wished Brent were there to help her during the week; he was so good with the children. Of course Evelina was a great help, and Mammy came up from the kitchen whenever she could to "tek keer uf mah babees" and to give Violet a little time to rest.

In another week Bonnie Anne was nearly well, but J.J.'s cold continued to drag on, with more feverishness, watering of the eyes, and irritation of the throat with much coughing. Satisfied that she was dealing simply with colds, Violet had not asked Will Anderson to return, but now, worried at how J.J.'s cold was lingering and the harsh sound of his cough, she sent Fabian to ask the doctor to come and take a look at J.J.

Approaching J.J.'s room, Will asked, "How long has this been going on?"

"Over two weeks, at least."

"Mm, let's have a look."

The doctor felt J.J.'s forehead, which was hot, looked at his eyes, which were weak and watery, and, with stethoscope, listened to his lungs, which were congested. "Now, young man, let's have a look at your tongue." J.J. promptly stuck out his tongue. "Now hold your tongue up; touch the roof of your mouth with the tip of your tongue. That's it. Mm...uh, huh."

"What is it?" Violet asked anxiously.

"Well, I'm afraid it is pertussis."

"Pertussis? What is that?"

"Whooping cough."

"Whooping cough? How can you be sure?"

"Well, the general symptoms are there, and then there is the tell-tale sign—open your mouth, J.J. and touch the top of your mouth with your tongue—look there, Violet, a sore there on the connective tissue of the tongue, on what we call the *praenum lingue.* All right, you can close your mouth now, J.J."

J.J. did as directed, wondering what kind of game the doctor was playing.

Will Anderson turned to Violet. "Shall we walk down the hall? I must be getting on my way."

As they approached the stairway, Violet asked, "Will, can't whooping cough be very dangerous?"

"Yes, Violet, sometimes. It is very dangerous for infants and often for children under five. How old is J.J. now?"

"Eight."

"Well then, he should overcome it all right, but we should take good care."

"How do we take care of him? What should we do?"

"Feed the little fellow lots of broth, have him drink lots of liquids–juice, milk, water–and give him a tablespoonful of cod liver oil each morning and evening. He probably won't like the taste, so try giving it with orange juice, a banana, or something."

"All right. Do you know what Grandmama says folks in the old days used to do for whooping cough?"

"No, but I can guess, Violet," laughed Will.

"They said a bag of ground little bugs around the neck, or white ant tea would help, or it would help to pass the victim through a horse collar three times, or mare's milk and tea made from blue clover blossoms might help, or even wearing a piece of stolen blue ribbon, or putting the victim in the hopper of a grist mill until the grist was ground."

"Now, Violet, surely you don't take any of those 'cures' seriously," chuckled Anderson. "Now, listen, in addition to what I've already told you, give J.J. a tablespoon of syrup of pepsin each day, and if he still needs a cathartic, give him a tablespoon of castor oil from time to time, but not more than necessary."

"All right, but Will, how long does whooping cough last?"

"Whooping cough has a way of hanging on, so you probably are in for a long siege. It usually goes through three stages. The first is the catarrh and so forth; he's probably about through that. Next comes the big one. This is when you have the coughing spells and the whoops. This phase usually lasts thirty to fifty days."

"Oh, my goodness. So long?"

"Yes, and then the final stage, a tapering off, may last another two or three weeks."

"Oh, dear, but, Will, can Bonnie Anne catch it from him?"

"She may have had just a touch of it and warded it off. If not, yes, she may well come down with it."

"Oh, I hope not. She's had enough sickness already."

They had reached the door, and the doctor was just stepping out on the porch when a thought struck Violet. "Will," she asked, "if J.J. is going to be sick for such a long time, shouldn't we–the children and I–just plan on staying at Fair Oaks for the rest of this legislative session? I don't want to move J.J. when he's not well. What do you think?"

"Quite right. By all means, do not consider moving J.J. I know it's hard on you and Brent to be separated like this, but right now, that's the way it must be. We've got to get that little fellow well again."

Near the end of January two of the older former workers, a man and a woman, died of pneumonia. Violet asked Reverend Jackson to come back and conduct a double funeral service. Violet had tried to take care with respect to the old folks on the plantation. When they were too old to work, she put them on one-fourth pay and continued to provide food and clothing, and she always arranged for someone to cook for them if they no longer could do it. She always was prompt to provide medical care, and she always was saddened when any of them died.

Then about the third week in February Violet began to feel a tingling and a rawness in her throat. She said nothing until after a couple of days of this the pain had developed in her throat to the point that she could not eat anything. This brought Brent into action. "I'll fetch Will Anderson right away," he said after dinner when she had not been able to eat.

"Oh, no," Violet croaked, "not now. Let's wait until morning to see if it isn't better."

By morning it was a lot worse. Violet felt a swelling and tightening in her throat. She felt severe pain in her neck and ears, and her neck was swollen. She could not even swallow and could hardly breathe. *Oh, God,* she thought *this is a sign of diphtheria. I know this can be very dangerous. I had better do something at least so I can take care of J.J. Oh, dear God, please help me to get well; please let me live and see my children grow up.* By now she was on the verge of panic. She could not even call to Brent. She had to lie there and wait for him to come back in the bedroom to inquire how she felt.

She shook her head. Tears fell from her eyes. She managed to whisper, "Awful. I'm afraid it may be diphtheria. Go get Will Anderson."

He pulled back in shock, and then, without a word, tore from the room. To Violet, it seemed that he was gone for hours, but actually he was back with the doctor in a little over an hour. Will Anderson examined her carefully without saying a word.. When he stood up she whispered, "Is it diphtheria?"

He shook his head and answered thoughtfully, "No, I think not. I think you have been having a severe case of tonsillitis, and now you have what we call quinsy."

"Quinsy? What's that?" asked Brent who was standing by the doctor and watching his every movement.

"That's a condition where you have abscesses around the tonsils."

"Can you do anything about it, Will? She seems so be in such pain. It tears me to bits to see Violet like this. You know, except for an occasional slight cold, she's never sick."

"I know, but she has literally worn herself out taking care of the children, and the sick workers, and keeping an eye on the sick pupils at her school. It would appear that the body can take just so much stress and fatigue, and then it breaks down so that it can get some rest. And yes, there is something we can do about these abscesses. I think to give Violet some quick relief we should lance that large abscess on her tonsil. How about it, Violet? Nod if you want me to do this."

Violet managed a nod. Something had to be done. She felt she could not take much more of this pain.

Will asked Evelina to bring a chamber pot containing water, a pitcher of warm soda water, and a glass. Then he told Violet to sit up, and when Evelina returned with the pot he asked that she hold it under Violet's mouth. He took a lancet from his bag, told Violet to hold her head back and open her mouth wide, and he went to work. Holding her mouth firmly with his left hand, he quickly and deftly reached into Violet's mouth and made the incision. Matter gushed out into the pot as she coughed.

"My, god," Brent exclaimed, "you had more corruption in there than Frank Moses has in the State House!" Will snickered, but Violet was unable to see the humor in Brent's remark.

After she had coughed out the last and vomited what was left in her stomach—mostly yellowish liquid since she had been unable to eat for several days—Will had her gargle and irrigate her throat with the soda water. Then she fell back on her pillow, completely drained. The doctor motioned Brent to sit down and wait quietly. He pulled a chair up by Violet's bed and waited. Within minutes Violet could say that she thought she was feeling a little better.

Will smiled. "Now, Violet, I want you to take some of this quinine twice a day, every other day. On alternate days, take this salicylic acid solution twice a day. I believe you said you had some carbolic acid?"

"Yes," she whispered, but louder than before.

He turned to Evelina. "Now listen carefully, Evelina. I want you to boil a five percent solution—that would be one cup of this in twenty cups of water—and then have Miss Violet breathe the steam from it. Do this several times a day."

"We do hit, Massuh Doctor, we do hit," burst forth Mammy who had followed the doctor upstairs to see what he said about her poor sick baby, Miss Violet. She had stood in the doorway watching his every move and listening to everything he said. She had never seen Miss Violet so sick in all her born days, and she had been beside herself with worry. She didn't approve of the way Miss Violet went down to the workers' cabins and nursed those sick folks and wore herself out and all, and now all that had made her sick, her sweet little baby.

Evelina nodded to the doctor and smiled at Mammy. "Doncha worree none, Massuh Doctor, we tek good keer uv Mis' Violet. Mammy an' meh watch ober her good."

"Don't forget to count me in on that, you all," chuckled Brent as the doctor and the two servants grinned. Even Violet managed a weak smile at her husband.

Each day that Violet was ill brought further deterioration of the smooth operation of the plantation and the household. Nobody had realized how much all hands looked to Violet for direction. Brent was there every day, and he had no hesitation to assert authority and leadership. The trouble was, he was not always sure what needed to be done, or how it should be done. Leo and the foremen knew well enough how to do their duties, and Mammy and Jarvis and the others knew theirs, but somehow they did not have that initiative for action for which almost unconsciously they depended on Violet.

Brent was restless and not sure what he should be doing, but he rode around and put in appearances. Both children were upset at the very idea that their mother should be sick. They became unruly and unsettled, even though J.J. was confined to his bed.

Within four days after the doctor's treatment, Violet was much improved, and in another five days she was back on her feet. She remained weak for several more days but everyone felt relieved that once more they could look to her for direction.

Violet's main worry now was for J.J. He was becoming even thinner, almost emaciated looking. She was startled every night by outbursts of his coughing and whoops, and found herself lying awake in bed waiting for another attack. Several times a day he went into such bouts of coughing that he was almost paralyzed for want of air until the relieving whoop came.

She realized that J.J. was only about midway through the second and most dangerous phase of his whooping cough. Then came a period of several days when the frequency of the coughing spells declined, but he seemed to be weakening and spending most of each day between spells in sleeping. When Doctor Anderson called near the end of that week, Violet searched intently for some sign of encouragement.

"He is a very sick little boy," the doctor told Violet and Brent as they paused with him in the library before he left.

"Will, isn't there anything else we can do?" demanded Violet.

"Just wait, and keep an eye on him. The next few days should be critical," he answered.

After Will had left, Violet turned to Brent, her voice breaking, "I don't know what to do. I just can't think of little J.J.–."

"Violet! Stop that! Our son is going to be all right." He softened his voice and repeated tenderly, "Darling, he *is* going to pull out of this."

"Brent, I'm tired of being brave and strong and optimistic. I'm just not up to that now. I'm scared and I'm tired. I just want to lie down and cry and cry."

He pulled her to him and held her in his arms, stroking her soft, dark hair with his hand. He smoothed a tendril back from her forehead and kissed her tears gently. "I know, my Darling, you have always been brave and strong, standing up to the Yankees and taking care of everyone. You were not afraid of the Yankees; you were very brave. Now you must be brave–for J.J., for Bonnie Anne, for everybody."

"But I didn't really fear the Yankees, Brent. I felt outrage, not fear. You can stand up to Yankees. That's different from disease. How does one stand up to whooping cough?"

"I'll tell you how. By doing all that the doctor told you to."

J.J. seemed a little stronger the next week, but he still was being difficult in taking his cod liver oil.

"Here, you *must* take your cod liver oil," Violet would say, trying to sound cheerful.

Predictably he would protest, "I won't, I won't! I hate it! It tastes awful. I won't, I won't!" and he would press his lips together tightly and turn his head away.

When she gave it with orange juice, his reaction was, "I don't like orange juice anymore. I don't like cod liver oil. I don't like orange juice with that awful stuff in it." and he would push the glass away.

When she tried bananas, it was with the same result. He always had liked bananas–one of his favorite foods. Now he would not eat any more bananas even without cod liver oil.

Still Violet kept cajoling, and one way or another she was able to get a couple of tablespoonfuls down him each day. She always breathed a deep sigh of relief when this was accomplished.

At last, by the end of March, J.J. was showing signs of getting stronger, and it appeared that he had entered the third and final phase of his illness. Now Violet felt free to give a good deal of time to the planting of crops and she resumed her twice-weekly visits to *The Joshua School.* Still, Brent worked out his schedule—the Senate, the railroad, the warehouses—to be at the house whenever Violet was not there.

Wednesday, April 16th, was the brightest, warmest day of the spring thus far—not a cloud in the sky, a warm zephyr gently tugging at bushes and boughs. Brent had returned to Columbia for the rest of the week, and Bonnie Anne was at her school at Edge Hill. Violet had spent the previous day at *The Joshua School,* and this morning she had ridden out to see how the crops were coming. It was a lazy day; it was a busy day.

J.J. still was in his bed, but he was becoming restless. Violet took his dinner, still mostly soup and milk, up to him shortly after noon. When he had finished, she inquired, "J.J., how are you feeling?"

"Oh, Mommy, I'm feeling good now," he answered with a smile, and then in a quite serious tone he informed her, "I don't think I need to stay in bed any longer."

Violet giggled, "Well, I'll tell you. I think this might be a good day for you to sit out-of-doors for a while. Would you like that?"

J.J. clapped his hands in delight. "Oh, yes, Mommy, may I, may I? Please, Mommy."

Violet laughed at her young son. It was so wonderful to see him in high spirits again. "You rest here for half an hour, and then Evelina and I will take you out." So eager was he to go outside that he immediately lay back in bed and let her pull the sheets up around his shoulders.

Violet kissed him and left to ask Evelina to get a couple of blankets. They took these downstairs and put them on a rocking chair in the office, and then together carried the chair out the back door and about thirty steps into the back yard. When they returned to J.J.'s room the boy hopped out of his bed and slipped into his flannel house shoes. Violet helped him put on his bathrobe, and Evelina brought another blanket as Violet went with J.J. down the stairs. Holding tightly to the rail, he made his way down, one step at a time, while Violet guarded him against any misstep. *He's gotten so very weak, not at all like the little boy who used to race up and down stairs as fast as he could go. These days we certainly won't have to caution him to slow down and walk up the stairs,* she thought sadly, but then she scolded herself, *Stop thinking like that. We are so fortunate that he is getting well now.*

They reached the bottom of the stairs, and Evelina threw the blanket over his shoulders. She joined Violet in clasping hands on arms to make a cradle seat for J.J. Together they carried him outside to the rocking chair, put him in it, and covered him with blankets, wrapping them securely around his legs and shoulders.

J.J. was beside himself with delight. He took a deep breath of fresh air. "Oh, it feels good out here." Looking down he noticed to the left of his chair a little portable fence that bounded a couple of square yards of grass. The fence formed a pen containing baby chicks. "Oh, Mommy, where did the baby chicks come from?" he exclaimed.

"They just hatched three weeks ago, pecked their way out of their shells, and looked upon the world for the first time. They live in the brooder house, over there by the hen house, where they can keep warm. But on a nice day like this they can come outdoors for awhile."

The chicks, little yellow fuzz balls, were running to and fro, chirping in competition while the old mother hen, a big buff Orpington, looked on with concern.

"I wish I could see them peck out of their eggs," J.J. said. "Mommy, may I hold one? Please, Mommy?"

Violet picked up one of the nervous chicks and handed it to J.J. He set it on his lap formed by the blankets and gently stroked the chick until it stopped trembling. J.J. smiled with pleasure and handed it back to his mother who returned it to the pen—to the obvious relief of the mother hen who had been clucking loudly the entire time. J.J. continued to watch in fascination as the chicks continued to run about looking for food and exploring in general their confined world.

After several minutes J.J. shifted his attention to a robin, hopping on the grass to his right front. Then a mocking bird, sitting in a nearby mulberry tree, displayed its white feathers of underwings and tail as it flew away.

Watching the mocking bird, Violet began singing, "Listen to the mocking bird, Listen to the mocking bird—." Suddenly thinking of Little Josh, she choked up, but quickly recovered before J.J. could notice. The chirping of a Carolina wren caught his attention, and then, best of all, a bluebird.

Leaning back in his chair, J.J. gazed all about. He looked out to the early blossoms of the flower garden, beyond the buildings to his right, and to the apple blossoms and peach blossoms of the orchards in the distance. He gazed over at the pond to his front and noticed the ducks and geese; he looked out toward the barns to his left front and left, and to the green meadows beyond. Then the flight of a bumblebee brought his attention to dandelions and violets all around him.

"Mommy, look at the flowers," he said.

Violet picked a large dandelion and a violet and handed them to J.J.

"These are the prettiest and best flowers of all," he announced. "The dandelion looks like the warm sun, and the violet looks like your eyes, Mommy, and that's your name, too." He gazed up at her with love. "And they're the best 'cause nobody has to work to make them grow and 'cause they don't have any stickers or anything. They're just pretty."

Evelina arrived with a cup of hot chocolate and a piece of buttered toast. J.J. thought these the best he ever had tasted. He quickly consumed the refreshments, to the delight of his mother and Evelina, and then leaned back in the chair again, breathing in all the warmth and beauty around him.

After an hour or so Violet announced that it was time to go in. J.J. protested just for a moment, but he felt so good that he was agreeable to anything. Besides, his mother promised he could come out the next day, if the weather continued to be so fair and warm.

Before starting back, Violet offered J.J. a banana. Without thinking, he began to protest, "No, I hat–", but this time he caught himself and stopped.

Violet smiled and said, "You may have this one without cod liver oil."

"But, Mommy, now all bananas taste like that awful cod liver oil."

"Just try it."

He took it, and much to his own surprise found it so good that he ate it with relish. When Violet broke into laughter, he looked at her sheepishly. She began removing the blankets from his shoulders and legs. "Now we really must go in. Do you think you can walk back to the house?"

"I think so, Mommy," he answered as he rose. Violet put one blanket over her shoulders, and took his hand. They started walking slowly while Evelina picked up the other blankets.

As they reached the house, J.J. stopped for another look all around. Turning back to his mother he said, "Mommy, this is the most beautiful, best day of my whole life."

"It is a beautiful day, but why do you say that?"

"Cause it's the day I got well, and I never will forget it." And he never did.

Chapter 54

Fishing, Hunting, Teaching

1873

"Mommy, Mommy, can I go fishing? Can I, can I?"

"*May* you go fishing?"

"Yes, yes, that's what I said, can I go fishing?"

"J.J., it's *may* I go fishing. How many times have I told you that when you ask permission to do something, you say '*may* I'?"

"Yes, yes, may I, Mommy?"

"Ah, yes, you used to enjoy fishing with Little Josh, didn't you?"

"Yes, it was fun being with Little Josh, but I never caught nothin'."

"You never caught *anything*, J.J.," sighed Violet. It seemed she had to correct J.J.'s grammar so often these days.

A touch exasperated, J.J. replied, "That's what I said, I never caught nothin'."

"I know, but repeat after me, 'I never caught *anything*,'" instructed Violet, emphasizing the word.

"I never caught *anything*," parroted J.J., mimicking his mother.

"Good boy, J.J., that's right, but Daddy will be back this evening. Why not wait until he can go with you?"

"No, I want to go now," he said stubbornly. "I want to surprise him. Please, Mommy, can I, uh, may I go now?"

"J.J., you know a fish hook can be very dangerous—"

"*May* be dangerous, Mommy," said J.J. impudently.

"No, nobody is asking permission; it's correct to say 'a fish hook *can* be dangerous'. But to go on, if you are not very, very careful, the hook may put your eye out, or get caught in your finger or your clothes. Anyway, you shouldn't get into Daddy's fishing gear when he is not here."

"I don't want to use Daddy's; I'll make mine. Little Josh taught me."

"What about a hook?"

"I'm gonna bend a pin."

"What will you use for fishing line?"

"Some strong thread."

"And what will you use for a pole?"

"I'm gonna make it from a little tree."

Violet realized J.J. had given some thought and planning to this, and, to tell the truth, she found she was proud of her little son and felt he should be encouraged. So she said, "Well, all right. I'll be working out in the flower garden. You can come along and we'll stop there and dig to see if we can find some fishing worms. Now, you go find Hattie and ask her to give you some straight pins and a spool of heavy black thread. And I think you had better not go barefoot. Wear your shoes so you won't be stepping on the pins or sharp stones or anything."

"Yes, ma'am," called out J.J. as he happily scampered upstairs to look for Hattie.

When he returned with pins and thread, Violet was putting on her sun bonnet. She handed J.J. a glass jar for the worms.

"Oh, Mommy, I'll need a bucket to put my fish in."

"Oh, of course. We'll pick up a bucket out in the tool shed; we'll have to stop there to get a shovel anyhow."

Down in the flower garden, they both felt the exhilaration of a beautiful day in mid-May. J.J. insisted that he dig for the worms. He was having trouble until his mother stepped on the shovel to force it into the ground, and then he turned the soil over. Three turns of the ground yielded half a dozen thick, juicy worms.

"Oh, Mommy, the fish are gonna like these worms!" he exclaimed delightedly as he held up the jar for her to see.

"That's enough worms, I think," Violet said, "Let's go." She went along far enough through the garden to a place where she would be able to keep an eye on J.J. on the creek bank without his being aware of it.

She watched as he hurried on toward the creek. *So like his father in so many ways,* she thought fondly.

Near the bank he found a sapling which he went to work on to make his fishing pole. After jumping up, grabbing it, and riding it to the ground, he twisted and pulled the sapling back and forth until it broke free. Then he pulled off all the branches and twigs until he had a flexible pole a couple of feet taller than he was. As Violet watched each movement, he got out the thick thread, pulled several feet off the spool, and tied one end to the small end of the pole. It took him a while to break the thread, but he managed. Then he got out a pin, and apparently dropped it for he was searching all around on the ground. Finally, he gave up the search and got out another pin, bent it into a V and tied the line tightly just under the large head of the pin. He found a small stick that he tied a foot above the pin to be a bobber, and then he took a worm from the jar and secured it on the pin. With his pole and baited line, he moved down the bank of the creek until Violet could see only his head. *Josh apparently taught him well,* she thought.

She continued watching. He dropped his line into the water and stood there waiting. For several minutes, nothing happened. Growing impatient, he brought out the line several times to take a look at his hook, and rebaited the pin.

Sensing that J.J. was exercising caution on the bank, Violet turned to her flowers for a while. Suddenly she heard a shout, "I got a fish! I got a fish! Mommy, Mommy, I caught a fish! All by myself!"

She looked up in time to see J.J. running toward her, carrying his pole and holding up the end of his line. When he got closer, she could see that he did indeed have a fish on the end of his line—a pretty little fish. J.J. had forgotten his worms and his bucket in his excitement. Violet held his pole and the fish while he went back for them.

He came running back, asking, "Mommy, can I, can I, *may* I ask Mammy to cook the fish for our supper tonight? Oh, Daddy will be so surprised, won't he?"

Violet smiled indulgently at J.J. "Yes, indeed, he will be so surprised, and so proud of you, and we'll see about having it for supper; maybe Mammy can cook it just for you."

So filled with excitement was J.J. that he could do nothing more as he waited impatiently for his father to get home. When the afternoon train stopped and then went on, J.J. went flying down the lane, now with the fish in a bucket half-filled with water. "Look, Daddy! Look, Daddy! Look at what I caught today! All by myself!"

When Brent saw the fish, his eyes lit up, and he patted J.J. on the back. "Well, son, you have caught your first fish, and all by yourself, haven't you? I'm mighty proud of you, that's for sure."

J.J. beamed at his father's praise. "What kind is it, Daddy?"

Brent took another look in the bucket. "Well, that's a little sunfish."

"Is it good to eat? Mommy said Mammy might fix it for supper."

"Sure. Sunfish are quite tasty. Come on, let's go give it to Mammy to cook for you." The two headed toward the kitchen, J.J. skipping alongside his father. Brent looked down at his son, and the thought struck him that J.J. had done a great deal of growing up over the last years. It was hard to believe that the little fellow was already nine years old. "Tell you what, son, this week-end we'll get out my fishing gear and take the rowboat out to the center of the pond where it's deep, and we'll do some more fishing. Just the two of us. How does that sound to you?"

"Oh, Daddy! Yes!" was all the little boy could manage.

The next week, Brent arrived home at Fair Oaks, from Columbia, with a weapon slung over his shoulder. Violet met him at the back door of the office. She stood on tiptoe to give him a hello kiss, then stood back to look at him, her eyebrows raised in question. "What in the world do you have there? Is Potter headed this way again or something?"

Stepping into the room Brent grinned and answered, "This, my dear, is a new sixteen-gauge, double-barreled, full-choke shotgun. Isn't it a beauty?" He slung it off his shoulder and held it up for her to examine.

"It's a beauty all right. How many Yankees could you get in one firing of both barrels?"

"Probably a whole platoon if they stand still; half that many if they're running sideways; twice that many if they turn tail and run," laughed Brent.

"Good! Let's keep it."

"Actually, I'm thinking more of ducks and partridges and rabbits and squirrels than I am of Yankees."

"That sounds appealing."

"Yes, I can't wait to try it out; I was thinking of taking J.J. squirrel hunting tomorrow."

"Oh, Brent, I don't know," responded Violet, a touch alarmed, "Do you think he's ready for that?"

"Now, Violet, you know we'll be very careful; this is an important part of every Southern boy's bringing up. It's important for him to learn how to use a gun properly and the caution that must be exercised at all times when handling any gun."

The next morning, J.J. was up and ready to go, ahead of everyone else. Knowing that he would be too excited to accomplish very much, Violet had excused him from piano practice that morning, to his delight—although he enjoyed playing the piano and was doing quite well with it. After all had finished their breakfast of fried eggs, hash brown Irish potatoes, grits, bacon, and hot biscuits sweetened with apple butter, Brent said, "Well, son, let's go."

"I'm ready," replied J.J., eagerly jumping up from his chair. They told the others good-bye.

Violet kissed them both and cautioned them to be careful. Brent told her not to worry.

"Oh, sure," she answered, forcing a smile.

On their way out, Brent stopped by the office to take his prized new shotgun from the rack of eight guns, and he picked up a box of shells, threw his game bag over his shoulder, and put on an old seaman's cap.

As they went down the steps, he said to J.J., "You can ride your pony, if you wish. I'll take Jeb."

Moving at a walk or slow trot they rode their steeds back toward the woods. A quarter of a mile from the edge of the woods Brent stopped and dismounted. "We'll tie our horses here and walk the rest of the way." he announced.

As J.J. brought his horse to a stop, he asked, "Why, Daddy?"

"Don't you like to walk?" asked Brent, helping J.J. to dismount, and then securing both horses.

"Sure, but why, Daddy?"

"Well, son, two reasons. We don't want the horses to frighten the game away, and we don't want the horses to be frightened by the sound of the gun. Blitzen, especially, would not be used to it, and he might shy and try to run away.

Brent took the shotgun from the saddle holster, wrapped his right arm around it so that the barrels would point to the ground, and they walked off.

"Daddy," said J.J., trotting beside Brent.

"Yes?" Brent shortened his stride and slowed his pace so that J.J. could keep up.

"Why do you carry your gun like that? My toy soldiers always have their guns up on their shoulders, pointing up in the air."

"Yes, that's right, but when no one is marching in front of us, it is safer to point it to the ground, so if it goes off by accident it won't hurt anybody. Remember that now."

They were walking along the lane between a big cotton field on their left and a cornfield on their right. A rail fence, punctuated now and then by a basswood tree or a cedar tree, bordered the cornfield. They were walking quietly when suddenly Brent stopped and put out his arm to hold J.J. back. "Look," he whispered, see up there on the fence?"

"Daddy, it looks like a little bear," J.J. whispered back.

"It's a raccoon."

"Yes, I know, a 'coon."

"They usually come out at night, but this is a young one, and he has decided to come out exploring in the daytime. Now I'll stand here, and you walk as softly as you can and see how close you can get to him."

J.J. had no more than started forward when the little raccoon stopped and looked straight at the boy. As J.J. kept walking slowly, trying not to rattle leaves, the raccoon froze in place. Then as J.J. came to within twenty feet, the raccoon jumped down on the other side of the fence. J.J. went up to where the raccoon had been and looked all around to try to see where it had gone, but could find no trace. While J.J. was still looking intently down at the grass, Brent came up and tapped him on the shoulder and pointed upward. J.J. looked up, and there was the raccoon, his small pointed chin resting in a fork of a tree, paws wrapped around the limb, eyes looking intently at the boy, not ten feet away. For a couple of minutes boy and raccoon just stared at each other. Then the raccoon quickly climbed down the tree and scampered off.

"All the time I was looking around on the ground for him he was up there in the tree watching me, wasn't he?" asked J.J., feeling a bit foolish.

"Like he was playing hide-and-seek."

"Yes! I wish we could take him home."

"Well, he's gone now, probably with his mother and brothers and sisters. He's happier with them and the woods than he would be in a pen at home, son. Wild creatures like their freedom; they don't like to be restricted."

"I don't either."

Brent laughed. By now they were approaching the woods. "Now, we are going to be looking for fox squirrels; they are the big gray ones. They're usually up in the biggest trees."

After a short while, Brent stopped and, placing his hand on J.J.'s shoulder, said in a low voice, "Hold it right here. I'll bet you there's a big fox squirrel up in that large tree right there."

J.J. looked intently and whispered, "I don't see any squirrel there."

"No, you don't, and I don't either. You see, whenever people approach, the squirrel always runs around on the other side of the tree to hide. Now, I want you to walk in a big circle around that tree there."

"But why, Daddy?"

"Because when the squirrel sees you he'll come around to this side, and then I can shoot him."

Without a further word, J.J. started walking in the prescribed circle. When he had reached the opposite side, Brent suddenly lifted the shotgun and fired. A big, gray fox squirrel came tumbling down. J.J. came running back to cheer his father's marksmanship. Brent knelt down and took out his hunting knife.

"You see, son, you want to gut your game as soon as you can, especially in warm weather. We all hunt to put additional food on the table, and we want that food to be as clean and fresh as possible; that way, it'll have a better taste. Meat that has not been gutted quickly can taste bad and make a person sick. Now watch carefully so you can learn what has to be done." He inserted his knife at the top of the squirrel's rib cage, under the throat, and quickly ran it down to the anal track. He reached in with two fingers, cleaned out the guts, and spilled them on the ground."

"Ugh, what are you going to do with that stuff?" J.J. asked, screwing up his nose in distaste.

"Leave it on the ground. It'll be gone before the day is over."

"Gone?"

"Yes. It'll be eaten by mice, raccoons, and other small animals. They'll leave nothing."

"Ugh!"

Brent laughed, picked up the squirrel, and put it in his leather game bag. He slung the bag back over his shoulder as he said, "We'll let Mammy skin it when we get home."

"What will she do with the skins?"

"Oh, she may give them to Hattie or to Rachel or some of the other women. They use these to make warm muffs and hats and fur collars for winter coats. Some of the workers have even made short coats out of the skins."

After five more such successes, Brent announced that that would be enough. "We'll have Mammy kill a couple of chickens and make us some of that delicious Brunswick stew of hers. You'll like that, won't you?" grinned Brent.

"Oh, yes, I *love* her stew, and this time it'll be *our* squirrels, not Aaron's, not Fabian's, not Leo's, not anybody's but ours!"

"Well, now, you know you've eaten stew made from squirrels your Daddy has shot," chuckled Brent.

"Yes, but this time it's different; I helped you shoot the squirrels!"

As they started walking back toward the edge of the woods, Brent asked, "Would you like to shoot my new gun?"

J.J. could scarcely believe his ears. "Oh, yes, yes!" he shouted in delight. "Can I shoot a squirrel?"

"*May* I shoot a squirrel?" corrected Brent.

"Yes, Daddy, that's what I said."

"Well, first, let's just take a practice shot and get used to the gun."

"All right, where?" he asked, jumping up and down again with excitement.

"Well, son, first of all, stop jumping up and down. You must learn that the hunter must always be cool, calm, and collected, in control of himself and of his gun."

They walked back through the gate, and Brent said, "Here, we'll shoot back into the woods."

He handed the unloaded gun to J.J., and the boy almost dropped it. "Pretty heavy, isn't it?" Brent said. "Here, rest the barrel on the top of the rail fence and hold the stock, here, back on your shoulder. Now, look down the barrel–aim at something–and pull the trigger slowly."

A click sounded as J.J. pulled the trigger. "Now put in a real bullet, Daddy."

"It's called a *shell*," Brent corrected him, and then loaded one chamber only. He put the shotgun in the boy's hands, again resting the barrel on the fence, and cocked the hammer. "Now pull it back hard—"

BANG!

"Ouch!" yelled J.J. as he fell flat on his back.

Brent turned aside to hide an involuntary laugh and then helped J.J. up, saying, "Are you all right, son?"

"Yes...well...just my shoulder hurts a little bit," answered J.J., a startled look still upon his face and tears in his eyes as he got up. He wiped his eyes with his sleeve as he said, "Wow, Daddy, that really hits hard." He rubbed his shoulder with his other hand.

"Son, I'm sorry. That's the kick. Actually, your falling down probably saved your shoulder from getting hurt more because that took up a lot of the kick. You didn't let me finish my instructions; I was trying to tell you to pull the stock very tightly against your shoulder so it wouldn't kick so hard. I wasn't saying to pull the trigger."

"Oh," muttered J.J. sheepishly. He didn't want his father to think him a baby. He might not want to take him hunting again, so he asked, "Daddy, may I shoot it again? I know I can do it right next time."

Brent felt badly about the incident. He wasn't sure J.J. should try again, but he was proud of his son's tenacity. "Isn't your shoulder too sore?" he asked.

"No, Daddy, I *want* to do it right this time. I need to learn if I'm gonna be a good shooter like you."

Brent smiled at that. "Here, put my cap over your shoulder for a cushion."

Before reloading, Brent repeated his instructions, "Now listen carefully to everything I say *before* you do anything. Hold the stock very strongly against your shoulder, look down the barrel, and when you are all ready, squeeze the trigger slowly. And another thing—spread your feet apart, with the left foot forward of the other one, like you stand on a wagon when a horse is pulling it at a rapid gait."

J.J. took the position as instructed, barrel of the gun resting on the fence. Brent loaded and cocked the gun. "It's ready now; be sure to hold the gun very, *very*, tightly against your shoulder...that's right; now aim down the barrel, and slowly squeeze the trigger. Now!"

This time at the loud bang J.J. stood his ground as some birds flew up.

"Good! That was good, J.J., and you scared up some partridges." He took the gun from J.J., saying, "That's enough for this time; let's go back to the house." He put his right arm around the gun, barrel down, and with his left hand took J.J.'s right to lead him around in the right direction.

As they turned toward the lane J.J. suddenly cried, "Oh, Daddy, look at all the pretty little flowers. Those are violets, like Mommy's name. Oh, Daddy, can we pick some to take to Mommy?"

"Indeed we can, and we should. These are among your mother's favorite flowers." He smiled at J.J., thinking aloud, "They are tender and soft and beautiful, and just the color of your mother's eyes at certain times."

"Is that why Grandmama and Granddaddy named her `Violet'?"

"Well, no, I really don't think so. As I recall, your granddaddy wanted to name all his daughters after flowers, but maybe he thought of these when he saw her; I don't know. Your mother is named Violet Lee, and her sisters—your two aunts—are named Charlotte Rose and Susan Phlox."

"Oh. But I don't call them Aunt Rose and Aunt Phlox."

"No, that's true. They're called by their first name, and your mother's happens to be Violet." Brent could see that this was getting deeper than he intended, so he said to J.J., "Come on, let's pick a handful to take to mother." It wasn't long before they had a handful.

Rising, Brent collected his gun, and they walked hand in hand toward their horses. J.J. consciously lengthened his stride, trying to match his father's. He felt at least a foot taller and ten years older.

After Brent and J.J. had left, Violet and Bonnie Anne drove into Sumter. On the way into town Violet asked Bonnie Anne if she would like to be a real teacher at the school, just for that day.

"Oh, yes, Mommy, I do. It will be such fun to be a real teacher, not a play teacher like J.J. and my dollies and I sometimes do. But, Mommy, I don't know how to be a *real* teacher. What will I do?"

"I was thinking that you could use your music to help teach the children new words."

"My music? How, Mommy?"

"Well, I was thinking, take a song that they know how to sing. You could play the melody on the piano while they sing the song. You might do this a couple of times. I'll write the words on the blackboard before you start, and then after they sing the song, you could use the pointer to point to the words as they sing the song again. Then you might ask if there are any words on the blackboard they know. If so, they could take turns underlining these, and repeating the word. Then they could sing the song again as you use your pointer to designate each word as they sing it. Then you might ask if any of them would like to try reading a whole line of the song, with everyone repeating the line as you point to the words. Then they could copy the words to the song, and look at what they have written as they sing the song over several times.

"Oh, I can do all that. That sounds like fun."

"Of course you can."

"And then may I read them a story from a book?"

"I'm sure they would like that. It's good to read to children."

"Why do you say it's good?"

"Well, honey, I mean that it's helpful for them to hear words in stories. They learn new ideas along with new words and ways of using words. Most of these children come from homes where the language is very limited."

"Limited?"

"Yes, that means the same words are used over and over again, so there's not much opportunity to learn new ones or to hear a more formal type of grammar. And I doubt that scarcely any of the parents or grandparents can read, so they don't get to have stories read to them."

"But, Mommy, they do get to *hear* stories. Colored folks are always telling stories when they get together and visit with family and friends. And they're good, too. Remember how Little Josh used to take J.J. and me with him to the workers' village to hear stories that the old people told."

"Ah, yes, and those stories are rich with colorful words and often instructive in their special way."

"Well, aren't they good for the children, too?"

Violet nodded and smiled, "Indeed yes, and they are important to the black folks heritage, but it's not quite the same as reading stories from books where the language is a bit different. We want our children at *The Joshua School* to be able to make something of themselves, and if they are going to do this, they will need learn much more than they have been getting."

At *The Joshua School,* Violet led Bonnie Anne into a class of students who were just learning to read. There the teacher told four children to go with Bonnie Anne into a small music study room for special instruction. Violet wrote the words to the song Bonnie Anne had selected on the blackboard and then went to a bench at the back of the room where she sat down to observe. She was amazed at what she saw.

Bonnie Anne stepped to the front and asked the children to listen to her carefully. "My name is Miss Sutler, and I will be your teacher for part of today. I have some activities planned which I believe will be interesting and enjoyable for you to do."

One of the boys began giggling. Looking at him, Bonnie Anne reprimanded him in a stern voice, "That will be quite enough. We will have none of that in this class." She slapped her pointer on the desk two times.

With a surprised look on his face, the young fellow closed his mouth and sat up straight. It was all Violet could do to keep a straight face and not burst into laughter.

"Thank you, young man," said Bonnie Anne, now giving him a smile. He relaxed at this and gave her all his attention. Then she explained what they would be doing. She walked over to the piano and began playing while the children sang. She remembered everything she and Violet had talked about. The pupils were attentive and participated eagerly; some knew words; some didn't, but they all tried. At the end of the lesson, they wanted to do it all over again. Bonnie Anne glanced at her mother, and Violet gave a slight nod. So the lesson was repeated, this time with even more eagerness and participation on the part of the children. Violet could see that some of the children had learned a number of words by the time the lesson was concluded.

Bonnie Anne's students had enjoyed her lesson so much, they chattered all through their meal about what fun they had. They told their teacher, their classmates, and other teachers. In the teachers' lounge, one of the teachers came up and asked Violet if it would be all right for Bonnie Anne to take a few of her pupils and do the same thing with them that afternoon after their rest period.

Bonnie Anne was enthralled. She felt so grown-up, and had a deep sense of accomplishment. "Oh, Mommy, may I? I really want to."

"If you aren't too tired, Honey."

"I'm not the least bit tired," she answered, sounding just like her mother.

The afternoon lesson was every bit as successful as the morning's. Word of Bonnie Anne's lessons had carried to Elijah and Esther, and both asked Violet if Bonnie Anne could return to help out whenever her own school was not in session.

Violet felt her heart would burst with pride as she and Bonnie Anne left the school to return home. *What a surprise I've had today. I had no idea Bonnie Anne has become so mature and self-possessed,* Violet thought, *and she's only ten and a half years old! Of course I knew she could teach the lesson, but I really thought she would need more help. I can hardly wait to tell Brent.* She clicked for Beau to pick up the pace.

When they arrived back at Fair Oaks, Bonnie Anne and J.J. competed with each other as their exciting experiences tumbled from their lips. Violet and Brent exchanged amused glances over their heads and listened with interest to the exchange between them, and then they filled in what the children had neglected to tell. Finally, everyone ran down, and Violet excused herself to go upstairs and freshen up.

As she entered the bedroom, a purple blaze caught her attention. Crossing to her dressing table, she found a bowl of violets. They were nestled in her mother's cut crystal bowl, the special vase she always saved for violets. Her heart stirred as she read the note: *When J.J. and I saw these spread over the field, we had to stop and pick them for our own beautiful Violet. We both love you very much. Signed: J.J. and Brent.* J.J. had written his own name in his little boy's scrawl.

She crossed to the writing desk and sat down. Dipping the pen in the ink well she began writing.

That evening, after the children had been bathed, said their prayers, put in bed, and kissed good-night, Violet and Brent went into their own bedroom. They had decided to go to bed early and read a while. Brent went into the dressing room to change into his nightshirt and robe. When he came out, Violet was still in the bathing room, and he crossed over to the bed to turn down the covers. There on top of his pillow lay a folded sheet of paper. Wondering what it could possibly be, he picked it up, and turned up the lamp wick so that a brighter light shone forth. On the folded sheet, Violet had written: *Darling, my flowers are perfectly beautiful. Thank you both so very, very much. I just had to write this poem for you.*

Brent unfolded the sheet and read:

Violets deep purple, with color so bright,
Petals encircle lavender with white.
You picked each flower slowly, one by one.
It took you a full hour until you were done.
Patiently, with love, because you well knew
My favorite of the deep purple hue,
And how every spring through meadows I'd roam,
Searching till evening for some to take home,
To fill mother's vase of cut crystal glass

With a purple blaze in one gorgeous mass.
So thank you, my sweet, for letting me know,
Of love so complete, like an old-fashioned beau.

And at the bottom, she had added: *P.S., I love you, too!*

Just then the door opened and Violet came into the room, looking delectable in a purple satin robe that had been a special gift from Brent. He stood there, holding out his arms. She melted into them, lifting her face for his deep kiss.

"Who's interested in reading," he muttered as he lifted her off her feet, his mouth still on hers, and carried her to their bed.

Chapter 55

Carolina Rail

1873

"There is panic on the Vienna Bourse!" exclaimed Brent a few days later in May, as he turned from the telegraph table in the Fair Oaks office toward Violet, seated at her desk.

Looking up from her day book she smiled and responded, "What's that? Too many people trying to crowd in for a ball of Viennese waltzes?"

"No, you silly gosling."

"Well, what then, you old goose?"

Patiently Brent explained, as he took out a cigarette paper, sprinkled tobacco in it, and rolled a smoke. "The bourse is the market."

"What kind of market?"

"Both a stock market, like the New York Stock Exchange, and a commodity market like the New Orleans Cotton Exchange and Board of Trade. They're having a crash in prices over there."

"What has that got to do with us?"

"Not much directly or immediately, but this is probably a symptom of financial stress all over Europe, and sooner or later I think that is bound to affect us over here." He took a puff of his cigarette, inhaling deeply.

"Won't the fall in prices over there be an advantage in your buying goods from France and Germany and England for the mercantile business?"

"Yes, it will until prices start to fall here, and we must move quickly and carefully to take advantage of that."

Her interest aroused, Violet closed her books and gave her full attention to what Brent was saying. After a pause, she asked, "Do you really think there is likely to be a financial panic over here?"

"There's no doubt in my mind, no doubt at all, and you know a panic usually leads directly to a more or less prolonged economic depression—a siege of hard times."

Now a worried look appeared on Violet's face as she asked further, "What makes you so sure that we are in for a panic and depression in this country? Oh, Brent, we've had so much of that in our lives this past decade."

"I know, Honey," he said sympathetically, "but if the panic on the Vienna Bourse is symptomatic of a situation generally in Europe, and I think it is, that means that European investors will be calling in loans from this country and unloading their stocks—and they have been essential in the expansion of railroads and industries in this country."

"And what else?"

"Well, all the watered stock in the railroads can be a big problem. Railroad stock has fallen into such disrepute that most investors now prefer bonds, but that only increases the huge amount of debt under which the railroads are operating and still expanding."

"Brent, you're getting me worried. What about the Carolina Central?"

"If depression comes it will be as much at risk as any of them." He took another puff, looking intently at Violet.

"What about the banks?"

"They are in a very risky situation. In the last four or five years even the new national banks have been lending many times as much money as they have taken in by deposits. I tell you, Violet, if a run starts on the banks, lots of them will just fold."

"That doesn't sound good."

"Certainly not. Three New York savings banks already have failed in the last year—and as you might guess, the small investors lost everything, but the officials of course saved themselves."

"Zounds! Any more good economic news?"

"Well, you know people who have money in insurance have been hard hit. They say the Chicago fire of two years ago has cost the insurance companies two hundred million dollars, and last year's fire in Boston cost them another seventy-two million."

Violet's face was clouded with worry. She sighed heavily and asked, "Darling, would you like some tea?"

"I think maybe scuppernong would be more appropriate, don't you?" He grinned at her.

"Maybe even rum would be better." Violet managed a grin, too.

"Sure, in the tea. Let's have Tiger Tea."

She reached for the crystal decanter containing rum and poured some into two china teacups. Then she topped that with hot tea that Ellie had brought in earlier in a warming pot. "We'll drink this concoction." Placing a teacup on a matching saucer, she stirred the mixture with a teaspoon, then handed it to Brent. She watched his face as he tasted the rum tea.

"How is it?" she asked.

"Delicious. Just what we need right now."

She took a sip of hers, nodded in agreement, and then went over to the needlepoint pull on the wall to summon Ellie.

Ellie appeared almost immediately, having anticipated the ring, and reappeared shortly with a tray of crackers, cheese, and peanuts to go along with their tea. Violet asked her to place the tray on the small table between the rocking chairs, and she and Brent moved to their chairs.

Taking another light sip of her rum tea, Violet asked, "Is there anything we can do to defend ourselves from all the dire developments you are predicting?"

Brent helped himself to a cracker and piece of cheese, chewing thoughtfully as he pondered Violet's question. He took a sip of his tea before answering, "Yes, there are some things we can do, and we must start doing them right away. Today. Our greatest hope will be in acting before others are aware of what is happening."

Brent set down his cup and rose from his chair. He crossed over to his desk and returned to his chair with pencil and paper with which to record notes as he spoke.

"The first thing to do is to sell all your cash crops on the futures markets. I'll check Charleston, New Orleans, and New York for best prices." He jotted some words on the paper.

"Why?"

"Because, if there is a financial panic, prices are likely to fall in the fall—"

"Yes, fall in the fall," she interrupted with sarcastic laughter.

Brent smiled in appreciation of her humor. "— and if we wait to sell then, it could mean big losses. *Big* losses."

"Yes, I see what you mean. Let's do it; do it now."

"And I shall order some goods from Europe right away, at their low prices, and try to sell them before the prices fall here." He jotted more notes down on his list.

"Won't that be risky?"

"Yes, but it can also be profitable."

"What else?"

"Quietly, very quietly, we must draw our money out of the banks and take all that money in gold, or gold bills of exchange and take only gold bills of exchange for our sales, and put all that in our safe right here at Fair Oaks."

"Oh, my goodness!"

"And we must do something about our railroad stocks and bonds."

Thoughtfully Violet looked at Brent, then out the window for a few moments. Turning back toward him she said, "I think we can do it. I think we'll be all right if those damned Vindictives in Washington and the local Yankee governor stay off our backs."

It was a busy summer for the Sutlers and for everyone at Fair Oaks. Brent spent several days each week in Columbia, staying at their town house, working at the warehouse, and working at the railroad office. He was taking much of his time in making the rounds of banks and merchants. Each week he would bring to Fair Oaks a handbag filled with gold bills of exchange and gold coins. At Fair Oaks he spent hours at the telegraph until he was able to complete futures sales on all the anticipated cotton and tobacco. He even bought up more cotton futures around Sumter County, and then sold them short.

On a Monday morning in mid-July, Brent went in to Sumter to see their friend, John Dargan, at the Citizens' Savings Bank.

Dargan greeted Brent cheerfully. "What can I do for you, Brent?"

Looking around quickly, Brent was relieved to see that there was no one else in the bank other than a young clerk. "May I see you for a minute in your office, John?"

"Of course, come on back," answered Dargan, leading the way.

Brent accepted the offer of a cigar and a chair as Dargan took the swivel chair at the roll top desk and turned toward Brent.

"John, I'm afraid I'm going to have to withdraw our funds from the bank."

"Well, Brent, how much were you thinking of?"

"All of them, John, all our checking and savings deposits."

Dargan could not conceal a look of serious concern that spread over his face. "What is it, Brent? What leads you to such a drastic step? I'm afraid if word of such a thing got out there would be a run on the bank."

"John, who is to know?"

"Of course, if you demand it, we'll have to let you have your deposits, but why the urgency?"

"I'll tell you, but it's got to remain between the two of us. You know of the panic on the Vienna Bourse in May—"

"All right. Yes."

"And now that has spread to Paris and Berlin, and, I understand, even to London." "I've seen some reports of those in the newspaper, but was not sure that would affect us here in South Carolina."

"Well, you know many of those European investors have big holdings in this country."

"Yes."

"And we are having a serious deficit in trade with Europe which means our gold continues to move over there, and so the price of gold keeps rising. Well, pretty soon the Europeans are going to begin calling in their loans and selling their American stocks. There is so much watered stock in our railroads and banks, and such big debts and over extension, that they are liable to go down like a house of cards."

Dargan gave a nod of understanding, put down his cigar, and said, "I'm afraid what you say is true, but quite frankly and just between us, I have greater worries closer to home."

"Oh, what's that, John?" asked Brent curiously.

"The Moses regime in Columbia is trying to put the squeeze on our central bank there, and, of course, on all its branches including this one. We'll be fortunate if we can survive until the panic you speak of actually hits us."

"Zounds! That makes it all the more important to get our money out as quickly as possible," responded Brent with a sense of urgency.

"Confidentially, I have to say you're right, and I'm afraid there is nothing I can do about it."

"Well, John, may I have our funds in gold? Now?"

"Well, Brent, that creates a problem. Of course you are entitled to gold, but if I send to Columbia for that amount, that would send up storm signals all over, and I'm afraid the Radicals would move right in."

Brent took another tack. "What about greenbacks? How much of a discount can you offer?"

"Well, they have been going at fifty cents or less on the dollar. If you can spread the withdrawals over a couple of weeks, I'll let you have three greenbacks to the dollar."

"All right. I'll risk the two weeks and the greenbacks," replied Brent. "The Republicans in Washington are pushing for resumption. If that goes through, I'll be back with those greenbacks to deposit them in your bank at one hundred cents."

"Good, good–if we still have a bank," Dargan said dejectedly as he rose and shook hands.

Over the next two weeks Brent was bringing bags of greenbacks to put in the safe at Fair Oaks. Then late in the afternoon of Wednesday, August 13, Brent, returning from Columbia, came striding into the Fair Oaks office where Violet was waiting for him.

Taking time for only an uncharacteristic cursory hug and kiss, his eyes flashing trouble, he grumbled, "Well, my dear, they've done it."

"Done what?" Violet asked, perplexed.

"Shut down the Citizens' Savings Bank."

"Oh, my goodness! What happened?"

"That damned Moses Ring in Columbia obtained an injunction against the bank, closed its doors, and liquidated its assets, that's what."

"Great scot! Did you get all of our money out in time?" Violet flung at him in alarm.

"Ah, yes, with two weeks to spare."

Violet took a sigh of relief and then asked, "Did you think the crash was coming this soon?"

"Honey, don't relax yet. This is not the crash, not yet. This is a preliminary round for us here, thanks to the Moses administration."

"Have you heard what John Dargan is going to do?"

"I have no idea, but I'm going in to see him tomorrow."

The next evening Brent returned from Sumter with a report that Dargan had anticipated what was coming and was able to save most of his own holdings. Now he was talking of trying to organize a national bank in Sumter, but Brent doubted that he would be able to raise the capital for such a venture, especially if hard times set in.

During the next few weeks of lie-by time, Violet, Brent, and the children saw more of each other than at any such time heretofore. It was almost a family holiday. Nearly every afternoon they would join for games on the lawn–tennis, croquet, and sometimes, with India rubber ball and hickory stick, a version of baseball. Each morning they all went horseback riding together around the meadows of the plantation and occasionally in the early evening they would ride over to Stateburg and perhaps pick up a bag of hard candy. Several times they took a picnic lunch down to the creek or pond and went fishing.

One morning late in August, after a family ride in the west meadow, Brent turned to Violet. "Let's get the kids back to Evelina and then ride over for a look at The Old Place, just the two of us."

"All right, but why?" she asked.

"Don't you think we should be keeping a closer watch on old Farley? Oh, I know that Leo and a couple of his foremen check regularly on Farley's doings, but I think he needs to know that we, too, are keeping an eye on him."

"Well, maybe you're right, Brent."

As they rode toward The Old Place, Violet continued, "I've really not been neglecting The Old Place completely. Leo and I did see that they got the crops in all right."

"Seeing how he's doing now may give us a clue about Farley's reliability."

"That's probably true, but knowing you, Brent, I have a feeling there's something else on your mind." She threw him a sidelong glance.

"Well, actually, I am thinking of something else."

She laughed triumphantly as she said, "I knew it! All right, what is it?"

"Well, if we can really count on Farley, we may want to use him as a stalking horse of our own for some business deals."

"What kind of business deals?"

"Relating to the Carolina Central," he answered slyly. Now he threw a sidelong glance at Violet, as if to read her reaction.

She returned his look and in an unsure voice said hesitantly, "Oh, Brent, you had better be careful."

"Don't worry, you may be sure I shall be careful, but I was just thinking of further steps to take in face of what I am certain is the coming financial panic."

"You still think a crash is coming?"

"More sure than ever."

When they arrived at the manager's house on The Old Place, Mrs. Farley told them that her husband was out on his daily inspection of the fields. As they rode out to find him, Violet and Brent were pleasantly surprised at what they saw. The cotton fields and tobacco fields were clean of weeds, the tenant cottages were neat and clean, the gardens were flourishing, the grass along the fence rows as well as on the lawns was trimmed and free of debris.

Near the east end of these farm plots, Farley spotted Violet and Brent and waved to them. He came riding up at a gallop with a proud smile. "Glad to see you," he said, with a ring of sincerity.

"Mr. Farley, the fields are looking good," commended Violet. "You are to be congratulated on the way you are caring for them."

"Thank you, Miz Sutler, thank you very much, "he said as his smile broadened, "I think all of the tenants are doing well. I try to keep after them as needed."

"We're really glad to hear that," Brent confirmed. Pausing as he looked all around, as much to see if anyone were in hearing distance as to review the crops, he added, "Blake, I would like to discuss some other business matters with you."

"What kind of business, Senator?"

"Well, maybe about some investments and financial arrangements."

"About the land here, or my store?" he asked in a worried tone.

"No, no, some other possibilities."

Visibly relieved, but puzzled, Farley replied, "Why, yes, of course."

"Well, Farley, could you come over to our Fair Oaks office tomorrow afternoon?"

"Of course; I'll be there."

On the ride back to Fair Oaks Brent explained to Violet what he had in mind for Farley.

Farley's arrival at the Fair Oaks office on the next afternoon was with an air of confidence completely missing on his call of ten months ago. He was wearing a new straw hat and light coat. He was clean shaven and exhibited a neat and completely different demeanor.

Both Violet and Brent greeted him with a welcoming smile. Violet offered tea, and Brent offered cigars as they sat roughly in the same arrangement as during that earlier meeting.

Obviously curious, Farley could not wait to say, "Well, Senator, what did you have in mind about some business matters?"

Before answering directly, Brent wanted to sound him out a little. "Tell me, Farley, have you had any further contacts with the Moses Scalawags in Columbia?"

"No, not really, Mistuh Sutler. I've been keeping my distance, ever since they done me wrong."

"Do you think you could still deal with any of their friends?"

"Yes, sir, probably, if necessary." Farley was wondering where Brent was going with this.

"Well, first of all. It has to be understood that what we are going to discuss must be kept in the strictest confidence. Can I count on you?"

"You know I will; you know you can, Senator. Without your help I don't know where I'd be now."

"All right then, I'll tell you, all the signs are pointing tȯ a financial panic, and we'll probably have a prolonged period of hard times after that."

"Oh, no!" gasped Farley in dismay.

"To guard against a fall in prices in the fall, I have sold all our cotton and tobacco and extra corn and wheat on the futures markets—."

"You have?"

"And I would like to sell all yours too, right away."

"All right, anything you say on marketing."

"Good, but now there is something else; I have a good many Carolina Central Railroad bonds. I would like to sell those very soon, but it would be better for the market if it were not known that I was selling, and I was hoping that you would sell them for me."

Farley hesitated only briefly before responding, "Why yes, of course. Should I try to sell them in Sumter?"

"No, in Columbia—to banks, to speculators, and so on."

"Yes, yes, I could do that."

"All right. Now, what I want you to do is to sell as many as you can in three or four days at ninety cents on the dollar. After three or four days, offer them at seventy-five cents, and after another few days, at fifty cents. Now, I want these to be spread out, not too many to one person. Got that?"

"Yes, sir."

"And do you know who are in the Railroad Ring?"

"Of course."

"Well, just for fun, whet their appetites with some bonds at fifty cents."

Farley smiled and nodded.

"Now, you see what is going to happen, I think, is that after the crash the value of those bonds probably will drop to ten cents or less. At that point we shall move in to buy them back."

The sparkle in Farley's eyes brightened as comprehension of what Brent had in mind became clear.

"Now, don't be getting any ideas of going off on your own," cautioned Brent.

"Oh, no, no," protested Farley, "as I said before, you can count on me. I mean it, Senator."

"Well, seeing how well you are doing with the tenant farms, I believe we can, Farley, and let me tell you, if all this comes out the way I hope, there will be a good share for you. You may count on that, and I believe you know that I am a man of my word."

"Oh, yes, sir, I won't worry none about that. I know you'll be fair."

"Good. Now, Farley, do you know John Fraser, the general manager of the Carolina Central?"

"Yes, sir, Senator, I've met him."

"And you know where his office is?"

"Yes, sir."

"Well, I want you to go to him, pick up his railroad bonds, and sell them the same way; I'll let him know you are coming."

"Yes, sir, Senator."

"And I want you to give me a list of everybody to whom you sell bonds."

"All right."

"Now, one other thing, Farley..."

"Yes, Senator, what is that?"

"Well, I think it would be a good idea for you to form a corporation."

Farley showed his surprise. "How? With whom?"

"It doesn't matter, so long as you retain control."

"Who should I bring in?"

"Doesn't matter, if you can trust them."

"Well, Senator, what about four or five of our tenant farmers?"

Brent smiled and nodded. "Sure, that's fine. Call your corporation Farley and Company, and get a charter for the purpose of owning and operating a general store and for other purposes. And, by the way, do you know a good lawyer in Columbia, maybe a Carpetbagger, to handle the incorporation and then later business matters?"

"Well, yes, maybe John Sullivan."

"You mean the State House lobbyist?"

"He's from New York; he's very clever; he has had lots of success in lobbying, is very personable, and easy to do business with."

"Mm, and can you trust him?"

"He has absolutely no conscience; he will move in whatever direction the grass seems greenest."

At that Brent grinned. "Sounds like our man. Offer him a good fee."

Brent moved over to his desk and took several envelopes of bonds, taken earlier from the safe, for which Farley willingly signed a receipt. Then Farley put them in his pouch.

Over the next three weeks Farley stopped frequently at the Fair Oaks office to report on his activities and to give Brent a list of buyers of the bonds, and to hand over the cash receipts from his sales.

On the most recent of these visits Brent asked, "Well, Farley, how have things gone with the Railroad Ring? Did they jump at your fifty-cent offer?"

"With some encouragement, Senator."

"How was that?"

"Well, I met with a couple of them in the State House saloon, and one of them said, 'You're a friend of Governor Moses, aren't you?' and I said, 'Well, yes,' and then he said, 'Are these bonds guaranteed by the state?' and I answered, 'They will be as soon as the legislature acts on them, and then, you can be sure the price will go right back up.' Then he said, 'So why are you selling them now for fifty cents?' and I told him, 'Cause I need the money now, and I can't wait for the legislature to act."

"And they took them?" Brent asked with a laugh.

"All I had left," Farley replied as he joined in the laughter.

At that point Violet, giggling, picked up the crystal decanter of scuppernong and poured each a glass to give a further flourish to the occasion. After Farley had departed, Violet shared with Brent the good news that, after a long and discouraging wait, Leo and Rachel were going to have a baby.

With the light-hearted living of those summer days, Brent had said that he felt as though they were living in the calm before a storm. The storm broke on Thursday, September 18th. As Violet came into the office that morning after seeing the children off to school with Evelina, Brent jumped up from the telegraph table and exclaimed excitedly, "I think this is it!"

"What is it?" Violet asked apprehensively, "The stock market?"

"A run on the New York stock market yesterday; the market closed at a record low, and I'll guess it will just keep going down, down, down."

"Oh, my goodness!" Violet gasped, drawing a chair up close to Brent as he resumed his place at the telegraph.

He remained fixed at the set all morning while Violet remained most of the time, though she went out from time to time to check on activities around the house and then brought in sandwiches and coffee.

"What does all this mean?" she asked.

"It means that probably lots of investors are going to lose fortunes and then probably that a lot of businesses will fail. You know there have been more failures than usual already this year, and just ten days ago the big New York Warehouse and Security Company failed, and there have been rumors all week of other pending bank failures."

A little after noon Brent cried out, "Zounds!" and he turned around to face Violet. "Jay Cooke—Jay Cooke's, the New York office of Jay Cooke's banking firm has closed its doors."

Violet was startled. "Jay Cooke? New York? He's a big one, isn't he?"

Solemnly Brent answered, "Just about the biggest of all. You know he practically financed the Yankee war effort. Now I guess he has gone too far in underwriting the western railroads."

"Can't anybody do anything?"

Brent shook his head and lit the cigarette he had just rolled. "Not much. Probably just have to let the storm blow itself out." He paused, thinking, and then went on, "And then will come the hard times—but wait, let's listen to see if there are more shocking bulletins." He turned back to the telegraph set.

Violet sat quietly, listening intently to Brent's reports as they came in. Within an hour Brent reported that Cooke's central office in Philadelphia had closed, and then, only minutes later, his Washington branch, and then the First National Bank of Washington. Through the afternoon came further bulletins of other bank closings and reports that these developments had accelerated the plunge of the stock market.

Two days later word came that all trading in the New York Stock Exchange had been suspended for an indefinite period.

Over the next few weeks Brent spent most of each morning monitoring the telegraph and most of each afternoon at his desk reading the Columbia *Phoenix*, figuring his next moves and then telegraphing orders to Cedric at the Columbia warehouse and exchanging information by telegraph with John Fraser at the railroad office. On the 29th he learned that the New York Stock Exchange had reopened, but business failures continued unabated. Unemployment was growing throughout the industrial North. Scores of railroads all over the country were defaulting on their bonds.

Early in November, Brent persuaded John Fraser that, since the railroad's business had fallen off sharply, it would be well for the Carolina Central to suspend payment of interest on its bonds. Soon the word was out that the Carolina Central was insolvent, and predictably its securities plummeted.

Meeting with Farley and Violet in the Fair Oaks office on Monday, the 10th, Brent announced, "Now is the time to buy back our railroad bonds."

"What are they worth?" asked Violet.

"We'll offer ten cents on the dollar." answered Brent.

Farley said, "I think I had better steer clear of the Railroad Ring. They're pretty mad at me since they got no legislative guarantee."

"Let them keep their bonds," Brent said with a laugh.

"What about your railroad stock?" asked Violet.

"Oh," replied Farley, "I didn't do anything about the stock."

Brent interjected to explain, "I didn't have enough to fool with, and it is practically worthless."

"Well, now, Senator, do you want me to buy up a lot of stock too for a few cents on the dollar?"

"Oh, no."

"No? Why not?" Violet asked. "Isn't that the way to get control of ownership, to get a controlling interest of the stock?"

"Yes, you are quite right," Brent answered. "Stock represents ownership and bonds represent loans. The stock holders are the owners; the bond holders are the creditors. But when a business is going down you don't want to be an owner, liable for the debts. Just between us, the best way to gain control is to be the principal creditors because when a company goes bankrupt they may liquidate its assets to distribute among the creditors."

"So how will all this work out?" asked Violet who couldn't help but be a bit worried, even though she knew Brent was smart about things like this.

Sensing her uneasiness, he smiled as if to reassure her. "Well, now Farley and Company buys up enough of the bonds to become the principal creditors of Carolina Central. Then Farley and Company sues to force the railroad into bankruptcy, and as principal creditor, we'll have first claim on the assets of the railroad, now appraised at a very low value. Meanwhile we form a new corporation."

"Who?" she asked.

"Well, you, and Fraser. And I shall approach Dargan and Shelby and Frierson, and of course, Farley here."

Enjoying this whole exposition, Farley smiled and nodded his concurrence.

"Then, Farley and Company will transfer to the new corporation its share of the assets of the Carolina Central, and the new corporation then will issue new stocks and bonds for additional capital and will become the operator of the Carolina Central Railroad."

Now Violet smiled, "Will it still be called the Carolina Central?"

"Oh, no, we shall have to find a new name."

"Well," Violet came back, "how about 'Carolina Rail'?"

"Carolina Rail," Brent repeated, "sounds good. I like it. How did you come up with that name?"

"You know, the sora, the little mud hen—"

"Of course! The game bird, the Carolina rail. That will be our emblem!" Brent responded enthusiastically.

Brent spent most of the week of December 15th in Columbia, scurrying about to complete his railroad scheme. On Friday Violet received a telegraph message from him: PLEASE BE IN COLUMBIA ON MONDAY FOR MEETING OF DIRECTORS OF CAROLINA RAIL.

Violet replied with a message: WILL ARRIVE ON MORNING TRAIN SATURDAY AND WILL GO DIRECTLY TO TOWN HOUSE.

When Brent arrived at the house that evening he greeted everyone as long-lost relatives. It was obvious that he was in a cheerful mood, though rather close-mouthed. Violet was beside herself with curiosity, but she did not press, figuring that he would talk business when he wanted to do so. The only thing he would volunteer was that plans had been going well, and both Farley and John Sullivan had been performing effectively, in part because the court judge thought that Farley and Sullivan were representing Frank Moses. Brent did say that the purpose of the meeting on Monday was to complete organization of the new corporation.

On Monday morning Violet and Brent arrived at the office of the Carolina Central just before ten o'clock, and they joined the others in the board room—all those whom Brent had mentioned in his earlier planning.

John Fraser took the chair temporarily and invited nominations for chairman of the board. Immediately John Frierson nominated Victor Shelby, and, with no further nominations, the election was unanimous. Then came the election of John Frierson as vice chairman and Violet Storm—to her complete surprise—as secretary.

Shelby announced that it was time to choose the operating officers for the railroad. The whole thing had been running as such a pre-planned thing that Violet wondered why Brent had not let her in on it. Apparently he wanted to surprise her with her selection as secretary of the board.

Now Farley nominated Brent Sutler to be president of the railroad, John Fraser to be vice president and general manager, and John Dargan to be treasurer, and all were accepted unanimously. Brent ventured a wink at Violet, and she smiled an acknowledgment. It was agreed that John Sullivan should be retained as counsel.

As they drove their buggy back to the town house, Violet turned to Brent and exclaimed, her heart in her eyes, "Oh, Brent, president of Carolina Rail, I'm *so* proud of you."

She leaned over and kissed him on the cheek and added, "A railroad president at age thirty-six; that is really something!"

Brent chuckled. "Well, I don't know about that. The Yankee general, McClellan, was president of the eastern division of the Ohio and Mississippi Railroad when he was only thirty-four."

"Oh, fiddlesticks! I'll take my Southern sailor at thirty-six."

"And there's something I'll gladly tell; I'll take my Southern belle."

And Violet came back with, "As Balzac says, 'a woman knows the face of the man she loves as a sailor knows the open sea'."

They broke into laughter, and Brent went on to say, "My congratulations to you, my dear, for being secretary to the board of a railroad at age thirty. I'll bet you can't find any example of any Yankee woman who has done that!"

"Likely not!" she replied tartly, her eyes twinkling.

Chapter 56

On Track

1874

After New Year's, 1874, Violet and Brent, with the children, Evelina, and Aaron returned to Columbia to spend the next four or five months. While she always loved being at Fair Oaks, Violet had missed having their winter months in Columbia last year, and she was glad to be back at the town house for a few months this year. Brent was more anxious than ever to get back, not so much for his duties as a senator, but especially to get on with plans for Carolina Rail. *He's like a child with a new toy,* thought Violet fondly.

Bonnie Anne was glad to return to school at the Female Academy and to renew old acquaintances after such a long absence. J.J. was glad to be back at Mr. Barnwell's school where there were nearly fifty boys this year. He was disappointed that Tommy Woodrow Wilson had gone off to Davidson College in North Carolina and would no longer be his monitor, but he was impressed when he was told that his new monitor would be William Barnwell, the son of the headmaster. Tuition at both schools was now eight dollars a month, but Violet considered the money well spent.

One of the first assets of the Carolina Central to attract Brent's attention was the headquarters office suite on the third floor of the National Bank Building, to convert it to headquarters for Carolina Rail.

As vice president and general manager, John Fraser would retain his old office, but the clerk in the alcove near the entrance to the central hall now would be replaced by a young lady who would serve as receptionist. On the opposite side, across from the receptionist, a long, narrow room was fitted for four office workers. A telegraph sat on one of the desks, a new typewriter on another, and on the third was a new mechanical adding machine. The fourth desk was for the office boy/messenger.

Brent set up his own office in a room across the hall from John Fraser's. Carter and Jonah at the plantation had made the swivel chair and flat-top desk which faced the door and the Bank of England chairs that surrounded the desk. On the desk was an abacus. Behind the desk was a table with a telegraph sitting on it. On entering the office, one could see banks of pigeon holes covering about a third of the back wall to the right of the desk. These were designed by Brent and constructed by Carter. Chests of drawers lined the two side walls. There was a big window with Venetian blinds on the wall to the right of the desk. An oriental rug, predominantly in blue and gold, covered the floor in front of the desk.

Hanging on the wall directly behind the desk was a large painting of the Carolina Rail emblem—the bird, artificially tinted in purplish blue, perched on just a suggestion of a black railroad track, with the background in shadings of pink and orange. A thin black line encircled the picture, forming an oval border. This was the original painting from which all the hand-painted copies, hand-drawn copies, lithographs, linoleum block, and stencils had been made. The painting had been done by a talented thirteen-year-old artist at *The Joshua School.* Students in the wood-working class had made the dark walnut frame.

At the end of the hall, and perpendicular to it, was a large room containing a fourteen-foot walnut table surrounded by a dozen wooden arm chairs—the table and chairs imported from England. This was the board room. In one corner was a small roll top desk for the secretary of the board. On either side of it were chests for the records of stockholders and bond holders, and for the minute books.

Outside the building, above the main entrance and on each side of the third-floor center window, were new flag poles rising at forty-five degree angles, and parallel to each other. One carried the South Carolina flag with its crescent and palmetto tree, and the other the new flag of Carolina Rail—white banner with the colorful bird emblem in the center. This new flag had also been made at *The Joshua School*—by a group of girls in one of the sewing classes.

Soon the emblem of Carolina Rail, the little marsh bird known as the Carolina rail and sometimes called the sora, was appearing on everything related to the railroad—every locomotive, tender, freight car, caboose, passenger car, water tower and fuel dump, on every bridge, every sign post at a railroad crossing, on the windows of the main office, even as the watermark on the company's stationery. It was on every railway station and decorated the plates, cups, and saucers used in their restaurants, and appeared in a corner of the cloth napkins.

One afternoon in mid-January while Brent was working at the desk in his railroad office, Blake Farley came bursting in, obviously agitated.

Looking up, a little irritated at the unannounced interruption, Brent asked, "Farley, what is it? Is something wrong?"

"Senator, we've got trouble," Farley managed to gasp between rapid breaths, brought on by his running up the steps. He slipped out of his heavy overcoat, tossed it and his hat over the back of one chair, and sat down in another. "The Railroad Ring are demanding payment on their Carolina Central bonds or a share of the assets."

Brent offered a cigar to Farley who nervously declined, and then took his time in lighting one for himself. He leaned forward over his desk and said, "Well, if they feel that way, go ahead and buy their bonds back at fifty cents on the dollar so they won't lose any money. Keep them happy."

Farley took a deep breath. "I'm afraid it's not that simple, Senator."

"No? Well, then what else do they want? We certainly are not going to pay them a premium on bonds that won't bring ten cents. Let them try to sell them somewhere else. They'll find out."

"But, Senator, they don't *want* to sell them," Farley protested. "They're playing for much higher stakes."

"Higher stakes? The Carolina Central no longer has enough assets to worry about."

"No, but they have brought suit to get a share of the assets. They say that all creditors are entitled to a proportionate share of the assets, and they are suing to get what they call their fair share." In spite of the coolness of the room Farley had to wipe his perspiring brow with his handkerchief.

"But that can't be much, can it? How many bonds did you sell them?" Brent continued to appear unruffled.

"Not enough for them to claim very much, but they went out and got more."

"More? Go on."

"Well, Senator, they picked up a bunch more bonds, even got some of the ten-cent ones right when we were buying them back."

Brent took a puff of his cigar and then set it on the ashtray. "Is that all?" he asked calmly.

"No, sir, they've done much more." Farley wiped his brow again before going on. "They picked up enough of that no-good stock to become principal owners, and on top of that, they've picked up a bunch of first-mortgage notes."

"How did they do that?"

"Mostly from the Citizens' Savings Bank when it was forced to close."

"Mm," muttered Brent as he got up and began pacing between his chair and the window. Farley waited quietly, watching. Then Brent stopped, excused himself, and disappeared from the room. In a couple of minutes he was back with John Fraser.

After Fraser had taken a chair beside Farley, in front of the desk, Brent said, "John, Blake here tells me that the Railroad Ring has acquired some first-mortgage Carolina Central notes and a good number of the bonds, and now are suing to obtain a share of the assets. Did we overlook something in those notes?"

"Maybe," answered Fraser with some apprehension, "but I didn't think there were enough notes to matter, compared to all our bonds."

"Trouble is," Brent muttered, "a first mortgage has priority over the bonds, and then if they have enough bonds to go with those notes, they might make things difficult for us. Damn, I wish we had those notes! Well, it's too late for that now." He turned to Farley and asked, "Any idea about how much they want, what they are demanding?"

"I have a very clear idea, Senator. They want a share of the Carolina Central assets to include all track and right-of-way between Columbia and Sumter."

"Zounds!" Brent exclaimed. "The rest of the line would not be of much value to us without that–but how can they get that? Carolina Central no longer owns those assets."

"No, Senator, but they are persuading the court that it was illegal to transfer all those assets without their getting their fair share."

Now Brent took out a handkerchief and wiped his brow as he responded, "But what can they do with that short section between Columbia and Sumter?"

"Well, sir, they can offer to sell it to us at an exorbitant price, or they might hold it hostage and extort a big ransom in the form of lease or rental fees, or they might sell it to the South Carolina Railroad or the Blue Ridge or the King's Mountain and Charlotte or somebody."

John Fraser frowned as he added, "–which might still give them a profit and leave us high and dry. Right, Brent?"

"Yes, except that most of the other railroads are in trouble too and probably could not pay much for it. I suspect the greatest likelihood is that they'll try to hold us up for it."

With a deep sigh of concern, Fraser asked, "Well, now, what can we do about all this?"

"We've got to find a way to head them off—and fast!" Brent declared. He slammed his fist down on the desk. Turning to Farley, he went on, "Blake, can you get our lawyer, John Sullivan, to meet with all of us here about this time tomorrow?

"Yes, sir, we'll be here," Farley promised as he reached for his hat and coat still lying on a vacant chair.

"And not a word about this to anyone else, not your wife, not your friends, not even your horse."

"Indeed not, sir!"

Brent held up his hand as if to stop him. "And, oh, Blake..."

"Yes, Senator?" Farley stopped in mid-action, one arm still to go into his coat.

"So you think we can still trust Sullivan?"

"As long as he gets a good fee, we can."

Promptly the next afternoon Farley and Sullivan joined Fraser and Brent in Brent's office. After only a few preliminary comments about current actions of the legislature and the most recent escapades of Governor Moses, they all lit cigars and got down to business.

Turning to Sullivan, Brent inquired, "John, are you familiar with what the Railroad Ring is up to?"

"Yes, Senator, I think so. I've heard several things over at the State House, and Farley has filled me in on the details," Sullivan answered as he brushed tobacco from his new dark green, lightly striped coat, ran his hand over his thinning sandy hair, and touched his luxurious sideburns.

"Can they get away with it?"

With a twinkle in his eyes, Sullivan chuckled and replied, "They might if I were handling it for them." The lawyer, in contrast to the worried dispositions of the others, radiated a confidence suggesting that he always expected to win for himself no matter how things came out for others.

Brent continued, "Well, we've got to head them off, but tell me, what can they do with the Carolina Central? Is it still in existence?"

"Yes," responded Sullivan, "but it doesn't have any assets to speak of, and it is bankrupt, but, yes, it is still in existence."

"All right," said Brent, "the first thing we do is to have the court appoint a receiver and put it in receivership; let the court appoint Farley and Company as receiver, before anybody else knows what is going on. Can you do that?"

"Well, yes, I think so, but what good will that do?" asked Sullivan. "The receiver will have to distribute the assets as the court says, and if the judge rules in their favor in their suit, and requires certain assets to be restored to Carolina Central and then handed over to them, they still win."

"Ah, but wait," Brent said as he held up his hand to regain the floor. "Are you familiar with receiver's certificates?"

"Well, yes, in a way. They are a kind of short-term note that a court may authorize when a company is in the hands of a receiver."

Brent nodded and went on, "And can't they have priority over even first mortgage notes and bonds?"

"They can if the judge so stipulates."

Getting a notion as to where Brent was headed, both Fraser and Farley visibly relaxed a little as Brent continued, "Now, here is what we do. We have Farley and Company appointed receiver of Carolina Central, and we persuade the judge to offer enough receiver's certificates to cover outstanding mortgage notes and bonds at about twenty-five cents on the dollar. Carolina Rail then buys all those receiver's certificates at a discount. When Carolina Central then is unable to pay off the receiver's certificates in thirty days, Carolina Rail demands that all remaining assets be turned over to cover the certificates, at which point the court will announce that all remaining bonds then outstanding are being defaulted, and that the Carolina Central is dissolved—out of business, period." Brent paused for breath and to observe the reaction of the others to his suggestions, especially the lawyer's.

With a broad smile of triumph, Sullivan exclaimed, "Senator, we can do it!" The other two joined in exchanges of reassurance, relieved that there was a good chance of getting out of this bind.

By the end of February the steps that Brent had outlined had been completed. The Carolina Central had been liquidated; Carolina Rail now was secure. Brent Sutler and John Fraser were secure in their positions. John Sullivan had received a handsome bonus. Members of the Railroad Ring knew they had been outwitted and were grumbling and issuing veiled threats against the new company. Blake Farley was known by everyone to be out of favor at the State House.

As Brent came into the railroad office on the first Monday in March, Fraser stopped him to tell him that Caleb Duprey was coming in the next afternoon and wanted to see Brent.

"What does he want?" Brent asked in an abrupt manner. He could never forget the part Duprey had played in Violet's difficulties while he was away at sea on the *Shenandoah.*

"Probably wants to mend fences, try to secure his position with the new regime. He has been serving as superintendent of the central section, Sumter to China Grove, you know."

Brent snorted derisively and replied, "Yes, I know. Don't you think he has outlived his usefulness?"

"Probably, though I must say he was quite efficient in getting the track laid quickly." Fraser knew of Brent's opinion of Duprey and considered the feelings justified, but he had to give the man his due.

"Sure, he got the track laid fast, but the way he ran rough shod over people created a lot of antagonism toward him."

"Yes, I heard about some of that later," Fraser answered rather lamely, "and I must say, I'm afraid that during the last couple of years he's been costing us more than he is worth."

"I've noticed that in the maintenance work; it's pretty bad," concurred Brent. "When he comes in, tell him to come directly to my office."

"Right."

That evening, over tea at their town house, Brent reported to Violet that Caleb Duprey would be coming in the next afternoon. "Don't you want to be there to see him" Brent asked with a poker face, but the mischievous look in his eyes gave him away.

Her eyes flashing in remembrance, Violet retorted heatedly, "Why, Brent Sutler, I don't ever, *ever*, want to see that blackguard again! Never!"

Brent ventured a grin at her response; she was such fun to tease. Actually, he did think it might be a good thing for Violet to be present during Duprey's visit, so he said in a serene voice, "Well, honey, I thought perhaps you ought to be there just to help straighten that rogue out. After all, you *are* secretary of the board."

Brent's composure had helped to settle her down. In a way, it might be interesting to see the effect her presence would have on Duprey, so she replied, "Oh, all right, I'll be there, if only to spit in his eye."

"Well, my Love, whatever happened to repentance and forgiveness?" He couldn't resist teasing her again.

"He's beyond all redemption. As far as I am concerned he can go straight to hell."

At that Brent exploded with laughter.

The next afternoon Violet was in Brent's office at the railroad headquarters several minutes before Duprey arrived. Presently Duprey came in. He glanced around the office, and when he saw Violet his face took on a look of shock and dismay. It was all Violet could do to keep a straight face. *This should be interesting*, she predicted to herself.

"Good afternoon, Mr. Duprey," Brent said without offering either a cigar or his hand. "I believe you've met the secretary of the board of Carolina Rail corporation, Mrs. Sutler. Brent's face was inscrutable.

"Yes, oh, yes, I have had the pleasure." He turned toward Violet, forcing a smile upon his nervous lips. The hand holding his hat was shaking. "Good afternoon, Mrs. Sutler."

Violet merely nodded, without even a trace of a smile, as Duprey took the chair toward which Brent waved, and then Brent sat down in his desk chair. Violet took a chair beside Brent.

"What is it you want, Mr. Duprey?" asked Brent.

Eyes shifting from one to the other and then around the room, Duprey responded in a low, husky voice, "Well, Mr. Sutler, sir, I just wanted to discuss plans for getting on with the work, and to express my hope that I can continue to be of service to the company..."

"Well, I'm afraid that I have been having increasing doubts about the extent of the service you ever have given to the company, and especially about your methods."

"Well, haven't I been effective in getting results?" He glanced at Violet out of the corner of his eye and remarked with just a trace of derision, "I hope you've not been influenced too much by the delicate sentiments of a woman on your board."

Violet jumped to her feet, pointed her finger straight at Duprey's face, and uttered forcefully, "Mr. Caleb Duprey I have had enough insults from you to last a lifetime!"

Duprey shot a fleeting glance at Brent. "Oh, Ma'am, I never meant no harm, I hope you've forgotten any little incident that I didn't mean; I sure hope—."

She cut him off with a scornful "Oh, no, of course not. You meant no harm. Every time a train comes roaring across my front yard I think of you and why you put the tracks there. A train almost killed our little daughter. How could I ever forget?"

Red streaks rose up Duprey's neck to become a full flush in his face. He lowered his head and stared at the floor.

Now Brent got up and poured more coals on the fire. He waved an unlighted cigar. "Duprey," he cautioned, "your insults to women and your rude manner toward everyone have been making enemies for the railroad for years. Your insolence has alienated customers and potential customers. Your high-handedness has created discontent among our workers—"

"But Mr. Sutler, sir," broke in Duprey, "I was just trying to do my job, and I promise I can do better—"

Brent went on as though he had not heard Duprey. "And now I find that you have been engaged in rake-offs, accepting inferior and unsatisfactory materials at premium prices and then pocketing the difference. When you put in faulty rails and inferior ties, you are not only jeopardizing property, but human lives..."

Duprey rose to his feet and protested vigorously, "Oh, Mr. Sutler, they weren't that bad; I didn't think they were dangerous. Please, I assure you I won't do any of those things again."

"No," Brent said, in growing exasperation, "I know damn well you won't, because you are finished here. It is time for you to pack your carpetbag and head back for Massachusetts or wherever you came from."

Duprey continued to protest, "But Mr. Sutler, sir, isn't there something I can do? I have a family, you know, and—"

"Well, that's a start," Brent came back, "I guess this must be the first time you ever thought of anybody but yourself. We'll give you a month's severance pay, but we'll send it directly to your wife. Now you clear on out of here. Now."

His eyes glittering with anger, Duprey muttered, "Damn you, Brent Sutler!" as he spun around and strode out of the room.

Violet and Brent stood and watched Duprey leave. Violet turned to Brent, took both of his hands in hers as she looked into his eyes. She said softly, "Bravo, my Darling! Bravo!"

The board of directors readily agreed to Brent's proposals for refinancing Carolina Rail. First they would issue fifty thousand shares of common stock at ten dollars par value. Fifty-one percent of this would be distributed to the officers and directors, partly as their compensation, but mainly to assure continued control of the corporation. Sixteen percent of the total issue would go to Brent, eleven percent to Fraser, and six percent to each of the other directors. They voted John Sullivan a five percent share, partly as a generous addition to his retainer, but mostly to give him a direct stake in the prosperity of the enterprise. All the remainder would be sold on the open market.

"No watered stock?" Violet asked impishly.

"No water," Brent replied, laughing.

In addition the board agreed to issue another fifty thousand shares of non-cumulative, non-participating, non-voting preferred stock, with a par value of twelve dollars and a stated dividend rate of five percent.

Still this would not be enough to finance all the improvements that Brent had in mind, and he persuaded them to agree to issue bonds for another million dollars at four percent interest.

This was becoming a little heady for directors who had been used to dealing in a few thousand dollars rather than millions, but Fraser assured them that, with recovery, the value of the physical property would be far above all that. And Dargan raised no protest. Shelby did ask him if he thought he could market all these issues.

"Well, I think we are in for a prolonged depression, but I believe if we play it right we can turn that to our advantage. Actually there has been a ready market for four percent bonds on the New York market in the last few weeks, and probably it can be done. Stocks will be a little more difficult in these times, I take it," Brent surmised.

"Yes, but we should be able to do a little manipulating among the various trust companies and investment bankers—those who are still solvent," replied Dargan.

Farley spoke up, "And the one to do that is Sullivan."

"Yes, if we can trust him," Shelby said wryly.

After a short pause, Brent narrowed his eyes and said, "I think we should send Dargan and Sullivan to New York—Dargan because he knows the finances, and Sullivan because he knows the ropes."

Shelby nodded in agreement and added, "And Jim Dargan can keep an eye on Sullivan, keep him out of mischief." At this the others also nodded.

"Aye," said Brent with a grin, "just keep him honest and to our advantage."

Dargan was pleased at the prospect of going to New York, and he expressed confidence that Sullivan could work in at the right securities dealers and they could accomplish their mission.

A month later Dargan was able to report enthusiastically to a meeting of the Board of Directors that their week in New York had been highly successful. By going around to several banking houses they had been able to place all the bonds at full value, less discounts, commissions, and fees. They had been able to sell half of the stock at only a dollar less than par value, and the other half they had deposited with Kuhn, Loeb, and Company, who had agreed to issue bankers' shares against it—which would make it easier for small investors to get in on the purchases at no major loss to the company.

"Good work!" Brent exclaimed when Dargan had finished. "Now we are in business. We've got to improve the track, get modern rolling stock, improve the system of fueling locomotives, improve the system of dispatching by telegraph, and dress up the stations. If necessary for some of these special projects, we still can go to the local banks for first and second mortgage notes. It may be necessary for a year or two to take additional loans, 'to rob Peter to pay Paul' to meet our interest payments, but after that I believe you'll see our revenues start climbing. While everyone else is engaged in cutting back and retrenchment, we'll move in to pick up their business."

A ring of almost involuntary applause greeted these remarks.

While the others engaged in rapid exchanges of congratulations and hopes for the future, Fraser stepped out and returned with a tray on which he carried a bottle of Madeira wine and wine glasses for everyone. With greater enthusiasm than he had shown all year, he called out, "To Carolina Rail, let our new trains start rolling!"

"Hear, hear!" Shelby called out, "Let our new trains start rolling out and our revenue start rolling in."

With gleeful laughter all drained their glasses and shook hands all around.

Chapter 57

Hopes and Fears

1874

Over the last several years the number of workers on the plantation had been gradually but steadily declining as a result of deaths, infirmities, and a few of the young people leaving for the cities. All these were more than the number of young workers who were coming of age and the arrivals of newcomers. Actually, additional machinery and improved farming methods had been adding steadily to production, so productivity in terms of production per person had been rising rather sharply. This had made it possible for Violet to raise the basic daily wage rate to forty cents.

The situation in the towns and cities was different. Hard times were slowing or closing factories and shops and stores, and the number of unemployed was growing dangerously. Violet was relieved to hear from Charlotte that so far the cotton mill where Leland and his father were working had been able to survive the depression fairly well. They were benefitting from a law of 1870 that provided that taxes on property for cotton or woolen manufacture should be returned to the investors for a period of four years. Now their plant was making number twenty cotton yarn at five cents less than the lowest cost in New England, and orders, both domestic and foreign, continued to come in.

A number of freed Negroes who earlier had left the plantations for the towns and cities began drifting back, hoping to be rehired. Violet adopted a policy of not turning away anyone who gave promise of hard work, until all the living quarters were filled and a few even overcrowded.

One of those arriving in quest of work was a young black man named Levi Smith. He was wearing threadbare clothing, but he was clean and he seemed anxious to work and to please. He had been a lad of seventeen, living with his father and mother as house servants in a Columbia house, when the city was burned. Since then he had worked at various odd jobs, but now he wanted a permanent occupation. He claimed to be skilled in carpentry and plumbing. Violet assigned him to Enoch, who, after a couple of weeks of observing his work, decided to make him responsible for maintenance of the big house and adjacent outbuildings. He would live in one of the basement rooms of the big house.

At the same time Brent was taking on as many workers as he could—black and white—to work on the railroad's section gangs.

There were moves in the State House to develop some kind of assistance for the unemployed, and some people were even suggesting that the Federal government ought to do something to relieve the distress of unemployment and economic hardship. Both Violet and Brent opposed the notion of looking to the government—state or federal—for this kind of relief. They admitted that the Freedmen's Bureau had been helpful to a degree in dealing with the needs of millions of suddenly freed slaves, but there had been too many deficiencies and too many unhappy results in that program to recommend that as a desirable way to deal with the poor or the unemployed. Above all, Violet and Brent shared with many of their colleagues a concern with creating a state of permanent dependency on the government on the part of those granted direct government assistance. This would be a dependency hardly better than the dependency of slaves on their masters.

In the State Senate, Brent offered proposals for a system of county poor farms with state support—farms to which unemployed people could go voluntarily where they would work regularly on the farm in return for food, clothing, shelter, and medical care, until they could return to work on a private farm or in a factory or on a railroad or somewhere. The county farm itself would produce as much as possible of the food and clothing needed for the inhabitants. However, neither Governor Moses nor the Carpetbagger and Scalawag members of the legislature were much interested in such projects. They were still more interested in providing state assistance for schemes for their own emoluments.

On one of the few days that spring when both Violet and Brent were in their office at Fair Oaks, Brent suddenly looked up from a sheaf of maps and papers on his desk and said to Violet who was seated across from him at her desk, "You know something, Honey, the first, the very *first* thing I'm going to do in our program of improvements on the railroad is to take up that track that runs across our front yard and reroute it around Fair Oaks plantation."

Violet gave a whoop of joy. "Oh, Brent, that would be wonderful! I can't tell you how I dislike that track through our yard—not just because of any memories as to why it was placed there, but it's dangerous and dirty and noisy and ruins our view from the house and the view of our house from the road—."

"I know, my darling, but there hasn't been anything I could do—"

"I don't just dislike that track, Brent; I hate, abhor, detest, despise, *loathe* that blasted track." Sparks seemed to be flying from her.

Brent chuckled. "I know," he repeated, "but first I had to get myself in the position of being in charge of the railroad. Now it's going to be removed from the front yard." He looked at Violet, drinking in her beauty. She was absolutely intoxicating when she became so electric with emotion. But as usual, he couldn't resist teasing her when she was like this.

"Still, I don't know," he went on, keeping his voice perfectly serious, "it really is convenient to have the track there when we want to catch a train; otherwise it would be much too far to walk."

"Fiddlesticks, Brent Sutler! How can you possibly say that, knowing how I feel?"

"So, I guess I'll move it so that it runs right by our back porch—"

"Brent! It'll still be dangerous and dirty and noisy and what about our beautiful gardens? How could you..." she stopped abruptly, realizing he was baiting her. She grinned and relaxed as she said, "Oh, Brent, you rascal, there you go again. Now stop this teasing; at first I thought you were serious."

He laughed, and then went on thoughtfully, "Well, you know, I am serious about putting the track out back."

"What?" she exclaimed. "Well, then, Brent Sutler, I shan't allow it. What will you do, get eminent domain? Now that you are a Senator, that should be easy." Her eyes were flashing with anger again, and she looked even more beautiful than before.

He wanted to take her in his arms, but he knew that to be an unwise move at this time; he'd likely get his face slapped. He grinned and answered, "Of course, and there is not a thing you can do about it."

Violet did an about turn. She picked up a paper and held it like a fan; her lovely eyes peered over it alluringly, her long eyelashes fluttering. In a provocative voice, she answered, "Oh, yes, there is; I shall resort to the method of the Athenian women under Lysistrata in demanding that their men end the war they were in."

Brent broke into laughter again. "Oh, come, come, my Love, that would be pretty drastic, wouldn't it? Too drastic for me. All right, I yield; I'm ready to compromise."

Now she grinned in triumph. "I do hope you mean to get that track out of here all together."

"Well, not quite. Remember I said I'm ready to compromise. Here's what I propose to do: re-route the railroad to run along the eastern border of the plantation and then curve around The Old Place to rejoin the present line at Providence—."

Violet took a deep, audible breath of relief.

"Then I want to put in a spur to run along the creek, past the cotton bailer and storehouse, the threshing shed and grist mill, the lumber mill, the tobacco sheds, and the corn cribs. Then we can ship out the crops without having to haul them either to Providence or Sumter."

She quickly saw the logic in this. "Why, Brent, that's a marvelous idea!"

"And then," he continued, "a little connecting spur right up to our back door—"

"Oh, no," she interrupted. "Not that."

"Now, Honey, hold on just a minute. On this back door spur we'll put a handcar, with canvas top to protect from sun and rain, which we can use to ride out to a shed beside the main track whenever we want to catch a train. We'll check on time of arrival by telegraph, and then we'll allow about ten minutes to propel ourselves out there on the handcar. How about that?"

"Oh, that's more like it. That's a marvelous idea!" She jumped up from her chair and ran around the desk to plant a kiss on the back of Brent's neck. He turned and pulled her into his arms and kissed her as he had wanted to moments before. He was confident this time his face wouldn't be slapped.

Within a month railroad construction crews had laid the new track around the east and north borders of the plantation. When a group of workers arrived to take up the track from the front, Brent grabbed a sledge hammer and with Violet trotting closely behind, he marched down to the track and symbolically swung the first blows to loosen the rails. Violet remembered how he had derailed the tracks on the night after Susan had rescued little Bonnie Anne from in front of the onrushing train—and she recalled how that incident had led to Brent's going to work on the railroad, and now, here he was, president of the railroad and taking up that damned track in the front yard.

When time permitted, Violet and Brent alternated that year between Columbia and Sumter for attending music concerts, lectures, and the theater. At the Music Hall, on the top floor of Sumter's new town hall, they attended concerts by the Sumter Orchestra and the Sumter Brass Band, and Lyceum lectures by Professor William James Rivers of the State University and Dr. James Carlisle of Wofford College.

In Columbia they attended several dramatic productions including *Maria Stuart, The Earl of Essex, Richilieu,* and *The Merchant of Venice.* They made it a point to be present for each performance of the *Little Brown Jugs* in a series of concerts at *The Joshua School.*

In addition, both were faithful in their church attendance, whether at Holy Cross in Stateburg or Trinity in Columbia. At Trinity, Violet was taking a greater interest in the various activities of the church. Almost without realizing it, she felt herself drawn more and more to the church, and a faith that had been weakened by years of tribulation and doubt seemed to be returning in a rather different form. It had a new depth without resulting in any hint of fanaticism or outward demonstrations other than in action. On the contrary, she kept most of her thoughts and feelings to herself as she meditated for new meaning and new understanding, and she wanted her life to reflect these.

"Well, we are in for a special treat come Saturday," Brent announced to Violet as he came into the town house late Monday afternoon, the last week of April.

"What is it? I can't wait to héar," said Violet as they took chairs in the parlor. She poured each a cup of tea and placed two sweet biscuits on each china saucer.

"A reception at the Governor's mansion–."

"What? Old Moses? I can hardly wait to go," groaned Violet, sarcastically.

"Oh, but Honey, we don't want to miss this."

She sighed, "How do we rate an invitation?"

"All the legislature is being invited."

"Just which is the Governor's mansion now?" asked Violet. "I've heard the rumors."

"Well, the rumors are correct. The official mansion is not good enough for Moses."

"No, I heard that, but I understand he uses several houses. Which is it this time?"

"Oh, the Preston Mansion, of course, the finest house in the city–which he bought for forty thousand dollars."

"On his salary of what?"

"Three thousand, five hundred dollars a year."

"Good lord! He must have major invisible sources of additional income."

"And some not so invisible," sneered Brent.

"Well, my dear husband, who will be at the Governor's reception?"

Brent made a face and answered, "Oh, the members of the House and Senate and their ladies, and members of the State Government–the State House Ring–and surely a lot of their favorite ladies."

"Oh, Brent, I can imagine," frowned Violet.

On Saturday afternoon Brent and Violet drove up to the Preston Mansion and entered. A colored band was playing *Rally Round the Flag* as crowds of men and women, black and white, milled around. Streams of guests continued to arrive and to add to the crowd and the confusion.

Violet tugged on Brent's arm and whispered, "Did you ever see such a bunch of bedizened creatures?"

"Hell, no."

Strains of *Hail to the Chief* signaled the arrival of the Governor.

Violet and Brent sought out Governor Moses who gave them a proper but cool greeting. He received a proper but cool greeting in return. Soon Brent was drawn off to a group of men who were discussing the relative situations of North and South during the period of economic depression.

Violet found herself entrapped in a covey of parvenues. A young white woman in fine pink silk, exaggerated accessories, and too much rice powder and rouge approached.

"Hello," she said, extending her hand like a man, "I'm Janice Jones."

"How do you do?" Violet responded graciously as she took the woman's hand, "My name is Violet Sutler, Mrs. Brent Sutler."

Miss Jones betrayed a note of shock as she inquired, "Mrs. Senator Sutler?"

"Yes, my husband is Senator Sutler."

With a little effort Miss Jones recovered her composure and led Violet to a corner where five other women were seated—another white who was from New York, and a brass ankle, a mulatto, and two Negroes from the vicinity. As Miss Jones introduced each, Violet replied, "How do you do?" and each in turn responded, "Glad to meetcha, I'm sure." Violet and Janice Jones took chairs with the group.

After a few observations on the weather and the beautifully decorated Governor's Mansion, and exchanges of compliments on their dresses, Violet turned the discourse to other conversational topics. "Do you like Victor Hugo's writings?" she inquired.

"Oh, yes, he's one of my favorites," one of the women responded enthusiastically.Violet added, "I think *Les Miserables* is fascinating, especially the way Hugo, with such dramatic effect, presents the problem of too strict enforcement of the law in some circumstances."

"Fortunately our Governor appreciates that," put in the one in red satin. "He don't favor enforcement of too much law."

"No, I should say he doesn't in many cases," replied Violet.

Another of the women spoke up, "Oh, I think it was very dramatic when Victor Hugo went to the guillotine for the woman he loved."

"You may be thinking of Sidney Carton in Dicken's *A Tale of Two Cities,*" Violet explained.

"Oh, yes, of course."

Violet ventured to go on, "What do you all think of George Eliot?"

"Oh, I think he's divine, don't you?" answered the woman in orange. She brushed back a strand of loose hair that was nearly the color of her dress.

I can't believe this! thought Violet. She went on to ask about a particular book, "Silas Marner?"

"I ain't never met him, I don't think," volunteered Janice Jones.

With a chuckle Violet responded, "No, I'm sure you wouldn't meet him around the State House; I doubt that anybody is saving and counting coins there."

Finding all this more entertaining than she had imagined, Violet pressed her advantage, "Another one of my favorite writers is George Sand."

"Oh, he is truly marvelous," said the woman in green.

Except for a slight smile, Violet maintained a poker face, "But don't you think that that affair with Chopin was scandalous?"

"Oh, very scandalous; that Chopin ought to be ashamed of herself!" exclaimed the woman in the blue dress. The others nodded their heads emphatically to indicate their agreement.

This is incredible, thought Violet, as she went on in a pleasant voice, "And speaking of scandal, what about the Tweed scandals in New York that they finally broke up. Wasn't that awful?"

"I'm not sure I remember," said the woman from New York. "Did that have something to do with the collection of customs duties on Scottish tweed cloth?"

With a sigh of resignation and frustration, Violet graciously excused herself to look for Brent. She found him just in time to gain the protection of his strong arms and sturdy body to protect her from the stampede when a call that supper was served brought on a melee toward the well-stocked tables in the great dining hall. Quickly, outstretched arms were competing in strenuous reaches across the table as guests swallowed grapes by the bunch, turkey and ham by the pound, cake by the loaf, and champagne by the bottle. Talking continued though mouths were stuffed. Rather than using the embroidered linen napkins lying beside each place, guests could be seen using their sleeves to wipe their mouths, and sometimes just the backs of their hands.

Brent turned to Violet. "Let's get out of here," he whispered above the din. His face reflected his repugnance with the situation.

"`Lead on, kindly Light,...Lead thou me on!" she quoted, and then added, "And quickly!"

Since they would be returning to Fair Oaks near the end of the month, Violet invited Charlotte and Leland, and Leland's father, Andrew Thompson, over for supper on Saturday, May 23rd. They were gathered in the parlor to await the dinner bell. Bonnie Anne and J.J. came in to say hello to their aunt and uncle and Mr. Thompson, and to play with baby Lee. They were disappointed when Charlotte told them that the baby had a few sniffles, and she had thought it best to leave him at home with Liza. After answering a few questions put to them by the grown-ups, the children were content to follow Evelina up to the playroom where they would have their supper on a little table set up there, along with their dolls and stuffed animals.

Violet watched the children as they skipped from the room, and then she picked up a letter from the side table. "I have a letter from our Susan," she announced with a happy smile. "It's addressed to all of us."

"Oh, wonderful! What does she say? We haven't heard from that little imp in ages," said Charlotte happily.

"It *is* wonderful to hear from her, and her news is even more exciting; she's expecting!" announced Violet to everyone in general.

"Oh, Violet," crowed Charlotte, clapping her hands in delight, "is she really in *that way*?"

"Well, her doctor thinks so."

"When? When is her time?" asked Charlotte, now beaming from ear to ear.

"Probably December, so I'm afraid they won't be able to spend Christmas at Fair Oaks this year."

"Oh, dear, I'm so happy for her!"

"Yes, yes..." "Good news, indeed..." "She'll be a fine little mother..." came from the men.

Violet went on, reading the letter to everyone. Susan said she and Gilbert were thrilled about the baby, and so were his folks. Gilbert was having the small back room repainted and fixed up as a nursery, and he treated her as if she were a porcelain doll. He just couldn't believe that she was strong and healthy and that having a baby was a perfectly normal thing. But it was nice having a husband who cared so much, so she knew she shouldn't fuss at him. They had been to several balls and formal dinners in the last month, and they were having a wonderful life together, and she was very happy, but she couldn't help but long for Fair Oaks, and please, everyone, keep writing letters full of the local news.

"Violet," interrupted Charlotte in a soft voice. She gave Leland a loving glance before going on modestly, "Leland and I have some news for you, too. We think...it's still a bit early...but we suspect...little Lee will have a new brother or sister sometime in January."

Violet jumped up from her chair and ran over to hug Charlotte. "Oh, Honey, that's wonderful! I'm so happy for you both. Oh, I hope you're right."

Brent added his congratulations to the young couple, both of whom were beaming with pride. Andrew, too, was grinning at the idea of another grandchild.

Just then they heard Mammy ringing the silver dinner bell. Violet folded the letter and tucked it into a skirt pocket as they all went into the dining room.

After everyone was seated and had placed their napkins on their laps, Violet looked around and remarked, "I must say, this is rather more orderly than the Governor's reception a few weeks ago".

"Did Susan have any other news?" asked Charlotte.

Violet took the letter from her pocket and unfolded it. "I'll have to read this line." She glanced at Brent and then read, " 'Tell the Commodore he had better watch out; we have heard of the Sutler scandal all the way out here."

All eyes riveted toward Brent. He flashed a nervous smile. Then a look of relaxed comprehension crossed his face as he laughed and said, "That little imp, she's not talking about me. It seems that sutlers—men who obtain concessions to sell goods of various kinds—have been bidding for concessions in Indian posts. Sometimes these payments have amounted to four times the annual profits, but the juiciest part is that

Grant's own Secretary of War, Belknap, has been receiving annual payments, through his wife as intermediary, from the sutler at Fort Sill in the Indian Territory."

Violet giggled. "Well, I'm relieved to hear that it is so far away." She glanced down at the letter. "But Susan also had something to say about the bad situation in Mississippi."

Andrew Thompson looked up with interest. "What's that?"

"Trouble with the blacks and with the state government."

"Mm, but I thought reconstruction was over for them, and they had been able to get out from under their Carpetbagger/Scalawag regime," said Thompson, frowning. He had relatives living in Mississippi, and he had been increasingly concerned about their well-being.

"Apparently the storm keeps coming back. Susan says they are still having trouble. She says they had a pretty serious race riot in Vicksburg in December, and the only thing that has eased a state of anarchy there has been local vigilante committees who have become tired of all the lawlessness and corruption of the Carpetbagger/Negro regimes."

"Well, I do declare!" sympathized Charlotte. "Those poor people! Seems like the situation is worse there than it is here."

"Except that the land owners have been able to work back into a measure of control in spite of the government," Violet responded. "In January the legislature voted impeachment against the governor, a Carpetbagger from Maine by the name of Ames, and against all of his executive officers. They think he may resign before it comes to trial."

Andrew Thompson turned toward Brent and asked, "Do you think there is any likelihood that Moses might be impeached?"

Jarvis had brought Leland's plate to Brent for another slice of beef. As Brent went to work on the roast, rather more vigorously than necessary, he responded, "No, not a chance in the world. Unlike Scott, he still has the legislature under his thumb. Our best chance to get out from under Moses is this year's election—not that the Democrats have any prospect yet, but I think he has about cooked his goose with his own cohorts. You saw where an Orangeburg County grand jury found a true bill against the Governor, and just last week the judge there issued a bench warrant and sent the sheriff to arrest the Governor. Can you beat that!"

"Can you arrest a governor?" asked Leland.

"Moses doesn't think so," Brent replied, nodding to Jarvis that he could take the plate back to Leland. "He called out his Negro militia and telegraphed the Chief Justice—his father—for assistance and declared that he could neither be arrested nor required to give bond so long as he was in office."

"I read something about that, but what was behind it?" inquired Andrew.

"Well, as usual his Excellency was running low on funds, and he applied to the Negro treasurer of Orangeburg County for a substantial loan, indicating to the treasurer that if he refused he would be removed from office. Moses gave the county treasurer a draft on the executive contingent fund, but then to the consternation of Moses, his own state treasurer refused to honor the draft and removed the county treasurer from office and charged him with malfeasance. This is where the county court came into action against the Governor, though I guess it did no good," answered Brent.

"This talk is about to give me indigestion," remarked Violet, smiling, "though I must say I relish any comment to the discredit of Mr. Moses."

The conversation turned to discussions of local economic conditions. The elder Thompson expressed concern that the cotton mill had been laying off more workers and cutting the wages of those who remained. Leland mentioned that he was thankful their own positions remained intact, though he was disappointed that income had not risen.

After desert Violet and Brent and their guests withdrew to the parlor where they enjoyed a small demitasse of hot chocolate, with a spoonful of the sweet cream floating on top.

Violet excused herself to run upstairs to the office and returned with a stack of newspapers.

"My goodness, what have you there?" asked Charlotte.

"Oh, just more dirt about Moses and the Carpetbaggers and Scalawags that I was afraid you might have missed. Have you been reading the Sumter newspaper?" Violet laid the papers on the needlepoint covered footstool in front of her chair.

Leland remarked pointedly, "I hope you don't mean Allen Gilbert's *Watchman,* that rag of the Radical Republicans."

Violet chuckled, "No, I mean *The Sumter News–*"

"No, not recently," Leland answered for both his wife and himself.

"Well, did you know that paper has changed its name?"

Charlotte showed her surprise. "No, what is it now?" she asked.

"They changed the name to *The True Southron–.*"

"Bravo!" exclaimed Andrew.

Violet held up a copy and read from the paper's own statement:

> *It is the organ, exponent and champion of the White people of the South...Like The News, it shall be the zealous guardian and defender of their honor and reputation, the fearless, independent, and incorruptible champion of their rights and liberties, and the uncompromising and implacable foe of carpetbaggers and renegades–of imported and domestic, official and unofficial corruption, venality and fraud.*

"I hope they don't go too far with that white supremacy emphasis," Brent stated, and added with a smile, "lest they offend a major part of my constituency."

"Oh, are you running again this year, Brent?" asked the inquisitive Charlotte.

Brent glanced at Violet as he answered, "I suppose so; it's that time, and I have a feeling that during my next term–."

"If there is one," interjected Violet with an acknowledging smile.

"Yes, if there is one, I have a feeling that there will be more radical changes around here than the Radicals have dreamed about. I have a feeling that the time is not too far away when we may be able to throw the rascals out."

"I certainly hope so," remarked Andrew.

"Brent, just what has been the extent of Moses' plunder?" Leland asked.

Brent slowly shook his head from side to side, his face showing disgust as he answered, "To tell the truth, Leland, nobody knows, but I can tell you this, he has been living at a rate of forty thousand dollars a year on an income of three thousand five hundred. He has sold state property and pocketed the money; he has sold appointments, commissions, and support for certain measures. He has sold pardons, over four hundred pardons in his eighteen months in power, and beyond that he has borrowed against everything he can get his hands on. They say that he owes a quarter of a million dollars. Add to that the plunder of all of his executive officers and Speaker Elliott of the House of Representatives and his core of followers in the House known as the Forty Thieves—and not to mention the antics of Honest John Patterson, our United States Senator."

Andrew groaned and added, "And just look at the condition of our State."

"Yes, just look at it," continued Brent, "practically bankrupt, and so are the taxpayers. Do you know that this year nearly three hundred and fifty thousand acres of land in nineteen counties went to the tax collectors, and another ninety thousand acres were sold for taxes? My father tells me that in Charleston alone, two thousand pieces of real estate have been forfeited for taxes this year. A delegation from the Taxpayers' Convention went up to Washington to see Grant just last month. Apparently Grant could not believe what he heard, and of course he did absolutely nothing about it."

"Isn't Grant himself having his troubles with fraud and corruption in the national government?" asked Leland.

"Indeed," Brent responded, "it's almost poetic justice, there seems to be as much graft and corruption going on all over the North as in the Carpetbag South."

"The Yankees seem to have a gift for spreading corruption all around" suggested Andrew.

This brought from Violet and Brent an antiphonal recitation of scandals they had been summarizing in their minds after reviewing back newspapers and copies of *Harper's Weekly*.

"Just to mention a few items," Violet began, "take Credit Mobilier, for instance."

"Yes," Brent joined in, "This was a development company, a device for which directors of the Union Pacific Railroad granted themselves construction contracts and by awarding shares to various congressmen and other government officials, the company obtained huge Government loans."

"And the affair of the Little Rock and Fort Smith Railroad," put in Violet.

"Yes, the Speaker of the U.S. House of Representatives, James G. Blaine, pushed through a favorable measure for support of the railroad, and then demanded a reward."

"Tell them about the Boss Shepherd Scandal in Washington, Brent," returned Violet.

"Shepherd was the power behind the governor of the District of Columbia in spending the District practically to bankruptcy by extravagance and corruption, and then when the head man in all of this finally resigned, Grant appointed Boss Shepherd himself to take his place."

"But all this is terrible, just terrible!" exclaimed a shocked Charlotte.

"Indeed," Andrew agreed solemnly.

"And, Brent, the Safe Burglary affair–." continued Violet.

"Oh, yes, there was a fellow by the name of Columbus Alexander who was trying to bring about some reform in the District of Columbia and an assistant Federal attorney and the Chief of the Secret Service conspired to injure Alexander and dissuade him from his activities."

"The Whiskey Ring."

"This is just coming to light, but it appears that revenue officers and distillers have been conspiring to defraud the Government of excise taxes, including some of Grant's cronies, and maybe even his own secretary.

"Revolting," declared Leland.

"Revolting, indeed," echoed his father.

"Tell them about the Sanborn contract," Violet went on.

"This involved Ben Butler–."

Violet broke in, "He was that Yankee devil in charge of the occupation of New Orleans; his brother made millions in illicit trade in cotton. Mary Chesnut called him a hideous cross-eyed beast."

Brent continued, "That's the one. Well, John Sanborn, Butler's stalking horse, got a contract from the U.S. Treasury Department to collect overdue revenue. According to hearings just this month, Sanborn collected four hundred and twenty-seven thousand dollars for which he received a commission of fifty percent."

"Now the Tweed Ring, Brent."

"You mean there's more? All this and more?" asked an incredulous Charlotte.

"Alas, yes, tell them, Brent."

"Well, over a period of three years after Grant became president, Boss William Tweed was running the city of New York, and he and his associates were dividing among themselves about eighty-five percent of the city's revenues. Finally this was broken up a couple of years ago by a brilliant prosecutor by the name of Samuel J. Tilden who now is Democratic governor of New York, and who may give us all some hope for the future."

"And just one more, the Salary Grab."

"All right, just this one, or we'll all be so depressed we won't be able to sleep tonight. But you're right, they should hear about the Salary Grab. This was another project headed by Ben Butler, now a Congressman from Massachusetts. It was an act of Congress at the end of its term last year, to give Senators and Representatives an increase in salary from five thousand to seven thousand five hundred dollars. Not only that, they voted to make it retroactive for two years!"

"Zounds!" Andrew exclaimed. "Is there no end to all this corruption?"

"Not as long as Grant and the Radicals stay in power, I should think," answered Brent. "Who knows what will turn up next? And please remember, this is only the public sector. In the private sector, there is as much going on in such things as the watering of stocks, attempts to corner the gold market and manipulate the stock market, the outright theft of corporations and railroads by securities and financial shenanigans, out from under one conniving group by another conniving group."

"And what about the more obvious outlaws," added Violet. "Don't forget them."

"Yes, those seem to be flourishing these days, too. What worries me most are the bands of railroad desperados that have been running loose. That sort of thing seems to have begun with the Reno gang of Indiana who were hanged by vigilantes a few years ago. Then there is Jessie James who robbed the Kansas City Fair of ten thousand dollars a couple of years ago, and he and his gang have been robbing banks and trains with immunity ever since. Trouble is, Jessie James was a fine soldier with Quantrill's raiders during the War. Then after the War he surrendered and went back home, but his Yankee-sympathizer neighbors had him declared an outlaw—which he proceeded to become. Actually more culpable, I think, is somebody like Sam Bass, who started out as a deputy U.S. marshal and then became an outlaw."

The grandfather's clock in the hall began striking ten o'clock.

"Oh, Lordy!" exclaimed Charlotte. "I had no idea it's so late; I just got caught up in all this fascinating conversation. Oh, Leland, we must get home as soon as we can. I've got to check on little Lee's cold."

"Yes, honey, now don't worry. The baby is fine," said Leland, smiling at Charlotte's concern.

Violet rang for Jarvis to bring Charlotte's cape. The weather was mild, and the men needed no wraps over their sack coats. The sisters kissed one another good-bye, and the men shook hands. Charlotte, Leland, and Andrew all thanked the Sutlers for the delicious supper.

"Do try to come down to Fair Oaks for a long week-end as soon as you can," Violet called to her guests as they descended the steps and crossed to the waiting carriage.

"We shall, I promise," called back Charlotte as Leland lifted her into the vehicle and they took off down the street.

Chapter 58

The Planter and the Railroad Magnate

1874

In late May of 1874, Monument Day in Sumter was a festive and colorful occasion. A large crowd gathered for the dedication of the Confederate Memorial monument near the center of town. Although General J.B. Kershaw was the chief orator of the day, Brent decided that this would be a good time to launch a few preliminary blows in his bid for re-election to the State Senate. At his suggestion, the committee invited him to be on the program to make a few remarks.

After the General had blasted the North for "first saddling us with slavery and then being willing to destroy us to free the slaves, and then holding us in armed subjugation while they rob us of our few remaining resources," and after he had brought tears to the eyes of his listeners with a recitation of the noble part the sons of Sumter had played in their struggle for states rights, Brent stepped to the lectern on the platform. He grasped the lapels of his light gray short coat, and with a smile he cast a sharp look all across the crowd. He flashed a special smile to Violet when he caught her eye in the audience. A light breeze ruffled his thick, dark hair so that a wisp fell across his forehead, giving him a youthful look. He unconsciously pushed it back with his fingers, but the breeze soon blew it back, and this time it went unnoticed by him. In a clear, well-modulated voice he began speaking:

"We must never give up the values that the brave men whose memory we honor today fought for. Justice and right and liberty must forever remain our goals. The time has come for us to reclaim this state and its government—."

He paused as the crowd cheered enthusiastically and waved their hats. Warming to his subject, he went on:

"It is time to root out the corruption from our state officials and from our counties [*More cheering*.] It is a disgrace that the treasurer of our county has been indicted for misuse of our funds. It seems that he has been very efficient in collecting our taxes, but very inefficient in handing them over to state agencies. It is a disgrace that our county school commissioner has been indicted for malfeasance in office. It is a disgrace that our county has been allowed to go bankrupt, with no work on bridges, no work on roads. It is a disgrace that all the public schools of the county have been closed for most of this year. It is a disgrace that the county has been doing nothing for the poor and the indigent during these hard times." *[Hear! Hear!]* He continued in this vein for fifteen minutes.

Loud applause accompanied the conclusion of Brent's remarks. He left the platform and joined Violet in the audience to watch the series of tableaux that followed.

The first scene was of a Confederate soldier, departing from his weeping family. The next depicted the soldier lying dead on the battlefield, shrouded by the Palmetto flag. Then followed a parade, across the platform, of the former Confederate states, each represented by a young woman in appropriate costume, appearing in mourning. Louisiana, Florida, and Arkansas wore chains to show that those states still had not been released from Federal military occupation and Radical rule. South Carolina, also in chains, was led by a sturdy Negro while Carpetbaggers and Scalawags were stripping her of her rich treasures.

In managing the planting and cultivation, Violet continued to emphasize the rotation of crops and the generous use of fertilizer. Recent discoveries of almost unlimited supplies of phosphate around Charleston provided a good source for fertilizer at low cost. Violet set a goal of getting a yield of one five-hundred pound bale of cotton from each acre under cultivation, and she felt sure that they could do better than that. Indeed she expressed confidence that instead of a bale to two acres, the fields would yield two bales to the acre.

She brought in a new kind of hay called alfalfa which was said to be very nutritious for cattle. It would withstand drought better than clover, and its deep roots drew up minerals which made it a good fertilizer for other crops. On the basis of what she had read, she figured that she would be able to get eight to ten tons to the acre, and what she sold should bring six to seven dollars a ton, which might make it almost as valuable as cotton.

To the cattle herd she added several Brahmins from Kentucky. She had been impressed by reports of how well these cattle, originally from India, thrived in warm, humid climates, how they were immune from ticks, were generally healthy, and were excellent for milk and butter as well as beef. She also was impressed by a report that when milk from Brahmins and from other cows were put in separate crocks and placed side by side in a dairy cellar, the milk from the Brahmins took at least two hours longer to turn sour than did the milk from the other cows.

Under Violet's attention and forcefulness, improvements continued on the plantation. Brent, as always impressed by her zest for improvement and creativity, supported her endeavors. She had him buy improved plows, harrows, reapers, and mowers, and to add better facilities to the cotton gin and press, the grain thresher, and the grist mill. She also added several things in the big house—a coal range from Perry and Company of Albany, New York, that, like the one in the town house, had four lids, a hot water reservoir on the side, an oven in the middle below the burners, and warming ovens above. She obtained a new Continental washing machine which contained a cylinder of wooden slats operated by handles to agitate the clothing through the wash water, and beside it she placed a newly perfected Reliance clothes wringer. She fitted all the beds in the house with the new woven wire mattresses which the manufacturer claimed were cleaner, more comfortable, and more durable than the old rope mattresses.

On a warm night in mid-June, Rachel gave birth to a baby girl. Although Leo had hoped for a boy, when he looked at the baby resting beside Rachel the beauty of the infant was remarkable. All traces of disappointment left Leo's face, to be replaced by a broad smile of unmitigated delight. It was obvious that he wouldn't trade this little girl for any boy in the world. Tenderly the big, burly, strong field boss leaned down, picked up his baby, and caressed her in his arms, smiling proudly at his wife and the others as if he, and not Rachel, had given birth to this remarkable child. Tired as she was, Rachel took a long, deep sigh of relief and her eyes shone with happiness.

A few days after Leo and Rachel's baby was born, Evelina knocked on the office door and asked if she could speak with Violet, who was working at her desk alone. Brent was in Columbia for the day.

"Miz Violet, may ah haf a word wif ya?"

"Of course, come on in and have a seat." Violet waved to one of the rocking chairs. "What is it?" she asked as she rose from her desk and took the other rocking chair.

"Wale, Miz Violet, ya know Levi."

"Yes, of course, he's a nice young man. Enoch tells me he's very good at his work and very dependable, too. What about him?"

"Wale, Miz Violet," began Evelina shyly, "he wants ta marry up wif me."

Violet was speechless with surprise. *My goodness, a love affair has been going on right in this house, and I didn't even know it! Well, that's to their credit. They have certainly been discreet.* She found her voice and with genuine pleasure she said, "Why, Evelina, this is wonderful! But do you love him? Do you want to marry him?"

Still in a shy voice, Evelina answered, "Oh, yas, Miz Violet, ah do want ta marry him, ah do, ah do—."

"Well, good then."

"Buh Miz Violet, ah 'fraid."

"Afraid? But why, Evelina?"

Obviously troubled, Evelina shifted her eyes, and then, tears welling up, she looked at Violet and explained, her voice barely audible, "Ya know, Miz Violet, whut dem Yankee sojuhs do ta meh after dey carry me off wif dem. Levi, he think ah be unspoil'd. W'en he find out ah be spoil'd, ah 'fraid he be mad wif meh."

Violet understood Evelina's concern. Slowly and sympathetically, she responded, "Evelina, I know that what happened to you was a terrible experience, but it was something over which you had no control. You couldn't help what happened, and we mustn't let that spoil things now."

The tears were running down Evelina's cheeks as she sorrowfully said, "Buh whut do ah do? Do ah tell Levi all 'bout dat or do ah keep hit uh secret?"

Violet sighed, "It's a difficult decision all right, Evelina. Probably...probably it would be best to keep it a secret, but that may not be possible. As you know, some others around here were at Fair Oaks at the time and have an inkling of what happened, although I'm sure none of them would want you to be hurt, ever." She stopped to think a moment while Evelina sat quietly, wiping off the tears on her cheeks with a handkerchief. Then Violet made up her mind. "Evelina, it might be better if I have a word with Levi. Yes, that's it. Now don't you say a word about this to Levi. Let me talk to him."

Evelina was visibly relieved that Violet had taken this burden from her. "Oh, tank ya, tank ya, Miz Violet. Ah know ya hep me some way."

Violet gave Evelina a hug and kissed her on the cheek. "Now don't you worry any more about this."

A couple of days later while Brent was gone on an errand to Sumter, Violet called Levi into her office and asked him to shut the door. She remained seated at her swivel desk chair as she invited Levi to take one of the Bank of England chairs beside the desk.

"Well, Levi, I understand that you would like to marry Evelina."

"Oh, yas, Miz Violet, ah sho do. Ah be wantin' ta come an' ask yo' permission ta do dat."

"Well, Levi, you have that, and our blessing. She's a wonderful woman; we consider her part of the family–."

"Ah know dat, yassum."

"–I don't know how I ever could have gotten along without her. She's been wonderful with the children, and they love her very much. And, Levi, you have been doing very good work since you came. Enoch is always telling me how pleased he is with you and how smart you are, and we don't want to do without you either."

"Tank ya, Miz Violet. Ah sho glad ta heah dat. Ah try ta do mah best."

"Levi, there is something I must tell you, and I hope you will understand."

"Yassum," he responded, wondering what Miss Violet wanted him to know.

Violet took a deep breath and began, "During the War Evelina was kidnaped, taken off by a group of renegade Yankee soldiers. They...they attacked her...they hurt her. It was a dreadful thing what they did to her, and I think she has been afraid of men ever since; she doesn't trust them, and for good reason. Now, Levi, you will need to be very gentle and patient and understanding with her–."

"Oh, Miz Violet," gasped Levi. He buried his face in his hands.

"–She feels a sense of shame for what happened, though it was none of her doing. She always has remained pure in her heart." Then she repeated, emphasizing the three words, "*Pure in heart,*" and added, "I hope you can understand that."

Levi looked up, a sad look in his eyes. He remained quiet for a few moments as though in deep thought, then rose from his chair. With a smile of sincerity he said, "Miz Violet, ah know she be pure in her heart. Ah do love her an' ah be very gent'l an' all wif her, an' ah unnerstan' whut you say, an' ah tank ya fo' 'plainin' all dis ta meh. Ah gonna be uh good husban' ta her, ah promise."

Violet rose and laid her hand on his sleeve. "And, Levi, I think it best that you never mention to her what happened. It will only bring back awful memories. Just let this be–let sleeping dogs lie."

"No, ma'am, ah say nothin' 'bout all dis. Ah wan' her ta forget dose bad tings an' jes' be happy wif meh."

The wedding was held on a bright, sunny Sunday afternoon. Every seat in the church/school was filled, and both side walls were lined with standees. Evelina had always been liked by everyone, and Levi had quickly earned the respect and admiration of not only the house servants but the plantation workers as well as he helped Enoch about the place. Charlotte and Leland, and little Lee came for the weekend, and Sarah and John Frierson and Mary and Will Anderson came for the ceremony. The doctor had worked very closely with Evelina during J.J.'s long illness, and he had become quite fond of the capable young servant who nursed the young boy with such genuine affection.

Elijah Jackson read the ceremony. Enoch and Aaron and Hattie and Mammy stood up with the young couple. J.J. was the ring bearer, and Bonnie Anne was the flower girl. The young couple, obviously deeply in love, stood proudly in their new clothes that Violet and Brent had given them for a wedding present. Immediately after the ceremony, the *Little Brown Jugs* led off for a festival of eating and dancing that lasted for the rest of the afternoon.

Violet gave the newlyweds Monday and Tuesday off and sent them in to Sumter where they stayed in a guest room at *The Joshua School.* They would return to a newly furbished two-room suite on the third floor of the big house.

While Violet was preoccupied with the plantation, Brent was initiating a whole series of improvements for the railroad in rapid-fire order. Now that the track in the front yard had been pulled up and relocated, the first priority was to begin replacing the iron rails of the remaining track with steel and to make adaptation to carry cars of different gauge. Like most railroads in the South, the Carolina Central had been built with a five-foot gauge. More and more of the northern and western railroads were being built at what was becoming the standard gauge of four feet eight and one-half inches. Freight coming into the South had to be unloaded and reloaded, or the cars had to be hoisted up on a different set of wheels when they came to a different gauge. Brent's approach was to lay a third rail inside one of the present rails to allow standard gauge, and thus permit cars of either gauge to move over the tracks. And he went on to make many other improvements to the railroad—new locomotives, passenger cars, freight cars, and new tank cars with expansion dome for carrying oil. Cabooses for the train crews would be added to all freight trains.

Brent's pride and joy would be two luxurious overnight trains that would operate between Columbia and Charleston. He would contract with Pullman of Chicago for new-type sleeping cars and dining cars, and a parlor car would be at the end, all lighted with new Pintch gaslights from Germany. Each car would have a lavatory and toilet. The trains could make the run in less than eight hours, but passengers would be welcomed aboard at six o'clock so that they could enjoy a leisurely supper if they wished. A newsboy would be aboard with the latest papers. The trains would pull out from each city about ten o'clock and arrive in the other at six in the morning. Passengers might remain on board until nine o'clock for a leisurely breakfast and a fresh newspaper.

Brent always discussed these plans with Violet. She did not simply concur, she reacted with enthusiasm.

John Fraser, too, maintained a positive attitude, and he was highly effective in putting the new plans into effect while carrying on current operations. Only on one point did he demur—the outlay for new passenger service.

With a sheaf of papers in his hands he came into Brent's office one morning to explain. "You know, Brent, passenger service never has been very profitable. If you will look at these figures you will see that the Carolina Central hardly broke even on passenger trains, and about as often as not ran at a loss."

Looking at the figures carefully, Brent responded, "I guess it depends a little on your accounting. I see here that a pro-rata share of the railroad maintenance, the telegraph, and so on has been assigned to the passenger trains. And that is proper, but on the other hand, if we took off all the passenger trains the cost of maintaining the track and so on would not decline at all. So those are really not out-of-pocket costs, and most of these losses are not out-of-pocket losses. I think passenger trains almost pay for themselves in terms simply of obtaining and operating the trains and the stations."

"Well, that may be true, but that still is an awful lot of effort for no profit. Besides that, passenger service is always a headache. People are always complaining—the train was late, or they were too hot, or too cold, and the cars were smoky and dirty—."

"There, John, you have hit on the point, precisely why passenger service should be expanded and improved."

"What do you mean?"

"It's public relations, John, public relations."

"Public relations?"

"Of course. Don't you see if we can turn all those complaints you're talking about into praise, that will be very much to our advantage. If every time a businessman rides one of our trains he has a good experience, if he is impressed by the speed and efficiency of the trains, and if he has good quarters and has a comfortable seat or berth, if he experiences all this, then when it comes to shipping freight, he'll be thinking Carolina Rail."

"Well, you do have a point there," conceded Fraser.

"And remember," added Brent, "we don't have to make a big capital outlay for the Pullman cars on our overnight trains. Pullman operates them and pays us a share for pulling them over our tracks."

"Yes, that's true."

"And another thing. We are going to be in a strong competitive position even on schedules. It's a shorter route to Charleston by the Columbia Branch and the South Carolina Railroad, but with our new equipment and new rails we'll be able to get there almost as fast as they can, and our more indirect route enables us to serve a good many more communities."

"Let's do it," John Fraser concluded. "Let's do all of it."

Chapter 59

This and That

1874

Late one afternoon in mid-June when Brent came pumping in on the handcar over the newly completed railroad spur, Violet greeted him with a hello kiss and led him into the office for lemonade and cookies and to chat about the day's events.

He looked around, expecting the usual deluge of children jumping on him in greeting and shouting, "Daddy's home! Daddy's home!" and being smothered with their kisses and hugs. "Where are the kids? I'm not accustomed to this peace and quiet."

Violet laughed. "I gave them permission to go visit Rachel and Leo's new baby. Evelina's with them. Come, sit down, enjoy this tranquility while it lasts."

He sat in one of the rocking chairs as Violet poured the lemonade.

"Camden again?" she asked. She placed several cookies on a small plate and handed these and a glass of lemonade to Brent. She had noticed that he had varied his regular routine by going to Camden on four successive days, and she was wondering what was up.

"Yes, Camden again," he answered. He took a bite of one of Mammy's sugar cookies as he concentrated on his lemonade.

She picked up her own lemonade and a couple of cookies and took the other rocking chair. "Well, how is the Charlotte extension of Carolina Rail coming?"

Brent hesitated, and without looking at Violet said, "Oh, that's coming along fine...fine."

You rascal, that's not what's on your mind right now, she thought. With an impish grin, she asked in a casual manner, "By the way, who won the last race?"

"Ladybird," he replied, without really thinking about her question, and then he caught himself quickly and continued, "Oh, uh, I don't know what you're talking about."

Violet giggled at his discomfiture. "Brent, when did the Camden Jockey Club revive its racing programs?"

In an innocent voice, Brent answered, "Oh, I believe they revived the races last year."

Violet set her glass on the table between the rocking chairs. "Brent Sutler, tell me, have your trips to Camden this week had more to do with horse races than with the Carolina Rail extension?"

Now a sheepish look came across Brent's face. "Well, maybe, almost as much."

"You aren't getting hooked on horse races, are you, Brent?" asked Violet, her voice rising slightly from worry.

"Oh, Violet, for gods' sake!"

A few days later Brent returned by horse and buggy from Sumter. He had decided to drive Beau into town to get the mail and newspapers. As Violet came out to meet him he said, "Do you remember Everett Duff?" A characteristic mischievous smirk on his face betrayed that he was hatching some kind of plot.

"Isn't he one of those Carpetbaggers at the Court House?"

"Precisely. Well, he was getting into his buggy alongside mine as I was leaving. Giving old Beau the once over, he sniggered and said, 'Kind of a worn out nag you've got there, isn't it?'

"'Oh, he does all right,' I replied.

"'I'll bet you he doesn't do well enough to keep up with my Morgan here.'

"'No, probably not," I said.

"'What's his name?' he asked.

"'Beauregard,' I answered.

"'Oh, a damned, worn-out Rebel general, eh?'

"'Damn you,' I said, 'I'll race you over a mile stretch for fifty dollars.'

"'Hate to take your money, but if you'll make it in greenbacks and not some of your worthless Confederate paper, I'll race any time you want, except today. I'm late for an appointment now.' How about tomorrow?'

"'Good,' I told him, 'I'll meet you at the railroad crossing on the Sumter-Stateburg road tomorrow at two o'clock, and we'll go for a mile, to the road junction.'

"'All right, I'll be there," he said.

Brent stopped and looked at Violet to gauge her reaction.

"Ha!" she laughed. "Do you think you have a chance? Isn't Beau getting a little old for that sort of thing?"

He flashed his mischievous grin. "Yes, I do, and that's where you come in, my dear."

"Me? What on earth do you mean?"

"Well, my dear, I want to borrow your Hermes."

"Brent Sutler, are you thinking about substituting Hermes for Beau?"

The roguish grin returned. "Sure I am. He's about the same color as Beau, and old Duff wouldn't know one horse from the other.

"But, Brent, that wouldn't be fair. That's not honest."

"Well, what if I had been driving Hermes instead of Beau today?"

"Then Duff would never have challenged you, I'm sure."

"Now, Violet, I don't know that, and anyway I just want to teach him a lesson. Wouldn't it be fun to beat a damned Carpetbagger? They sure have done their best to beat the hell out of us."

"You're right about that. A damned Carpetbagger. Yes! Let's do it!" Her conscience was clear; after all he was one of those diabolic Carpetbaggers who had tried to drain the life from her family and her people.

The next afternoon Violet walked with the two children to the road to watch the great race go by. A little after two o'clock she told them, "I think I hear the horses. Watch and see who's ahead."

Presently Hermes, pulling the buggy with Brent in it, flashed by. Brent gave a quick wave and continued urging Hermes on, leaving a cloud of dust behind. The children and Violet yelled with excitement. It seemed ages before the other buggy driven by Duff came by, almost hidden in the cloud of dust. Violet couldn't believe how far ahead Hermes was. *What a magnificent horse,* she exulted, *and he's all mine!*

Within a few minutes the two buggies returned. Brent invited Duff to come in for a glass of scuppernong. Violet and the children, clapping and chattering with excitement, climbed into the buggy with Brent and rode up to the house.

Sending the children out with Evelina, Violet and Brent led Duff into the office. Before accepting refreshments, Duff handed over fifty dollars to Brent. Brent took the bundle to his desk and carefully counted the money. Then with a chuckle he handed it back.

"Duff," he said, "I pulled a fast one on you today. I did a switch, just to show you what a Southern horse can do. Actually, Hermes—that's his name—is a pacer, a standard bred horse. He belongs to my wife." Violet beamed with delight—at her husband's declaration of the switch, and because her horse had done so well.

"Well, I declare," Duff responded, "you probably should keep the money anyway." Then, accepting it, he went on, "But I do appreciate your candor, Mr. Sutler. Indeed I do." He looked around the parlor and added, "This is certainly a beautiful home you have here. It's fortunate you've been able to hold on to it."

Violet could only nod. It would be neither courteous nor gracious to comment on the difficulties and barriers that had threatened their very existence.

After wine and cheese, and congenial conversation, Duff took his leave, saying, "Senator, if you ever race that nag, let me know: I'd rather put my money on him."

After he was gone, Violet turned to Brent, "Imagine! He called my Hermes a *nag*! *A nag*! How do you like that!"

Brent just shook his head and roared with laughter. It had been a great afternoon.

While Violet got a kick out of Hermes' race, she still was concerned about what she perceived to be a gnawing addiction on the part of Brent for horse racing, but the more she fussed at him the more he denied it and the more ill-tempered he became. Worst of all, he had even mentioned that they were working on a system of placing bets on distant tracks by telegraph. *Lose thousands in the comfort of your own office,* she thought. *Oh, Brent, my dear husband, I would never have thought this could happen. I wonder what I can do; I must do something.*

Then one morning over breakfast, after the children had excused themselves from the table and run out to ride their ponies with Fabian, Violet approached Brent from a different tack.

"Honey, I've been wondering. Can't betting on the horses be rather expensive?" she asked in a mild tone.

"Oh, I suppose so...sometimes," he answered, sipping his second cup of coffee.

She took a deep breath and went on, "Tell me, Brent, have you lost much?"

She had his attention. He looked at her more intently than usual. "Well, now my dear, I wouldn't say that."

Violet persisted, "Well, have you broken even?"

His eyes shifted to the coffee in his cup, "Well, no, not exactly, but I do get a certain enjoyment out of betting on the horses."

"Well, Brent, tell me. I really want to understand. Do you enjoy it mainly for the betting, for the taking of chances, the gambling, or do you enjoy it more for the horses themselves?"

Brent leaned back in his chair and thought a long time. Finally, after he drained his cup of coffee, he answered her question. "Well, my dear, to be honest, maybe a little of both, but I think I get my greatest kick out of watching the horses run."

"Brent," Violet went on, "it might not be much more expensive and a lot more fun to raise some horses of your own to race—and forget the betting. Just win the purses."

Again Brent thought for a while, then with a big smile he turned to her, "Maybe you've got something there. Mm, and you know something, we'll do a little pioneering around here. We'll go in for harness horse racing, the pacers and the trotters. We'll start with Hermes..."

"Well, now, I don't know about that—."

"Just this year, honey, just to get a start, and then we'll put him back into your sole service."

I don't much like the idea of using my Hermes for this, but if it'll get Brent's mind off of betting, I think I'd better go along on this, she thought, so she said somewhat reluctantly, "Well, all right then, but couldn't we build a track to train him here?

"Of course. That's what we'll do!" he replied eagerly, already caught up in this new undertaking.

Over the next week Brent and Violet got Leo to get a crew of workers to build a track. It was a half-mile oval laid around forty acres of the west meadow. The workers plowed it, built banks on the curves, then harrowed the track and dragged it and rolled it to a smooth surface.

In Camden, Brent bought another pacer, a two-year old black colt called Midnight Star and a bay trotter, only a yearling, called Bay Rum. Violet thought them both beautiful. She found herself as excited as Brent about all this, and the children were nearly so. They were finding it hard to understand why their ponies couldn't be used, too, and Brent tried patiently to explain to them the differences without slighting their pretty little ponies. He did tell Bonnie Anne and J.J. that the two of them could race their ponies against one another when the track was not being used—but only with permission from him or Violet, and that they always had to be very careful.

Jason, the plantation's animal husbandman, brought up four young black workers, Charles and Benjamin, to be drivers and trainers, and Joseph, to be the groom, and the oldest, Martin, to be the swipe. Charles and Benjamin's responsibility would be to give the race horses daily workouts pulling the high-wheeled sulky. Joseph would curry the horses and keep the harness and sulky in good repair, while Martin's job would be to walk the horses around the walking circle to cool off after a workouts, feed them, and keep their stables clean.

Violet found that she was enjoying as much as Brent watching the horses work out each day, and just for the fun of it, each took a turn at driving from time to time, and even racing with each other while the children cheered them on. Violet, with Hermes, invariably won.

Actually Violet encouraged wholesome recreation of all kinds, though she wondered at times if people caught up in the oppressive darkness of the Reconstruction were too frantically seeking diversion. Still, she was convinced that hard play made hard work more effective. Further, the more one had suffered in the past, the more each little moment of enjoyment meant. Each moment was all the more precious, and each joy all the more magnified.

Grandmama Lee arrived for a visit. She tutored the children on their manners, but she also read stories to them, played games with them and took them picnicking along the creek. She even took them fishing at the pond several times. She never seemed bored and always seemed to be enjoying herself thoroughly. Violet was relieved that her health continued to be good and amazed at her high level of energy and interest—especially as the older woman watched or participated in new activities.

Almost daily, weather permitting, the children and their great grandmother watched Charles and Benjamin exercise the horses on the track. Sometimes in the late afternoons, the family would play croquet, now becoming a rage all over the country, and played here with a fine set of equipment that Brent had imported from England. In this game, Grandmama Lee could hold her own.

But she remained an interested spectator in another lawn sport. This was lawn tennis. On the southwest lawn, Brent had Fabian cut the grass short, and then directed him in laying out lines of watered lime to mark off the court. The court was of a trapezoid design on each side of the net, where the baselines were four feet longer than the net, and the sidelines angled from the net posts back to form the corners at the baselines. Brent and Violet frequently played singles, and then at times Bonnie Anne would join Brent, and J.J. would be Violet's partner for some doubles.

One special occasion for J. J. was when Brent took him to the Fourth of July baseball game in Orangeberg , though he was disappointed when the Carolina Club of Charleston defeated the Orange club, 41 to 23.

At the end of July, Grandmama Lee lovingly kissed everyone goodbye and left to spend a week in Columbia with Charlotte and Leland and little Lee before returning to Virginia. They all missed her terribly. As they had done before during her last visit, and Violet in her letters, Brent and Violet beseeched her to move down from Richmond and make her home with them at Fair Oaks. Catherine Lee appreciated their invitation, but patiently explained to them that while she loved them all very much, South Carolina was just too far from Virginia. That was her home, and she declared she was too old to make new adjustments. Besides, when she passed away, she wanted to buried by her beloved husband, Fitzhugh Randolph Lee in the family's private cemetery. She reminded them that her mother and father, her two sisters, and two of her own babies were also buried there. Disappointed, Violet and Brent told her they understood and respected her wishes.

On a Friday morning, just two days after Catherine Lee had departed, Violet rode up to the house with a worried look on her face. She dismounted and strode quickly to the porch. Out to greet her, Brent inquired instantly, "What is it? Has something happened?"

"Oh, Brent, we've got trouble," declared Violet, her voice breaking.

"Trouble? What kind of trouble?"

"Caterpillars!"

"*Caterpillars*?"

"Yes, caterpillars."

"Where?"

"In the cotton fields and in the tobacco. Millions of them! If we don't get them out, they'll destroy the whole crops! Oh, Brent, this is awful, just awful!" she exclaimed plaintively.

"All right, let's have a look," Brent told her as he ran out to the carriage house to get his horse. Violet mounted Hermes again and followed him. She waited while he saddled Jeb, and then they rode out to the cotton fields.

Arriving at the edge of the field, Brent jumped down for a closer look. With his hands he spread first the stalks of one plant and then another apart, peering closely. He straightened up and looked at Violet, a serious look on his face. "I see what you mean," he said. "Is this the first time you've had these?"

"No, there have been some before, but this is the first time on any scale like this. They don't come every year, you know, only when the weather and other things are just right—old timers used to say it depended on the phases of the moon. At any rate, this is the first time they have threatened total destruction like this."

"Mm, well, the question is, what can we do about them? What about turpentine?"

"I don't think so. I read a report where somebody plunged caterpillars into turpentine, and they emerged as ravenous for their all-day meal as though they had been sprinkled with pure water.

"Burning?"

"We can't burn a whole field, and if we just burn a section where the pupae are it seems to make no difference."

"Lime?"

"Lime will kill them all right, but how are you going to put lime on four hundred acres of cotton and two hundred of tobacco and not hurt the cotton and tobacco?"

"Mm, would birds help?"

"Yes, they might help if we could get them into the fields." She looked down at the ground and then across the fields, in thought, and then exclaimed excitedly, "Wait a minute. Come on, to the grist mill!"

"The grist mill? For what?" he asked, puzzled.

"For some cracked corn to entice the birds!"

They returned in a few minutes with a large bag of cracked corn. They scattered some along the end of the field and then pulled back and watched. In about half an hour a couple of blackbirds—actually purple grackles—appeared, and then a few more. Silently, motionless, Violet and Brent watched while the birds pecked at the corn, and when that was gone they looked around and began working on the caterpillars.

"Come on, let's find Leo and tell him what we've discovered," she called as she moved up to a gallop.

It was past noon, and they found the overseer at his house just finishing his dinner.

"Leo," Violet cried, "there are caterpillar worms all over the cotton and tobacco fields!"

"Yassum, Miz Violet, ah know dat. Henry, he done tole meh 'bout dem.. Ah wen' wif him ta de fields ta tek uh look, and ma'am, ah ain't nebber see nuttin' like dat befo'. Ain't nebber see so many climbin' like dat all ober de plants befo'. Whut ya tink ussan oughta do?"

"Leo, I think we're on to something that will work. Now listen to me carefully. I want you to get some men and go to the grist mill and get several bushels of cracked corn—and have them start cracking more, too, right away.

"Yassum," he nodded, wondering what he was supposed to do with all that corn.

"Take the corn and sprinkle it all across the fields where the caterpillars are. That will make the birds come, and they will eat the caterpillars off of the plants. My husband and I have already tried this, and it worked just fine."

With a huge grin of comprehension, Leo nodded again as he walked off quickly to follow her directions, calling back, "Yassum, Miz Violet, and don'cha worry none no mo'."

"Leo, wait a minute," she called after him. As he stopped and turned around, she went on, "That probably won't be enough. After the birds have done all they can, we'll probably have to get everybody and clear out what remains by hand. I'm afraid we'll have to have some of the men work all day Sunday after church spreading the corn. Tell them they can have Monday off."

"Yassum, ah do dat. We work hard, don'cha worry."

Violet smiled and waved him on. She knew she could always depend on Leo.

When Violet and Brent rode up to the fields on Monday it was clear that the birds had gotten the word. Blackbirds by the hundreds were all over the fields devouring caterpillars. The blackbirds were taking care of the upper branches. Hundreds of crows had come in to share this unexpected feast, working mainly on the mid-areas of the stalks, and scores of wild turkeys were taking what they could reach from the ground.

Three days of this made a tremendous difference, but now the birds were thinning out, going elsewhere to seek their fortune, but a number of caterpillars remained. To complete the job, Violet had Leo mobilize everyone who could do anything, including nearly all the women, old folks who were no longer working regularly, and children down to the age of eight or nine. J.J. even insisted on helping, saying it was time he learned how to be a planter, but Bonnie Anne refused to consider even touching a caterpillar, and she stayed back at the house with Evelina. Everyone moved through their assigned rows to pinch the remaining caterpillars with their fingers.

Finally crews of experienced workers moved along and cut off the tops of the plants and the ends of the tender branches where the eggs of the cotton moth or butterfly were usually deposited.

After five days of this all-out effort, the fields were clean. The cotton and the tobacco crops had been saved, and Violet declared a holiday for everybody.

Violet and Brent and the children began looking forward to the Sumter County Fair to be held at the end of September, and to the introduction there of harness horse racing, and to the debut of Hermes and Midnight Star as professional racers.

A crowd of thousands gathered to watch the big event. Midnight Star, in the trotting race for two-year-olds, finished out of the money though he showed promise. It was a different story for Hermes. With Charles driving superbly, Hermes won the premier pacing event in two straight heats, at times of 2:19¼ and 2:20.

Brent was beside himself with enthusiasm and pride. "That was fantastic!" shouted an excited Brent. "That was only two seconds slower than the record of Pocahontas and only five seconds behind the record of Willy Boyce, but Willy Boyce was pacing under a saddle, didn't have to pull that cart."

Ever mindful of his role in South Carolina politics, Brent took further advantage of the fair to move among the voters shaking hands, telling jokes, and kissing babies.

For the November election, Brent, with the assistance of Violet, renewed the strategy that had won for him four years previously—mobilizing all the friendly blacks of the area and carrying them to the polling places. The results were even more decisive. This time Brent carried a big majority of both the white and the black voters.

Nevertheless, in the state as a whole, the Radical Republicans still were in control. They had majorities in the legislature almost as one-sided as before.

The race for Governor had taken a bizarre turn. Frank Moses was not even renominated, but the Radical Republicans had an internal battle for his successor. When they finally nominated Daniel H. Chamberlain, carpetbagger former attorney general, the "moderates" held another convention in Charleston and nominated John T. Green for governor and Martin T. Delany for lieutenant governor.

Chamberlain, a native of Massachusetts, had been educated at Amherst, Yale, and Harvard. He had served as a lieutenant in the Union army and had come to South Carolina in 1866. He had been involved in the "printing ring" and other questionable activities and had been a supporter and secret promoter of Honest John Patterson. His running mate was the mulatto incumbent, Richard H. Gleaves, who had come to South Carolina from Pennsylvania in 1866.

Green was a native South Carolinian from Sumter, and though now a Republican, was highly regarded. Delany was perhaps the most remarkable black leader in the state. He had been a scientist, an explorer, a newspaper man, a major in the Federal army, and a member of the Freedmen's Bureau. Shortly after the War he had written to President Johnson, "What becomes necessary to secure and perpetuate the Union is...a recognition of the political equality of the blacks with the whites in all their relations as American citizens." But he had no time for the white Carpetbaggers whom he regarded as exploiting the blacks of South Carolina, and in his eloquent oratory he did not hesitate to denounce Chamberlain and his associates.

The Democrats did not nominate anybody for governor or lieutenant governor, but they urged their followers to vote for the reform candidates.

Brent told anybody who would listen to vote for Green and Delany. Unfortunately, Green was too ill to campaign. The day after the election Brent was disappointed, though not surprised, to learn that Chamberlain and Gleaves had won.

After weeks of anticipation, Violet got Bonnie Anne and J.J. ready to go into Columbia on Thursday the week after the election, to attend the state fair sponsored by the State Agricultural and Mechanical Society, and a special attraction this year, the Stone & Murray's combination circus.

Brent had been in Columbia all week taking care of railroad business and mercantile business in the mornings, and attending the horse races and visiting mechanical exhibits at the fair in the afternoons.

Violet had sent a note to Miss Simons at the Edge Hill School to let her know that Bonnie Anne and J.J. would be away on Thursday and Friday. Violet and Evelina got the children ready, and propelling themselves on the handcar out to their little wayside station, they caught the afternoon local train for Columbia.

The next morning, Brent insisted that everyone get up before dawn to go out to the siding of the South Carolina Railroad to watch the circus unload. It was beyond anything they had imagined. In unflagging excitement they watched the brightly colored wagons come down the ramps of the railroad cars. They watched elephants push wagons around with their heads and trunks and then teams of horses pull them away. There was a vast assortment of animals and people, but all moved methodically in a way that demonstrated that they knew what they were supposed to do and had the training and discipline to do it.

When that task appeared to be nearly finished, Brent rushed the family back to the carriage and quickly drove over to the fairgrounds. There men already were at work putting up side-show exhibits and various booths. In the center of the field a big canvas tent lay spread out on the ground. All around it men were driving big stakes into the ground with sledgehammers—two men at each stake, swinging their sledgehammers alternately in perfect time and perfect rhythm. Then men set up tall poles at openings in the tent. Eight elephants, spaced at intervals all around the tent, with a heavy rope harnessed to each, stood motionless. Even Brent watched in awe as the chief gave a signal and all the elephants, each led by a handler, moved outward, lifting the big tent into place. Until just recently, circuses generally had been held in the open air, and were at the mercy of the weather. Now the big tent provided a spectacular improvement.

On Saturday afternoon, Violet and Brent and the two children and Evelina went to see the big show itself. Attracted by the posters, they looked forward to seeing Signorina Ella Eugenie, the "Lion Enchantress" demonstrate how lions could be conquered by a woman, to acts by trick ponies, educated mules, acting monkeys, sagacious dogs, lions, panthers, leopards, Bengal tigers, and an unusually large aviary, and various giants, dwarfs, and monstrosities.

Bonnie Anne and J.J. clapped their hands in glee as the brass band struck up *The March of the Gladiators* and the parade of animals and performers began as the prelude to the performances. As the children and Evelina chattered in wonder at each element, Violet and Brent began playing games of recognition.

"Look, the hyena," announced Brent.

"Well, I do declare, if that doesn't appear to be Frank Moses," laughed Violet.

"Indeed, I believe it is he," agreed Brent with a bigger laugh of his own.

"What is that?" asked Violet as another smaller animal came by in its wagon cage.

"That's a jackal–why that must be our U.S. Senator, Honest John Patterson." Brent let out such a loud guffaw that surrounding people turned to stare.

"Sh, not so loud, honey," cautioned Violet.

Pointing to a big gorilla being led by its trainer, Brent exclaimed in a lower voice, "There's our esteemed Speaker of the House!"

A barrel of monkeys came by next, and Violet giggled, "Oh, look, that must be our state legislature all together."

"Yes, yes, the Forty Thieves," Brent agreed.

Beautiful teams of horses and of mules went by. When the elephants marched by them, Brent noted, "Well, well, the Republican elephant. By the way, did you see Nast's cartoon in this week's *Harper's Weekly* showing the elephant as the symbol of the Republican Party?"

"Oh, no, I didn't see that, but I can imagine it–the Radical Republicans just walking all over everybody."

"And look, there is the poor little Democratic donkey."

"I do remember that cartoon, where Nast called it the symbol of the Democratic Party—a live jackass killing a dead lion."

When a tiger came by Brent called it "Tammany Hall."

Finally, Violet said, "Look, Brent, there's Wade Hampton!" and she pointed to a majestic lion, sitting high on a pedestal in a magnificent wagon drawn by six white horses with red plumes.

At the end came a group of clowns going through their antics. "*Vox populi*!" Brent cried out. Violet giggled again. Surveying the whole scene, she remarked, "Well, as Shakespeare wrote, 'All the world's a stage, and all the men and women merely players."

"Or as Shakespeare might have written, 'All the world's a circus, and all the people are merely clowns or ringmasters." came back Brent.

"And you can't tell one from the other," added Violet. She went on, "Ha, or you might say, 'All the world's a barnyard, and all the people merely mules or mule skinners."

"And you can't tell one from the other," he added.

"Oh, Brent!"

Neither could contain their peals of laughter as the band played on and the show went on.

Chapter 60

On to Vicksburg

1874-1875

"Here's a Western Union telegram from Susan," Violet exclaimed as she went through the morning mail that Levi had just brought in to the Fair Oaks office.

"What does she say?" asked Brent as he looked up from his desk.

"I hope it's good news about a new arrival," said Violet as she tore open the envelope. "Yes, yes, listen: *HAPPY TO ANNOUNCE ARRIVAL OF HEALTHY NEW SON DEC 21 STOP NAME GEORGE GILBERT.*

"December 21st. They should have named him 'Winter."

"Hah, yes, that was day before yesterday. He'll be the best Christmas present of all." He paused a moment and then laughed. "Maybe 'Noel' would be an appropriate name for the little tyke."

"Oh, you silly goose. Now George Brent Sutler, you know the baby has been named after you and Gil."

Christmas at Fair Oaks was small that year. Susan, of course, was in Vicksburg. Charlotte was expecting and the doctor advised her not to travel, and neither Grandmama Lee nor Brent's mother felt up to traveling this year.

On Tuesday, January 5th, Violet and Brent and the two children, with Evelina and Levi, went into Columbia for what was becoming their regular winter season.

They celebrated Twelfth Night with a kind of second Christmas at Charlotte and Leland's. The after supper festivities took a surprising turn when Charlotte suddenly announced that her time had come. Without a word Leland dashed out, without coat or hat, and returned in a short while with Doctor Ramsey who presided over the birth of a little girl.

When it was all over and everyone gathered around, Charlotte said softly, "Coming at this time, she will just have to be called Mary, and she'll be named Rosemary, after Mama."

"And we shall be the wise men," added Brent, laughing.

"Thank goodness for this postal service," Violet said as she came in from the front porch of their town house with a bundle of mail one day in mid-January, 1875.

"And thank goodness Columbia is big enough to qualify for home delivery," answered Brent who had just arrived home for his noontime dinner. "I'll have to admit that's one of the few good things the Yankee government has done since the War."

Stopping near the stairway for a look at the mail before running up to the office with it, Violet exclaimed suddenly, "Hurrah, here's a letter from Susan! Should be more about the baby. I've not been able to keep from worrying about my little sister, you know, and how I do wish she didn't have to live so far away."

Brent followed Violet into the dining room and took a chair beside her as she tore open the envelope. "Yes, I know you've been concerned about her, and she's not so little any more, my dear," he replied, smiling at Violet's happiness at receiving the letter.

Beaming as she scanned the sheet of note paper, she announced excitedly, "Honey, do listen to this:

> *I am happy to report that both our new baby and his mother are doing very well. You know his name is George Gilbert, and we call him 'G.G.' for short. We do hope that you can come out and see us and your new nephew very soon. Oh, Violet and Brent, I do miss you all just so very much, and maybe it's having the baby and all, but I surely do want to see you. I need to see you, especially since we weren't together this past Christmas. Oh, do come!*

Violet stopped and looked at Brent, her eyes shining, "Oh, Brent, let's do—and soon."

Hiding a smile, he asked innocently, "Do what?"

"Oh, Brent! Go out to Vicksburg for a visit with Susan and Gilbert and see the new baby, that's what!"

"Mm, well now, when are you thinking of going? About lie-by time this summer?"

"No, I really don't want to wait that long. Brent, I want to go soon—now."

He got up, walked around the table, and stood at the window looking out. After several moments of apparently deep thought he turned to face her and asked, "What about the children? Were you thinking of taking them?"

Her surprise showed as she answered, "Why, yes, of course. I wouldn't want to be away from them for so long."

"But what about school?"

"Oh, Brent, it would be worth it. They would learn more in two weeks on a trip like this than they would in probably the whole year in their classrooms. Education isn't just done with books, you know, and I'm sure we could arrange for their absence. They can practice their reading and arithmetic on the train ride, and we can help them. It'll be fun for all of us," she concluded optimistically.

He looked out the window for a minute and then turned back toward her with that special grin of his. "Darling, how about a second honeymoon?"

"Why, kind sir, what can you mean?" she said coquettishly. Then she added with a sigh, "Remember, Honey, the kids will be with us. I can't imagine them with us day and night while we do—uh, all that you have in mind—."

"Why, lovely lady, do I detect a faint blush upon your soft cheeks? What can you have in mind?" He laughed, and then became more serious. "Now, listen, I was just thinking. Maybe we could work it so that we could leave the children and Evelina with Susan for a few days while we take the steamboat, maybe the *Robert E. Lee,* down to New Orleans—."

Violet ran to him and threw her arms around his neck, and between kisses and hugs she cried, "Oh, wonderful, wonderful, my Darling Husband!"

After a few minutes of savoring this special attention, Brent went on, "But wait, Honey, you 'ain't' heard everything yet!"

"Oh, 'ain't' I? Tell me, what else?"

"Well, maybe we could time it right to get there for the end of Carnival and the big Mardi Gras celebration—you know, the big parade, grand balls, and all that."

Violet was nearly beside herself with excitement. She was almost afraid to believe all this. "Oh, Brent, does the Carpetbag government let all that sort of thing go on down there now, like it used to?"

"Sure, they wouldn't dare not to." He loved to see Violet caught up like this. She glowed with excitement and her beauty was breathtaking.

"Oh, Darling, it sounds more wonderful all the time. Keep talking."

"Well, you know Bruce is in Shreveport now—."

"Yes."

"—Working for the Texas and Pacific Railroad. He writes that he spends lots of time in New Orleans. I'll telegraph him of our plans and ask him to make arrangements for rooms, tickets, invitations, everything."

"When is Mardi Gras?"

Well, you know it's the ending of Carnival, and Mardi Gras is Fat Tuesday—."

"Oh, of course. It's the same as what the English—and we—call Pancake Tuesday, and what the Church calls Shrove Tuesday, the day before Ash Wednesday and the beginning of Lent, but when does it fall this year?"

"I think it's early this year, the second week in February."

"That won't give much time to get ready. I guess we will have to leave about the first in order to have a few days with Susan before going on to New Orleans."

"We'll take the overnight Carolina Rail—the Charleston Express—from here to Charleston, have a day's visit with Mother and Father and Phoebe, and then go on by way of Augusta, Chattanooga, and Corinth."

"It all sounds wonderful!"

Brent hesitated a moment, but then went on, "Honey, there's something I've been wanting to discuss with you. I know Aaron was the Major's man, and he's taken good care of me since I came home from the Navy, but now I think it's about time he started training someone to assist him, and eventually take over his duties—although we'll always have something for him to do here in the house so he won't feel neglected, of course."

"I know, and to tell the truth, I've been terribly worried about how his arthritis pains him. He never complains, but I can tell it hurts."

"Well, Levi seems an intelligent man; he knows the ways of the house, and he's certainly been good to Evelina—."

"Oh, yes, so kind, so understanding—."

"Well, what do you think of having him eventually take over for Aaron? My thinking is—I'll talk with Aaron, of course—is that Levi could accompany us on the trip—"

"But not to New Orleans with us–."

"No, my love, not on our second honeymoon, but he can help Evelina with the children and help with our baggage, and help Susan and Gilbert if they need him."

"I think it's a wonderful idea. I concur completely. When are you going to talk with Aaron, and then to Levi?"

"Aaron, this evening; Levi, sometime tomorrow if all goes well."

"I know you'll be tactful–."

"You don't have to worry about Aaron's feelings. I'll be diplomatic."

On Monday, Uncle Job drove them to the station in time to board the Charleston Express at 6:30 p.m. The children were jumping with exhilaration, and Violet and Evelina were nearly as excited. Brent and Levi hid their excitement behind big grins and a controlled demeanor. Aaron had actually been pleased that he did not have to accompany Brent on the long train ride. He liked Levi and was pleased that Levi would be learning to take over his duties, and that he, Aaron, would be sharing more of Jarvis's duties.

Evelina had been nearly in tears when Violet first told her about the trip, but the tears of sadness quickly turned to tears of joy when Violet mentioned that Levi would be going along.

Uncle Job and Levi took care of the baggage as the others boarded the new train. "Oh, Brent, it is a beauty," Violet exclaimed. "I've seen it pass in the moonlight, but never had a good look at it. I'm glad to get a chance to try it out."

"So am I. I need to keep an alert watch on our railroad operations," answered Brent. Brent, of course, had inspected the cars before, but Violet was taken completely by surprise when she saw the interior of the Pullman sleeping car. It was lighted by Pintch gaslights, heated by hot-water heaters, and it was furnished with hand-carved walnut woodwork, plush red carpets, and fine mirrors. The seats were obviously plush and comfortable, and Brent explained how they could be folded down into beds, and another berth overhead, now folded up out of sight, could be pulled down when needed. Heavy green curtains, now folded back between seats, would be spread across the berth openings to provide privacy. Green curtains at the windows helped screen the dirt. Violet was amused to see a placard near the door, *Please Take Off Boots Before Retiring.*

"Seems to me a good idea," she said pointedly.

Brent broke into laughter.

The porter had welcomed them all properly and helped Uncle Job and Levi stow their baggage near their places in the sleeping car, and then they said goodbye to Uncle Job and, while the train would not leave the station until ten o'clock, they went directly to the diner. The tables were covered with clean linen and decorated with paper flowers. On each side of each table was a bench with a back, like short church pews. Violet took a place near the window, and Brent slipped in beside her. The two children sat across from them, and Evelina and Levi sat at a table across the aisle.

After supper, they all went to the parlor car to sit and talk some more, while Violet and Brent read the newspapers. Brent asked the porter to make up the berths for the children and those for Evelina and Levi, but to wait awhile for his and Violet's.

After the children were in their beds, still much too excited to sleep, but with Evelina and Levi to keep them reasonably quiet, Brent and Violet took a tour of the other cars—another Pullman sleeper, a day coach, a baggage and express car, and a railway post office car. They had to make their tour before the train left, because there were no covers between the cars and passengers were forbidden to go from one car to another while the train was in motion.

The train pulled out promptly at ten, and Violet and Brent decided to stay up until they passed Fair Oaks. They could barely make out the plantation through the trees in the partial moonlight, but they gained some reassurance from its tranquil look.

When all was quiet except for a few light snores up and down the aisle from other sleeping passengers, Brent slipped out of his berth and into Violet's.

"Just thought you might be lonely and needed some company," he whispered. "Move over just a bit."

"Oh, Brent, you *are* a rascal!," Violet giggled softly, taking him into her arms.

"I'll slip back before dawn," he said, kissing her.

The next morning they awoke to two pairs of round blue eyes staring at them from between the slits in the privacy curtains.

"Children! What are you doing here. You're supposed to be asleep!" exclaimed a startled Violet. She and Brent glanced at one another. Violet felt a warm flush rise upon her cheeks.

"Daddy, is something wrong with your bed upstairs?" asked Bonnie Anne, curiously.

"How could great big you fit into Mommy's berth?" asked J.J. "Aren't you afraid of falling out?"

"Sh!" cautioned Violet, "or you'll wake up the other people."

"Uh, I got a little chilly up there, and I thought Mommy's bed might be warmer," grinned Brent, slipping out and stepping up to his berth.

"Well, *were* you warmer, Daddy?" asked J.J. solicitously.

"Definitely."

"Oh, Brent!" giggled Violet.

"Well, I was."

"Well, he was, Mommy," echoed J.J., sticking up for his daddy.

Just then, down the aisle, a head of rumpled white hair appeared outside its curtain and in a loud whisper said, "For heaven's sake, stop that noise and go back to sleep! Can't you keep your children quiet?"

Sheepishly, they all watched the head disappear from sight. Now peering down from between his curtains, Brent told the children to hop back in their berths and try to go back to sleep. Instead, they looked at one another and, as if on cue, Bonnie Anne hopped in her mother's bed, and J.J. climbed up and crawled in bed with Brent. Giggling, they each turned on their side and pretended to fall asleep instantly and thus couldn't hear the whispered commands to return to their own berths. Their parents sighed and gave up, hoping to catch a bit more sleep before getting up. Noting their parents' capitulation, the children were full of whispered questions and comments. Eventually, all was quiet again.

After breakfast, they left the train and walked along the platform toward the station.

"Daddy," said Bonnie Anne, pointing, "look at the big letters on that black car behind the engine. They say *Carolina Rail.* Why, Daddy?"

"That car is the tender that carries coal for the engine, and *Carolina Rail* is the name of the railroad company, and guess what, your Mommy is the one who thought up the name."

"Mommy did? Well, I like that name, but why do they have the big picture of a bird on the tender and on the engine?"

"Honey, that bird is also called the Carolina rail, and since that is the name of the company the bird makes a very good symbol or badge for the company, don't you think?" He fondly ruffled her hair with his fingers.

She smiled and nodded her understanding. "Oh, yes, I like the bird and it looks pretty on the train." She looked up at her mother who had been standing by quietly, enjoying listening to Brent answer the children's questions. "You did a good job, Mommy," said Bonnie Anne proudly.

Violet smiled and thanked her little daughter. "Yes, I did, didn't I?" she agreed.

It didn't take long for Brent to find a driver and large carriage to pick up their baggage and then to take them all to his parents' house. Soon they were being enthusiastically and lovingly greeted by Isabel and James Sutler and Brent's sister, Phoebe.

The next morning at seven-thirty, Violet and Brent, Bonnie Anne and J.J., and Evelina and Levi said goodbye to the elder Sutlers and Phoebe, and then boarded a train of the South Carolina Railroad for Augusta. The train was made up of all day coaches. They found seats together near the middle of the second car. The upholstered seats had been red, but were now discolored by wear and smoke. The day was a cool one, but the car was overheated by the stoves in the rear and front of the car.

Soon after the train was underway, Brent observed, "Do you know that this railroad line, which then was the Charleston-Hamburg, had the first scheduled passenger train in America, in the 1830's?"

Violet wrinkled her nose in distaste. "If you ask me, we are on one of their original cars!"

"Well now, honey, you're just spoiled by the *Carolina Rail*" he responded.

At Augusta, they changed trains to the Western and Atlantic, and had lunch at the station restaurant while they waited. They stopped overnight at Chattanooga, staying at the railway inn, and departed at seven in the morning. With changes to the Illinois Central at Grand Junction, Tennessee, and to the restored Southern Mississippi at Jackson, they arrived in Vicksburg after dark.

Gilbert was waiting for them at the station with his and Susan's buggy, and he had hired a driver with a large carriage to help transport everyone and the luggage to the house. Violet and Brent rode along with him, and the children and two servants rode in the carriage.

The first order of business, after happily greeting Susan and assuring themselves that she looked just fine, was to see little G.G. Susan and Gilbert led them proudly into the nursery that they had fixed up for the baby. He proved to be all that was expected—pretty and plump with his mother's fair skin, rosy cheeks, and blue eyes; contented and alert and uttering sweet little cooing noises. They looked at him in rapture, but Bonnie Anne, especially, was enthralled at this beautiful, little, live doll. Instantly she wanted to pick him up and hold him, and moved to do so when Violet restrained her gently, saying, "Now, Bonnie Anne, you know it's important for babies to get used to the strange people around them."

"But Mommy, I'm no stranger; I'm his *cousin*—his *first* cousin. And he's so cute and cuddly," she replied with disappointment.

"I know, darling, but let's wait until later. Perhaps tomorrow Aunt Susan might let you sit in the chair and hold him for a few minutes. We'll see."

Susan and Gilbert showed them to their rooms—Violet and Brent were in the main guest room, the two children each with a bed in the back bedroom, and Evelina and Levi in a small bedroom off the kitchen downstairs.

After they had freshened up, Susan served some vegetable soup that had been simmering on the stove, along with crackers, for supper. Seeing that Susan had no one to help her, Evelina volunteered to help serve. Levi offered his help, too, and suggested that Miss Susan sit down with her family whom she hadn't seen in such a long time. Susan looked at Violet as if to ask if that was all right. Violet smiled and nodded.

Violet had noticed that no one accompanied Gilbert to the station to help with the luggage, and had observed no servants in the house. She had concluded that perhaps Susan and Gilbert were now using "day help" as so many were doing these days. "Don't you have any regular servants any more?" she asked her sister.

Susan shook her head. "Well, no...trustworthy help has been difficult to find lately, so we have learned to do without. I'm thankful that I learned a little about cooking and housework during those trying times during and after the War at home."

Violet smiled and replied, "Well, I must say, you seem to be doing very well. This soup is delicious; the baby looks healthy and happy; the house looks neat and clean. I must say, I'm proud of you, Susan."

"Well, thanks, Violet. We manage—and of course Gilbert helps me some, too." She threw a glance at Gilbert and went on, changing the subject and flooding Violet with questions, "But now, tell me, what's going on at Fair Oaks? That business of the caterpillars you wrote about was horrible. How is Mammy's health? How are Charlotte and Leland and little Lee? Tell us about their new little baby. Have you seen them lately? Does Leo's baby look like him or Rachel? What are the Carpetbaggers and Scalawags up to these days? Have they raised the taxes on Fair Oaks again? Oh, dear, I hope not—."

"Hold it!" laughed Violet. "I'll take one question at a time, please." She proceeded to answer all of Susan's questions, with Brent interjecting here and there as needed. Gilbert had a few of his own, mostly about business and politics. The children were hungry and tired, and for once, seemed more focused on eating than anything else, although they listened with interest to the conversation swirling around them. Occasionally they would make a few comments of their own under their breaths to one another, which, fortunately, went unheard by the grown-ups. In time, the conversation ran down, and the weary travelers opted for early to bed.

The next day while Evelina and Levi stayed behind to care for the three children, Susan and Gilbert led Violet and Brent on a walking tour of Vicksburg. They walked along Greek revival, prewar mansions on Cherry, Crawford, and Grove Streets. They were impressed by the Duff Green house on Locust and First Streets, a brick house with iron grillwork galleries, that had been used as a hospital during the war. All this was very attractive, but signs of the wartime siege were still all around. Indeed the cupola on the county courthouse, riddled by the Yankee Commodore Farragut's gunboats on the Mississippi, still remained unrepaired. They visited some of the caves, such as Hough Cave on Lover's Lane, where the people had huddled to escape the weeks of bombardment during the siege.

Brent insisted on treating everyone to an appetizing lunch in the dining parlor of the Washington Hotel, only three blocks from Susan's house. They placed their orders, and soon the conversation picked up.

"I see that they are paving Washington Street out here," Brent commented. "Everywhere else in town I've seen only gravel or dirt."

"Yes, but with stepping stones at the corners for wet days," put in Susan with a smile.

Gilbert nodded, and added, "But haven't you seen the kind of pavement they're using? Wood blocks. Can you beat that?"

Violet, Susan, and Gilbert went on back to the house, while Brent walked down to the riverfront to see about steamboat schedules and pick up the tickets for his and Violet's trip.

Violet scrutinized each of their faces before going on, somewhat hesitatingly, "I appreciate your offer in your letter to let us leave the children with you. Evelina and Levi will stay here to take care of them and to give you whatever help you might need."

"That'll be just fine," smiled Susan.

"Indeed, yes, it'll be fun to have the children for a while just to ourselves," chimed in Gilbert. "Stay as long as you wish."

"Oh, thank you," said Violet. "But there's one thing, there's Evelina and Levi—two adults—and Brent insists on our helping out with food and such."

"Why, Violet, that isn't necessary," said Susan.

"Indeed not," agreed Gilbert.

"Well, then, we just can't go. You're a young couple, just starting out, and with a new baby. No, that's asking too much of you these days."

"Why, no it isn't, Violet," said Susan.

"Indeed not," Gilbert again agreed.

"I'm sorry, but you've just got to let us do this; otherwise, we wouldn't feel comfortable about going off on this trip."

"Well, if you put it that way," said Gilbert.

"Well, all right," said Susan reluctantly, taking her cue from her husband.

"Good, then that's settled, and thank you both very much."

That evening, after both Bonnie Anne and J.J. had taken turns holding their new little cousin, they gathered in the dining room where Susan, with Evelina's and Levi's help, served a supper of vegetable stew and Johnny cake. Then Evelina and Levi went into the kitchen where Evelina had set places for the two of them.

After a pause in the conversation of small talk about the day's events, Brent asked, "What is the political situation now? I think you wrote something about some kind of race riot a couple of months ago."

"Oh, yes," Susan answered quickly and in a whisper, darting a look at the kitchen door, "they say that seventy darkies were killed when they attacked the courthouse."

"Well, what was behind it?" Brent asked.

Gilbert answered in a low voice, "What happened was, the old-line white residents had become sick and tired of the inefficiency and corruption of the so-called Carpetbagger sheriff, so they browbeat him until he gave up his office. But the blacks thought that the sheriff was their protector, so they rioted at the courthouse. The whites came out to break up the riot with gunfire, and I guess seventy or more of the blacks were killed."

Violet glanced apprehensively at the children and asked, "Have things settled down now? Is it safe around here? Everything looked all right today when we were out."

Gilbert answered, "Yes, fairly safe. Vigilance committees have been patrolling the streets ever since."

"Zounds!" exclaimed Violet. "I thought Mississippi had been readmitted into the Union five years ago, and the so-called Reconstruction should be over. This sounds worse than Columbia right now. I guess...I guess maybe we have less violence, but probably more corruption."

Noting her sister's concern, Susan went on, "I think it's safe here now, but there is still a tenseness in the atmosphere, and we find a number of our supposed friends—even some of those at the church—rather cool toward us. I guess Gilbert and I are sort of caught in the middle. The Carpetbaggers and the blacks think we are Bourbons, and the Bourbons—the conservative and traditional white planters and so on—look upon us as Carpetbaggers."

"But that's awful!" gasped Violet, shocked at the idea that her sister, descended from the Lees and Randolphs and Clarks of Virginia, not to say the Storms and Pinckneys of South Carolina, might not be accepted by the traditional white planters in Mississippi, or for that matter, even looked upon as a traitorous Carpetbagger.

Gilbert added, "Well, I'm from Indiana, but I must say I hold no brief for this Carpetbag state government that we still have here in Mississippi. Actually, in 1865 the

Democrats had elected a governor, Benjamin Humphreys, but the Federal troops threw him out in 1868 and installed a general from Maine by the name of Adelbert Ames as military governor, where he remained for a couple of years. Then Ames went to the U.S. Senate along with—and get this—a Carpetbag Negro from Indiana by the name of Hiram Revels. After four years as U.S. Senator, Ames was elected governor as a Republican. However, the Democrats were able to win control of the legislature this year, and there is a move there to impeach Ames as well as the Negro lieutenant governor, Davis, and all the other state officers who surround Ames."

"Sounds interesting," said Brent, "but he can't be as bad as our Frank Moses, our distinguished governor from Sumter. Tell me, how much have the Carpetbaggers and Scalawags cost the state?"

Gilbert shook his head and heaved a deep sigh as he answered, "Brent, nobody knows, but I can tell you the state printing cost has gone up from eight thousand dollars a year to as much as a hundred and twenty-eight thousand a year."

"Whew!" exclaimed Violet, "sounds like South Carolina."

"But I'll bet their railroad scandals can't match ours," put in Brent.

"Probably not," agreed Gilbert, "because the state constitution forbids state aid for the railroads. Nevertheless we have another outlet for plunder—the river. Improvements on the river have cost more than the railroads ever could have, is my guess."

Susan looked glum. "One wonders, is there no end to all of this?"

"To tell the truth, I would say that corruption in the local county and city governments is even worse than in the State House," Gilbert told them.

"To anticipate something more pleasant," said Brent, changing the subject, "the *Robert E. Lee* is supposed to be on schedule to leave Vicksburg tomorrow in the early afternoon, and we hope to be aboard." He turned to Susan and Gilbert, "Violet told me that you two are willing to take on our little rascals so that we can take this special trip alone. We surely do appreciate this."

"That's wonderful about the *Robert E. Lee*," grinned Susan, with a touch of her old impishness showing, "and we're thrilled to have the children just to ourselves. And, of course, it's nice to have Evelina and Levi's help, too. We'll all get along just fine. Now don't you worry yourselves about anything, you hear?"

Chapter 61

Down the Mississippi

1875

On the day of departure for New Orleans, as Violet and Brent completed their packing, Bonnie Anne and J.J. began to raise objections.

"Mommy, Daddy, I want to go, too. Why can't J.J. and I go with you?" asked a tearful Bonnie Anne.

"I wanna ride on the steamboat, too. Oh, please, Daddy, please let me go with you and Mommy. I'll be good, I promise. I'll be the best little boy you ever had," cried J.J.

"I'll be good, too, and I promise I won't argue with J.J. Not at all, I promise!" added Bonnie Anne.

Violet looked up from her packing in distress. As a look of helplessness and discomfort crept over Brent's face, Susan came to their rescue. "Come, come," she said to the youngsters, "I promise, we'll take a steamboat ride ourselves while Mommy and Daddy are away. How about that? And I do need your help with little G.G."

"Well, all right, Aunt Susan," replied Bonnie Anne, who really loved her young aunt very much and was thrilled to be visiting her.

Seeing that Bonnie Anne had acquiesced, J.J. surrendered reluctantly, "All right, if you promise you'll take us on the steamboat."

"I promise," said Susan, and the frowns were replaced by smiles of anticipation.

That afternoon, Bonnie Anne and J.J. and Susan went along as Gilbert drove Violet and Brent to the quay. As they went down the steep road to the river, J.J. clapped his hands in glee as a dozen tied-up steamboats came into view. Bonnie Anne stood up for a better view as she looked at them in awe. Most of the vessels were taking on bales of cotton that had been waiting in the warehouses since fall for better prices. The *Robert E. Lee* sat there like a queen in the midst of her court. Secured high on the front of the pilot house was a set of gilded deer antlers, emblematic of racing superiority. The *Lee*'s record for the run from New Orleans to Saint Louis set in its race against the *Natchez* nearly five years earlier had never been equaled. Small tugs plied back and forth to deliver messages and to push or pull coal barges in and out.

Even Violet could not contain her excitement as they all went aboard. They were impressed by the decor and appointments of all that they saw—the mahogany paneled saloon on the boiler deck, polished brass trimmings everywhere, and thick wool carpets on the interior decks. As they followed a steward up the grand open staircase to find their stateroom, they admired the mahogany railings over gilded iron grillwork, lighted by sparkling chandeliers. Their room was on the hurricane deck, forward of the great paddle wheels, aft of the tall twin chimneys.

As the steward held the door open for them to step inside, Brent flashed a grin and explained, "What do you think of this? It's the bridal chamber. You see, they combined the regular staterooms to make this into a bedroom and parlor. It's eight feet by sixteen all told."

Everyone thought it beautiful. It had a wall-to-wall red carpet, big windows trimmed with red and white curtains, a double brass bed, chair and desk with a kerosene lamp covered with a flowers-on-white translucent shade, large mirrors, and marble-top wash stand with pitcher and bowl. Sitting on the desk was a silver bucket holding a large bottle of French champagne.

After goodbye hugs, Susan and Gilbert took the children back to the quay, and Violet and Brent went out to the rail to wave to them. Violet signaled to them to go on without waiting for the steamboat to leave. She knew how restless the children could get when they had to stand a while in one place. They waved a last goodbye, threw kisses, and took their leave.

Violet confessed to Brent that she felt a little sense of loneliness and emptiness at leaving the children, but she was happy to be with her husband on such a beautiful and famous steamer as the *Robert E. Lee,* whereupon he planted a big kiss upon her soft lips.

As the boat got underway, a fresh breeze made the cool air feel cold. Violet and Brent put on their coats and hats and found rocking chairs on the outside decks to watch the sunset over the Louisiana shore, where the dark green and brown of the river bank separated the quiet colors of the sky from the shimmering colors of the reflection on the moving water. Only two or three other people were out on this deck, occupying Bank of England chairs close to the bulkhead.

Turning toward Violet, Brent said, "You know, my Love, we are lucky to be able to get on the *Robert E. Lee*."

"What do you mean, sold out?"

"Well, just about, but that is not it; I understand that the *Lee* is to be turned into a wharf boat later this year."

"What's that—a wharf boat?"

"Retirement, like a horse being put out to pasture."

"Oh, no! But it's so beautiful; it doesn't look that worn out."

"No, but these steamboats only last five years or so, and the *Lee* now is over nine years old."

"Well, it's a lucky break for us that she's still operating."

In about an hour and a half, as the boat approached a big bend in the river, Brent called out, "Look, this was Jefferson Davis's plantation." He pointed in the direction.

"Oh, my goodness, just imagine, the home of our Confederate president."

"Yes, you see how the river has cut through and formed a new channel? Made the whole thing an island. I understand that Jeff Davis's brother, Joseph, who had been a lawyer in Natchez, bought this whole area, about ten miles across in each direction."

"That's a lot of land."

"Yes, it sure is. Joseph became wealthy as a cotton planter here and built a house that he called 'Hurricane.' Later he gave a section to his young brother—you know Jeff was twenty-four years younger than Joseph."

"Well, I'd heard there was a big age difference between the two, but I didn't know exactly how many years."

Brent went on, "So Jeff built a house there and called his plantation 'Brierfield."

"And here we are, right at the place. You know Jefferson Davis had a very enlightened attitude toward his slaves. Daddy used to tell how he emphasized self-discipline, set up a kind of system of courts of their own, and he never allowed any whipping of any of his slaves."

"So I've heard."

When Venus, the first star of evening, appeared, Violet rose and stepped to the rail and gazed at the water. Brent came up and put his arms around her waist. Ignoring the crushing of her hat, she leaned her head against his shoulder. The sound of the paddle wheels, at first a distraction, now had a soothing and sensual effect.

"Oh, Brent, darling," she whispered, "it's so beautiful, so peaceful here, just what we need as a respite from all our pressures. Thank you for making this possible."

He kissed her lightly on her cheek in a way to reflect that he was sharing her thoughts, feeling her feelings. It was as if they were sailing through the air in a tranquil world on their own.

The first gong for supper interrupted their reverie. They returned to their stateroom, changed to formal attire, and then went to the dining saloon. A long table, covered with white linen, English bone china, and silver flatware, extended down the middle of the long room. A string of waiters brought them in turn the elements of an elegant seven-course meal, which they ate ravenously.

After dining, they paused in the lounge to enjoy several glasses of red wine and several waltzes to the music of a black band. Then they got their coats and returned to the outer deck to drink in the night sky punctuated with its distant sparkling diamonds and crescent moon, the sounds of the boat's paddle wheels turning through the water, the soft, cool refreshing breeze, and the glimmers of light from the boat that lighted the foam and spray around the paddle wheel. Here and there a reflected star could be seen on the otherwise dark river.

"When I see the crescent moon, I think of South Carolina," Violet said softly.

"Why?"

"Oh, you silly goose, you know the crescent is on our state flag, but I wonder, why do we have the crescent as well as the palmetto on the flag?"

"I guess because during the Revolution the Carolina soldiers wore a crescent on their caps."

"Oh."

"The crescent should also make you think of New Orleans since it's called the crescent city."

"Why is it called that?"

"I suppose because the river makes a great bend there, like a crescent moon, right in front of the city."

"That must be it."

They stood quietly by the railing, enjoying the fresh breeze and the moonlight and the sounds of the boat moving through the water, and in a short while, they returned to their room to enjoy the cool champagne awaiting them, the warmth of their bed, and their love and passion for each other.

During the night the boat reduced speed, as a precaution against snags, as a contribution to the comfort of the passengers, and to allow more sightseeing during daylight hours. The next morning, it arrived at Natchez. Here there would be a three-hour delay for passengers to disembark and others to embark, and discharging and loading cargo. Brent and Violet went out on the promenade to watch the boat tie up.

"They call the waterfront area there 'Natchez Under the Hill'," Brent said, taking a quick side-wise look at Violet, his eyes dancing with mischief, "and since we are going to be here a while I thought I might go off and have a look around. I heard from some of the crew that that place right over there, *The Blue Cat*, has some very interesting attractions."

"Oh, no you don't, you silly goose, you're not going anywhere without me, and I certainly shall not be going over there!"

Brent laughed and replied with pretended woefulness, "Oh well then, I suppose my second choice might be for us to hire a rig and see a little of the town."

Violet grinned. "Now that sounds better, much better. Let's do it."

As they drove up to the town they were impressed by its size and beauty and by the number of great mansions in the vicinity. The first to come to their attention, around a curve near the top of the bluff, was Rosalie, a large, red brick house with two-story Greek revival portico and balcony, four columns each on the west and east fronts and a one-story veranda extending all across the two fronts.

They turned up a lane to the southward, still overlooking the river, and approached a long bungalow. "I understand this is The Briars where Jefferson Davis was married," explained Brent.

"*And* Varina Howell," added Violet.

"Who?"

"Varina Howell also was married here—she became Mrs. Davis, the second Mrs. Jefferson Davis.

Brent flashed his characteristic grin, acknowledging Violet's point. "Of course, my dear, it takes two to tie the knot. I revise my comment: This is where Jefferson Davis and Varina Howell were married. How's that?"

"That's better."

They turned back and then a short distance to the east they came upon the magnificent Dunleith, a big white house completely surrounded by a two-story colonnade and galleries.

Now they turned toward the center of the town and drove past Magnolia Hall, a large, red house distinctive for its four tall Ionic columns at the front. Behind it, across the street to the east was Trinity Episcopal Church, built of white limestone in the form of a Greek temple. On down, on the corner of High Street and Pearl, they saw what they decided was probably the greatest house of all—the all-white Stanton Hall, with four tall Corinthian columns and balcony in front, and an enclosed berkeley, or what Brent called a Widow's Watch, rising above the hipped roof at the center.

Brent suggested that they stop for some refreshment. Turning into Franklin Street, Brent noticed a hotel, The Jefferson, and he pulled up in front. He tied the horse to a hitching post and they went into the dining room.

"After all the food on the boat last evening and this morning's breakfast, I really don't feel much like more food now," remarked Violet, "but I am a bit thirsty."

"Of course not," Brent agreed as he went on to order a ham sandwich for each, a glass of sarsaparilla soda for Violet and a glass of ale for himself.

Violet took a sip of her soda and then a deep breath of relaxation. "This is all amazing, absolutely amazing. I've never seen so many beautiful, great houses in one area. Thank God, Grant didn't come through here destroying everything in sight like he did in Vicksburg. At least there's all this."

"And we have seen only a fraction of them here."

"There's more to come, down the river," smiled Brent.

"But all these stand for the Southern culture, the civilization that we talk about all the time. Of course I realized that Mississippi shared these things with the rest of the South, but I am surprised to see so many testimonials to Southern civilization this far west."

Brent chuckled. "My dear, you betray your Atlantic orientation. People here don't think of themselves as being so far west of the ocean; they think of being only a short distance north of the Gulf."

Violet nodded with a smile, and granted, "I suppose so."

"And don't forget the first white men, those with DeSoto, came to Mississippi only about twenty years after the first exploration of the Carolinas, and the first settlement by the French on the Gulf coast was less than thirty years after the first settlement by the English in South Carolina. The second settlement by the French, right here at Natchez, was only fifteen years or so after that. Did you know that Wade Hampton is about as big a land holder in Mississippi as in South Carolina?"

"Yes, I've heard something about that. Well, I just can't believe that all the civilization that this represents has been completely swept away, even by the War and Reconstruction."

"No, of course not, but you must remember that only about a tenth of the population depended on the great plantations even before the War. Most of the people in the South were small farmers."

"That's true, but those small farmers believed enough in that civilization to fight for it, didn't they?"

"Yes, they did."

"Why?"

"Probably because they all dreamed that one day they would be great planters, plantation owners, based on the fact that many of them did rise in that manner. But that's not all. They thought they had the right to secede, and they resented it when the North invaded the South to deny it. They shared the view that the Southerners did not have a fair shake, and they were fighting for the right to govern themselves."

Violet's brow was furrowed with thought. "Brent," she said slowly, "Was our War really so very different from the American Revolution?"

"What do you mean?"

"Well now, think about this. Was not the American Revolution but a secession of the states—all thirteen of them—from Great Britain?"

"Yes, of course it was."

"The early Americans were burdened with the Stamp Act and other taxes; the South was burdened with the unfair tariff. In 1776 the English were bossy and arrogant; we had the hostile abuse of the Northern abolitionists. The English considered any talk of American independence as treason; so, too, the attitude of the North was that any mention of separation from the Union was sedition, even though earlier many of them assumed a right of states to secede. Indeed, you know that after the War there was even talk of trying Jefferson Davis for treason. And another thing, the British used their army and navy to keep the colonies from breaking away from the Empire; the North used their army and navy to keep the Southern states from seceding and to hold them in the Union." She placed her hand on his arm with intensity as if to punctuate what she had just said. "Well, what to you think. Don't you agree?"

Brent was always entranced when Violet got caught up in her thoughts this way, with her cheeks flushed and eyes shining with emotion. He knew that this topic was a serious one for her, so he answered somberly, "I agree on every point. I just wonder why all this has not been stressed more. I guess it all depends on whose ox is being gored."

"Daddy said there were those who tried to point out the similarities, but their ideas were put down as quickly as they arose. The North didn't want their people to even consider such notions."

"No, certainly not."

He drained the rest of his ale and placed a few coins on the table, saying, "And now, my Love, it's time to get back to the boat."

On the way out Violet noticed that Brent picked up some pamphlets that were set out on a side table in the hall. "What have you there?" she asked curiously.

"Oh, some writings from the works of John James Audubon—."

"You mean the painter of birds?"

"Yes, that one, and by others who have traveled down the Mississippi."

"Oh, good, they'll be interesting to read and a souvenir of where we've been," she said agreeably.

That afternoon they missed some of the shoreline sights, for they chose to have a siesta in their stateroom. Their sightseeing had tired them just a bit, and the refreshments at the Jefferson Hotel and the heavy dinner on the boat relaxed them a lot. But, as always, their energy soon rebounded.

Brent was fascinated by the differences in navigating on the river from sailing on the high seas, and he was a welcome visitor to the pilot house. He mingled with the officers on the Texas deck and with the deck hands on the main. He visited the engine room, chatting with the engineers. And he stopped for an occasional ale and smoke and a friendly game of poker in the bar, forward of the men's saloon, and for conversation in the barber shop. Violet spent a great deal of this time catching up on her reading, and some time, but not much, conversing with other ladies in the delicately appointed ladies' parlor, but she much preferred to be with Brent on deck enjoying the scenery or in their bridal chamber stateroom enjoying each other.

In the evening, after another sumptuous supper, they enjoyed more Viennese waltzes and wine. Violet coaxed Brent away from the gaming tables and agreed to join him for some hands of whist with several other couples. It was an enjoyable evening all around, and when they retired to their stateroom they were full of chuckles and good humor.

By early morning on Monday they were at Baton Rouge. After breakfast, as the boat got underway, Brent said to Violet, "Come on, let's get our lap robes and go find some rocking chairs on the outer deck. Soon we should be seeing some more of the old plantation houses passing in review.".

On the deck, as Brent tucked her lap robe securely around her, Violet asked, "Are we still in Mississippi?"

"No, it's Louisiana on both sides now," he answered, settling into his deck chair and spreading his robe out over him. He picked up a tourist guide by his chair.

"I wish we could see all this in both the spring and fall," Violet ventured in mock anguish.

"I thought you wanted to come down here now," he reminded her.

"I did. I didn't want to wait any longer to see Susan and the new baby."

After half an hour or so, a deck steward pointed out that they were coming up on Magnolia Mound, one of the oldest and most beautiful of the great plantations.

"Says here," Brent noted as he read from a pamphlet, "they started out growing tobacco and indigo at Magnolia Mound, but later changed to sugar and cotton. Probably one reason was that they found out indigo was not healthy for their workers."

"I'm sure that was a wise decision," Violet responded. "I remember Daddy mentioning that indigo could make the workers ill. And the demand for cotton increased so much back then. Everybody began putting it in."

In a while they saw Nottoway. Brent referred to his pamphlet again and announced that it was often called the White Castle by river travelers and was built shortly before the War by a Randolph from Virginia. "It says here that it took ten years to build, and it took fifty-seven house servants to run it. Says it is probably the largest and most spectacular of any in the South."

"Great Scot."

"And here, listen, it has a solid white grand ballroom, with hand-carved cypress interior Corinthian columns, white marble fireplaces, and crystal chandeliers. Says Mrs. Randolph wanted it all white so that the ladies' gowns of any color would look good in it."

"Smart lady. I bet she had dark hair."

"Why do you say that?"

"Dark-haired women stand out in a light background. I probably shouldn't tell you this, but why do you think all our wallpaper and paint are light-colored?"

"I never thought about it. So that's why you look so beautiful at Fair Oaks...and all the time I thought it was you," he said, grinning mischievously and reaching over to pull a lock of her hair.

"Oh, you rascal," she laughed, turning her head quickly so that the hair slipped from his fingers.

The steward came by again to suggest that they might want to go back over to the portside for a look at the Houmas House. Brent returned to his literature, and then announced, "Now, look, there it is, the big Houmas House. See the columns and verandas all across the white house? And look at those oak trees. This pamphlet says they are two hundred years old. The plantation consists of ten thousand acres now, but it used to be twenty thousand. Surely you've heard of this place before, Violet."

She lifted her eyebrows in query. "I have?"

He grinned. "Of course. This is the house that John Preston and his wife came out from South Carolina to build."

"You mean the daughter of the first General Wade Hampton?" she asked in surprise.

"Exactly. This is the land that old General Hampton acquired when the Army sent him out here after the Revolution."

Violet was delighted at seeing this place. "It's amazing that the house survived the War so well. I heard from the Prestons in Columbia that John Preston sold the place to an Irishman before the War, and when that Yankee devil, Ben Butler, came up to take over the house for his headquarters, the owner defied him—said he was a British subject and the general would create an international incident with Queen Victoria if Butler tried to destroy the house."

"Sounds like my Violet," Brent said, chuckling.

"But what about that Atlantic orientation you were speaking of earlier?" asked Violet, her eyes twinkling.

"Atlantic orientation? What do you mean?"

"Why, Brent, here you've been telling me of the great plantations of the Prestons of South Carolina, the Randolphs of Virginia, and of Wade Hampton's great land holdings in Mississippi."

"Oh, yes, yes, but you see, these are all late comers. I was referring more to the early settlers when I mentioned the Atlantic orientation." He chuckled again. His sharp witted little wife wasn't about to let him get by with that.

"Oh, Brent, here is where I wish we could go ashore. I'd so like to see Houmas House, and some of the others, too."

Brent turned toward her. He'd noted the wishful tone in her voice. "If this were the middle of the cotton shipping season, we could, honey. Then the boats stop at all the plantation landings until their decks are stacked full of bales of cotton. We picked up some in Natchez, but the boats are not making the plantation stops now."

Early in the afternoon, now a bright, sunny day, they hurried out to the starboard deck for a look at what was probably the best known place of all, the place that river travelers had named Oak Alley for the avenue of twenty-eight enormous live oak trees that led up to the big house with six white columns all along the front and three dormers in the sloping roof.

Referring to his pamphlet again, Brent told Violet, "That avenue of trees was planted by some unknown French settler for his log cabin a hundred and thirty years before Jacques Telesphore Roman III built his great house there. Did you ever see such big trees?"

"Never."

"That settler planted them forty feet apart, and the avenue is eighty feet wide at the beginning but narrows as it approaches the house, so the trees have had plenty of room to grow in these hundred and seventy-five years."

"And they certainly have."

As they approached New Orleans late in the afternoon, they took short notice of San Francisco plantation house that Violet said looked like a steamboat that had climbed up on the bank. They did notice the historic Destrehan plantation where, they had read, such celebrities as the pirate Jean Laffite and the Duke of Orleans, later King Louis-Philippe of France, had been guests. The house had a marble bathtub that supposedly was the gift of Napoleon.

"I've heard that the Freedmen's Bureau operated a colony for freed slaves at the Destrehan Plantation," remarked Brent.

"Well, I hope they did better for them than they did in Sumter," was Violet's only comment.

Just before sunset, about five o'clock, they were standing at the rail, waiting to disembark, when they saw Bruce on the quay waving vigorously with his hat. Violet and Brent waved back, happy to see him again after so many years, and eagerly anticipating what arrangements he had made for them in the beautiful and romantic old city of New Orleans.

Chapter 62

Mardi Gras

1875

They ran down the stage to greet Bruce. It took a while for the excitement of greetings of reunion after years of separation to subside. While the two brothers were busy tossing questions at one another, Violet studied Bruce. It always amazed her how much he and Brent resembled one another in looks and intelligence, though not in personality and character. Like Brent, Bruce had dark hair that was slightly wavy, the same wide smile and even white teeth, but his eyes were grey instead of sea-blue. He was three inches shorter and a tad heavier than Brent. His moustache was slightly fuller and his sideburns slightly longer. He had a roguish air about him and was nattily dressed in a grey flannel sack suit, a gray top hat, gray gloves, and gray shoes. He sported a silver walking stick that Violet suspected had a hidden flask inside.

In a short while, after the questions diminished somewhat, Bruce led them to a hackney that he had hired to carry them and their baggage to the St. Charles hotel. He pointed out the sights as they drove up the curving St. Charles Avenue eastward past Audubon Park, near the river, and northeastward through the Garden District, northward past Lafayette Square and on past the striking Ionic Greek temple that was the city hall. They arrived at the hotel, just short of the French Quarter.

"What a magnificent hotel!" Violet exclaimed as they drove up.

"You should have seen the original, as the people here say," remarked Bruce. "It burned down in 1851, and then was rebuilt."

Violet and Brent looked in awe at the projecting portico of fourteen Corinthian columns and as they gazed upward at the gleaming white dome supported by a marble colonnade.

Pointing to an open turret atop the dome, Bruce said, "That's the place to do your sightseeing. You can see the whole city of New Orleans from there."

As they entered the high front door, Violet looked around and whispered to Brent, "Oh, my goodness, their lobby is as big as most hotels!"

Bruce led them to the front desk so that Brent might register, and then took his leave, saying that he would rejoin them here at the hotel at seven o'clock for dinner, and at that time he would tell them what Mardi Gras plans he had been able to make for them.

Violet and Brent were pleased to find that their third floor suite reflected the grandeur of the public rooms they saw on the way up—plush, dark blue carpet, blue and white velvet brocade draperies, white silk brocade wall covering, white woodwork, ornamental gold-framed mirrors, brass fixtures, and a settee and two large chairs covered to match the draperies. A mahogany end table was on either side of the settee. On the wall, over each end table, was an ornamental brass gas lamp. A brass kerosene lamp sat on a round, walnut coffee table in front of the settee and chairs.

Violet led Brent into the bedroom to show him the handsome pecan tester bed. The hangings and bed ruffle were of white crocheted lace, and the bedspread was of silk brocade figured with gold flowered designs. The two pecan chests of drawers were covered with white runners, embroidered with flowers. Mirrors covered the two doors of the large walnut wardrobe. The walls of the room were covered in the same material as the parlor–white silk brocade, but here the draperies were of the same fabric as the bedspread.

Sunlight streaming into both rooms was reflected by the white walls, providing a bright, cheerful, glow throughout.

"Oh, Brent, have you *ever* seen hotel rooms so lovely?" breathed Violet in ecstasy.

"No, I'll have to admit I never have. I also hereby submit that I will no doubt faint when I get the bill."

"Oh, Brent! There you go."

"Just joking, just joking, my dear," he responded hastily.

After the maid had come in, unpacked, and hung up their clothes, they were glad for a chance to rest until time to dress for dinner.

They met Bruce downstairs in the lobby promptly at seven. He led them to the beautiful large dining room that was almost filled with nearly five hundred brightly dressed guests. The maitre d' led them to a small round table covered with starched white linen and heavy silver flatware. Multicolored fresh flowers gave off a sweet aroma from the center of the table.

Animated conversation accompanied the courses of crawfish bisque, *filet de sole bonne femme* and rice, white wine, and peach cobbler.

"Any lady friends?" Brent asked his brother. Brent was of the opinion that it was high time his brother settled down.

"Oh, sure, several, but still no special one for me. There's Marie in New Orleans; you'll meet her tomorrow evening, and Madeline in St. Louis and Barbara in Sacramento–."

"I get the idea," grinned Brent, but he was disappointed. Bruce still seemed to be sowing his wild oats.

Looking at Violet, Bruce said in mock seriousness, "Well, brother dear, you've got Violet. What other woman is there? Now if she has a twin sister hidden away somewhere–."

"Oh, Bruce," laughed Violet. "But really, with so many lady friends here and there, you sound like a sailor to me–."

Bruce came back quickly, "Sure, and there's Ching-li in Shanghai–."

Brent said, "I remember you writing about going over there, but you spared us the details in your letter."

Incredulous, Violet asked, "What in the world were you doing there?"

"I was recruiting workers for the railroad."

Still incredulous, Violet asked, "Bruce, do you mean you were shanghai-ing Chinese coolies?"

"Well, I wouldn't say I was shanghai-ing them; I was contracting workers."

"Do tell us about it. How did the Chinese take to all this? How did it work out?" The questions tumbled from Violet's lips. She was fascinated upon hearing this news.

"Well, it all started with the Central Pacific when they were pushing eastward to meet the Union Pacific in the sixties, and they were hard pressed for workers. There weren't many white workers to begin with, and most of them kept taking off for the gold fields. Finally one of the owners told the construction chief, Jim Strobridge, to hire some Chinese workers from California. Well, old Strobridge was hard-boiled, and he had no use for Chinamen–said they were strange little heathens who ate unchristian food like seaweed and mushrooms, and they even washed themselves everyday, like women–."

Violet interrupted sarcastically, "Oh, we couldn't use men who washed everyday, could we?"

Bruce went on, "And Strobridge refused to hire any Chinese, but then, with his shortage of labor he began falling far behind schedule. He had no choice. With great reluctance he agreed to take on fifty as a test trial. He was amazed when they built a better, longer rail bed, than white crews in the same time. Then they began taking on Chinese by the hundreds. When they could get no more from California, they began recruiting in China. That's where I came in–I made one trip to Shanghai and Canton. Before it was over the Central Pacific had ten thousand Chinese at work through the mountains, grading rail beds, pounding spikes, building snow sheds, everything. Near the end, when they were racing toward the finish, a mostly Chinese crew laid ten miles of track in twelve hours and won a ten thousand dollar bet for Mr. Crocker, who was the one of the big four who was in charge of construction."

Violet broke in again, "I don't mean to be critical or anything, but just how does the use of coolies differ from slavery?"

"In some places, it doesn't," Brent spoke up, "especially in Peru, Guiana, and Cuba, and other West Indian colonies. After slavery was abolished there, most of the blacks refused to work on the sugar plantations and so on, so the planters simply brought in coolies."

"How do they persuade them to leave their homes in China?"

Brent answered ironically, "They entice them with great promises, or they buy them from local warlords who have taken them prisoners, or they simply pay head-money to people who kidnap them. They call the depots where they collect them *barracoons,* the same thing they called the collection points in the West African slave trade. When they get the Chinamen to Cuba or Peru, they often sell them at auction.

"Well, now hold it, big brother, my system was to take along a couple of our Chinese workers to explain to their compatriots the great opportunities here," explained Bruce.

Brent nodded but continued on, explaining to Violet, "The coolie trade to the West Indies supposedly was abolished about ten years ago, but they find ways to get around it. And I tell you, the conditions on those coolie ships are as bad as they were on the slave ships. The British finally adopted some strict regulations on the number of coolies that could be carried on a ship, and for sanitation, but then the Portuguese stepped in and took over the coolie trade."

"I suppose their working conditions were not very good either," Violet ventured.

"Terrible," Brent answered. "I heard about this while sailing on the *Shenandoah.* Worst of all was the fraudulent consignment of many of them to the foul guano pits of the Peruvian islands. Overseers herded them with cowhide lashes. They said that of four thousand Chinese workers consigned to the guano pits by 1860, not one survived. Those who did not die naturally committed suicide."

"How awful!" gasped a shocked Violet.

Bruce turned to her, "Violet, you asked how this differs from slavery," he resumed. "As you see, not at all in the West Indies, though workers there were on seven-year contracts, supposedly, and not life commitments. Our workers on the railroad here generally were given a minimum daily wage, and they were promised passage back to their home countries in three years, though I must say most of them have opted to stay. Another thing is, that family units have been preserved to a considerable degree; they maintain close family ties, wherever they are."

"What about their working conditions?" she asked.

"Well, I'll tell you, when it comes to working through the mountain passes I would say they endured more hardship than any slave on a Southern plantation."

By now they had all finished their desserts, and Bruce suggested that they withdraw to the lounge chairs in the lobby. As they took comfortable chairs near a large side window, Violet remarked, "I must say, this hotel is like a palace."

"You know how the visiting politician from New York, Oakley Hall, described the original St. Charles?" asked Bruce.

"How?"

"Just what you said. He said if you would set the St. Charles down in St. Petersburg you would think it a palace; if you put it in Boston you would think it a college; if it were in London you would think it the stock exchange, but in New Orleans it is all three."

Looking around, Brent commented, "Well, I must say, it does not seem that Reconstruction or the depression have had much of an impact around here."

"Well, now, hold on, big brother. Most of this is Carpetbag money. This is where the pirates spend their plunder taken from us southerners."

"How about the state as a whole?" inquired Brent.

"I guess every Southern state thinks that it has suffered worse from the Reconstruction than the others. Certainly the Louisianians think that. In four years, from 1868 to '72, the Carpetbag/Scalawag/Negro legislature increased state expenditures by ten times. They made enormous increases in taxes and still managed to create a fifty-seven million dollar debt. There has been lots of factional fighting among the Republicans. In '72, two governors and two legislatures were installed, and they set up a rival capitol here at the famous St. Louis Hotel in the French Quarter—and which you must see, by the way. The Democrats supported the Liberal Republicans, but of course the Federal government recognized the Radicals who do not have the support of a majority of the people. There have been several violent clashes between the two groups, the most notable here in New Orleans was between the White League and the Republican police last September. Local people talk about that as a kind of battle for independence. But then, nobody fights during carnival; everybody has a wonderful time."

"I surely hope so," said Violet, a bit perturbed.

"The biggest attraction around here, and the biggest opportunity for graft, has to be the Lottery," said Bruce.

"The Lottery?" Violet asked in surprise.

"The Lottery?" asked Brent, "Tell me, where do the lines form?"

"Now, Brent!" exclaimed Violet hastily.

"You can buy tickets at any saloon, tobacconist, hotel, and so on, but the big public drawings are up at the Auditorium, twice a month for medium drawings, twice a year for the grand prizes. Some barber won three hundred thousand dollars at one of those, and people have been going crazy ever since. There are even small daily drawings for the big public events. Two of our famous Confederate generals, Beauregard and Early, sit up on the stage and preside over the drawings. They each get paid thirty thousand dollars a year for this service," Bruce ended, rather sarcastically.

"Beauregard is a native of New Orleans, isn't he?" inquired Brent.

"Yes, he is," answered Bruce.

"But, Bruce, how did all this get started?" asked Violet.

"Well, I'll tell you. Six or seven years ago a group of men made a deal with the Carpetbag government for a twenty-five-year charter to operate a lottery, and they paid the legislature three hundred thousand for their approval. The operators agreed to hand over to the state half of their take; the usual arrangement is three quarters."

With some irony, Violet observed, "I trust that this payback goes for education, hospitals, poor relief, and the like."

"Well, the Lottery itself pledged donations to all those kinds of things, but I'm afraid not much has come of it. Many people call the Lottery the "Golden Octopus." They've been raking in—or raking off—millions each year," responded Bruce gloomily. He paused and turned to a more immediate subject. "But I have some good news for you two. I've been fortunate enough to get a membership in the Carnival Krewe called *Rex*, which was founded just three years ago to rival the older *Comus*. We have tickets for the grand ball tomorrow night, and I also have reservations for dinner for all of us at Antoine's tomorrow afternoon. How does that sound?"

"Oh, it sounds exciting!" exclaimed Violet, smiling in expectation.

"Now to see the festivities," continued Bruce, "you will want to get an early start in the morning. You can see lots of the activities from your room balcony. About eleven o'clock you may want to walk down to City Hall where our *Rex* parade will be ending."

"We'll be there," said Violet.

Bruce added, "Good, and after the parade I'll meet you about two o'clock at Antoine's. That's on St. Louis Street in the French Quarter, only a five or six block walk from here. Just go north of Canal, and continue north on Bourbon Street, and then turn right on St. Louis."

"We'll find it," Brent promised.

"You'll need some kind of mask and costume for the ball, you know."

Violet nodded "We're prepared. We brought them with us."

"Where are you staying?" Brent asked Bruce.

"I have a place out on west Canal Street. I'll be going now and I'll see you tomorrow. Now, you two may want to take a look around the French Quarter before you turn in. Lots of revelers out, as there have been all month."

Following Bruce's suggestion, Violet and Brent went up to their rooms to get their coats and hats and then left the hotel for a walk up Bourbon Street. Crowds of people, of all ages and backgrounds, all in colorful attire and in a festive mood, were in the streets. Music floated or blared from all directions. Suddenly Violet recognized the beat of the specialty numbers of the *Little Brown Jugs,* and tears came to her eyes as she remembered Little Josh. Brent looked down at her, acknowledging with his eyes that he, too, was thinking of Little Josh. She smiled bravely through her tears, tightened her grip on Brent's arm, and went on.

The next morning they climbed the steps all the way to the turret above the dome of the hotel for a look around at the city. People in all kinds of costumes and wagons with all kinds of decorations were moving in all directions. It was a beautiful day with blue skies and bright sunshine. The sun picked up the bright colors of the moving people and wagons, turning them all into a kaleidoscope of luminous hues and tints. New Orleans was electric with waves of reflections.

They returned to their suite and went out on their balcony to watch the activities from there until time to leave for the *Rex parade.* At eleven they were at City Hall and just in time to see the dozen or so beautiful floats, each drawn by well-groomed and plumed teams of horses. As the parade passed by, Violet and Brent tried to pick out Bruce among the masked marchers, but could not be sure which was he. At the end of the parade Rex himself, seated high on a canopied throne drawn by six white horses, came along waving to the people and then saluting his Queen.

Crowds in the streets made the walk to Antoine's take much longer than they expected, but they were there in time to meet Bruce at two o'clock. The place was so crowded that they had a difficult time finding him.

In due course they did, and while the three waited in the anteroom, Violet pointed out the prints of Audubon paintings on the walls. "That one," she said, pointing, "is called *Pheasants and Dog* and is just about my favorite, I think."

"Oh, yes, I like that one especially," said Brent. "I've seen pheasants that look just like those in our fields, and the dog is so realistic looking. I almost want to reach out and pet him."

After a while they were shown to a table, and the maitre d' seated Violet. She admired the cut-out work on the white linen table cloth, the blue and yellow fresh flowers nesting in a silver pitcher, the Haviland china service plate, the scrolled silver place setting, and the crystal wine glasses. She could not help but stare at the paintings on the brocaded walls; she recognized a Rubens, a Rafael, a Rembrandt; two French paintings, Fragonard's *The Swing* and Carot's *Dance of the Nymphs*; and two paintings by American artists, Edward Hicks' *The Peaceable Kingdom* and Benjamin West's *Penn's Treaty with the Indians.*

"This is like a museum—so many beautiful paintings; surely, they must be copies," commented Violet.

"I wouldn't know," said Brent looking around. "Very French, indeed."

"Yes," agreed Bruce, "the owner is a man from Marseilles who came here by way of New York. He served at the St. Charles Hotel for a while, then opened a pension of his own near the St. Louis, and then twenty-five years ago he opened this place."

They continued their animated conversation of the day's adventures over *jambalaya,* a specially seasoned combination of shrimp, oysters, tomatoes, rice, and other ingredients, and then the specialty of the house, *Dinde Talleyrand,* a unique turkey dish. When they had finished, Bruce said that Violet and Brent probably needed some time to rest and then to get their costumes ready, and that he and Marie would meet them about seven o'clock in the hotel lobby to go out to watch the *Comus* parade, and then they would all go to the grand ball of *Rex.*

Violet had packed a hooped crinoline which she wore under her own lavender brocade gown, and with her accessories and powdered wig, she became a colonial dame. Her all-face mask was white. Brent had brought along items that he combined to create a Sir Walter Raleigh costume. He wore a black half mask, and carried a large, white silk handkerchief.

Violet thought he looked quite dashing and didn't hesitate to tell him so; he thought her a beautiful eighteenth-century lady and told her so.

At seven they met Bruce and his companion, Marie. He was dressed as a pirate, and she as a *fille à la cassette.* Marie was a Creole of rather dark complexion, and Violet thought her quite attractive.

The *Comus* parade, with the benefit of torchlights, was even more colorful than the others as the scarlet and yellow decorations seemed to change hues as the floats moved and their shadows played on the walls of the buildings along the way.

"I've been enjoying the Mardi Gras parades for most of my life," remarked Marie, "but I do believe that this year they have been the most colorful and beautiful of all."

"Fantastic!" exclaimed Violet, breathing in the beauty of it all, "This is my first. It's wonderful; everything is wonderful!".

The two couples followed the crowd up Royal Street and then along Orleans Street toward the auditorium where the *Comus* would have their ball. Bruce led his guests over to the French Opera House for the ball of the *Rex Krewe.* Here, on the lower level, people in all kinds of colorful attractive or grotesque costumes were singing, and playing pranks, and dancing to music ranging from Viennese waltzes to old favorite songs and new compositions and improvisations.

During a break, Bruce said, "Now for a lanny-yap."

"What on earth are you talking about?" demanded Violet.

"A lagniappe."

"Is that something to eat?"

Bruce laughed and answered, "No, no, it's spelled *l-a-g-n-i-a-p-p-e*, pronounced *lanny-yap*—real New Orleans, meaning something extra, like a little gift a merchant may give you when you make a purchase, or like the thirteenth doughnut in a baker's dozen, or just about anything you can think of as something extra. People even say it when a waiter drops his tray in a restaurant."

"Just what extra do you have in mind?" wondered Violet.

"Follow me and see," smiled Bruce. He led his party up to the lobby for punch. They sipped the refreshing drink and then decided to take a look around the grand building—an opera house with a thousand upholstered armchairs on the main floor and with four curved tiers of boxes and seats above for another thousand patrons.

They returned to the ballroom where everyone was singing the Mardi Gras theme song, a song of many improvised verses: *If ever I cease to love, If ever I cease to love, May the fish get legs, And the cows lay eggs, If ever cease to love...*

Brent lifted Violet's mask and stole a kiss. "Oh, darling," sighed Violet, "what a wonderful time we are having! I just want this evening to go on and on."

Brent laughed. "Well, it will for a while, my love."

Shortly before midnight, Rex and his court, with the crowd following, marched over to the auditorium to salute the other king, Comus. After a promenade by the two courts, everyone joined in a grand march and concluded with a sumptuous feast that seemed to go on course after delicious course until Brent leaned over and whispered in Violet's ear, "Well, you know, you said you wanted this evening to go on and on—and it certainly has."

"Yes, what an evening, but now I think I'm ready to go home and go to bed." she whispered back, giggling a little.

"Well, I'm willing to go to bed with you any time," he grinned.

Still giggling, she replied, "Oh, Brent, that isn't what I meant."

"I know it isn't, now, but it will be soon," he answered with a gleam in his eye.

Chapter 63

Heaven and Hell

1875

"Quite a difference from last night, isn't it," Violet said to Brent as they walked along Bourbon Street on Wednesday morning.

"There certainly is; I guess most of last night's revelers are sleeping late today."

They walked on up the street, now more crowded with litter than with people, past the Absinthe House where supposedly Andrew Jackson and Jean Lafitte met to plan the defense of New Orleans in the War of 1812. They strolled by shops, banks, restaurants, saloons, and stucco or brick houses with double-tiered iron-lace balconies, always built right on the sidewalk, or *trottoir*, but with trim, private courtyards hidden within.

As they approached the three-spired St. Louis Cathedral on the northwest side of Jackson Square, Violet suggested that they go in. "It's Ash Wednesday, and I think we should attend a church service of some kind," she ventured.

"All right, if you say so."

"Of course this will be Catholic. I hope you won't mind."

Brent smiled. "I guess the question is, will they mind us?"

"Well, we won't take communion, although that's something I've never understood. We Episcopalians welcome those of other faiths to take communion with us."

As they entered, people were coming out—not many, but enough to indicate that early morning Mass had just ended.

"Well, so much for the service, but let's look around anyway," she said. Pausing at a table in the narthex, Violet picked up some leaflets, and then a small, leather prayerfold caught her attention. It had a metal likeness of St. Francis on the right and a prayer on the left. She glanced at the words quickly, dropped a coin into a box, and picked up the prayerfold.

"I was much impressed when Father Roberts of Holy Cross first read this to me during a call—about nine years ago, before you had come home from the War. Come, let's go on in."

With Brent at her side she entered the nave, paused to admire its beauty, and then walked down past a few rows of pews. They entered one and knelt. Taking Brent's hand with her left hand and holding the open prayerfold with her right, she softly read the Prayer of St. Francis.

Brent gently squeezed her hand in communication, and she returned it. They remained silent for a few moments, then rose and went out into the cool, sunny day. They took deep breaths of the temperate river breeze and felt completely refreshed.

They sauntered over to the grassy center of the square to look at the statue of Andrew Jackson, a duplicate of the one in Washington, D.C. They read the words on the monument in honor of how the Battle of New Orleans was fought in January 1815, two weeks after the treaty of peace had been signed.

Then they walked toward the river, along the magnificent Renaissance-style, block-long Pontalba apartment building. They noticed that a similar building framed the square on the opposite side. Attractive shops on the ground floor of the Pontalba building caught their attention. They stopped to buy souvenirs for themselves, family, and servants. For himself, Brent found a handsome, polished wooden walking stick with a carved, ivory knob, and he insisted that Violet not only purchase the jeweled hair combs that caught her eye, but also a beautiful silver bracelet with stones of lavender amethyst and blue sapphire.

Arranging to have their many purchases delivered to their hotel, they walked on up on the levee and found a bench where they stopped to rest and survey the river front and chat a while. They watched tugs and barges, shrimp boats and private rowboats, river steamboats plying back and forth, and ocean-going steamers—even though it was another hundred miles down the meandering river to the mouth at the Gulf.

They walked along the waterfront northward to the French market where they bought a few more souvenirs, including a Creole doll for Bonnie Anne and a model steamboat for J.J., several boxes of maple pralines, and had a lunch of oyster stew—chock full of delicious huge oysters.

To go back to the hotel they returned southward along Decatur Street, then west on St. Louis Street. As they came to their hotel, Violet stopped for another look around. "Oh, Brent, I do so very much hate to leave this beautiful hotel and this beautiful city. But, I guess it's time to get back to the real world where so many depend on us."

They boarded the steamboat, *James Howard,* at six o'clock at the foot of St. Charles Street. Violet was amazed to find that this boat was even bigger and more palatial than the *Robert E. Lee.* Indeed it was the biggest boat on the river—capacity of 3,000 tons, 320 feet long, 53 feet wide, its twin chimneys rising high toward the sky. When it got underway it swung its two landing stages out in front where, forming a V, they protruded at an angle like a pair of great horns.

Violet and Brent found their stateroom, again a bridal suite even larger than on the *Lee,* but this time on the boiler deck. A door on one side opened to the outer deck while a door opposite opened into the giant, ostentatiously decorated saloon. Here, when they went in for supper, they found individual tables with settings for four, six, or eight diners, in contrast to the long, consolidated table where they had dined on the *Lee.* Violet thought the cuisine not quite as good; Brent claimed he could tell no difference. He ate everything put before him with gusto. In addition to the three regular meals there was mid-morning coffee, afternoon tea, and midnight buffet. Brent tried to miss none of them while Violet opted out of the extras except for tea.

The return voyage was as pleasant as had been the one down to New Orleans, though being upstream it took a half day longer.

When they arrived back at Vicksburg Saturday morning, Susan and Gilbert, with Bonnie Anne and J.J., were there with buggy and carriage to meet them. Violet and Brent were no more than off the landing stage when Bonnie Anne and J.J. came running up to tell excitedly of their *own* steamboat ride. Susan explained that on Sunday afternoon they had taken the children for a two-hour ride on a local excursion boat.

The next morning a messenger arrived at the Hudson house. After he had left, Susan and Gilbert bounded into the parlor to find Violet and Brent.

"Good news!" Susan exclaimed enthusiastically.

"What is it?" asked Brent. "Has Grant resigned the presidency, or has the Radical Congress taken a recess?"

Susan and Gilbert laughed. Susan went on to explain, "To tell you the truth, Gilbert has not had a steady position for the last year. There's been practically no railroad building during this depression, but today Gilbert received word that he is to go to work making route surveys for the Vicksburg, Pensacola & Ship Island."

Violet ran over to Susan and hugged her. "Oh, Susan, that's just wonderful! I'm so happy for you."

Brent rose from his chair and crossed over to shake hands with Gilbert. "I'm sorry to hear you've been out of work, but that's great about the new job. Sounds interesting. And congratulations!"

After a supper that was more bountiful than previous evenings, Susan and Gilbert joined Violet and Brent in the parlor while Evelina got the children ready for bed and Levi went out to feed the horse. Brent had arranged for an opened bottle of champagne in a bucket of ice to be waiting on the fireplace table.

"My goodness, what's this?" asked Gilbert, looking a bit startled.

"Oh, it's champagne!" exclaimed Susan.

"Just thought we might have a toast to your new job," smiled Brent.

"Wonderful idea!" agreed Violet.

Brent poured each a glass of the bubbling liquid and then, holding up his glass, said, "Here's to the new job and better times all around."

After all had sipped the wine in toast, they took chairs and settled back comfortably.

"I really think business is going to pick up this year," said Brent, setting down his glass.

"I hope so," responded Gilbert. "There are all kinds of plans for railroads through here, but none of them has been able to get any major building underway."

Susan, with a glimmer of her old self returning, added, "Well, Commodore, I'm sure that—."

CRASH! The loud noise of splintering glass interrupted as a brick came through the front window and rolled toward the fireplace. Instantly Brent sprang from his chair, instructing the women to lie down on the floor, and dashed out the front door with Gilbert close behind him.

As the sisters followed Brent's instructions and remained on the floor, Violet reached over and took Susan's hand. "What's happening?" she whispered.

"Probably some young black hoodlums out to get revenge," Susan whispered back.

"But why here? Why your house?"

"Probably confused. Somebody must have told them that we were some of the whites who were involved in the massacre at the courthouse."

By now Bonnie Anne and J.J. had come bounding down the stairs crying, "What is it, Daddy? What was that loud noise?" They stopped suddenly when they saw their mother and aunt lying on the floor.

"Mommy! What are you and Aunt Susan doing there?"

Violet hopped up and ran over to reassure them. She told Evelina who had followed them down the stairs to take the children back upstairs, get the baby from his crib, and keep them all in the center hall, away from any window. She gave a warning glance in response to the questioning look in Evelina's eyes, and motioned for her to go. "Go quickly, quickly, Evelina." Evelina turned and, taking each child's hand in one of hers, fled back upstairs with them.

Levi came running in from the carriage house in back. Violet told him to go up and stay with Evelina and the children in the center hall. "She'll need your help with the three children," she told him, "and Brent and Gilbert have gone out to see what's happening."

Just then they heard two or three rifle or musket shots at some distance up the street. Disregarding instructions to stay on the floor, Violet and Susan ran out on the porch. They could see dark shadows moving and hear footsteps running back and forth. Seeing neither Brent nor Gilbert, they went back in the house to wait. This time they dutifully lay back down on the floor. Violet knew Evelina and Levi would follow her instructions with the children upstairs.

A few minutes later they could hear a rumble of steps on the front porch. They jumped up, and Susan ran to the door, opened it, and peered outside. She was surprised to see a group of men carrying someone.

Suddenly she shouted in a shrill voice, "It's Brent! He's been hurt!"

"Oh, dear God, no!" exclaimed Violet running to the door.

Gilbert, with Brent's head in his hands, was leading the way in. Four other men were helping to carry Brent.

"Can you get him upstairs to his bed?" Susan asked as she dashed up the steps to prepare the way.

Violet called out to Levi to come downstairs quickly. The tone of her voice told him that something bad had happened, and he nearly flew down the steps.

"Bring water and pans upstairs—as soon as you can, Levi. It's Brent!"

"Dear Gawd!" he gasped, and disappeared in the kitchen.

At the head of the stairs, Bonnie Anne and J.J. were watching what was happening, Evelina behind them with the baby in her arms. As they recognized their daddy being carried up the stairs Bonnie Anne and J.J. broke into loud wails of terror. Violet gave them a quick hug, tried to reassure them, and sternly told Evelina to take the crying children back to their beds and make them stay there.

By the time they got Brent to the bed in the guest room, Susan was almost in an uncharacteristic state of hysteria, as though somehow it was her fault to have induced Brent and Violet to come out to Vicksburg, although she had had the presence of mind to throw the covers back so the men could lay Brent gently on the sheets.

As Violet went to work, Susan got control of herself and became the cool, efficient assistant that was more characteristic of her, with a display of the same kind of courage that she had shown in racing to the rescue of little Bonnie Anne on the railroad track.

Violet kneeled at Brent's side and asked Gilbert to bring a lamp close by. Brent was conscious, but apparently weak from loss of blood. Eyes not sharply focused, he looked at Violet and murmured feebly, "Well, looks like we have a little mess here."

She struggled to maintain a calm demeanor. "Yes, you old goose, what did you mean, going flying down the street like that? No, don't answer, save your strength. Let me see what we have here." Right away she could see that he still was bleeding profusely from an ugly wound that appeared to be just above his heart.

"Levi, where's that water?" she called loudly, and to Susan she said, "Get some towels, quickly."

Susan was back in a minute with towels, followed by Levi with water.

Violet grabbed a towel, rolled it up, put it over the wound, and applied pressure. "We've got to stop the bleeding," she explained to the others. She looked up at Gilbert and asked, "He's got to have a doctor. Is there one near?"

"Yes, just a couple of blocks away. I'll run get him." He turned and started running toward the stairs.

"Gilbert, wait!" called Violet. Turning to Susan she asked, "Susan, do you have any carbolic acid in the house?"

"No, I'm afraid not. Can we get some?"

"I hope so, and I'm sure you don't have any chloroform."

"Oh, no."

"Gilbert," Violet called. As he reappeared at the door she asked, "Is there any way we can get some carbolic acid? We need to get it quickly to prevent infection."

"They should have it at the apothecary, which doesn't open until eight in the morning. But I'll see if I can rouse Mr. Hooker, the owner, to go down and open up for that."

"And see if you can get some chloroform too—and some Vaseline."

"All right, Violet. I'll run by to get Doc Brown to hurry over, and then I'll run on to Hooker's."

"And be careful and don't get yourself shot, too," Susan admonished him.

He grabbed his service revolver and ran down the stairs and out the front door, letting the door slam after him.

Violet continued to apply pressure to the wound, with the towels soaking up what seemed to be a great deal of blood. She murmured terms of endearment and encouragement as she worked on Brent's wound. His eyes remained closed, and he made no reply other than a moan now and then. It seemed ages before Gilbert returned. Actually, he was back in forty-five minutes with the required materials, though the doctor had not yet arrived.

"What happened?" Susan asked.

Still breathing hard from his race to the doctor's and the apothecary's, Gilbert answered, "Doc Brown was out on another case, but Mrs. Brown assured me that when he returned she would urge him to get here as quickly as possible."

"What took so long at the apothecary," Susan asked.

"I didn't know that it did," he replied between deep breaths. "Mr. Hooker got up right away and ran downstairs with me to the apothecary. There were a few hoodlums there, and they weren't going to let us in. 'A man's life may depend on this,' Mr. Hooker said. 'We don' care,' one of them said, 'yall keel uh hundred uf our brudduh, an' we gwine ta git revenge.' Well, I took out my revolver, shouted 'Stand aside,' and fired three shots over their heads in rapid succession, and they fled in short order."

"Oh, Gilbert, how brave," sighed Susan in both admiration and dismay that her husband may have been in danger.

Violet already was pouring carbolic acid into a vessel of warm water to make what she estimated to be a five percent solution. Then, removing the towel, she began sprinkling the carbolic acid solution on the wound. Brent remained quiet, eyes still closed.

It was another hour before the doctor arrived. Apologizing for his late arrival, Doctor Brown examined the wound. Taking note of what Violet had been doing, he said, "That carbolic acid probably was a good idea. Now, there are four big dangers here. One is infection; another is gangrene, caused by loss of blood to the soft tissues; another is the loss of blood to the general system, and finally, there is always the danger of pneumonia or pneumonitis, which may be more acute if the lung has been punctured."

Probing further, the doctor said, "Mm, the bullet is still in there, and we have got to get it out; otherwise this will never heal, but getting it out will cause considerable pain and may cause further loss of blood."

Just then Brent opened his eyes and whispered in a voice barely audible, "Go ahead with whatever you have to do, Doc."

Violet looked at the doctor and said, "We were able to get some chloroform. Will that help? Is he strong enough to take it?"

The doctor nodded and replied, "I believe he is strong enough, and the chloroform should be a help in relieving him of the intense pain. It will make our probing for the bullet near his heart—near the aorta and the pulmonary artery—much safer by enabling him to lie still. Can you administer the chloroform, Mrs. Sutler?"

"I used to give it sometimes in the soldiers' hospitals during the War, though we were out of chloroform most of the time."

"Yes, I know. Well, all right, let's get a clean cloth, fold it like a handkerchief, soak it with chloroform, hold it over his nose and mouth, and ask him to breathe deeply until he falls asleep. Keep a sharp lookout—not too much at first, then a little more if he wakes up too soon."

Violet did as she was told while the doctor began probing with his forceps. No further chloroform was necessary before he triumphantly held up the bullet and dropped it in a pan. Then he applied sutures.

He walked away from the bed and said to Violet, "I think we have stopped the bleeding though he still is dangerously weak. We should tell within a day or two whether any infection has set in, and it may be another four or five days before we know if pneumonia is going to develop."

Violet sank into a chair, weak with relief that the worst was over, that the doctor had been able to remove the bullet from such a dangerous location, and that Brent was still alive. She found herself praying silently, *Dear God, how could I live without this man; please, please don't let him die. I need him so; the children need their father.*

She looked up at the doctor and said, "Doctor Brown, thank you so much for your prompt and skillful attention. Thank you for helping my husband."

"Glad to do whatever I can, Mrs. Sutler."

They both looked anxiously toward the bed as Brent began talking, "Commence firing, Mr. Hawkins; get the damned pirates; keep them away from the cannon!"

The doctor smiled faintly and said, "He's beginning to come out from under the chloroform."

Violet watched patiently, stroking Brent's forehead with her soft hands, occasionally wiping his face with a damp, cool cloth. In time his eyes opened with a flutter. He looked around without turning his head until he saw Violet. She held his hand firmly.

"Welcome back to the real world," she said with tenderness.

"That was quite a battle," he whispered weakly. "I think the damned pirates got me right here. He started to point to his left shoulder with his right hand, but a sharp pain caused him to let it drop at his side as he let out a moan.

The next day Violet sat in vigil at Brent's side. About noontime she wrote out several messages and asked Gilbert to take them to Western Union to send by telegraph—one to the lieutenant governor at the State House in Columbia; one to Charlotte with a request that she get word to Leo and Mammy at Fair Oaks and to Beulah and Job at the town house; one asking for prayers to the church ministers in Columbia and Stateburg; one to Cedric at the warehouse in Columbia; one to John Fraser at the railroad office; one to Reverend Jackson at *The Joshua School* in Sumter; and one to Brent's father in Charleston—notifying them all that Brent had been injured and their return to South Carolina would be delayed for a week or so.

All afternoon she kept praying for Brent, and each time she prayed she recalled their talk in New Orleans that when one prayed, something should be done about it, and then she would sprinkle more carbolic acid on his wound.

Toward evening, Brent's condition took a turn for the worse. He became perceptibly weaker, his pulse rapid but feeble. He slipped in and out of consciousness.

"Oh, God, no, not this," Violet said, only barely audible as she burst into tears. She ran into the hall and called, "Gilbert! Gilbert! Run for the doctor. Quick!"

"I'm leaving now," he called up, grabbing his coat and hat off the lower hall clothes tree. He was out of the house in a flash.

Susan came upstairs and waited with Violet. Gilbert returned in a few minutes with word that the doctor was out on another call and was not expected back for two or three hours.

Violet was alarmed. "Can't you go find him? Isn't there another doctor you can get?"

Gilbert looked at Brent lying white and still upon the bed. "There's one on the other side of town. We don't know him very well, but I'll try to get him." He took off again, this time to get his horse and buggy to carry him across town.

Brent opened his eyes again. They seemed to be getting that dreaded glassy look.

What more could the doctor do, even if he were here, Violet asked herself.

In a feeble whisper Brent asked if he might see the children. Violet nodded to Susan who went out and returned shortly, leading the two children by their hands. Obviously they had been coached to put on a brave front.

Bonnie Anne stepped to the right side of the bed, trembling a little. She leaned over and kissed him on the cheek. He gave her a weak hug with one arm, forced a smile, and asked, "How's my little girl? Now, I may be away for a while, will you help Mommy all you can—"

She nodded.

"—and be a good girl?"

Bonnie Anne nodded again and turned away to hide her tears.

J.J. stepped up. Brent grasped his hand and tried to squeeze it hard, but his illness had sapped his strength. "Well, young man, I may be away for a while. While I am away, will you look after Mommy and Bonnie Anne—"

J.J. nodded and put his cheek on Brent's, then stood up and answered, "Yes, sir, but Daddy, please don't be gone long."

"—and be a good boy?"

"Yes, sir," J.J. said bravely, and he turned and ran out of the room. The last person whom he had seen who had been shot was Little Josh.

Chapter 64

Goin' Home

1875

After about an hour, Gilbert returned with the news that the doctor across town was not there. His housekeeper reported that he had gone on a trip to New Orleans and wasn't expected back for five days. Gilbert then rode over to Doctor Brown's office again, but he was still out on a call. The doctor had sent a message to his wife that he would likely be up all night with his patient. Gilbert left a written note for Mrs. Brown to give her husband, as soon as he returned. In it he asked the doctor to come over to the Hudson house right away, that Mr. Sutler appeared to have taken a turn for the worse.

Searching for some spark of light on a dark night, reaching out for some ray of hope in a possibly hopeless situation, Violet sat for hours at Brent's side, holding his hand, checking his pulse, whispering heartening and supportive comments, kissing him gently, and reassuring him of her love and faith that he would be all right. Finally, from sheer exhaustion, she allowed herself to lie down beside Brent, on the right side of the bed so as not to disturb his wound.

When she awoke sunshine was flooding through the window and Doctor Brown was standing at the foot of the bed. Startled, she sat up and looked at Brent. His eyes were open, and he managed a slight smile. She rose from the bed, ran over to the washstand and splashed cold water on her face. She returned for another look at Brent and dared hope that he was much improved. A bit of color had returned to his ashen face, and his eyes seemed clearer.

"I had no intention of falling asleep," she explained to the doctor. "I thought I would just lie down for a few minutes and rest."

"I liked your warmth beside me," murmured Brent.

The doctor smiled in understanding and said that he would call again the next morning. He motioned for Violet to accompany him out to the hall. When they were out of hearing of the bedroom, Violet whispered, "Oh, Doctor Brown, last evening I thought we had lost him. Now he seems much better. Is he going to be all right?"

"Mrs. Sutler, I will be honest with you," the doctor replied softly. "He is a very weak man. Get him to eat as much soup as possible, a little at a time, all through the day. If he continues to show improvement till evening, then I believe he will have overcome the initial loss of blood. I see no sign of infection so far, but you may want to continue to sprinkle a little of your carbolic acid solution through the day. If all goes well until tomorrow, then we still have to worry about pneumonia for another three or four days. Keep up your good work and don't give up hope now—and don't let *him* give up hope." He patted her shoulder in reassurance and took his leave.

All during the morning, Violet encouraged Brent to eat a little soup. She fed him several small bowls of chicken broth, creamed potato soup, and creamed tomato soup—trying to vary the menu so he would eat more. In the afternoon he ate some milk toast, and continued to show marked improvement. In the evening she was able to get him to eat a little more soup, after which the children came in to pay their daddy another visit. They noticed his voice was stronger, and their mother seemed happier and more relaxed. After kissing him good-night, they skipped to their rooms, with the feeling that now their world somehow seemed more secure.

The next morning Doctor Brown confirmed that indeed the first crisis had passed, and there still was no sign of infection. He advised Violet to continue giving him small meals of soup or milk toast whenever Brent would eat it.

Brent continued to improve steadily. The doctor said that Brent's naturally healthy and strong body and his stamina were all working to his advantage. On the third day, Brent was sitting up and asking for real food, something that would stick to his ribs longer than soup, and on the fourth day he was complaining that he couldn't afford to stay in bed much longer; he had to take care of his business.

That afternoon when Doctor Brown stopped by, Violet asked, "Do I dare inquire when Brent may be able to travel? He's beginning to chaff at the bit, and he does seem so much stronger now, though he still tires quite easily if he sits up in bed too long."

The doctor considered her question thoughtfully. "It's a long trip, isn't it? Well, I would say that in three more days, if he continues to show improvement, and there is no sign of pneumonia, and if he feels up to it, he can go. Of course, you must try to find a way to allow him to rest comfortably while traveling; he'll need to be able to lie down during the day as well as the night. And he must not carry anything."

"Doc, I feel up to it right now," Brent declared.

"Well, now I wouldn't exactly say that, not quite yet," laughed the doctor, pleased at the progress of his patient. He had become rather fond of this young couple from South Carolina.

After another couple of days had passed without setback or relapse, Violet announced that they would plan to leave for home on Monday, February 22nd. Gilbert volunteered to arrange to have two cots for Violet and Brent to be installed in the baggage car of the Illinois Central at Jackson. Since the local Vicksburg train had no baggage car, nor much of anything else, it would be necessary for Brent to sit up the two hours from Vicksburg to Jackson.

The trip to Jackson was rough on Brent. Violet could tell the shaking and jerking of the car intensified his pain, but Brent assured Violet that it was no more difficult for him than for the others. At Jackson they were pleased to find that they were expected, and cots had indeed been installed in the baggage car. Evelina and Levi and the children found seats in the day coach next to the baggage car, though they all joined Violet and Brent in the baggage car for the picnic lunch that Susan had prepared for them, and they remained together until the first stop an hour later. Brent then was glad for the chance to rest quietly on the cot, and Violet was too.

At Grand Junction, Tennessee, they had to change trains, and some railroad baggage men obligingly transferred the cots to the other train. At Chattanooga they again stopped at the inn for overnight while the cots were stored in the station. Brent admitted that he was glad to rest in a real bed for a change.

The next morning they returned to another train with the same arrangements. At the lunch stop and then at an afternoon stop, Levi brought food for Violet and Brent while Evelina took the children to eat in the station restaurant. *What on earth would we do without Evelina and Levi's help,* Violet thought. *We are so fortunate they are part of our family.*

Again they had to change at Augusta. When they pulled in to Charleston, James and Isabel Sutler and Phoebe were at the station to greet them. Isabel Sutler was visibly worried about her son, though she never had been fully informed about the extent of his injury. She was horrified when later the details of the incident in Vicksburg were explained to her.

Brent was showing fatigue and discomfort from his travels, and Violet was glad for the chance to have him rest at the home of his parents for two days before continuing on the final leg of their journey home. The return of his energy and improvement in his physical condition after rest relieved his mother's solicitous worries.

Brent was elated when they transferred to a Pullman on the *Columbia Limited* on Carolina Rail. He was feeling better and he and Violet decided, rather than requesting a special stop at Fair Oaks because of his injury, they would continue on to Columbia. She knew that Mammy would be distressed that they had not gotten off there, but Brent wanted to talk with Cedric about the business. The night run to Columbia seemed a luxury after the previous days' travel.

Cedric and Uncle Job were there at the station in Columbia to meet them when they got off the train at seven o'clock in the morning. Both had brought carriages to transport everybody and their baggage. When they got to the town house, Charlotte and Leland were there to see if they could help. Slowly, and with some pain, Brent made his way up to the bedroom. There he slept all day, awoke for a fairly hearty supper, and then slept all night.

Satisfied that Brent's strength was holding up, Violet decreed that in two days they would move back to Fair Oaks for the rest of the year. It would be quiet and there would be more help to look after Brent, and when he felt like it he could work in the plantation office and keep in touch with his activities by telegraph.

They returned to Fair Oaks on an afternoon train. The handcar was at the shed and with Bonnie Anne and J.J. pumping furiously on the other end of the teeter-totter-like handle, Levi propelled the car with all the people to the house. He then returned for the baggage.

Brent was happy to be back at Fair Oaks. Will Anderson was at the house when they arrived. He wanted to examine Brent's wound and make sure everything was healing satisfactorily. When he had finished he announced to his waiting audience just outside the bedroom door that Brent's wound was coming along nicely but that it would be a while before Brent could engage in any vigorous activity.

Rex, the collie, slipped in the door and lay beside Brent's bed, where he remained day and night except for brief trips outside. He would not leave Brent even to eat, and Levi had to bring food and water up to the faithful dog.

Within a week Brent was up and around enough to take his dinners and suppers regularly with the family and to spend a few hours each morning in the office—at the telegraph, answering his mail, reading papers, and making plans, and everywhere that he went Rex was sure to follow along as though fearful of letting his master out of his sight. Brent arranged for regular mail service—for clerks on the railway post office cars to drop a bag with his mail and newspapers at the little shed each time they passed. For outgoing mail he had Enoch and Levi rig a device for hanging a mail bag on a pole, with an arm and latch catch release, where the mail car, with a retractable steel arm, could snatch the bag while the train was traveling at full speed.

Now Levi, in addition to his other duties, became the chief courier. Each morning and evening he would take the handcar out to the shed by the railroad to pick up the bag of mail that had been dropped and to hang the bag of outgoing mail on the release pole.

Violet was able to devote more of her attention to the plantation. On the basis of her reading and thinking she decided to double crop the corn this year. If it worked out satisfactorily, yield per acre might be doubled. On the basis of her own record keeping she knew that the last killing frost very seldom occurred after about March 14th, and the first frost of autumn was not until about November 21st. This gave a growing season of at least 252 days. This should allow ample time for two crops, especially if she changed from the common dent corn to the flint corn that was grown in New England and Wisconsin where the growing season was shorter.

Further, she decided that it would be wise to double-crop the corn with the alfalfa so that the second crop of corn would be planted in the field where the first crop of alfalfa had been grown, because corn used up the nitrogen while alfalfa replenished it. It still should be possible to get multiple cuttings of alfalfa from each crop, she reasoned.

As for fertilizer, she was a little reluctant to use more of the Peruvian guano after hearing in New Orleans from Bruce and Brent about the use of coolie labor to bring it out, though she was not sure to what extent such exploitation still was going on. Instead she would rely more on the relatively cheap Charleston phosphates.

Finally she decided that she would put three of the big fields in cotton, totaling six hundred plus acres. She would double crop corn with the alfalfa and with the winter wheat now coming up in bright green, for one hundred acres each. The fifth field, half plowed during the autumn where corn had been grown the previous year, now would be harrowed and oats planted, and after the harvest in late June would stand fallow. The rest of that field would remain fallow all year.

This year she planned no tobacco on the main plantation. The Old Place, the plots under Farley's supervision, would be planted in two hundred acres of tobacco and two hundred acres of cotton.

Once the crops were in, Violet turned to a special project largely for Brent's benefit. She arranged for Enoch, with half a dozen helpers, to build beside the training track a small barn for the race horses. It had four stalls facing out on a covered porch that ran the length of the barn, an accessory room, feed room, and sulky shed. It was all finished before Brent had any idea it was being done.

On a warm, sunny day in April, Brent walked out to a chair in the back yard and sat there for a couple of hours. Bonnie Anne and J.J. came out to be with him.

"Is this your get-well day, Daddy?" asked J.J. "I 'member my get-well day when I had the whooping cough, and I got to sit out here with the baby chicks."

Brent smiled and answered, "Yes, J.J., now I know just how you felt. I guess I won't forget this day either.

Violet came up, winked to the children who had been very good about keeping the secret, and led Brent around to where he could see the new race horse barn.

"Surprise, Daddy! Surprise!" shouted the children, jumping up and down in delight.A broad smile spread across Brent's face. "Great day of the morning! Is that what I think it is? Let's go have a look."

She shook her head, grinning, "Honey, that's not a short walk, and you've been up too long already today. We'll go out in the morning, first thing after breakfast, I promise."

"As you say, nurse," he responded in pretended meekness. The children giggled in appreciation.

Chapter 65

Rabbit Tobacco

1875

One warm afternoon during the first week of June, after Violet and Brent had been working for a while in the office, she suggested that they go for a walk. Without hats or scarves they went out the front door, by the magnolia trees with their large, cream, sweet-scented blossoms, and then around to the flower garden near the east lawn. Brent took her hand as they walked along brick paths lined with beds of brilliantly blooming roses—red, pink, yellow, white—and jasmine, pansies, anemones, larkspur, bachelor buttons, gardenias, phlox, chrysanthemums and paperwhites.

They paused quietly to listen to the song of a Carolina wren. Violet walked ahead a few steps and then turned to face Brent. A gust of wind disheveled her shiny hair. Another gust restored it. Imitating Brent's smirk that he put on when he was about to introduce some special development, she asked, "How are you feeling now?"

"Oh, fine, fine," he answered, "strong as an ox."

She giggled softly and glanced up at him from under her long lashes. "Maybe you should be saying strong as a bull."

"Why do you say that?"

"Well, darling, New Orleans must have done it."

"Done what?"

"Done gonna make you a daddy again!" She answered, laughing at her own vernacular.

"Again? My God, that bullet must have been more potent than I thought!" Then, recuperating his aplomb, he put his arms around her tenderly and said, "Darling, that is wonderful, just wonderful." He kissed her gently.

"I think so, too," she whispered back between kisses. She was happy that Brent seemed as pleased about the prospect of another baby as she had found herself to be.

Holding hands, they walked on along the garden paths. Brent asked, "Just when do you reckon this new arrival to join the family?"

"December, I should think."

"What a wonderful Christmas present for us all. Have you told Mammy yet? You know how she loves babies around the house."

"No, of course not, I wanted to tell you first, silly goose, but if I don't tell her soon, she'll be suspecting. You know how observant she can be. And I know Evelina will be excited; we'll need to give some thought to getting her more help now."

"True." They walked on a little farther, and then he added protectively, "Well, I don't think it would be wise for you to be riding Hermes over the plantation from now on."

"I know, but I thought maybe I could use the buggy for another month or so."

"Ah, Honey, you know that can be just as rough and bumpy, especially by the fields and through the orchard, and over by the pond. Let me make your inspections for you."

She was pleased that he wanted to take on this responsibility for her, though she would miss this part of her work and especially her conversations with the workers and their children. She knew that Leo would come to the house regularly to keep her abreast of developments and to discuss what should be done about the place, but her regular inspections were a part of her life on this land she loved so much. Still, a healthy baby would be worth it all. So she said, "Oh, Brent, that sounds good. Thank you. I'm sure you'll do fine, and I'm willing to bet that you will come to enjoy your inspections."

"Mm, likely." After another walk and pause, Brent turned as a thought struck him. "Violet, I just thought of something." He grinned mischievously.

"Oh, dear, I recognize that grin on your face, the one that always makes me wonder what's coming next. Well, what is it?" She gave him a wide smile of encouragement.

"Well, my Love, well...since you won't be riding around any more this year...I was just thinking...that maybe we could allow Hermes to race one more season—"

"Why, you silly goose, is that all you're thinking about?"

"No, no, my little gosling," he grinned, "but we really should be getting the best use that we can out of that beautiful new horse barn, don't you think? After all, you did build it."

She laughed at his logic. "Why, of course, but what about poor Midnight Star and Bay Rum?" she reminded him.

"Oh, of course we'll race them too, but you know that Hermes is a real winner, and whenever I take him anywhere that he's not known, everybody will bet against him because he has four white legs, and we can clean up"

She reacted with a giggle to that comment. She knew the old saying about a horse having four white legs being no good was ridiculous, but she also knew that lots of people believed that myth, and she found herself agreeing with Brent that they ought to take advantage of it if they could.

"All right," she said, "go on and race Hermes for the rest of this year—as long as you don't lose money. Remember, my dear husband, the whole idea is to make our gains by winning the purses, not at the betting windows."

"Yes, ma'am, I consider myself forewarned," he chuckled.

Brent was riding Jeb out toward the training track one hot August afternoon when he saw a wisp of smoke drifting out of one of the side windows of the big horse barn. Riding quickly up to the window, he peered inside. There were J.J. and two little black boys sitting in a pile of straw in an empty stall, smoking. Their backs were to the window, and behind them the straw appeared to be smoldering. Quickly Brent galloped around to the main door, leaped from his horse, grabbed a water bucket, filled it from the horse trough, dashed down to the burning stall, and threw the water on the fire, drenching the boys in the process.

"What's going on here?" he shouted angrily.

The two black boys, their eyes as big as saucers, jumped up, took off at a dead run, and disappeared. With a look of startled dismay on his face, J.J. jumped up and put his hand behind him. "Nothin'," he said guiltily, his eyes not meeting Brent's.

"Nothing, indeed, "Brent shot back, "don't you know you had set the straw on fire? You could have burned the barn down! And what do you have in your hand, young man?"

"Nothin', Daddy," J.J. answered, his hand still behind his back.

"Show me!"

Hesitatingly, J.J. held out his hand to show the butt of a clumsily made cigarette.

"And what's that?"

"A cigarette."

Brent turned and walked over to the charred straw and stomped on it to make sure that all the fire was extinguished. Then he picked up a shingle from near the outer wall. Turning back to J.J., Brent said, with exasperation in his voice, "Bend over, son."

Trembling, J.J. complied, and Brent lifted the shingle and administered a sharp blow to the boy's posterior. Immediately J.J. burst into tears. Brent handed him the water bucket and said, "Now take this and run back to the water trough and fill it up, and bring it back here and throw the water on the straw so we can be sure the fire is out–quickly!"

J.J. did as he was told and then broke into uncontrollable sobs. Brent could see that this was not because he was hurting from the blow, but because he had disappointed his father.

"Now tell me about this," Brent demanded. "Where did you get those cigarettes?"

Between sobs the boy answered, "Made 'em."

"From what?"

"Just some of your paper and rabbit tobacco."

"Where did you find the rabbit tobacco?"

"Erasmus and Seth found it in the fallow field, and they said it was all right to smoke."

"Son, one important lesson you must learn is that you don't do what other boys tell you; you do what you yourself know is the right thing."

"But, Daddy," gulped J.J., "I didn't think there was anything wrong with smokin' 'cause you smoke all the time."

At that Brent was taken aback for a minute, then he went on, "Well, if you thought there was nothing wrong with it, why were you hiding in the barn to do it?"

"Cause I was afraid Mommy wouldn't like it. She don't even like it very much when you smoke."

Brent flashed a grin–which he concealed quickly. "Well, son, you shouldn't do it until you are a little older. Actually, I guess rabbit tobacco will not hurt you much, but you see, the big danger here was in starting a fire in the barn. You might have burned up the barn and the horses."

J.J. replied, sadly, "Yes, sir, I never thought of that. Oh, that would be awful, Daddy, just awful. Oh, Daddy, I won't do it any more, I promise."

"Good. Now I will say you shouldn't smoke until you are eighteen; then I shall raise no objection. Understand, J.J.?"

J.J. nodded. "Yes, sir," he said meekly.

Brent took a cigar from his pocket, lit it, and handed it to J.J. "Here, now smoke this."

J.J. looked at his father in surprise.

"Take some puffs."

J.J. took some quick puffs and began coughing.

"Take some more puffs."

J.J. obediently did as he was told. This time he coughed until his eyes began watering and tears slid down his cheeks. After a minute or two he said, "Oh, Daddy, I don't feel so good. Please don't make me smoke any more. I don't like it."

"Well now, smoking is not so good, is it? Do you think you can wait until you're eighteen?"

"Oh, yes, Daddy, it's awful!" He had another coughing spell.

Brent paused to give J.J. a chance to gain his composure and stop coughing. Brent placed his hand on the boy's shoulder and said in a gentle voice, "Son, we all make mistakes, all of us. And when we make a mistake, the only thing to do is to own up to it, say we're sorry, promise not to do it again, and make amends for it."

The boy looked up at his father, his heart in his eyes, "I'm sorry, Daddy."

Brent smiled. "Yes, I'm sure you are."

"And I want to make amends like you say, but," J.J. hesitated, "Daddy, what's *amends*?"

Brent smiled again. "Making amends is repairing the damage, if we can. Now, you run out there by the door and find a pitchfork and fetch it."

Without another word J.J. ran out of the stall and was back quickly with the pitchfork.

"Here," Brent said, "take the pitchfork and pick up all the straw around where it was smoldering, take it outside, and throw it on the manure pile. Then take your fork and bring in some fresh straw and put it down here."

The boy quickly and diligently went to work and in only a few minutes had all the charred straw out and the fresh straw in.

"All right," Brent told him, "that's fine. You've make your amends. Now we can just forget about this."

"Thank you, Daddy," said J.J., with a bit of his customary sparkle returning to his eyes.

"And I want you to know that, most of the time, Mommy and I are very pleased with your deportment and your helpfulness. We know you are a good little boy." Brent patted J.J.'s shoulder again and added, "And son, I am very proud of you."

J.J. looked up with a smile, and with the back of his hand he wiped away the remaining tear streaks. "And Daddy, I am very proud of you."

Now Brent's eyes sparkled. He felt a foot taller as he led his son to the horse, helped him on, and they rode back toward the house.

Bonnie Anne and J.J. now ate at the dining table with their parents for most meals. Now twelve and eleven, they had outgrown their child's table and chairs, as well as the sibling rivalry that used to permeate their conversation at mealtimes. Sometimes Violet would keep them at the table after the noon dinner or after supper for instruction in table manners and in etiquette in general. She much preferred this approach to constant correction in table manners during the meal itself. Habitual errors would be noted in these sessions, and she would give directions for improvement.

In one of these sessions after the noonday meal, Violet referred to rules of etiquette that George Washington had learned when he was a boy. She read, "Every action done in company ought to be done with some sign of respect to those present...Sing not to yourself with a humming noise or drum with your fingers or feet."

Violet looked directly at J.J. who abruptly stopped drumming with his fingers on the table.

Violet resumed her reading: "If anyone comes to speak to you while you are sitting, stand up though he be your inferior...Persons of low degree ought not to use many ceremonies to lords and others of high degree, but respect and highly honor them, and those of high degree ought to treat those of low degree with affability and courtesy, without arrogance..."

She explained that the purpose of good manners is to make others feel at ease, that no one should be made to feel uncomfortable. She emphasized that one should not take advantage of anyone of a lower station, and that one should always be kind, calm, courteous, and considerate toward others, and in particular to all servants, even the most humble of them.

Violet also had been continuing piano lessons for the children and in more or less subtle ways encouraged them to read books. Bonnie Anne took to both of these avenues with enthusiasm. J.J. enjoyed reading, but he was beginning to object more and more to the piano lessons although earlier he had shown an adeptness for this instrument.

One day after dinner he blurted out, "I would rather pitch horse manure than take these old piano lessons."

"Well, you may get your chance to do that," Violet shot back. Then, thinking better of it, for she didn't want to alienate him from music altogether, she said, "No, if you really don't want to continue to learn to play the piano, I don't want to force you to, but I hope you will come in sometimes and listen to Bonnie Anne and me play."

"Oh, yes, Mommy, I'll do that," he assured her, relieved that he didn't have to take lessons any more. He just didn't like to sit still for such long periods, he told her.

Brent then suggested that J.J. fill the void by learning to be a really good telegraph operator. J.J. was thrilled that his father wanted to teach him to use the telegraph, and he promised to take twice weekly telegraph lessons and to practice daily, completely forgetting that these demanded sitting still, too.

"You can be a great help to me, son," Brent told him, "if you can monitor the telegraph for messages and for news, and if you can send messages for me."

J.J. clapped his hands with excitement. Now *this* was something really important. This is what *men* did, business men like his daddy.

Several days later Violet suggested to Bonnie Anne that perhaps she would like to learn a little bookkeeping—how to keep accounts of receipts and expenditures. To this too, Bonnie Anne enthusiastically agreed. When it came time to call a meeting of the Board of Directors of Carolina Rail, Violet had Bonnie Anne assist in preparing the letters and addressing the envelopes in her neat, well-formed handwriting.

With the cotton harvest in October and November, Violet gave her attention to more efficient reclamation of the cottonseed—the pressing of the seed for oil and the use of the residue as feed and fertilizer.

The big event in November was Hermes' appearance in the race at the state fair in Columbia. Violet was not traveling, but she couldn't conceal a sense of excitement as the groom and swipe loaded Hermes onto a railroad car and Brent and the two drivers joined them as Hermes was on the way to the greatest race of his life.

Five days later, J.J. came running out of the office with a report that there was a message from Daddy on the telegraph: HERMES WINS IN THREE HEATS IN RECORD TIME.

Chapter 66

A Hunt for the Old Days

1875

On the second Saturday in November, Violet heard a horse galloping up the lane. Soon there was a knock on the door. She opened it to find Ramey, the Frierson's house servant, with his hat in one hand and a note from Sarah Frierson in the other. She greeted the elderly man with affection, for she had known him all her life, and suggested he go around to the kitchen where Mammy would give him something to refresh him while he waited for Violet's reply.

She carried the note into the library where Brent was relaxing, catching up on his newspaper reading.

"Who was that?" he asked.

"Ramey. He brought a note over from Sarah." She took the note out of its envelope, unfolded it, and read it aloud to Brent:

My dear Violet and Brent,

John and I would like to stop by tomorrow afternoon, about three o'clock, if this is convenient with you. We have two guests with us for the week-end and would like to bring them with us. You, of course, know Patricia Rutledge, Susan's schoolmate at Edge Hill. Indeed, she was one of Susan's wedding attendants, wasn't she? Well anyhow, you will recall that shortly after Susan's wedding Patricia went to visit some relatives in Virginia and ended up marrying a fine young man from Norfolk, who turned out to be John's second cousin once removed. Anyway, Harrison, that's Patricia's husband, has somehow managed to purchase Midlands Plantation from that Yankee Carpetbagger Smith who took it over when Archibald Martin disappeared after his second wife died. So they'll be your neighbors! Of course the partly burned house and fields are in great disrepair—that Yankee didn't know a thing about running a place like Midlands, and of course he sold off a great deal of the land, but Harrison wants to talk to Brent about some possibilities he has in mind, and to meet Susan's "folks". The two girls correspond fairly frequently, as you no doubt know. And Patricia is so anxious to see all of you and Fair Oaks again.

So do let me know if this time is convenient. Until then, dear friend, I am,

Most cordially,
Sarah Frierson

"Well, how about that!" exclaimed Brent. "It'll be nice to see Patricia again and to meet her husband, and I must say, I am delighted that the old Midlands place will be fixed up again."

"Me, too, but have you seen it lately?"

"Oh, yes, I've ridden over that way a few times when I've had nothing else to do. It's always kind of worried me that old Archibald just up and disappeared. Not in his nature. He was too set in his ways to behave in that manner."

"True. I never thought it like him to do that."

"Don't think I never noticed how he looked at you out of the sides of his eyes, literally drooling, after his first wife died, and before I joined the navy. No doubt, he was probably hoping I'd not return from the navy."

"Why, Brent!"

"Nevertheless, I bet he was. After all, my dear, you are an absolutely beautiful woman, and to tell you the truth, I can't say I blame old Archibald one bit," he replied laughing.

"Well, stop talking that nonsense, you silly goose." She suddenly recalled those sly looks Archibald Martin used to give her at church. I always wondered if that Yankee Carpetbagger had something to do with his disappearance. It wasn't long after that that Midlands was picked up for back taxes by that Yankee, Smith, you know."

"Yes, and after he moved in I rode over to offer my help and made a few tactful suggestions on running the place, based on our successful experiences here at Fair Oaks. He had a tantrum, told me to get off his place and never set foot on it again, that he didn't need any advice from any dumb southerner. So I did and I didn't, until I heard he'd left town, then I rode over to see what condition the place was in. I just know I'm damn glad he's gone."

The Friersons and Stuarts arrived promptly at three o'clock. Fabian took the horse and carriage around back, while the guests were ushered into the parlor by Bonnie Anne and J.J. who had rushed to the door before Jarvis to greet them with hoops of joy. The Friersons had always made much over the children and never failed to bring them a small delicacy or little present.

Jarvis had followed to take the wraps and then left to hang them up. Violet gave Patricia a welcoming hug and Sarah a kiss on her cheek. Then she stepped back to take a look at Susan's best friend.

"Why, Patricia, you're even lovelier; you're like a flower in bloom!" exclaimed Violet warmly. Patricia had indeed grown into a lovely young woman. Her soft brown hair fell in natural curls that framed her sweet face. Her eyes were slate gray and now sparkled with pleasure at Violet's remarks, and her lips were full and pink. She wore a becoming gray dress that matched her eyes, and the pink trim of the dress matched the glow on her cheeks.

Patricia proudly introduced her husband. "Violet and Brent, I want to present my husband, Harrison, and I know you'll come to love him just as I do. He's made me so happy, deciding to move back here and all." She turned to the tall, smiling young man with reddish hair and deep brown eyes. "Harrison, meet Violet and Brent."

He bowed slightly, saying, "Miss Violet, Mister Brent, I consider it an honor to be presented to you. I've heard so much about you from my wife, and from Susan's letters, too. Needless to say, we are all delighted that we shall be your neighbors, and I hope we'll be seeing each other right often."

Violet invited her guests to be seated, called Ellie and asked her to bring more hot chocolate for all, including the children, and then, turning to Patricia she said, "Oh, it's so good to have you back home and to meet you, Harrison. It'll be wonderful having you for neighbors, and what fun for Susan when she comes for a visit! Susan told me that you had written that twice when in Richmond, you called on Grandmama Lee. How did you find her?"

"Fine, hale and hearty, full of energy and doing all kinds of charitable things as usual. She's truly a remarkable woman, isn't she?"

"Oh, indeed," breathed Violet, "and I do miss her so."

"Well, she misses you all, too. She told me that you and Brent wanted her to move here to Fair Oaks—on a permanent basis. She says she loves you all with all her heart, and it would be wonderful to be close to you and the grandchildren, but she just has too many memories there, and she's too old to change, and she does have lots of friends there—though she says they are getting old!"

"I know. She's told us all those things; perhaps it's selfish of me. And I do worry about her being alone..."

"Oh, my goodness, Violet, from what I hear, she's always has company or is going some place to help somebody. I tell you, she's an inspiration to us all."

For the next hour, they talked of Patricia's stay in Virginia, her marriage to Harrison, and their decision to move to Sumter County. She wanted to hear about Susan and Leland and baby George Gilbert—"G.G."—, and about Charlotte and Leland and their baby, little Lee, and if Edge Hill school still existed.

Although Harrison had grown up on a large plantation in the tidewater area of Virginia, it had been some years since he had farmed, and he wanted advice and suggestions from Violet and Brent on revitalizing the sandy soil of Midlands and which crops they had found to be most successful, and where he might find some dependable workers.

John Frierson helped himself to another cookie, looked over at Violet and then at Brent, and said, "Speaking of horses, Harrison asked me last night if we had revived our old habits of fox-hunting in Sumter County." He settled back in his chair, savored a bite of his cookie, and continued, "Ah, Violet, my dear, many a morning your father and I used to race across these fields with our hounds, and with either the huntsman or one of us yelling 'Gone away!' or 'View, halloa!' or 'Tally ho!' Those were the more carefree days for the Major and the rest of us young knaves." He let out a big sigh at the thought of those days.

Sarah broke in. "Not just you men, my dear. You will recall that Rosemary and I and some of the other wives used to hunt, too, although we never liked it very much when the hounds actually ran a fox down. Thank heavens that didn't happen very often."

Violet grimaced, "Or the pads and mask! Daddy told me one time when I complained I thought all that was so gruesome, that most of them rode just for the thrill of riding fast over the meadows and fields, jumping the fences, chasing after the dogs, and the camaraderie of it all. He said, to tell the truth, that he didn't care if they ever seized the fox."

"Neither did my father when we hunted around Charleston," put in Brent, "but, frankly, I always liked the hunt better when we did seize the fox. To me, it was the challenge, the success of getting the best of a smart animal like the fox. Oh, I know, some critics say it's unfair, but I note they don't balk at slaughtering chickens or lambs or calves, which they eat with relish and don't give a chance of escaping, and they don't mind wearing skins in coats and hats or shoes or sitting on furniture covered with skins. And then there are those who hunt deer, and bear, and 'coons, and 'possums, and turkeys and ducks and other birds, and throw hooks with bait in the water and catch innocent fish. What's the difference, I say."

"You've made a point," said Harrison.

Brent mused, "What a shame we don't still have those two English thoroughbred hunters the Major used to own. I never saw horses jump fences and travel at such speeds over the meadows, er, that is of course, except Hermes on the race track. He smiled at Violet."

She grinned, "Let's have a fox-hunt! It's true that many of the big estates have been broken into 'forty-acres' and smaller farms, but we've got all of Fair Oaks and The Old Place, part of the Midlands, and all of the Frierson's Cherry Vale."

The fox-hunt was scheduled for the first Saturday after Thanksgiving, a week after the Stuarts moved into the Midlands old plantation house. Jason, in charge of animal husbandry at Fair Oaks, had been approached for the position of Huntsman again, as he had been years ago for the Major. He accepted with alacrity, reminding everyone of how the Major had relied on him to train and care for the hounds and arrange for the hunts. Brent had acquired a pack of fox-hounds, as had John Frierson, and Harrison Stuart brought his hounds down from Virginia. In all there were twenty-four fox-hounds ready for hunting.

Violet was excited and told Brent she was not going to miss this hunt after so many years. He informed her in a no-nonsense voice that in no way was she to mount a horse, with the baby due in a couple of weeks or so. She would have many opportunities in the future for hunting, and he absolutely would not allow her to put either herself or the baby in a dangerous spot, and that was that.

Looking at his sea-blue eyes, suddenly dark with anger and alarm for her well-being, she capitulated, acknowledging that he was right, but she insisted on taking charge of the Hunt Breakfast at Fair Oaks.

Bonnie Anne and J.J. wanted to mount their ponies and ride along, but here, again, Brent balked, telling them that they might hunt after he had purchased them larger horses. They were older, now, and actually getting too large for their ponies. The children were disappointed, but at the same time they were thrilled at their father's promise to give them new horses. He also planned to get two English thoroughbred hunters for himself and Violet. For these fields and fences he wanted horses of speed and leaping power.

Those living in the vicinity were eager to bring the sport of fox-hunting back and a group of about twenty riders had turned out, on whatever horses they could bring. They had held several meetings for planning the chase. Most everyone wanted Brent to be the Master of Foxhounds, but he gracefully declined, stating that the honor should be John Frierson's since he was senior to Brent in experience. John agreed with cheerful willingness, and then selected other experienced hunters as the Whippers-in, of which Brent was one. It would be their job, along with the Huntsman, to see that the hounds worked properly in the field.

They agreed not to be concerned with "Proper Hunt Attire" for the first chase. The pink (scarlet) coats of the Huntsman and Whippers-in had been long gone, either stolen by Yankee renegades, eaten by moths, or the cloth used for other purposes during the War. If the group decided that hunts would be held on a regular basis, this matter could be taken up at a later time. No one wanted such riding attire to be hastily thrown together.

At the appointed time, the hunters, men and women, mounted their horses, and Violet, the children, and a few of the other wives who were not riding, along with the house servants, gathered in the area west of the carriage house for the Blessing of the Hounds and to see the chase take off. Charlotte and Leland, and Andrew Thompson, had come for Thanksgiving and were taking part in the hunt. Brent's mother and father and his sister, Phoebe, had come from Charleston, but only James Sutler and Phoebe were riding. Will and Mary Anderson came over from Stateburg, and John Manning of Milford House brought along two of his cousins. Charles Rhett and Scott and Edith Carson came over from Sumter. Farley heard about the plans and asked Brent if he might be allowed to join in on the hunt. Brent told him that of course he would be welcome, the more the merrier.

With Brent and Harrison on either side of him, John Frierson held up his hand for silence. A hush quickly fell all around, though inner throbs of excitement brought short breaths to all. "Father Wilson will now give us the blessing," he said simply.

The men removed their hats, and everyone bowed their heads. The priest moved his horse up to the center of the group while all waited.

The hounds looked restlessly about and then at Enoch as if begging him to give the order for them to move on. Brent looked down at the dogs, admiring their compact, muscular bodies, their full heads with broad brows and long, wide muzzles with open nostrils. Their ears were set low and laid close to the cheek. Their eyes were soft and brown. He noted their broad chests, their ribs deep so as to provide plenty of breathing space. Their legs were straight and strong, and their feet were round and cat-like. Their black and tan and white coats were hard and smooth and glossy.

"Let us pray," the priest intoned, "Oh Lord, from whom all good things do come; Grant to us thy humble servants, that by thy holy inspiration we may think those things that are good, and by thy merciful guiding may perform the same; through our Lord

Jesus Christ." He paused a moment as everyone said *Amen* and then he continued, "Bless these hounds who run before us, and all horses and riders who follow; keep them safe from harm and adversity. And thank thee for the privilege of participating in this sport again." Loud *Amens* concluded the prayer.

The hunters, accompanied by the pack of hounds, were led off by the Huntsman toward the place in the field where he expected to find a scent. There he loosed the dogs. Everyone waited with baited breath as the hounds ranged about sniffing and searching for scent-traces in the air and on the ground left by the recent passage of an unsuspecting fox. Soon a hound gave tongue, indicating that it had found a trail, and the other hounds ran over to join him and the pack dashed away following the scent. With a cry of "Gone away!" and another of "Tally-ho!" the riders followed the racing hounds as straight and fast as possible, taking care to remain behind the field of hounds and Whippers-in, and keeping to lanes and gates where possible—but where needful, they jumped fences and rode over fields and meadows.

Several times the cry of "View! halloa!" rang out, signaling the fox had been sighted and invoking new excitement on the part of the hunters. Then suddenly the hounds halted and began giving tongue and milling about a deep hole.

"Damn! He's gone to earth!" exclaimed Brent, taking off his cap and wiping his forehead which had become heavy with perspiration from the frenzy of the chase.

"Well, that's bad luck for us, good luck for the fox, I guess," said John Frierson, riding up to join Brent and watching the hounds scratch at the dirt in frustration. He looked over at Enoch. "Any more chance of finding another one?"

They were now on the back side of Frierson's property. Enoch looked around and nodded, "Yassuh, jes' lemme git dese hounds up and away to yonder, an' ah'll see whut ah kin do." After some effort he was able to calm the hounds and lead them some distance away where they soon began ranging about again, searching for scent-traces. In time, one gave tongue, and the pack took off again, with the riders racing to catch up. After two fences and over a shallow hollow in the ground, they heard "Tally-ho!" ring out.

In the hunters' absence make-shift tables and benches had been set up on the front lawn. These were covered with white tablecloths and decorated with camellia and magnolia leaves and yellow chrysanthemums. Under the wide-spreading branches of one of the oak trees, a refreshment beverage table was filled with goblets and glasses for the varied wines and bourbon set out. This would likely be the first stop of riders for they would be hot and thirsty when they arrived. Aaron and Levi would serve the drinks to the guests.

As soon as Violet heard the sound of hooves coming up the lane, she called to her helpers to begin bringing out the food for the Hunt Breakfast. Mammy, Ellie, Evelina, Jarvis, Levi, the children, and those wives who had not joined in the hunt came carrying baskets of fruit and breads and pastries, and platters of sliced roast beef and roast pork and fried chicken, and egg omelets with Johnnie cakes, and baked pumpkin, and bowls of Brunswick stew, and spinach salad. There were cherry and apple and pumpkin pies.

Fabian and Joseph, with Enoch's help, had trained some of the boys from the worker's village in the care of horses, how to cool them down, rub them down, clean them up, and they all stood waiting to take the horses as the riders dismounted. Harrison and Patricia's two stablemen were also there to help with this. They had brought over two additional horses that the Stuarts lent the Thompsons.

The hunters crossed from the lane through the line of live oak trees and over to the front lawn. Violet and the children ran to Brent. "Well, how did it go?" she asked.

"Daddy, Daddy, did you catch a fox?" the children wanted to know, jumping around in their excitement.

He shook his head. "Not this time, I'm sorry to say. We had two really good chases, but one fox went to earth and the other just plain outsmarted the hounds. Lots of fun, though. Next time we'll get one," he added as he dismounted and handed the reins to Fabian, thanking him for taking the horse.

He put his arm around Violet and led her over to the refreshment table, while the children left to run over to Charlotte and Patricia and ask them about the chase.

"Whew, I need a drink. Haven't had that much exercise in a couple of years."

"You mean, since before you were shot. Do you feel all right?" Violet asked anxiously.

"Feel great, my Love," he said, taking the glass of wine that Aaron had poured. He finished it quickly and handed his glass to Aaron for a refill. By then, the table was crowded with thirsty horsemen and Brent and Violet moved away from the group.

They all stood around, enjoying the invigorating drinks and resting up from their spirited riding, but soon the aroma of the feast awaiting them drew them to the food tables. The early hour of rising and the morning hunt had whetted everybody's appetite. Everyone heartily agreed that even though they came back without a brush, they had had a marvelous time and hoped the hunts would be scheduled on a regular basis.

Chapter 67

Centennial

1876

Five days after the hunt, on Thursday, December 2nd, Violet gave birth to a healthy little boy. Violet had been fearful that the birth would not be easy, since so many years had passed since J.J. was born, but that turned out not to be the case. Little Wade Hampton Sutler decided to make his entrance into his new world as quickly and effortlessly as possible. Consequently, Violet was confined to her bed for only a week, and she was soon up and about, taking care of her family as usual, though she did find the need for a short nap each afternoon for a while. Brent and the children were enchanted with the new baby. J.J. was thrilled to hear that little Wade looked exactly like he did when he was born. Bonnie Anne was disappointed at first that the baby wasn't a girl, but she soon fell in love with her "new little baby doll brother." The house servants were thrilled to have a new baby in the house again, especially Mammy and Evelina.

As the hour approached midnight on December 31, 1875, Violet and Brent sat alone in front of a glowing fireplace in the library of Fair Oaks. They generally had taken little notice of New Year's in recent years, but tonight they were sitting up after everyone else had gone to bed. Rex was snoozing at his customary place by Brent's feet. Violet and Brent were sipping wine, enjoying each other's company, just relaxing.

That is, Violet was trying to relax. She knew it wouldn't be long until little Wade would wake up crying for his next meal. What a hungry little rascal he had turned out to be! And he was already growing–so fast that Brent claimed he could sit and watch him get longer. She smiled at the thought of how much he made over the baby, and then felt sad at the thought that because of the War he had missed ever seeing J.J. as an infant; indeed he missed the first two and a half years of J.J's life. And Bonnie Anne was only a little over thirteen months old when he left, and he didn't see her again until she was four. Ah, a void in time, precious time missed from his children's lives. But that was war and nothing could be done about that. She was sure he thought of this; perhaps that was why he coddled the baby so. She thought herself fortunate, for her experience had shown that most men seemed uncomfortable, even unsure around babies. She had observed that her friends' husbands did not seem to pay much attention to their children until they were about six or seven years old.

Twelve gongs from the grandfather's clock in the hall interrupted their dreamy relaxation. Faintly, across the backyard, sounds of a slight commotion drifted through the shuttered windows.

Violet raised her head to listen. "I guess the workers have begun their celebration of what they've come to think of as their Emancipation Day."

"Ah, this is 1876, the year of the centennial," Brent said as he reached to refill his glass.

"Centennial of what?"

"Centennial of the independence of the United States of America, you silly gosling."

"Oh, my goodness, we've been so busy I hadn't thought much about that."

"Ha! I'm thinking that this year may have another significance; it may be another year of independence. It may be the year of the independence of South Carolina from Northern occupation."

"Well, I'll certainly drink to that!"

Which they did.

Then Brent went on, "You know they're planning a big Centennial Exposition in Philadelphia, a world's fair."

"For South Carolina's independence from Yankee slavery?"

He broke into laughter. "No, my little gosling."

"All right, you silly goose, I've read something about a world's fair in Philadelphia in the paper, but I've not given much thought to it." A copy of Brent's special smirk appeared upon her face as she continued, "Now, if it were in honor of the South's freedom from—."

"I've been thinking, maybe we ought to go up for a look."

The smirk was quickly replaced by a look of surprise. "What? Up to Yankee land? To Philadelphia?"

"Sure, it would be safe, and I'm certain there will be lots to see there."

"I don't know," she replied slowly, "I'm not sure I'm interested. We haven't been paying a lot of attention to the Fourth of July lately. You know the Negroes are making that practically a second Emancipation Day. Think what they'll try to make of a centennial."

"But, Honey, that needn't concern us about a trip to Philadelphia. There'll be lots to see and do there."

"Like what, for instance?" she asked, not convinced she wanted such a trip. *My goodness, it hasn't even been a month yet since I had the baby!* she thought.

"Like the latest Paris fashions, like the continental cuisine, like the latest developments in agricultural machinery—."

"Well now, you do make it sound more interesting. Let me think about it. And keep in mind that we have our precious little Wade to think about now."

On New Year's Day Mammy set out an especially tasty dinner featuring the traditional serving of hoppin' john to assure good fortune for the coming year.

Over the next several weeks Violet and Brent continued to think and talk about the Centennial. Newspaper articles about construction of exposition buildings and facilities and articles about plans of various foreign governments to have pavilions and exhibits more and more commanded Violet's attention. Her health, energy, and strength returned, and the baby was eating well, growing, and showed a happy, contented, but lively disposition.

"Well, you've talked me into it," she said to Brent at breakfast one morning in mid-March. "When do we go to Philadelphia, and what are the logistics arrangements for us all?"

She was not surprised when he answered, "Well, I've been thinking about that. I would say that the trip will take maybe five days—most of a day and part of a night going, three days there, and half a day and a night returning. You know, we'll be boarding and disembarking right here at Fair Oaks. When would be the best time to get away from the plantation?"

She folded her hands and let them rest in her lap. "How about going in June, after school is out but before the early harvest?"

"Sounds good to me. I'm thinking that I might have a special railroad car fixed up—beds, tables, chairs, icebox, everything. We move it up there and park it on a siding near the station, and that could be our living quarters, our hotel while we are there." He looked at Violet triumphantly.

Her face broke into a wide smile. "Why, Honey, that sounds like a marvelous idea."

One afternoon a couple of months later, Violet looked out the back window of the office in disbelief. It appeared that a freight train was coming right up the handcar track toward the house. Looking more closely as it came nearer, she could see that it was a single boxcar being pushed by a small donkey engine.

As she ran out the back door, followed by a barking Rex, Brent came bounding off the car. With a wide grin he shouted, "Violet! Come see our excursion car!" The car came to a halt just a few feet from the back porch, and Brent bade the crew to uncouple and withdraw the switch engine.

Brent returned to Violet and lifted her up through the side door in the forward third of the car, rather than in the center, and jumped up beside her.

"This is the parlor," Brent explained with a note of pride. She was amazed as she glanced about the sizeable room that she had entered. Thick green carpets covered the floor. Several framed pictures hung on the white walls. The entry door actually was fitted with double French windows, with French windows also opposite, and there were rows of six-pane, colonial-type windows along either sidewall, all covered with sheer green curtains. On the left Violet noticed a narrow aisle and wall that indicated separate rooms. She walked around to her right for a closer look at two upholstered chairs bolted to the floor, and two wooden rocking chairs with flanges on the rockers, fitted to rails bolted to the floor.

"I call these railroad rockers," Brent explained.

There was a dining table, a work table, and in the center a library table with lamp—all bolted in place. There were several loose single chairs. At the far end was a small galley with kerosene stove and icebox.

Coming back the other way, they walked down the narrow aisle past, on the right, a double bedroom with a crib for little Wade. Then the aisle went around corners to become a center aisle with two single bedrooms on either side—single, but with an upper berth overhead in each.

"Like the forecastle on a ship," explained Brent, "only more privacy and more room. You see, it sleeps ten people comfortably."

Beyond the bedrooms, at the end of the car, were double washrooms and a luggage storage room.

"Brent, this is marvelous! What ingenuity!" exclaimed a delighted Violet.

"The men down at the shops did it. Took one of our new forty-foot boxcars and put in all this. I call it the 'Wayside Inn'."

"A most appropriate name," she laughed. "I say, this is the way to travel!"

"We'll leave it here, where we can bring our things on board whenever we want until departure time."

When June 5th came, the excitement of the adults nearly matched that of the children. Evelina and Levi were coming along to serve as stewards, housekeepers, cooks, baggage handlers, and children lookouts, but they also were assured a chance to see the fair, and they were as excited as anyone else. Claribel, who had moved up to the big house when the baby was born, would continue to be little Wade's nurse on the trip. Brent and Violet had promised her that she, too, would have some time off to see the fair.

All the house servants, plus Leo and Rachel, were lined up on the back porch to bid the travelers farewell. Rex kept running up and down the porch, barking in protest of being left behind.

"Now, y'all have uh good time an' doncha worree none," called Mammy.

"Dat's righ'. We tek keer uf ebberting jes' fine," said Leo, his large, kindly face alight with his huge smile.

The little donkey engine pulled the car out to the switch along the main line where the eight o'clock local train hooked on to it, pulled it to Camden whence another took it to Charlotte. There, by prior arrangement, a train of the *Richmond and Danville* picked it up for as far as Staunton, Virginia, where the *Baltimore and Ohio* hooked on to take it to Baltimore, and thence the *Pennsylvania* took it to Philadelphia.

They arrived at the siding outside the fair in the middle of the night, and everyone was sound asleep. Not until they awoke in the morning did they realize they had reached their destination, and then their excited voices filled the car.

Immediately after breakfast, Brent and Violet, Bonnie Anne and J.J., and Evelina and Levi, leaving Claribel with little Wade, took off to find the entry to Fairmount Park, site of the exposition. The *Pennsylvania* depot through which they walked was by far the largest train station any of them ever had seen. Throngs of people were arriving in waves from all directions–by special trains, by steamboats over the Schuylkill River, by horse-drawn streetcars on tracks, by hackneys, by private carriages, by walking from nearby temporary hotels.

Noticing that the exact amount–either a silver half dollar or a paper half dollar, was required at all of the thirty-three money-gates at the main entrance, Brent stopped at a change bureau and came away with a bagful of silver half dollars. It was a warm day, though not as oppressively hot as it was likely to be later in the summer. Still, Brent, like most of the men, was fully dressed in coat, matching trousers, light waistcoat, ascot, and gray top hat. Violet wore a pink flowered muslin dress, a white straw hat with a large brim, and white crocheted lace gloves. To help ward off the rays of the sun, she carried a flowered parasol that matched her dress.

Bonnie Anne was in a blue and white checked gingham dress that was partially covered by a white lace pinafore. Streamers of blue and white checked ribbon circled and fell from the back of her white straw hat. She, too, wore gloves, but hers were of plain white cotton. Her parasol matched her pinafore. J.J. wore his navy cotton sailor suit with a matching sailor hat. Evelina and Levi were dressed in their Sunday best, he in a dark suit, white shirt and tie, and she in a yellow dress with white buttons and trim.

On entering the grounds the first thing that Brent did was to buy an official catalogue for a dollar and a half. Right away they saw that the exhibits numbered in the thousands, and it would take many days to see them all. As they gazed about they were overwhelmed by the size and number of the buildings, the bright red, white, and blue decorations everywhere, the continually flowing fountains, the lines of beautiful, varicolored garden flowers, and the smooth asphalt walks. People were everywhere, but the place was not overcrowded. Sounds of engines, music, laughter, and talking blended to sustain a festive mood for everyone.

One of the first facts that Brent noted from his catalogue was that the fairgrounds occupied a tract of 285 acres in Fairmount Park. The park itself covered over four thousand acres, and was said to be the largest fully landscaped city park in the world.

Then, discovering that a little narrow-gauge railroad ran a four-mile circuit of the grounds, Brent suggested that they ride the train all the way around for an overview. In delighted expectation they all clambered aboard the next time the train came by. It followed a curving course between a series of model factories, past an encampment of West Point cadets, then it looped around the Agricultural Building on the north side. From here the passengers could see the big Memorial Fountain. Erected by the Catholic Total Abstinence Union, it featured a sixteen-foot marble Biblical Moses and smaller statues of Europeans who had come over to serve with the Revolutionary Army in 1776. Beyond that was the Horticulture Building. Looping back to Belmont Avenue, the railroad made a turn to pass between the U.S. Government Building on the right and the Women's Pavilion on the left.

"Think of that," said Violet, "a whole big building devoted just to women."

"Yes, how about that," grinned Brent.

Approaching a special monument they got off the train for a bird's-eye view of the grounds. The monument was a replica of the forearm and torch of the Statue of Liberty then under construction in Paris by Gustave Eiffel, as a special centennial gift to the United States from the French people.

"If just the forearm and torch are this big, how large will the whole statue be?" asked Violet as they began climbing up the narrow steps.

Bringing up the rear, Brent replied, "It'll be the biggest statue in the world—maybe the biggest ever."

"Bigger than the ancient Colossus of Rhodes?"

"Half again as big, they say."

Climbing now intervened to capture all available breath so that talking was reduced to a minimum. Attaining the summit, they joined half a dozen other sightseers on the balcony of the torch where they all marveled at the view.

"Lawdy, lawdy, jes' look at dat!" exclaimed Evelina to Levi whose eyes were big as saucers as he glanced all about.

"Ain't nebber seen nuttin' like dat!" he exclaimed, drinking it all in.

Peering over the railing, J.J. remarked in wonder, "Mommy, Daddy, look at the people down there. They look like little toy soldiers and dolls, don't they?"

The rest of the day was devoted to visiting the various state exhibits, in buildings of their own or in wings of the Main Building, and the exhibits of foreign nations.

The only Southern states–Southern being former members of the Confederacy–to have exhibits were Arkansas and Mississippi. Arkansas featured sheaves of wheat and oats, large bolls of cotton, bundles of timothy and red-top grass, corn and beans and other products. The Mississippi building was a small log cabin in Gothic style, with an exhibit of products crafted from various kinds of Mississippi wood.

Brent suggested that since it was shortly after noon they all must be hungry and why didn't they go to the New England Log House for something to eat. The children let out whoops of joy. When they arrived they found that twenty young ladies in costumes of the 1750's were serving Boston baked beans, brown bread, and New England boiled dinner, all cooked in the fireplace. Everyone was hungry and when they had finished, all agreed that the food was almost as good as Southern cooking.

Of the foreign exhibits, that of Great Britain was the biggest and, Violet thought, the best. Brent preferred the Belgian crafts. Both thought the French exhibit of Lyon silk, bronze work, and other artifacts might have been better, but agreed that it all was beautifully displayed. For the children it was no contest. Nothing could compare with the German toys and dolls.

Then Violet called Brent's attention to another German presentation among works of art. "Can you imagine the nerve? What kind of taste for a world's fair?" She pointed to a big canvas depicting the French surrender at Sedan in 1870. It showed a weak little Frenchman who was creeping up a hill toward the dominating figures of Kaiser Wilhelm I and Chancellor Otto von Bismarck.

Further along they paused at two buildings given to Belgian, German, and Swiss teachers in demonstrating their methods of kindergarten education for young children.

Late in the afternoon Brent told Violet that he would go with Levi and Evelina to take the children back to their railway car quarters, and he would meet her on the terrace here and then just the two of them would go to a special restaurant for dinner. While waiting, Violet walked slowly around the terrace and regarded the coming and going of people across the lengthening shadows. She felt a certain strangeness, as though she were in a foreign country. *This is Pennsylvania,* she thought, *the state of Gettysburg, where Christopher is buried.* At the same time she felt a certain elation in seeing what Americans had accomplished in a hundred years, and she felt a certain sense of reassurance in how this exposition itself was a kind of representation of reconciliation between North and South. People here were showing no negative attitudes toward her and her family as Southerners. In contrast to the statements of political leaders that she had read and in contrast to so many of the Carpetbaggers in South Carolina, people seemed friendly and considerate.

"Ready to go?" Brent's voice broke into her thoughts.

"Yes, yes, but where? Is everything all right at our railroad inn?"

"Yes. I'll tell you about it while we're eating. I passed what looked like a good French restaurant over this way. Shall we try it?"

"Oh, yes, I'm famished, you know, and I'm in the mood for some really fine cuisine—like we had in New Orleans."

Going into the *Trois Frères Provençaux*, they were promptly and tastefully served a five-course dinner based on Chateaubriand with béarnaise sauce.

"You said that you would tell about our Wayside Inn," Violet reminded Brent as the waiter cleared their soup bowls.

"Yes. No problem, but when I got there several railroad men and others were walking around looking at it. They acted like they thought it was one of the exhibits."

"What did you do?"

"Showed them in."

"Oh, my goodness, what did they think?"

"Some of them wanted to know where I got it. I explained it was finished in the Columbia shops of *The Carolina Rail.* Then they wanted to know if they could buy some."

"And of course you said, 'Of course'."

"Of course."

When he received the dinner check, Brent exclaimed, "Great Scot! I'll have to find some new sources of revenue to meet this kind of extravagant pricing."

The next day, Wednesday, Evelina stayed in the railroad car with the baby while Claribel took her turn to see the fair and to help with the older children. Levi came along to help keep an eye on Bonnie Anne and J.J. and to help with parcels. They visited the Main Building and Machinery Hall. A band was playing on a bandstand in the very center of the Main Building. When the band fell silent, one of three great organs in different areas of the building filled the void. Violet and Brent and the others looked at pottery and cutlery and hardware and lamps and clothing and clocks and glassware and jewelry and all kinds of other artifacts until everything was becoming a blur. In the art gallery they were favorably impressed by the showings of American artists in comparison with European. One of their favorites was a work of Thomas Eakins, *Chess Players.*

But Violet was shocked by another painting that she considered atrocious. It was *The Battle of Gettysburg* by Rothermel that showed a horrible slaughter of Confederate soldiers. Memories of Christopher flooded back, and the idea that her young brother may have died in such a carnage made her feel faint. Turning from the repulsive painting in disgust, Brent saw the color drain from Violet's face and her lips beginning to tremble. Quickly he put his arms tightly around her to steady her and turned her away from the picture. With his hand, he pushed her head to his shoulder, and they stood that way for several minutes until he felt her trembling stop and heard her draw a deep breath.

As she drew away, he kissed her lovingly and said, "Come on, let's get out of here. We've seen enough of this place."

One of the most attractive exhibits was of wheeled vehicles, from the most primitive cart and wheelbarrow to the most modern Pullman palace car. This appealed especially to J.J. and his father. Violet was interested, but she was having a difficult time getting the Gettysburg painting out of her mind, and several times she had to fight tears. She did not want to cast a shadow on everybody else's enjoyment of the fair, so she wiped her eyes surreptitiously and maintained an effort to keep a smile on her face.

The children gravitated toward the numerous ice cream stands and soft-drink fountains. These featured flavored water or soda, but most impressive were the demonstrations of Charles E. Hires showing how he made Root Beer and sold it for three cents a glass. Brent was more impressed when they wandered over to the Brewers' Hall and saw mammoth vats of beer.

One of the most popular attractions of the fair dominated the Machinery Hall—the huge Corliss steam engine whose twin cylinders rose several stories high and which provided power for all the other machinery in the building. Brent was intrigued by a pre-rolled cigarette machine developed by Major Lewis Ginter of Richmond, Virginia, and operated by the Allen and Ginter Tobacco Works.

"Don't you think this is going to add to the demand of tobacco?" asked Violet.

"No doubt about it. I suggest you double your tobacco crop as soon as possible," Brent replied.

"Won't everyone else who sees this be doing the same thing?"

"Likely so, but most of them will wait a year or two to see how it works out; we *know* what it will do, and we will get the jump on them."

"Immediately," Violet agreed. "I'll see if we can add to this year's crop."

"Good idea—and I'll start selling."

They continued their tour, looking at Germany's exhibit of Krupp guns, but perhaps the most novel of all was Alexander Graham Bell's telephone.

"What do you think of that?" Violet asked. "Just imagine being able actually to hear someone's voice over a machine, and then to talk as though that person were in the same room. It's amazing!"

While Claribel had found the fair interesting, she had missed and worried about her young charge, even though she knew Evelina was perfectly capable of taking good care of little Wade. She thanked Violet for giving her the chance to spend the day at the fair, but now she had seen it and would be content to spend the rest of the time at the railroad car. Besides, Bonnie Anne and J.J. were accustomed to being with Evelina, she said. Violet acceded to the nurse's wishes, so early the next morning, this time with Evelina, they took the narrow gauge railroad to the Women's Building. Ever since she had glimpsed it from the little tour train on the first day, she had been eager to visit it.

"Why a Women's Building? Where's the Men's Building?" asked Brent, taking a quick look again at his fair catalogue.

"Oh, you silly goose, all these other buildings are men's buildings."

"Well, you seemed to be enjoying all those exhibits immensely." A mischievous look came into his eyes as he went on, "And, my dear, you are most definitely a woman."

"I did, indeed," laughed Violet. "Come on, you silly goose, let's have a look at what women have been doing." They entered the large building, the children skipping on ahead with Evelina and Levi close behind.

It had a big central hall, reaching up to an open dome, and with four wings radiating from the center and forming a broad cross. In one wing was a section of a textile mill, with neatly dressed women operating the shiny new machines. A young lady from Iowa, educated in engineering, operated a sixty-horsepower steam engine that ran all the machinery in the building. In the art wing there were paintings and sculptures by women. There was one that Brent lingered by—a high-profile bust of a beautiful girl, sculptured in butter, and created by a Mrs. Brooks of Arkansas.

"Now, Brent, come on," grinned Violet, "look at these exhibits." She led him past exhibits of needlework and embroidery to a complete *materia medica* from the Women's Medical College of Philadelphia. It was all fascinating to Violet.

It was past their accustomed noon dinner time, and the children were getting restless and hungry. Brent suggested that they dine at the American Restaurant which was in front of the Agricultural Building. They found the food better and cheaper and the surroundings cooler and cleaner than any of the others they had seen as they moved about the fairgrounds.

After they had eaten, they visited the Agricultural Building. Here they saw the kinds of things one usually found at county fairs, though on a vast scale. The new and improved reapers and binders and drills caught Violet's attention, and she was especially impressed by a steam traction engine that could pull forty plows across a field at once.

"You use steam engines to pull trains; why not steam engines to pull plows and planters and reapers?" she asked Brent.

"Indeed, why not?"

"Brent, do you think that someday such engines might replace horses and mules on the plantations and farms, and in so doing reduce the need for hand labor in cultivation?"

"Why not? Yes, I do think that's a possibility."

Here, in the Agricultural Building, everyone was pleased to find the only exhibit they had seen from South Carolina—a display of rice from Georgetown. At the tobacco exhibit there were Perique from New Orleans, leaf, plug, and smoking tobacco from Durham, North Carolina, and various brands of cigars, cigarettes, and snuff.

Leaving the Agricultural Building they made their way to the Southern Restaurant, at the far end of the Belmont Avenue crosswalk, for an early supper. Here, they found that the restaurant was managed by a man from Atlanta and run entirely by Negroes, and they encountered many other people from the South. Violet and Brent, the children, and Evelina and Levi, all agreed that the food prepared here was the most delicious of any that they had eaten.

Chapter 68

The Red Shirt Campaign

1876

"What in the world are you doing with all that red flannel?" Violet asked as Brent entered the back hall door of Fair Oaks. He was carrying several yards of red cloth.

As soon as he dropped it on a chair in the hall he answered, "I'm getting ready for the political campaign."

"For goodness sake, what on earth has this got to do with a political campaign?"

"You know Wade Hampton's campaign for governor begins next week, September 2nd, in Anderson, and the Democratic rifle clubs and saber clubs and other groups are going to wear red shirts as their uniform—as their symbol of full support. Frankly, my dear, I was hoping that you would have Hattie and her helpers make this flannel up into shirts for me."

"Of course we'll do that." Violet walked into the office, Brent following, and both took rocking chairs in front of the empty fireplace. "But tell me, why red shirts?" she asked.

"Some of the Radical leaders in the North, mainly that senator from Indiana, Oliver P. Morton, like to 'wave the bloody shirt' for political effect—that is, they accuse the Democrats of rebellion and so on—like to keep fighting the War against the South to arouse antagonism and gain support for the Radical Republicans, so they think. Well, now we are defying them; we're going to wave their bloody shirt right back at them. Some of the clubs in Charleston and some others around Aiken started this about the same time. Now everybody is taking to it."

"Well then, we'll make all the shirts you can use."

"Yes, make some extras for me so I can change once in a while, though I don't know why, we used to go for months at sea without changing clothes." He looked at her, his eyes twinkling.

"Ugh!" She wrinkled her nose at the thought.

"Anyway, let's make up some extras so I can pass them out to other men who are willing to wear them."

"We'll make all you have goods for."

"Thank you, Violet."

On the following Wednesday, August 30, with the help of Levi who would be going along, Brent loaded their faithful horses, Jeb and Feather, into a railroad car on the siding behind the house, and stowed their equipment and some food supplies. Violet hurried back and forth to bring little items that might be of use.

Brent put on one of the new red shirts, and Violet handed him his old seaman's cap that she had fitted with a red plume.

"Now, my handsome Red Knight, be off to the wars for righteousness, and do be careful. I shall expect you back in a month?"

"Yes, my Lady, I'll try to do my part in slaying the dragon in that time. I'll help organize the meetings until we end up here. Then I'll stay here to try to organize the vote in this area. Get ready to help with the big day in Sumter."

"Oh don't worry, I shall do everything I can to help turn the rascals out."

Violet followed with interest and excitement the newspaper accounts of the opening of the campaign in the northwest corner of the state. It was reported that a mounted escort of 1,600 red-shirted horsemen escorted General Hampton into Anderson. There a crowd of over six thousand heard speeches by Martin Gary, Samuel McGowan, Wyatt Aiken, and others as well as Hampton. In his address, Hampton pointed out that he was the first white man in the South to advocate giving the vote to Negroes "as they proved themselves capable of using it." He concluded with his slogan, "Reconciliation, Retrenchment and Reform."

Reports on succeeding days told of the growing enthusiasm of the Hampton campaign as it moved from place to place. At the little town of Greenville, three days after Anderson, another escort of fifteen hundred mounted men met the General and a crowd of five thousand gathered to hear him speak in the afternoon and another for a meeting that night.

A Northern reporter wrote:

> *Such delirium as they arouse can be paralleled only by itself even in this delirious state. Their whole tour is a vast triumphal procession; at every depot they are received by a tremendous concourse of citizens and escorts of cavalry. Their meetings draw the whole white population, male and female, for scores of miles around, and have to be held invariably in the open air. They are preceded by processions of the rifle clubs, mounted and on foot, miles in length, marching amidst the strains of music and the booming of cannon; at night there are torchlight processions equally imposing. The speakers arouse in thousands the memories of old, and call on their hearers to redeem the grand old State and restore it to its ancient place of honor in the Republic. The wildest cheering follows. The enthusiasm, as Confederate veterans press forward to wring their old General's hand, is indescribable.*

Others reported of processions three miles long, with as many as three thousand mounted men, including hundreds of Negro Democrats who withstood the insults of their fellow Negroes. They reported of the participation of numerous brass bands, choirs of young women, massive floral decorations, and colorful, dramatic tableaux.

South Carolina had seen nothing like this since the Revolutionary War or since the boys had gone off to fight the War in 1861. It was as though a great forest fire had been ignited in the north country and now was sweeping across the state.

Several town elections on September 11 seemed to point toward Democratic success—Kingstree elected its first conservative Democratic municipal government since the beginning of Reconstruction. In Abbeville, seventy-five out of 143 black voters voted the straight Democratic ticket. Other towns were showing similar trends. General Hampton announced at Cheraw, "There are already colored men enough in the Democratic party to carry this election."

The Radical Republicans did not hold their state nominating convention until September 15. Violet was amused to read that Governor Chamberlain's name had been offered for renomination by none other than Honest John Patterson, and the convention had duly nominated the Governor for reelection. She was rather more shocked in reading of the nominations for the rest of the state ticket—Robert B. Elliott, the notorious black speaker of the house who had opposed every tentative step of Chamberlain toward reform, for attorney general; Richard H. Gleave, the mulatto from Pennsylvania, renominated for lieutenant governor, and T.C. Dunn of Massachusetts and Wisconsin, renominated for comptroller general.

It was a great relief to Violet when Brent and Levi, and the horses, returned to Fair Oaks by a freight train on Friday afternoon, September 29. She greeted him with the same fervor and enthusiasm that she had shown when he returned from the War and when he had returned from his voyage to the West Indies six years ago.

Fabian came running up to take Jeb and Feather around to the carriage house. Brent went on into the house with Violet, as Levi followed with the bags.

"Well, my dear husband, according to the papers you have been on one grand parade and celebration all this time," she said, taking his arm and looking up at him with a big smile.

"Yes, indeed," he answered, leaning down to give her another kiss.

Just then the children came bounding in to throw themselves on their father and give their greetings and kisses and hugs. Rex, the collie, not to be outdone, was doing his best to welcome his master, barking in delight, licking Brent's hands, and standing on his hind legs and trying to lick Brent's face.

Evelina flew into the room, said hello to Brent, and flung her arms around Levi. It had been a long month for her, too. Then Evelina and Levi slipped from the hall, hand in hand, to have some quiet time just to themselves.

As soon as things had quieted down and the children had returned to their activities, and Brent had said hello to Mammy and Jarvis and Aaron, Violet said, "Let's go into the library and you can tell me all about it. I know you must be tired, and a cup of tea will refresh you a bit." Before she had even finished, Ellie appeared with the tea tray. Ellie welcomed Brent home, curtsied, and returned to the kitchen.

Violet poured them each a cup of tea, placed a buttered scone on each saucer, and handed Brent his, saying, "Now tell me all about it."

He chuckled at her impatience "First let me tell you what's coming up."

"What's that?"

"One week from tomorrow, Saturday, October 7th, will be Hampton Day in Sumter."

"That sounds exciting."

"It should be a great day. Do you think we might have the Friersons, Stuarts, and the Andersons, and maybe the Shelbys and the Dargans, come over here Sunday afternoon to talk about plans?"

"Of course. If you'll send telegraph messages to the Shelbys and Dargans, I'll send Levi with notes to the Friersons, Stuarts, and Andersons the first thing in the morning."

"I'll do that."

"Now, Brent, how has the campaign really been going?"

"It beats anything I have ever seen. You can just feel the electricity in the air. I don't see how the Radicals can stop us. Even lots of blacks are crossing Jordan, coming over to the support of Hampton."

"I've been reading about that in the papers. The Democrats have even been winning some of the town elections."

"True."

"Have you heard about the riot at Ellenton?" she inquired.

"Yes, saw it in the paper, heard some talk about it."

"That would make it sound like a lot of the blacks are going on the warpath."

"Some of the men around Hampton think that that is exactly what the Radicals want—riots that would justify sending in more Federal troops. They seem to think that the presence of more Federal troops would intimidate the voters and would be an advantage to the Radicals."

"I can see that, but don't you think we ought to meet violence with violence? Now we seem so close to getting the Radical Carpetbaggers out that it would be a shame to let them stay in by threats of violence, don't you think?"

"Yes, it would, but I doubt that violence is the answer. Now Martin Gary would say yes; he favors any means to keep the blacks from the polls, including threats of violence. Hampton says 'No'. He says the only way is reconciliation, moderation, persuasion, and absolutely no violence."

"Well, I'm with Gary. I say hold on to this advantage and don't let them take it away from us."

"Now, Violet, I'm not so sure about that. Hampton has been doing pretty well, and it seems to me that his way is the only way to assure some kind of peaceable future."

She shook her head in protest. "There won't be any future if we keep letting the Radicals take it away from us. I say that any darkies that are not safe votes for us ought to be kept away from the polls. We all agree on the ends, even though there may be some differences on the means."

"Now you're sounding Machiavellian, my Dear. I say the means are the essence of politics. The ends often are so obscure or often so broadly stated that everyone agrees with them, and the only essential difference is in the means."

"Well, I think we need a bit of Machiavelli around here; I think we ought to use the means necessary to get the results we want. If they shoot, shoot back. If they threaten to vote against you, don't let them vote. Brent, things have *got* to be changed in the South; they're grinding us down; we have no real freedom any longer. Frankly, it seems to me that Hampton is sounding like too much milk and cider and not enough fire! I think Gary has the right idea"

With a look of some surprise Brent replied, "That doesn't sound like my sweet, compassionate, understanding Violet."

"You haven't seen me under fire."

"But you always have gotten along well with the Negroes—certainly with all the workers here, certainly with all those at the school, certainly—."

"Those are different. I also have been attacked by stray Negroes in my own house. I have seen the illiterates up at the State House trying to lord it over everybody. I have seen my husband shot by Negro hoodlums for no reason other than that he is white, and now we have the report of a white woman and her little boy being attacked and beaten by Negro robbers over at Ellenton."

"But we also have seen some of those in the legislature who have been rather decent, have had a pretty good attitude. There are more and more now who see through the manipulations of the Carpetbaggers and Scalawags to use them for their own, I mean the Carpetbaggers' own advantage, and look how many of them have crossed Jordan to support Hampton in spite of all the invectives and threats from the Radicals and their black sheep."

"Oh, I don't know."

On Sunday afternoon the invited guests joined Violet and Brent on the front porch where pitchers of lemonade and plates of small sandwiches and cookies had been set out on small tables within a semicircle of rocking chairs. They were there to talk politics and to make plans for Hampton Day in Sumter.

Taking a long sip of cool lemonade, John Frierson turned toward Brent and asked, "Brent, how has the campaign been going on the hustings?"

"I tell you, I never have seen anything like it; it's been like a Roman triumphal procession all the way."

"And what about the national ticket?" asked Victor Shelby.

"Tilden and Hendricks seem to be popular everywhere, and the Republican Hayes seems to create little enthusiasm. Frankly, though, I've found there is more interest in the state contest than in the national."

"To be expected, I should say," replied Shelby. "Well, it's a great gain that at least we have a candidate this year."

"I think we have a winner," Brent said, looking around for the agreement of the others. All nodded.

"What is the most effective strategy in this campaign?" Will Anderson asked.

Brent quickly responded, "The Sutler strategy—win all of the native white votes and win enough of the black votes to neutralize the Radicals' black majority. And that is Hampton's strategy too, though I must say Gary and Tillman disagree with that. They think the only way to win is to keep the blacks away from the polls, by whatever means."

"What do you think about that?" Virginia Shelby asked.

Brent glanced toward Violet. She avoided his look as he answered, "I think that can never work in the long run; that is simply using Carpetbagger methods. Frankly, I think that Ben Tillman may be a dangerous man. He is always stirring up racial animosities, especially between the upcountry small farmers, the po' buckras, and the blacks. I say in the long run we've got to convince the blacks that their true interests are with us."

"Aside from moderation and persuasion of the blacks, can anything else be done?" asked Sarah Frierson.

Brent nodded and answered, "Let me tell you about three special tactics we have been using. One is *dividing time*–."

"Dividing time? Never heard of it; what's that?" interrupted Victor.

"Actually I think this started with Gary as a result of some correspondence he had with friends in Mississippi. He refers to it as the 'Mississippi Plan.' There the idea was to have all Democrats form clubs, all armed, and each club under a competent captain. Members of these clubs then go to Radical meetings to shout 'liars, thieves, rascals' at any false statements and so on."

Violet interrupted to say, "And those clubs in Mississippi have become local vigilance committees–that was all they had to maintain law and order, and we have seen some of the results of that first hand."

"I guess we have," murmured Mary Anderson.

Brent continued, "Now whenever the Radicals have a meeting here we have a contingent of Red Shirts, saber club members, ride over to the meeting, and without any violence or threats, simply demand equal time for their spokesmen to speak to the issues. That creates quite a stir, but there has been no violence." He paused a moment as if a thought had just occurred to him. "But you know something? Chamberlain must feel a little intimidated or unsure of himself. He's not made a public speech since his nomination."

John Frierson spoke up, "Yes, the division of time started as a device of Gary to intimidate the audiences, but Colonel Haskell sent to all county chairmen instructions to the effect that we might send our men to these meetings, but they must remain perfectly quiet, they are to keep order, and to request a division of time. If they are rejected they should follow rules of procedure, but they may indicate their pleasure or displeasure by applauding, or hissing, but must never make any demonstration or threat of force."

"I must say," said Brent, "that has been working very well. You know Hampton's main concern is not to arouse excessive enthusiasm but to control it. Anyway, the Union League and other Radical Republican groups have been convening meetings of Negroes that are kind of weird mixtures of Voodoo rites, warped Christianity, and politics. They tell the blacks that if the Democrats win, all the Negroes will either be shot or returned to slavery. By division of time we've been able to expose the lies and neutralize exaggerations."

"And you were saying that there are a couple of other tactics that you all have been using?" asked Victor.

Brent nodded again. "I wouldn't say that we all are using them, but one that supports in a way our approach is the 'one-man-apiece policy.' The way that works is that in many counties each white voter assumes a promise to pick one Negro and then to persuade him, by reason, or I'm afraid sometimes by bribes or threats, either to vote for Hampton, or just not vote at all. And another tactic is 'preference, not proscription.' This is to appeal to the Negroes' needs for jobs. Instead of telling them that they will not be given a job if they vote Republican, which would clearly be against Federal law, qualified Negro Democrats are given certificates that promise them preference over Radical Republicans in employment. I guess you might call that affirmative action on behalf of Negroes if they vote right. I don't think Hampton encourages this one, but I'm sure it's effective in some quarters."

"No doubt," agreed Victor.

"But when it comes to threats and intimidation and taunts, you should see how the Radical Republicans, and especially the Negro Republicans, treat the Negro Democrats. I think you have to hand it to all those Negroes who have crossed the Jordan and openly support Hampton and Tilden."

"That's certainly right," John Frierson agreed.

Violet made sure that everyone's glass was refilled with lemonade and that the sandwich and cookie plates had been passed before she spoke up, "Have you heard how some of the black women have been intimidating their men? It's a fright. Lots of those Negro women refuse to hear Hampton or any other Democrat speak, and they do everything they can to prevent the black men from listening. Wives and mothers refuse to wash their men's clothes or to cook for them if they are Democrats. A Negro landlady in Columbia ran a black lawyer out of the house because she saw him wearing a Tilden button. And a Negro wife locked her husband out, said she wouldn't have any Democratic nigger sleep with her as long as she lived. And when black men put on red shirts, enraged black women sometimes run out and tear them off. I heard that when one Negro man shouted 'Hurrah for Hampton' a bunch of women tore all his clothes off. Even some of the Negro churches turn out members known to be Democrats."

"I do declare!" gasped a shocked Virginia Shelby, fanning herself.

"Indeed!" exclaimed Mary Anderson.

John Frierson smiled at the two women as if in reassurance, then turned to Brent to ask, "Have you been following the Radicals' exploitation of the Ellenton riot?"

"Can you believe that?" exclaimed Brent.

"What is it?" Harrison Stuart asked. "Don't forget, I'm still kind of new to this area."

"I have it right here in the papers," answered Brent as he reached for some newspapers beside his chair. "Chamberlain has called for a disbanding of the rifle clubs, but he has said nothing about disbanding the Negro armed organizations. He issued a proclamation full of exaggeration and asked Grant to send in more Federal troops."

"But that's awful!" protested Patricia.

"Indeed it is," agreed Victor, "and I've heard that Honest John Patterson is supposed to have said that the Ellenton riot was worth thousands of votes to the Radical Republicans, and supposedly he said, 'We've got to raise hell with these niggers and get Federal troops down here or the damned Rebels will carry the state in spite of anything we can do."

"Well," said Dargan, "you remember how Chamberlain tried to make political capital out of the so-called Hamburg massacre last July."

"They talk about massacre," Victor added, "they should think about what happened to General Custer a month earlier, in June, when he went up against the Sioux of Sitting Bull."

"Indeed," agreed Brent.

"I must say," Frierson said, "Colonel Haskell, the State Democratic chairman, has been following Hampton's policy of conciliation to the letter. He issued instructions to all county chairmen that they should resort to no threats, no intimidation, no violence whatever."

"And now," said Brent, "we must think a little bit about the business immediately at hand, Hampton Day in Sumter, next Saturday, October 7th."

"Well, what are we supposed to do?" inquired Harrison Stuart.

Frierson spoke up, "The County Committee is making the arrangements, and they have subcommittees working on all different aspects. John Dargan, our good friend here, is to be the grand marshal, and he will have twenty-one assistant marshals to help organize the parade. They would like for us to help with decorations and some kind of tableau in connection with Hampton's appearance."

"What kind of decorations have they been having, Brent?" asked Patricia Stuart.

"Every kind of flower you can think of, in every formation you can think of—in rows along the street, in big arches near the speaking area, in clusters around the speakers' platform, and then red, white, and blue bunting everywhere, and sometimes big poster pictures of the candidates."

"We should be able to manage that," said Violet. "We'll call on all the neighbors for flowers and take whole wagon loads into town." All the other ladies agreed to help.

Then Victor Shelby suggested, "As for the tableau, why not use the motif they used at the Monument Fair, but instead of all the states, why not a Miss South Carolina, in chains, to greet General Hampton as her liberator?"

"I like that," said Sarah Frierson, "and I hereby propose Violet to be our Miss South Carolina."

"Hear, hear!" said the others.

Blushing, Violet folded her arms across her chest. "No, no, not me. You want some pretty, young girl, not an old matron."

"Nonsense," said Dargan, "we don't want a pretty, young girl; we want a beautiful lady; that's Carolina."

"Hear, hear!" everybody said, and by acclamation, Violet was it.

Recovering her composure, Violet thanked them for the compliment and went on to ask, "One more thing. What about school children? Should they be encouraged to attend?"

"By all means they should see the parade, and they should see General Hampton," Shelby said quickly.

"Yes, indeed," Brent added.

Violet smiled and said, "I'll have the sewing classes at *The Joshua School* make as many small state flags as they can so that the children and others can wave them at the parade."

The next day Violet told Leo that all the workers should have the day off on Saturday to go into town to see the big parade, and he might arrange for horses and wagons to carry them in. Then she and Brent drove into Sumter. While Brent visited various people at the Court House and around town to make further plans, she went to *The Joshua School* to get the flag-making project started.

On Friday morning, Violet and Brent, Bonnie Anne and J.J. and Evelina, and with Levi at the reins, drove the carriage into Sumter. They used the guest quarters at *The Joshua School* and spent the rest of the day in preparation for the morrow.

Hampton Day was a bright, sunny, October day. By early morning hundreds of people were milling about on the streets decorated profusely with flowers and banners. At nine o'clock Brent joined a detachment of horsemen to ride out to the county line to meet General Hampton and escort him into town. They led Hampton to the depot where the great parade was forming. Meanwhile Violet was marshaling the pupils at *The Joshua School* to march down to where they could view the parade.

With military precision, Dargan, as grand marshal, and his assistants, all wearing red, white, or blue sashes and carrying red, white, and blue batons, got the parade moving. General Hampton, accompanied by General James Connor, led off in a great, colorfully decorated carriage drawn by four white horses. The long line of marchers moved to the music of bands from Columbia, Timmonsville, Darlington, and Stateburg. Six thousand cheering spectators lined the streets of Sumter. Hundreds of school children, including others besides those from *The Joshua School* with whom Bonnie Anne and J.J. stood, were wildly waving their blue state flags.

Many of the crowd were women, and many of the women were wearing red trimmings. As a Columbia newspaper reported in a ditty:

Red ribbons round their waists,
Red ribbons in their hair,
Red ribbons to their tastes,
Pinned to them everywhere.

The parade passed through a great arch of flowers at the intersection of Liberty and Main Streets, through a second in front of the newspaper office of *The True Southron,* and a third near the home of Charles H. Moise where the speakers' platform had been erected. Here was a big picture poster of Wade Hampton, *Savior of South Carolina,* and another of Tilden, *Savior of America.*

The last element in the parade drew more wild cheers from the crowd—a column of fours of two thousand mounted Red Shirts, including over three hundred Negroes, all shouting in unison, "Hurrah for Hampton! Hurrah for Hampton!"

When Bonnie Anne and J.J. spotted Brent near the head of the column, they shouted above the noise of the crowd, "Daddy! Daddy!" He acknowledged them with a smile and a wave. At that point, Violet, leaving Bonnie Anne and J.J. in the care of Evelina and Levi, excused herself to walk rapidly up to the Moise house to get ready for her special part in the ceremonies.

With Red Shirts forming a circle all around the square, the spectators moved up to the vicinity of the speakers' platform. After preliminary speeches by M.P. O'Connor, James Chesnut, and J.B. Kershaw, the chairman, Thomas B. Fraser, stepped up and introduced Hampton who was waiting at the steps below the platform.

As Hampton approached the steps, a bowed figure draped in black robes and wrapped in chains emerged from behind a screen of flowers at the rear of the platform and walked toward him. As he walked up the steps the dark figure, waiting for him near the top of the steps, threw off the chains with a loud clang and then threw off the black robes. There stood a beautiful lady in pure white silk, a golden coronet with the words `*South Carolina*' resting on her shining dark hair, blue eyes sparkling as she looked skyward, arms outstretched. It was South Carolina liberated. It was Violet Lee Storm Sutler at her most beautiful best. A hush fell over the whole crowd as General Hampton kissed the hand of the lady. Then the people burst into wild applause as Violet walked in a stately manner to the rear of the platform and disappeared behind the screen of flowers.

The General had become used to this kind of thing over the last several weeks, but this seemed to make the deepest impression on him. Unashamed, he had to wipe a tear from his eye and clear his throat before speaking.

In moderate but clear tones, projecting his voice so that it could be heard by the thousands without his shouting, he summarized his views. He appealed for the support of everyone, black and white alike, in the interest of peace, liberty, and prosperity. Among other things he said:

> *The only way to bring about prosperity in this state is to bring the two races in friendly relations together. The Democratic Party in South Carolina, of whom I am the exponent, has promised that every citizen of this state is to be the equal of all; he is to have every right given him by the Constitution of the United States and of this state...And I pledge my faith, and I pledge it for those gentlemen who are on the ticket with me, that if we are elected, as far as in us the power lies, we will observe, protect, and defend the rights of the colored man as quickly as of any other man in South Carolina...If there is a white man in this assembly who, because he is a Democrat, or because he is a white man, believes that when I am elected Governor, if I should be, that I will stand between him and the law, or grant him any privilege or immunity that shall not be granted to the colored man, he is mistaken...Not one single right enjoyed by the colored people today shall be taken from them. And we further*

> *pledge that we will give better facilities for education than they have ever had before... We pledge free men, free ballots, free schools.*

After the speeches all the people were invited to a great barbecue. This gave General Hampton and the other state and local candidates opportunities to shake hands with multitudes of voters and voter's wives, relatives, and friends. The only sour note was that although special provision had been made for the Negroes, many of them stayed away on account of a rumor spread by the opposition that the food had been poisoned.

Later, in the early evening, Violet and Brent had a chance to accompany Hampton, James and Mary Chesnut, and several local leaders when they went to Moise's house for dinner. During the dinner a telegram came announcing that Governor Chamberlain had issued a proclamation declaring martial law in Aiken and Barnwell and ordering that all rifle and saber clubs immediately disband. After dinner the gentlemen withdrew to the shade of a chestnut oak on the lawn to discuss the situation.

"We have to obey the law, and we don't want any violence," Hampton declared.

"But we've got to have organization if we are to see this campaign through to a successful conclusion," protested James Chesnut, "and the rifle clubs are the key to our organization."

"Why not just disband the rifle clubs and then immediately reorganize them?" suggested Brent.

"I doubt Chamberlain and his henchmen would stand still for that," remarked Moise.

"Oh, but listen," continued Brent, "we organize them as different clubs, different names, same function. Many of them are represented here, and we can get word to the others. You see, the Columbia Flying Artillery might become the Hampton and Tilden Musical Club, for instance; another might become the First Baptist Church Sewing Circle; our Sumter club can become Mother's Little Helpers; another may become a Mounted Baseball Club, and so on."

By now everyone was breaking out in laughter. Hampton said, "Senator, I believe you have something there. Let's do it."

That night a big torch-light parade, now featuring Violet standing on a wagon as "South Carolina Liberated," and more speeches at the Court House concluded the celebration of Hampton Day in Sumter.

Chapter 69

Disputed Elections

1876

During the rest of October, Violet was giving most of her attention to the picking of cotton, while Brent was giving a good deal of his attention to the continuing political campaign in Sumter County. Both were following the progress of Hampton's campaign across the rest of the state through the newspapers that Levi brought in daily from the mail drops.

On Saturday morning, a week after Hampton Day in Sumter, they were in their office reviewing the news and discussing the latest events.

"I see here that they are still arresting prominent Democrats around Aiken for alleged participation in the Ellenton riots," remarked Brent. "Now they are using the Federal Courts to reduce the strength of the Democrats."

"How far are they going with that?" Violet asked.

"No doubt as far as they can. Some of my sources in Columbia have told me that Honest John Patterson is boasting that they have arrested seven hundred Democrats during the campaign—for rioting, intimidation, and so on—trying to break up our dividing time tactics. They say that Negroes have been selling affidavits against Democrats for a dollar and a half apiece or eighteen dollars a dozen."

"Why Brent, that's terrible. Is Wade Hampton's popularity going to be able to stand up against all that?"

"Yes, I think so, but they are trying everything." His voice was heavy with sarcasm. He glanced down at his paper and then said, "Can you believe this—ex-Governor Scott has crossed Jordan."

She glanced over at Brent to see if he was joshing her. "No, I don't believe it. Anyway I'm not sure we want his support."

"Ah, but it's a good sign. He didn't do it very gracefully, but he has come out in favor of Hampton, and you know another who has crossed Jordan and may be even more significant, is Martin Delaney."

"Martin Delaney? I don't think I've heard of him. Who is he?"

"Oh, you remember, the Negro who was candidate for lieutenant governor on the reform ticket two years ago."

"Oh yes, now I recall him. That *is* good news."

A week later Violet and Brent were back at their desks, again reviewing the newspapers and mail.

"I see there has been another so-called massacre, this one at the village of Cainhoy, near Charleston," Brent said.

"Oh, dear, what happened there?"

"It was supposed to be a joint meeting. Apparently it was going all right until someone fired a shot in the air. Then the Negroes ran outside, grabbed weapons that they had stashed away there and started shooting everywhere, while the whites returned their fire. Six white men and one black man were killed."

"How awful!"

"Honest John will be pleased—thinks this will mean more votes for the Radicals." He picked up several envelopes and glanced over them. "Look, here's a letter from Father." He set the others down, reached for his brass letter opener, and ripped open the envelope.

"What does he say?" She waited patiently while he skimmed through the letter.

"Says there's lots of enthusiasm for Hampton in Charleston—tells about the Cainhoy riot—says in Charleston people are afraid to pass in front of a lighted window at night, even behind a drawn shade, lest their shadow become a target for a rock or even a bullet."

"Oh, Brent, that sounds like Vicksburg, doesn't it? Oh, I do hope your mother and father and Phoebe will be all right. Perhaps they might like to come stay with us for awhile."

"Good idea. I'll get off an invitation by telegraph in a little while, but don't get your heart set on it, Violet. You know how independent all three are."

"Yes, I know, like father like son."

"What's that?" He had returned to his pile of newspapers.

"Oh, nothing, nothing at all."

"Hear this from the Columbia paper. Chamberlain has appealed to Grant for help, says the rifle clubs have not been disbanded as he ordered, and he asks for more Federal troops, and so now we have a proclamation from Grant. He says the native whites have banned together in lawless combinations 'who ride up and down by day and night, in arms, murdering peaceable citizens, and engaging in unlawful and insurrectionary proceedings,' and he calls upon them to 'disperse and retire peaceably to their abodes.' I tell you, Violet, this is getting harder and harder to believe."

"I know."

"And listen to the reply by the State Democratic Committee, with Hampton's blessing. 'We are not engaged in unlawful and insurrectionary proceedings. We cannot "disperse," because we are not gathered together. We cannot "retire peaceably to our abodes" because we are at home in peace, disturbed only by the political agitations created by the Governor and his minions. But we resignedly, and cheerfully, in the performance of our duty, suspend the exercise of our individual and private rights in order to prevent evil to the whole people."

"Pretty good, I must say."

"I tell you, Violet, that Colonel Haskell, the state chairman, is a reasoned, controlled, alert gentleman." Returning to his paper, Brent said, "But look, Grant already has ordered more Federal troops anyway—all available forces of the Atlantic District to report to General Ruger in Columbia, quote, 'to help enforce the authority of the United States.'" A sarcastic smile appeared on his face as he continued in a tense voice, "What they really intend, of course, is to enforce the authority of the

Radical Republicans. Their feeling is that the more Federal troops there are around, the more the Democrats and especially Negro Democrats will feel intimidated and will fail to vote."

"I'll be glad when the election is over—the closer it gets the more stress and the more danger of violence."

"True, and one of the worst things they have done was to try to get Hampton himself involved in a riot at Aiken just three days ago. Right in the middle of a big Hampton meeting. a U.S. Marshal and a squad of soldiers swept in with a lot of noise and commotion and arrested eleven prominent Democrats on conspiracy charges. If Hampton had given the word the crowd would have torn the intruders to pieces, but, as always, he urged against violence and asked the victims to accept their arrest peaceably."

Violet frowned. "Well, Brent, I think that's another case where his restraint went too far."

"No, my dear, I must disagree with you. In the long run it will pay off. Everyone knows he was a great war general; everyone knows he has great courage. So they know he is urging restraint and nonviolence out of principle and certainly not out of any taint of cowardice."

"No," said Violet, now smiling, "I don't think anyone would accuse Wade Hampton of cowardice even though some of us would like to see him be a little more forceful at times."

Holding several papers, Brent went on, "Here is something else interesting. Our papers have several quotations from a number of Northern papers that are voicing sympathy for the South and criticism of the tactics of the Radical Republicans. Here is a quotation from the New York *Sun*: 'This attempt to overawe the vote of South Carolina by Grant's soldiers will react against the party in whose behalf it is made.' And from *The New York Herald*: 'Chamberlain has no real wish for order,' and from the New York *World*: 'Nothing...will be for one moment weighed in the balance by the men who rule this country today, against the perpetuation of their power."

While Brent was reading all this, Violet was shaking her head in agreement with the quotations he was excerpting from the papers. When he stopped, she remarked, "Well, that's encouraging to see that at last at least some of the Northerners are seeing through the tactics of the Radicals."

The State Democratic Committee proclaimed Thursday, October 26th, a special day of fasting and prayer, "not for Hampton, nor for the Democratic Party, but for South Carolina, stricken, troubled, her civilization and life at stake."

Violet and Brent joined with a hundred friends and neighbors in a prayer meeting at Holy Cross Church. Such meetings were being held in Protestant churches all over the state. Catholics were forbidden to hold such meetings, but their churches remained open for individual prayers. Violet made sure that Jesse Wallace held such a meeting at the church/school building in the workers' village for all of Fair Oaks' plantation workers—with time off from their regular work.

Election Day, November 7th, was a gloomy, rainy day. Violet was up early to see that Leo was getting his wagon trains ready to carry Negro voters to the polls from Fair

Oaks and from the other plantations and villages in this part of the county—with instructions that they should vote for Hampton for Governor and for the Democratic presidential electors. "To make your votes count in the right way, just call for a Democratic ballot and put a cross beside each name on the ticket—and that ballot is the one with the picture of the rooster on it," she told everyone.

Brent went by horseback to ride the circuit from Stateburg to Manchester to Privateer to Sumter, helping to get out the vote and helping in any other way that he could.

Violet saw to it that a good supper of corn bread and ham and beans was ready when Brent returned from his cold, wet ride that evening. After he had had a chance to wash up and change clothes, the family gathered at the dining table.

"How did it go?" Violet inquired of Brent. She waited patiently while Brent took several bites of his supper before replying. The day's work had whipped up his appetite, and he was hungry.

Finally he laid down his fork and leaned back in his chair as he replied, "Lots of excitement everywhere, but to tell you the truth, I'm worried."

"Oh, my goodness, why? Has Hampton's support been melting away?" Now she, too, set her fork down, to give him her full attention.

"I'm afraid it has among a good many of the blacks. I think the Radicals have most of the blacks intimidated in this county. I saw whole lines of blacks asking for Republican ballots, and you know we just have to have a good many black votes to have any chance of winning."

"Yes, I know. Oh, Brent, that is bad news. When will we know something?"

"It'll take some time, especially if it's a close election. You know the ballots have to be counted, then the precinct managers send their results to the county election commissions, and these report to the State Board of Canvassers."

"But Brent, aren't all those people Radicals?"

"Yes, they are, but for the first time since the War there will be Democratic representatives at the precincts when the votes are counted and at the county commissions when the results are received."

"Well, that's good, because I certainly do not trust those Radicals one bit," she said, and then asked, "Did you hear of violence anywhere?"

He buttered a piece of his corn bread and took a bite before answering, "So far I have heard of none. You know there are contingents of Federal troops in every county seat and major town to assure a so-called 'fair' election."

"Including Sumter?" Painful thoughts of Little Josh being shot by the Yankee soldiers in Sumter flashed through her mind. She shook her head as if to shake away those sad memories.

Brent knew Violet was thinking of the tragic incident with Little Josh, and he went on in a calm voice, "A detail of Blue Bellies arrived in Sumter last Thursday. The word went out to give them the royal treatment—greet them in a friendly manner, give them samples of southern cooking, and so on. Seems to have worked out rather well, except I'm afraid lots of our Negro supporters may have stayed away and failed to vote."

"Oh, dear, that *is* too bad. Well, when will we hear the results?"

"As I said, it may take several days, but we should begin to get some returns by about midnight by way of news bulletins on the telegraph. Why don't we take a nap until about midnight, and then go in and listen to the telegraph."

"Good idea. Let's do that."

It was an hour after midnight by the time Violet and Brent got down to the office with a good supply of ham sandwiches, cheese, and coffee.

"Let's see if we can find out anything yet," said Brent as he turned on the telegraph sounder.

"Reminds me of when we were listening for news of the stock market and the bank closing at the onset of the panic in '73," remarked Violet, pulling up a chair and sitting by Brent at the telegraph table.

Brent smiled and lit a cigarette. He concentrated on the *click, click* of the telegraph. Suddenly he turned to Violet and reported, "Sounds like New York is going for Tilden; that's good news."

"Yes, I could make that out, but is there anything yet on the state? On Wade 7Hampton?"

"Just wait a minute...here's a report going in from Sumter to Columbia...well, my dear, it's as I feared...looks like Sumter is going for Chamberlain..."

"*Oh, no*!"

"Hold on...a report from Columbia to the Sumter newspaper...the state is very close, but Hampton has a slight lead..."

"Whew, *that's* good."

It was another hour before there was anything more substantial. Then Brent announced, "Indiana is for Tilden, or perhaps I should say for Hendricks, the vice-presidential nominee who is from there." A little later Brent reported, "Pennsylvania, Illinois, and Ohio are going for Hayes. Of course Ohio is his home state."

"Does that make the race close?"

"Yes, fairly close, but listen...Connecticut and New Jersey are for Tilden. Now you know he is likely to carry all the South and the border states. If he does, and if he holds on to those Northern states, he should be in."

"Hooray! Now have another sandwich and more coffee to celebrate that."

"Hold on, I'll take another sandwich and a refill, but I doubt if we can be sure of Tilden's success until tomorrow. Let's wait a couple more hours to see if there's any change."

"Let's do. You know what Daddy always said, 'Don't count your chickens until they hatch."

"Sound advice, especially in politics."

With a growing drowsiness and diminished conversation, they continued to munch on cheese and unleavened biscuits and sip coffee.

Then about dawn, Brent sat up and listened intently. "Violet, listen to this—the morning *New York Tribune* says 'Tilden elected'!"

"Hurrah! Hurrah! Hurrah for Tilden!"

Brent jumped up, grabbed Violet, and they danced around the room in utter delight at the news of Tilden's success. When they stropped to catch their breath, Brent suggested that it was time for some sleep. "Let's invite the Friersons, the Stuarts, and the Andersons over in the afternoon to listen for later returns while we open some champagne."

"Yes, let's do that!" agreed Violet, elated over what looked like a big Tilden win.

When John and Sarah Frierson, Harrison and Patricia Stuart, and Will and Mary Anderson arrived about four o'clock that afternoon, newspapers from Charleston, Sumter, and Columbia had arrived, and reports still were coming over the telegraph. Jarvis and Aaron served each guest and the hosts a glass of the bubbling champagne.

"How does the situation look now?" John Frierson asked.

With a smile, Brent answered, "So far, so good. Wade Hampton still has a lead, and I think he is elected. And it looks like all the Tilden states in the early returns still are holding up, and it appears that Tilden is going to have a plurality in the popular vote of more than a quarter of a million."

"Bravo! To Tilden!" responded everyone else as they lifted their glasses in toast.

"How does Tilden's electoral vote look?" asked Harrison.

"Quite good," said Brent, "with New York, Connecticut, New Jersey, Indiana, West Virginia, and all the border states and all the South, that should add up to two hundred three for Tilden and a hundred sixty-six for Hayes."

More "Bravos" and another round of champagne. An excitement, built up from long anticipation of liberation rose with each report and each hopeful comment for the future.

After a short respite from the self-congratulatory comments that animated the group, a period of relative silence set in when the group seemed to be searching for a second wind with which to resume the celebration. Brent, still at the telegraph table, suddenly shouted, "Zounds!"

"What is it?" asked Violet.

Brent turned to the group and announced, "Can you believe this? Now *The New York Times* has put out a second edition in which they claim the election is in doubt. The Radicals are going to challenge the votes of South Carolina, Florida, and Louisiana, and the *Times* says if the Radicals can get those three states, with a total of nineteen electoral votes, Hayes will win the presidency by one vote."

"But that's ludicrous!" exclaimed Violet.

"Why those three states?" Will Anderson asked.

John Frierson answered, "Don't you see, Will, those are the three states still under Federal military occupation, where the Radicals have the best chance of manipulating the vote. Undoubtedly the Republicans there will send in a second set of returns"

"That's ridiculous," Sarah said, "surely they can't get all those votes."

"They will if they can," Brent replied tersely, "but there's more."

"Oh, Brent, what is it?" asked a worried Violet.

"Chamberlain is refusing to concede the election of Hampton. Claims he is still governor for another term. Looks like we may be in for a real donnybrook all around."

On Friday, November 10th, Violet, Brent, and the children, with Evelina and Levi, returned to Columbia with the intent to remain this year until May. Brent was anxious to follow developments at the State House, and Violet wanted to get the children back in their schools. The situation with respect to the elections was becoming more muddled each day.

As they moved their baggage into the town house, Brent said, "The State Board of Canvassers is scheduled to meet today, and I want to hurry over to the State House to see what they are doing."

"Who's on the Board?" Violet asked.

"Would you believe five elected Radical state officials, three of whom are running for reelection?"

"You mean three who are up for reelection are actually serving on the Board? Oh, dear, what chance has Wade Hampton with them?"

"Honey, he wouldn't have any, but the verification of the election of the governor and lieutenant governor is up to the General Assembly, not them. So I mustn't miss any of the sessions of the Senate."

"I should say not."

Ten days later, Brent reported that the Board had determined the election of the Radical Republican presidential electors, three Republicans of five state officers, and presumably a majority of one for the Democrats in the General Assembly, though that remained in doubt. "And that is crucial for determining the governorship," he explained to Violet. "There's talk that they are going to try to throw out the votes of Edgefield, Barnwell, and Laurens counties."

Violet led Brent into the library for a cup of tea as she tried to understand what was going on. "Now what?" she inquired.

"Well, the Democrats are applying to the state Supreme Court to require the Board of Canvassers to do their duty properly."

"Will that do any good?"

"Honey, I doubt it. They are all Radical Republicans, and you know who is the Chief Justice?"

"Don't tell me it's still Frank Moses, Senior?"

"Indeed, the father of the renegade former governor."

"Do you think there really were any irregularities in the voting?"

"No doubt. In some counties there were more votes counted than there were voters according to the census. And they say there was lots of stuffing of the ballot boxes, multiple voting, and so on, though no violence to keep people away." Then, with a twinkle in his eye, Brent added, "There may have been a few Georgians who came across the borders to vote, and they say some of the Red Shirts may have ridden around and voted in several different precincts."

"Oh, my goodness. Well, was it just the Democrats doing that sort of thing?"

"Of course not. The Republicans did just as much, but the thing is, that Republican Board of Canvassers has no right to pick out three or four counties and throw their votes out. They'll throw out whatever they need to assure themselves of a victory. And please remember, my dear, all the election boards and officials from the precincts up, were Radical Republicans, and they had Federal troops overlooking the voting. And still, everyone agrees—except for Chamberlain himself and a few Radical extremists—that Wade Hampton won a majority of the votes for governor."

Another week passed as turmoil mounted. On Friday evening, the 25th, Brent came running up the steps of the town house where Violet greeted him at the door. Breathless, he threw off his hat and great coat, walked into the parlor, and stood by the fire.

"Now what's happened?" Violet asked.

That characteristic smile appeared on his face as he replied, "The Supreme Court has put the State Board of Canvassers in jail!"

"What? Does this call for more champagne?" Her face was alight with her excitement at his news.

"Not yet, but there is hope. I must say, Chief Justice Moses is a credit to that scoundrel son of his."

"But why did the court put the members of the Board in jail?"

"For not carrying out its duty in giving certificates to those elected to the legislature and other offices."

"Good! Now what about the governor?"

"That will have to wait for the legislature to confirm the returns."

"When does the legislature meet?"

"Next Tuesday."

"I'd like to go over and sit in the gallery."

"Why don't you?"

Tuesday Violet walked up across the State House grounds with Brent through an atmosphere that seemed charged with electricity. When they arrived at the door they found Federal soldiers there, and a man who claimed to be acting as sergeant-at-arms told Violet that she could not enter, though Brent could go to his Senate seat. Brent told her to wait across the street, in front of Trinity Church, and he would join her there as soon as he could to let her know what was happening.

About noon Brent came walking across the street at a brisk pace. "The Senate was able to meet with its new and hold-over members, but the House is in turmoil—only half of them there. The Democrats have not been seated."

Looking across the way, Violet spotted a double column of men marching down Richardson Street toward the State House. Pointing toward them she asked, "Who are those men, Brent?"

Brent squinted in their direction. "Those are the Democrats of the House of Representatives, I think. I understand they've been holding a caucus over in Carolina Hall. Let's walk over and see what happens."

As they neared the State House, Brent said, "Look, Violet, they're letting them in the door."

But only a few minutes later the Democratic legislators were coming back out. Brent stopped a legislative friend, General William Henry Wallace of Union and asked, "What's going on here, Henry?"

"They blocked the doors to the House chamber and wouldn't let us enter. They've got Federal troops in there to preserve order, they say. So, the Radicals, without our presence, already had gone ahead and organized. Elected Mackey as their so-called speaker."

"How can they do that?"

"Pure brass and Federal soldiers."

"Well, what are you going to do now?"

"We have a quorum ourselves if we admit the men from Edgefield and Laurens, and we are going back to Carolina Hall and organize ourselves as the legal House. And you know something? That Republican House in there is all Negro except for Mackey of Charleston and your two men from Sumter, Thomas Johnston and John Ferriter."

"Whatever has happened to the Board of Canvassers?" Brent wanted to know.

"They got a writ of *habeas corpus* from the Federal court and were released."

"Oh, damn, but I guess we do have to hand it to the State Supreme Court for applying the law without political bias."

"Yes, that we do, surprising, isn't it?"

"Well, Henry, I hope you stand your ground."

"Don't worry, I assure you we shall."

Violet broke in, "Look, there's Wade Hampton going up to the State House."

"It *is* Hampton," said Brent.

"And watch," commented Wallace, "they are not letting him enter either. Looks like he is going to say something. Come on, let's move over where we can hear."

Wade Hampton stood on the capitol steps as the crowd, growing in hostility toward the occupants of the State House, gathered in front of the tall, impressive figure. The throng fell silent as he raised his hand for attention, and then began speaking:

> *My friends, I am truly doing what I have done earnestly during the whole exciting contest, pouring oil on the troubled waters. It is of great importance to us all, as citizens of South Carolina, that peace should be preserved...Keep perfectly quiet, leave the streets, and do nothing to provoke a riot. We trust to the law and the Constitution, and we have perfect faith in the justice of our cause.*

The next afternoon when Brent came in to the town house, Violet greeted him with rather more anxiety than usual. As he took a chair in the parlor and gratefully accepted a glass of scuppernong, she asked, "What's the situation down at the State House now?"

"The Democrats of the House, meeting over in Carolina Hall, organized and elected Wallace as speaker."

"So now we have two houses of representatives?"

"Yes, two, both claiming to be the house of representatives of the General Assembly."

She shook her head in wonder as she said, "What a mess."

"It is, indeed." He held out his wine glass for a refill.

Pouring the wine, she asked, "Brent, I can't help but worry, do you think there is any danger of violence?"

"Probably. We likely would have had a forceful entry of the State House already had it not been for the influence of Wade Hampton."

"Have you seen the report from the *New York Herald* in the afternoon paper?"

"No, haven't seen the afternoon paper."

Picking up a newspaper, Violet took a chair opposite Brent and said, "Listen to this:

> *The bearing of South Carolina citizens in the great trial to which they were subjected yesterday was admirable. There has never been a more critical and dangerous conjunction in the history of American politics. The whole country had its attention focused on the proceedings at Columbia and there was a great strain of anxiety and apprehension lest scenes of violence and bloodshed should set the whole country on fire and inaugurate a new civil war. Public passion was in so inflamed a state that a mere spark might have kindled a conflagration of which the consequences might have been appalling. As no spark fell into the dry tinder there we felicitate the country that the period of danger is past.*
>
> *The credit of preserving the peace at Columbia yesterday is due to General Wade Hampton, Democratic candidate for Governor. He had only to lift his finger, he had only to signify the slightest assent and the State House would have been rescued from the Federal soldiers and his supporters could have controlled the organization of the Legislature...It is fortunate that they have a leader so strong, so sagacious, so self-possessed, and so thoroughly trusted as Wade Hampton. He perfectly understands the situation, and as we may judge by his conduct yesterday, he will make no mistakes...His supporters have so much confidence in him that they will do nothing against his wishes and he understands the situation too well to permit any resort to violence.*

"That is well done," Brent said.

"Yet I can't help but wonder if the period of danger is really past," she sighed.

"On the contrary, Violet, there will be a danger of violence as long as Chamberlain insists on holding the State House by the force of Federal arms."

She sighed again. "Were there any more developments today?"

"Something new every day. The shirt-tail Republican House, presided over by Mackey, voted to unseat the five Democratic members from Barnwell County, even though the Board of Canvassers had conceded their election, and they held valid certificates from the secretary of state, and then they proceeded to seat the five Radical Republicans who had been defeated."

"But Brent, how can they do that?"

"They can't. I don't think the Supreme Court will allow it."

"Tomorrow is supposed to be Thanksgiving, you know. Anything special?"

"Back to the State House, early, but I thought you paid little never mind to Thanksgiving as being too much of a New England relic."

"That's true, although Grandmama Lee claims that the first Thanksgiving was held at Berkeley Plantation in Virginia, on December 4, 1619, before the Pilgrims even left England. I know that we don't pay very much attention to it here, but you know our Protestant Episcopal Church in 1789 recognized Thanksgiving and set the first Thursday in November as the date for it, unless civil authorities should set another date–which some states did, and then in 1863 President Lincoln proclaimed the last Thursday in November as Thanksgiving Day. Anyway, there'll be a service at Trinity."

"I suppose so."

"Why don't I plan to go to services at Trinity Church, and then you can meet me there about noon."

"Sounds good, but I don't think you should take the children over there. We still may have trouble, and, Violet, stay alert and clear out if it looks like anything is developing."

Chapter 70

Double Trouble

1876 - 1877

The next morning Brent was out of the house at dawn. Violet drove alone to Trinity Church in time for the eleven o'clock Thanksgiving service. When it was over she went outside to wait for Brent. She waited for an hour with no sign of him. Another half hour, nothing. She could see a few soldiers around the State House and only a few people going in and out. She determined to go over and see if she could find her husband.

No one delayed her at the door—obviously she was no legislator since only men could vote. As she walked by the House chamber she heard shouting and talking and pounding in pure bedlam. As she hurried over toward the Senate chamber, Brent came running up to her before she had spotted him.

A little grimly he asked, "What are you doing here?"

"Looking for you, you silly goose. Did you think you could stand me up and get away with it? Church has been over for an hour and a half."

He looked surprised. "Is it that late already? Come here and listen." He led her over to a corner in the corridor.

"What in the world is going on?" Violet looked up curiously and tilted her head toward the noisy House chamber.

"General Wallace and the Democrats, insisting that they have a quorum of the House, all arrived here earlier, brushed the doorkeepers aside, and took their places in the House, with Henry Wallace in the speaker's chair."

"Good for them."

"Then an hour or so later, the Radicals arrived, claiming that they constituted the House. They moved in right alongside the Democrats, and Mackey, their alleged speaker, went up to the speaker's rostrum and refused to leave when Wallace invited him to do so."

"Amazing, but what has that got to do with your failure to meet me at noon?"

"You see, if they ever get settled into voting on confirming the election of the governor, that is a joint vote, and I dare not miss that, and there may be other critical votes. Nobody dares to leave, lest he miss a vote."

"Of course not, but Brent, do we dare go up in the gallery and see what is going on in the House?"

"I think so. Several of the senators are up there watching."

When they got to the balcony the noise on the floor of the House was more raucous than ever.

"I see General Wallace down there on the rostrum," Violet said, "Is that Mackey beside him?"

"Yes, it is," Brent answered, "Look, both are presiding as Speaker–and the Democrats are paying attention only to Wallace, and the Republicans to Mackey, and men are speaking on both sides at the same time, neither paying the slightest attention to the other. What a muddle."

They watched for several more minutes before Violet said she probably ought to be getting home to the children. "Any idea when you will be getting home?" she asked.

"Not the slightest. Probably late. Who knows what voting may come up, and we Democrats don't dare leave because they likely would not let us back in. The military commander already has notified Wallace that at noon tomorrow the Democratic members from Edgefield and Laurens counties would be evicted. Some of the other senators and I have lodged a strong protest against this. The Army is supposed to be here to preserve order, not to take sides, though, of course, Chamberlain is using them to hold on to the governor's office. Anyway, we may be here late tonight. I'm not planning to go anywhere else, so as long as I'm not home, you can assume I'm here."

Violet delayed supper for an hour, and then another hour, but Brent did not come. She waited up until midnight, and still he was not there. She decided to go on to bed and get some rest while she waited. Her prayers were longer than usual this time, and she drifted off to sleep before finishing.

When she awoke the next morning, Brent still was not there. She resolved to go back to the State House, and decided to take Levi along to tend the horse so that she could leave quickly if there was any trouble.

Arriving at the State House she entered without difficulty. Tired, bedraggled men were milling all around the halls. She found Brent near the entrance to the Senate chamber, looking as bedraggled as all the others.

She came up beside him and clasped his hand. "For goodness sakes, Brent, have you been here all night?"

"Of course, what do you think?" he answered in a tired voice.

"You look exhausted. Have you had anything to eat?"

"Last evening we emptied the Solons' Saloon, but we've had nothing since. I certainly could use a cup of hot coffee."

She gazed at him even more closely. She brushed her hand lightly across his cheek. "You're getting that scraggly beard again that makes you look like General Sherman–."

He ran his hand over his face. "My god, Violet, do you think you could fetch me a razor?"

"And your eyes are so red you look like you've been with Don Juan in hell. Have you had any sleep at all?"

"No, not much. Tried to sleep at my desk, but it was pretty cold and uncomfortable."

"I'll be back as quickly as I can," Violet said as she spun around and headed down the hall and out the door.

Taking the reins herself, she and Levi sped back to the town house, quickly jumped out, and while Levi tied the horse to the iron hitching post, she ran into the house.

In half an hour she came out with Evelina and two big pots of coffee, a basket with three loaves of bread, several jars of jam, and half a dozen coffee cups. In another basket she had a razor, soap, and a towel.

Back at the State House, Brent greeted her with a new enthusiasm as she delivered her supplies. After emptying her basket, Violet promised to return in the early afternoon with more victuals.

"Thank you, Violet. I was really famished, and I certainly don't want to go around looking like I've been at sea a month. When you come back will you bring a blanket? We may be in for several more nights of this nonsense."

"I hope not! Yes, I'll bring the blanket." She stood on her tiptoes to give him a light kiss on the cheek and then left.

That afternoon she returned, and with the help of Levi and Uncle Job, brought in a big pot of baked beans, corn bread, butter, ham, baked Irish potatoes, sugar cookies, a couple of blankets, and a clean shirt. Dozens of other men and women were carrying food into the State House when she arrived. Brent's spirits rose as each dish was uncovered, and he was glad to have food to share with some of his colleagues.

"This reminds me of how we used to take food down to the soldiers at the railroad stations during the War," said Violet, "and we used to come up here to work in the hospital at the old State House."

"Darling, you really are an angel of mercy, and I'll try to think of as many errands for you to run for me as I can, just so I can see you again—."

"Oh, you silly goose!" laughed Violet.

Violet, with Levi and Uncle Job, returned to the State House on her errands of mercy morning and afternoon for the next two days. On Saturday afternoon, Brent told Violet to have Levi and Uncle Job wait with the rig while they would go up and have another look at the House. He had heard that it might be interesting.

"How have things been going?" she asked as they walked up the stairs to the balcony.

"Better than you might think. There are lots of acid speeches and shouting of epithets during the day, but last night the blacks all joined with the whites in singing, *Listen to the Mocking Bird,* and *Carolina,* and the whites joined them in singing Negro spirituals, and they listened to each other tell stories."

"Did the Army evict those Democrats as they threatened?"

"No, they did not. Our protest held firm." Waving down toward the floor of the House, Brent whispered, "Listen."

A distinguished looking black man had risen from the Radical Republican side to speak. In contrast with earlier sessions, a hush fell over the hall. Everyone leaned forward to listen more closely.

"Who is it?" Violet whispered.

"That's Tom Hamilton from Beaufort. He was one of Chamberlain's strongest supporters at the Republican convention in September," Brent answered in a low voice.

"What is he up to now?"

"Listen."

Hamilton went into a scathing speech against what the Radical Republicans were doing in blocking the will of the people as expressed in the election. Then he walked up to the rostrum, faced Speaker Wallace, held up his hand and took the oath as a member of the Wallace House. Head high, he looked defiantly all around the chamber and returned to his seat on the front row, while his Radical Republican associates cowered and the Democrats broke into cheers."

"Can you believe that?" exclaimed Brent softly. "One of the most outstanding black Republican leaders in the House has just crossed Jordan!"

Sunday afternoon, as Violet was preparing baskets of food to take to the State House, Brent suddenly came bounding in the door. He brushed Violet's cheek with his lips as she ran to meet him and continued upstairs, two steps at a time, and into their office.

Violet ran up after him, calling, "Brent, Brent, what on earth is it? What's happened?"

"Just a minute, my dear. I've got to get some telegraph messages off. Then I'll explain."

Violet had never seen Brent so agitated. She watched quietly as he took paper and pen and wrote a series of messages. Taking these to the telegraph table he began operating the key. After he had finished the first message he handed it over to Violet. She read:

CAPTAIN JONATHAN WELLS STOP GREENVILLE STOP SHIP FIRST TRAIN 200 CHICKENS STATE FAIR WITH SUFFICIENT GAFFS.

She wanted to cry out, "What does this mean?" but she controlled herself while Brent continued to work at the telegraph. At last he shut down the instrument and turned around.

With a worried look on his face, he said, "Hampton received an anonymous letter this afternoon saying that seventy-five to a hundred members of the Hunkidori Club of Charleston—."

"What is the Hunkidori Club?"

"A bunch of mostly black ruffians and thugs. They say the plan is for Chamberlain to appoint them as constables, and then they will help expel the Democratic representatives from Laurens and Edgefield, and in effect, make the Wallace House inoperative."

"Oh, my goodness, do you think they really will come, or was the note just an act of some crank who wants to make trouble?"

"We checked around the State House and found over a hundred Hunkidoris already in there—and they are armed."

"Zounds, no! Now what did that strange message mean?"

"That meant to mobilize two hundred Red Shirts, armed, and get them to Columbia as quickly as possible. Other messages are to Sumter, Fairfield, and Lexington counties. Couriers are rounding up the clubs in Columbia and Richland County."

Violet shuddered. For the second time that week flashes of Brent's being shot in Vicksburg by hoodlums and carried into the house close to death haunted her. She struggled to control her voice. "Oh, Brent, do you think there will be violence?"

"There will be if the Red Shirts don't get here in time. We hope we can overpower the Hunkis so that they will not dare open fire. Now, Violet, I think I had better get back to the Senate. Try not to worry, my Love."

"Are you going to wear your red shirt?"

"No, I had better go as a Senator, but I'm taking no chances," he said as he strapped on his revolver under his coat and filled his pockets with cartridges.

Again a kaleidoscope of fearful memories flickered through her mind. "Do you think it will be another all-night stay?" she asked in a small voice.

"Probably." He knew what was going through her mind, but he could not lie to her. To get her thinking of something else he asked, "Honey, can you get some food for me to take along?"

"Of course," was all she could manage. She turned so he could not see the tears of fright in her eyes, and she headed quickly toward the kitchen.

During the night Violet found herself listening for gunfire. She heard none. Intermittently she sent up little prayers of thanks for the silence.

Brent was back early the next afternoon, before the children came home from school. When he strode in, Violet ran up and flung her arms around him in relief. He kissed her and held her tightly for a few moments. He knew that it had been a difficult night for her, too.

She drew back, looked up into his weary sea-blue eyes and asked him anxiously, "What happened?"

He smiled and answered, "First of all, my Love, as you can see, I am all right. So wipe that worried look off your face." He gave her a gentle kiss before going on, "Now as to what happened, come on upstairs with me. After not seeing a bed for four nights, I'm ready for a nap. I'll fill you in while I'm cleaning up and undressing."

They walked up the stairs and into their bedroom together.

"Brent, you've got to tell me what happened. I know you are tired, but I just can't wait any longer."

He sat down in a chair to remove his shoes and began to describe what had gone on since he had last seen her. "Well, Wallace's House decided to leave the State House and go back to Carolina Hall–."

"Oh, does that mean they have given up?"

"Not at all. They still insist they have a legal, legislative quorum, and that that legality does not depend on where they happen to be sitting."

"What about the Hunkidories and the Red Shirts? Did they clash?"

"Beats anything you ever saw. By noon today there were three thousand Red Shirts all around the capitol, and they are still pouring in, coming on horseback or by railroad boxcars. Probably be twice that many by tonight. They had secret instructions, which they were careful to let the Radical Republican so-called Speaker Mackey overhear, that if the Hunkidoris fired a shot, the Red Shirts immediately would shoot Mackey—and no shot was fired."

With a great sigh of relief, Violet breathed softly, "Thank God for that."

"But now Mackey and his shirt-tail Republican House have called for a joint session with the Senate to vote on the election of the Governor."

"Are you going?"

"Oh, yes, I'll go. We'll be outnumbered, and with the Radicals acting on their own as the House, it will all be completely illegal, but I want to keep up with what they are doing."

The next afternoon Brent reported that, as predicted, the illegal legislature had voted confirmation of Chamberlain as Governor. Brent said that there was to be a meeting that night around Choral Hall, and he planned to go.

On returning from that meeting, he reported that five thousand men were there cheering Hampton. "Somebody yelled, 'Give us the word, General, and we'll tear down the State House with our bare hands.' But Hampton urged peace and moderation, said he would lead them into the State House when the time comes."

On Thursday, December 7th, Violet and Brent went to the State House, out of curiosity, to join the small crowd there for the "inauguration" of Chamberlain. They remained for a speech by Hampton that evening, out on the street, when he said, "The people have elected me Governor, and by the Eternal God, I will be Governor or we shall have a military governor."

A week later, Brent attended a joint session of the Wallace Democratic House and Democratic Senate, and voted that Hampton had been elected Governor.

Chamberlain held on to the Governor's office, and that afternoon Violet and Brent joined a crowd in the street for a colorful ceremony for the inauguration of Hampton. In his inaugural address, Hampton said:

> *A great task is before the conservative party of this state. They entered on this contest on a platform so broad, so strong, so liberal, that every honest citizen could stand upon it. They recognized and accepted the amendments of the Constitution in good faith; they pledged themselves to work reform and to establish good government; they promised to keep up an efficient system of public education; and they declared solemnly that all citizens of South Carolina, of both races and of both parties, should be regarded as equals in the eye of the law; all to be protected in the enjoyment of every political right now possessed by them.*
>
> *To the faithful observance of these pledges we stand committed, and I, as the representative of the conservative party, hold myself*

bound by every dictate of honor and good faith to use every effort to have these pledges redeemed fully and honestly. It is due not only to ourselves but to the colored people of the State that wise, just and liberal measures would prevail in our legislation. We owe much of our late success to these colored voters who were brave enough to rise above the prejudice of race and honest enough to throw off the shackles of party in their determination to save the State. To those who, misled by their fears, their ignorance, or by evil counseling, turned a deaf ear to our appeals, we should not be vindictive but magnanimous. Let us show to all of them that the true interests of both races can best be secured by cultivating peace and promoting prosperity among all classes of our fellow citizens...

That evening Violet brought in wine and cheese for a little relaxation with Brent in the parlor of their town house.

"Quite a ceremony today," Violet remarked.

"Now we have Hampton inaugurated."

"Will it stick?"

"I think so. Yesterday the Army General announced that he would uphold the Mackey Republicans and would deny the Wallace Democrats entrance into the State House, but also yesterday the Supreme Court recognized the Wallace House as the legally constituted House of Representatives."

"What was the final popular vote for Governor?"

"According to the Republican canvassers themselves, the vote for Hampton was 92,261 to 91,127 for Chamberlain. Hampton reckons that he got 17,000 Negro votes."

"Then what is the problem? Why doesn't Chamberlain step down? We can't have two Governors."

"Chamberlain claims that there were enough fraudulent Democratic votes that should be thrown out to give him the victory."

"What about the vote for President?"

"I'm afraid that the same canvass shows about the same margin on the other side—in favor of Hayes, the Republican, but the Democrats are contesting that."

"So I guess the national election still is in doubt. I guess our toast with champagne was a bit premature."

"Very much so. The Democratic National Chairman, Abram Hewitt of New York, has asked all Democrats to hold mass meetings in their local towns on January 8th to let their congressmen know where they stand on resolving the presidential election."

"Why January 8th?"

"Give time to get the word, I suppose. It may be because that is the anniversary of Andrew Jackson's victory at the Battle of New Orleans."

"Of course, that's it."

"But Tilden has canceled that. He is just like Hampton in calling for moderation and no violence."

"So right now South Carolina has two Governors and two Houses of Representatives, and we don't know who is going to be President."

"That's about it, though I must say Chamberlain is on shaky ground, and Tilden has such a big lead in Louisiana that I don't see how they can throw out enough votes to count him out there, and with just that one doubtful state, he will be in."

Violet and the family returned to Fair Oaks for the celebration of Christmas and for the payment of year-end wages and Christmas bonuses to all the workers. Charlotte, Leland, little Lee and baby Rosemary, and Andrew joined them there the day before Christmas, and Brent's mother and father and Phoebe came over from Charleston. Grandmama Lee in Virginia could not come down, but she promised a long visit in the Spring when traveling would be more comfortable. The Friersons and the Stuarts joined them all for dinner on Christmas Day.

There was an even deeper closeness among the family members; the children seemed to enjoy Christmas even more as they got older; games of whist and Brent's new chess game were as popular as ever, and conversations were lively and stimulating with all the political doings and undoings going on, though everyone was now fearful that Hampton and Tilden might not come out the winners in the elections.

During the next few weeks Violet and Brent followed closely the continually unfolding political news. On January 30th, they read that in Columbia the Supreme Court had recognized Wade Hampton as Governor, and in Washington, Congress had established an Electoral Commission to review the disputed votes for President of South Carolina, Florida, and Louisiana, and one questionable electoral vote in Oregon.

On February 10th, they read that the Electoral Commission, by a strictly partisan vote of eight to seven, had awarded the electoral votes of Florida to Hayes.

On February 24th, Brent looked up from his paper as he and Violet read in their town house office. With a deep sigh he said, "Well, Violet, I'm afraid it's all over for Tilden."

She let out a little cry of protest. "Oh, no! Louisiana?"

In a grim voice he answered, "Yes. Would you believe that by votes of eight to seven the Commission threw out thirteen thousand Democratic votes in order to steal Louisiana?"

"That's awful, simply awful! Those blasted crooked Radicals! Oh, it all makes me feel so...so *impotent*!"

Violet looked out the window as a carriage pulled up in front of the town house.

"Who is it? Brent asked.

"John Frierson and two other men. Oh...I think that's Charles Rhett, and the other one is Scott Carson. You remember him, he was a captain in Hampton's Legion, knew Daddy there."

"Sure, I remember Scott, and it'll be good to see my old buddy, Charles, again. Wonder what they're doing in Columbia."

Jarvis was occupied in the kitchen, and both Violet and Brent were at the door to greet the visitors. They invited them in to chairs in front of the parlor fireplace. Brent moved up additional chairs while Violet ordered tea.

Charles Rhett was the same handsome, dashing, debonair figure that Violet remembered, except today there was fire in his eyes and an unusually serious disposition. His dark hair was neatly combed and his thin moustache closely trimmed.

Scott Carson, his blond hair a little mussed, affected a rather more calm disposition, but he, too, was agitated and upset.

After all had settled in a semicircle around the fire, John Frierson spoke the concerns of everyone. "We have just come from Sumter where we heard that they've given Louisiana to Hayes."

"Yes," Brent nodded, "I know."

"By God, I say let's march on Washington," said Rhett, his dark eyes flashing. "We're going around the county to see if the Red Shirts are ready to march again."

Brent frowned and said, "But Wade Hampton is advising peaceable approaches."

"Well, what about a peaceful march?" asked Carson. "Henry Watterson, you know, the editor of the newspaper in Louisville, Kentucky, is calling for a hundred thousand Tilden men to march on Washington unarmed."

Violet showed her alarm, "Oh, but don't you think that would likely lead to fighting?"

Rhett answered sharply, "I say if it does, so be it."

As Cora brought in tea and Violet poured for everyone, Frierson said, "I understand very unofficially of course, that some of our Southern leaders have been meeting privately with some of Hayes' men to try to work out a compromise."

"Compromise?" Rhett responded. "How can you compromise an election? Either Tilden wins or he doesn't. What is there to compromise?"

John Frierson turned to him and answered, "Some think it may be possible to get some concessions from Hayes in favor of the South in return for the Democrats not obstructing his inauguration."

"Sounds like a pretty heavy price," said Carson. "It seems to me it would be better to get Tilden in office and be sure of fair treatment of the South."

"Of course it would," Rhett said. "You can't trust those damned Radical Republicans, no matter what they say."

Brent got up, walked around the room in deep thought, and returned to his chair. "I think we may be able to trust Hayes," he said. "It may be a deal can be worked out–if we let them steal the election then Hayes would withdraw the Federal troops from Louisiana and South Carolina and give us all more of a free hand in running our own affairs."

"Do you think something like that could really work?" asked Frierson.

Brent looked around the group before answering. "You know, there is a peculiar thing about politics. You might call it the *political inversion* principle. Sometimes when one party or leader has been criticizing an opposing leader or has been opposing policies of the other party, that leader may turn around and do those very things and get away with it, while the party that originally held that position might be severely criticized for doing the same thing."

"How do you mean that?" inquired Carson.

Brent explained, "It may well be that Hayes might do more for the South than could Tilden. If Tilden eased the Reconstruction Acts and withdrew the troops, the northern Vindictives would scream bloody murder. They would be waving the bloody shirt all over the place. Hayes, being a Republican, could do it with less screaming from his own party."

John Frierson nodded his concurrence in these sentiments. "Our main interest is in getting Wade Hampton installed as Governor and getting the Federal Government off our backs. It's just possible that we may be able to assure that more quickly with Hayes than with Tilden."

After further conversation, and with some reluctance, Rhett and Carson came around to Brent's view—reflecting Hampton's—that no march on Washington was indicated, and there still was real hope of regaining control of the State Government.

At the end of February Violet and Brent read that, as preordained, South Carolina's vote had been reviewed, and by another vote of eight to seven the Commission had awarded South Carolina's electoral votes to Hayes.

"But didn't you say that South Carolina probably did vote for Hayes?" Violet asked.

"Yes, I did, though one cannot be sure. The South Carolina Democrats had a pretty good case before the Commission. Their contention is that the South Carolina vote should not be counted at all, and of course, that would give the election to Tilden."

"On what did the Democrats base their contention?"

"On the following: One, that the legislature had failed to provide a registration law as the Constitution requires; two, that more than a thousand deputy United States marshals, appointed under an unconstitutional law, had interfered with voting rights of the people, and third, that there really was not in operation a republican form of government in the state as guaranteed by the Federal Constitution."

"That all sounds pretty convincing to me."

"Sure, and to seven Democrats on the Commission, but that won't do it," he said sarcastically.

"So that does it for the Radicals," she replied with resignation.

On Monday, since the regular date for inauguration, March 4th, fell on Sunday, March 5, 1877, Rutherford B. Hayes, Republican of Ohio, was inaugurated President of the United States.

And D.H. Chamberlain still held to the State House in Columbia.

Chapter 71

Faith Renewed

1877

During this winter of 1876-77, Violet found herself attending church regularly more and more as a matter of conviction than merely as a matter of habit or to set an example for the children.

For his part, Brent thought that vestry meetings and committee meetings were largely a waste of time. He conceded that somebody had to do what they did, but not he. Still, he surprised even himself at the regularity of his attendance at church services. He saw this more as support for Violet and for his admiration of Wade Hampton, who was a regular attender at Trinity, than out of any deep sense of personal commitment. He was a major financial contributor both to Holy Cross Church at Stateburg and Trinity Church in Columbia. He preferred to make contributions in kind when practicable. If there was a need for some new pews or carpet or choir robes or certain repairs, he would use his connections to get good prices and then donate them.

Meanwhile Bonnie Anne and J.J. had been attending a class at Trinity for instruction in the catechism in preparation for confirmation. On Wednesday afternoon, Violet stopped at the church to pick them up. She walked by the room in a wing where the instruction was going on. They were learning *The Apostles' Creed.* She walked on to the nave of the church and sat in one of the pews to wait. She glanced around at the beautiful stained glass windows, as she had many times before, but this time, with the sunshine streaming through the bright colors, a new sense of awe spread through her.

"Good afternoon, Violet." It was Father Shand, standing by the pew, his admiration for his parishioner reflected in his kindly brown eyes.

Rising, she smiled and said, "Good afternoon, Father."

He motioned with his hand. "Please, keep your seat. Isn't this a beautiful first day of spring?"

"Indeed it is, and just look how the streams of light are coming through those lovely windows."

"Ah, yes. You have come for the children?"

"Yes, they were working on *The Apostle' Creed* when I walked by."

"Yes, Father Henley is working with them."

Violet fidgeted in the pew. She looked up at Father Shand and said, "You know something, I have a confession to make."

"My goodness, what is that?"

"I never have really understood the significance of the Creed."

"What do you mean, Violet?"

Violet looked up toward the altar where tablets on either side bore the words of *The Ten Commandments, The Lord's Prayer,* and *The Apostles' Creed.*

"Look," she answered, " *'God the Father Almighty, Maker of heaven and earth,* is fairly straightforward,' but then what is the significance of *'Suffered under Pontius Pilate...descended into hell,'* and so on? How is any of that going to affect my behavior or my attitude? And why do we give Pontius Pilate so much attention, to always repeat his name?"

"Perhaps to give it a time reference."

"Does that really matter?"

"Well, Violet, all this is leading up to the resurrection. Don't you think that is fundamental? Especially at this time of the year when we celebrate the renewal of life?"

Her smooth forehead creased into a frown as she pondered his questions. "Yes, I suppose it is, but if the Creed is supposed to be a summary of the essential elements of the faith, I don't see it there."

"Do you prefer *The Nicene Creed*?"

"Not really. That has the same difficulties. It also talks about Pontius Pilate and all of that. It sounds good, but I don't know what it means—'*Very God of very God, Begotten, not made'*, and so on, and I don't know how accepting it changes my behavior or attitude. Neither does it express the fundamental Christian teachings as I see it."

"Well, Violet, what do you think are the fundamental teachings of Christianity?"

"I think it is love, *agape*, and I don't see it even mentioned there."

"Isn't it? Perhaps not the word specifically, but think, my dear, what greater love than to join us here on earth, to take the form of man, to suffer as man upon the Cross, to take our sins upon His shoulders, and then to rise from the dead and ascend to heaven and leave us with the comforting and reassuring thought that life goes on after death. Ah, love and caring are evident throughout both creeds. God is the epitome of love."

"I haven't thought of it in that perspective, Father," she admitted.

A gentle smile came upon Father Shand's face as he said, "I tell you, Violet, why don't you have a go at composing a creed the way you think it ought to be."

Violet laughed nervously and blushed. "Now, Father, that would be presumptuous. You are mocking me."

"Oh, no, no, not at all," Father Shand said hastily, "I am sorry if it came across like that. I was not suggesting that you might *replace* the traditional creeds. No, indeed, but I believe it is a very useful exercise for anyone to jot down the essentials of his belief in a kind of personal creed. Why don't you do that and bring it to me in a week."

Now Violet managed a giggle. "You sound like a schoolmaster."

He laughed fondly, "Of course, why not? Will you do it?"

Violet hesitated a few moments, then smiled and replied, "Of course, why not?"

During the next few days Violet spent every free moment in thinking about her assignment. Each day, when her chores were done, Brent and Bonnie Anne and J.J. were away, and the baby was napping, she went to the office, closed the door, put her *Bible* and *Book of Common Prayer* before her, and wrote down her thoughts. She discovered that she looked upon this exercise as a stimulating challenge. *The Nicene Creed says, "I believe in one God the Father Almighty, Maker of heaven and earth, And of all things visible and invisible," and that is good. But the Gospel of St. John also says, "the Word was God," and the first epistle of John says, "God is Love"...And in the Gospel of John, Jesus says that He is "the light of the world"...*

True to her word, Violet was back at Trinity Church with a copy of her personal creed within a week. She found Father Shand in his study and handed him her paper. She took a chair and eagerly waited for him to finish reading what she had set down. She was not disappointed in his reaction.

"Why, Violet, this is well-done, well-done, indeed." He proceeded to reread it, this time aloud, and Violet listened to the words that were indicative of her deepest beliefs, beliefs that she was unaware of until Father Shand had given her this assignment:

> *I believe in one God, the Father Almighty who is Love and who is the Word, Maker of heaven and earth, and of all things visible and invisible; the Son, manifest in Jesus Christ, the Light of the world, who was endowed with such love that he laid down his life for it, and dwells in the hearts of all men, and the Holy Spirit, the Comforter, the Giver of life, the Spirit of loving-kindness, and the source of truth, wisdom, and inspiration.*
>
> *And in the worship of Him in spirit and in truth, and in loving Him with all heart, soul, and mind. And that this love expresses itself in love for one another, in serving Him through serving others, in doing to others as one would be done by, in offering more than is asked, in doing good to enemies as well as friends, and living in faith, hope, and love, amongst which the greatest is love.*
>
> *I believe in the blessedness of the humble, the happiness of the merciful, the felicity of the peacemakers, the beatitude of the pure in heart, and the favor of them who seek righteousness for its own sake.*
>
> *I believe in the fatherhood of God, the brotherhood of man, and the fellowship of the church; the freedom of the mind, the forgiveness of sin, and the life everlasting. Amen.*

"Very well done," Father Shand repeated. "May I keep this?"

"Of course," she replied, pleased that he liked it so much that he wanted to keep it. She had made another copy for herself, which one day she would show Brent.

"How did you find the task?

"Difficult, challenging, thought-provoking, intimidating, scary, comforting, revealing, exciting, searching," she rattled off. "All of these and more. I understand why you asked me to do this. The exercise forced me to *think*, to admit to myself what's in my heart and soul and mind. It forced me to analyze and pull together my deepest beliefs; indeed, to admit these beliefs to myself. It wasn't easy, but I'm glad I did."

Pre-dawn on Easter, April 1st, was clear and slightly cool, with the promise of a sunny day. Bonnie Anne and J.J. made strong protests at such early rising, but soon they were thrilled to be getting into their new clothes. Bonnie Anne wore a new blue dress of poplin dotted with magenta. Her sash was solid magenta. Her boots were made of gray wool and black patent leather. Her hair, now deep brown in color, but with red and gold highlights, was parted in the middle with bunches of long curls held close to her neck. She wore a blue straw hat trimmed with magenta ribbon and carried white cotton gloves.

J.J. wore a white linen waist with a ruffled collar, and navy full pleated pantaloons which tapered to cuffs just above his ankles revealing his side-button leather shoes. He wore a broad-brimmed straw sailor hat with navy ribbon and short navy streamers.

Violet's dress was deep rose, with trimmings of pale pink ruffles and ruchings. The overskirt of her dress was split in front and turned back to show the pale pink lining while her separate back overskirts were puffed and draped. A green velvet bow on the back of her overskirt formed the bustle. Under the deep v-necked bodice of the dress she wore a pale pink tucked blouse. Hoops were still being worn, but now her hoop curved out at the sides and back only, leaving the front flat. Violet was happy with this change because it made it easier for her and other ladies to kneel at the altar rail when taking communion. Her gloves were of white lace.

Violet had pulled her hair up away from her face, with curls on the top of her head and down the back. Short curly bangs fringed her forehead and half-way down the sides of her face, giving her a piquant look. Brent liked her new hair style, and protested her wearing her pert light green straw hat.

"But, Darling, you know it isn't proper not to wear a hat outside, and besides, I *have* to wear a hat to church, and *especially* on Easter."

"I guess so," he agreed reluctantly, "but you just look so adorable. Well, promise me you'll take it off the minute we get home, and don't put on any of those lace house caps either."

"All right."

She looked at Brent in his new outfit, thinking, *I declare, he gets more handsome and elegant-looking with each year.* She admired the studied look of his long gray sack coat. Although it had four buttons, in line with the mode of the day, he fastened only the top button, so that it opened to reveal his matching vest and the upper part of his checked trousers. His shirt had a stiff collar, and he wore a blue checked ascot with the jeweled stickpin that Violet had given him. He carried a walking stick with a silver head.

"Brent, you just look so...so...handsome this morning."

"And you look absolutely gorgeous, my Love. Listen, I have a great idea. Let's send the children and the servants to church, and let's you and I stay home this morning." He raised one eyebrow wickedly and looking at her with an invitation in his eyes.

"Oh, you silly, silly goose, you know we can't do that!" giggled Violet, and then she added, "But I agree, it's a great idea."

Levi and Evelina, Uncle Job, and Cora and Raymond came along. Only Aunt Beulah stayed at home to take care of baby Wade. It took both the buggy and the carriage to transport everyone to church.

As they entered the church, the twenty-year old organ in the west gallery filled the whole place with Handel's music, and the rising sun lit up the stained-glass windows along the east wall in sparkling colors that reflected across the nave.

During the processional hymn, the crucifer, the large choir of men and boys, various altar boys, and Father Shand, with his assistant, Father Henley, came down the long center aisle and found their places. After the preliminaries, Father Shand read the Easter Story from St. Luke—of how Mary Magdalene, and Joanna, and Mary the mother of James, and other women had told the apostles of the resurrection. A hymn followed this, and then he read the Prayer of St. Francis of Assisi. After another hymn, he invited the congregation to stand and read together from a leaflet that had been inserted in each hymnal. It was a neatly printed sheet with the title, *A Christian's Creed, by Violet Storm Sutler.*

Brent nudged Violet with his elbow. "What's this?" he whispered. "Did you write this?"

"Yes, shush, listen," she admonished him, surprised at this turn of events.

"Please read this in silence," Father Shand instructed the congregation. "If it seems to represent your own beliefs, then join me in reading it aloud.." After a pause for the silent reading, voices throughout the church merged into one as they repeated Violet's creed.

Brent nudged Violet again. "Very good; even I can buy that," he whispered.

Violet smiled at his approval even as she frowned for him to be quiet.

Then, much to Violet's surprise, Brent got up and went to the lectern. He turned the pages of the Bible and began reading the Second Lesson, Proverbs 31:10-29:

> *Who can find a virtuous woman? for her price is far above rubies.*
>
> *The heart of her husband doth safely trust in her, so that he shall have no need of spoil.*
>
> *She will do him good and not evil all the days of her life.*
>
> *She seeketh wool, and flax, and worketh willingly with her hands.*
>
> *She is like the merchants' ships; she bringeth her food from afar.*
>
> *She riseth also while it is yet night, and giveth meat to her household, and a portion to her maidens.*
>
> *She considereth a field, and buyeth it; with the fruit of her hands she planteth a vineyard.*
>
> *She girdeth her loins with strength, and strengtheneth her arms.*

> *She perceiveth that her merchandise is good; her candle goeth not out by night...*
>
> *She stretcheth out her hand to the poor; yea, she reacheth forth her hands to the needy.*
>
> *She maketh herself coverings of tapestry; her clothing is silk and purple.*
>
> *Her husband is known in the gates, when he sitteth among the elders of the land.*
>
> *She maketh fine linen, and selleth it; and delivereth girdles unto the merchant.*
>
> *Strength and honor are her clothing; and she shall rejoice in time to come.*
>
> *She openeth her mouth with wisdom, and in her tongue is the law of kindness.*
>
> *She looketh well to the ways of her household, and eateth not the bread of idleness.*
>
> *Her children arise up, and call her blessed; her husband also, and he praiseth her.*
>
> *Many daughters have done virtuously, but thou excellest them all.*

Violet was dumbfounded. When Brent returned to the pew she grasped his hand, smiled, and whispered, "Thank you."

In his short sermon, Father Shand stressed Easter as a time for hope. In his conclusion he said, "One of our daily newspapers has taken the name, *Phoenix*. The phoenix, of course, was a legendary bird of ancient Egypt, and later adapted in Greece and Rome, that was consumed in flames when its nest burned, but from which emerged a new phoenix.

"This also was connected with the palm tree in the sun worship of ancient Egypt. The palm tree was called the phoenix in Greek; the scientific name for the date palm is still phoenix dactylifera, and of course we have the South Carolina palm, the palmetto. Here we see a tradition of hope for a new life at last culminated in our Easter. We are seeing the rebirth of Columbia and South Carolina."

During the Communion service, Father Shand led the congregation in saying in unison *The Nicene Creed.* Violet found herself joining in with all the fervor of a new convert.

A few days later, Violet was surprised, but pleased, to receive a letter from Dr. J.L. Jones, president of Columbia Female College. It was a request for her to speak for the senior convocation at the college.

She thought about her talk over the next several days. She decided she would focus on the attributes of maturity and the changing role of women.

On Friday morning, Dr. Jones escorted Violet, Charlotte, and Bonnie Anne up to the chapel, on the second floor of the building. It was an attractive room about fifty-five feet by thirty-five. It had a ceiling of at least twenty-four feet, and the windows were treble-size. Only senior students were required to be present, but all students were invited, and nearly all were there. They had just changed to their spring uniforms of white muslin or lawn, trimmed according to individual taste.

Charlotte gave a whisper of good luck to Violet, and she and Bonnie Anne found their two seats on the front row that had been reserved for them by Mrs. Jones.

After an introduction by Dr. Jones who presented her as one of Columbia's most respected alumnae, Violet stepped up to the lectern. She looked lovely and cool.

She surveyed the audience deliberately, smiled, and began speaking in her most pleasant, melodious tones, "Dr. Jones, Mrs. Jones, Faculty, and Students—It is a special pleasure for me to be able to share this occasion with you. You remember how as a result of the War women found themselves having to run plantations, run offices, run businesses, and do all kinds of things in addition to caring for their families and running their households. These kinds of activities are bound to continue in the years ahead.

"Last year I had a chance to visit, with my family, the Centennial Exposition in Philadelphia. It was a remarkable collection of exhibits and demonstrations, and one of the most remarkable of all was the Women's Building. There, a whole, huge building was devoted exclusively to women's activities; there a young woman engineer was operating the great steam engine that powered all the machinery in that large building. In addition to exhibits of needlework and embroidery, there was a complete *materia medica* from the Women's Medical College of Philadelphia, a section of a textile mill operated by women, and art exhibits of paintings and sculpture by women.

"Women were granted the right to vote in the Wyoming Territory over seven years ago, and I am sure that it is only a matter of time until women will have the vote in all the states.

"Now women must prepare themselves for all these things—and the first requirement is that they grow up. You know, some people just grow old without growing up at all. What are the attributes that mark maturity in a person? I have turned this question over in my mind for some time. I jotted down what I thought were ten characteristics of a mature person—faith, humility, skepticism, equanimity, sensitivity, courtesy, patience, flexibility, responsibility, and courage. Then a remarkable thing struck me—that each of these had the backing of St. Paul in the famous thirteenth chapter of his first letter to the Corinthians.

She went on for the next fifteen minutes to expand upon these.

Loud and sustained applause erupted at the conclusion of the talk, and a lively discussion followed in the dining room on the first floor, where Violet, Charlotte, and Bonnie Anne joined students and faculty for dinner.

Chapter 72

Little Joey

1877

A few days later on a cool, cloudy afternoon, Violet asked Levi to drive her downtown for some shopping. Before returning to the town house she decided to drive up through the slummy Negro area that she had seen some time earlier, but lately had been avoiding. Memories of what she had seen had remained in the back of her mind, never completely out of her thoughts, always hovering, always nagging. She wanted to know if the situation had improved.

"Miz Violet, ya sure ya wanta go up dere?" asked Levi, turning around to look at her. "Dat ain't no place fo' uh lady, beggin' ya pardon, ma'am."

"Yes, Levi, I have my reasons," she answered.

When they got there, to her disappointment Violet saw no improvement at all—still the decrepit houses, refuse in the streets, stench in the air. Her first impulse was to turn about at once. Then she noticed a little black boy, about seven years old, standing on the curb crying. Violet asked Levi to stop and wait while she went to see what the matter was.

She walked up to the little boy and put her hand gently on his tattered shoulder. "What's the matter, young fellow? Why are you crying?"

Without looking up he answered in a trembling voice, "Ah be lost, ah be lost."

"Tell me, what is your name?" she asked in a soft voice.

"Ah be Joey, Ma'am," he ventured, wiping his nose on his sleeve.

She took him by the hand and, with Levi following along with the buggy, she led the little boy from door to door asking if anyone knew him. At the fifth try, a woman recognized him and told Violet that he lived over on the other street, second house from the corner. They walked over to the street, still hand in hand, with Levi following and shaking his head from side to side and muttering to himself.

Arriving on the street corner, little Joey tugged at her hand and pointed, "Look lady, dere be mah house!" Violet restrained a shudder as she observed the litter and other trash strewn about the grassless yard. They went up the fractured walk to the porch nearly filled with pieces of broken furniture, and miscellaneous debris. Violet knocked at the door. At first there was no answer. She knocked again, this time much harder. Soon the door opened slowly. Peering through the opening was a thin black woman with a dirty, faded kerchief tied around her head. She was balancing a baby on one hip and a toddler on the other. The blank look on her face when she saw Violet quickly changed to one of consternation when she saw the boy.

"Whar ya be, boy, whar ya be? Ah tole ya ta keep yasef ta de fron' yard. Ah gwine whup ya hard, ah sho' is." She did not inquire as to whom Violet might be, why she was standing there with the boy, nor did she invite Violet into the house. She just glared at the child.

He did not seem intimidated. It was as though he was accustomed to being talked to in that tone and hearing such threats. "Ah got lost, muvver, an' ah no kno' how ta git home, an' dis nice lady foun' meh an' heah ah be," he explained, holding tightly to Violet's hand. Then suddenly, he pushed open the door with his other hand and, as his mother stepped aside, he pulled Violet into the darkened front room. She gasped as the stench of unwashed diapers and dishes and old dirt and dust hit her. She wanted to place her handkerchief over her nose to filter out the fetid air, but she didn't. She felt sorry for Joey. She sensed something special about him, and she was determined not to embarrass him—or his mother.

"Dis lady, she be mah frien'," he told his mother. He turned to Violet and flashed a big, friendly smile. "Ah be Joey, ma'am, an' dis be mah muvver, an' de baby be Sue, an' dat li'l boy on muvver hip be Lorenzo buh we call him 'Lo' an'—" he pointed to other dim figures lying around on the floor on what looked to be old worn quilts or blankets, "an' dose mah udder brudder an' sistuh, Mary an' Wayne, an' Clare, an Charles. Sit down, Ma'am," he said, pulling the only chair in the room that was not broken in some way from the corner.

Violet did as bidden, and even though she knew Levi, waiting outside, could not see into the house, she could feel his disapproving eyes boring into her back.

Little Joey sat down on the floor beside her, beaming with pleasure at his guest. The other children had sat up and were now staring at her in silence. As Violet's eyes became accustomed to the murkiness of the room, she could make out the children of varying ages and sizes and the room in general. There was a small wooden table against the back wall. Chipped dishes containing dried food, and stained cups and glasses were lying about the table and on the floor here and there. She saw small dark movements on some of the plates in the corner—and prayed they weren't what they looked like, little scurrying bugs trying to taste the dried food. Tattered shades covered the windows, admitting only slender rays of light here and there through the tears and slits. Beside the table at the back was a door leading into another room which Violet assumed to be the kitchen and dining area. Part of a table was in sight, and she watched in dismay as a chicken suddenly hopped up on the end of the table, deposited a dropping, and then hopped down with complete indifference.

Joey's mother had said nothing, but now she set both the baby and the toddler on the floor and disappeared into the kitchen only to return with a wooden stool. She dragged this across from Violet and sat down on it. She, too, stared and looked at Violet in silence. Only Joey seemed to have command of his tongue.

"Whut be yo' call'd by, ma'am?" he asked, looking up at her with an unassuming air.

Never, never have I seen people living like this, not even on the poorest plantations, thought Violet. *The dirt on their bodies and clothes and in the house, and the foulness they breathe, and the trash in the yard and on the porch does not seem to faze them. And that chicken walking around in the house! What kind of "freedom" is this? But this little boy, this little Joey, he has a spark; he seems different. I wonder why.*

"I am called 'Mrs. Sutler.' And my driver is Levi. We live on the other side of town."

"Ya got chillun?"

"Yes, three."

"Whut be dey?"

"A girl named Bonnie Anne, a baby boy we call Wade Hampton, and another boy, named Jonathan Jackson, but we call him J.J.."

Joey broke into an understanding smile. "Jes' like Lorenzo, he be call'd Lo."

"Yes."

"Ya gotta man?"

"A man? Oh, you mean a husband. Yes, my husband's name is Brent."

"Muvver got no man. Ya man yo' chillun fadder?"

Violet could feel her face flush. *This is only a child talking like that!* "Yes, he's my children's father."

"Mah fadder, he daid."

Suddenly the woman spoke up, "He git kill'd daid. He git in uh figh' and de udder man, he hadda big knife. Joey fadder, he good man, treat meh an' de chillun nice. Ah sho' do miss him. He gib me Joey an' de two bebbies fo' he git daid."

Violet didn't quite know what to say, but the woman seemed to expect a reply. "I'm sorry, especially for little Joey. He seems like a good little boy, and so bright, too." She smiled down at the little fellow who had taken her hand in his again.

Violet wanted to ask the woman how did she and the children get by, if they had a spring or well for water, and the like, but everything that came to mind could have been interpreted as an intrusion of privacy or a criticism—so she asked no questions.

But the woman seemed to read her thoughts. "Mah fust man, he gib meh de udder chillun. He be good man, buh he be sick mos' uf de time, and he git consumpshun an' de good Lawd done tek away fo' his las' bebe done git born. Den ah meet Joey fadder an' marry up wif him, an' tings bettuh 'til he done git kill'd. Now de chillun an meh...," she took a deep sigh and went on, "wale, we git by, we still heah. Ah wuks w'en ah can, hep'n de ladies in town wif dere cleanin' and ironin', buh lately, dere ain't bin much uf dat. De two chick'n gib us uh couple egg a day, an' ah tel de chillun we no eat de chick'n 'cause den dere be no mo' egg. Wunz de chick'n gone, we got nuttin'. An' las' week de well buck't sprung uh leak an' we git jes' 'nuff wadder ta drink uh li'l. Can't wash nuttin'. Lady, ya need some hep a' ya house? Ah be hard wukker."

Joey broke into the conversation, "When ah git jes' uh li'l bigguh ah gonna git meh uh job and wuk, wuk hard an' hep mah muvver an' ebberone. Mah muvver man, de man whut be wif ussans now, he no git wuk; he try, buh dere ain't no wuk fo' him."

Well the little fellow answered some of my questions, I guess.

She rose and said she must be leaving, that she was expected at home. The woman picked up the baby and the toddler and, except for Joey, with the children gathered at the door. Joey accompanied her to the buggy, and she gave him a hug and a kiss upon his smudgy face before taking off with a still disapproving Levi.

Riding back toward the town house, Violet could not get the Negro slum out of her thoughts. Somehow Little Joey reminded her of Little Josh. *I pray something can be done to improve the Negroes' lot,* she thought. Suddenly the sun broke through a rift in the clouds. *Oh, God,* she thought, *there I go—I have just been praying for their improvement; now I am committed to doing something about it. I'll send some food over this afternoon, and a couple of well buckets, and a dishpan and soap, and tomorrow, I'll send more food and see about some clothes and a bit of furniture, but what these people need is not handouts, but steady work. And they don't need ridicule, but education. And they don't need intimidation, but love and understanding.*

When Brent came home later that afternoon, Violet, fresh from a warm bath and a change of clothes—having been fearful that the unpleasant odor might have clung to her hair or dress—greeted him in the parlor with tea and biscuits. Brent explained how Chamberlain still was holding the State House in spite of everything, and that President Hayes had asked both Hampton and Chamberlain to meet with him, separately, in Washington.

"Really? Brent, something happened to me today that has stirred me deeply. I think I've had what some people call an epiphany experience."

He looked at her in surprise. "Epiphany? I thought that was when the Magi came bearing gifts for the Christ Child, you know, Twelfth Night."

"Yes, that's the Epiphany; an epiphany experience is sort of seeing the light on something, of—."

"You mean like Saint Elmo's fire?"

"What's Saint Elmo's fire?"

"You know, that kind of a ball of fire or lightning that appears on the top of a mast of a ship sometimes during stormy weather; we saw it on the way to the West Indies."

"No, not that, I mean seeing something in a different perspective. I guess the most extreme example of seeing the light was Saint Paul on the way to Damascus."

"Then what has dazzled you, my Love; I hope you haven't discovered that the Carpetbaggers have been right all along," he teased.

"No, you silly goose, I'm serious. It's more like Wade Hampton has been right all along."

"Well, well, this *is* interesting. In what way?"

"In avoiding violence, in calling for moderation, in recognizing rights for the Negro."

"Well, well," he repeated, "I'm glad that you've seen the light in that regard, though I must warn you, the political crisis is not over yet."

"Brent, I told you that I've had an unusual experience. I want you to come and take a ride with me through the Negro slums."

"Why?" he asked in surprise.

"Just so you can see how bad off they are."

"Violet, my dear, I don't need any Saint Elmo's fire to know that."

"No, but you don't sense the real impact unless you go over and see it," she persisted.

"When?" he asked, already setting down his cup in anticipation of her answer.

"Right now. It won't take an hour."

"Oh, all right, let's go."

Levi brought the horse and buggy around, and Violet asked Levi and Uncle Job to load the provisions Aunt Beulah had assembled, along with the buckets, pan, and soap. She had had Uncle Job fetch some new rope, just in case it was needed for the well, and a lamp and a bottle of oil. All these they placed in the space at the rear of the buggy.

Brent took the reins and headed off in the direction of the area about which Violet had spoken. On the way she told him about finding Little Joey lost and then taking him to his house where she met his mother and brothers and sisters, and the condition in which they were living. She guided him to the house. Brent picked up a basket of provisions, and she carried the two water buckets, the dishpan, and soap.

Little Joey himself opened the door. When he saw it was Violet, he let out a yell of joy and called to his mother that the pretty lady was back. Everyone was happy to see her, and they were elated at Brent's basket of provisions. Joey's mother was almost as happy to see the well buckets. Violet introduced Brent to Joey and his mother, and then with Joey's help to the other children.

"Dis be ya man? He sho' be big," said Joey, looking up at Brent with admiration in his eyes.

"Yes, this is my husband, Joey. He wanted to meet you."

This made Joey even happier. The fact that this nice lady's man wanted to meet him made him feel important somehow. He gazed at Brent with the same adoration that he gave Violet.

Brent smiled and looked down at the little fellow. Instantly he felt what Violet had sensed in the boy. "Joey, come help me bring in the rest of the food, and then take me out to your well so I can check the rope." He took Joey's hand in his, and the two went out to the buggy.

Again the odor grabbed at Violet and she caught her breath, but this time since it was expected, it didn't seem quite so bad. She entered the house to help unload the basket. Brent and Joey brought in the rest of the provisions and went out back to the well. Brent noticed that a rickety outhouse stood not far from the well. Soon he came through the kitchen, nodded to Joey's mother, and remarked to Violet that the well did, indeed, need the new rope. He went on through the front room and out to get the rope from the buggy.

After Brent, with Joey's "help", had attached the new rope securely on the well spindle, Joey showed him around the small, three-room house, then they rejoined the others in the front room. Joey sat down on the floor by Violet, and Brent leaned against the wall, his eyes scrutinizing everything in sight.

On the way home Brent was thoughtful, as if reviewing in his mind what he had seen and heard. Violet left him to his thoughts for a while, and then broke in to urge him to do all he could to get more support for the education of the Negroes through the legislature. He told her he needed no persuading on that score, but he noted that would be much easier to accomplish if ever they could get Hampton installed in the State House, for that was one of the things Hampton had promised.

"I think that tomorrow I'll talk to Mrs. Shand at Trinity Church about having the ladies of Trinity take the lead in mobilizing support from all the churches in the city for Negro food relief for those unable to get work."

"Good idea. Do that; those poor people desperately need help."

Shortly thereafter, on another day, she drove again over to the slum area to take some more foodstuffs and necessities to Joey's family. Now they had a settee and several chairs and small tables in the parlor, clean mattresses on the beds, curtains at the windows, and unchipped glass and pottery dishes, and staples on the food shelf. And now that they had sufficient water and a supply of soap, Joey's mother and her oldest daughter had scrubbed the windows and floors, washed the blankets and quilts, and cleared the porch and yard of debris. As though proud of what was inside the house, they had left the windows open to the sunshine and fresh air.

As Violet drove back, more thoughts kept crowding her mind. *Yes, some wherewithal is necessary before freedom can be real. If a person has no money, he is bound to the soil just as much as is a serf or a slave, but there is more to it than that. The ills of the Reconstruction and the Yankee occupation were not simply in the plunder of resources; something far worse was the suffocation of liberty, the robbery of the spirit. Perhaps, too, that was the way the slaves had felt. Now it was necessary not only to enable the freed slaves to find means for existence. It also was essential for them to build their spirits, and the best way to do that, in addition to schools, was for them to have a church, a church that they can call their own.*

She stopped at Trinity Church again, this time to see Father Shand. He was walking among the camellias and poinsettias in the churchyard. When he saw her approaching, he smiled and asked if she would like to go inside.

"Oh, no, Father Shand, it's too beautiful out here."

"He motioned for her to take a seat on one of the wooden benches lining the path. "Then what can I do for you, Violet?"

"I've been concerned about the Negroes up in that slum area."

"Yes, I know. Mrs. Shand told me about how much they need our help. She is already organizing the ladies for rescue missions over there to insure the Negroes have food and other necessities."

"That's good, but Dr. Shand, I've been thinking...they need something more than that. We don't want any new Federal bureaucracy like the Freedmen's Bureau. Even our church charities must not go too far. You know, as Thomas Jefferson said, 'Dependency begets servitude.' Sometimes they have accused us of reintroducing slavery on the plantation, but I think a greater danger of restoring slavery would be an extended system of poor-relief dependency. That could become the equivalent of slavery without the benefit of any labor."

"I see what you are saying, Violet. Well now, what do you have in mind?" smiled the gentle priest.

"A church."

"A church? There are already many churches in the city. You know the Negroes are free to attend them, any one of them they wish."

"Yes, that's true, but I think it would mean a great deal to them to have a church of their own. I was thinking that maybe we, and some of the other churches, could act as sponsors to get them started."

"Mm," he murmured thoughtfully, "You think that would help?"

"No doubt of it, Dr. Shand. Let it be an African Methodist Episcopal Church. Let them build it themselves, with their own hands. They have enough skilled carpenters and brick-layers and glaziers, and other workers, from off the plantations. Then they would think of it as their very own. Such a church could become a kind of community center for them and could be a force for moral instruction and for uplifting the spirit. I think most of all, they need an uplifting of their spirits, a sense of self-reliance and independence."

"Mm," he perused, "a church of their very own, that they build themselves. That might be an excellent idea, Violet. What do you think should be the first step?"

"The first thing to do is to get representatives from our churches together to adopt a plan, where we help to get it started. Secondly, get Negro representatives to help plan the building, organize the workers, and supervise them. I think it's important that we do not try to control their church. They must see it as *theirs.*"

"Right. I think, though, we might bring in a good AME minister and arrange for the people to appoint him as pastor of the new church even before they start working on it. For that matter, he could be their chief organizer, and in the meantime he could carry on prayer meetings in their homes and minister to their spiritual needs while developing an enthusiasm for this project."

"Yes, that might be the best way to go. Brent knows some good black ministers in the legislature. Maybe they could recommend someone, and he could get started right away. Brent and I will try to increase our contribution to Trinity to help finance their minister, and I'm sure others will want to do this, too. But I think support should come from the church and not only individuals."

Father Shand looked at Violet with pride and delight. "Excellent. If you will start moving in that direction, I'll see what I can do to build a fire under the church leaders of Trinity and the other churches to get to work on this. You know, the AME has made a good start in Charleston, and has organized a South Carolina conference. I'm certain they would help."

"Oh, I hope so."

"There are a number of prosperous black merchants in town who ought to be enlisted for support, people like Joseph Taylor, William Taylor, Junius Moody, and Augustus Cooper."

"Yes, yes, indeed."

"They say that William Taylor has such a big grocery business that he has to call in the police on Saturdays to handle the crowds."

"So I've heard. He should be a strong source of help. I'll ask Brent to see him about it."

Violet rose and extended her hand. She thanked Father Shand for his time and his support in this matter, and with a smile and a wave she was off. As she walked quickly back to her buggy to return to the town house, she was filled with a sense of elation and anticipation.

Chapter 73

Ratification Ball

1877

When Brent came into the town house late one afternoon a few days after Easter, he told Violet that there might be some important news coming and they should go up to the office and listen to the telegraph.

"What's happened, Brent?" Violet asked.

Concentrating on the telegraph sounder, he replied without looking up at her, "Rumors are flying that Hayes has agreed to withdraw the Federal troops from the State House, but nobody has any confirmation. If it's true, it should mean that Wade Hampton would be able to walk into the State House and take over."

He leaned back in his chair. Violet pulled one over beside him and sat down. While they waited for further news, Violet reported that a letter from Susan had arrived that morning.

"Anything interesting?" he asked, still watching the telegraph.

"Most things are going well there, but they all were disappointed at what they are calling 'The stolen election' of Hayes.."

Now he looked at Violet with a smile. "Aren't we all, but we still may get the main thing, with Hampton."

After a few minutes of near silence the sounder began clicking. Brent turned to the telegraph, listening intently. "Listen, this is it! Federal troops are to withdraw from the South Carolina State House at noon tomorrow, April 10!"

"Thank God! That's wonderful!" Violet exclaimed.

Violet and Brent were at the State House grounds the next morning. There was a large, enthusiastic crowd there when they saw a scowling Chamberlain, giving up his claim to gubernatorial authority, walk out of the State House, get into his carriage, and drive away amidst jeers and catcalls of the onlookers. Shortly afterward the company of blue-clad United States soldiers filed out of the State House and marched to their barracks in total silence.

The next day Violet and Brent joined a crowd of fervent citizens who this time were attracted by the arrival of a triumphant Wade Hampton. He and his fellow state officials marched into the State House amidst wild applauding and roaring "hoorays" and "bravos."

Violet nudged Brent, saying, "I can understand how the French felt when the German occupation forces marched out of eastern France in 1873."

He nodded. "Yes, and their occupation was only for two and a half years. Ours has lasted twelve years...twelve long years. What a day this is for us!" He picked her up and twirled her around, giving her a big kiss before setting her back down on her feet.

Violet was filled with emotions of joy and thankfulness and excitement and elation. "Yes, what a day! Oh, Brent, let's celebrate this occasion. Let's have a ball, a grand ball at Fair Oaks!"

"That's a great idea, my Love; indeed, let's have a ratification in celebration of the liberation of South Carolina."

"When can we have it?"

"As soon as you can get ready."

"How about a week from Saturday, the 21st?"

"That sounds good to me, Violet. We'll run a special train out from Columbia to bring people from here, including, I hope, Governor Wade Hampton."

"There'll be people coming from Sumter and Stateburg and all around the county, and surely some will stay overnight."

"Yes, I expect so. Mother and Father, along with Phoebe will want to be here, and of course Charlotte and Leland and Andrew." He paused a moment and then went on, "I wish Susan and Gil could make it. Do you think they might? Shall I get off a telegram to them?"

"Yes, do that, Brent."

By special train, by scheduled train, by carriage, by buggy, by horseback, a hundred and twenty guests poured into Fair Oaks on the evening of Saturday, April 21, 1877. Brent's parents and sister arrived from Charleston; General Hampton and a number of political leaders came from Columbia, and friends and neighbors from all around the area were there. The Stuarts, Friersons, and Andersons had sent over groomsmen, cooks, maids, and other servants to help those at Fair Oaks, and Charlotte and Leland brought Aunt Beulah and Uncle Job with them. In addition to the house servants, Rachel had lined up half a dozen young women and as many young men to help out. Jarvis and Aaron, Fabian, and Hattie and Aunt Beulah took charge of any special training necessary. In Columbia Violet rented extra attire for those helpers who needed it.

For the preliminary dancing and entertainment, the *Little Brown Jugs,* seated in the orchestra balcony at the far end of the ballroom, provided the music. They began with their favorite syncopated rhythm versions of *The Little Brown Jug, Aura Lee, Listen to the Mocking Bird,* and *Oh, Susanna.* Some of the guests as they arrived, attracted by that special style of music, hurried to the dance floor. Others tarried by the table and sideboards, filled with food, in the dining room, or the punch bowls and small platters of food in the parlor. After half an hour, Brent strode down to the front of the ballroom, beneath the orchestra, and called upon everyone to join in a grand march. He directed them as they marched down the room, first in column of twos, then in fours, then in eights, while the *Little Brown Jugs* played in succession *Dixie, The Bonnie Blue Flag,* and *Carolina,* each of which everyone greeted with shouts of delight.

When all had formed their eights, Brent called for a halt. The *Little Brown Jugs* took their leave, and waiters with trays of champagne moved through the crowd. Then Violet reenacted her tableau of Hampton Day at Sumter. Completely shrouded in a black robe and hood and with chains around her shoulders, representing South Carolina subjugated, she mounted the stairs to the orchestra balcony. Brent lit a flare that poured a dazzling light upon her. Then she threw off the chains and threw off the black robe and hood, and stepped out as South Carolina liberated in her gleaming white silk dress and golden coronet, bearing the words *South Carolina,* on her dark shining hair. As she stretched her arms upward, Brent escorted Governor Hampton up the steps. The Governor kissed her hand and waved to the crowd. A great cheer went up "Hurrah for South Carolina! Hurrah for Hampton!"

Brent stepped up and called for attention. Raising his glass, he said, "I propose a toast—to South Carolina liberated, may she ever be free!"

There were shouts of "Hear, hear," and the people sipped their champagne.

Then Brent raised his glass again. "Here's to Governor Hampton and to his long good health that he may lead us in making it so!"

Again, "Hear, hear!" and "Hurrah for Hampton!"

Someone in the back shouted, "Here's to Mr. Chamberlain, may he enjoy a long retirement." Roars of laughter greeted this toast.

And another, "Here's to Honest John Patterson. May he receive a warm reception in Tartarus!"

Then came laughter and more shouts of "Hear, hear!"

With the *Little Brown Jugs* leading off, Violet and Brent, standing together beside the band in the balcony, led the whole crowd in a thunderous singing of two verses of *Carolina*—

Thy skirts indeed the foe may part,
Thy robe be pierced with sword and dart,
They shall not touch thy noble heart,
Carolina! Carolina!
Girt with such wills to do and bear,
Assured in right, and mailed in prayer,
Thou wilt not bow thee to despair,
Carolina! Carolina!

At this point Brent directed everyone to move outside to the front lawn for a ten-minute display of pyrotechnics. After that an orchestra from Sumter, mostly strings, with a couple of horns and a snare drum, took its place in the orchestra balcony. First came a Virginia Reel in which nearly everyone joined. After that, it was all Viennese waltzes. For some of the people the waltz was still a little too shocking for dancing, but even those few admitted that they enjoyed listening while the others danced round and round. Violet hardly missed a waltz, alternating between Brent and guests who were lined up waiting a turn with her.

Each piece she thought better than the previous one—*Artist's Life, Tales from the Vienna Woods, Du und Du,* and the *Blue Danube* which everyone acclaimed. But Violet declared that her favorite was Strauss's *Roses from the South.* She asked the orchestra to play that waltz three times, and each time she let all those around her know the title, *Roses from the South.*

About eleven o'clock the music stopped, and Governor Hampton and other state officials led the way to the special train for Columbia, and then the other guests began leaving, all with laudatory comments about the occasion and what it celebrated.

After most of the others had gone, the house guests and several neighbors remained in the parlor for further conversation. James and Mary Chesnut were there, and the Stuarts, the Friersons, the Frasers, the Shelbys, the Dargans, the Andersons, the Farleys, the Carsons, Charles Rhett, Charlotte and Leland and his father, and Brent's parents and sister, and Susan and Gil.

Several side conversations were going on all at once until Andrew Thompson began repeating some of his earlier lines, and everyone turned to listen.

"It's been a great occasion, and it is wonderful to see South Carolina supposedly free again, but I'm afraid we may be kidding ourselves."

"What do you mean, Father?" Leland asked.

"Well, as others have said, 'The Old South is not what it used to be, and never was.'"

Violet quickly responded, "That probably is true; things often seem much better in the remote past and in the distant future. It's like Macaulay said in his *History of England* where he likens our view of history to the view of travelers on the Arabian desert who see far to the rear a lake where hours before they had been toiling through hot sand, and far ahead the mirage of a lake toward which they are going. He says that in a similar way people now speak of merry old England of ages ago when things were really bad and suggests that probably in the future, in the twentieth century, men will be speaking of the reign of Queen Victoria as a time when England was truly merry England."

"Very profound," Shelby said, "and I dare say he was right."

"But there is more to it than that," Farley said. "Whatever was real about Southern civilization now is probably gone forever, swept away by four years of war and twelve years of Yankee military occupation and Reconstruction."

"Nonsense," said Violet. "Do you remember that some time before Aristotle's time, the Greeks had a great war between North and South?"

Charles Rhett spoke up, "Of course, the Peloponnesian War, where Athens was leader of the North and Sparta of the South."

"Of course," Violet answered, "and who won that one?"

"The Spartans," two or three people responded.

"And whose civilization do we now remember and honor, the Athenian or the Spartan?"

Rhett replied, "I guess the leaders of our South should have paid more attention to the Spartan war-making capabilities."

"Ah-hah!" said Violet, "and that is all we have to remember of the Spartans—that they were great warriors. Don't you see, what we consider the superior culture prevailed even though it suffered military defeat. Can you name any other legacy of Spartan civilization?"

Silence. Everyone looked at one another as if expecting the other to answer, but no one spoke up.

She smiled and went on, "Look what we still appreciate and are influenced by from the Athenians—the statecraft of Solon and Pericles; the sculpture of Myron and Phidias, the architecture of Callicrates and Ictinus; the painting of Zeuxis; the philosophy of Zeno, Socrates, and Plato; the drama of Aeschylus, Sophocles, Euripides, and Aristophanes; the oratory of Isocrates and Demosthenes; the science of Anaxagoras and the science and philosophy of Aristotle, and the histories of Herodotus and Thucydides. I tell you, Southern civilization has *not* been swept away by the Yankees any more than the Athenian civilization was swept away by the Spartans, or than the Greek civilization was swept away by the Romans, or than the Roman civilization was swept away by Attila the Hun or the Visigoths."

"Bravo!" rang out from several listeners.

Again Violet smiled and continued, "Our Southern civilization, which cultivates good manners and good morals and good taste, an appreciation for fine art and music and literature, continuous development of the intellect, and a devotion to individual liberty, self-reliance, responsibility and a high sense of honor—this must persist."

"Hear hear!" others cried out.

Violet called for refills of everyone's champagne glasses.

John Frierson smiled and said, "Now is our chance to begin our own Reconstruction—to reach out and recapture what is best in the spirit of the South, and build on it."

Mary Chesnut raised her glass for attention. "Look at the irony of the situation. It is just like the playing out of a Greek tragedy. The Radical Republicans were bent on perpetuating themselves in power, but the means they chose to do it have guaranteed that they will not be elected again."

Brent raised his glass and said, "Right you are. I'll bet you South Carolina will not vote Republican again for a hundred years."

"I'm sure of that," said Mary, "but I'm afraid the big question now is, can Wade Hampton last four years?"

"Why, what do you mean?" asked Violet.

"You know there's a lot of pressure against his moderation and his policies for racial equality."

"Yes, I know," Violet responded, "and I must confess that I've had some misgivings on that score myself, but now I am sure he is right."

John Frierson spoke up, "You know General Gary was one of Hampton's original supporters, but I'm afraid now he is headed for a break with Hampton on those very questions."

Brent frowned, shook his head slowly in assent, and added, "The one who scares me is young Pitchfork Ben Tillman. Already he has been stirring up antagonism of the back country poor farmers against the Negroes. This could undo all that Hampton may do in promoting racial harmony."

"Nothing human is ever permanent, is it?" sighed Violet.

Acknowledgments

The authors want to express their appreciation to all who gave support and assistance in the completion of this work. Special thanks are due those who read the manuscript, in full or in part, and offered valuable suggestions: Raymond and Martha Stokes, Robert and Lou Womack, Reba Logwood, son James W. Huston, and sister Lois Ann Huston. Thanks are due daughter Elizabeth Exum for her long-time support and for the authors' photograph. Josh's song was composed by daughter Nita Diane Huston.

Among those who were especially helpful during our several visits to South Carolina were Margaret Dinkens and Robert Witt of the Sumter county Historical Museum; the Rev. J. Edwin Pippin, rector of Holy Cross Episcopal Church in Stateburg; Joan Carigan and Sara Hempley of Trinity Cathedral in Columbia; Allen Stokes, director of the South Caroliniana Library, and Carol Tobin, head research librarian at the Thomas Cooper Library, the University of South Carolina; Loure Hall, overseer and caretaker of Milford Plantation; members of the Lenoir family who continue to operate the Lenoir Country Store and Post Office, established by their forebears before 1825, near Sumter; the staff of the Dixie (Oakland) Plantation, and the Information Service of Columbia College.

For making materials available for us locally we are indebted to Carol Pollack, reference librarian, and Virginia Dunn, archivist, of the Knight-Capon Library, Lynchburg College.

Our principal sources for historical events and background were the following;

W.L. Fleming, ed., *Documentary History of Reconstruction: Political, Military, Social, Religious, Educational and Industrial 1865 to Present Time (1906)*; W.L. Fleming, *The Secret of Appomattox: A Chronicle of the Reunion of the State (Chronicles of America, vol. 32)(1919); The South and the Building of the Nation,* 13 vols.; Edgar Wallace Knight, *The Influence of Reconstruction on Education in the South* (1913); Paul Luison, *Race, Class, and Party, A History of Negro Suffrage and White Politics in the South* (1932); Ella Lonn, *Reconstruction in Louisiana After 1868* (1918); James S. Pike, *The Prostrate State: South Carolina Under Negro Government* (1874); Whitelaw Reid, *After the War, A Southern Tour* (1866); John S. Reynolds, *Reconstruction in South Carolina (*1905); Robert Somers, *The Southern States Since the War* (1871); Alrutheus A. Taylor, *The Negro in South Carolina During Reconstruction* (1926); Harvey Wish, *Reconstruction in the South: First Hand Accounts;* Ulrich B. Phillips, *Life and Labor in the Old South* (1929); Paul H. Buck, *The Road to Reunion* (1937); C. Vann Woodwward, *The Strange Career of Jim Crow* (1957); Charles Joyner, *Down by the Riverside: A South Carolina Slave Community* (1984); Sidney Andrews, *The South Since the War* (1866, 1971); Claude G. Bowers, *The Tragic Era* (1929); Katherine M. Jones, *Heroines of Dixie* (1955); Allan Nevins, *Ordeal of the Union,* 8 vols. (1947, 1950, 1959, 1960, 1971); Douglas Southall Freeman, *Lee's Lieutenants,* 3 vols. (1945); *Official Records of the Union and Confederate Navies in the War of the Rebellion* (1921); Francis B. Simkins and

Robert H. Woody, *South Carolina During Reconstruction* (1932, 1966); Claude G. Bowers, *The Tragic Era: The Revolution after Lincoln* (1929); William A. Dunning, *Reconstruction, Political and Economic, 1865-1877* (1907); Myrta Avary, *Dixie After the War* (1906); James W. Garner, *Reconstruction in Mississippi* (1901); J.G. Hamilton, *Reconstruction in North Carolina* (1914); David Chalmers, *History of the Ku Klux Klan*; Allen W. Trelease, *White Terror: The Ku Klux Klan Conspiracy and Southern Reconstruction;* Burton J. Hendrick, *Statesmen of the Lost Cause* (1939); C. Vann Woodward, ed., *Mary Chesnut's Civil War* (1981); Joseph T. Derry, *Story of the Confederate States* (1895, 1996); Richard Taylor, *Destruction and Reconstruction* (1879, 1998); Ervin L. Jordan, Jr., *Black Confederates and Afro-Yankees in Civil War Virginia* (1995); William J. Cooper, Jr., *Jefferson Davis, American* (2000); Felicity Allen, *Jefferson Davis, Unconquerable Heart* (1999); Twelve Southerners, *I'll Take My Stand* (1930, 1977); Julie Saville, *The Work of Reconstruction* (1994); *History of the State Agricultural and Mechanical Society of South Carolina* (1916); William B. Hesseltine, *The South in American History* (1943); J.G. Randall, *The Civil War and Reconstruction* (1937); Harnett T. Kane, *Queen of New Orleans* (1949); George Benjamin West, *When the Yankees Came, Civil War and Reconstruction on the Virginia Peninsula,* edited by Parke Rouse, Jr., (1977); John F. Marszalek, *Sherman* (1993); Anne King Gregorie, *History of Sumter County* (1954, 1974); Jerold J. Savory, *Columbia College, The Ariail Era* (1979); John Osborne, *The Old South* (1968); T. Harry Williams, *The Union Restored* (1963); J.C. Furnas, *The Americans, A Social History of the United States, 1587-1914 (1969);* Cassie Nicholes, *Historical Sketches of Sumter County.* 2 vols. (1975), John R. Poindexter, *Sumter County, A Photographic Chronicle;* Thomas S. Sumter, *Stateburg and Its People* (1922, 1930, 1934, 1949, 1982); Allen Carpenter, *The New Enchantment of America: South Carolina* (1979); Janie Revill, *Sumter District* (1968); Jim Dan Hill, *Sea Dogs of the Sixties* (1935); Seth M. Scheiner, *Reconstruction, A Tragic Era?* (1968); John D. Barnhart, "Reconstruction on the Lower Mississippi," *Mississippi Historical Review* (1934); William B. Hesseltine, "Economic Factors in the Abandonment of Reconstruction," *Mississippi Historical Review* (1935); Francis B. Simkins, "Race Legislation in South Carolina Since 1865," *South Atlantic Quarterly* (1921); Robert H. Woody, "The Labor and Immigration Problem of South Carolina During Reconstruction," *Mississippi Historical Review* (1931); Mary Celestia Parler, *Word List from Wedgefield, South Carolina* (1930); Sylvester Primer, "Charleston Provincialisms," *The American Journal of Philology* (1888); Guy S. Lowman, Jr., and Raven I. McDavid, *Linguistic Atlas,* and contemporary newspapers: *The Daily South Carolinian, Columbia Phoenix, The Daily Phoenix, Daily Carolinian, The Sumter Southron.*

About the Authors

James A. and Anne Marshall Huston make their home in Lynchburg, Virginia. He is a native of Fairmount, Indiana. A great grandfather served in the Mississippi cavalry and a grandfather in the Indiana infantry in the Civil War. James was educated at Indiana University and New York University, with terms at Oxford in England and at Fribourg in Switzerland.

Anne Marshall was born in High Point, North Carolina. Later her family returned to her mother's home state of Virginia where Anne spent a large part of her life in Williamsburg. Two of her great grandfathers served in the Army of Northern Virginia. At present, she is the Recorder of the Military Service Awards for the Capt. Sally Tompkins Chapter of the United Daughters of the Confederacy, Mathews Court House, Virginia. She is a graduate of the College of William and Mary and completed her doctoral studies at the University of Virginia.

During World War II, James was operations officer of an infantry battalion in Europe. He taught history at Purdue University for twenty-five years, and for twelve years was Dean of Lynchburg College in Virginia. Anne Marshall has been an elementary school teacher, reading specialist, and reading consultant. She has taught graduate courses at the College of William and Mary and the University of Virginia, and undergraduate and graduate courses at Lynchburg College where she was professor of education and director of the graduate reading specialist program.

Both have professional books and articles published in their respective fields. In addition, James is the author of an earlier historical novel dealing with the rivalry of Tecumseh and William Henry Harrison. Together the Hustons wrote a short novel, set in the Battle of the Bulge in the Ardennes during World War II. But so far as they are concerned, *Violet Storm* is their *magnum opus.*

Printed in the United States
7069RDAM110609422800001B